AUTUMN ON ANGEL STREET

They waited, all the women who had come to the yard.
They stood, ignoring the slanting rain, facing the silent
winding wheels and willing them to move, to bring up a
cage with their men inside. They willed their husbands,
sons, fathers and sweethearts still to be alive and not to
have been blown apart by the blast, not to have been
burned or crushed or choked or drowned. There were so
many ways to suffer and die in the tunnels under the
ground, and they imagined them all.

They all wished for it to be over; wished they were at
home, talking, cooking tea, laughing maybe, or moaning
about the children or the leaking roof. They wanted it to
be Sunday so they could go to chapel and later sit at
home and not think about what could happen
underground.

All the women waited because there was nothing else
they could do.

About the author

Born in North London in 1945, A. R. Davey now lives in
Wellingborough, Northamptonshire. Hodder & Stoughton will
publish *Winter in Paradise Square*, the sequel to *Autumn on
Angel Street*, in 1996.

Autumn on
Angel Street

A. R. Davey

CORONET BOOKS
Hodder and Stoughton

First published in 1995 by Hodder and Stoughton
A division of Hodder Headline PLC

First published in paperback in 1996 by Hodder & Stoughton
A Coronet Papaerback

10 9 8 7 6 5 4 3 2

British Library Cataloguing in Publication Data

Davey A. R.
Autumn on Angel Street
I. Title
823 [F]

ISBN 0 340 63974 1

Typeset by Avon Dataset Ltd, Bidford-on-Avon, Warks

Printed and bound in Great Britain by
Cox & Wyman, Reading, Berks

Hodder and Stoughton
A division of Hodder Headline PLC
338 Euston Road
London NW1 3BH

To Shirley
For her unflagging encouragement

PART ONE

PART ONE

CHAPTER 1

London, autumn 1891

The evening sun was low, casting long shadows across the streets, and somewhere, blocks away, a clock chimed seven.

Seven? She was late.

She had left home at six in the morning and now she was late and Rose might be worrying; but she could not rush, her feet and legs would not let her.

She was tired, and not only from the long day's work but from near-sleepless nights and from worrying. Worrying about Rose and her twins, about Edward, and to some extent about herself. And about the autumn; it was almost over and the leaves were nearly gone.

Her mind drifted and she forgot about the pains in her legs and back as her feet plodded on. Turned left, started the long slog up Mile Hill. Pavement hard, feet heavy, eyes heavy, head heavy; on and on, slower and slower, boots beginning to drag.

A distant call: 'Miss Forrester?'

Whoever was calling was a long way away, might leave her alone if she ignored him.

Raw vegetables and oil lamps, damp sacks, leather, fish, beer, wooden crates. Smoke. Everything, it all smelled so real she could see it, in her dream.

Smelled horses and wet oats and axle grease. Heard a heavy cart.

'Miss Forrester! *Miss Forrester!*'

Hands grabbed her. She fell backward. Her basket was yanked away.

She jumped, instantly alert, not properly awake. Saw the iron wheel rim above her eyes; heard it grind on the cobbles inches from her toes. Saw her basket bouncing behind the wheel's wooden spokes.

'Miss Forrester? Are you all right?' A man's voice, rough, then apologetic. 'I'm sorry to grab you like that, miss, but you look real queer.'

She could hear but she could not speak. She felt shivery and her brain and eyes seemed loose in her head. She squinted. The world spun, tilted, steadied, and settled, blurred and misty and then clear. And then she saw the overloaded four-wheeled wagon trundling away and her basket lying in the road. Saw the market barrows, housewives with their own baskets, strings of children, and knew she was at the top of Mile Hill, only yards from her turning, Angel Street.

'Miss Forrester, you nearly had it then, stepping out in the road like that. You all right? You look worn out.' She recognised the man wearing a leather coster's apron.

'Oh, Sam, I'm sorry. Yes, I'm all right, thank you. A bit weary, I think, that's all.' She nodded and concentrated on a barrow's oil lamps, forcing her eyes to stay open. 'I've been out all day, Sam, over in St George's.'

She rubbed her face and eyes and clambered on to her knees, then feet.

'A bit weary? You look half asleep, if you'll pardon me for saying so,' Sam said respectfully and steadied her with one hand while he shook dust off a potato sack and folded it over the edge of a cattle trough. 'Sit down for a minute, miss, before you fall down.'

He picked her basket up and she sat down and massaged her calves through her skirt, then stretched and rubbed her back. Her head was itching but she deliberately did not scratch it.

'You say you've been over in St George's? Worst slums in London.' Sam shook his head. 'Dangerous too, especially for a woman on her own. A young lady like you shouldn't be sent to places like that. Can't the mission find a bloke, sorry, miss, a man, who could go?'

'No, Sam, but thanks for being concerned.' She smiled at him. 'Anyway, I'm not that young any more and I'm certainly no lady. It's safe enough really. They know me over there and the women who need help most wouldn't talk to a man. They'd be scared he'd take advantage, one way or another.'

She unlaced a boot and rubbed her foot. 'No, St George's in the east is all right; if you don't have to live there, that is.'

'Rather you than me, miss.' Sam moved to join her on the trough but she motioned him away.

'Don't get too close. I think I'm lousy.'

He peered at her hair, and shuddered.

'Oh yeah, I can see the little bleeders. Rather you than me,' he said again, and stayed an arm's length away.

'I'd better get home and have a bath.' She laced up her boot, thanked him again for his concern, and stood up to leave.

'Do you want me to walk home with you?' He picked up her basket.

'No, but thanks, anyway. I'll be all right.'

'Here, take these, miss,' he said confidentially, and dropped a few pieces of fruit into her basket. 'Only be wasted otherwise, and perhaps it'll help. Looks to me as if you've caught the flu from Mrs Shelley.'

'Mrs Shelley?' she said clumsily and realised her mistake. 'Oh, Rose.'

She hoped he had not noticed her confusion, or would put it down to her being tired or feeling ill.

'Haven't seen her or her kiddies for a week or more.' He handed her the basket. 'Are they better now?'

'Yes, thanks. The children are fine but Rose is still weak.'

'Takes it out of you, the flu. And my missus reckons your sister always looks a bit pasty, anyway. Never really looked right, Mrs Shelley, not since you found her, Miss Forrester. Needs building up, my Agnes reckons. We were wondering if—'

'I think Agnes is probably right, Sam,' she interrupted him, thanked him again and turned away before he could ask any more questions.

He was a kind man but he would gossip with anyone and she did not want to be drawn into a conversation about Rose and the children. She was tired and felt ill and might easily say something he could pass on; and innocent comments had a way of finding their way back to the wrong people.

There had been enough trouble in the past, even before she found Rose again. She did not want any more. There were too many secrets to keep hidden, too many dangerous dogs that strangers might unwittingly unleash.

She had found Rose, hiding with her babies in one room in a dirty Shoreditch slum, almost four years ago. They had been friends for years but when she found her, Rose was so battered and frightened, so thin and damaged that it was not until they sat close and talked that she recognised anything familiar about her.

There were no clues in the voice, the words were too few and too whispered, and the face was too bruised and cut and swollen to be recognisable. But the eyes!

Rose's green eyes, not bright and alert as they once had

been, but dull and lifeless and constantly shifting with short, erratic movements, like her hands; but they were Rose's eyes.

'Rose?' She still remembered the shock she felt when she realised who she was talking to, and Rose's lack of response. 'It's Elizabeth, Rose. Elizabeth Forrester. Don't you recognise me?'

The blank stare hurt then and hurt again every time she remembered it.

She should have followed the rules, written a report about Rose and the children and arranged for them to stay at the mission, but she did not even think about that. The mission did not have the facilities to take care of someone like Rose; she would have been sent to hospital and the children would have been passed to an institution where they might have been kept even after their mother recovered, if ever she had.

No, she decided there and then that Rose needed to be taken care of, and a proper home to recover in, protection for herself and the children in case her husband came looking for them. She remembered the impulsive decision, typical of the sort Rose would once have made under similar circumstances.

She had the house in Angel Street all to herself, and although by Rose's standards it was small it was big enough for Rose and the children to live with her, so without telling anyone she simply took them home.

It was easy at first. Anyone could see that Rose and the twins had been beaten and no one was able to argue that she was not Mrs Shelley, even though it was simply a name Rose had taken to help her hide.

But it was later that the awkward questions started.

She and Rose thought of themselves as sisters but it was not only their backgrounds which were so different: they looked nothing like each other.

Rose was soft and pale, short with heavy copper curls, and when the cuts and bruises healed she had the beauty

and gloss of a porcelain figure. It was improbable she
would have a sister who was taller than most men, gypsy
dark and gaunt, and with a brisk no-nonsense attitude that
had come from a lifetime of working.

It was Rose who found the solution and told everyone
they were really half sisters, same father but different
mothers, born into different circumstances. An ingenious
invention, Rose insisted, and it had solved the problem.
The questions stopped immediately, the gossips satisfied
that they had forced a family skeleton out of a cupboard;
their attention diverted from the real secret, Rose's real
identity and the real reason she was scared her husband
might find her.

So Elizabeth hoped Sam had not noticed her fumbling
reaction, left him in mid sentence and walked towards
Angel Street. As she moved along the pavement people
stopped her to ask about her and her sister and the twins;
and several costers gave her more fruit or a few vegetables
or fish wrapped in paper, always saying they were glad it
was her and not them that had spent the day in St
George's.

The basket was full and heavy by the time she reached
the corner of Angel Street, and she leaned against the
green tiled wall of the Angel Inn for a final rest. As always,
she glanced up at the inn's gilded wooden angel. It peered
down from the corner niche where it was trapped, its nose
permanently turned up as if it did not quite approve of the
vinegary smell coming from the alehouse it was meant to
advertise.

She was fond of the little angel; its offended expression,
cracked wings and general shabbiness gave it an air of
patient defiance she could commiserate with.
Occasionally, when the mood took her and there was no
one around to overhear, she stopped to talk to the angel;
and sometimes she fancied it answered her with the sort
of sensible, unbiased advice she would expect from an

angel carved out of wood that was a hundred or two hundred years old.

This evening the angel looked pale in the last of the evening light. It looked as tired as she felt.

'Goodnight, Angel,' she whispered and smiled as she turned the corner into Angel Street.

Then she saw the street's only tree and her heart stumbled.

It looked ragged. Yesterday it had been decked out with golden leaves. Now it was in tatters, a few clusters of limp leaves clinging on to the last days of autumn.

It was only a little tree, a scraggy little lime planted where there was no paving slab, but for her and Rose it was the most important tree in the world.

She stared at it. She had watched it calendar the seasons for five years but this was the year that mattered, the autumn that she and Rose had waited for. And now the tree they loved was telling her the autumn was almost finished, and perhaps their hopes were finished, too.

Her energy drained down through her legs until her feet felt heavy. She limped to the tree and touched it tenderly as if it were an old friend in need of forgiving.

Then she turned through her front gate, took the three paces to the front door and remembered to renew her smile.

She had hardly stepped into Number Fourteen when the twins, Helen and Jamie, bundled along the narrow passage and tugged her skirts.

'Aunty Lizzie!' Helen was the first to speak. 'Come and see our puppy! Mama found it in a sack and she said we could keep it. Come on!'

She put down the basket and the children pulled her through the small scullery and out into the back garden. The dog was a small brown mongrel, not a puppy but not much larger. It cowered in a wooden box, looking up at her.

It had frightened eyes and its ribs showed through its

mangy coat. She understood immediately why Rose had taken it in.

Jamie lifted the dog up and cradled it like a baby, and she suddenly thought that the boy seemed much older than his few years.

'I had to bathe him.' Jamie fondled the animal, and added quietly, 'He was lousy.'

'So am I, children,' she remembered, 'so keep away from me and ask your mother if there's any hot water left.'

'There is.' Rose appeared by the back door. 'And the shed's ready for you.'

The shed was a wooden shelter which leaned against the back wall and housed a tin bath and disinfectant for her to delouse herself whenever she came home after a day spent on mission visits.

'Get undressed and I'll bring out the water and some clean clothes.' Rose sounded tired.

'Are you all right?'

Rose shrugged and smiled. 'Yes. Don't worry. Just tired like you. I'll feel better soon.'

'The dog? Do you think it's a good idea?'

'It won't eat much, Lizzie,' Rose answered defensively, reached down to the bundle Jamie was cuddling and tickled the dog's ear. 'Just scraps.'

'I wasn't thinking of that,' smiling because Rose's practical reply was so predictable. 'I'm more concerned about your asthma.'

'He'll have to stay outside. Mama's told us that,' Helen said quickly.

'Yes, Aunty Lizzie, and I'm going to build Kitchener a proper kennel to sleep in,' Jamie added.

'Kitchener? After the kitchen range?' she teased.

'No, Aunty Lizzie, of course not. After General Kitchener,' Jamie answered solemnly.

She laughed, and Rose joined her in the joke. It was difficult to imagine anything less like General Kitchener than this timid little stray.

The laughter, the bath and the promising smell of supper cooking revived her, and the ragged little lime tree was forgotten.

They ate in the warm kitchen and after they had finished and the supper things had been washed and put away she sat around the kitchen table with Rose and the children. She spread out some papers and pulled the oil lamp close so she could see to write her reports on the day's visits. Rose sat opposite. Jamie and Helen snuggled close against her.

'So you want a story? Which one?' Rose asked, and Elizabeth watched her lean back and put her arms around the children. 'Only one tonight because I'm feeling tired.'

'One about a dog,' Jamie demanded, but Rose told him she did not know any stories about dogs.

'The Princess and the Pauper.' Helen asked for her favourite. 'You haven't told us that one for ages.'

'Not again,' Jamie argued, 'it's a girl's story.'

'But it's a nice story. Please, Mama?' Helen wheedled.

'Oh, all right,' Jamie conceded immediately and folded his arms on the table ready to listen.

She smiled as she listened to the children. Helen usually asked for the same story and Jamie always protested, but never enough to stop the story being told. She thought he probably liked it as much as his sister but something in his make-up stopped him from admitting it. A sign that he was growing up, thinking of himself as the man of the house? Already?

She looked away and concentrated on her work as Rose told the familiar story.

'No, Mama, you've gone wrong!' Helen said quietly. 'That's the second time since you started.'

'Of course, I'm sorry.' Elizabeth heard Rose retell the scene she must have told a thousand times before.

She moved the lamp slightly, not enough to attract attention but enough to light up Rose's face. It looked pale, almost waxen, and a dull, washed-out greyness had replaced the green sparkle in her eyes. Once the children had gone to bed she would try to persuade her to see the doctor; but she knew Rose would insist that she was not ill, just tired, still recovering from influenza which had been made worse by the asthma attacks that seemed to be returning more frequently now.

Then her sight blurred as her own tiredness crept back, and she rubbed her eyes and continued with her notes before she forgot what she had to report.

'You've gone wrong again, Mama,' she heard Helen interrupt once more, and listened as the child finished the story they all knew so well. 'The pauper tells the princess about the magic tree and a spell he knows which can turn its leaves into real gold. He can only work his magic in the autumn so he has to go away until then, but he promises the princess that when he comes back he will be rich enough to marry her. And he does come back, in the autumn and just in time to stop her dying from a broken heart. Then they are married in cloaks made from the golden leaves and they live happily ever after.'

She looked up and saw tears form in Rose's eyes, flow over her pale eyelashes, and wash down her cheeks, and as Helen asked her not to cry she heard Rose whisper, 'But the autumn's almost over, darling, and there's hardly any leaves left on our little tree.'

She saw Helen frown and saw Rose's arms fall away from the children's shoulders, but she was not quick enough to catch her as she slumped forwards. Rose groaned, slid off her chair and crumpled on the floor.

'Mama!' she heard Helen scream. 'It doesn't matter. Really!'

'Helen, it's all right.' Elizabeth lifted the girl away from her mother. 'Jamie! Go next door and get Uncle Jack. Quickly!'

She pulled Rose clear of the table and chair and laid her flat on the floor. Rose was breathing erratically, and too lightly. This was not just another asthma attack; she was thin, bony, and her skin seemed loose.

Moments later Jack Cutler appeared and instantly decided they needed help. 'I'd better fetch the doctor, Lizzie.'

'Help me to get her on to a chair, first.' She turned a dining chair around and they sat Rose on it the wrong way around, with her arms hanging over the chair back. 'It'll help her to breathe.'

'Is it Kitchener's fault, Aunty Lizzie?' Jamie cried.

'No, Jamie. Kitchener couldn't have caused this.' She tried to sound calm. 'Go on, Jack. I can manage.'

She rubbed Rose's back and wrapped her free arm around both the children.

'Don't worry. Your mama will be all right. Both of you go up to your bedrooms. It'll be all right in the morning.' She squeezed the children comfortingly. 'Go on now. Be good.'

They backed away, holding hands, turned and ran up the stairs.

It was half an hour before Jack returned with the doctor. Rose had been sick. Half conscious, she was breathing fast.

The doctor was in evening dress. He felt Rose's pulse and put his cheek against her forehead.

'Your sister's burning up and her pulse is very weak. I'd better get her to hospital.' He looked worried. 'How long has she been ill, Miss Forrester?'

She was frightened and confused, and gabbled her answer. 'She had the flu a couple of weeks back. And a bad asthma attack. She's been tired and out of sorts since. I didn't realise she was this ill, Doctor.'

'She's very weak. All the symptoms of consumption. I don't know how she stayed on her feet.'

'Willpower, probably, Doctor. Rose has a lot of willpower.' She heard her own voice tremble. 'Consumption?'

'I think so. Has she lost much weight?'

'Yes, but I hadn't noticed until tonight.' She touched Rose's face. 'How can we get her to hospital?'

'I was on my way to the theatre. My cab's outside.' The doctor picked up his bag. 'Can you carry her out for me, Mr Cutler?'

Jack lifted Rose and started toward the door, the doctor leading him.

'We'll let you know, Miss Forrester,' the doctor said quietly.

'I'll come with you, Doctor. Jack, can you or your Ada stay with the children?'

'I'm afraid there's not enough room in the cab, Miss Forrester, my wife's still outside,' the doctor said calmly. 'Anyway, I think it's best if you stay with the children, they'll need comforting. We'll send for you if we need you. Now, Mr Cutler, let's go.'

They moved along the passageway and the children suddenly appeared on the stairs.

'Mama!' Helen rushed forward to grab her mother's trailing hand. 'I'm sorry, Mama. Please don't go!'

Jack quickly lifted Rose out of Helen's reach. 'Lizzie?'

She caught hold of the girl and held her against her skirts but Jamie almost edged past her and in stopping him she pushed him over.

'Mama!' he screamed. 'Mama!'

Rose lifted her head and stared. 'Lizzie, tell Edward where I am. Tell him where to find me.' She slumped back unconscious as Jack carried her out through the front door and placed her in the cab.

As Jack moved away she revived enough to call out again, a plaintive, thin, urgent plea: 'Don't forget, Lizzie!'

'I'll tell him.' The children were crying and edging towards the front door. 'Back to bed, both of you. Your mama will be all right. But she's very tired and has to go to a special place to sleep. You'll see her soon, and I'll be up in a minute.'

She stepped outside and pulled the door almost shut behind her, hoping the children could not hear. 'How ill is she, Doctor?'

'She's ill, Miss Forrester, and that's all I can say.'

'But do you think she'll recover?'

'She's very weak, Miss Forrester, and if it is consumption, well . . .'

'I see,' she said, and as the cab drove away she wondered how she could have been so preoccupied that she had not noticed how ill Rose was; especially as it was not the first time she had not seen what was right under her nose, and realised her own exhaustion was to blame.

She agreed to let the children sleep with her; she needed their comfort as much as they wanted hers. She watched as, unprompted, they knelt down together and prayed for their mother. Helen began to sob and Jamie immediately wrapped a protective arm around her and begged her not to cry. Even when they had climbed into the bed Jamie still held her until her sobbing eased into a miserable whine and finally subsided to a snuffle.

Elizabeth lay beside the children, feeling ill and desperately tired but unable to sleep, her mind erratically picturing what had happened and imagining what might happen in the next days, weeks, even years.

The curtains flapped in a sudden wind and rain pelted against the part-open window. She pulled back the bedcover and sat up but before she could move towards the window Jamie stirred.

'Aunty Lizzie, who's Edward?' he asked suddenly.

'Edward?'

'Mama said to tell him where she was. You haven't forgotten, have you?' he reminded her unnecessarily. 'Is he our father, Aunty Lizzie?'

'Edward's my brother,' she answered without thinking.

'Is he coming here?' Jamie asked after a moment's thought.

'He may.'

'When?' Jamie persisted.

'You do ask a lot of questions,' she said evasively because she did not know if he would come. 'Now, I think you should both go to sleep.'

Helen stirred and sat up, and showed that she had been listening. 'Why hasn't he been here before?'

'He couldn't come to see us before, Helen, or I suppose he would have done. He had to live a long way away.' She kissed them both and settled them into the bed. 'Now go to sleep.'

They seemed ready to sleep, but then Jamie asked yet another question. 'Is our father dead, Aunty Lizzie? I suppose he is, otherwise he'd be here living with us, wouldn't he?'

She squirmed as she heard the question Rose had always avoided answering.

Helen sat up again, thought for a moment, then said suddenly. 'He's not dead, Jamie. We don't live with him because he doesn't like us. And he hurt Mama, didn't he, Aunty Lizzie?'

It was a shocking statement, impossible to answer, something Helen should not have known about.

'Is that true, Aunty Lizzie?' Jamie shrank down under the blanket as if he were trying to hide.

'Will we have to go and live with him if Mama dies?' Helen added her own fears.

'No, of course not.' She was reluctant to say their mother would not die, it was a promise she might not be able to keep.

'But is what Helen said true, Aunty Lizzie?' Jamie was crying now.

It was impossible to answer. Helen had obviously heard something that she should not have and it would be wrong to make her out to be a liar. But the children were very frightened and worried and if she did not satisfy them they would worry all the more.

How could she explain to two small children why their mother had run away from her marriage? It would mean telling them all about Edward, Sebastian, Charlotte, John, Joshua, and Adam Marriott and all the other people who had a part in what happened; people they did not know, some of whom they could never know.

How could she tell two very young children what had happened in a way they would understand? It was a long story, and so much had happened she was not sure she understood everything herself. And she certainly did not know how to start the story. Once upon a time did not seem appropriate.

'Aunty Lizzie' – Jamie reached out and squeezed her hand – 'is it true?'

'All right. I'll tell you everything.' She tucked both children back under the covers. 'But not tonight because it'll take a long time and it's already late. And I'm very tired.'

She yawned, a theatrical yawn to convince them she really was too tired. 'But you mustn't worry about anything. There's nothing to be frightened of. I'm here, and I love you both too much ever to leave either of you.'

'Promise?' Jamie asked quietly.

'I promise, Jamie. I promise you both that I'll never leave you. Now, try to sleep, and I'll tell you all about your father tomorrow.'

'And about your brother?'

'And Edward, but now you must go to sleep.'

She sat on the edge of the bed, relieved that they did not argue any more, but knowing that tomorrow they would remember and expect answers. Answers she did not know how to give them.

The wind blew the curtains again and a cold draught made her shiver. She padded across to the open window and leaned against the sash for a moment, too weary to lift it shut. The fresh air revived her and she stood still for several minutes, looking out into the night.

A sudden squall hammered against the front of the
house and before she could step back or close the window
pellets of hard, sooty rain blew into her face.

Soot. She could smell it, even taste it on her lips.

A distant train hooted into the night; short, echoing
blasts that went on and on and on.

It all seemed to have happened before. The rain, the
smell of soot, the whistle.

The old, always lurking fear came back. Senses ran
together; stomach and mind reeled. Pincote was never that
far away; it was always there in her head.

She slammed the sash shut. Rain rattled against the
window.

She slipped into the bed, hardly disturbing the children
who were already asleep.

'Oh, Rose, Rose,' she mouthed silently and tasted her
own tears.

She did not know how the story would end, but now, at
least, she remembered how it started.

CHAPTER 2

Pincote Colliery, early 1885

Elizabeth looked out from her mother's bedroom window, but for something to do rather than to see anything. It was early, before dawn, but even if dawn had already come the heavy sleeting rain would still have kept the valley dark.

Not that she needed light to know what the valley looked like. She had looked out of the same window almost every day for eighteen years, until she had moved out to lodgings a mile away in Pincote Market. Even then, over the past four years, she had still come home once or twice every week, always coming upstairs to look out of the window to see the same familiar view.

Roofs. The window looked down the hill over roofs. Row after row of grey slate roofs, creased ribbons of them sagging between blackened chimneys and following the line of North Hill; row after row of roofs, like steps, leading down to the valley bottom and its sprawl of colliery buildings and yards. The high walled-in pithead with its two large wheels mounted above the mine shaft, piles of coal, railway wagons waiting to be filled or towed away, shiny rails and rust-stained wooden sleepers. Beyond the railway line, the river, sluggish and black, filled with the devil's sweat, the legend said; the river's green slime and the fact there were neither fish nor weeds seemed proof for most. And beyond the river there were the Dead Lakes where the ground had subsided above old underground workings and water had filled up the hollows; stinking, stagnant water that seeped down through the earth until it drained off into the mine and on to the men who mined coal for a living. And finally, on the far side of the valley, South Ridge, still gorse-covered except where the never-stopping, endless train of cable-hung buckets swung across the valley to toss out slag on two waste spills.

The view was ugly, dirty, constricting: but the very fact that it was so ugly, so completely dirty and seemed to mark the passage of so many people's lives, made it fascinating. A mile away, from her bedroom where she lodged in the headmaster's house, she could see the clean stone school building where she taught, and beyond that the pretty back gardens between two parallel rows of three-storey villas. It was a very pleasant outlook, people commented on it, but she did not find herself drawn to her own bedroom window to stare at that view.

Perhaps she did not feel part of the world she saw from that window, whereas she still felt a part of Pincote Colliery. Miners said you had to be born into mining to understand the people, but she knew otherwise. She had not been born into it, she had been adopted, taken in unofficially by Minty and Joshua Forrester, when she was a baby. She had grown up as a miner's daughter, not been born into it, unless, of course, her parents had been miners. There was no way of knowing who they were.

A steam whistle shook her out of her reverie.

'Is that you, Lizzie?' Her mother spoke for the first time in three days. 'What are you doing here, lass?'

'You've been very ill, Ma.' She leaned over the bed and

tried not to breathe in the stench of germ-laden sweat. 'But you sound a bit better now, like.'

She tucked the blankets tight around her mother's shoulders, and noticed the mint green eyes that usually sparkled were faded and dull. 'Do you want anything, Ma?'

'Aye, lass. Some tea?'

'I'll get you some, now.'

'The men. Are they working?'

'Just leaving, Ma, whistle's just gone. I'll tell them you're feeling a bit better.'

She dropped down the steep, ladder-like stairs, into the living room, rushed through the back kitchen and into the yard.

Her father, her 'twin' brother Edward, born about the same time as her, and the slightly older real twins, Thomas and Simon, were already in the back alleyway, but they turned back into the yard as she called.

'Ma's awake, asking for tea.'

'Thank God for that.' Her father looked relieved and she thought she saw him hesitate. 'But I cannot stop now, Lizzie, we're late and I've got to get the gangs sorted. Tell her I'll get home as quick as I can, like.'

'We'll cover you, Da,' Edward said immediately, 'if you want to see Ma first. Joey can sort the men out.'

'No, lad, I'm happy for Lizzie to tell me she's all right. We've got the doctor's bills to think of now, so I cannot afford to pay fines for being late to work, like.'

'I'll pay your fine, Da.' She heard Edward's offer but knew their father would refuse it.

'Thank you, lad, but I'll pay me own way, if you don't mind. Honest day's work for an honest day's pay.'

'Honest day's work, right enough, Da,' Edward said quietly, 'but I . . .'

'You moaning again, boy? Thousands'd be glad of your job. You should be happy you're still able to earn a wage, lad, not moaning about what you get.' Her father spoke angrily, in bursts, and she noticed the way he leaned close to Edward as if he was deliberately trying to provoke a full-blown row. 'What makes you think you're so bloody special?'

Edward looked directly into his father's eyes, but he clamped his jaw shut and did not say anything more.

Elizabeth stood and watched them, her father and her favourite brother, the tension building as neither man moved nor spoke. Simon and Thomas looked helplessly towards her and she sensed she was the only one who could speak without making the situation worse.

'Tell Joey and Paul about Ma, when you see them,' she said quietly, more concerned to stop a row than to remind them they should tell her two married brothers.

'Aye, we will.' Edward nodded, and the tension passed.

She stood by the back gate and watched the men trundle off down the back alley. They were lost in moments, hidden by curtains of sleet and the early morning gloom, but before they disappeared she saw what she expected to see; Edward storming off ahead of the others, choosing to be alone to relieve his frustration with their father.

She stood still for a moment, wondering if Edward and his father antagonised each other so much because they seemed to be so different, or perhaps because deep down they were so similar. Whatever the reason, it was driving them further apart each day and she wondered why her father felt the need to bully Edward so much, and how much longer Edward would submit.

She heard the back gate bang and as she turned the wind whipped her face with sleet. She lifted her hands to shield her eyes and realised she was trembling. Family rows, any rows, even the threat of one, always churned up her stomach and her hands.

The fug of a near-sleepless night cleared as she shut the gate and crossed the yard, and she remembered that it was Edward's birthday. He was twenty-two. In a sense it was her birthday too; she did not know exactly when she had been born but she was roughly the same age as Edward and they always shared the day. This was the first time she had forgotten it.

She went indoors, dried her face and made tea.

'They've gone on to work, then?' She thought her mother sounded disappointed that no one had come up to see her.

'Aye, Ma. They were already late.'

'I heard your da shouting. What was that about?'

'Nothing. Just Da and Edward. It's over now.' She saw how her mother shrivelled back into her pillow and wished she could have avoided saying anything.

'I suppose Edward said they ought to come and see me,' her mother said astutely.

'Something like that, Ma, but Da's worried about losing money for being late on shift.'

'I can understand that, lass, but I wish he wouldn't treat Edward as if he was still a little lad. It worries me.'

'Have you told him?' Perhaps that was the answer, if Ma said it worried her.

'It's your da's way, Lizzie. He doesn't mean anything by it. He won't think of Edward as anything but a lad until he's married and given his wife a child.'

'Edward married, Ma? I can't see it, not really. He's too much of a dreamer.'

'Be better if he wasn't, lass. His da'd think more of him if his head wasn't always in a book. Or if he didn't preach politics the way he does. Nothing but trouble, them unions and the Miners' Association. We don't need them here, not in Pincote.'

'Maybe you're right, Ma, but perhaps Edward's right too, in some of the things he says. He's not the only one who reckons the association might help make things better.' She could have said more but she could see her mother was already tired and she did not want to risk starting an argument or making her feel bad again.

Weeks of near-constant rain had swollen the river and

filled the Dead Lakes to their brims. The water was seeping down into the workings and Edward had said the left face could soon be waist-deep in water and might have to be abandoned until the water level dropped. That would mean lost wages because there was not enough coal on the right face to keep all the men working.

Worse than that, Edward had overheard one of the maintenance foremen telling his gang that water was seeping into the shaft and that the whole mine might be closed until the shaft was repaired. If that happened there would be no wages at all.

Her mother sighed. 'Mining's a dangerous job, lass. A union won't change that and anyway, Pincote's no different to any other mine Mr Laybourne owns.'

She was tempted to argue that Pincote was one of the few mines Mr Laybourne owned which still had only the one shaft, but that was another thing best left unsaid. That was where she and Edward differed. She knew how to keep quiet and disguise her real feelings, whereas Edward might not always speak out but he could never hide the fact that he was not saying what was on his mind.

She helped her mother to sit up so she could drink her tea.

'How long you been here, lass, looking after us, like?' Her mother blew on the hot tea before sipping it.

'Three days, Ma, ever since you got taken real bad.'

'How about your work, then?'

'School's closed for a week. Bit of a holiday, like.'

She noticed her mother's expression change, and hoped that did not mean she was going to ask about Saul.

'And how's your young man been getting on? Has he been up here to see you?'

'No, Ma, he's not been up.' Suddenly she was not so sure she could hide the way she felt.

'Nothing wrong, is there? Between the two of you, like?'

'No, Ma.'

'You would tell me, if there was?'

'Aye, of course.' She knew she had answered too quickly, knew that this time she had given herself away.

There was a moment's pause as her mother seemed to be thinking, then, 'Well, if you don't want to discuss it, lass, then I'll not interfere. So long as you're sure, like?'

She smiled at her mother. 'Last night, Ma, we were all worried that you were at death's door. We took it in turns to sit by you, all through the night, like. Then this morning you're as chirpy as a bird and canny as a fox.'

'I'd have hoped you'd be glad enough, lass, not complaining about it,' her mother said sharply, and immediately softened her voice. 'So what's wrong, then, Lizzie? You going to tell me or leave me to think the worst, like?'

She knew she might as well tell her mother the truth she had been holding back.

'I didn't tell you before, Ma, because you were ill and I didn't know if I'd make you worse.'

'Well, carry on, lass, now you've started, like.'

'Saul's applied for a master's post at Alnwick School and he's going off today for an interview. He'll be back on Saturday.'

'Alnwick?' Her mother pursed her lips as she considered the prospect. 'Posh school, isn't it? Fee paying?'

'Aye.'

'And what's our Edward say about that? Special education for the privileged classes. Not what he preaches, is it?'

'No, Ma, nor me neither for that matter,' she admitted, and added, 'If Saul gets it we'd have to move there, of course. There's a house with the post.'

'Well, lass, you have to go where your man's work is. That's only natural, like.'

'But I wouldn't be allowed to teach. I'd just be a housewife.' She knew she had used the wrong words as soon as she said them.

'Something wrong with being a housewife?'

'You know what I mean, Ma,' she said awkwardly, 'a schoolmaster's wife in a posh school. I don't know if I'd fit in.'

'You're as good as any others, Lizzie, and better than most, I reckon.'

'Well, Ma, I don't know if I really want to fit in.'

'Ah, well, that's a different matter, lass, and you're the only one who can decide on that. Saul's sure, though, is he?'

'He'll take it, if it's offered.'

'Even if it means leaving you behind, like?' her mother asked shrewdly.

She shrugged. She did not know for certain but she was almost sure Saul would go without her.

'Well, lass, wait until you know if he's got it before you start worrying about what to do.'

That advice was easier to give than to take.

She crossed to the window and looked out. Grey dawn was washing the valley and South Ridge was just visible as an indistinct hump beyond the mist. A single buzzard circled over the colliery. Seconds later it was joined by its mate. They dipped their wings in an unconscious salute and sped across the river and the Dead Lakes, heading south.

She envied them their freedom, forgot them immediately, and turned back to ask her mother if she wanted more tea.

CHAPTER 3

South Ridge, the long, high hill with steep slopes dropping away to the north and south, marks the southern extreme of the moors and high ground that reach down from Hadrian's Wall and the Borders. It shelters a flat farmed plain from the worst of the north winds, and protects Laybourne Manor and its walled estate from the sounds and smells of the mining valley behind it.

The manor sits comfortably on the lower southern slope of the ridge, looking over a curved gravel drive and sheep-grazed parkland to the farmed land beyond. The sternness of its grey stone walls is softened by old ivy and a creeper which turns bright red in the autumn. The house is surrounded by trees, oak, elm, ash, pine, cedar; and only the rooms in the third storey and the servants' attic rooms above them have clear views of the country to the south.

Rose Laybourne sat at the writing table by her bedroom window and stared out over the lawns and the rhododendron bushes which smothered the high estate wall, over the sheep-dotted fields of the nearest farm, and over the horizon where the ground and sky merged in a watery haze.

She was dreaming.

Miss Smith, her governess and tutor, had told her to write a composition about *Hamlet*; but *Hamlet* was depressing and as a poem about spring had come into her head without any effort she had written that down instead. Miss Smith would not mind, she was sure of that. The dear old thing loved poetry, and by tomorrow she would have forgotten what work she had set anyway.

A pair of buzzards settled on a branch of a leafless oak, had a brief discussion, then launched themselves off on a swooping flight.

It must be wonderful to fly, to be free to glide and dive, to climb even higher than South Ridge and look down on its rocky crown, King's Crag, and perch there, up on the crag, and see the world spread out below.

Suddenly, in her imagination, she was in the air, a bird soaring along the top of the ridge, rising easily to rest on the rocks at the summit of the world. She looked down on the view she knew so well, remembered so well even though she had only managed the climb half a dozen times in her life; always alone, always kept secret.

She remembered it well because she saw it often, in her mind. It was part of her best dream, when she was standing on top of King's Crag in the arms of the man she would love.

In her dreams she knew the man she would fall in love with. She had no idea what he would look like, how tall he would be or even how his voice would sound; but she knew him well enough to recognise him the moment she saw him. She was certain of that.

She stopped dreaming.

What was love like, really? Outside of dreams. How did you know when you were in love?

The answer was important; especially since Hubert
Belchester had asked her to marry him, because although
she knew she liked him and enjoyed being with him, she
did not know for certain if she loved him.

Hubert was tall, pale and gracefully beautiful, and he
was wealthy and would inherit even more when his
family's estate passed to him. He was amusing, attentive,
and she was certain he loved her.

Hundreds of women would have accepted his proposal
immediately, but she had asked for time to think. And now
she would soon have to make up her mind. Her birthday
was in two months' time and she had promised to give him
her answer by then. He was not the man she dreamed
about; but did that really matter if they could be happy
together?

She had asked her parents for advice and although they
told her she must make up her own mind her father made
his own opinions clear: she would be eighteen soon and
eighteen was a very sensible age for a girl to marry.

His first wife had been eighteen when she had married
him, and Rose's mother, Charlotte, had been eighteen
when he had married her twenty years later. Rose's half
sister, Catherine, was sent away to Manchester to find a
husband when she was eighteen, but she had been too
particular and had prevaricated until she was twenty-two
years old and had to make do with a man twice her age
who had failed her in almost every way.

So, Father said, she should be sensible and think of all
the advantages of marrying into the Belchester family: the
security and the pleasures of living on their lovely estate
on the Dorset coast and in the town house in London. She
should be grateful that a man like Hubert Belchester had
asked her to marry him. Who else might she meet, living
in a small and remote town like Pincote; who else could
offer her the life Hubert could give her?

In Pincote Market? Who else indeed?

But when Father told her to be sensible and think of all

the things Hubert could give her he forgot to ask her what she could give Hubert. Even forgot to ask her if she really wanted the things Hubert could give her, or if she wanted something else entirely.

'Rose, darling,' her mother called through the bedroom door, 'Mr Hopkins has the carriage ready. He's waiting to take you into town.'

'I'm coming, Mama.' Time to stop dreaming and go into Pincote Market to try on the new dress Mrs Lumley was making for her to wear at her eighteenth birthday party ball.

Her ball, but her brother John's as well, a joint celebration of her birthday and John's safe return from America.

She wondered if John had changed as much as she had, and decided immediately that was not possible. Men did not change, not obviously. He was fully grown when he went away, twenty-one. She had been sixteen, dumpy as a flour sack and with long lank hair and a face full of freckles.

John might not even recognise her now, not since she had turned into a woman. Sometimes she hardly recognised herself, the change had happened so quickly and so recently. Within just a month, it seemed, her soft fat became firm and she changed shape. Her thin hair thickened and her freckles faded away.

It had been fun turning into a beautiful swan like her mother, suddenly realising that men would look at her in a different way.

Until her father had spoiled it by saying that now she was grown up she should think about choosing a husband, and she would not find one in a small town like Pincote Market.

The carriage breasted the saddle of land where the western end of South Ridge joined a range of lower hills then followed a road across common land blanketed with sheep and new lambs. Sheep and their wool was the reason

Pincote Market existed, and it was sheep and wool that had made it rich and confident.

The road turned and Rose saw the town sprawled across the valley below, the angled hardness of the grey stone buildings diffused by the rain. It was a small town, she thought, and perhaps her father was right to say that she would not find a suitable husband there, but what made him think she was ready to look for a husband?

If he had thought to ask her she would have told him she wanted another two years to herself, two years to spend at her mother's old school in France, two years to learn so many of the things she wanted to know and to spend with girls of her own age.

Two years to see just some of the exciting places her mother had seen during her childhood. Two years to become acquainted with people who had not spent their entire lives in Pincote Market and on the family estate. Two years to learn to grow up independently, away from the family and the servants and parochial Pincote Market where everyone treated her as though she were a princess.

After all, her brother John had been away at Alnwick School for six years, then spent two years in Europe and then another two in America; ten years altogether. And she wanted just two.

She shuddered, and suddenly realised how lucky John was to have been born a man. He had been allowed to travel alone for four years and even though he would be expected to breed a son to carry the Laybourne name on to the next generation he would not be pressured into marrying before he felt he was ready.

Quite the reverse; he had become engaged to Lillian McDougall before he left for America but because he was a man no one expected him to rush into marriage the moment he returned home, although they all assumed that Lillian, as a woman, would devotedly wait first for him to return and then patiently wait until he felt he was ready to marry her.

It was unfair that men and women should be treated so differently; should not women have some rights, too?

She loved John dearly, and understood why he preferred to wait before settling down, but surely she should be allowed to spend a little time deciding what she wanted to do with her life? Surely that was not too much to ask? She might even decide that Hubert really was the man she wanted to marry after all, but at least she would have made the decision herself, and in her own time.

She gathered up her long copper curls in both hands and twirled before the full-length mirrors.

'The dress is beautiful, Mrs Lumley. Quite beautiful.' Rose twisted in the opposite direction and saw how the deep green satin swayed from her hips and lifted just enough to show her slim ankles.

She stood still and let her hair tumble over her shoulders, then ran her hands over the fine material, felt how it was moulded under her round breasts and hugged her slim waist before it spread out softly over the layers of petticoats that emphasised her hips. Looking at herself in the mirror she was proud of the way her body had fattened where it should have fattened, and slimmed where it should have slimmed. Proud of the way her lips had filled out and her face had thinned to emphasise her cheekbones and her large green eyes, the way her hair had grown thick and long and its waves had taken on the colour and lustre of the copper pans Cook used in the kitchen.

'The gown is beautiful, quite beautiful.'

On impulse she suddenly threw her arms around Mrs Lumley and kissed her cheek.

'Thank you so much. It's perfect.'

Mrs Lumley seemed embarrassed by the impulsive kiss. 'It's not quite finished yet, but it's a pleasure to make a dress for a beautiful young lady like yourself, Miss Laybourne.'

She did not respond to the compliment, but quickly

wiped away small tears of joy and stood and looked at
herself for a few moments longer, modestly amazed that
she looked as beautiful as she did, even with her hair loose
and without wearing the necklace and earrings her parents
had promised to buy to match the colour of the dress.

'Thank you, Mrs Lumley. The dress is very beautiful
and I'm sure my mother will approve.' She smiled and ran
her fingers along a seam. 'The stitching is so fine that it
hardly shows.'

'That's Annie's work, Miss Laybourne. Annie Darling.'
Mrs Lumley beckoned to a thin, grey-haired woman with
old eyes set deep in a young face.

'Thank you, Mrs Darling.' Rose bowed towards the
woman who was busy sewing another dress. 'Your work's
incredibly fine.'

'Thank you, miss.' Mrs Darling looked up from her
work and smiled, and seemed unduly grateful for the
recognition she was given.

She agreed when she would return for another fitting
and was about to leave when a high, wailing sound echoed
from the buildings outside. The sound stopped suddenly,
then started again. Stopped and started once more.

'What's that noise?' she asked as she reached for her
bonnet.

'It's the colliery whistle, Miss Laybourne,' Mrs Lumley
answered quietly. 'There must have been an accident.'

She saw Annie Darling suddenly suck a finger she had
pricked with her needle, and noticed how the woman's
hands were trembling.

'Are you feeling unwell, Mrs Darling?' She touched the
woman's shoulder.

'The whistle startled me, miss.' Annie Darling looked at
her with twitching, terrified eyes.

'It is an awful sound.' She listened to the whistle. 'Quite
terrifying.'

'Especially as my son's underground.' Annie Darling
looked away towards the window.

Mrs Lumley placed a hand on the woman's other shoulder. 'Do you want to go to the colliery?'

'May I?'

'Of course. You must.' Mrs Lumley was already reaching for Annie Darling's coat.

'I'll take you,' Rose insisted. 'Our carriage is outside. It'll be quicker than you walking.'

'I can't put you to that trouble, miss.'

'It isn't any trouble. Come along.'

Hopkins opened the carriage door and pulled down the step, 'The manor, Miss Rose?'

'No, Mr Hopkins. There's been an accident at the colliery. I'd like to take Mrs Darling there. Her son's working underground.'

'I'm sorry, miss, but I was told to take you directly home.' Hopkins looked worried.

'I know, Mr Hopkins,' she said firmly, and helped Annie Darling into the carriage, 'but I'm sure my mother will understand.'

She listened to the familiar sound of the carriage creaking and rumbling, listened to the horses' hooves thudding on the roadway, and watched Annie Darling pulling nervously at her fingers or plucking at her hair and clothes.

She could see Mrs Darling was almost overcome with worry and she wanted to help her but she did not know how; and suddenly it occurred to her that she had always been so protected from real life that never before had she been left alone with a virtual stranger.

'Mrs Darling?' She thought she ought to say something but when the other woman's eyes flicked towards her she did not know what to say.

'Yes, Miss Laybourne?'

'I . . . I'm very sorry.'

'What for?' Mrs Darling looked puzzled.

'I think I ought to know how to help you, but I don't.' It seemed better to admit the truth than allow Mrs Darling to think she did not care about her anguish.

'You are helping, Miss Laybourne. You're here.'

'But that doesn't seem to be enough. Not to me.'

'It is, really. There's not much anyone can do, Miss Laybourne, but it's better to be with someone than worrying alone.' Mrs Darling shrugged, then apparently felt she should explain. 'That's why the women all go to the pithead whenever there's an accident. We can't do anything to help our men, but just being together helps us, like.'

'It must be awful.' She thought how inadequate she sounded, how inadequate the words were, and knew she would never understand how awful it really was.

'Aye. You never get used to it, waiting, like. It drains everything out of you, the fear and the worry.'

'I don't know how you manage to live with it. You must be scared every time your men go to work.' She shuddered at the thought.

'No, miss. You do get used to that. Other things on your mind most days. Ordinary things. It's just when . . .'

She saw the tears come into Annie Darling's eyes and some inbred instinct made her reach out to hold the woman's hands. Mrs Darling looked surprised, unsure, and began to pull away but gentle pressure on her fingers and a caring smile seemed to reassure her.

'You're very kind, Miss Laybourne,' she said and released just one hand to wipe away her tears.

'No, Mrs Darling, not really.' It was an embarrassing moment and she wondered what else she could say. 'How old is your son?'

'Billy's only thirteen, but he's a big lad, and strong, so they let him work up at the face.'

'Thirteen?' She could not hide her shock; she knew children worked in the colliery but she had not thought much about it before; had never thought about them actually going underground to help cut the coal.

'Oh, I don't like him doing it, miss, but we need the

money and the men he works with don't mind.' Mrs
Darling sounded so defensive that she wished she had
thought before speaking out.

'Please, Mrs Darling, I was not criticising you. I can see
you'd prefer he didn't have to work in the mine, and I'm
sure he works hard and he's a credit to you.'

'Aye, miss. I'm very proud of him. Proper little man, he
is.' Annie Darling seemed to relax a little, and having
relaxed she talked freely for several moments. 'He goes
under with a couple of lads from our street and they treat
him like he's their younger brother. William Wright, he's
one of our next-door neighbour's sons, and Edward
Forrester who lives two doors away. Elizabeth Forrester,
Edward's sister, was Billy's teacher when he was at the
school and now Edward's teaching him how to be a miner.
The lads know we need the money now my husband can't
work, and I know they'll take care of Billy for me. As much
as they can, anyway.'

'I'm sure they will, Mrs Darling.' She almost told the
poor woman not to worry, but stopped herself and instead
asked about Billy's father.

'He was crushed by a rock fall, miss. Cracked his head
and his back. Should've died, but he didn't, though I
sometimes think he'd be better off dead, poor man. He
can't move and he never speaks. Just sits on his potty chair
all day, staring out of the window. Needs feeding and
washing like a baby. But his mind's all right, miss. You can
see it through his eyes. That makes it worse, really,
knowing he knows what he's like.'

'That is awful!' That word again, not enough to express
how she felt.

'Aye, miss. There's a lot of awful things happen down
there.'

The carriage turned into Murdock Street, the street
which separated the terraces of cottages that made up the
village called Pincote Colliery from the colliery itself.

Rose was astonished by the number of people pouring

from the side streets into Murdock Street. She had no idea so many people lived in the little village. Men, but mainly women and children were rushing along the narrow street, overflowing from the pavements into the road so the carriage was forced to move at walking pace.

She looked out at the faces of the women, and realised that for all she knew about the way these people lived she may as well have been looking at an illustration in one of her geography study books. Shame made her look away. She knew more about how people lived in far-off countries than she knew about life on the north side of South Ridge. That could not be right. The carriage turned through tall iron gates set in a high brick wall and stopped.

She opened the carriage window to see better and her stomach and heart churned. In front of her was a high structure topped by two enormous wheels. Cables ran at an angle from a nearby building, looped over the wheels then plunged down into the earth. Below the wheels but still ten feet or so above the ground was a platform which seemed to reach out from another building that had wooden steps leading up to a door on the first floor.

There were another two identical two-storey buildings either side of the windings and they extended back almost to the high wall. The windings, the buildings and the wall surrounded a large yard which was already crowded with women standing in groups. The women all turned as she opened the carriage door, then turned away as a door opened at the top of another flight of steps which led up the outside of the left-hand building. She looked up and saw Mr Speake, the mine manager, standing on the landing at the top of the steps.

'Miss Laybourne,' Mr Speake called out. 'I'll come down to you.'

She waited as he came down the steps and waddled across the yard, his collar turned up against the rain and his short, round body contrasting with the thin bodies of the waiting women who followed him to the carriage.

'What's happened, Mr Speake?' one of the women called, but he ignored her and hauled himself into the carriage.

The women pressed tight against the carriage and Hopkins, the driver, had to settle the horses which suddenly became fractious.

'Miss Laybourne.' Mr Speake doffed his round hat and glanced at Mrs Darling but did not acknowledge her.

His actions irritated Rose and she heard an unusual sharpness in her voice as she asked, 'What has happened, Mr Speake?'

'There's been an accident.'

'A serious accident?'

'Aye. A big gas explosion up near the main face. It's brought down a lot of rock and there's flooding.'

She did not know what to say. He said it was serious, and it certainly sounded as though it was, but because she knew nothing about the mine she could not judge the circumstances for herself.

Annie Darling leaned forward. 'Are there many men hurt, Mr Speake?'

'A few score, we reckon, but we don't know yet.'

The carriage door was open and the nearest women, those who could hear what was being said, passed the news back to the others.

'What are you doing to get them out?' a woman asked brusquely.

'Everything we can,' Speake answered irritably.

'But what exactly?' the woman demanded.

'I told you. Everything we can. But we cannot get to the face because the main road's flooded.'

'So our men are trapped down there? Maybe drowning?' another woman said sharply.

'Drowning? Oh, God. Billy!' Annie Darling fell forward. Rose grabbed her and held her back against the seat.

'Mr Speake, Mrs Darling's fainted. Help me get her up to your office, please.'

As she struggled to keep the woman off the floor a strange thrill excited her.

She moved aside to allow Mr Speake and another man to lift the unconscious woman from the carriage, then asked Mr Hopkins to drive back to the manor and tell her parents what had happened.

'Shouldn't you come back with me, Miss Rose?'

'No, Mr Hopkins. I'll stay here.' She was too excited to leave, but she was careful to hide the treacherous feeling.

'Are you certain, Miss Rose?' Hopkins looked worried. 'Your father might not . . .'

'Simply tell him that I'm needed here. Mrs Darling will need someone to take care of her.' The excuse, an acceptable reason for staying, stemmed the rising feeling of guilt.

She wanted to stay. This was the most exciting thing that had ever happened to her, but she was disturbed about the way she felt. It was wrong to be excited, to be pleased to be present at something which would bring tragedy to so many families.

She left Hopkins to turn the carriage and hurried up the steps to where Mrs Darling had been placed in a large chair in the manager's office.

'I'll look after Mrs Darling now, Mr Speake, but can you please bring me some drinking water?' She saw the relief on the manager's face as he left on his errand, and the gratitude in Annie Darling's eyes as she recovered.

'Thank you, Miss Laybourne. For all your help.'

'Thank you for allowing me to help, and for telling me about your family,' she answered, and she meant what she said.

That was why she felt excited. She was learning things no one had ever thought she should know; and, for the first time in her life, she felt she was being useful.

Elizabeth was sitting in a small upright chair by her mother's bedroom window, the warmth of the room and the random rattling of rain on the window glass lulling her into a fitful sleep. She woke with the whistle's first blast, stepped to the window and pulled up the sash.

The rain blew against her face; she tasted soot and coal, then heard the whistle scream again.

'Ma! There's been an accident!'

'Lizzie! Oh God!' Her mother sat up, suddenly awake.

'I'll go, Ma, then come back and tell you what's happened.'

'No. I'll come with you.'

'No, Ma, don't be daft. You've been very ill and it's cold and raining hard out there. Stay here in the warm.'

'No, lass, give us me clothes. I'm coming with you.'

There was no point in arguing so she helped her mother to dress and they set off towards the pit yard, arms around each other for mutual comfort and support.

The yard was crowded but friends pointed to where Flo and Mary, Joey and Paul's wives, were waiting

'Ma, Lizzie.' Flo nodded, asked Minty if she would not be better back indoors, and explained what she had heard. 'A big gas explosion on the left face has brought down a lot of rock, collapsed the end of the main road and no one can get to any of the men who were working up there. And there's flooding.'

Flo spoke in the flat, matter-of-fact tone the women always used when they did not know how bad things were.

'Bad flooding?' Elizabeth noticed a tremor in her voice; the thought of drowning terrified her.

'They reckon it's enough to fill the bypass.' Flo shrugged.

'Is that bad?' a young woman holding a small baby asked timidly. 'We've only just moved here. My husband's first week underground.'

'Aye, lass, it is bad.' Elizabeth drew the woman into the family group and tried to explain as simply as she could. 'The bypass is a small tunnel, very small, mind. It's meant to help drain water out of the workings and to let the fans suck air in, so it's not very big but men can crawl along it if they have to. If it's the only way out, like, and with the main road collapsed it is the only way out. But if it's flooded—'

'The men can't get out, and fresh air can't get in?' the woman interrupted her. 'And a man who's trapped might drown or suffocate.'

'Aye,' Flo said.

She did not say any more. No one did.

They waited, all the women who had come to the yard. They stood, ignoring the slanting rain, facing the silent winding wheels and willing them to move, to bring up a cage with their men inside. They willed their husbands, sons, fathers and sweethearts still to be alive and not to have been blown apart by the blast, not to have been burned or crushed or choked or drowned. There were so many ways to suffer and die in the tunnels under the ground, and they imagined them all.

But until the wheels began to move they had to wait, and while they waited they did the only things they could do; hope, pray and worry. They hoped that their men were helping in the rescue, and were not amongst the trapped. They prayed their men were not already dead or hurt, and that they would come up alive. And they worried that their hopes and prayers were already wasted.

They all wished for it to be over; wished they were at home, talking, cooking tea, laughing maybe, or moaning about the children or the leaking roof. They wanted it to be Sunday so they could go to chapel and later sit at home and not think about what could happen underground.

A few prayed for their daughters or mothers and some prayed for themselves; that they would have strength to cope, whatever happened.

All the women waited because there was nothing else they could do.

It was dark by four o'clock. The women did not talk and now they tried not to think.

After her almost sleepless night Elizabeth kept sliding into a cosy nap, broken each time she felt herself falling over. Other women did the same, some holding children who were already asleep. The waiting was worrying and uncomfortable. And it was boring. The inactivity made the waiting worse, piled up the frustration of not being able to do anything to help.

In the distance Pincote Market's Town Hall clock struck five. The women stirred when a carriage arrived and Sebastian and Charlotte Laybourne rushed up the steps to the manager's office, but nothing more happened and they settled back to the waiting.

Later – it seemed much longer than an hour since it had last chimed – the distant clock struck six.

The winding wheels turned at intervals, taking down men and equipment to repair the damage and bringing up equipment which had been smashed. But few men came up, and that meant there was little news about the men trapped below.

And then the cage came up and four stretchers were carried out, along the landing stage and into the lamp room, and then down the lamp room's wooden steps into the yard. A clutch of women pushed forward as their men's names were called out.

Their men were dead.

Four new widows and ten fatherless children.

How many more?

The women waited but now they did not want to know how many more. Now they did not want to know because they had seen what could happen.

And the Town Hall clock struck the half hour. A single sound, it dominated the suddenly silent yard. Somehow it seemed to signify the mean way the men had died; each one drowned as he worked in the dark to provide food and shelter and warmth for his family.

The sense of shock spread.

The Town Hall clock struck seven. Braziers were

brought out and lit and the women moved around them, children and older women pushed up close to benefit from what warmth there was. Rain hissed against the hot coals and an unpleasant, sulphurous smell wreathed about the night air.

Mugs of tea were passed around.

'Miss Forrester.' Her eyes seemed to see the sheets of paper before she saw the man holding them.

'Aye, Mr Trenchard.' She looked into the assistant manager's face and knew what he was going to ask.

'You're a school teacher,' he said, 'so you can read.'

'No better than you, I shouldn't think.' She did not want this task.

'It'll come better from you, a woman, like,' he said awkwardly, 'especially as you know most of the . . .'

There was a moment's silence as she hesitated.

'Besides' – he spoke again – 'I need to get back underground. I can't stay up top. There are things to do, like.'

'Aye.' She took the papers and the lamp he gave her to read them by.

She scanned the list headed 'Missing' first. Her father, all her brothers and William Wright who lived next door were on the list. Her heart pounded and made her light-headed. She took a deep breath and quickly read the second sheet, the list of dead men.

'Pru.' She moved across to where Pru Wright, William's mother, and Nancy, his pretty sister, were standing. 'William's on the Missing list, but it looks as if Ned and the boys are all right. They're probably helping with the rescue.'

She saw the relief on Pru's face as she realised that her husband and three of her sons were probably safe; then she turned back to her own mother and sisters-in-law and told them the bad news.

'Only missing, that's something, isn't it?' Minty said hopefully, and Flo and Mary nodded but said nothing.

'Miss Forrester.' She felt someone tugging at her coat.

'Alice?' She looked down and saw Alice Darling, one of her pupils. 'What are you doing here?'

'Looking for me mam, miss.' Alice looked frightened. 'It's me da, miss. He's fallen off his chair and he's too heavy for me to pick him up, miss.'

'Don't worry, Alice.' She took the child's hand and passed the lists to Flo. 'I'm sorry, Flo, but can you do this while I help Alice to find her mam?'

'Aye.' Flo did not hesitate. 'I heard someone say Annie arrived with Rose Laybourne. I haven't seen her down here so maybe she's up in the manager's office.'

'I'll try there first.' She began to lead Alice away but Flo called her back.

'Lizzie? Billy Darling. He's on the Missing list.'

'Aye,' Minty said. 'He was working with Edward and William, Lizzie.'

'Of course.' She nodded, squeezed Alice's hand and led her up the steps to Mr Speake's office.

She knocked on the door and waited.

'Come in,' Mr Laybourne barked.

She opened the door and pushed Alice into the office.

'Alice. What's wrong?' Annie Darling rushed to her daughter who promptly hid in her skirts.

'Miss Forrester?' Mr Laybourne ushered her into the office. 'I'm sorry. Trenchard showed me the lists. I see that all of your family are unaccounted for.'

He was chairman of both the Higher School and of the Lower School where she taught, and she was glad he recognised her and associated her with her family; it gave her more confidence to talk to him.

'Good evening, sir, and thank you. At least they're only missing.' She felt her voice begin to break so she swallowed and told him why she had come. 'I'm sorry to bother you and Mrs Laybourne but Alice is frightened because her father has fallen and she can't lift him off the floor. She needs her mother.'

'Of course.' Mr Laybourne looked out of the window. 'Obviously you're needed at home, Mrs Darling. There's nothing you can do here so I suggest you go home and look after your family. We'll send news as soon as we have any. You'll take care of that, Miss Forrester?'

'Of course, sir.' She nodded and turned to Annie. 'I'll come and help you, if you like.'

Before Annie could answer an inner door opened and Rose Laybourne appeared, crossed the office and bent low to look at Alice.

'This must be your daughter, Mrs Darling. She looks so much like you.' She fondled the child's hair. 'Have you come looking for your mama?'

Annie Darling told her what had happened.

'I'd like to go home with you, Mrs Darling, to help you with your husband,' Rose suggested immediately.

'Thank you, Miss Laybourne, but Miss Forrester's already offered to do that,' Mrs Darling explained.

'Please, Mrs Darling. I'd like to help. To do something useful rather than simply wait here.' Rose reached for the coat she had left draped over a chair.

'I don't think that's a very sensible idea, Rose,' her mother said quietly. 'It's cold and wet and we don't want you to catch a chill and bring on a breathing attack.'

'Please, Mama.' Rose turned her big green eyes on to her mother. 'Please.'

'I don't think so, my dear,' her mother said firmly.

'Mama?' Elizabeth noticed a powerful insistence in Rose's voice.

She had often seen the Laybournes in church, but never close enough to see how similar mother and daughter looked. The likeness was striking even though Mrs Laybourne had smooth silver hair against Rose's tumble of copper-coloured waves, and calm grey eyes against Rose's vivid green ones. Now the green eyes and the grey eyes seemed to fence with each other. Rose Laybourne looked determined, but her mother seemed unwilling to submit.

'There's no need,' she intervened, and wilted as Rose turned the pleading eyes on to her.

'But I'd like to, Miss Forrester,' Rose said eagerly.

Mrs Laybourne seemed to hesitate for a moment, then she smiled. 'Oh, go on if you want to, but don't get too cold.'

'Thank you, Mama.' Rose slid into her coat. 'Are you ready, Mrs Darling, Miss Forrester?'

'Aye,' Elizabeth said and opened the door and as the wind thrashed rain into the office she saw Rose turn back as if she had changed her mind.

A moment later she realised she had misjudged her.

'Mama, there are a lot of ladies and children standing outside and the weather's awful. Don't you think we should open up the store rooms so they can wait under cover?'

'Certainly, Rose. We should have thought of that earlier. Perhaps some of the older ladies might like to come up here, where it's warmer for them?' Mrs Laybourne was already rearranging chairs. 'If they wouldn't feel too uncomfortable sitting up here with us? What do you think, Miss Forrester?'

'We can ask them, ma'am.'

'I'd rather wait here, with me friends, if you don't mind, miss.' Elizabeth noticed the way her mother hunched her shoulders and tightened her shawl as if to emphasise her words.

'Of course, Mrs Forrester, I understand.' Rose appeared to accept the refusal, then tried again. 'But I understand it could be a long wait and it seems a pity to let all that heat go to waste. Anyway, I think my mother suggested that you and some of the other ladies might like to join her because she would appreciate other women's company and the chance to talk. Isn't that right, Miss Forrester?'

'Aye,' she answered, impressed and grateful that the lie had been delivered so graciously that her mother had no choice but to accept the offer. 'Go on up, Ma. You'll catch your death if you stay out here much longer. I'm sure Pru'll go up with you.'

On impulse she turned to the young woman who had only recently moved into the village. 'You too. It won't do your baby any good at all to be out in this weather. And you can get to know Ma and a few other women.'

Then she heard Alice pleading with her mother to go home and she turned towards the gates, glad that she had something to do, something to take her mind off her father and Edward and her other brothers.

Edward bit the inside of his lip and felt pain. Pain! He was alive, not dead! His heart thumped and as the blood rushed into his head he swallowed hard until the consoling muzziness cleared and his brain began to concentrate again.

He could not see and he could not hear, but he could move his feet and hands, arms and legs, and his head. He was surprised to find himself standing up, his back against rock; then he remembered, remembered William had left him and Billy working in number three pit and remembered cursing him for leaving them short-handed.

Remembered cursing even more when William called him. 'Edward, I think I can smell gas! Come and see, man. Quick!'

Remembered leaving the cave-like pit and jumping down from the small opening into the gob tunnel that ran behind all the pits. Remembered jumping into ankle-deep water and thinking it would not take much to flood the workings. Remembered that the gob tunnel between him and the main road had been widened and ten or more pits had been combined into one big chamber so the water could flow away quicker.

Remembered thinking how unsafe that could be if there was an explosion but that false alarms had stopped work three times already that shift and the men would not treat William kindly if he were wrong . . .

Remembered the scream the gas made as it escaped into the tunnel, the flash, the way the air became solid, the feeling that the world was turning somersaults and throwing him about inside itself. Remembered pressing himself against the solid gob wall.

Remembered hearing tearing rock crashing down around him. Remembered men screaming, for hours it seemed; then they had stopped screaming and he had not heard anything more or felt anything more. He thought he was dead like the men who had stopped screaming.

But now he knew he was not dead, he was still alive; and although he must have stood against the gob for a long time, hours or maybe days, that did not matter. All that mattered was that he was safe there.

The muzziness returned. He was grateful; it dulled the fear that remembering brought back.

The darkness, solid, total blackness, paralysed him. Even when the water he was standing in chilled him so his feet and legs ached with cold the darkness still held him hard against the gob, too scared to move.

His throat was sore and he swallowed thick, foul-tasting saliva gritty with coal dust. Swallowing cleared his ears again and somewhere, not far away, he heard water falling against rocks; a constant, echoing, pouring rush.

He became aware of water pressing against his calves, cold and tight; and then he felt a slow, slopping wave lick his thighs. The water was rising. It was relentless, and he knew he was going to drown.

The water would not stop rising; but it would take hours to creep up and up. He thought about how he would feel when it reached his chest, his throat, and then his mouth and nose; the final moments of terror and panic. There was no way to avoid it, no one could get to him in time.

He wished he had been crushed like the others. At least that was a quick end.

Then he thought he heard someone cough.

'Who's there?' he asked quietly, scared that even the

sound of his voice could bring down more rocks, but even more scared that he might have been mistaken.

No answer. Just the lapping water and the darkness.

Pounding heart, pounding head. Try again, hearing desperation in his own voice. 'Is there anyone out there?'

A wave slopped in the dark tunnel.

Silence, then, 'Is that you, Edward?'

William. Unbelievably it was William's voice.

'Aye. Where are you?' His mouth asked sensibly but his brain reacted to the ridiculous situation and he wanted to laugh.

'Against the gob.'

'So am I.'

He inched towards William's voice, feet shuffling sideways, back loose against the wall, arm outstretched and fingers feeling the gob until they brushed cloth and he felt William's shoulder.

Suddenly his arms were around William and William's were around him. They embraced each other like lovers for a moment, then, embarrassed, moved apart; but the spell the dark and the water had cast was broken.

'Are you all right, William?'

'Aye. I'm not hurt, Edward, but I am shit scared, man.'

'That makes the two of us.' He was glad William admitted being scared, it somehow made him feel better. 'We've been in some scrapes together, since we were boys, like, but I reckon this is the worst, man.'

'Don't reckon we'll be home for tea,' William joked unsteadily, 'and there'll be poor old Nancy up there waiting for us. I forgot to tell you she's promised you a kiss for your birthday, man.'

'Aye.' It seemed ironic to die on his birthday. 'Reckon there's anyone else down here?'

'Don't know. James and me Uncle Gordon were in two pit.' William accounted for his own family first. 'We left Billy in three. The McKenzies were in four and the Johnson brothers were working number one with Adam.'

'Adam Marriott?'

'Aye.'

Adam! He felt a surge of hope. Adam Marriott preached in the town's chapel, or in the market place or anywhere he felt he should. Adam was different; not only because of the way he spoke, some said he was from the West Country, but because he was special, everyone felt it.

He was a giant, six feet nine at least, and a yard across the shoulders, and his uncut red hair and straggly beard made him look like an Old Testament prophet. He was the gentlest of men, calm and quiet until roused to preach, and when he preached everyone listened, not only because his voice seemed to come from a cave deep down in his chest but because he did not preach like anyone else they had ever heard. He talked about God as if he knew Him, and it was that which caused the surge of hope.

Surely God would not kill Adam? And if they could find Adam perhaps they would be saved, too, but they could not find him without light.

The need to do something, and a sense of shame at being so frightened, helped him to concentrate.

'I've still got me flint box!' He slipped his free hand into his pocket and touched the small metal container. 'Daft bugger, I should've thought about that earlier.'

'What about gas!' William sounded scared.

'Cannot smell any. I reckon the blast cleared it pretty well. Anyway, what does it matter? We're not going anywhere without a light.' He pulled out the box and flicked the little iron wheel.

The wadding in the box smouldered and he blew on it until it caught fire and gave off as much light as a small candle. He noticed that William's eyebrows and hair were frizzled; then realised he was wearing a shirt.

'Give us your shirt, man, and that stick that's poking through the gob.'

He tied the shirt around the stick to make a torch and lit it. The extra light showed that the collapsed roof had sealed the end of the gob tunnel and was damming the water which was still pouring in from somewhere back along the tunnel.

'Well, William, there's no way back to the main road.' He lifted the torch so he could see around him.

The part of the gob tunnel they were standing in was still intact even though the wooden support props had been knocked down. He moved the torch, saw the step leading to the entrance to number four pit, and decided to look for the McKenzies before searching for anyone else. There was no sound from any of the pits and he thought William might find it easier if he saw other bodies before finding his own family.

The props and sacking curtain that should have supported and covered the entrance to four pit had disappeared. He crawled through the opening and saw why. Everything was burned. The collapsed wooden props were all seared black and the pit walls were grey where the dust had ignited with the heat of the flash fire.

There was a huge hole in the wall which had separated four pit from the chamber where most of the other men had been working. He guessed the gas had exploded in the pit and blown the hole in the wall, and then ripped through the open chamber the miners had created as they pulled down the individual pit walls.

The three McKenzie brothers were sprawled on the pit floor, all face down, their hair frizzled and their trousers partly burned away. The men's bare backs were blistered and he did not turn them over or check their pulses; it was obvious they were all dead.

He turned away. Water was already seeping down the walls, staining the grey black again. The unsupported roof groaned.

'Come on, out!' He pushed William back into the gob.

'That's where it started, Edward.' William sounded furious. 'I could smell it outside, man, so I don't know why they didn't.'

'Perhaps they had colds,' he heard himself say, and added without thinking, 'they won't catch any more, poor sods.'

There was no point in blaming the McKenzies.

He grabbed a lamp which was still hanging from a spike near the entrance, and lit it, grateful that the wick caught before the rag torch burned out.

He dumped the torch into the water and led William towards number three pit where they had been working with Billy. The entrance had partly collapsed but the pit itself seemed almost untouched. And it looked empty.

'Billy?'

There was the faintest sound, a small animal noise.

'Billy?' He scrambled through the entrance and crossed the floor.

The furthest wall, the face he had been working when William called, had collapsed into the crevasse he had cut, the coal naturally broken into lumps which had stacked themselves neatly as they fell. It was something he should have been proud to see, it showed his skill as a miner, but it meant nothing.

'Billy!'

Then he saw him, curled up in a ball in a corner of the pit, his head covered by his arms, sobbing like a child. He was relieved and angry, puzzled by his own emotions, guilty. He stopped himself from telling the boy to stop bawling, stubbed out the temptation to remind the boy he was alive when others were dead, and for the first time since he had brought the boy underground, he remembered that Billy was still a child.

'Billy, thank God you're all right.' He put his arm around him and helped him to his feet. 'We've got to go, lad.'

'Where?' The tears had washed away the coal dust and left white rings around Billy's eyes. 'Up top?'

'No.' He did not know where they were going but as the roof groaned and fragments of coal scattered down he knew they had to leave the pit before it collapsed on them, and he led the way back into the gob tunnel.

He waded down the sloping tunnel towards two pit and noticed the water was well above his knees. He could hear more than he could see in the dim lamplight. The waterfall sounded only yards away and suddenly water sprayed across his bare chest and shoulders.

'Wait a moment.' He held out his hand to stop the others, then moved on a yard or two, the lamp held as far forward as he could manage. 'Oh Christ!'

A section of the roof had fallen in and a jumble of rocks formed a mound blocking the tunnel just beyond the entrance to the second pit. Water was pouring out from the hole in the roof, splashing across the natural dam and flooding the tunnel. The pit floor was three feet higher than the gob tunnel floor but the floodwater was only inches below the step and it was rising fast. In a few minutes it was going to spill over and flood the pit.

'James! Gordon!' he yelled, not really expecting an answer.

There was not one.

He glanced at William who had moved up beside him, and shrugged. 'It doesn't look too good, man.'

'Let's have a look anyway,' William said.

'Aye, but then we'd better try to get over that blockage.' He paused, wondered if he should say what was on his mind, and decided he had to. 'If we can't get out that way, William, then we've had it.'

'Even if we can get over, we still mightn't get out.' William glanced towards the fall. 'But if we have to shift the rocks it'll be easier with two more to help us, Edward.'

'That's right enough,' he agreed and waded waist-high towards the second pit.

A small boulder half blocked the pit entry. He handed the lamp to William and pulled the stone into the flood. The water was lapping level with the step into the pit.

'James! Gordon! Can you hear me?' he yelled loudly as he scrambled up on to the step.

'I can hear you.' Adam Marriott's big voice boomed over the sounds of falling water. 'Who's that, then?'

'Edward. Edward Forrester. And William Wright and Billy Darling. Where are you, Adam?' He could not tell what direction Adam's voice was coming from.

'Well, you're very welcome, Edward. We're behind the fall,' Adam yelled back. 'We didn't expect to be rescued just yet, but never mind, we'll not turn you away.'

'Sorry Adam, we're trapped too,' he yelled back. 'Tunnel's come down behind us so there's no way back to the main road. And it's flooding.'

'Well, that's not a lot of use, is it, my friend?' Adam boomed again. 'Can you get to us?'

'Maybe. We're going to try anyway. Who's with you, Adam?'

'A very small congregation: William's brother James, Peter and Luke Johnson, and Charly Walker. We're all well apart from James whose arm's snapped.'

'That all? What about Gordon?'

'Haven't seen him, I'm afraid,' the answer came back. 'The rocks haven't closed the tunnel completely and you may all be small enough to squeeze over but it's a narrow gap and I don't trust what's left of the gob roof. It's very loose and I think that if we try to wedge in props we'll probably bring more rocks down.'

'Does James know where Gordon was?'

'James was in the gob when it blew and he was knocked out for a few minutes. Reckon Gordon's still in the pit but we can't get to him because we're all too big to get over the roof fall.'

'All right,' he called back, 'we'll look for Gordon, then we'll decide what to do. But first we'll send young Billy through to you.'

Billy looked at the mass of fallen rock and pulled away from it.

'Come on, Billy,' William said soothingly. 'You'll be safer on the other side. Think of your ma and sisters.'

Billy stood still, petrified. The roof groaned and stones fell on to the mound of rock.

'Edward?' Billy's voice sounded thin.

'Come on, man, follow me up,' Edward climbed on to the rock fall, grabbed Billy's hand and pulled and pushed him through the falling water into the narrow gap under the broken roof. 'Go on, man. Wriggle. Adam's waiting for you over there.'

The boy kept moving, slowly and whimpering all the time, but he kept crawling forwards.

'We've got him,' Adam called out, and joked, 'and I promise that we'll wait for you.'

Then the roof groaned and a black crack ran towards the hole above the fallen rock. Water seeped through. The roof settled. A loose prop toppled, slid into the flood and suddenly a huge chunk of roof smacked down on the floodwater. A vicious wave raced up the tunnel. The waterfall turned into a torrent.

'Come on.' Edward grabbed William and hauled him into the pit.

The floor was awash now. Water sloshed against walls and fallen coal, its sound echoing off the ceiling somewhere above the lamp glow.

'Gordon!'

'Uncle!'

Nothing.

The pit was long, and high because the seam was thick at this end, much higher than the low entry suggested. The lamp lit no more than three feet.

'Gordon! Gordon!' Urgent because the water was already rising.

'Here.' A whisper in the darkness.

'Where?'

Nothing but slopping water. And a creaking roof.

He took the lamp from William and prowled around the pit, stumbling over debris in the black water. Then he saw two eyes glinting in the dark, reflecting the dim lamplight.

'William, over here.' Edward stood the lamp on a pile of coal and knelt down.

Gordon was sitting against a side wall, legs trapped under a long slab of coal, half-strangled sounds coming from his open mouth, his hands fluttering against the flood.

'Try to shift it off him.' Unnecessary words; William was already heaving at the slab, but it would not move.

The pit roof creaked and a few rocks fell somewhere near the entry. A fallen prop floated into the lamplight.

He grabbed the length of wood and levered at the slab. 'It's lifting.'

The prop snapped. Gordon jerked and screamed.

More rocks fell, splashing into the water. The roof creaked again.

'Quick, William, before the bloody roof . . .' Edward ducked instinctively as he heard the roof give way.

It cracked and rumbled like thunder as a huge section of rock tore away and thudded down on to the pit floor. The pit shuddered and filled with dust and spray. Momentary silence, then the roar of even more water pouring directly into the pit through the broken roof.

The devil's sweat. The pit was going to flood. He knew, and he hesitated, until he saw Gordon's arms thresh against the water.

'Let's try . . .' A wave smacked across his legs, pushed him down on his knees and slapped across Gordon's face.

He yanked at the slab. It moved a fraction, enough for him to pull Gordon's head and shoulders above the rising water but not enough to free him.

'For Christ's sake, William, pull!' he screamed.

They pulled together and the rock lifted some more.

'I can't hold it, Edward! It's slipping.'

He felt pain as the rock slipped and trapped his hands. 'William, I'm stuck.'

He tried to force the rock away but it had settled and would not move. He flinched as more of the roof fell in, and as he glanced back towards the pit entrance he guessed that it was almost shut off by boulders.

More water gushed out of the collapsing roof. He felt it rise up his back and he saw it cover Gordon's face, only inches from his own. Air bubbles streamed out of Gordon's mouth and as the water flooded over Gordon's head strands of his hair rose and moved like river weed waving in a current. Gordon's eyes were still open, staring at him through the water. He stared back, his hands trapped, unable to help Gordon or himself.

The water erupted as Gordon's arms thrust upwards, clawing at the air he needed to breathe.

The lamp hissed as the rising water put it out. The darkness closed in again.

He tried to free his fingers but they were stuck fast. Then he felt Gordon's fingers in his hair, pulling his head lower. Panic as he felt the water running over his shoulders and creeping into his open mouth.

'Pull! Pull!' he spluttered at William.

Suddenly the water was in his ears and eyes and nose and running down his throat. He was going to drown with Gordon!

The shock gave him strength. He pulled hard. The rock moved. His hands slipped free, but Gordon's fingers still pulled him down. He grabbed a deep breath and reached under the water again, found Gordon's shoulders and tried to lift the man above the flood.

He could not get a firm grip. His hands slipped until they rested either side of Gordon's head. He reached down again and his own face went below the surface, but Gordon was still stuck.

He wrenched his head free from Gordon's clutches and stood up to gulp more air, plunged down again, head under water, water in his nostrils. His hands ran across Gordon's face. His fingers slid into the man's open mouth and felt his teeth and loose tongue.

He stood up again.

'William, your uncle's had it. Get out!'

Suddenly he could not think of anything other than escaping from the pit and getting back into the gob tunnel. If they could climb over the fallen rocks they might get above the flood. Might be able to get to the other men.

He had seen Gordon drown, seen the panic and terror he feared more than death itself.

He stumbled through the darkness and collided with William.

'Edward! Follow me. Hang on.'

He felt William grab his hand and he let himself be led through the darkness, felt the water rise up to his chest. Then he stumbled. The water closed over his head. He surfaced but William had gone.

'William!'

'This way. I've found the entry.'

He worked towards his friend's voice but the splashing water and echoing sounds confused him.

'This way, man. I'm out of the water,' he heard William call again.

He reached out and touched solid rock. Ran his hand as far as he could in both directions but he could not find the opening. The water was up to his neck and he could not find the way out. A crash and a wave as more rocks fell.

He worked along the wall, both hands feeling the rock, but he could not find the opening. Perhaps the fall had blocked it, shut him in. The water was up to his chin and still gushing into the pit. He had the awful thought that it might already have risen above the pit entrance. He would never find his way out. Then he stumbled and the water closed over his head.

He surfaced. Did not know where he was. The dark and the water terrified him.

He panicked and thrashed his arms.

He felt William's hand grab him and he reached up to get a firm grip on his friend's arm.

'Steady, Edward! I've got you, man! Don't struggle or you'll pull me in.'

He fell back into the water as William's grip slipped; surfaced again and thrashed about in the black flood.

'William!'

'I'm here, man. I've got you.' Their hands locked. 'But don't panic. Don't pull me, man. Edward!'

He felt William splash into the water beside him and he heard a flat crack like two rocks hitting each other. William did not try to climb back out of the water, did not speak, did not do anything.

He turned and William's head bumped against his. He grabbed his friend instinctively and held him tight; struggled to get them both out of the water. His shin cracked against a large rock. He stepped up on to it, dragging William with him. Then another rock, and another. His head knocked against something hard and he stumbled into an open space. The pit entrance? He struggled forward, blind in the darkness.

Suddenly he was under falling water and thought he could hear men shouting. He took a deep breath and plunged through the deluge, crawled blindly up and across the scattered rocks until he was clear of the waterfall. He stumbled higher, squirmed under the jagged roof, dragging William behind him. Ducked instinctively as he heard the roof groan and crack above him.

Something hard banged against his head and pink lights seemed to dance before his eyes. He heard another section of the roof collapse, but it was behind him and he wriggled on, stubbing his free hand against rocks and debris, ignoring the pain in his head. Suddenly the pink lights gave way to the hazy yellow of oil lamps. He stopped and blinked the grit-filled water out of his eyes.

Hands reached out and lifted William away, then someone grabbed him and hauled him on to his feet and he realised he was in the end of the gob tunnel on the far side of the rock fall.

'Edward?' Adam Marriott's voice. 'Well done, boy. Risking your neck like that.'

'We thought you'd had it.' Luke Johnson helped him to reach a pile of coal, and made him sit down. 'We were trying to get to you when the roof fell in. Crushed Charly. Didn't stand a chance. Then we saw the fall had dammed the bloody tunnel and reckoned you'd be drowned in the pit even if the roof hadn't already come down on you.'

'I couldn't get Gordon out,' he said simply, unable to explain any more.

'You tried, man. Cannot ask any man to do more than that,' Luke said reverently, then turned as his brother, Peter, spoke.

'William's pretty bad. Side of his head's bashed in,' Peter said bluntly. 'May have risked your neck for nothing, trying to save him, Edward.'

He wanted to tell them that if he had not panicked William might not have been hurt; but as he was about to speak William's younger brother, James, came out from the pit entry and stepped into the gob. He stopped as he saw his brother laid out on the pit floor. 'Is he dead?'

'No,' Luke Johnson said. 'Would've drowned if Edward hadn't got him out though. Bloody hero. Don't know if I could've done it.'

'Thanks, Edward, for trying, like.' James knelt down beside William.

The praise was embarrassing. He was not a hero and he did not want to be called one. William was the hero. He was a coward who had panicked and sooner or later he was going to have to explain what had really happened, but he was too tired to do that now.

There was silence for a few minutes, then he heard someone ask, 'Well, what do you reckon we should do now?'

No one replied and as he looked up he realised that they were all waiting for him to answer. Even the older and more experienced men were looking to him as their leader.

'No one knows we're here and even if they do try to get through it'll take a week or more to reach us. We'd be drowned by then.' He pointed towards the pile of rocks he had dragged William over. 'That lot's holding back the flood, for the moment anyway, but if the water keeps pouring in the level's sure to rise enough for it to flood over the fall. We've only got one chance, and we can't afford to waste it by waiting here and hoping someone'll come for us, because they won't. We've got to try and get through the bypass and hope that we can find one of the old gobs that's still solid enough to lead us back to the main road.'

'But the bypass might be flooded too,' James said nervously, and another voice agreed.

'And it might not be,' he insisted, 'and anyway, if we don't try we'll starve, suffocate or drown. And I've got to get William to a doctor, and Billy back to his ma.'

He rested for a while. Now he was over the rock barrier he was grateful for it. The random way the rocks had fallen had dammed the flood, and might just give him a chance to escape from the devil's sweat that was drowning the world he thought had him trapped. Thank God the rocks had fallen as they had.

Thank God? It was an expression, not a prayer, but he looked across to Adam and wondered if Adam had offered a prayer which had anything to do with it. Then he thought about all the men who had not escaped, and the women who did not yet know their men were dead, and wondered why any God would allow that to happen.

Perhaps God's power did not count underground; perhaps this really was the devil's world.

Suddenly, in that moment, he knew he had to leave Pincote. There was nothing for him here, only mining, and he had finished with that.

If he got out alive.

Rose coughed and felt sick.

The smell stuck in her throat and closed her nostrils

and she had to turn back into the street to avoid embarrassing herself and Mrs Darling; but worse than the smell was the look in Mr Darling's eyes as he stared up at her, uncomprehending but hostile.

She took several deep breaths and steadied herself, turned back through the front door, stood on the threshold and tried to absorb what she saw.

Poverty. She had heard about it but had never seen it. It was offensive. Her father's horses lived in better conditions. She had seen farm pigs living in better conditions.

Mr Darling had been lifted and settled back on his chair. She had assumed it would be a proper commode but this was a plain wooden scullery chair with a hole cut in the seat. A white china pot stood beneath it. The pot was chipped and stained with urine and worse. The mess had spilled over on to the bare floor.

Mr Darling wore a shirt without a collar and had a heavy grey blanket draped from his shoulders. Wasted white legs stuck out beneath the blanket. His feet were bony and bare.

She looked at his face and tried to smile. He stared back from dark eyes sunk back in black eye sockets. Wrinkled skin, yellow and blotched with brown, clung to his skull. His neck was scraggy. White stubble stood out on his chin and jowls and wisps of longer hair trickled down his windpipe.

She looked away.

An iron-frame bed took up a quarter of the room, pressed into a corner along a wall which held a framed religious text. The walls were sepia-coloured except for where two candles in holders had burned them deep brown. The ceiling was almost black. It was boarded and she realised she was looking at the underside of the upstairs floorboards.

Thin curtains hung from a length of string.

The floor was bare apart from a home-made rag rug which lay rucked in front of a small fireplace where a tiny fire smoked; more smoke was blowing into the room than was escaping up the chimney.

'Come into the back kitchen, Miss Laybourne,' Miss Forrester said, and she followed her across the room and through a rough door into a room even smaller than the first.

A scrubbed pine table with drawers under its top, four three-legged wooden stools, a simple cabinet, two buckets under a stone sink and a half-sized range almost filled the room. Two shelves held small baskets of vegetables and a few pans, plates and mugs.

There were nails driven into the door which led to the back yard and a single towel and children's coats hung limply from them.

Two pretty little girls with scared expressions tried to hide in a corner.

She did not know what to say to them, not even when Miss Forrester encouraged them to step forward and be introduced.

All she could think of was that this was awful, that word again, and that she should try not to look or sound shocked.

Miss Forrester turned as Mrs Darling came through the door. 'I'm afraid we can't stay, Annie. I must get back to see if Ma's all right.'

'Thank you for helping,' Annie Darling said. 'Are you sure you won't stay for some tea?'

Rose found her own voice. 'No, thank you, Mrs Darling. We should both go back to see if there's anything we can do, but thank you for allowing me to come home with you. I'm sorry I wasn't much help.'

'You were, Miss Laybourne, and you, Lizzie. You were there when I needed someone. I'll not forget that.'

Her gratitude was overwhelmingly genuine.

As they returned through the front room she saw Mrs Darling had managed to lay her husband down on a piece of oiled cloth on the bed.

'Goodnight, Mr Darling.' She smiled at him once more, and this time she thought his look seemed less hostile.

Then she noticed the ladder-like staircase which led from the front room up to the first floor and wondered how poor the upstairs must be, turned to wish Mrs Darling goodnight, promised to let her have any news about Billy as soon as possible, and held her breath until she was back in the street.

As they walked back along the dark, empty, rainswept street, their steps making the only sounds, Elizabeth realised Rose Laybourne was crying.

'Are you all right, Miss Laybourne?'

'Yes.' The answer was sobbed more than spoken.

A few more yards of uncomfortable silence, then Rose Laybourne spoke again, very quietly, as if she was talking to herself. 'I didn't realise people lived like that.'

'Not too many do, Miss Laybourne, though none live a lot better. Annie Darling's had especially bad luck. That's why her house is so poor. It's not her fault, mind.'

'No. I'm not blaming her. I admire her and I feel so sorry for her, especially now. What will happen to her if Billy . . .'

'If Billy's dead or cannot work when he comes up?' Elizabeth felt these were matters which should not be avoided. 'Well, she won't be able to pay her rent and your father's agent'll probably evict her. He'll need the house for a family that's working, you see? Mr Darling'll probably go into an institution and die. I reckon it's only Annie that keeps him alive. Once they're homeless the girls will almost surely be taken by the parish, and Mrs Darling'll have to do the best she can on her own. At best she and the girls might go into the workhouse, I suppose. At least they'd be together that way.'

'I feel so guilty, Miss Forrester.'

'Well, you shouldn't, Miss Laybourne. It's not your fault, not at all, and you did try to help Annie.' She pulled her collar up as a squall whipped along the street.

'I really did very little, Miss Forrester, but I must

confess I'm surprised that people are willing to live that sort of life. Don't they resent us, my family, for what we have?'

'Some do, Miss Laybourne, but most don't.' This was a rare opportunity to say things that would normally stay unsaid. 'Most people aren't envious of you, Miss Laybourne. They don't want to take away what you have but they would like just a little bit more for themselves. Better homes and more food, and the chance to put a bit of money aside so they wouldn't risk losing everything just because they're ill or have an accident. That's exactly what I'd like to see. That and better education so people could do more with their lives.'

'Is that what you call' – what did Papa call it? – 'socialism, Miss Forrester?'

'That's what I like to think it means, Miss Laybourne, though there are others like my brother, Edward, who think it's as much about changing the way the country's run.'

'My father says socialism would lead to revolution, the way it has in other countries.'

'I doubt it would, Miss Laybourne, not in England. You've seen the people here. I don't suppose they're much different from people all over the country. They don't want a revolution. It's true there's a few who do want to make things change fast, but most people are more patient. They don't want to cause any trouble, Miss Laybourne. They just want to live their lives as best they can. They've got families and enough to worry about as it is.'

They reached the end of Albert Street and turned down North Hill, the steep street which led down to Murdock Street and the colliery. A steam winch chuffed and the winding wheels chattered then sang as they dropped one cage deep into the mine and pulled the other one up.

Rose looked at the young woman who seemed to know so much, and envied her knowledge and understanding. Elizabeth Forrester was young, that was obvious, but she talked with a sureness which made her seem much older than she looked.

'Thank you, Miss Forrester, for explaining everything so well. Your pupils must be very happy to be taught by you.'

'My pupils have to listen to me, Miss Laybourne, but I'm not sure they enjoy it. I've enjoyed talking with you, though, and I hope you don't think I've said anything out of place.'

'No, not at all. It's been most' – she sought the right word – 'enlightening.'

She walked on down the steep hill, her head low to keep the rain off her face. Yes, the conversation had been enlightening; and disturbing. In a few hours she had seen and heard about a way of life she had not known existed, learned that the miners and their families lived a far harder life than she had ever imagined; but that was not what disturbed her.

Her father believed these people wanted a revolution, and he was wrong. She had never known him to be wrong before, and that was what disturbed her. She had always thought he was infallible.

And if he was wrong about socialism, perhaps he could be wrong about other things. About her marrying Hubert Belchester.

She discarded the thought immediately. How could she worry about her small problems when she was amongst women who were facing up to imminent disaster? Women like Mrs Darling and Miss Forrester's mother and sisters-in-law. Women she could no longer think of as anonymous miners' wives.

'Miss Forrester?' Another question jumped into her mind. 'Miss Forrester?'

She turned around and saw Miss Forrester had stopped and was standing very still and seemed to be listening.

'Is something wrong, Miss Forrester?'

'Aye. The winding wheels've stopped and they shouldn't have.'

'How do you know?'

'You get used to the noise they make. You know how long they should keep turning to bring the cages the full depth of the shaft. They haven't been turning long enough, Miss Laybourne, and there's no reason to stop the cages anywhere but at the bottom or the top.'

Suddenly the cables screamed as though they were in pain. The sound came from deep down in the earth; an agonised, primeval groan.

'Miss Forrester?' She sensed the schoolteacher's fear and saw it in her white face, her hands which stiffened then clenched into tight little fists, and in her still, staring eyes.

Below the hill, down in the colliery yard, the cluster of lights and the red glowing braziers gave the workings an odd and almost shameful beauty.

'Miss Forrester.' She reached out to take Elizabeth Forrester's hand, then stopped.

Another groan, deep, long, tearing; an enormous, tortured, inhuman roar that threw itself from one side of the valley to the other as if it were trying to escape its torment.

'Miss Forrester?'

But Miss Forrester did not move, apart from her lips which did not stop moving as they spouted unheard words.

'Miss Forrester?' Then the wind stumbled and she heard the words.

'Thy Kingdom come, Thy Will be done, as . . .' and the wind picked up and blew the next words away.

'Miss Forrester, what's happened?'

'The shaft's collapsing.'

'But how will the men get out?'

'They won't, Miss Laybourne. Not if the shaft's gone. There isn't another way out.'

Then they both began to run down the hill, together, holding hands without thinking, forgetting the differences between them.

Because at that moment the differences did not matter.

All that mattered was the safety of the men who might be trapped.

And as Rose ran she prayed the same prayer as all the other women who waited in the rain.

She prayed that the shaft was not collapsing.

CHAPTER 4

Rose was stunned by what she saw in the colliery yard.

The women who had been so quiet were in a frenzy. They were crowded around the bottom of the lamp room steps, shaking their fists and screaming at Mr Speake who was standing at the top of the steps, his hat lost and his rain-soaked hair plastered tight against his head. His face twitched and he was ashen. His arms were raised and even at a distance she could see that his hands were shaking.

He kept looking towards his office as if he expected her father to come to his rescue but the office door was shut.

A large woman suddenly rushed up the steps as if she were going to attack him but at the last moment she turned and raised her own hands to silence the crowd.

The yells died down, faded away altogether.

'Now, Mr Speake,' the woman said loudly, 'tell us what's happening. And none of your lies, mind. We want the truth, whatever it is.'

'The shaft,' Speake began quietly, then raised his voice

so it carried across the yard, 'the shaft is lined with blocks of stone which hold the earth back. Some of those blocks have broken away and jammed against a cage so we cannot raise it.'

'Is the shaft going to collapse?' the woman asked.

'Not if we can shore up the damage,' Speake said quickly.

'Can you do that?'

'I don't know. We're lowering someone on a cable to see how bad the damage is.'

'How soon will you know?'

'Half an hour. Maybe a bit longer.' Speake paused, then added, 'I'll let you know as soon as I can. Now you must let me go so I can supervise the work.'

He did not move. It was as if he were waiting for the women's permission to leave them.

'Aye, go on then,' the large woman said.

'Wait a minute,' a voice yelled from the crowd. 'I heard that you knew the shaft was dangerous. You knew it needed repairing.'

Speake did not answer.

'Did you know, Mr Speake?' the large woman asked bluntly.

'We've already carried out some repairs.' Speake shifted his feet and sounded uneasy. 'We think it may be those that've broken up again.'

'Then why didn't you close the works until you knew it was safe?' another woman shouted and others called out their agreement.

'We didn't think it was necessary,' Speake yelled back, an edge of panic in his voice.

'You mean Mr Laybourne doesn't think it's necessary to put a second shaft in?' someone shouted sarcastically. 'Not like in the new mines he's sunk?'

'The law says we have to put two shafts only in new mines. This mine's quite legal,' Speake yelled and edged towards the lamp room door.

'The law?' The sarcastic voice was filled with disgust. 'Bugger the law, Mr Speake. Laybourne's put extra shafts in his other old mines. Why not in Pincote?'

'You'd have to ask Mr Laybourne, Mrs.' Speake stepped backward into the lamp room and slammed the door, ending the need to talk any more.

'I'll tell you why,' Rose heard one of the women say, 'because the men in the other mines could go and work for someone else. There's only one mine in Pincote so we have to put up with whatever Laybourne wants to give us. The greedy sod won't pay out any more'n he has to. Not here.'

Rose was shocked, by the accusation and by the woman's language.

She turned to Elizabeth Forrester. 'Is that true?'

'Well, it's what everyone thinks, Miss Laybourne. That's why my brother wants the men to join the Miners' Association. Edward thinks that's the only way they can make your father improve the mine.'

'I see,' she said, and her chest tightened and warned her that she might be about to suffer another attack of asthma, 'but I think they're wrong.'

'Miss Laybourne' – she noticed the concern in Miss Forrester's voice – 'I think that maybe you should go back to your parents. It could get nasty down here. I wouldn't want to see you get hurt.'

'Perhaps.' She did not want to run away. 'But if I stay, will you stay with me, Miss Forrester? I'll understand if you'd prefer not to.'

She studied Miss Forrester's face and saw her indecision, then saw her chin rise up and a determined expression settle in her eyes.

'I'd be proud to stay with you, Miss Laybourne, but will you call me Elizabeth? I'd feel more comfortable if you would.'

She smiled. 'Of course, Elizabeth. And please call me Rose.'

'I'd rather call you Miss Laybourne. If your father heard me using your Christian name he might think it impertinent.'

'Then don't let him hear you, Elizabeth.' She grinned.

'Aren't you scared, being down here, like?' Elizabeth looked even more concerned than she had moments earlier.

'Yes, more scared than I've ever been,' she admitted immediately, then remembered that was not true. 'No, I was even more scared, once.'

'Aye? When was that?'

'Oh, years ago. Twelve years ago, when I was only six, and lost in an even bigger crowd than this. Although I suppose everything seems so much bigger when you're small.' It was obvious that Elizabeth was interested so she began to tell her the story, and as she told it her chest grew even tighter with the memory, squeezing her lungs and closing her throat until it seemed that the memory itself was suffocating her.

The Midsummer Fair. She remembered how she begged her father for permission to explore the fascinating maze of colourful stalls and tents, exciting shies and noisy rides and had promised faithfully, so faithfully, that she would hold tight to her older brother John's hand and never let go.

It was hot, she remembered, so hot she was dressed in the simplest white cotton dress, and it was so sunny that she had been told she must never remove her new hat with its green ribbon and wide brim.

The fair was packed with people, she had never seen so many people packed so tightly together; and the wide-brimmed hat was a nuisance because it was constantly being knocked askew as people brushed past.

She had held on to her hat with one hand, and John's hand with her other; and as the crowd grew more and more dense she could not walk by John's side any longer but had to trail behind him, her arm stretched out further and further until only her fingers were locked into his.

Then her hat was knocked off. She grabbed it off the ground before it was trodden on; and John was gone.

Her stomach churned as she remembered the feeling of being left alone in a foreign, suddenly unfriendly world.

She remembered screaming when the crowd pushed her and John apart. Screaming louder as he disappeared and legs and skirts closed around her; half suffocating her. Then the fear of being trampled and realising she could not walk against the flow; having to turn and let the crowd jostle her even further away. Being shoved, pushed, prodded and swept along until she did not know where she was, the hat lost anyway; the fear of being lost herself and of being found and being punished for losing her hat.

Confusion. Fear and guilt. The first ever feeling of not being able to breathe.

The noise of steam organs, whirling carousels, raucous laughter; gaudy colours, strange smells, strange faces grinning down at her, a man with black teeth grabbing her and asking questions she could not understand until someone thrust a jug in his hand and pulled him away.

Remembered standing in front of a gypsy caravan, terrified she would be taken away and never see her mother again; the terror of choking when her throat tightened and she could not breathe. Sobbing and being ignored.

She remembered it all, even after twelve years; the noise, the smells, the colours, the terror of it all. And she remembered how it had ended. How she saw the boy looking at her, his hands in his pockets, his head rolled back and cocked to one side. He had smiled and crouched down in front of her.

'I'm on me own, too.' He did not ask her name. 'Would you like me to tell you a story while we look for your ma and da?'

She did not remember telling him who she was, but she remembered the story, the safe feel of his firm grip as he

led her through the crowds until she saw John and her
mother waiting by their carriage, and she remembered
running to them. Then she turned, and the boy had gone.

She remembered it all so clearly, and how she had
refused to go to the fair for several years after; and then
how she had insisted on going each year so she could
search for a face in the crowd.

But she never saw him again and even began to wonder
if her parents were right; if she really had imagined there
was a kind young boy who had taken care of her and told
her a story she still remembered.

'Frightening, aye, but a lovely story for all that, Miss
Laybourne.'

'Rose, please, Elizabeth.' She smiled and was pleased to
see Elizabeth smile back, a sign that at least for a few
moments she had forgotten the horror and stopped
worrying about her father and brothers.

'My father said that you teach at the school?' she said,
determined to divert Elizabeth's mind a little longer, and
to learn more about her new friend. 'Do you enjoy it?'

'Oh, aye, Miss Laybourne, Rose. Very much.'

'And you live with your parents?'

'They've only two bedrooms and it was difficult with
three brothers still at home, like, so I lodge with the
headmaster and his wife in the schoolhouse. At the
moment, anyway.'

'Does that mean you're thinking of leaving?'

'Maybe. I'm engaged, sort of. My young man teaches in
the Upper School in Pincote but he's applied for a master's
post at Alnwick School. There's a house goes with the
position, and I suppose we'll move in there if he's offered
the post.'

'My brother John went to Alnwick School, Elizabeth.'
At last she had found something they had in common. 'It's
a lovely little town with a wonderful castle. Do you
know it?'

'No, I've never been far outside the valley. Have you?'

She thought carefully before she answered. In spite of her grievances she enjoyed far more privileges than Elizabeth and it seemed unfair to say too much, but she sensed that nothing she might say would make Elizabeth envious.

'I haven't travelled as much as my brother. He's due to come home tomorrow after spending two years in North America, and before that he travelled all over Europe. I've been fortunate, though, because I've paid occasional visits to my half sister in Manchester and to family friends in London and on the Dorset coast.' She saw the interest in Elizabeth's eyes and decided to test out her real ambition on this impartial stranger. 'But I'd like to travel more and see some of the things my mother's seen. Her father was in the Foreign Service and her mother was French, and when she was a child she lived in France, Sweden and Italy as well as in London. She travelled with them at first, but then they were posted to India and she was sent back to school in France to finish her education. She never saw them again. They were killed in the Mutiny.'

'That's awful, Rose. I had no idea. So you never met them?'

'No, nor my father's parents. They died long before I was born. Are your grandparents still alive, Elizabeth?'

'My grandparents? I don't even know if my parents are still alive, Rose, or who they are.'

She listened as Elizabeth explained that she had been abandoned as a baby and Josh and Minty Forrester had looked after her even though they had five sons of their own. 'Edward and I think of ourselves as twins and I think of the Forresters as my real parents. I've been really lucky. I could have been left to die or been brought up in an institution, or perhaps have been taken in by a family which wouldn't have been so kind to me.'

This was a different life to any Rose had heard of and she was grateful again, this time because Elizabeth was allowing her to share what so many women would have kept secret.

Elizabeth was impressed by Rose. Not many girls of her age and background would want to spend an evening waiting in the cold in a rainswept yard for news of men she did not even know. Not many would have thought about providing shelter and warmth for the waiting women and children, and even fewer would have refused to use the shelter themselves. And very few girls of her age and background would be able to talk with anyone, know when to speak and when it was best to stay silent.

There was more to Rose Laybourne than was immediately obvious.

The rain kept falling, chased by cold winds which eddied around the yard. The women who preferred to wait in the open gathered around the braziers, stamping their feet and rubbing their hands to keep their circulation going, talking about things which did not matter and would not remind them too much about what was happening below ground.

Snatches of news were brought to them at intervals, much of it worrying, and the winding wheels stayed obstinately still.

Elizabeth knew she should go to see how her mother was feeling, but she realised that Rose would go with her and then find it difficult to leave, so she waited in the yard, hoping that the men would be brought up soon.

Her head tipped forwards as she fell asleep standing up.

'Elizabeth.' Rose's hand grabbed her arm. 'Why don't you sit down and rest?'

'Aye, I think maybe I will, in a moment.' She saw Ben Clements, the maintenance foreman, standing in a corner smoking his pipe, and she led Rose across the yard to ask him if there was any news she could pass to the other women.

'The cage is still jammed, Lizzie.' He looked tired and

worried. 'I've been down to look at the cladding and I
reckon we can make a temporary repair, but first we need
to make up a cradle big enough for meself and two other
men to work from.'

'You'll lower it into the shaft?' she heard Rose ask.
'That's dangerous, isn't it?'

'Aye, Miss Laybourne, but we've no choice if we're to
get the men out.'

'But if we had a second shaft you could get them up
through that?' Rose said quietly.

'Aye, miss, but we don't have one.'

'I know.' Rose seemed to be considering something. 'It
would be very expensive to sink another shaft, I suppose.'

'Very expensive, and it'd take a long time. Much longer
than we've got if we're going to get these men out alive.'

'Yes.' Rose nodded, and as Ben Clements excused
himself and turned to leave she touched his arm. 'Good
luck, Mr Clements.'

'Thank you, miss.' Ben looked surprised and excused
himself again as an urgent shout called him up on to the
landing stage.

'Rose, I wouldn't say too much about another shaft. People
might misinterpret your meaning.' Elizabeth thought it
wise to warn Rose that the comments she was making
might compromise her position as the owner's daughter.

'Thank you, Elizabeth, but once John's home I think I'll
talk to him about a second shaft. He may be able to
influence my father, especially as he was trapped underground while he was working in America.'

'He was?' It astonished her that John Laybourne would
have put himself in a position where his life might be in
danger.

'Oh yes, Elizabeth. He was trapped for several days and,
although he was quite safe when he wrote and told us what
had happened, I still feel ill and frightened simply thinking
about it.' Elizabeth heard a tremor in Rose's voice. 'So you
see, I can understand a little of what you're feeling. Only a

little, of course. It doesn't compare with what you're suffering now, I realise that, and I don't know how you remain so calm, Elizabeth.'

She saw Rose reach up and rub tears out of her eyes, not for effect or daintily with a handkerchief, but surreptitiously and with her bare fingers.

Her earlier feeling was confirmed; there really was much more to this girl than was obvious, and perhaps the same applied to her brother.

She wondered what John was like now. Her last memory of him was as a shy and gangling young boy who had come to see her and a few of her school friends recite poetry and set pieces of Shakespeare at the school's annual St George's Day celebrations.

The conversation with Ben somehow swept away her tiredness and Elizabeth decided that instead of resting under cover she would stay outside in the yard, and she was pleased when Rose said she would wait with her.

The braziers were refilled with coal, and more tea was made and passed around. Somehow the night grew even darker, even more hostile.

A long time passed, the hours marked by the distant chimes. No one spoke now; she noted that Rose and all the other women seemed to be contained by their own thoughts and, although she was grateful for the simple privacy the lack of conversation proffered, she tried hard not to think too much about her father and brothers.

The waiting seemed endless and the night's silence tangible, intimidating.

She stared at the wheels, stationary and difficult to see in the slanting rain, and wondered how the men trapped in the cage felt, knowing they were only a hundred feet or so from the surface, knowing there were several hundred feet of nothing waiting below them. Knowing that if the shaft collapsed on top of them the cables would never hold the extra weight.

She wondered how long it was until dawn.

Then she heard a cautious shout: 'Try her now.'

The winch engine turned faster and she thought she saw the wheels begin to turn.

'Take her steady, man. Don't rush her, there's some bad injuries in the cage.' The order was shouted above the engine's din.

She stood below the landing stage where the rescued men would step out to safety. The cage lifted into sight and stopped and someone slid bolts into place to lock it in position. The iron grille which acted as a gate clanged as it was swung aside, and dark figures stepped out slowly on to the stage.

She sensed that everyone should have cheered the men as they came up, but this was not a moment for celebration, there were still too many men trapped far below and there were too many men who would never step out into the night air again.

Wind flicked along a row of lamps hung to light the stage and the gantry, making shadows sway unsteadily, making it difficult to see who had been brought up first, but giving just enough light for Elizabeth to see that her father and brothers were not amongst the men.

Her heart fell; she felt jealous of those who cried out names of men they knew were safe, and ashamed of herself for feeling that way.

Everyone in the yard watched the men who dragged their feet along the platform, men who looked lost and small in the large grey blankets which were thrown around them. Tough men who suddenly looked like sleepy children.

The men staggered through the lamp room and down the steps into the yard. Six of them carried three stretchers, and all the others had bloody bandages wrapped around their heads or arms, or had hurt their legs so they needed support from someone fitter.

There was a moment's confusion as women rushed

forward to see if it was their own men who had been brought up, then recognised someone else's husband or father or brother and turned away to call a friend's name.

It was difficult to recognise the men at first: the dark, the shadows, the black dust caked on their faces even thicker than usual, but also because the shock and strain seemed to have changed the shape of each man's face.

The men being carried on stretchers were identified and placed in a covered wagon which rolled out of the yard and turned towards the infirmary in Pincote Market, the mothers and wives sitting alongside the stretchers.

She saw a man talking to the young woman who had only just moved to the village, the woman whose husband was spending his first week underground, and saw her hold her baby even tighter, turn and walk towards the gates. She did not need to hear what had been said, she could see it in the woman's face and the way she walked. She was a widow.

'Aye, lass.' The first man Elizabeth asked was happy to leave his fussing wife for a moment so he could talk. 'And I can tell you this, mind, I'll be happy to work with your brother Edward any time. Any time at all, like.'

'Edward's safe?'

'Aye, lass, he's safe. So are the half-dozen he led from behind the fall. All except William Wright, that is. Doctor reckons he's real poorly, but by all accounts he would not even have got out if Edward hadn't risked his neck to save him. Proper hero your brother, lass. Surprised me, I'll tell you. Never thought he had it in him, like. Neither did your old da, I reckon. Set us all thinking, has young Edward.'

'Do you know when they're coming up?'

'They were carrying William out along the main and that was slowing them down a bit but I reckon they'll be in the next cage. Anyway, they shouldn't be long now, lass.'

She rushed back to tell her mother the news and to let

Pru know that William was badly hurt but still alive and on his way to the surface.

As she spoke the winding wheels began to turn, slowly dropping the first cage back into the shaft and pulling the second cage up to the surface. They turned slowly, very slowly, then they stopped altogether.

The wind carried the sound of urgent shouts and the crowd moved forward again. The temporary shoring had slipped and the second cage was jammed against the shaft's broken cladding.

Edward knelt beside William's stretcher, pressing a pad against the side of his friend's head. His hand was sticky with the blood which seeped through the cotton cloth and his arm ached from applying pressure to stop the bleeding.

'Only a few more yards and we'll be up top,' he told his unconscious friend. 'You've made it this far, lad, a few more minutes and we'll get you to the infirmary.'

He could actually feel the wind blowing down the shaft, bringing the scent of the moors into the damp coal-smelling mine. He had thought he would never smell the moors again, never see them again.

He had been convinced he and the others would not get out of the bypass drain before the water level rose and the flood filled it, but he had kept on and refused to let the others turn back even when the water reached their chins because he had to do everything he could to save William. Turning back would have sentenced William to die. He and the others might have been able to try again if the level dropped, but he knew William would not live long enough to try again. William was not going to live without a doctor's help.

'Just a few more minutes, lad, and we'll be up top.'

William did not answer, he lay still and did not even respond when a large rock fell loose from the shaft's cladding and crashed against the top of the cage.

'Soon be there, lad.' His arm was aching so much he

changed hands, careful to maintain the pressure.

'He's gone, Edward,' he heard Simon say but refused to believe him.

'No, he's still bleeding, Simon. He'll be all right once he gets proper treatment.'

'He's dead, son.' His father held him by his shoulders and lifted him up. 'Been dead ten minutes or more. You cannot do any more for him. You did all you could. It's not your fault.'

'Aye, lad,' he heard Ned, William's father, say from the corner of the cage. 'He's been dead a good ten minutes.'

He saw Ned's face in the lamplight and noticed the streaks where Ned's tears had washed away the coal dust.

'I'm sorry, Ned,' was all he could say, and he almost choked when Ned wrapped his arms around him and hugged him tight.

He looked down at William, blood now running out from his nose and mouth. He had killed his best friend because he had panicked. He wanted to say it was his fault, but he was too numb to speak.

Then the cage began to lift, water sprayed out from the broken shaft lining and soaked him again, and minutes later the cold night wind cut through the cage and made him shiver.

'It's Josh Forrester with his boys and Ned Wright and his lads,' Elizabeth heard someone call and pushed her mother through the gap which opened in the crowd.

She moved aside as Mary and Flo stepped forward, both reaching for their husbands' black-streaked faces before their eyes dropped to the stretcher the men carried between them.

As Paul and Joey lowered the stretcher and threw their arms around their wives she saw Ned, and noticed how he tried to stop Pru pulling back the blanket which covered the stretcher.

Then Edward moved forward and she and her mother

hugged him, aware of the bandage around his head but more aware of the body on the stretcher.

'Who's that?' she asked quietly.

'William,' he answered unemotionally. 'He died while we were on our way up.'

A sudden wind whipped across the yard. Rain hammered down. She turned her face into it and saw Pru Wright crouch across her dead son as if she were trying to protect him from the cold and the wet.

'Always scared of the dark when he was a boy,' Pru said as if it mattered. 'Daft for a miner, like.'

Her shawl lifted in the wind then settled back over her and William's heads. No one reached out to remove it. No one was jealous of their last moment of privacy.

'Lizzie.' Simon touched her shoulder and she turned away and let him hug her, held him with one arm while the other went out to Thomas.

Then her father was there, allowing his emotions to show for once, and the whole family seemed to huddle together in a welter of arms and tearful faces.

Except Edward.

She saw him standing apart, by himself, and she knew he needed to be alone so she left him and even warned Nancy, with her eyes, not to bother him.

Nancy looked devastated. William was her favourite brother, and Edward was probably the only one who could have comforted her at that moment, but it would not have been fair to let Nancy intrude on his grief.

James appeared through the wet night, one arm splinted and supported in a sling. He put his good arm around his sister's shoulders. 'He didn't suffer, Nance. He was unconscious all the time Edward was trying to save him. Edward risked his life to get William out, to stop him drowning. It's so bloody unfair!'

Elizabeth heard him break down into incoherent sobs and saw Nancy hold him tight and try to soothe him, stroking his head gently as he buried it in her small shoulder.

The cage dropped away without her really noticing it; her attention was taken up by the mixture of grief and joy that was surging through her own family and their friends, but she turned towards the dock as the next cage came up and watched the men come out through the lamp room and down the steps to join the crowd in the yard.

The first person she recognised was Billy Darling. She sighed with relief that another family had been spared a tragedy, and was surprised when Billy made straight for Edward and shook his hand.

'Thank you,' he said simply. 'I'm real proud to be working with you, Edward. You're a real hero, everyone says so.'

'I'm no bloody hero, Billy,' she heard Edward say softly, as if he were talking to a child. 'You'd better get home, boy. Your ma must be worried sick.'

She watched young Billy walk away, and saw the pride in the way he moved. He was probably entitled to feel proud, she decided. He could not be more than twelve or thirteen years old but he had all the responsibilities of a grown man, and had probably acted like a grown man over the last few hours.

She turned back towards Edward and suddenly found herself crying. She took the handkerchief which was offered without realising that it was Rose Laybourne's.

'Is that young man standing over there your brother?'

'Aye,' she muttered absently, then noticed who had asked. 'Yes, Rose. My brother Edward.'

'What a coincidence – he's the boy I told you about. The boy at the fair.'

'Edward? Are you sure?' Edward had never mentioned meeting the owner's daughter.

'Oh yes, I'm sure. It's twelve years ago but he's hardly changed. He's a man now, of course, but he's almost as I remember him.'

It was him; she was sure, even though she had not seen him for twelve years. It was the way he stood, feet planted apart and at an angle to each other, hands in his trouser pockets, his head rolled back and slightly cocked to the left, his back arched as if he were leaning against a bow. And his voice, quiet and steady in spite of the noise and confusion all around; local but different, not as harsh as the usual dialect, softer and more precise as if he thought words should be used carefully. He looked arrogant, but his eyes and voice were gentle. That was what made him memorable.

It was him, the boy who had taken care of her after John let go of her hand in the Midsummer Fair crowd.

And now he was standing only a few yards away from her, just as he had been that day, his hands in his pockets and his head rolled back and cocked to one side.

And, as her heart beat fast, she realised she did not only recognise him from that day at the fair when she was still a child.

She had been with him since then. She had been with him up on King's Crag, in her dreams. She knew now. She knew who her unseen lover was. Edward Forrester.

'Elizabeth, will you introduce us? Please.' She ought to thank him, show him she still remembered.

'Of course, but are you sure it was Edward?'

'Oh, yes. I'm sure, Elizabeth. I remember how he looked, how he stood, the way he spoke. Every time I think about the story he told me, about a princess and a pauper and a magic tree with real gold leaves, I hear his voice.' She paused, feeling that she needed to explain but she did not know how to. 'I know it sounds silly but . . .'

'No, Rose, it doesn't sound silly, not at all. He told me the story, too. I think he made it up to amuse me when I was ill a long time ago. The story about a magic tree, a magic autumn . . .' Elizabeth's voice trailed off. 'He did not tell me about finding you, though, about helping you, but then he wouldn't. He wouldn't tell. He'd think it was too much like boasting.'

They moved forward but stopped as Edward was

suddenly surrounded by a group of grateful men.

He saw Ned coming for him and tried to move away but
Ned's arm came round his shoulders and held him tight.

'Quiet everyone, please.' Ned raised his free arm. 'My
William died in the cage on the way up but I want you all to
know that Edward risked his own life trying to save him. I
just want everyone to know that, like.'

Ned stopped suddenly and began to cry again. It was
embarrassing and Edward wanted to tell Ned and
everyone what had really happened but his father stepped
up to him before he could speak.

'Well done, lad, I'm real proud of you.'

The words stunned him, words he never thought he
would hear his father say, not even in his wildest moments,
and a sudden temptation crept up on him. The temptation
not to say anything, not tonight. Just enjoy the glory for a
while longer, and then maybe some of it might rub off and
stay for good.

Suddenly someone called for three cheers and he was
hoisted up on to men's shoulders. Lanterns were held high
on long poles and he was paraded for a few minutes before
they lowered him to the ground beside Elizabeth and a
young woman he did not recognise.

'It's not your fault that William died.' Elizabeth laid a
sympathetic hand on his arm but he could not tell her that
she had misread the look on his face.

He shrugged. It was too late to say anything, for now.
He felt numb but in pain, but it was not a physical pain, it
was worse than that, an agony deep in his heart and his
soul, and he just wanted to get away from everyone and be
alone.

His mother put her arm around him. 'Let's go home, lad.
You look worn out.'

'Edward.' Elizabeth stopped them. 'I'd like to introduce
Miss Rose Laybourne.'

The young woman nodded a greeting before she spoke.

'How do you feel, Mr Forrester?' She pushed back the wet curls the wind blew across her face.

'All right, I suppose, miss.' He felt awkward; he could not say how he really felt, certainly not to the owner's daughter, and he wanted to go home.

'I'm glad.' She hesitated, then added. 'I'd like to thank you.'

'You've nothing to thank me for, miss.'

'Oh, but I have. Not for what you did today, especially. But you took care of me a long time ago, when I was a child. At the Midsummer Fair.'

She annoyed him. After what had happened, and only God knew how many men were dead or maimed or still dying, all the Laybourne girl could think of was how he had helped her find her parents at a fair years ago. Something trifling he had forgotten about immediately afterwards.

'Aye, I remember, Miss Laybourne. Anyone would have done the same, miss.' He tried to sound dismissive and show her he wanted to leave.

'But they didn't,' he heard the irritating girl insist as he turned away, 'but you did and I'd like to thank you for it. If there's ever anything I can do for you . . .'

'Well, as a matter of fact, miss, there is something you can do,' he heard himself say sharply.

'Really?' He was pleased to hear how excited she sounded, pleased because he knew he was going to spit in her patronising face.

'Aye, Miss Laybourne. You can persuade your father to sink another bloody shaft like he's already done in his other mines. That way, more men like William Wright mightn't have to die before we can bring them up.'

It was good to see her embarrassment and the way the colour sank out of her face. It was not often you had the chance to wrongfoot a Laybourne.

'I'm sorry, Mr Forrester.' She turned and began to walk away.

He watched her, already feeling guilty, shocked by his

outburst and ashamed at the cheap trick he had played on her.

Then he heard Elizabeth explode. 'That was bloody rude, Edward, even allowing for what you've been through. Bloody rude and unforgivable. She was thanking you for something which happened years ago. Most people in her position wouldn't have bothered even if they'd remembered. Just think on that. Boy!'

It was the way she fired the last word that hurt.

'Your sister's right.' He felt his mother take her arm away from him.

He hesitated; the girl was almost invisible in the dark and rain.

'Miss Laybourne!' He rushed after her, shouldering people aside. 'Miss Laybourne! Wait!'

She stopped and as she turned he could see she was crying. He reached out without thinking and rested both hands on her shoulders. It was an instinctive gesture, meant to be apologetic, but immediately he touched her he felt possessively protective.

'I'm sorry, Miss Laybourne. I shouldn't have said those things. It was very rude, and I apologise.'

'Please don't apologise. I think I can understand how you must feel.' She smiled and did not try to hide the tears which mingled with the rain on her face, did not fuss because the wind was tugging at her hair.

Suddenly, incredibly, the pain he felt in his heart began to ebb, drifting away as if someone was soothing him with gentle words and caresses. His eyes stared straight into hers and he wanted to kiss her. Wanted to wrap his arms around her and hold her tight because there was something about her that made him think he had known her a long time, a long time. The fact that she was beautiful did not matter, there was something else, something indefinable that made him want her.

But whatever it was did not detract from her beauty. She was beautiful, not artificially beautiful, but naturally, wonderfully beautiful. Those eyes, the way she tilted her head, her smile and the small dimples in her cheeks. Her soft mouth smiling at him.

She was standing there, not moving away, just standing still, smiling at him. Everything else seemed remote. The only thing that mattered was that she was content to stand there with him, not to move away.

He had never felt like this before.

The wind tugged her hair off her face, streaming it behind her so he could see her throat below her upturned chin. He wanted to pull her into his chest, lift her up so he could kiss the softness of her throat, her chin, and those full, smiling lips. He wanted to enjoy her, but to take care of her.

He felt clumsy and dirty and inadequate. Tried to speak, saw her eyebrows raise in anticipation, but no words came.

Instead he lowered his hands and let them run down her arms, reluctantly releasing his hold on her, reluctant not to touch her any longer but conscious that he should not be touching her at all.

His fingers trailed across the backs of her gloveless hands, along her fingers; slowly, anything to prolong contact, his eyes still matching her full gaze, his fingertips lingering.

Suddenly she turned her hands over and gripped his. Tight. And she did not let go. He closed his hands around hers. She squeezed and he felt a surge of excitement spread through him until it nearly choked him. It made his groin ache.

He did not speak. Neither did she. They stood, looking into each other's eyes.

The ache in his groin turned into a real pain. He had to do something to ease it, and all he could do was to speak, almost croaking. 'It's my birthday, today. Twenty-two.'

He said it simply because he had to say something, the actual words did not matter.

'Oh, your birthday.' A quiet, husky voice which he

thought reflected his own lack of interest in what was being said. 'It's mine soon. Middle of May. I'll be eighteen.'

'I've made a mess of your coat, miss.' His hands had left black marks on her shoulders and sleeves.

'It doesn't matter.' She shrugged, and their hands parted with the shrug.

She placed hers behind her back, and took a step backward. She looked quite lost.

He could see her better now they were not standing so close, see how her breasts thrust up under her coat. The pain in his groin grew more intense.

'Well, I suppose I should join my parents.' He heard her words and thought she seemed reluctant to leave.

'You can manage that, can you? Now you're nearly eighteen?'

'I think so.' She looked down at the ground, then looked up into his eyes and smiled. 'Goodbye, Mr Forrester.'

'Goodbye, Miss Laybourne.'

And she turned and walked away.

And he stood and watched her go, even after the rain closed after her and the crowd packed around him and demanded his attention.

CHAPTER 5

—————

During the night the rain stopped falling, and even the wind, after a final, petulant shove, turned away. It was as if they had both decided to save their energies for later.

Thick, still clouds shut out the moon, and the darkness which blanketed the town seemed to smother activity and deaden sound. Nothing moved. The engines which slung the waste buckets across the valley had stopped when the coal stopped coming up. The pithead winch was quiet and even the main pump engine was still. The wagons in the railway sidings were empty and did not need to be moved. The valley was dark and silent.

Unlike normal nights there was no shift, no work and no one about.

The streets were still empty when dawn came, and, unusually, they stayed empty and quiet. So quiet that Edward did not wake until noon.

He had not expected to sleep. He thought his mind would be full of nightmares, blackness, fear, screaming men, drowning men. And guilt; for killing William, for not admitting the truth when everyone thought he was a hero, and guilt that he had looked into Rose Laybourne's eyes and temporarily forgotten all that had happened.

But he slept well and when he woke, twelve hours' sleep had already put some distance between then and now. He had caused William's accident, he would never deny that to himself, but he had not killed him.

That was what he told himself, and he tried hard to believe it, to suppress the inner voice that kept telling him he was to blame for everything and that he should redeem himself by staying to fight the miners' cause.

He had avoided Pru and Nancy last night but they could not be avoided for ever so he went next door before he ate any breakfast, keen to get that misery over before he faced the rest of the day. Nancy was not there, she had gone to buy food for a family which did not feel much like eating, and he was thankful that he had only to face one tearful woman at a time.

'I didn't thank you for trying to save him.' Pru wrapped her arms around him and cried on to his shoulder.

'He would've done the same for me,' he said awkwardly because that other voice was trying to make him say something different.

'The bloody shaft,' Ned said viciously, 'that's what killed him. They knew it was dangerous, only having one. If we'd had another shaft we'd have got him out alive. Bastards!'

'Aye,' he heard himself agree, his mind grabbing at a way of shifting the blame, 'we've got to make Laybourne see sense.'

'I liked the way you spoke up to the Laybourne girl,' Ned continued. 'Took guts, that did.'

Took guts to talk to a girl? The guilt rushed back. He excused himself and left quickly.

He went the back way, through the yards, and into his mother's kitchen.

'Been next door?' His father was hanging his jacket on a nail on the back door.

'Aye, Da, I thought I'd better.' He took the mug of tea Elizabeth offered him and noticed the sharp look she gave his father, and the way his father shuffled his hands and feet; but he ignored that for a moment. 'Where's Ma?'

'In bed,' Elizabeth said, without looking up from the bread she was sawing. 'Ill again. I knew yesterday'd be too much for her.'

Elizabeth handed him two slices of bread and as she did so he caught her scowl and the curt way she nodded at their father, as if telling him to get on with something.

His father looked from him to Elizabeth, and back again, and seemed to wilt before he spoke. 'Look, son, I'm sorry I argued with you about stopping to see your ma yesterday. Reckon I was wrong. Reckon I might've been wrong about a few things.'

It was an embarrassing moment for both of them. It would have felt better if they could have hugged each other, or at least shaken hands, but that would have been going too far; best to let it pass without any ceremony.

'Never mind that, Da.' He shrugged. 'What's important now is to decide how we're going to get Laybourne to make the mine safer.'

'Aye.' His father looked at him and some sort of understanding passed between them. 'Get some food inside you, and I'll tell you what's been happening this morning.'

It seemed that the workings would be closed for at least a week, maybe longer, while the shaft was repaired and the main road was made safe from further flooding by sealing off what remained of the lower gob tunnel. The men who were buried in the collapsed workings would be left there, it was too dangerous to recover their bodies. Once the flood had been pumped out of the main road a new face would be cut beyond the disaster, well beyond it so there would be a thick wall of solid coal left to isolate the un'stable rock from the new workings.

'Seems sound enough to me, son,' his father said when he finished explaining the details of the entire repair operation.

'That's fine, Da, but they won't need everyone to work on the repairs. What's the company doing about paying the men that aren't working? They'll still need wages to keep their families fed.'

'You know the rule, son. No coal, no pay.'

'Wonderful.' He meant what he said.

Most of the families lived hand to mouth and could not afford to lose even a day's pay, let alone a week's or more; so now had to be the right time to canvass for the association, when the men were still shocked by the accident and were angry because they were not being paid.

'Anyway' – his father hesitated and looked embarrassed – 'Mr Speake's promised there'll be work for all of us. And he wants to see you when you feel ready. He wants to hear what you've got to say about the collapse.'

'He'll hear, all right.'

'Steady, son. He wants to know for the inquest, like.'

'So he and Laybourne know what lies to tell the coroner?'

His father shrugged. 'You'll get your chance to stand up in court, you and all those who got out.'

'Aye, Da, after a few months when things've settled down and it's all past and half forgotten. After so many stories have been told that the men aren't really sure what they remember any more.' He grabbed his coat and cap. 'I'll go and see Speake now. Get it over, like.'

There was not much activity around the colliery yard, just groups of men standing around talking, almost in whispers. Every so often a quiet argument would break out as one man corrected another's memory of what happened the day before; the truth was already being distorted, either innocently or to give someone standing they did not deserve.

His inner voice told him he should not be scornful, not him who had not told any lies as such, but had kept back the truth just the same.

Then the voice became smug as men recognised him and came across to praise him and shake his hand.

He gave every man the same response, and in a sense he hoped that what he said was true: 'You would have done the same, man, I just happened to be there.'

And they all grimaced their agreement in the same way, and nodded in the same way, but they all avoided looking him in the eyes.

Unlike Rose Laybourne, last night. He was standing roughly where he had stood with her. The yard looked different now, in daylight and without rain, and last night's drama suddenly seemed stale. He wondered how the owner's daughter would react if she saw him now. Would she still grip his hands the way she had under cover of the dark, when she saw him as the night's hero?

Of course she would not. She would have forgotten him already. In a few years' time she might remember the magic of standing in the wind and rain with a tired miner, if something reminded her; and she might be amused and tell her friends and they might laugh with her.

He shoved his hands deep into his pockets, hunched his shoulders and idly tapped a loose cobble with the toe of his boot.

And thought about the way she had looked at him. It was the sort of look, well, if she was not who she was and he was not just a miner . . .

No point in thinking like that; he threw the mood away as if it was burned bread crust. Thinking about her had helped him sleep last night, helped him to adjust to what had happened. She had done that without knowing it, and he could not expect any more from her. Not as the owner's daughter.

He crossed the yard and as he reached the bottom of the steps leading up to the manager's office the manager's voice boomed down from above, 'Forrester!'

'Yes, Speake,' he felt like saying, but instead showed his defiance by looking up but not moving towards the steps.

He detested Speake's arrogance and the self-important way the round little man strutted about the yard. He detested Speake's authority to rule the lives of so many men and women. He detested the way Speake was always spotless and smelled as if he had been bathed in scent.

'We'll see you now, as you're here,' the mine manager barked down at him but he stayed still and did not move until Speake conceded a reluctant, 'When you're ready.'

He sat in the chair in front of Speake's desk without waiting to be asked, and was irritated that Speake did not seem to notice the small sign of insolence. The fat little manager asked prepared questions and Mr Trenchard, the assistant manager, younger and leaner, wrote the replies down into a thick book.

He noticed that when Trenchard occasionally asked for answers to be repeated or clarified Speake became annoyed, so he deliberately took his time, mumbling and constantly referring back to things he said he had overlooked, apologising to Trenchard each time. He caught Trenchard's eye at one point and was sure he saw a conspiratorial wink of encouragement.

'So, in your opinion the accident was caused by igniting gas, an unexpectedly large amount of gas?' He noticed Speake give a quick, almost nervous glance at his pocket watch, suggesting that he was trying to finish the interview in a hurry. 'Is that right, Forrester?'

'Aye,' he said carefully, wondering why Speake was in a hurry.

'And George Willis, one of the company's deputies, had already warned the men to be careful?'

'Aye, that's right, and the men were being careful. We were all being careful, Mr Speake, and I don't reckon there's any man who'd say the accident was due to a miner's negligence.'

'I don't suppose any of them would, Forrester. I don't suppose any of them would admit to that,' Speake said sarcastically and looked away.

He heard the words and felt himself stand up. Saw his hands raised and open, and saw them trembling with the anger which stopped him saying anything. He slammed his palms down on to Speake's desk and kept his hands there; better to be insolent than to put them around Speake's neck and wring the smugness out of him. He glared at the manager, saw him jerk back, out of arm's reach, eyes darting to Trenchard, imploring his support, then back, trying to judge the level of anger he had released.

He stared at Speake, heard the office door open and close behind him but ignored it, and concentrated on forming his thoughts into words that might make Speake understand how he felt. When the words did come they came in a torrent.

'Mr Speake' – he leaned even harder on his hands to hide a worse tremble – 'George Willis is a friend of mine, a sort of uncle even and I'd not choose to do him any harm or question his judgement. Normally, mind. Given a free hand, like, he'd have closed the workings until he was sure all the gas had been cleared. He told me that, good as, anyway. But he knew what you and Mr Laybourne would say, and he knew what the men would say if they lost wages because of the "No coal, no pay" rule. Now, a load of those men are dead and the rest aren't going to get any wages anyway. It's no good trying to blame the men or George Willis. It's you and Mr Laybourne who're responsible because of the way you force me and the others to work. So don't you tell me that it's our fault. Especially when you won't even pay the men who can't work because the bloody mine that killed their kin and their mates still needs repairing.'

'Mr Forrester.' The voice came from behind and he
spun around, saw Sebastian Laybourne; and instinctively
reached out and shook the hand that was offered. 'My
compliments, Mr Forrester.'

He felt foolish as his anger ebbed away.

'Sit down, Mr Forrester, I'm sure you must be
exhausted after yesterday.' Laybourne looked towards the
manager. 'Mr Speake, I think you and Mr Trenchard
should leave me alone with Mr Forrester.'

He sat down, unsure what would happen next, not so
confident now that his outburst was spent. He watched the
managers leave; neither of them spoke but he thought that
Trenchard was only just holding back a smile. It was quite
obvious that Trenchard did not have any respect for
Speake and that Speake resented the younger man, but
that did not explain why Speake had been trying to rush
the interview or why Trenchard was happy to see it
prolonged.

Sebastian Laybourne sat in Speake's chair, leaned on
the desk and started immediately. 'A fine speech. I'm glad
that you were able to come here this morning, Mr
Forrester, and I'm sorry that I'm rather late.'

'You're late? I'm sorry, sir, but I don't understand.'

'Mr Speake did ask you here to meet me?' The way the
owner's voice trailed off told him that Speake had not
followed orders, and that was why he wanted to rush the
interview.

'No, sir, I came here of me own accord, like, and
because me da said the managers wanted to see me.
Sometime, but nothing specific, like.' He hoped he was
nailing down Speake's coffin.

'A misunderstanding, I suspect,' Laybourne said calmly.

'You wanted to see me then, sir?'

'Yes, because of my daughter.'

The answer threw him off guard and he could not
respond. He thought about what had happened between
him and Rose and began to panic.

'You look surprised, Mr Forrester.'

'I am, sir.' What the hell had she said about him?

All they had done was to hold hands, and she seemed as keen as him.

'She tells me that you're quite a passionate young man.' His blood pounded and he was not sure whether it was the anxiety of waiting for Laybourne to pounce or the sudden thought of being passionate with the man's daughter.

'Aye?'

'You demanded that she spoke to me about sinking a second shaft.'

'And I apologised for being rude to her, sir. I shouldn't have said it in the way I did.'

'Perhaps you should not have said it at all.'

'I said what needs to be said, sir. I only apologised for the way that I spoke to your daughter, not for what I said. You owe us a second shaft, sir, there's no denying that.'

'And it seems from what I overheard a few moments ago that you also think I owe you quite a lot more. How do you propose we pay for these things?'

'I'm sure there's a way, sir.'

'I wish there was, Mr Forrester.' The words seemed to be said with real regret.

'I don't understand what you mean.' He eyed Laybourne and tried to judge the man's honesty.

'I mean that there's a limit to how much the company can afford to spend on the mine, Mr Forrester. Pincote Colliery is only one of our businesses, and quite honestly, any further investment could be very unwise. I don't need to tell you how remote Pincote is. It's far from the markets and we have to transport the coal for miles, unlike the mines at Shearton and in the Newcastle coalfields, where the transport costs are much lower. It may be cheaper just to close the Pincote mine.'

'Are you serious, sir?' The question slipped out without thought. 'That'd be a disaster for Pincote.'

'Quite.' He saw the owner's grim expression. 'And that's

why I feel honour bound to try to keep it open. Closure would destroy Pincote Colliery and the lives of every family that lives here. Therefore, we must try to find a compromise. It is important that we look for ways to improve safety, but without incurring vast cost. That's why I wanted to talk to you, particularly as I believe my family owes you a debt.'

'Owes me a debt, sir?'

'For taking care of my daughter some years ago, Mr Forrester.' He was disarmed by Laybourne's smile and soft laugh. 'My wife and I thought this mysterious boy was someone Rose had imagined, but now I understand it was you.'

'It was nothing, sir, and it was years ago.'

'It's proof that you have an innate sense of responsibility, Mr Forrester. Proof endorsed by the way you behaved yesterday. Most men would have waited to be rescued, or if they had seen an opportunity to escape they would have gone immediately. They would not have stopped to search for possible survivors. We need men who are prepared to act on their own initiative, not just in Pincote but in our other mines. And not only underground. This country will always need coal, Mr Forrester, and it will always need natural leaders like you, to manage the mines and make them as safe as possible.'

He heard the words but he was not sure what the owner was really saying. 'I'm not sure I understand, sir.'

'I'd like to offer you a position, Mr Forrester, to be trained as a deputy under your friend, George Willis. Later, if you're interested, of course, we would train you to become an assistant manager either in Pincote or one of our other larger mines, or perhaps even as manager of a smaller mine. Eventually you might even manage Pincote Colliery.' Mr Laybourne paused, his face creased into a warm smile. 'Well, what do you think of my offer?'

'I don't know what to think, sir. I never thought of meself as ever becoming a manager.'

'I cannot say that I had, either, Mr Forrester, but my daughter suggested you might be better employed, and having considered what she said I realised that you really do have a great deal to offer us.'

His heart was pounding and his head felt light with excitement, not only because of the offer but because Rose Laybourne had recommended him. 'I don't know what to say, sir.'

He was keen to accept, both to please Rose and to satisfy the ambition which had suddenly been lit, but he was cautious enough to realise how his brothers, and William's father and brothers, might see the sudden change of loyalties. 'I ought to tell you, sir, that I've been talking to the men about joining the association.'

'Yes, Mr Forrester, I know you have.' Mr Laybourne stopped smiling, stood up and slowly walked to the window. He stood looking down into the yard and did not turn around as he spoke again. 'I can understand why you may have thought it necessary but I can assure you it isn't, not if you accept my offer. Believe me, I'll place you in a position where you can do far more for the men than any representative of the National Miners' Association. I won't have strangers interfering in the way I manage my collieries, Mr Forrester, not when I have local men like you to help me.'

It was flattering to think the owner had such confidence in him.

'Well, Mr Forrester?' Laybourne turned around, his face smiling once more. 'I've explained why we cannot afford to sink a second shaft and I've offered you a position which will enable you not only to help the men but also improve your own circumstances. I can't do anything more. The rest is up to you.'

'Well, sir, I didn't expect this.' He tried to hide his excitement, and to suppress an instinctive sense of unease. 'I'm interested, of course, but I need to think about it.'

'I understand.' Mr Laybourne nodded, then laughed

quietly. 'But please don't take too long. My daughter's sure to think it's my fault if you don't accept.'

The outside door opened and as he looked towards it Rose stepped into the office. His heart pounded; he stood up too fast and heard the chair skid away behind him, and wondered if he should offer Rose his hand or if that would be taken as being offensive.

'Mr Forrester.' He heard her low voice and saw her smile as she crossed the room, her hand held out for him to take. 'I didn't think we'd meet again. Not this soon.'

She was wearing gloves but he could feel the soft strength in her fingers as she shook his hand and held it for a fraction longer than was formally polite.

'Miss Laybourne.' He cursed himself for his earlier doubts, and suddenly wished that they were alone and could talk.

'As you can see, on this occasion I found my parents without any trouble.' Her green eyes glanced mischievously out from under her long lashes, and stayed with him as she introduced her mother.

'I'm pleased to meet you, Mrs Laybourne.' He shook her hand and knew exactly what Rose would look like in twenty years' time; still beautiful but poised and elegant rather than impulsive and youthful.

'Rose's mysterious boy prince.' Mrs Laybourne nodded and smiled.

'Mama!'

'I'm no prince, Mrs Laybourne.' He caught a strange, distant expression in Rose's eyes, and felt too unsettled to say anything more.

'It's time we left.' Mrs Laybourne nodded towards the office clock.

'We're meeting John, my brother, at the station,' Rose explained breathlessly. 'He's coming home from America. He's been away for two whole years, Mr Forrester!'

'Aye.' He laughed; her excitement amused him. 'My

sister, Lizzie, Elizabeth, told me he's been digging coal out there. Is that right, sir?'

'That's correct, Mr Forrester. He's been trained in mine engineering and I decided that he should spend some time in the United States to gain experience which would not have been possible in England. You will be working directly under him before very long, if you accept my offer.'

'You will accept, won't you, Mr Forrester?' Rose pleaded, and he knew that if he did not look away from those green eyes he would accept the job just to make her happy.

'I thank you for the opportunity, sir,' he said to her father, and immediately turned so that he could look at Rose. 'I'll certainly think about it. Very seriously.'

Then he was outside, walking towards the gates, hoping not to be noticed by a group of men gathered in the far corner of the yard.

'Edward!' His heart beat fast as he heard Henry Wright, William's twin, calling. 'Come over here, man. We need to talk to you.'

'Not now, Henry. I've had enough today, man.'

'Come on. It's important. Won't take long.' Henry left the group and came across to fetch him.

'I'm buggered, Henry. I just want to go home.'

Henry grabbed his arm and pulled him towards the other men. 'You've been up there a long time, Edward. What was it all about?'

'I had to talk to Speake about yesterday,' he said, and saw from Henry's nod that he did know Speake had left some time earlier.

He heard Henry lecturing him but his mind was not on what was being said, he was thinking about the offer Mr Laybourne had made. 'Sorry, Henry, say that again.' He forced himself to concentrate.

'We've been talking and we've agreed we want you to lead us into the association, Edward. We don't want any more truck with Laybourne. We want to force him to put in a second shaft, better pumps, better ventilation, and we want an end to the "no coal, no pay" rule.'

'Aye?' He wanted to warn Henry about the dangers of making the demands but did not feel he should repeat what Mr Laybourne had told him, it would have seemed like a betrayal of a confidence.

'It's only what you and William wanted,' Henry said firmly. 'The things you and William and me agreed about.'

'Aye, Henry, and there's a lot who didn't agree so I'll have to think about it.' He tried hard not to sound too evasive.

'Think about it!' Henry exploded. 'What's there to think about, man? What's the matter with you?'

'Henry, I'm tired.' He looked over Henry's shoulder and saw Rose and her mother as they walked down the steps from the manager's office and were helped up into the four-horse carriage that was waiting.

'Aye, well don't take too long deciding,' Henry said brusquely. 'We cannot bring William back but if we get what he wanted we can at least say he died for a reason. If we don't, then I reckon he'll always be there, Edward, haunting us, like.'

And as he watched the Laybournes' carriage drive towards the gates and saw Rose smile at him he knew he was heading into a conflict and sensed that, perhaps, William had already started to haunt him.

CHAPTER 6

The wind pounced at half past four, hurling hailstones through the early evening gloom, turning the black railway sleepers white and whipping the railway's telegraph wires until they whined.

Elizabeth grabbed at her bonnet and looked along the platform. The station seemed empty apart from the station-master who was sitting in his booth, drinking tea and reading; too absorbed to care that she was standing in the open even though he had seen her.

The station looked unusually well lit with additional oil lanterns strung up between the fixed lamps, and the platform seemed to have been swept clean, even before the wind attacked anything that was loose.

Best of all there was an oil lamp and a coal fire in the first-class ladies' waiting room, and no first-class passengers waiting.

She slipped inside, took off her outdoor coat and the jacket she wore over her white blouse and made herself comfortable in the winged chair nearest the fire. Outside the wind moaned and thrashed hail against the window, but inside it was warm and cosy, smelled of leather, polish and chimney smoke; and the loudest sounds were the oil lamp's stutter, the hiss and shift of the coal fire, and the steady tock, tock, tock of a wood-cased clock. Quiet. Comfort. The chance to be alone. Peace after yesterday's drama and a week of nursing her mother. She opened the book she had brought to read while she waited for Saul's train to arrive.

Concentration ebbed, the book felt heavy and difficult to hold, the coals burned and settled and the lamp stuttered, stuttered, stuttered again and glimmered down to nothing. She slipped into sleep, still and warm like a heavy cloak.

A cold draught disturbed her. She woke slowly, not sure where she was. She did not move until she heard someone moving behind her; then she shook herself awake and stood up ready to apologise for being there.

A match flared.

The station-master looked at her, oddly, she thought. He did not move, just held up the burning match until it scorched his fingers.

'Jesus Christ save me.' She saw him back off through the door, vaguely crossing himself as he went.

'Watch what you're doing, man!'

'Mr Laybourne, sir, don't go in, there's a spectre in there.'

'Don't be a fool, let me pass.' The tall shadow of Mr Laybourne bundled the small, plump shadow aside. 'Who's there?'

'Elizabeth Forrester, sir.'

'What are you doing in here?'

'I'm waiting for Mr Beckett and I sheltered here from the wind,' she began and thought that she should explain fully. 'It was warm and I'm afraid I fell asleep. The lamp must have gone . . .'

'Don't sound so apologetic, Miss Forrester,' Mrs Laybourne said kindly. 'I'm not surprised that you fell asleep after all that's happened to you over the past few days. Your mother, how is she?'

'Back in bed, I'm afraid, ma'am, but thank you for asking. Last night was too much for her, even though you kindly allowed her to wait in the office.'

She turned as Mr Laybourne spoke. 'Nothing particularly kind about that' – the lamp glowed and settled as he lit it and replaced the glass funnel – 'nothing at all.'

She saw Rose for the first time, holding herself and covering her face as though she were ill. Before she could ask what was wrong with her she heard Mr Laybourne call the station-master.

'Here, man, here's your spectre. Come and look.'

The station-master peered around the door, then advanced, slowly, towards her. She watched him come, looked past him at Rose and realised the girl was not ill, she was convulsed with laughter. The station-master stopped a few feet away, obviously nervous and embarrassed. She smiled at the little man in his tight uniform and was tempted to say 'Boo,' but instead she apologised for frightening him.

Rose spluttered.

The station-master looked even more embarrassed, then tried to assert himself.

'You shouldn't have been here. This is for first-class ladies.'

Rose spluttered again.

Mrs Laybourne frowned criticism at her daughter, then said charmingly, 'I believe Miss Forrester is a first-class lady, Mr Timmins.'

She heard Rose splutter even louder and had to put a hand up to hide her own face as she tried hard to stop herself laughing.

'No right to go jumping out on people like that,' Mr

Timmins said pompously, 'especially when you don't have a ticket.'

She saw Rose with tears running down her face, ready to collapse with laughter, and bit her own lip hard.

'That's all, Timmins.' Mr Laybourne excused the wretched little man and she was relieved when he closed the door behind him and she could laugh without embarrassing him more.

Rose came to her, held on to her and roared with laughter which would have seemed more appropriate if it had come from a man. Rose looked girlish, nothing like as mature as she had been last night.

'That was unforgivable, Rose,' her father said sternly.

'But it was very funny, Papa.'

She felt awkward, being the cause of the incident.

'Nevertheless.' She heard the stern voice again and stopped herself laughing, but noticed the smile that Mrs Laybourne was trying to hide and felt better.

'You're waiting for Mr Beckett.' Rose composed herself and moved away. 'Your young man who's hoping to go to Alnwick, Miss Forrester?'

'Yes, Miss Laybourne.' She was surprised that Rose should have remembered their conversation. 'He's returning from his interview today.'

'Oh, Miss Forrester.' Mrs Laybourne moved aside and motioned towards a young woman standing in shadows just inside the door. 'Forgive me. I haven't introduced Miss McDougall.'

The woman stepped forward and offered a dainty nod in acknowledgement. She was pale, slim, small and very pretty, a delicate frond of a woman.

'My son's fiancée.'

The girl smiled and nodded again. It was obvious that she did not want to become too familiar.

'I'm pleased to meet you, Miss McDougall,' she said clumsily to the girl's half-turned face.

A train whistle blew, the waiting room door banged

open and Rose disappeared in a flurry of skirts and long coat, one hand clutching her hat.

The locomotive arrived in a rush of steam and smoke which added to the confusion on the platform. Three women eager to see a son, a brother and a lover they had not seen for two years and wondering, she guessed, how much he had changed in that time.

Elizabeth felt guilty. Saul had been gone for three days and she could not say that she had missed him particularly. She was only waiting for him because she felt it was her duty to be there and because she wanted to know if he had been offered the post in Alnwick; if she would be forced to make a decision which would affect the rest of her life.

The station-master had wasted his time stringing up the extra lanterns; the wind had put most of them out and left pools of darkness all along the platform. The train's carriages and wagons reached almost to the platform's canopy, shutting out the wind but enclosing the smoke and steam so that it was impossible to see anything clearly. Everything was foggy or shadowy.

A shadow she had not noticed moved suddenly. She stepped aside too late; the shadow collided with her and immediately she felt strong arms wrapped around her, holding her tight.

'I'm real sorry,' a strange voice apologised, 'I hope I didn't hurt you.'

'Not at all.' She was breathless from the impact and the hold the man had on her.

The smoke cleared and she saw a tanned face smiling at her. The man was even taller than her, a head taller. His teeth were white, his eyes grey and his hair the colour of sun-bleached straw. His shoulders were wide and he had strong arms that held her against his hard body. He was John Laybourne, there was no question, but he was not the nervous boy that she remembered seeing a few times years earlier.

'I am real sorry, miss,' he said again, but not sorry

enough to release her, she thought and immediately realised that she did not mind being held by him.

'John!' Rose called, and he was gone, swinging his sister off the ground and kissing her full on the mouth.

She watched, and felt cheated. Then she saw the way he pecked Miss McDougall's cheek and the feeling mellowed.

Then Saul was there, pecking her cheek, but she did not notice what he said, her attention was focused on John Laybourne greeting his mother and shaking hands with his father, laughing and talking all the while in his strange deep voice. He had changed.

'Elizabeth?' She heard Saul and turned to him. 'Are you pleased to see me?'

'Yes. Of course.' She hoped she sounded convincing.

'John Laybourne,' he explained the obvious, 'we travelled together from Newcastle. Quite an interesting young man.'

'Yes, I expect he is,' she answered enthusiastically, and thought how pompous Saul sounded.

He could not be more than two years older than John Laybourne, certainly not senior enough to refer to him as a young man.

'Miss' – she turned away as John Laybourne touched her shoulder – 'are you sure that I didn't hurt you?'

'Quite sure, thank you, Mr Laybourne.'

'Mr Laybourne.' He seemed to ponder the name. 'I can see I'm back in England.'

She thought he sounded disappointed to be back, but then he smiled. 'You must be Miss Forrester, Saul's fiancée. You teach in the Lower School where you used to be a pupil. I remember watching you recite Shakespeare at a St George's Day parade, you and your brother, when you were quite young.'

'That was years ago,' she said, trembling because he had remembered her.

'You were good, but your brother, well.' He shook his head. 'What was his name?'

'Edward.' She laughed, and because he seemed so friendly she added quickly, 'It still is his name.'

'And he's the town's hero.' Rose put her arm through her brother's. 'Yesterday he saved several men from dying underground.'

'An accident? Was it bad?' She noticed the way his smile disappeared instantly.

'I'm afraid it was.' Mr Laybourne tried to pull his son away and Elizabeth was pleased to see John resist.

'Any of your family . . .' He did not finish the question and suddenly she was embarrassed by the way he looked directly into her eyes.

'No, thank God, but our neighbour lost a son and a brother.'

'Many dead?'

'Fifteen, and two dozen injured.'

'Oh.' It seemed that he did not know what to say and she felt sorry for him. 'Dangerous business, mining.'

'Aye,' she answered and nodded farewell as the delicate Miss McDougall led him away.

He looked back, nodded, shrugged, and she was alone with Saul.

Rose sat facing rearwards, Lillian sharing her seat, but sitting away in the corner, and her parents either side of John on the back seat.

She was tired from the effort of last night and the excitement of John's return; and her chest felt a little tight, warning that an asthma attack might start if she did not rest.

So she sat back, listened to the conversation and looked at John. He had told her that he would not have recognised her because she had changed so much; but he had changed too, more than she had expected. Not physically, but in some invisible way. He looked like her brother but he was different, a man in his own right, a little distant, almost a stranger.

She wondered what Lillian thought about him, and remembered the way she had stretched her neck for John to peck her cheek when they met again. It was not the way she would have wanted to be greeted by her fiancé if he had been away for two whole years. She would have wanted to be picked up and kissed firmly, on the mouth. A long, passionate kiss that told her how much he had missed her.

Then she remembered that was almost how John had kissed her and her mother. Perhaps he was satisfied just to peck Lillian's cheek rather than kiss her properly.

And Mr Beckett? He had given Elizabeth Forrester a similar peck, as if he was meeting her again after just a few hours instead of three or four days. Was that how engaged couples were meant to behave? It was not very romantic.

Would Hubert kiss her like that, she wondered, and decided he probably would. Very politely, very gently.

Her chest tightened a little more. Poor Hubert; polite, handsome, Hubert. He was all the things that Edward Forrester was not, yet it was Edward Forrester she had thought of the moment she woke up that morning.

The carriage pulled round a bend and started the slow climb out of the valley. She remembered how slowly it had climbed last night, or was it early this morning, when she had sat back and tried to remember everything about Edward, every movement he had made, everything that he had said. Meeting him today had confirmed what she remembered.

He was not handsome, in fact he looked rather stern. He was short and too broad for his height, he had untidy hair, and he was not particularly well mannered; but there was something attractive about him. Something in his eyes or his voice, or in his gestures? Something indefinable.

Elizabeth waited for Saul to collect his bag, and then let him take her arm and lead her out of the station, into the wind and sleet.

'The previous master has died and they've offered me the position,' Saul said without any preamble, 'on very favourable terms which I've accepted.'

'You've accepted?'

'The salary is very reasonable, quite generous, and of course there's also a house provided in the grounds, although we cannot move in until the widow and her children vacate it, of course.' Her question went unnoticed.

'That's rather inconvenient,' she said, mimicking his mood, 'the widow wanting to stay there until she finds another home.'

He did not seem to notice the edge to her voice and he continued without pausing. 'I'll have to find temporary lodgings until the house is available but I suppose it'll save me employing a housekeeper until you can move in. I thought a June wedding would be best. You're excited, I suppose?'

She did not answer, but it did not matter, he was excited enough for both of them. They walked on and she tried to listen as he told her in detail about everything that had happened or had been said during the last three days.

They parted when they reached the house where he lived with his parents. They invited her to tea but she refused, using the excuse that she must go to her own parents as her mother was ill again; but neither Saul nor his parents seemed to listen. They were all too impressed by the thought of him teaching in a private school, and none of them seemed to consider the inconvenience Saul would cause Pincote Higher School by leaving in the middle of a term.

She had been walking with one arm held captive by Saul and the other raised to hold her bonnet. Now, alone, she took her bonnet off, stuffed it inside her coat, and walked with her hands thrust into her coat pockets. Spikes of ice stuck in her hair until the wind blew them out or they melted and ran down her face and neck. She did not care, she had too much on her mind to worry about small things like that.

She turned towards Pincote Colliery and people she could understand. People without ambitions, perhaps, but people who cared about each other.

People like Edward, who had risked his life to save a friend and resented being called a hero. Who put up with his father's moods to save his mother worrying. Who had not yet realised that Nancy Wright was in love with him and would do anything for him. He was typical of the people she knew. People who did not take advantage of each other's weaknesses. People you could trust.

The wind blew on her back, pushing her onwards, lightening her steps, and she wondered if it was symbolic.

CHAPTER 7

'You're a fraud, Edward Forrester,' Henry yelled at him across the yard. 'You say one thing and you do something else.'

'Maybe I am, Henry,' he shouted back and felt the pain banging into his head again, 'but at least I'm not trying to prove a point by stopping the mine from being repaired. Call your lads off the gates, man, and let anyone who wants to work on the repairs do it with a clear conscience. They need the wage the company'll pay for the repairs and we all need the mine working so we can start earning again. The company as well as us.'

'Aye? Repair a damaged shaft when what we really need is another one?'

'Well, you'll not get anything if you stop the pits producing, which is why me da and me brothers are working. I would be too, if I felt up to it, like.' He walked over to the gates so he could talk to Henry without shouting. 'I told you yesterday that I wasn't sure if the

association was the right thing for Pincote. I still want to
think about it, but I can tell you we'll get no support for the
association if the men think it'll cost 'em their jobs or even
if they think they'll lose wages. So do yourself a favour,
man, and either work on the repairs or go home.'

There was a murmur of support from the twenty or so
men Henry and his mates were keeping out of the yard.

'Aye, come on, Henry,' one of the men said. 'I've got me
wife and five bairns to keep and I cannot do without the
work, man.'

Several more men agreed and Henry suddenly stepped
away from the gates and without speaking motioned his
mates to follow him down Murdock Street.

'Thanks, Edward,' several of the men said as they filed
through the gates.

He nodded, then began to walk home.

He walked slowly, glad to be alone for a few minutes.
One of the problems of living five to a two-bedroom house
was that there was no privacy, few opportunities to be
alone, few opportunities to think without being
interrupted.

But he could not think, not clearly. His head was
hurting and he suddenly felt very tired, too tired to make
sense of the muddled thoughts which kept jumping up and
fading away. The conversation he had with Mr Laybourne,
the association, Henry, and Rose Laybourne's smile: they
all rushed about in his head and made him angry with
himself for not being able to settle them into some sort of
order.

He walked along the alley behind the houses and stood
in the back yard for several minutes, in the dark and away
from the window where he might be seen, composing
himself not to be irritated by the cosseting Elizabeth was
sure to give him when she saw his head was bleeding
again.

When he opened the kitchen door he was surprised to
see Nancy Wright sitting at the table. He had not been

avoiding her deliberately, but that did not stop him feeling guilty that he had not spoken to her about William, and he assumed that was why she was there.

'Edward!' She jumped up to look at the cut on his head, her cool fingers gentle on his face. 'Looks nasty, lad. And it's bleeding.'

'Aye, it's hurting a bit.' He winced as she prodded. 'Reckon I just need a bit of a lay down, like.'

'Aye, but you'd best let me put a fresh bandage on that first, mind. And there's tea if you want some. I made it for your ma. Lizzie asked me to keep an eye on her.'

'How is she?'

'Asleep, again.' Nancy grimaced. 'She's sleeping an awful lot, Edward. She doesn't look well, not at all.'

'Tough old bird, is Ma,' hiding his fear, 'and the doctor said she needed plenty of rest. Anyway, where's Lizzie?'

'Gone to meet Saul off the train. To find out if he got his job, like.' She reached up to a shelf and took down a clean bandage the nurses had passed on. 'Sit down, and I'll clean that cut and bandage you up a bit.'

He did as he was told and enjoyed being fussed over, which surprised him. Nancy had always liked to take care of him, even when she was little. She was always there, a devoted little puppy, eager to do anything to make him happy, except go away when he wanted to be alone.

Now she was sixteen, and not so little, he noticed as her breasts brushed against him. She had turned into a woman. He was not sure when it had happened; it must have been a sudden change because she was still a little girl the last time he noticed her. But now she was a woman, an attractive woman. Ned would have to watch over her.

'There.' She tucked the loose end of bandage into the binding. 'Now stand up.'

He did as he was told.

'I nearly forgot something,' she said and wrapped her arms around his neck. 'Your birthday kiss, even though it's a day late.'

Her soft lips pressed against his. She held them there for a moment, and then, just as he began to enjoy it she pulled away.

'Nice?' Her pretty round face, full lips, grey eyes and golden hair seemed to fill the room.

'Aye, quite nice, for a young lass,' he admitted and prepared to grab her if she flounced away, which she did. 'Just teasing, Nance.'

'Teasing?' Her eyebrows arched up, and suddenly she was back, her hands behind his shoulders and head, pushing his lips down on to hers, her tongue thrusting his aside as it searched his mouth.

He did not know what to do with his hands so he rested them on her hips, round firm hips that suddenly drove her body hard against his, so hard that he was pushed against the wall. Feelings burst through him, confusing him. The pain Rose had caused yesterday came back into his groin, and as Nancy's tongue left his mouth his tongue chased it, thrusting deep into her.

She whimpered; his heart beat fast and he slid his arms around her and crushed her into him, felt the push of her breasts against his stomach. He held her hard until neither of them had any breath left, then he lifted his mouth off hers but kept his grip on her body.

Her head rolled back, exposing her soft throat, gurgling with laughter. 'Was that better then?'

'Aye.' Nothing more to say, just get ready to kiss her again.

'Do you like me better than Rose Laybourne, then?'

'What?'

'I saw the way you looked at her last night. You've never looked at me that way.' She looked wounded, suspicious.

'Don't be silly, Nance, she's the owner's daughter.'

'And wouldn't look twice at a miner?' Her eyebrows arched again.

'Nor even a mine manager, lass. Not in her class.'

'So you don't like her?'

'I did not say that. I like her fine enough.' It was good to tease her again, good to hold her as she tried to wriggle away. 'And she really cares about people like us, Nance.'

'Aye? And what makes you think that?' The wriggling stopped and she looked serious. 'You saw her for a few minutes yesterday and you reckon you know what she's like?'

'I want this kept secret, Nance. It might upset a few people, especially your ma and da, so keep it to yourself.' He felt her relax against him. 'She's persuaded her father to offer us a post as a deputy, and then to train as assistant manager. Manager perhaps, in time.'

He was still excited by the feel of her body against his but he saw the passion drain away from her, and he let her step back.

'Are you sure?'

'Aye, lass, I've been talking to Laybourne himself, like, this afternoon.'

'That'd mean more money, I suppose.'

'Aye, I suppose so.'

'Enough for you to leave home? Get married?'

'Aye, maybe.' He had not thought about the details of his possible future life.

'Edward, you must know how I feel about you, and always have.' He watched her as she sucked her lips and tried to compose herself. 'But do you love me?'

God, what a question. On top of everything else!

The back door opened before he had to answer and the wind and Elizabeth rushed in.

'We're in for another night of it, I reckon.' She took her wet coat off. 'Thanks for watching Ma for me, Nancy. Is she all right?'

'Aye, sleeping.'

'That's good. Oh, your ma wants you, lass,' she said above the sound she made shaking her coat.

Nancy shrugged and moved towards the door and he was glad Lizzie had come in when she had.

Did he love Nancy? Much as he did Lizzie he would have said until a few minutes ago, but now he was not sure. There was one thing he was sure about: he was sorry they had stopped kissing.

He wrapped his own wet coat around Nancy's shoulders and squeezed her gently, hoping that might mean something to her, then slapped his cap on her head and opened the door for her to run next door the back way. She turned and waved as she went through the high back gate, then she was lost behind the seven feet of bricks which separated the yards.

He stood by the open door for a moment, enjoying the freshness the wind and sleet brought off the moors, then Elizabeth complained about the draught.

'Everything all right?' she asked and he watched her eyes and knew something had made her suspicious. 'Between you and Nancy?'

'Aye, just talking, like, and Nance bandaged me head again.'

'Making your peace with her, about William?'

He shrugged. He did not want to lie, especially to her, but he needed time to think.

'How did your Saul get on over at Alnwick?' He took the opportunity to change the subject, and wished he had not.

'My Saul? Oh, wonderfully well,' she answered flatly. 'They've offered him the post and he's accepted it. Yes, Saul, my Saul, has done extremely well.'

'So well that you're upset?'

'Saul's ambitious,' she said, shrugged and turned away.

'Aye, and what's wrong with that? You're always telling me to try to improve myself, lass.' He reached out and turned her around so he could look at her face. 'You're a teacher, Lizzie. I thought education was all about giving people the chance to improve themselves.'

'It is. Of course it is, but you've got to be responsible about it.'

'And Saul isn't? I'd have thought he was about the most responsible person alive, lass.'

'He's doing it for the wrong reasons, for his own gain.'

'But that's why people do most things, Lizzie. Anyway, you'd gain too.'

'Not if I don't marry him.'

'Sounds serious.' He squeezed her shoulders.

She nodded, and said quietly, 'I'm not sure I still love him, Edward. In fact, I'm not sure I even like him very much.'

'That does sound serious.' He let his hands drop. 'But you've known him for two years now. What's changed?'

'Nothing, not really. He's a good man at heart, like, honest, careful, responsible, intelligent . . .'

'And boring, Lizzie, and stuck up.' He tried to make her smile but the ruse did not work.

'That's just his way, he doesn't mean any harm. He can be very considerate, always was to me. Never treated me as though I was just big, gangly, bossy Elizabeth, the woman who's got a mind of her own and terrorises the menfolk for miles around.'

'That's not how you are, Lizzie.' He defended her against herself. 'Fair enough, you speak out about things that matter to you, but there's nothing much wrong with that.'

'Maybe not in a man, but if a woman does it men get scared and run away. Men like their women to be quiet, obedient little souls, and I reckon Saul might be my only chance of finding someone who'll put up with me. I'm twenty-two, older than most single women around here. I want a home and I want children. I don't want to grow old on my own, Edward. Do you understand that?'

'Never thought about it, lass.' He took hold of her hands. 'Have you ever discussed all this with Saul?'

'No, not really. We've talked about getting married, but only as if it was just something we would get around to one day. Something inevitable, like summer or autumn.' She shrugged. 'We never really talk much, and now I think about it I reckon he's as desperate to find someone who'll put up with him as I am to find someone who'll put up with me.'

He held her as she cried on to his shoulder. 'You're just tired, Lizzie. You'll think differently tomorrow.'

'I don't know, Edward, lad. I can't stand ambitious people, not if they're prepared to let everyone else down just so they can make themselves look good, like.' She hugged him and pulled away. 'I'm glad we can still talk like this. Glad you're not like Saul.'

He avoided her eyes as she looked at him. She knew him too well and he was scared she might look into his eyes and see the troubles inside his head. He did not want the added complication of her opinion, not at the moment, especially as she suddenly seemed biased against ambition.

He had an opportunity to change his life, an opportunity he had not thought possible, an opportunity which could put him in a position to help men and women who needed his help; so what instinct told him he would be wrong to take it? Why did he sense that Mr Laybourne was trying to trick him?

CHAPTER 8

———————————◆———————————

Its real name was North Hill Cemetery but the people who knew they were destined to go there called it the boneyard.

North Hill formed the northern slope of Pincote Valley, the side opposite South Ridge. It was steep, and above the terraced cottages that were Pincote Colliery, above the fringe of fields that had reverted to scrub, was the beginning of the North Moors; reedy marshes lying between bracken-covered islands and outcrops of rock.

The burial ground was on the lower edge of the moor, just above the scrubby abandoned fields. It was an exposed patch of ground which grew larger every year as more and more graves were needed. It grew upwards, away from the town below, and it was enclosed by low walls made from rocks hewn out of the ground when new graves were dug. The walls were built dry, without mortar, so they could be demolished and rebuilt as the boundary was moved.

Some of the graves were not graves at all, just grey granite headstones made to mark the life and death of someone whose body lay entombed in the mine under the valley floor.

Apart from, perhaps, a posy pinned down on the day of burial there were no flowers on the graves. The weather on North Hill beat down anything but the toughest gorse; there were no trees or bushes and even the spindly grass trembled constantly as it tried to keep its grip on the thin soil.

The road which led up North Hill was cobbled on its lower length, but beyond the highest row of cottages it continued as a rutted track, climbing past a derelict barn and up to and beyond the cemetery. It was possible for a horse to drag a cart up to the cemetery when the sun or frost made the ground hard, but otherwise coffins had to be carried.

It was grey, overcast, a morning made for funerals; and William's was the first of the day. There would be four more, all the dead men whose bodies had been recovered from the mine on the day the left face collapsed.

William's coffin was carried out of Pru's parlour and loaded on a cart pulled by an old nag. Both horse and cart were covered in black crepe tied down with blackened rope.

The mourners lined up, Edward in a place of honour, walking arm in arm with Nancy, in line with her brothers and a few paces behind Ned and Pru. He would have preferred not to have been there, but he was expected to pay his respects and he had more reason to respect William than anyone else in town.

The remaining mourners followed and the cart was driven the short distance from Pru and Ned's house to the end of Albert Street, then it stopped and the coffin was lifted from the cart and William was carried up North Hill on the shoulders of men he had played with as a boy and worked with as a man: his brothers and the men who had tried to save him by carrying him through the bypass tunnel.

The bearers struggled along the rutted track. The slippery mud made their job difficult but they somehow kept William's coffin on their shoulders. As they passed the old barn where all but Adam had played during younger summers they turned and held the coffin up as though they were showing William the ramshackle structure for the last time, then they turned away for the final climb. The procession of mourners straggled along behind, helping each other as more and more mud stuck to their boots.

The vicar should have come up from Pincote Market, but he did not arrive and no one missed him. Everyone assumed that he had either drunk too much brandy to warm him against the cold or that he had simply forgotten to come; and they all agreed that Adam gave William a better farewell than any vicar could have offered.

Adam knew William as well as any of them, and his words sounded more honest for that. 'We wish you weren't dead, my friend, but you are and there's nothing any of us can do about that,' Adam said simply, 'so we hope that if there is another life, you'll be happier there than you were here. Meanwhile, there's Pru and Ned, and your brothers and sister to think about, and we ought to be trying to comfort them and helping them live through their grief and anguish. You were a good man, William, and all of us liked you and trusted you, but you aren't with us any more so we should all think about those who're left. No point in wasting our concern on you, old friend, not now, so let's help your family to get on with their lives.'

It was a much more practical lesson than the usual mutterings about God giving and God taking away.

William's coffin was lowered into its hole, into the water which had already seeped into the bottom, and two men shovelled a mixture of earth and stones on top of the box to stop it floating. And, Edward thought, that was it; the water was going to claim William after all.

He left Nancy at the graveside and walked down to the

lowest wall, stood and looked over Pincote Colliery, the town and the mine. The weather was cold and windy, but at least it was not raining.

He looked at the old barn and remembered some of the times they had all spent there and the myths they had weaved around it. The ghost stories, credible because the cemetery wall was full of holes that the wind moaned through, the ghosts, they had said, of the men and women buried in the graveyard. Now William, the first of them to die, was buried here and his ghost was free to roam, and he knew beyond doubt that William's ghost would not be content to stay in the graveyard.

William always had a persistent spirit and his death would not change that. His ghost would demand justice, as William always had.

'Don't cry.' Nancy was there, brushing away the tears he had not realised he was shedding.

'You don't realise the truth, Nancy,' he blurted out. 'He mightn't have died if it hadn't been for me.'

'Hush,' she said softly. 'Adam told me what you told him. How you and William found each other standing by the gob. If you hadn't found him he would have died anyway, alone and frightened. At least he had you with him at the end. And you did try to save him, and Uncle Gordon. You mustn't feel guilty about what happened. You did your best.'

He let her turn his face to her and she kissed him, just a fleeting, soft, compassionate kiss, nothing like the adventure they had shared in the back kitchen a few days earlier or the short-lived fumble her mother had interrupted in her back yard the following night, when he had still managed to avoid saying the incriminating words 'I love you'.

'Are you coming back to the house, or would you rather be left alone?'

He was astonished by how grown-up she seemed, this sixteen-year-old woman who suddenly showed she knew him as well or better than he knew himself.

'I'd rather be alone, if you don't mind.' He tried to stop his voice breaking but failed.

'Of course I don't mind, and neither will anyone else.' She squeezed his arm. 'We all love you, Edward, in our different ways. Everyone will understand.'

He took her back to her house, kissed her as he left her in the back yard, and walked away, glad to avoid Henry and another almost inevitable argument.

It was impossible to walk around Pincote Colliery without someone stopping to talk, especially on a day like this, so he turned his back on the town and on North Hill, used the railway bridge to cross the river, and headed towards South Ridge.

The slope above the mine had been spoiled where two continuous trains of buckets crossed the valley on cables and dumped debris and black slag, creating enormous arrowheads of rubbish which grew year by year, but he turned away from the mine and climbed a narrow path up the unspoiled, gorse-covered slope leading up to King's Crag.

The sun had begun to shine and although it did not warm the air it did bring clean light into the valley and seemed to brush colour into the hillside. The climb warmed him and the wind blowing into his face refreshed him. He walked steadily and did not stop until he was on top of the ridge, staring across the valley and the moors to the north. He did not look back towards the mine or the cemetery where William's grave was being filled in. He had come up here to be on his own, not to bring ghosts with him.

He stood for a long time, just looking, not thinking, until he began to feel cold. The only shelter on top of the ridge was in a miniature valley which lay inside King's Crag. The crag itself was formed by a three-quarter circle of rocks which jutted out from the ridge like a part-rotted giant tree stump and apart from shelter it offered seclusion. He ambled across to it, lay down on the grass in the crag's lap, and stared up at the high white limitless sky.

He was tired. He had felt tired ever since the accident; tired but full of edgy, restless energy which, after his first night's exhaustion, stopped him sleeping. Now the climb had used up the energy and he needed to sleep.

He woke up several times, always in a panic, water rising up his chest, rocks falling around him; then he fell back into another sleep, and back into the strange world which seemed so real.

His family and friends found him asleep and gathered around him, threatening, shouting, accusing him of being a liar, a traitor. Then he noticed William and Gordon standing apart from the others, calling him, urging him to escape with them. Suddenly they dashed into the crowd and picked him up, carried him away, took him into a tunnel with a bright light at the end; but the light was reflecting off water. He tried to tell them they would all drown but they would not listen, would not put him down. Then he realised they were dead; skeletons with hair which waved like weeds as they walked along the river bed.

And he looked up through the water and saw weeping willows and his mother alone on the riverbank, trying to reach him, and then the men he worked with running along the bank, jeering at him.

The world tipped up and all he could hear was the sound of someone crying, moaning, like the wind.

He drifted awake, relieved that he was dry and safe, and listened to the wind cutting through gaps in the rocks, low, mournful moaning; the ghostly sounds he remembered from his childhood days.

'Edward?' The voice was as soft and low as the wind, and it terrified him. 'Edward?'

'Gordon? William?' he cried out and sat up, scared he was still dreaming but terrified he was awake and they were there, waiting for him.

All he could see were rocks and grass and sky.

'Edward?' There was a voice, behind him.

He rolled over and saw a hatless figure in a wide-collared coat, dark green and almost invisible against the grass.

He strained to see who it was. Not William or Gordon, they were dead, very dead, but the woman who was watching him was alive. She was sitting on a small rock, her shining copper tresses not quite resisting the pull of the wind. Rose Laybourne!

'You scared the hell out of me!' He resented her intrusion, invasion, watching him sleep, catching him off guard.

'I was worried about you, Mr Forrester. You were shouting and threshing about and I was scared either to wake you or leave you alone up here, so I waited for you to wake up properly.'

'I'm sorry.' He knew he had reacted badly. 'I didn't mean to be rude.'

They studied each other for a moment.

'Is this the way you usually start a conversation?' she asked mildly and with such comic mock exasperation that he laughed with her and at himself.

'Only with you, Miss Laybourne.' He was happy to watch her laugh with him, and he stood up and walked closer to her.

She reached out and brushed something off his sleeve, an unconsciously intimate gesture that somehow made her seem as though she had always been a familiar part of his life, and asked, 'What are you doing here?'

'I wanted to be alone.' He looked into her quiet eyes. 'And you?'

'I wanted to be alone,' she answered, flashing a smile which was instantly replaced by a blush of embarrassment and downcast eyes.

'Then perhaps we should ignore each other,' said lightly in the hope that she would argue.

'You're a very difficult man to ignore, Mr Forrester,' he heard and his heart beat harder.

He looked at her and knew what he had to say. 'Miss Laybourne, I don't think anyone could ever ignore you.'

She looked even more embarrassed and he felt awkward and clumsy. He should not have spoken to her like that. 'I'm sorry, Miss Laybourne, I shouldn't have said that.'

'Please don't keep apologising.' There was a moment's pause as she seemed to look for something on the ground, then she glanced up from under her eyelashes. 'It was a very nice thing to say, Mr Forrester, and I'm glad you said it.'

The world fell away and for a moment there was just her and an impression of peace. The wind tweaked her hair and lines creased into her square forehead as she spoke in her low voice.

'I don't mean to pry, but you did not seem to be sleeping well.' It was a question more than a statement, but said in a way that suggested he did not have to answer if he did not want to.

'I think I was dreaming.'

'Bad dreams,' she said quietly, 'about the accident?'

'Aye. We buried my friend William today.'

'I understand. Was he a close friend?'

'Close as my brothers. We grew up together, next-door neighbours since I can remember.'

She nodded and looked away and he knew that she was giving him a few moments to control his feelings.

A big bird flew above them, turned and glided across the gorse, let out a mewing cry and rose up as it was joined by its mate. The birds circled, chasing each other in a rising spiral until they were indistinct dots against the white sky, then they swooped down and raced across the lower slope towards the large manor house.

'I'm surprised you come all the way up here to be alone, Miss Laybourne.'

She turned to watch the birds, and as she turned her head back again he sensed that the quietness in her eyes had spread through her whole body.

She shrugged and he could see that she felt embarrassed. 'It's so, so peaceful up here. I know that probably seems silly when there are warm rooms down there in the house, but there's a special peace up here that I can't find anywhere else, so I come here when I've anything important to think about. Or when I really want to be sure I'll be alone.'

'That's not silly, Miss Laybourne. I can understand. I like to get away meself, sometimes. I walk over North Hill and sit on the moors up there.'

'But you came here today? Why was that? Oh, of course.' She reacted to her own question immediately and seemed almost to panic. 'I'm sorry, that was a stupid thing to say under the circumstances. The cemetery's on North Hill, isn't it? I didn't think.'

'No, you're all right, Miss Laybourne. I'm over that now. William's dead and there's nothing to do but get on with things. Adam Marriott, our chapel preacher, said we ought to concentrate on looking after the living, and I reckon he's right.' He watched her watching him, nodding and waiting for him to continue. 'It's how you do that. That's what I've got to think about now.'

'I don't understand what you mean.'

'I'm not even sure I understand what I mean, Miss Laybourne, but I suppose it's really a matter of me conscience.' He sat down in front of her.

'I still don't understand.' She was still sitting on the rock but she leaned forward, elbows on her knees, chin in her hands, in a way that told him she really was interested in what he might say. 'Do you want to explain? Or isn't it any of my business?'

'Oh, it's your business all right,' said half jokingly to ease what had to be said, 'in more ways than one, mind. Look, Miss Laybourne, it's all right us sitting here and talking like this, but it's unusual, isn't it? I mean, I'm a miner, grew up mining and living with miners. I owe it to them to stick by them, and they reckon they want me to help them get the association in to make your father improve conditions. For my part, well I'm keen to take up your father's offer but he's told me he'll not abide the association under any circumstances. Now, do I look after meself like, join forces with your father and your family and say to hell with whatever me family and me mates think? Or do I thank your father and you but stick with me own kind?'

'But surely there's no question? Papa will never allow the Miners' Association to come into Pincote. He'd rather close the mine. You'll never persuade him, or force him, to change his mind, and you'll only be able to help your family and friends if you accept his offer.' There was a note of insistence in her voice.

'Aye, that's what he told me, but maybe . . .'

'No.' She shook her head and looked nervous. 'I know my father, Mr Forrester. Once he's made up his mind nothing will make him change it. Believe me!'

She sounded almost as if she was frightened and he wondered what else was on her mind. Perhaps he might find a way to ask her later, but first he had to explain his own fears so she could understand. It seemed very important that she did understand what a sacrifice he might be making if he took up the offer. The managers had no friends in the colliery town. Even George Willis, born into mining and related to miners, had few real friends since he had become a deputy and in Laybourne's direct pay.

'I'd like to believe what your father told me, Miss Laybourne, but it's all a bit cosy for my liking. The day after the men show that they'd take me for a leader, and the day it comes out that William and I've been trying to get them to join the association, your father offers me a nice job with a future, so long as I support him and persuade the men to forget the association. He never offered me that sort of job before.'

'But you hadn't come to his notice before.' She stood up. 'Don't you understand that? The same day he heard that you had led men away from probable death I recognised you as the boy who took care of me years ago. That's all there is to it. It's not "cosy" at all. It's simply that the two events coincided, but it's what happened and you've no reason to be suspicious.'

'I'm glad to hear you say that, Miss Laybourne.' He was happy to believe her; there was something in her eyes, in her face, that encouraged trust.

'Then you'll accept the position Papa, my father, has offered you?'

'Change sides? That's how most of the people I know will see it, Miss Laybourne. They'll look on me as a traitor. They'll think I've only taken the job because I want to get on, to better meself, like.'

'But even if they think that at first they'll soon see that you're also helping them,' she insisted, 'so surely they won't begrudge you your own opportunity, Mr Forrester.'

'People only see what they want to see, Miss Laybourne, and if I take on your father's job they'll see me in almost the same light as they see your family. Worse, maybe.' He knew he had said too much but it was too late; her expression showed she had noticed.

'And what do people think of my family, Mr Forrester?' There was an edge to her voice.

'I'm sorry, I shouldn't have spoken out like that, not after all your generosity.'

'Mr Forrester, please don't feel beholden to us, we don't deserve it. I've simply thanked you for a kindness you once did me, and my father has offered you an opportunity which he believes will benefit everyone, so I'd like you to explain what you meant.' Her green eyes were hard and cold.

He shifted uneasily. 'It's time for me to leave, Miss Laybourne.'

'I didn't think you were the sort to run away, Mr Forrester.' Her bluntness caught him off guard.

'I'm not, but I don't want you to think I'm rude, Miss Laybourne.'

'Oh, I don't.' Now she sounded defensive. 'I don't think you're rude, Mr Forrester, but I did think you spoke your mind. Your sister told me what she felt people thought about us, and I'd value your opinion. Please tell me what you meant.'

The green eyes were appealing, too appealing to be ignored no matter how much the truth might hurt her.

'Your family's very rich, Miss Laybourne, and most people reckon you've made your money by making them sweat, by paying low wages and keeping them in poor conditions you wouldn't live in yourselves.' He could not look at her as he spoke, and that made him feel even worse.

She did not speak, and when he did look at her he saw that she looked dismayed.

'I can understand that, Mr Forrester, especially after seeing Mrs Darling's home, but is that how you feel?'

'Aye, if you really want the truth, I reckon it is. You live a very privileged life, Miss Laybourne.'

'So you don't feel we do enough to deserve what we have?'

'It's not my place to say . . .'

'Please, Mr Forrester, don't stop now. Tell me, honestly, how you feel. It is important that I know.'

'Well.' He felt uncomfortable, but he forced himself to look into her eyes. 'It's not just you, your father anyway, but generations of your family. Your family's sucked the life out of the people here and—'

'Have you ever heard the story of King's Crag?' she interrupted him.

'King's Crag?'

'Yes. That's where we are. King's Crag.'

'I know that,' he began, but before he could say anything

more she stood up, grabbed his hands and pulled him on to his feet.

'Come on. You told me a story the first time we met but I'll tell you one this time, a real one, not a fairy story.' She tugged him towards the highest of the rock outcrops. 'When we get to the top I'll tell you something which may help you to understand the truth about our family and what we've already done to improve people's lives around here.'

When we get to the top? He stared at the bare rock, thirty or forty feet high and steep-sided, not much less than a sheer cliff; then at the girl, short and soft and dressed in a heavy coat, a hand muff and shiny boots. Then he saw the way her face was set and he knew she was going to climb and that he had no choice other than to follow.

She did not wait for him and started scrabbling her way up. He watched for a minute, ready to catch her if she fell but she went up like a cat up a tree. He followed.

He caught up with her and they climbed side by side, five or six feet apart.

The wind constantly curled around the rock, tugging one minute and blowing the next, freezing fingers, watering eyes and stinging ears.

'You all right?' He was level with her and she seemed to be stuck, looking for a handhold to steady her.

She nodded and he hoped he looked as confident as her. He looked down and saw thirty feet of cliff below his boots, and several hundred feet of steep hillside below the cliff. If either of them fell they would drop three or four hundred feet before the gorse and fallen boulders stopped them.

He looked at the girl again. The wind had flapped her wide collar against her face and she was reaching for a handhold which was too far away.

'You sure you're all right?' he yelled again but the wind screamed and she did not seem to hear. 'Stay where you are!'

She was balanced on one foot, only a toehold, one hand gripping the rock and the other stretched out six inches from the next handhold. She looked as though she were preparing to jump towards it.

'Don't!' he yelled desperately and edged across the rock face towards her.

She jumped. The wind caught her and lifted her away from the cliff.

'Oh Christ!' He froze.

Loose stones scattered down the cliff. She slipped, hands scrabbling at the rock, then suddenly she found a grip, clawed her way back and there she was, grinning at him.

'Come on, not far now,' she yelled back and stretched out for another handhold.

His hands shook as he reached up, grabbed the rock and pulled himself on. He reached the top and rolled over the edge, then reached back and offered her his hand to help her up the last three feet.

Her fingers closed on his and her mouth opened in a joyous laugh as he pulled her over the edge and on to the flat top. Suddenly he wanted to kiss her, hold her and kiss her on the mouth the way he had kissed Nancy. But he did not have the nerve so he steadied her until they moved away from the edge, then let his hands drop.

She smiled. She did not look like the sort of girl who would climb a rock face but there was obviously much more to her than her appearance suggested.

The top of the crag was bare and as flat as a table. She led him across to the far side and stood a few yards away from where the crag's south face fell almost all the way to the bottom of the ridge.

The wind was savage, threatening to throw the pair of them down into the valley. Their clothes flapped and her hair streamed out but she did not seem to mind.

It was impossible to hear each other talk unless they stood close together and he held her hand at first, instinctively and without thought, then wrapped an arm around her shoulders. Their heads came together and as her hair rustled up into his face she brushed it backwards, trapping it between their heads, not minding that their cheeks were touching.

He still could not hear her properly so he stood behind her, his arms wrapped around her waist, and she leaned her back against him. He held her tighter and felt the weight of her breasts on his forearms, pressed his face against hers and smelled the scent of her tousled hair and the faintest perfume.

She did not appear to mind and his earlier feeling that she seemed always to have been a part of his life grew stronger. She was the owner's daughter and he knew he should not be standing here alone with her in his arms, but everything had happened so naturally and without contrivance on either part that he did not feel that it was wrong or even that their different status should not allow for it to happen.

It was natural, and innocent and wonderful that they should be there together, alone. And he wondered what she was thinking.

'What do you see around us, Mr Forrester? Tell me.'

He looked in every direction. The afternoon had cleared and all the horizons sat sharp against the sky. Pincote Colliery, the town and the mine were hidden in the valley, but he could see empty moors stretching away to the north and east, the remnants of forests and vast tracks of grazing land beyond Pincote Market to the west, and the field-covered plain with its clusters of farm buildings reaching as far as he could see to the south.

'Describe it,' she ordered and he did his best, but she was not satisfied.

'You're telling me what you think you see' – her breath passed warm across his face – 'but what do you really see?'

'I don't understand.' He gave up after a few moments.

'You're seeing the Laybourne Estates. We own everything you can see, and do you know why?'

He did not, and he listened carefully as she told him.

'The moors have always been there, and you must know how marshy and dangerous they are. Only good for grazing sheep that can grow coats heavy enough to keep out the weather.' She lifted her right arm and pointed away to the west. 'There used to be nothing but thick forest that way. Forests packed with wolves and even bears. Intractable forests with hidden bogs which could drown even a man on horseback. South of here, this farmland, was dangerous marshland and only the local people knew the tracks which led through it.'

'Aye?' The wind caught her coat and flapped it against his knees. 'Go on, it's interesting.'

He listened to her, his head close to her mouth so he could catch her words before the wind stole them; and his imagination imposed his own pictures on the country spread below. He saw it as he thought she saw it, a dangerous, almost impenetrable wasteland.

'Old reports say that sometimes the marshes would glow in the dark, reflecting the fires of hell. Very few people lived here, but those who did raised good crops of reeds and flax, sturdy little horses, cattle and sheep, and later, of course, panned for coal in the river. But they were constantly attacked by bands of robbers and rustlers. Men who did not just steal but who extorted money and kidnapped women and girls and murdered and raped at will. The Romans never succeeded in controlling this area because their armies needed roads to march on and any roads they tried to build just sank into the bogs. Later, the Normans had similar problems and could not extract taxes from the people up here, or control the bands of robbers who knew the secret paths. But the Normans found another way to police the area. The King sent an emissary to talk to the leader of the strongest band of outlaws and they met here, which is why it's called King's Crag.'

The sudden gust of wind took away her breath and she paused.

'Go on, it's fascinating.'

'It was a clear day, like today, and the emissary ceded everything in sight in return for regular payments of taxes and the promise that the leader and his band would no longer be outlawed. The leader was called John Lateborn.'

'Lateborn?'

'Yes. The name changed over the years, so you can see that my forefathers were thieves and murderers, hardly the privileged ancestry you obviously thought we have. The family ruled the area without interference from the Crown, maintained local peace, administered a sort of justice, and imposed and collected taxes for the Crown and for themselves. And gradually, over hundreds of years, the family changed their attitude to the people they ruled, and the land they owned. It took centuries but they drained the marshes and settled tenanted farms across what became a fertile plain. They filled the worst of the forest bogs and cleared the bracken and spindlewood so the natural trees, oak, elm, larch, beech and pine, could grow unchallenged, and they planted yew and willow along the riverbanks to shelter sheep and cattle during the long winters. The river had always carried pieces of coal and pans were built to make it easier to collect. Cotes, cottages, were built for the workers who worked the pans.'

'Pancotes.' The origin of the town's name became clear.

'Of course. We call it Pincote now. A monastery was built and during Tudor times the monks discovered a cave system which led down to a deep underground seam, the beginning of Pincote Colliery. So you see, without our family this land would never have become what you see now. All the people who live here have the Laybournes to thank for the livings they earn. We have grown rich, I won't deny that, but I won't let anyone tell me that we haven't put back more than we've taken, and even now most of the money that comes from the estates is invested to improve conditions here.'

'You must be very proud.' He was glad she had told him history he had not known, and humble when he thought about his own family's small part in what had happened.

'I am, and so is my father, which is why he doesn't want to allow you or anyone else to force him into giving outsiders a say in what happens here. That's why he doesn't want the Miners' Association. Do you understand, now?'

'Aye.' He was so taken aback he hardly noticed the way she carefully removed his arms from her waist and turned to look at him.

'And do you understand why I think you've a part to play by working with John and my father instead of against them? My father doesn't want to fight with the people who live here, Mr Forrester. He feels responsible for them, and I'm sure that by working with him you can help make a better future for everyone.'

'I do understand, now.' He saw the same concerned look in her eyes that he had seen before.

'You could have been killed last week. From what I've heard, if the rocks which dammed the tunnel hadn't fallen as they did you would have been drowned.' She pushed aside her hair as the wind whipped it across her face.

'That's right, we were lucky.' He remembered his own thoughts as they walked through the bypass, and added awkwardly, 'I remember thanking God at the time.'

'Lucky, Mr Forrester? You're special, I'm sure of that. Perhaps all this was meant to happen. Perhaps your life was saved for a purpose.' She said the last words quietly, almost as if she were speaking to herself, and the way she spoke and looked away from him drew his attention to her embarrassment in talking the way she was. 'Perhaps you've a bigger part to play than you think.'

He wanted to say that there was nothing special about him, but that would have seemed to deny everything that she believed and he did not want to deny her anything.

'Thank you, Miss Laybourne.' It seemed strange to be so formal with a girl he had held close in his arms and who had apparently been happy to share a sort of innocent intimacy with him, but he wanted her to tell him exactly what she thought he should do. 'But what part do you think I've to play in all this?'

'I . . .' she began, and he knew she was not going to say what he wanted her to say. 'I think you'll be good at whatever you want to do because you care. I think you'd make a good manager, if that's what you want to do, because you care about people and their feelings.'

'And what do you want to do?' He pressed the question, hoping she would say more, hoping they could talk a little longer, and when she did not speak at all he tried to lead her. 'What part do you think you'll play?'

'In Pincote? The estates?' A wistful look flashed across her face and was replaced immediately by an expression he had not seen before. 'The estates will pass to my brother, John, and I don't mind that. He'll look after them and the people who live here. He's a good man. An exceptionally good man.'

'But you?' he persisted, unwilling to accept such an evasive answer.

'Me? I'm just a woman.'

She looked deflated, as if she were about to cry, and although he almost reached out to hold her he thought that would be wrong and kept his arms by his side.

'Just a woman?' he said in a light, forced tone. 'I don't think my sister Lizzie'd accept any woman saying she was "just a woman", not without an argument.'

'Miss Forrester is free to do whatever she wants with her life.'

'I doubt she'd agree with that.' He thought about Lizzie and Saul.

'Well, as free as any woman can be.' She looked away again. 'For instance the freedom to decide when and whom to marry.'

'It's not quite that simple, not for Lizzie.'

'But she'll not be forced into marrying her schoolmaster unless she wants to, will she?' As she spoke he regretted what he had said, Lizzie had spoken in confidence, but then Rose added, 'I saw your sister meet her young man at the station. She said something which suggested she was not entirely committed to him.'

'I see, but that's Lizzie. I was asking about you.' He knew he had no right to press her for an answer, but he needed to know what she would say.

'My situation is rather different.' It was not the answer he wanted, not an answer at all but more a remark which begged even more questions. 'And I think we ought to leave, before people begin to wonder where we are.'

His heart leaped as he heard her refer to herself and him as 'we', then he realised that she meant them as individuals and he felt a distance come between them and his excitement turned sour.

He helped her climb down the steep rock face and they stood in the shelter of the crags to say goodbye.

'Should I see you home?' he asked. Anything to prolong the time alone with her.

'I don't think so,' she said evasively and he could tell that she was wondering how her family would react to learning she had spent time alone with a man from the colliery, 'but thank you for offering to take care of me.'

'I'd like . . .' He was going to tell her that he would like to take care of her for ever, but common sense stopped him.

'Yes?' Her eagerness almost pushed sense aside.

'I'd like to thank you for telling me about your family.' It was not a total lie but when he saw the look it brought to her face he wished he had been more honest.

'I hope it helps you to make up your mind to accept my father's offer,' she said and he noticed uncertainty in her eyes and suddenly wanted to hold her again, to be as close as those minutes on top of the rock, but she stepped backwards, away from him. 'Good afternoon, Mr Forrester. I hope we'll meet again, soon.'

And she was gone, gone from the miniature valley, gone

from the world she had weaved about them, gone from the magic of the time they had spent together. But the magic seemed to linger amongst the rocks, and he stayed with it, hoping that by remembering everything they had said to each other he could capture it for ever.

He climbed back to the top of the crag, stood where he had stood with her, and tried to remember the words she had used, tried to remember how it felt to have his arms around her, the feel of her leaning against him. He had held other girls, not many, but enough to realise none had ever affected him like this before. Even the earlier frenzy with Nancy, exciting as it was, amounted to nothing compared with the quiet, yearning excitement that he now felt for Rose. The longing for a fulfilment which could be met simply by her smile, the casual brushing of his sleeve, a shared idea.

He sat down; his knees really were weak and unsteady. They had met three times, not counting that day years ago, and after three brief meetings he was in love with a girl who was several classes out of his reach. He was in love with her, and it was ridiculous.

And how did she feel, if it mattered? She had let him hold her, but they needed to stand close in order to talk and she seemed far more interested in talking than in being close. She had even unwrapped his arms and stood apart, he remembered. She had said he was special, but she meant he had something more than other men from the valley, not that he was special to her. She had said she hoped they would meet again, but she was well brought up and perhaps she was just being polite.

He looked up. The horizons were already indistinct in the late afternoon light. The dream was disappearing.

He stood up again and wrapped his arms around her imaginary body. There was no satisfaction in the embrace, but then he remembered the look in her eyes and the wistful expression that had crossed her face. She had done nothing to encourage him, and she was right not to do so.

They were classes apart, and by deliberately saying
nothing she had made it clear that even if she did have any
feelings for him they must be futile feelings.

Anger purged any guilt he felt about William or the
association. Anger and frustration. And regret that, alone
together on top of their personal world, he had not made
himself clear to her while he held her in his arms, his face
close enough to hers to have taken a kiss, her body close
enough, perhaps, to have given more.

The frustration of the opportunity lost suddenly drove
through him, stirring up the strange restlessness again.

There was no sunset to embellish what was left of the
dream. The day simply died, and as its life flickered away
he dropped down from the ridge, crossed the river on the
iron railway bridge, and let the dark and narrow streets of
Pincote Colliery assimilate him as they always did.

He turned into the alley that ran behind the terrace
where he lived and stopped at Nancy's gate. He had a half-
formed idea and he knew it was wrong, but something
inside was driving him. Something he could not resist. He
opened the gate, and stopped dead.

He could just see through the window into the Wrights'
back kitchen. The curtain had not been closed properly
and he could see Nancy washing herself. She was half in
shadow but as she moved he saw her breasts, heavy and
white and full. A second later she closed the curtain
properly, but instead of dissipating, the energy he had built
up seemed to increase to a fervour.

He reasoned quickly that if she was washing like that
she was probably alone, certainly her father and brothers
must be out of the house; and he walked to the back door,
intending to knock and walk in as neighbours always
did. He did not see a pail until he had kicked it against a
wall.

'Who's there?' A sharp, nervous question and he
imagined her rushing to cover herself.

'Only me, Edward.' His mouth was dry.

'Come in.'

He opened the door and saw her, already covered by a petticoat, but although it covered her it was wet and did not conceal her.

'I'm sorry,' he lied, and stood with his hand on the open door, ready to leave if she told him to.

'Come in and shut the door, it's draughty.'

'I didn't realise,' he lied again and closed the door behind him.

'I don't mind.' She smiled and kept her lips apart. 'If you don't.'

'I don't mind at all, lass.' The wetness spread and the petticoat formed itself to the shape of her breasts, stomach and hips.

'Where've you been, then?'

'Just walking.' He could not take his eyes off her.

'See anyone?'

'Not to talk to,' he lied once more, knowing that any mention of Rose would be disastrous, and telling himself that Rose would not want anyone to know they had met. 'Family out?'

'Aye. Lads are on a wake with Da, and Ma's gone to Uncle Gordon's to sort out his things. Agents'll want the place back now it's empty.' She moved enough to make her breasts swing, and he knew she was teasing him. 'Like what you see?'

'Aye.'

'Well, d'you just want to look, then?'

His hands reached out and lifted her heavy breasts, felt their weight and softness, then he pulled her to his chest, kissed her mouth hard and squeezed her breasts gently until she whimpered just as she had before.

'I love you, Edward,' she said and he moaned as she rubbed her hand over his flies.

'I love you, lass,' he lied, knowing that was the only way she was likely to give him what he wanted.

He ran his hands over her hips and reached down until

he could pull the petticoat up enough to feel her thighs and the hair between her legs.

'You feel ready, lad. I was beginning to think it'd never happen.' She bit his ear.

'It'll happen, now.'

'No.' She pulled away sharply. 'Not here, it's not safe.'

He felt angry and peculiarly relieved at the same time, but then as she tried to turn away he grabbed her and held her as he had held Rose, and the rush came back to him. One hand travelled up to feel her breasts and the other sank back between her legs. He crushed his mouth against her neck.

'I know where we can go, where it's safe.' She moved in his arms but did not try to escape. 'But you'll have to let me dress.'

He let her reach for her clothes but as she dressed he managed to keep hold of her, never completely releasing her, feeling her and keeping both of them aroused all the time.

Even as they walked along the alley and turned up North Hill, he used the cover of the night to keep his hands on her, satisfying himself and ensuring he did not lose any further opportunities that day. Once they were away from the terraces they stopped often, embracing and kissing, his hands always inside her coat, enjoying her promising, warm, body.

She led him under cover. He smelled straw and damp stone, rotting wood, familiar smells from a childhood that was and seemed years gone. Then in a darkness he was accustomed to he turned her around so that her back leaned against him and slowly removed her coat and dress and still damp petticoat. He ran his hands over her body until he had felt every inch of it time and time again, and as her legs began to quiver he laid her down on the straw. He kissed her and felt her until she clawed his clothes off him and begged him to enter her.

He did not know how long the frenzy lasted, but

suddenly it was over and he was resting on his elbows, her nipples brushing his chest as she gasped for breath.

'I love you, Edward.'

He knew how he should have responded, but now it was over he could not bring himself to lie again.

CHAPTER 9

———————

Rose lay back on her pillows and felt the breeze blow in from the open window. Her room was dark, the house quiet.

She had been excused supper and allowed to eat a light meal in her room because everyone thought she looked and sounded as though her asthma were about to recur. She did not want them to worry about her but she could not reassure them she was quite well without explaining that she had over-exerted herself climbing King's Crag. That would have worried them even more and they would have scolded her for taking risks alone on the ridge, and probably they would have forbidden her to go there again.

She chuckled, and imagined their faces if she had also told them she had been held safe in Edward Forrester's arms.

Safe in Edward Forrester's arms. She cuddled herself and tried to remember exactly how it felt to be held by him. She had never felt so safe in her life. Or so excited.

She remembered how she had trembled as she stood on top of the crag, not because she felt scared or cold, but because he was holding her; and as she trembled he had tightened his grip and that had simply made her tremble even more. She remembered the feeling, and trembled again.

She remembered once asking her mother how she would know if she really was in love and her mother had laughed and given an answer which did not help in the least: 'You'll know, Rose, when it happens.'

But her mother was right after all. You did know when you were in love, and she knew she was in love with Edward Forrester.

The name suited him. A good, honest, strong English name.

Rose Forrester, another good English name, but it was not possible, not as things were. If the Lateborns had not been outlaws the family would probably have been given a title, but even without a title the distance between her and Edward could not have been greater. Her parents would never accept him as a son-in-law, not a miner.

Things might change in time but they would not change soon enough for her and Edward; that was not possible.

If only he was the adopted child, not his sister, then perhaps he might find he was like the magical prince in his story and come and claim her, carry her off to be happy ever after; but magical princes and happy ever after only exist in fairy stories, not in towns like Pincote.

It was more than South Ridge which separated her from Edward, it was a whole social attitude.

Yes, things might change, and she would help them change, but not soon enough.

Of course they could run away together, if he wanted to. But would he want to? Did he feel the same about her as she did about him? Surely, if he had he would have tried to kiss her, or at least said something?

The warm feeling she basked in cooled.

It sounded as though he was going to say something, once, but then he seemed to think of something else to say; but perhaps that was because he was unsure of her. She had deliberately not done anything to encourage him, or to discourage him either, so perhaps he really was unsure

Yes, that was why he did not say anything, almost certainly. He did not want to offend her, appear too forward.

And, she was sure, there was something in the way he held her, as if he felt he knew her as she really was. And there was something in his eyes, not just today but when they stood in the rain after he came up from the mine.

Yes, she had confused him, she was sure of that. If they could meet again, alone, perhaps they could talk more openly. And if they could talk they might find a way; after all it was not as if she would inherit the estates, John would, so did it really matter who she married, within reason? A mine manager, perhaps?

Yes, if Edward could prove himself and become a manager then it might be possible; but when would she know?

She tried to sleep, but an energy she had not known before made her impatient; an energy which made her more restless every time she thought about the way he held her, or spoke, or looked at her.

Eventually she stopped trying to sleep, lit the lamp by her bed and took out a sketch pad. She screwed up her eyes to help remember exactly what he looked like, and an hour later she had a sketch she was happy with.

'Rose, are you awake?'

'Yes, John. Come in.' She stuffed the pad under her bedclothes and smiled as her brother sat down beside her.

'How are you feeling?'

'I'm well, John, honestly. Just tired, I suppose.'

'But not tired enough to sleep.' He paused. 'Are you worried about anything, Rose? Papa told me about Hubert Belchester's proposal.'

'Oh, you know about that?' She felt that she should have told him herself.

'Do you want to marry him?'

If he had been there to ask that question a few days earlier she would have been evasive and non-committal, but now she wanted him to know the truth.

'No, but Papa thinks I should. He says I won't find anyone suitable in Pincote.'

'Well, that's true, I suppose.' His answer hurt more than it should have. 'And Mama tells me that Belchester is totally besotted with you. But Rose, Hubert Belchester? Really?'

She laughed at the way he wrinkled his nose and felt bound to make a small joke in Hubert's defence. 'Do you mind? That could be my future husband you're laughing at.'

'No wonder you're feeling ill, little sister.' He laughed but immediately became serious. 'Hubert's a good man, Rose, but there's nothing to him. He's got no character, no backbone and whatever Papa says you mustn't marry him unless you want to.'

'I might not have much choice. Papa thinks I should marry him, and soon. Even Mama thinks I'll grow to love him when I know him better.' Tears welled up and she tried to sound calmer than she felt. 'They've told me I must leave home or I'll never find anyone suitable, and I suppose they're right.'

'Perhaps, but why such a hurry?'

'I'm eighteen in two months, John.'

'Not exactly an old crone, though.'

'Papa thinks I will be if I don't marry soon. He's determined I must leave Pincote this summer.'

'I don't understand the urgency. What difference will a year or two make?'

'Papa thinks it will make a difference, and that's enough. It's not something he's prepared to discuss, John. He's made up his mind, and you know what that means.' She knew John would understand.

'How's your reading coming along?' he asked suddenly and she was so confused that she answered without thinking.

'Slowly, I'm afraid. I love books but I'm still very slow.'

'And your sums?' He frowned and when she wrinkled her nose he laughed.

'History?'

'I know all about our family.' She almost told him she had given Edward Forrester a brief history, but stopped herself. 'And a lot about England and the Empire.'

'Geography?'

'Why do you want to know?' His questions were exasperating.

'Never mind,' he said brusquely, a trait inherited from their father. 'French, art, sewing?'

'I'm fluent in spoken French and can read quite a lot. I'm good at art and needlework.'

'Because Mama teaches you?' he asked and she nodded.

'But you're not very good at the subjects Miss Smith teaches?'

'But that's not really her fault, John.' She defended the old lady who had taught her and John, and Catherine before them. 'I was ill so often when I was small, and now Miss Smith's so old she doesn't seem able to help me much. And I'm not as bright as you.'

'That's rubbish. Perhaps you should go away to school for a year or two. You're fluent in French, so maybe you should go to Mama's old school until you've caught up with your education. I can't think Mama would object if you did want to go. Think, all that's left of our family live near the school and she hasn't seen most of them for years. When she visited you she could also visit them again.' He sounded excited and his new accent became more pronounced as he spoke. 'Think about it, little sister, and let me know if you like the idea. It might be the answer if Papa insists you leave home soon. Better to go away to school for a couple of years than to marry Hubert if you don't love him. Anyway, you never know, you might even meet a handsome Frenchman who'd whisk you off your feet.'

He kissed her and left, and she settled back on the pillows, wondering if it was really something he had only just thought of or whether he or Mama had guessed it was what she wanted to do.

Then, as she thought about going to France, and how she would not be able to see Edward, a vague plan began to form. Two years! A lot might happen in two years, if Edward would wait for her. Everything could change. Perhaps he could make something of himself in two years, just enough for her parents to accept him as a suitable beau; that would be a start.

If he was interested, of course. They must meet again, and before she went to France. She could not go without knowing how he felt about her. If she went to France, of course.

It was all very complicated, she thought, as she drifted into and out of sleep. Anyway, two years in France would give her an excuse not to accept Hubert's proposal.

Hubert! He was handsome, but John was right. Now that she had met Edward she could see that Hubert had no real character. He was too nice, too shiny, too perfect. Not rugged and awkward and difficult like Edward.

She thought about him for a few moments, remembered his arms and snuggled into them under her blanket, drifted away into sleep and half woke up as she remembered that everything depended upon what her father said. Her whole life depended on what her father said.

Then she remembered the sketch and looked at it.

'Good night, darling. Sleep well.' She kissed his lips and tried to imagine how a real kiss would feel.

CHAPTER 10

———◆———

Pincote Colliery was served by three Methodist churches which everyone called chapels, and the largest stood on the corner of Inkerman Street and Alma Street.

It was a functional building, modern and simple, with a slate roof, plain glass windows and red brick walls. The red bricks could still be seen inside the chapel but outside the walls and the windows were stained black by the coal dust which blackened every building in Pincote Colliery.

The chapel did not have a bell; none of the chapels had bells of their own. Everyone who went to chapel knew the times of the services, and if their clocks or watches had stopped or been pawned they had only to listen out for their neighbours or for the single bell that tolled over St George's in Pincote Market and which regulated worship in both towns throughout the Sabbath.

The remembrance service for the men who had died in the accident was held in the Inkerman Street chapel the day after the burials in the North Hill Cemetery. It was

held on a Wednesday, so no bell tolled for the dead men,
but at the appointed hour the chapel filled with novice
widows, weeping mothers, fathers, brothers, sisters and
friends, until the congregation overflowed on to the
pavements and along both Inkerman and Alma Streets.
Everyone wore black or dark grey and it was as if the
building itself had spread out to touch and comfort the
surrounding terraces of flat-fronted cottages, a number
now missing the men who had given them life.

Those outside could not hear the lessons and tributes,
but they could hear the swell of the prayers and the roared
hymns, so they picked up the words, moments late
perhaps, and joined in the service as best they could.

Elizabeth had not visited the chapel since she had
become a schoolmistress. Her position obliged her to
worship at St George's in Pincote Market, always
accompanied by Saul and his parents. She had asked Saul
to join her in chapel but was not surprised when he gave
several quite plausible reasons for not being able to do so,
and as she held Edward's hand she felt treacherously
pleased that Saul was not there.

The front pews were given over to the families who had
lost men. She sat six rows back, next to Edward who was
sitting by the aisle, ready to play his part in the service.
Pru, William's mother, was sitting one row in front, across
the aisle, black, veiled and sobbing so much that her body
shook and her heels rattled against the pew.

'Edward Forrester will now read the roll of honour.' She
heard Adam's words and smiled encouragement into
Edward's taut face before he rose, tugged at his sleeves
and the bottom of his jacket, and walked stiffly towards the
pulpit.

She listened as his boots crunched on the flagstone
floor, the sound somehow emphasising the noise of Pru's
sobs and the constant, half-muffled coughs which marked
every meeting of men who worked in dust underground.

She watched as Edward turned and took out a slip of

paper, his precaution against his emotion making him
forget to mention any man's name.

'Charles Andrews.' His voice sounded rough, thick and
emotional. 'Norman Cartwright.'

Several women lowered their heads and a few cried
tears they tried to repress.

The list continued, punctuated by an occasional howl as
the strain overcame someone's efforts to hold back their
feelings.

'Gordon McKenzie.' She saw Edward stiffen and shake
his head as Adam whispered into his ear and reached for
the list. 'Ian McKenzie. Stuart McKenzie.'

She remembered Edward had almost burst into tears
when he told her how he found the McKenzie brothers,
and now she could see again just how hard it was for him
to stay composed after speaking their names.

'Gordon Wright.' His voice broke. 'William Wright.'

She saw how quickly he turned his face away from the
congregation, and she instinctively looked towards Pru.

'William!' She heard Pru sob and saw her slump
forwards.

'Pru.' She moved fast enough to stop her falling off the
seat but too late to stop her head cracking against the pew
in front.

Blood streamed down Pru's face.

'Nancy, help me get your mother outside.' She pushed
her handkerchief against the cut and together with Nancy
managed to help Pru along the aisle and towards the
chapel door.

'Allow me, Miss Forrester.' Rose Laybourne, black-
coated and veiled, stepped forward.

'We're all right, thank you, Ro, Miss Laybourne.' She
was surprised to see Rose, and even more surprised to see
Rose's parents and John standing unannounced at the rear
of the chapel. 'We don't want to make a fuss.'

John Laybourne nodded towards her and stepped back
to open the door.

'And that concludes the roll of honour.' She heard the words from the other end of the chapel and noticed the relief in Edward's voice.

As she moved Pru towards the door there was a moment's silence, then Henry shouted, 'And where's the honour in dying in Laybourne's bloody mine? Tell me, Edward. Where's the bloody honour in that?'

She turned and looked back.

'Not now, Henry. Not here,' Edward said firmly. 'This isn't the time, nor the place for—'

'I don't agree,' Henry stood up and yelled back. 'We're all together in this place. And we're all here for the same reason. Because Laybourne killed twenty of us. While we're here we might as well decide what we're going to do—'

'Stop it, Henry,' Adam's voice boomed out. 'Edward's right. This isn't the time or the place for politics.'

'When is the right time?' Henry shouted and banged his fist against a pew. 'Where's the right place? This seems good enough to me.'

'Calm down, Henry.' She watched Edward walk forward. 'We're all upset and—'

'Upset? Upset? Edward, me brother and me uncle were killed because Laybourne won't pay out to make the bloody mine safer.' Henry moved into the aisle and stood no more than a foot away from Edward.

'I know that, man.' She saw Edward reach out.

'You know nothing. Bugger off!' Henry's arms flew up and suddenly Edward was stumbling backward against Adam.

'Henry,' she yelled and started down the aisle but Pru grabbed her and held her back as men and women left the pews and packed around the three men.

'This—' she saw Edward's list of names was in Henry's hand – 'is all that's left of twenty men. We're insulting them if all we do is come to chapel, sing a few hymns, say a few prayers, then bugger off back to our homes. They deserve

more than that. They deserve to know that we're doing
something to stop their brothers, their uncles, their sons
from dying the way they did.'

A chorus of voices shouted support.

The minister banged his heavy black Bible against the
pulpit in a useless attempt to quieten the tumult, and
simply added to the noise.

Suddenly Henry appeared above the crowd, standing on
a pew, his arms held out wide.

'I reckon we should march on the mine. Now. Make
Laybourne listen. Let's make that murdering bastard give
us what we want. What he's already given his other mines.
Why're we any different?'

'Yes!' Another roar went up and the chapel rang as
boots scuffed against the stone floor.

She turned towards the Laybournes and saw that John
and his father were trying to push Rose and her mother
through the door but that neither woman was willing to
leave.

'Right,' Henry yelled and she turned as he jumped down
from the pew. 'Follow me!'

Her eyes went straight to where the Laybournes were
standing.

'*Stop!*' Mr Laybourne stood tall, taller than anyone
except Adam who was trapped at the far end of the chapel.

Silence, except for a whimpering child.

Mr Laybourne strode to the door and slammed it shut.

The silence lengthened, everyone watching, waiting.

'I am prepared to talk,' he said, his face red with anger,
'but not here and certainly not now. I'll talk to you when
you're calmer, more rational. But I'll not be intimidated by
threats of a riot. I came here with my family out of respect
for the men who died, and I expected you all to honour
your fellows in the same way. I'm disgusted that some of
you had other intentions.'

He turned and threw the door open again. 'You may go
to the colliery if you wish, and I promise that I won't try

to stop you. But I also promise you that any man who steps into that yard this afternoon will never step into it again.'

'You can't threaten us, Laybourne,' Henry screamed.

'I'm not threatening you, Mr Wright. You may do as you wish, but now I'd like to speak with the families who are mourning. Outside, away from the stench you have brought into this place of worship.'

'You're the only thing that smells in here,' Henry retorted. 'You smell like a butcher. A rich butcher.'

There was a roar. It was impossible to hear whether it was in agreement or not.

'Henry, that's *enough*.' She heard Edward, his voice trembling with anger. 'Give me that.'

The crowd parted and she saw Edward storm through the gap, the list of dead men once again in his hand. He stopped at the door, threw the list on the floor and ground it to shreds with his boot. The men and their families gasped, and then fell silent.

'Why're you all so shocked? That's no more shameful than anything you've done. You should be ashamed of yourselves.' He glared into the mass of faces and singled out several men by name, embarrassing them into looking away.

The individuals' embarrassment spread and the only sound was the noise of shuffling feet. Even Henry was told to keep quiet when he tried to speak.

The crowd's fury had been stemmed.

She watched as Edward turned to Mr Laybourne and apologised on everyone's behalf, then clumped out of the chapel and turned along Inkerman Street, pushing his way through the crowd that had gathered close to the door.

She started after him but a hand reached out and held her arm.

'I'd let him go, Miss Forrester,' John Laybourne said quietly, and she knew he was right. 'Let's move outside.'

She allowed him to lead her away but as she passed

Rose their eyes met and Rose's hand brushed her arm.

'Miss Forrester, please pass on my regards to your brother,' Rose said quietly, picked up the pieces of shredded paper and handed them to her.

John led her away from the crowd before he spoke.

'It's fortunate that your brother kept his head, Miss Forrester.' He reached out and took the shredded paper from her. 'And that he's a consummate actor. Quite a dramatic conclusion.'

'He wasn't acting, Mr Laybourne. He meant what he said. Every word of it.'

'Yes.' He nodded and looked away for a moment. When he looked back he was smiling. 'Well, I doubt you'll ever experience such drama in St George's or the church at Alnwick. Far too respectable.'

'They're all God's houses, Mr Laybourne.'

'Of course, but there are some who wouldn't feel quite so righteous worshipping in a simple chapel. That doesn't bother you?'

'I grew up as a miner's daughter, Mr Laybourne. I smelled and tasted coal in everything, the air, my food, my clothes and even my hair. I'm not ashamed of that so I don't think I should be ashamed of worshipping God in a chapel that smells of coal. We worship the same God, whether we do it in a chapel or a grand cathedral.'

'That's not what I asked,' he said, and she thought he sounded patronising. 'I asked if you'll be bothered by people thinking there's a difference.'

'I try not to be, Mr Laybourne. After all, I've been going to St George's for years.'

His sudden loud laughter took her by surprise.

'Have I amused you, Mr Laybourne?' She was annoyed by the primness which had slipped into her voice.

'Your honesty has, Miss Forrester.' His laughter died to a chuckle. 'Mr Beckett didn't accompany you today?'

She nearly replied immediately, but realised there was a subtle inference in the way he asked the question.

'Are you suggesting that he chose not to come because the service was held in a chapel?'

He carefully placed his hand over his heart and looked offended, but his eyes were still smiling. 'Of course I'm not, Miss Forrester.'

His smile spread to his lips, and she felt it infecting her own mouth.

'Good day, Mr Laybourne.' She turned and walked away, with a treacherous lightness of mind that was just a little disturbing.

She walked across the road to where her father was waiting outside the chapel.

'Bit of a mess, wasn't it, lass?'

'Aye, Da, but it could have been worse, mind.' She noticed how she made herself use the local dialect when she was talking to her family or the neighbours, and realised for the first time that she now talked naturally in what her mother would call a refined accent.

It bothered her that she had not noticed the change.

'You all right, Lizzie? I saw you talking to young Mr Laybourne.'

'He was just being polite, Da. I met him at the station when I went to meet Saul. Remember? I did tell you.' There was a half-conscious need to explain, almost to apologise, but she did not want to tell him what had been said.

'Aye.' She noticed how her father glanced towards John Laybourne who was calling up the family carriage. 'Got a lot about him, that boy.'

'Aye, Da, and his sister, I reckon.'

Her father nodded, and told her how Rose Laybourne had fussed over Pru and given her a clean handkerchief to cover the cut on her forehead.

'How is Pru?' She had forgotten all about her.

'Upset. Henry's just told her that he doesn't want to live with her and Ned any more. Reckons they're letting William and Gordon down because they won't stand up to Mr Laybourne.'

'He'll calm down. He probably just got carried away . . .'

'Maybe, but the damage is done and you know what Ned's like, and Henry said some nasty things about him. And Edward, and you too. I can't see Ned forgiving him that easy.'

She guessed what Henry had said about Edward, but she could not imagine what he had said about her and she did not think it was the time to ask.

The streets were clearing and the chapel was almost empty. She watched as John went inside and then reappeared with his parents and Rose. He nodded towards her and doffed his hat, and Rose gave her a brief wave before climbing up into the carriage.

Elizabeth's mother appeared, looking weak and ill and leaning on Simon's arm.

'It's over then.' Her mother sounded tired.

'No,' her father said. 'I reckon it's just about started. Look at Mr Laybourne. I don't reckon he's going to forget this. Not yet.'

She looked into the carriage as it passed and saw a tight expression on Mr Laybourne's face.

'Well, Edward did the right thing, at least,' she said and turned back to her father.

'Aye, I'll give him credit for that, but I reckon he might just have bitten off a bit more than he can chew.' Her father slipped an arm around her mother's waist and helped her walk away.

'Young Forrester' – Rose glanced across the carriage as her father spoke, and the anger in his eyes frightened her – 'd'you think we can rely on him, John?'

'I think so, Father, from what I saw today. I think the men prefer him to that other character, Henry Wright.'

'Yes, Forrester acquitted himself well, very well.'

She felt her chest swell. Her father really did approve of Edward, but he still looked angry and there was an intimidating hardness in both his voice and his face when he spoke again. 'And you gave Hopkins directions, John?'

'Yes, Father. We'll stop on the way home.'

'Stop where?' Her mother seemed puzzled.

'The police station, Charlotte. The men have got to learn that I'll not allow them to behave the way they did today. We all went along to pay our respects to the dead men and their families, and they spat in our faces. I'll not allow that, especially in chapel, and now they're going to have to pay for what they did.'

'Is that wise?' Her mother looked worried. 'And the police?'

'I'll not be bullied.' Her father's face set even harder.

'But, Sebastian . . .'

'But nothing, Charlotte. You run the house, I'll run the mine. I'll lock the men out until they give me their written agreement not to join the Miners' Association and not to bring politics into the chapels. If necessary I'll shut the chapels, too.'

'Sebastian!' Her mother gasped. 'Close the mine if you have to but you can't shut them out of the chapels.'

'I can do what I like, Charlotte, and don't you forget that.' Rose shrank back as her father's temper exploded. 'I'll put police into the yard to keep out any troublemakers, and if necessary I'll put a police guard on the chapels, too. That's an end to it!'

She felt her chest tighten, and noticed the way John looked at her mother, as if warning her not to say anything more.

The afternoon had been a disaster. She had looked forward to seeing Edward again, and had hoped they might be able to talk, even for only a few minutes. He had not spoken to her, had hardly seemed aware of her being there, and she was sure he had not noticed the special way she looked at him, a silent look that was supposed to show how much she admired him for what he did.

After the evening meal Edward wanted to be alone so he

walked up North Hill, sat amongst rocks above the cemetery and tried to decide what to do, but he could not concentrate; Rose kept slipping into his mind.

He had noticed the way she looked at him in the chapel, and wished he had not left so quickly. It seemed the right thing to do at the time, the only thing he could do to calm the situation, and he hated walking away from her without saying something, anything; but once he had left he knew he could not go back. That would have spoiled the effect.

But now he could not think of anything without thinking of her; did not want to think of anything without considering how it might affect her. Then, slowly, he realised all he really wanted was to see her again to find out if her feelings for him were as strong as his were for her, ridiculous and impossible as they might be.

But there was no way to meet her again, not alone.

Then without warning it started to rain. Huge blobs of water soaked him before he could scramble away from the rocks. He raced across the grass, turned on to the track that led past the cemetery and ran down the hill until he saw the black mound of the barn. At least he could find some cover there, and have the opportunity to be alone for a while longer.

He sprinted across the field and into the barn, and sensed that someone else was already there.

'Who's that?' His heart sank as he heard Nancy call out.

'It's me, Edward.'

'Oh, darling.' She found him and threw her arms around him. 'I hoped you'd come.'

He held her and returned her kiss without much enthusiasm.

'Da's thrown Henry out of the house.'

'I know.'

'He's staying in Uncle Gordon's old place. I took his things there. Noakes and a few more of his friends have moved in with him.'

'The revolutionary headquarters, I suppose,' he said, and followed her down on to a thick layer of straw. 'He's stupid. The agent'll find out they've moved in without permission and he'll tell Laybourne and they'll all get thrown out. Then there'll be trouble.'

'That's what Da said.' She spoke quietly, then added cagily. 'I had hoped we would take the place on.'

'What?'

'For when we're married,' she said simply, and he did not have the heart to tell her that he had never thought of marrying her.

They lay on the straw and listened to the rain drumming on the barn's roof. After a while she kissed him and tried to interest him in doing more but he pushed her away.

'Sorry, Nance, but I just don't feel like it, lass. Today's been a right bastard and I need to think, like.' He sensed she felt rejected but he could not offer her any comfort.

A long time passed without either of them speaking. Her being there irritated him; it stopped him thinking clearly. Eventually he stopped trying and stood up.

'Nance, look, the rain's not going to stop, so we may as well make a run for it and go home.'

'We could stay here the night,' she suggested timidly.

'Oh no. It must be past midnight already and your ma and da'll be worried about you by now.'

He felt like telling her that directly or indirectly he was responsible for Ned and Pru losing two of their sons and he did not want to add their daughter to the list.

'Just a bit longer, Edward, please.'

'No. Come on. Now!' he said sharply and shoved the door open. 'Come on, Nance, I'm in no mood for buggering about.'

She followed without speaking. He apologised for his rudeness by holding her hand as they ran off the hill and into the alley behind the houses, but he did not speak and he was glad she kept her own silence. When they reached her back gate they kissed goodnight. She tried to make it a lingering parting, but he quickly opened the gate and pushed her into the yard.

'Goodnight, Nance.'

'Goodnight, darling. I love you.'

'Yes,' he answered non-committally, and shut the gate between them.

It had been a disastrous day and a worse evening. He already felt bad because he had used Nancy and abused her trust, but now he felt worse, now that she assumed he loved her enough to marry her. He should have told her the truth but he was wary of saying any more than he had to; the truth had a way of turning itself around.

And he still had not decided what he could do to bring Laybourne and the men together. If only, instead of pretending to be a hero, he had admitted that he had not deliberately risked his life to save William, no one would have thought any worse of him. And they would not have thought he had the qualities and the ability to be their leader. He could have stayed anonymous.

But the inner voice laughed cynically and reminded him that if he had not played the hero his father would still treat him like a little boy, Laybourne would not have offered him a future as a manager, and Rose would not have had any reason to take him up on to King's Crag.

And, he realised as the voice taunted him more, he actually enjoyed feeling different from the other men. He enjoyed the feeling of importance that came when men whom he had once thought of as being better and wiser treated him as an equal, or more.

Yes, he realised, half ashamed of himself, he enjoyed being important. It gave him his own identity. He was not just any other man now; he was Edward Forrester, and although at the moment he was a miner that would change. He was sure.

He slept well and waited until after his father and brothers left for work before rolling off his mattress; his head injury meant he would not help with the repairs and without any work to do he could have stayed in bed for hours, but he felt restless as soon as he woke up.

He still had to find answers to his problems: how to accept Laybourne's offer without upsetting his family and friends and, more important, how to see Rose again, preferably alone.

His mother was feeling worse and he persuaded her to spend another day in bed, then went downstairs to make breakfast for them both. He had just brewed the tea when the back gate banged open.

Ned rushed into the yard, Nancy just behind him, the left side of her face swelling into a bruise, and he could easily guess why Ned looked so angry.

He opened the door and began his apology. 'I'm sorry I didn't bring Nance home earlier, Ned. I didn't realise how late it was until I'd got in meself.'

'I shouldn't think you did. We were bloody worried, waiting up till that time. Still, we sorted that out with the girl, and anyway, she explained she was with you and that you've asked her to marry you so that makes a difference.'

Asked her to marry him? He glanced towards her but she was looking away from him and obviously scared that he would deny it and prove her a liar.

He was stunned, but even so he could imagine the scene when Nancy had walked through the door after midnight and her parents had gone for her. He could not blame her for saying the first thing that must have come into her head even though it meant there was even more to undo, but before he could think what to say or do he realised Ned had something else on his mind.

'We're all pleased, Edward. Pru especially, after what happened to William, like, but all that can wait. There's trouble and you'd better come quick. Laybourne's locked us out and shoved up notices telling us what he expects us to do if we want the mine opened again.'

'And what does he want?'

'He wants us to sign to say we won't join the association and that we'll all go back on his terms.'

'I cannot say that surprises me, Ned, not after yesterday. How have the men taken it?'

'They want you, Edward. They reckon, after yesterday, like, you're the only one Laybourne'll listen to. You're our only chance, man. Will you go up to the manor and speak for us?'

'And say what? Say we still want another shaft? We still want—'

'No, lad,' Ned interrupted him. 'Get what you can, but most of all, get Laybourne to open up the gates. Laybourne's stopped the bloody pumps and if we don't get them started again, real soon, the workings'll flood and we won't have a bloody mine to work in.'

'Henry reckoned we'd be insulting William and Gordon if we didn't force Laybourne's hand, and even you said we had to stand out for another shaft. Are you really telling me that doesn't matter any more? I need to be sure, Ned. I don't want the men saying I sold 'em down the river, like.'

'When we buried William, Adam said we had to look after the living. I reckon he's right, and we cannot do that if we make 'em starve.' Ned looked and sounded dejected. 'We know it's a lot to ask, lad, but will you speak to Laybourne? Go up to the manor for us?'

'Aye, Ned. Of course.'

Of course. Of course he would go up to the manor.

Rose was there.

CHAPTER 11

Elizabeth was standing in the corridor outside the teachers' rest room, or Common Room as Saul insisted on calling it since Alnwick had confirmed his appointment.

The sound of children's playground laughter was muted by the closed windows. That was just one of the things which made teaching enjoyable. Actually helping the children to learn was satisfying, unless the class was particularly inattentive, but there were so many other things she knew she would miss if she was forced to stop. She liked to hear the children play and laugh, she enjoyed the sound of them singing or even chanting their multiplication tables, and she liked the way the schoolrooms echoed, and the very smell that was peculiar to school.

'You look very pensive.' Saul came to stand beside her.

'Yes.' She did not want to be drawn into a conversation with him, not while there were others who were close enough to hear what was being said.

'Are you worried about something?' Saul persisted, but before she had to answer a whistle blew and the children began to form lines, ready to file back into school.

'I must go.' She turned away as a door opened at the end of the corridor and Mr Peebles, the headmaster, appeared leading several members of the school board.

She stood aside as the group came along the narrow corridor.

'Bad business, Peebles. Bad business,' one of the men blustered. 'Near riot, I heard. Poor example to their offspring. I seriously recommend you keep an eye on any of their brats who attend here. Don't want them disrupting morning assembly.'

'I don't believe there's any serious danger of that, sir,' Mr Peebles said awkwardly, caught her eye and grimaced apologetically.

'You never know, sir,' the man insisted, 'you never know, sir. I'd birch the lot of 'em, men and women. Tan 'em so they cannot sit for a week or more. Would've done that in the old days, you know. That and fine them a few days' wages.'

'I've heard,' another man spoke up quickly, 'that Mr Laybourne's closed the gates against them. Brought the police in, too.'

She felt her face flush and her heart thump. The first man came level with her, half a head shorter. He stopped, looked her up and down.

'D'you teach here, young lady?'

She nodded, unwilling to speak for fear of saying more than she should.

'Hm,' he murmured dismissively, then noticed Saul. 'Mr Beckett! Congratulations. I've heard much about you and I understand from your father that you're to teach at my old school.'

'Yes, sir.' She watched Saul preen himself as the man was effusive with praises.

'Wonderful school, you know. Fertile ground for the

university. *The* university. You know, not the other one, the place that calls itself a university.' The man laughed and she felt ashamed as Saul laughed with him. 'Your father tells me you'll be glad to shake the smell of coal dust off your shoes, eh? Get well away from that sort?'

'Yes, sir.' Saul did not even hesitate.

She moved forward, saw Mr Peebles silently imploring her not to say anything, and stopped; her mind a jumble of fury, humiliation, and worry about her family if Laybourne really had locked the mine's gates.

Then Mr Peebles shepherded the group on through a door at the far end of the corridor.

She had Saul all to herself.

'So you've decided I'm not to come with you?' She challenged him to find an excuse without humiliating himself as much as he had humiliated her.

'Elizabeth, dear, of course I still expect you to come with me, but Mr Charlesworth's a governor of this school and a director of the bank my father works for. My father works directly under him. What could I say?'

'Quite a lot, Saul. Quite a lot.' She paused, fuming, trying to think of something he could have said. 'You might have introduced me. As your fiancée. I was standing only a few feet away.'

'I simply didn't think it was appropriate, Elizabeth.'

'Why? Because you didn't think he'd approve of me? I'm surprised your parents approve of me, Saul, me being a coal miner's daughter.'

'Well, you're not, are you?' he snapped. 'Not really.'

'What do you mean?' She heard her voice rise and thought that everyone in the school must be able to hear, but suddenly she did not care.

'Elizabeth, the Forresters aren't your real parents, thank God, and only He knows who they are.' She heard the words but she was too hurt to reply. She felt herself wilt as he advanced towards her, his tone simultaneously sharp and patronising. 'You're a foundling, so remember that, Elizabeth, and forget you were brought up as a miner's daughter. You're intelligent, and quite presentable when you bother so there's no reason why anyone should suspect you're anything less than they would expect of my wife.'

'Less than they'd expect of your wife?' She found her voice. 'Are you really that ashamed of me, Saul?'

'Not of you, Elizabeth. I understand the circumstances and don't really mind about your past, but other people don't have to know, do they? Especially after we're married.'

'You patronising, pompous' – she struggled to find a word – 'bastard.'

She had never sworn before and she was astonished how the word relieved her feelings; and pleased at the stunned way Saul stared at her.

'Marry you? I wouldn't marry you if you were the only man in the universe.' She took a deep breath and thought of a suitable final insult. 'Not that you'll ever be a man, Saul, your mother's seen to that.'

She turned away, still angry with Saul and frustrated with herself because she was leaving without having expounded the fury which made her hands tremble and her legs weak.

Then she saw the fire bucket hanging from a bracket on the wall.

She turned to look back at Saul. He was standing very still, his face blank, his arms half raised. He did not speak, and did not even seem to notice as she turned away again and heaved the bucket of water off the bracket.

She knew it was a childish thing to do, but she could not stop herself. The water hit him full in the face and the shock seemed to push him up against the wall. The rest room door opened slowly and two faces looked out, but no one spoke, not even Saul.

Her energy expounded she felt drained, and very embarrassed.

'Just so that there's no further confusion, Saul' – she handed him the empty bucket – 'No, I'm not going to marry you.'

She knew she had behaved badly, completely out of character, and she knew she would bring down the wrath of the school governors and might even lose her job: but at that moment she did not care.

For once she had hit back against the prejudice and bigotry she usually submitted to, and she felt proud of herself for doing so.

She felt the same lightness of spirit she had felt when she walked away from John Laybourne the previous day, and she smiled as she imagined how he would laugh when he heard how she had flushed the pomposity out of Saul.

'My name is Edward Forrester and I'd like to see Mr Laybourne, please.'

Previously he had only ever seen the manor from the top of South Ridge; now, close up, it looked enormous, nigh on half the length of an entire Pincote Colliery street and three times as high as any cottage. He guessed there was as much living space in the manor as there was in all the Albert Street cottages put together.

He waited outside the front door while the woman who had answered the loud jangling bell went to find the master, as she called him, and ask if he were free to see 'someone from the colliery', as he had described himself. He stood on the top step of the flight, close to the high door with its polished brass and felt conscious of his poor clothes and boots, his background, and the difference between him and Rose.

When he had thought about that before it had been as something abstract, but now he was standing outside her home it suddenly seemed a very real difference.

What could he offer someone like Rose Laybourne?

The answer was very little.

'Mr Forrester.' The woman reappeared. 'Please come

in. The master will see you as soon as he's free.'

He waited in the large hallway, cap in hand, alternately hoping he would see Rose and that he would not. The house overwhelmed him, not just because it was so large but because it seemed so permanent; it carried the feeling of having been there for centuries and the certainty that it would remain for centuries more. That, and the thought that the same could be said of the Laybournes, was daunting and made him feel very small and insignificant.

He looked up at the sound of someone almost running down the stairs, and was aware of them passing and shutting the front door before he realised the man could have been Mr Speake.

'Mr Forrester, please come up.' It was Mr Laybourne, calling down from the galleried landing.

He ran up the stairs and was surprised when Sebastian Laybourne shook his hand.

'Please follow me, Mr Forrester.' The owner led him along a wood-panelled corridor and into a book-lined study where John Laybourne was in one of two chairs placed behind a large desk. 'Mr Forrester, I'd like to introduce you to my son who's just taken over management of Pincote Colliery from Mr Speake.'

John Laybourne stood up and they both leaned across the desk to shake hands. It was a dry, firm handshake, and he noticed how rough John Laybourne's hand was; a hand used to physical work.

They exchanged a few words but he did not ask what had happened to Mr Speake. The man had been a bad manager, mean, ineffective and unfair. He was not sorry to see him leave, and he hoped that he had played a part in his dismissal.

'Please, Mr Forrester, sit down.' John Laybourne pointed to a chair in front of the desk. 'What's brought you here without an appointment? Come to accept our offer?'

He waited until both the Laybournes were seated before he sat down, and then came straight to the point. 'Aye, sir, in a sense, and because most of the men and women who work in the colliery have asked me to come and talk to you. I'm here to tell you that they want to go back to work.'

'I'm impressed.' Sebastian Laybourne leaned forward. 'You obviously warrant the considerable faith my daughter appears to have in you.'

He felt awkward and wondered exactly what Rose had said about him.

'Thank you, sir.' He could not think of anything else to say.

John Laybourne also leaned forward. 'You say the men want to return to work, but yesterday their mood rather suggested they wished to impose certain conditions on us. Before we discuss reopening the mine I'd like to know what those conditions are,' he said without any preamble, and took up a pen and piece of paper to make notes.

'They understand, sir, that they're not in any position to force you to do anything.' He thought he might as well be honest. 'Well, most of them do.'

'It's amazing how soon they've seen sense,' John Laybourne said, with a sideways glance at his father, 'but pressed men don't work as well as volunteers, so tell me what sort of improvements they would really like. Not that I'm offering to do anything other than listen, you understand.'

'Of course, sir.' He was surprised at John Laybourne's openness, but cautioned by the stony look on the older Laybourne's face. 'Well, sir, we want a second shaft, a bigger pump and better ventilation. They're the improvements to our working conditions. We want compensation for wages lost during stoppages, and better compensation for injuries and for the widows of men who die working. And the men want the freedom to join the Miners' Association,' he added, deciding that John Laybourne would respect his bluntness.

He waited for a response, but the father remained stiff-faced and the son simply studied the list of demands.

'We think they are reasonable requests, Mr Laybourne,' he said as the silence lengthened, noticed Sebastian Laybourne's slight nod and tried to judge what he was thinking.

John Laybourne spoke first. 'We'll install a better pump and improve ventilation. That'll make your working conditions better and reduce the stoppage times so you'll earn more. It should also reduce the risk of accidents, although we will increase compensation anyway. But I must retain the no coal, no pay rule. Can we agree on that?'

'I think the men will agree to that.' He already knew the men would compromise but he sensed it was better not to accept the proposal immediately.

'The company will begin to remedy those items almost immediately.' John Laybourne scribbled notes on to another sheet of paper. 'In return I want the workers' agreement not to join the Miners' Association.'

'That may be more difficult.' He knew he sounded evasive but he did not want to surrender everything until they had discussed the second shaft. 'But if you agree to another shaft—'

'That's not necessary,' he was interrupted, 'because I've a better and much less expensive alternative in mind.'

'Better?'

'Yes. I don't suppose you know there was a mine here in Elizabethan times, worked by Catholic monks who had a monastery on South Ridge. The original entrance was down an old watercourse and through a series of caverns. The monastery was dissolved and its ruins and the original entrance are buried under one of the waste spills.' He waved a hand airily. 'We intend to find the old entrance and reopen it. That would give us the second entry you want and also allow us to open up new workings to mine the coal we know is in South Ridge itself. It'd also increase the number of jobs. Do you agree?'

'Aye.' There was nothing to argue about.

'And if we can always talk like this and reach agreements,

then I think you'll also agree that there's no need to join the Miners' Association? So, do you agree, Mr Forrester?'

He knew he had been outwitted, but there was not any reason to argue; the men were getting almost everything they wanted.

'Aye, sir, it makes sense.'

'Good.' John Laybourne stood up and reached out his hand. 'Then we'll reopen the works on Monday morning.'

They shook hands and as they moved towards the door he trembled with excitement. They were going to get most of what they wanted, and they were going back to work. He had done it, and the men surely would not begrudge him his new position, not now.

Then Sebastian Laybourne spoke again: 'There's just one thing my son omitted to mention, Mr Forrester.'

His enthusiasm wavered. Sebastian Laybourne's eyes were still cold, still intimidating.

'I want the men to sign agreements not to join the Miners' Association, and I think the best time for them to sign is when they visit their chapels on Sunday. They can then begin work on Monday as usual.'

His stomach churned. The men would see that as unfair and feel humiliated, and although he knew they would sign if they were forced to he thought that as a sign of good faith Laybourne should be willing to accept their word. 'They've given their word, sir, as you have. Isn't that enough?'

'No. I want their written agreements, and I want them made in chapel.'

'I'm sorry, sir, but I'm not sure I can ask them to do that. They'll be happy to accept your word, sir, so cannot you accept theirs?'

'Mr Forrester, let me make myself clear. I require every worker to sign a document agreeing not to join the Miners' Association.'

'Half or more of them cannot write their signatures, sir.' He knew that was a lame excuse, but he needed time to think.

'Then their marks will do. I'll ensure that sufficient forms are left at each of the chapels and I'll expect every man and woman who visits the chapel to sign.'

'That'll be seen as a humiliation which'll do you no credit, sir.' He felt he had to speak out, whatever the consequences.

'I believe that's for me to decide, Mr Forrester. I assume that you will accept the position I offered you last week?'

'Aye, sir, if it's still open to me.'

'Of course it is, but then you must accept my instruction to obtain the workers' signatures as your first duty, Mr Forrester. I trust you won't let me down.' Then, having set and sprung the trap, Laybourne smiled and left.

'Forgive me, sir' – he turned to John Laybourne – 'but I don't think your father is being wise, not if he expects the men to work without resentment.'

'He's insistent, Mr Forrester. This isn't something he's prepared to negotiate. The men humiliated him and he intends to take his revenge.'

'They didn't intend to humiliate him, sir. It was just something which got out of hand, like.'

'Maybe, but he doesn't see it like that, so I suggest you do as he told you. Oh, there is one other thing, Mr Forrester.' Edward's stomach churned as he wondered what the next surprise would be. 'I'd appreciate you passing my best regards to your sister, and advising her that I'll be presenting this year's prizes at the St George's Day celebration.'

'Thank you, sir. I'll certainly do that,' he answered and wondered if he would be allowed to meet Rose.

'Two more things, Mr Forrester. First, please don't call me sir. It sounds servile and that doesn't suit you. I'm sure you're as proud to be a Forrester as I am to be a Laybourne. Let's each respect each other's names and use them. Secondly' – he hesitated and seemed to change his mind about what to say – 'secondly, Mr Forrester, I understand that I must thank you for taking care of my sister years ago, when she had been left in my care. You're the prince she's been babbling about for so long.'

'I'm no prince, Mr Laybourne.' He wondered what Laybourne had first intended to say.

'I know that, Mr Forrester. I know that, but I'm not so sure my sister does.' The words were spoken in a way which implied more than they said.

Not a threat, not even a warning as such. More a passive suggestion that Rose might need protecting from herself. A plea, perhaps, that they should both look to protect her. A statement of trust? But why was it made? Just what had Rose said to him and their father?

'Now, Mr Forrester, I'm sure my sister will never forgive me if I don't allow her the opportunity to meet you again before you leave.'

'Why, Mr Forrester, how lovely to see you.' Rose looked soft and enchanting, and untouchable in her mother's company.

It was embarrassing to be talking to her in her own home, especially with her mother present, and agonising to be so close but unable to touch her, and not to be able to talk the way they had on King's Crag.

He noticed the way her eyes watched him, never leaving his face so that whenever he looked at her their eyes met, and the way she seemed to be restless, always leaning or inching towards him but never coming any closer; and he thought that if he had noticed her mother certainly had. He was almost glad when it came time to leave. The embarrassment and his own feelings were rising to a level where he was finding it difficult to restrain what he said.

They shook hands as they parted, and he was excited to feel her fingers squeeze his, to hold them for slightly longer than was normal while her eyes looked directly into his and her lips moved slightly but made no sound, as if she were preparing for a kiss.

He walked towards home and climbed South Ridge

without even noticing the slope; his mind was on Rose, her eyes, her touch, and her lips. There was no question in his mind that he loved her, no matter how improbable the situation was, and he was sure she felt the same for him.

It was a ridiculous situation, difficult to imagine how anything could possibly come of it, but it was enough at that moment simply to feel the way he did. He thought about climbing on to the top of King's Crag but decided not to; it would not be the same without Rose, and anyway he had to get home and talk to his father and the others.

The little house seemed to be packed with people waiting to hear about the outcome of the meeting, but although they all congratulated him on what he had achieved there were two matters he was not sure they would be pleased to hear.

'I'm not going back down to cut coal, Da.' He thought that if he could make his father understand then no one else would complain. 'John Laybourne's taken over as manager, Trenchard will be the under manager, George'll be deputy manager in charge of all the firemen, and I'll be George's assistant. You could argue that I'm joining the other side but it'll give us a chance to know more about what's happening generally and get more involved in the safety of things. To make sure the improvements are made properly.'

'Well, I reckon it'll be good for us to have one of our own in their camp, like.' His father nodded his acceptance, and everyone else agreed.

'And there's one last thing, and this is something I'm not happy about because it's just Laybourne getting his revenge.' He told them what Laybourne wanted, and about how he thought they should outwit the owner.

'Bit risky, son. If we don't do as he wants he might keep the gates locked,' his mother warned.

'Aye, Ma, but I reckon we've got to show him that if we give our word we expect that to be enough. If he really wants us to sign papers promising not to join the association then those who agree can always do it away from the chapels. That way he doesn't get to humiliate us, but if we're going to do as I suggest, then we'll have to get moving so everyone in town knows the plan.'

'Leave that to me, Edward,' Adam Marriott volunteered. 'You've done enough today, your head still bad and all, and anyway this is something I need to do.'

Edward left Adam to organise everyone, his mother went back to bed to rest, and the house emptied until he was left alone with Elizabeth.

He saw Elizabeth smiling at him. 'Edward, I'd never have thought you'd have it in you to do all you have, lad. What's happened?'

'Love of a good woman.' He spoke without thinking, but only half regretted what he said; he needed to talk to someone and Lizzie was the only one he could afford to talk with.

'Nancy, is that?' she asked.

'No, Lizzie. Not really.' It was embarrassing enough to explain why Nancy had lied, but it was even worse to admit how he felt about Rose Laybourne and to say that he thought she felt the same for him.

'Rose Laybourne? You certainly don't make life easy for yourself, do you, lad?'

'It's not something I set out to do, Lizzie. In fact, if you remember, I was bloody rude to her and you told me so.'

'Aye, lad, I remember all right. But as you've admitted, it is pretty ridiculous to think of you and Rose Laybourne and I'm sure you've either misunderstood her or she's just playing with you. Think about it, Edward, you and the owner's daughter.' Lizzie talked sense as usual, and he knew she was right; although it did not help the way he felt it did encourage him to distract her by teasing her about John Laybourne.

'I know it's ridiculous, Lizzie. Just as silly as you and John Laybourne.'

'What do you mean?' There was an edge to her voice.

'He especially asked me to pass on his regards to you, and to tell you he'll be presenting the prizes at the St George's Day celebration at your school.'

'Well, that doesn't mean anything, lad.'

'Maybe, but you didn't see the expression in his eyes when he spoke about you, lass.' He grinned to see her look uncomfortable, and quickly reminded her of all she had told him about meeting John Laybourne at the railway station. 'Don't tell me you weren't keen on him, Lizzie. I reckon he feels the same way about you.'

He had no reason to suppose anything of the sort, he had only wanted to tease her, but the way she flushed suggested that he might be right about her feelings for the owner's son. 'Edward! Don't forget he's engaged! You shouldn't joke about things like that.'

'Well, you're engaged too, aren't you, Lizzie? To the honourable and boring . . .'

'No. No, I'm not. Not any more.'

He did not know what to say, so he apologised for teasing her about John Laybourne.

'Don't apologise, Edward. Maybe John Laybourne is to blame, in a way. Seeing him made me realise how small-minded Saul is, but that was only part of it. There were lots of things I wasn't sure about, and then Saul told me that one of the advantages of moving to Alnwick was that no one knew us. He said they needn't ever know that I was brought up as a coal miner's daughter and I wasn't ever to admit to it.'

'The bugger!' He suddenly felt angry for her, for his parents, and for all the mining families who were looked down on by people like Saul Beckett. 'The bloody bugger.'

'Aye, that's pretty well what I told him, and a bit worse, I reckon.'

'Good for you, Lizzie.'

'Not really. We had our row at school, in front of everyone. Children, teachers, the headmaster and three of the governors, mind. I think I could be in trouble, Edward, and no one'll take my side, apart from the headmaster, maybe.' She grimaced. 'I don't know what I'll do if I lose me job, and I reckon I might. Anyway, lad, you've enough problems of your own. When are you going to tell Nancy you're not marrying her? More to the point, how're you going to tell Pru? She's real happy about it, and it's taken her mind off William and the accident, and Henry.'

They were good questions, but he did not have answers. All he had was Lizzie's advice that it was better done sooner than later.

That evening Nancy asked if he would walk with her and they trudged through the rain up to the musty old barn.

'Kiss me,' she demanded, and he did as he was told without any enthusiasm. 'That wasn't much of a kiss, Edward.'

'I'm sorry,' he said, irritated but too scared to say what he knew he should.

'I thought you said you loved me,' she said quietly, 'but I saw the way you looked when Da told you about us getting married.'

'What do you expect, Nance? Your da comes and tells me he's glad we're getting married and I don't even remember asking you?'

'Not in so many words, but after the other night when we . . .' She stopped and he could see she was finding it difficult to put her thoughts into words. 'I didn't think you'd have done that if you didn't reckon on us getting married.'

'You seemed as keen as me, lass.' He knew it was a cheap comment, and unfair, and he felt mean and dirty for saying it, but it was true and much less brutal than the full truth, that he did not love her but did love Rose Laybourne, the owner's daughter.

'I was keen, Edward, because I love you and I thought you loved me too. Enough to want to marry me.' She moved away and he heard her voice, very small, and

sounding very hurt, say simply, 'But you don't, do you?
You never did. You just used me.'

'That's not true, Nance. I just need time. Everything's
happened so fast. I need more time, that's all.' It was easier
to say that than admit the truth.

'All right, Edward, I'll give you time.' The door creaked
open and he knew she was crying as she walked away.

Sunday. Edward stood opposite the locked gates in
Murdock Street and heard the bell at St George's in
Pincote Market start its slow, ponderous toll. His heart
leapt. He would soon know what the men and their families
were going to do. Whether they would support him and
stand up to Laybourne, or whether they would simply go
to chapel and sign the agreements which would confirm
their humiliation. And his.

He thought about Rose, just briefly, and wondered what
she would think. Whether she would think he was right or
wrong, and he supposed it would depend on where her
loyalties lay.

The bell stopped tolling.

And high on the hill above the mine the small rebellion
began. All through the maze of terraced streets front doors
were opened and slammed shut in a steady deliberate beat.
The miners' war drums, the signal that they were ready to
march. The beat grew faster and faster until the noise
broke down into a chaotic cacophony. Then it stopped.

Suddenly.

Silence. Even he found it intimidating.

He watched the remaining policemen, only six of them,
move closer together. They did not speak but they looked
around and they waited. And listened.

Then it came, the new sound, distant, from the top
terraces and spreading down the hill through the streets
and alleys where the miners lived. The steady scuff of
boots against cobbles. The noise grew louder as more and
more people joined the throng on the march.

'Mr Forrester,' Sergeant Craddock, the man commanding the guard, called across the road, 'don't give us any trouble, lad. You cannot win by causing trouble for yourselves.'

'We're not here to cause trouble, Sergeant, only to prove that we can be trusted not to cause it, and to show that we'll keep our word.' He hoped that was true, that Henry and his crowd would not spoil the peaceful demonstration.

'Just you remember, lad, one word from me'll bring in reinforcements. Horses and rifles if need be,' Craddock shouted.

'They'll not be needed, Sergeant. You have my word on that.'

The tramp of boots increased.

St George's bell began its second toll, the last chance for sluggards to rush into worship. Its sound hardly pricked through the clatter of marching feet.

He saw the head of the crowd move into sight and noticed the policemen move several paces backward even though they were protected by the high wall and gates.

People were still marching steadily and for a moment he wondered if, even now, once they saw the policemen, their courage would fail and they would walk past and go on to chapel as usual. Then he saw the other procession coming from the opposite end of Murdock Street. Men dressed in worn suits and women wrapped in shawls, children, miniatures of their parents, and babies swaddled in cut-down blankets. And beyond them a rippling sea of caps and headscarves and small clutches of black bonnets, once bought for men's funerals and now bobbing together like tarred corks as widows clung to each other for mutual support on this decisive day.

It looked as though every household had turned out and he felt proud of them all.

Then he saw his mother, flanked by his father and Joey, Flo close behind with Paul and Mary and the children.

Simon and Thomas were there, and Ned and Pru and even
Nancy, doe-eyed and serious. Her brothers, Albert and
James, were with the other men outside the cottage Henry
had taken over, assigned to keep Henry and his mates
away from the service.

Then he saw Lizzie pushing her way through the crowd.
She was perhaps more courageous than any of the others
because she usually went to St George's and her absence
would be noticed at a time when she could not afford any
further criticism, or obvious association with the miners
and their families.

St George's bell had stopped tolling but the crowd
tramped on, their boots forming a steady beat backed by
the dragging sounds made by those who took shorter
steps.

'Forrester?' Sergeant Craddock shouted.

'Just an open-air Sunday service, Sergeant,' he called
back. 'Please join us if you'd care to.'

And to confirm his story the ministers from the chapels
arrived to show their unity with their congregation.

The tramping broke down into a rough shuffle as the
two processions met and spilled out to fill the street. The
crunch of boots faded away. People pressed together, arm
against arm. Children were lifted on to fathers' or mothers'
shoulders so they should not be crushed and so they could
see what was happening. The crowd filled Murdock Street
and spilled up the side streets. The pressure of bodies
pushed him and his family up against the colliery yard
gates.

Eyes avoided looking at the policemen inside the yard.
Nothing was said. No one wanted to do anything which
might provoke the police into calling for reinforcements;
Murdock Street was packed and trouble would mean
carnage.

He smiled as he saw his mother looking brighter than
she had for weeks, one hand gripping his father's arm and
the other clutching her Bible.

Then he saw Adam wading through the crowd, the box he used for street preaching on his shoulder, and he shook Adam's hand before saying simply, 'Adam Marriott will lead us in prayers and hymns.'

The final hymn died away, sung by the men and women and children in the crowd and by the policemen in the yard, and as it faded a commotion started at the far end of Murdock Street and spread through the crowd.

'What's happening, Adam?' he asked, sure that Adam, standing on his box, could see.

'I think Mr Laybourne's just arrived, Edward.'

Moments later he saw the Laybourne carriage edging through the crowd, driven slowly by an old driver who was obviously being careful not to hurt anyone. The carriage stopped in front of him. Sebastian Laybourne and his son stepped down and he could see Rose and her mother sitting upright, watching.

'What's the meaning of this, Forrester?' Sebastian Laybourne looked severe.

'We decided to hold a combined service here, Mr Laybourne.' He looked up into the owner's eyes and tried to judge if his expression showed his real mood. 'We've done no harm and we've worshipped God as we always do.'

'But you haven't signed the agreements.' Laybourne stated.

'Only because you wanted them signed in chapel and none of us went to chapel, sir. We'll sign them tomorrow, in the works, like, but we all feel that chapel is a place we go to worship God and shouldn't be used for political ends.'

It was a provocative statement; he wondered how Laybourne would react and his glance went instinctively to Rose. She smiled back, and nodded, a sure sign that he had her encouragement.

'But you have used the chapel for political ends, Forrester,' Laybourne blazed at him.

'Not me, sir, nor any of the moderate men here. I grant

you that a few troublemakers did and if you look over there
you'll see that they're not part of this service, we wanted
them to have no part in this.'

Laybourne turned towards the house where Henry and
a few of his cronies were pressed against the windows
which had been nailed shut from the outside.

'So I see, Mr Forrester.' Laybourne turned back to face
him. 'Once again I'm impressed by your abilities. I think
you could be a very dangerous man, Mr Forrester, and I'm
glad to know that you're on our side.'

'I do what I think is right, sir, but I'm on no one's side. I
think we should all work together, not against each other.'
He found himself looking at Rose as he spoke and he saw
the open expression which encouraged him even more,
then he glanced back at her father. 'The men'll sign the
agreements tomorrow, sir, when we start work.'

'There's no need, Mr Forrester. It's quite obvious that I
can trust you.'

He was astonished and did not react as the owner
jumped back into the carriage. He looked at Rose, they
smiled at each other, and then his attention was taken by
John Laybourne and Elizabeth.

'You chose the miners' service to St George's,' he heard
John say to her, 'in spite of the recent trouble you've
landed yourself in.'

'Aye, because I thought it was right,' Lizzie answered
bluntly.

'Or because you wanted to make a statement that you
don't care for authority, Miss Forrester?'

'Maybe that too,' she admitted, and added, smiling, 'or
maybe I just find the service here is less boring.'

'Miss Forrester!' John Laybourne sounded shocked.
'You must take every opportunity of learning how to deal
with boredom if you're to become a schoolmaster's wife at
Alnwick. You will be bored out of your shoes,' he said
pedantically.

'Aye, and maybe that's why I'm not going. If you've

heard about the row I had with Saul,' Lizzie said openly, 'then you must know that I'm no longer engaged to him and I cannot understand why you would therefore suggest that I'm still going to Alnwick.'

'Whoah,' John Laybourne countered, as if he were restraining a horse. 'A woman who speaks her mind. Wonderful! I thought they only existed in America, Miss Forrester, and not too many there either. I apologise for being rude, and I simply wanted to be sure of the facts.'

'Perhaps, but I don't understand what business it is of yours, Mr Laybourne.'

He noticed the edge had returned to Lizzie's voice, and the way her eyes blazed, and thought it best to intervene before she and John Laybourne had a full-scale row. 'Come on, Lizzie.'

'No.' She rounded on him, but before she could say any more John Laybourne interrupted.

'You're quite right to be upset, Miss Forrester. My teasing sometimes goes too far, as my sister could confirm. I do apologise, most humbly.' He watched as Lizzie allowed John Laybourne to take her hand, raise it to his lips and kiss it. 'I promise to be more gentlemanly when I visit your school for the prize-giving.'

'I may not be there myself,' she answered.

'Then I won't attend either, Miss Forrester. Good day. Good day, Mr Forrester. We'll meet in my office first thing tomorrow morning.'

'Yes, Mr Laybourne,' he said, and wondered exactly what sort of man he would be working for.

CHAPTER 12

───────◆───────

Rose stood in the miniature valley where she had watched Edward sleeping. Primroses that were growing by the rock she had sat on were almost ready to flower. She must remember to come and sketch them or, even better, bring her watercolours and paint them.

She wondered if Edward liked drawing, or painting, or reading. Wondered how he spent his evenings. If he thought of her as often as she thought of him.

It was four weeks since they had stood together on the crag and she still remembered the feel of his arms round her, the sound of his voice, deep and soft. The arms and the voice she had dreamed about for years without knowing who they belonged to.

Four weeks without being alone with him.

She sat on the rock by the primroses and imagined he was there with her, imagined what he might say to her. What she might say to him.

'I'll be away for two years, Edward, if my father allows

me to go, but I'll come back to you. Will you wait for me?'

'Of course I'll wait,' he would say, 'because I love you.'

'John says you'll be under manager in less than two years, and the manager eventually. I heard him telling my mother that he thinks you might eventually become the general manager responsible for all the company's mines. Anyway, even as assistant manager I'm sure John would let you take the company house on Bridge Road, the nice one with gardens reaching down to the riverbank. It should be John's but he's going to rebuild the old lodge for when he marries Lillian McDougall. And of course Lillian doesn't have any brothers so one day she'll inherit all her family's mines so perhaps you'd run all of them, too.'

And he would laugh and say modestly, 'I think you're looking too far ahead, Rose.'

'But we need to plan ahead, Edward, if we're to be married. And I'm sure Papa would agree, if you asked him. He respects you so.'

And he would hold her and kiss her and say that of course he would ask her father for her hand.

But she was dreaming again, she remembered, dreaming about something that might never happen. Edward was not there, and perhaps he had already forgotten about her.

And perhaps Papa would not agree to her going to school, or she would fail the entrance tests or they would not think her French was fluent enough! The worries tumbled over each other. Perhaps, even, Papa would still insist she married Hubert Belchester!

She took out her handkerchief to dry her eyes. She would never marry Hubert Belchester, not now she had met Edward. She would rather become an old maid, because she would still have her dreams of what might have been if only . . .

If only what?

If only she had run away with Edward. She would leave a message in their secret meeting place, King's Crag, telling him he must be there at sunset, and they would run away together under cover of darkness.

She hugged herself, pretending it was his arms around her. And then she thought she was a silly girl, the silly romantic girl her father had accused her of being when he tried to make her accept Hubert's proposal. Not the sort of girl Edward would want. He would want a sensible, dependable woman. The sort of person she really was. When she was not dreaming.

But was that the sort of woman he wanted? Would he think of King's Crag as their secret meeting place?

The miniature valley was gloomy. The afternoon drawing into evening. Time to go home.

She tucked her handkerchief into her pocket and turned to leave, unsure of herself and of Edward. Then she stopped.

There was a test. A way, perhaps, of knowing. If Edward came to the crag he would notice the primroses, she was sure of that. She took out her handkerchief, wrapped it around a small stone, and placed it amongst the wild flowers. If he loved her he would understand, and replace her handkerchief with his own. Then she would know. She would know for certain.

She thought of nothing other than Edward as she walked back down to the manor. She was half happy and half sad and she did not know which she enjoyed most.

As she entered the vegetable garden behind the house she saw John. He looked agitated.

'Where have you been?' He grabbed her arm as if he was angry with her.

'Just walking,' she explained. 'Is something wrong?'

He paused and his hesitation frightened her.

When he spoke she heard the tremble in his voice. 'It's Miss Smith. She's ill.'

'Again? The poor dear.' She opened the rear door. 'I'll go to her now.'

'She's very ill, Rose. She collapsed an hour ago. Mama's

with her and Hopkins has gone for the doctor.' He seemed
to turn pale. 'And I think you should prepare yourself. She
looks awful.'

She threw her coat off, ran up the stairs to Miss Smith's
room and entered without knocking. Miss Smith was in
bed, still wearing her day clothes but weighed down with
blankets. Her white hair, normally fiercely tidy, was
splayed across the pillows in an untidy fan. Her mouth was
open and dripping saliva.

'Miss Smith!'

There was no greeting from Miss Smith, just a flicker
from eyes that were sunk back and half covered by
drooping lids. A hard rattling sound came from the
drooping mouth.

'Miss Smith!' She threw herself on to the bed, opposite
her mother.

A hand clawed at her hair and pulled her close to the old
lady's face. A horrible stale smell made her screw up her
nose before she could stop herself.

'You're beautiful, Rose. Leave here. Leave like
Catherine did.'

'I don't understand,' she said quietly, but Miss Smith did
not answer.

'Miss Smith? Miss Smith?' Her mother was shaking her
head, and she realised the old lady was dead.

An awful stench filled the room as she tried to untangle
her hair from the lifeless fingers, and as she sat up the
hand which had so often held hers warmly grazed coldly
across her face and neck.

'I'm sorry, darling,' she heard her mother say, and she
looked from her mother's tearful eyes to Miss Smith's
staring ones.

'I don't understand what she meant, Mama.'

Her mother did not answer, she just reached across and
pulled Miss Smith's eyelids closed.

'Did you understand, Mama?'

Her mother shook her head and said there was nothing

they could do and they should go. Her father came into the
room as they were leaving and as they shut the door
behind him she was surprised to hear him sobbing, but as
her mother reminded her, Miss Smith had been the tutor
governess to his three children for thirty-nine years.

That was the last time she saw Miss Smith. The
undertakers collected the body and after they embalmed
it they asked if any of the family wanted to pay their
respects before the coffin was closed but she refused. The
cold hand, rattling breath and staring eyes had already
obliterated the warmer memories of the old lady who had
been stern but honest with her all her life. And seeing the
embalmed body was not going to explain the reason for
Miss Smith's final instruction to her.

'Leave here. Leave like Catherine did.'

She puzzled over it for a while, and decided that it was
Miss Smith's way of telling her she should leave Pincote to
find a husband. There was an element of comfort in
thinking that the old lady's final act was to give advice to
her, even if it was the wrong advice. Edward was in
Pincote, and it was Edward that she was determined to
marry.

She wished she had the comfort of Edward's company at
Miss Smith's funeral; and slipped her hand into her pocket
so she could feel the sketch of him she had drawn.
Everyone else had someone to accompany them, only she
and Miss Smith were alone.

She watched the coffin lowered into the grave in St
George's churchyard next to Anne Laybourne, her father's
first wife, and amongst the graves of various Laybourne
servants. The funeral service had been short and simple.

Miss Smith had no family and no friends outside the
manor's household and few inside. Apart from Hopkins,
the coachman, she was the longest-serving member of the
household and had always demanded that her fellow
employees respected her seniority. When she did not eat

with the family she ate alone in the room she had occupied since she first came to the manor. A maid carried her food to her and collected the empty dishes. A chambermaid cleaned her room and tidied her bed. Miss Smith was never more than formally civil to either.

'Are you all right, Rose?' John asked as they turned away from the grave.

'Yes, thank you.' She pointed to a headstone which had already been carved and was standing a few feet from the grave. 'But I think the wrong date's been put on the headstone.'

'No, Rose, that's right. She was fifty-eight years old.' John confirmed the date.

'I thought she was much older. That means she was a few years younger than Papa.' The thought simply reinforced what she had suddenly realised, life was fragile.

They returned to the manor immediately the funeral was over. Everyone was quiet, and she noticed that her father was quietest of all. He had been unusually withdrawn since Miss Smith died.

'Papa?' She tried to sit on his lap to comfort him, something she had often done until recently, but he pushed her away.

'Well, we've buried Miss Smith. Now we must decide what we're to do with you, young lady.'

'Papa?' His rejection hurt and the implications of what he said worried her.

'Now Miss Smith's gone, we must decide. The Belchesters will be here in a few weeks and you owe Hubert an answer. What will it be?'

'I'm not ready to be married, Papa, not yet,' she said cagily, trying not to upset him any more. 'But I should like to go to the Annecy Collegiate, if I may.'

'Come to my study.'

She did as she was told, scared that he would tell her that she must either marry Hubert or go to live with her half sister in the hope that there she would find someone who suited her as a prospective husband. Catherine had come for the funeral and as she was returning home by train that afternoon their father would no doubt think it convenient for his daughters to travel together. Her mind raced over all the possibilities and implications and she was astonished when he told her to sit in front of his desk and handed her a letter from her mother's old school.

'Read it,' he said grimly, 'aloud and in English.'

The letter was written in French. She read it quickly, translating as she went, grateful that the handwriting was clear but only half aware of what it said.

'Well?' She knew she was expected to answer and scanned the letter again, reading the details and assimilating them this time.

It said that there were opportunities available in the collegiate, but only for healthy young ladies with fluent French who could pass the entrance examination and the interview to assess their suitability.

'I would like to apply, Papa,' she said, her head light with excitement.

'Why, Rose? Why do you want to improve your education when you'll never need to earn your living, and why do you want to go to France?'

'I believe that whatever I do in my life, Papa, I'll enjoy it more if I've had a better education, and I'd like to go to France as part of that education and because I'm sure the experience of living away from home would be good for me.' She gave the answer she had rehearsed so many times.

'I see.' Her father nodded and she thought he seemed satisfied. 'It's not because you see it as a means of not marrying Hubert Belchester?'

'No, Papa, not at all.' She hoped she sounded convincing.

'Good. Your mother, and even your brother, seem to think it will be good for you to extend your education, young lady, so I propose to allow you to apply, upon one condition.'

'Yes, Papa.'

'You agree to marry Hubert and become officially engaged to him before you leave. That way you'll always have the security of knowing that he's waiting for you when you return.'

Her heart fell. The only way she could avoid marrying Hubert now was to promise herself to him in two years' time. It seemed wrong to make him a promise she would never fulfil, and disloyal to Edward to expect him to wait for her when she was engaged to someone else.

But she had no choice.

Elizabeth felt sick when Mr Peebles asked her into his office. The headmaster looked very nervous and when he asked her to sit down she feared the worst.

'Miss Forrester, Elizabeth' – he looked down at his desk – 'I told you that several of the school's directors have expressed doubts about your suitability to remain here after your recent experiences.'

'You mean the row, Mr Peebles?' she asked bluntly even though she felt sorry that he had to speak on their behalf.

'Yes.' He looked wretched and continued slowly. 'I'm afraid that I've been instructed to remove you from school immediately, and without references.'

'I see,' she said, and thought that there was little use in arguing with him. Whatever she said would not change the situation and would only make him feel worse; and she could not do that to someone who had always been kind to her.

'However, another opportunity has arisen for you to take a temporary position.'

'Without references?'

'Quite so. Do you think you may be interested?'

'It depends upon the opportunity, Mr Peebles, but I need to earn my living so I suppose I'll have to consider anything that's offered.'

She hardly understood what the headmaster said next,

and it was not until he was already at his door that she realised what was happening.

'If you'd just wait here for a few moments,' he said, and closed the door behind him.

When it reopened she saw Mrs Laybourne.

'Good afternoon, Miss Forrester, are you keeping well?' It was a brisk introduction and she watched Mrs Laybourne walk behind the headmaster's desk and sit down.

'Quite well, thank you, Mrs Laybourne.' She did not have time to say any more before the visitor began to explain the reason she was there.

'I understand the board have dismissed you and I must make it clear that my husband had no part in that. Both he and I understand the position you found yourself in, Miss Forrester.' She saw a faint smile on the other woman's lips. 'You're obviously a very strong-willed young lady and we wonder if you're strong-willed enough to teach another strong-willed young lady? My daughter, Rose?'

'I don't understand.'

'Of course you don't. Allow me to explain.'

The sun was shining as she walked to her parents' home. She was excited and nervous. Excited at the thought of living in the same house as John Laybourne, and because of the challenge Mrs Laybourne had set her. And nervous because the thought of living in the manor frightened her, and because she did not know what her parents would say when she told them what she was going to do.

'Lizzie, we didn't expect to see you today,' her father said and immediately leaned across to where her mother was dozing in front of the fire. 'Minty, wake up, love. Our Lizzie's come to see us.'

She kissed them both, and noticed her mother's slow reaction and the concern in her father's face.

'I've got some news for you, and I don't know whether or not you'll like it,' she said bluntly.

'Go on, lass,' her father said, and sat back, his concerned face looking even more grim.

She explained what had happened and waited for their reaction.

'I'm sorry you've been sacked,' her mother said, and waited until she could take in enough breath to continue, 'but it sounds grand, what you're going to do.'

Her mother sat back, breathing through her mouth to overcome the effort of talking so much.

'Aye, lass, your ma's right. Good luck to you.'

'You don't mind me working for the Laybournes?' She was relieved that they had not criticised her for taking the job without asking them first.

'The whole family works for the Laybournes, one way or another,' her father said quietly, and then added in an even quieter voice, 'at least, they did.'

'What do you mean?' she asked, alerted that another crisis had broken.

'It's Joey and Paul,' he said, and she could tell that he was angry even though he was trying hard not to show it.

'Yes?' she demanded and noticed the way he looked at her mother then stared down into the small fire. 'Tell me, Da.'

He did not answer so she turned to her mother, and saw that she was shrinking into herself, tears rolling out from the hollow eye sockets.

'Da! Tell me what's happened.'

'They're leaving Pincote, Lizzie. Going to work on the railway.'

'Where? When?'

'America, Lizzie. Next month.'

CHAPTER 13

—————————◆—————————

Edward climbed fast, his boots thudding on the rough path and his heart thudding in his chest.

'Your ma's dying, son.' His father had told him what he knew but had tried to ignore. 'And nothing you or anyone else does can make any difference now.'

He felt as though he was partly responsible, he should have done more; but now there was nothing he could do except wait and be with her at the end.

He paused below the top of the ridge and looked back across the valley, beyond the mine and its buildings to the threaded rows of tiny cottages which were stuck on the opposite hillside. Pincote Colliery. The cemetery caught his eyes for a moment, then he glanced at Pincote Market before sweeping his sight across the river and along the steep north slope of South Ridge.

In less than a minute he had seen his entire world.

'Come with us, Edward. There's grand opportunities for a man who's willing to work.' He heard Joey's words as if he were still standing beside him. 'Come with us, lad, there's nothing here for you, no matter how hard you work. America's a new country, a big, open land where anything's possible, man. You can have anything you want if you work for it.'

Anything. Except Rose and peace of mind. But could he have either even if he stayed?

He moved along the slope until he could see King's Crag.

It started as a sheer cliff but three gullies had formed in the top thirty feet or so and the late afternoon sun cast them into shadow. In that light the crag looked like the back of an enormous hand reaching up for the sky. Reaching for something it could never have.

He was going to the crag to think, and hoping by some miracle that Rose might be there, but the appearance of the giant hand depressed him even more than he had already been. Even King's Crag, with all that its memories meant to him, seemed to have turned against him. It had built up his expectations, and now it seemed to be telling him something different: that he would always be reaching for something he could never have.

He looked across the valley again, North Hill on one side, the side where he belonged, King's Crag on the other, from where he had glimpsed a world he wanted to be part of. A world where Rose Laybourne lived.

And now there was another world open to him, one he had never considered, waiting across an ocean.

He reached the miniature valley, desperately hoping that Rose would be there, but the little valley was empty.

'Rose!' The rocks repeated her name but she did not appear.

He stared at the small boulder she had sat on when she watched him sleep. A single shaft of sunlight, like a length of clean timber, leaned across the valley. Its end rested against the boulder and illuminated a clutch of primroses which had opened at its base. Wild flowers for his mother.

A simple token but something which would brighten her day.

Then the miracle he had hoped for happened. He knelt down to pick the flowers and saw something white and lacy nestling amongst them. A handkerchief wrapped around a stone?

He unwrapped it and saw the initials embroidered in fine gold thread. R.C.L. Rose Charlotte Laybourne!

A shiver of excitement shook off the depression and in that moment he decided anything was possible. Rose had sent him her favour, just as a medieval lady would the knight of her choice. In that moment he knew what he wanted was in Pincote. There was no need to go to America.

He picked just one primrose, took out his own handkerchief, a rough square of rag, and wrapped it around the stone and the primrose. His first present to her. He settled it amongst the primrose leaves and picked several flowers but left enough not to desecrate the place. Then he turned towards home.

'Edward.' Elizabeth smiled as he walked into the kitchen. 'Flowers for Ma?'

'Aye, a few primroses, like.' He was surprised to find her at home. 'Didn't expect to see you here.'

'I came with some news, lad, but instead I got more than I bargained for.' She shrugged.

'You've heard then, about Joey and Paul?'

'Aye. What do you think?' she asked quietly, pulling the door shut so their parents could not overhear what they said.

'Bad timing, with Ma as she is, but I cannot blame 'em, Lizzie. They've got their wives and bairns to think about.'

'Aye, and you, lad? I hear they've asked if you'll go too?'

'I'm sticking here, lass. But you? They'd take you if you want to go.' He noticed her surprise and realised that she had not even thought about going with them.

'No.' She shook her head and turned to the pans on the

range. 'America sounds fine, but not for me.'

'I'm with you there, lass, but what brought you up here?'

'I've been sacked. Because of the row with Saul.'

He was stunned. 'Christ, Lizzie, I'm sorry. That's not bloody fair, especially after Saul, like.' He felt his anger boil up and was about to explode when he saw her smiling. 'But you're not worried about it?'

'I've been offered a position at the manor.'

'Laybourne Manor?'

'Aye, teaching Rose Laybourne.'

'What?' He was suddenly aware of Rose's handkerchief in his pocket and he closed his hand around it as if it needed to be better hidden.

He listened to her explain what had happened and as he agreed to help her move her belongings into the manor he almost shouted with delight. He would surely meet Rose again and might even see her alone for a while.

'But where's this school she's going to and how long will she be away, like?' he asked without thinking, and Elizabeth's expression told him he had asked too much.

'You're very interested,' she said.

'Just interested, lass, that's all.'

He noticed her hesitate before she answered. 'Somewhere in France. She'll be away for two years.'

His confidence crumbled. Going to France for two years? But she had left him her handkerchief. It did not make sense. He had to see her and taking Lizzie to the manor offered the opportunity.

'I did warn you, lad, that you'd probably got it wrong – but you'll still borrow a cart and help me move in?' he heard Elizabeth ask again.

'Aye, of course, I'll be pleased to.' He turned away, to take the flowers to his mother, and then something else occurred to him. 'You're moving in on St George's Day. I seem to remember John Laybourne saying that if you weren't at the school he wouldn't go to the prize-giving for the recitals.'

'Aye, his mother told me he's already sent his apologies to the school and to the board of governors. I understand it'll be the first time that a member of the family hasn't attended since the tradition started years ago.'

'So he's keeping his word?'

'Yes, lad, it looks like it.'

He borrowed the same cart and nag that had carried William's coffin. It was more than big enough to carry Elizabeth's three large bags but it saved the long walk to the manor and meant it was easier to talk as they travelled.

It was a beautiful day, sunny although the air still carried a spring chill.

'Can you smell the trees and the hedges, Lizzie? It's a wonderful day.'

'You sound happy. Why's that?' She grinned and held on as the cart rode over a dip.

'Because it's St George's Day and Shakespeare's birthday and this is a grand English morning and I'm glad I'm English. That's why.'

'They the only reasons?' he heard her ask and avoided giving an answer; which could only be that he was looking forward to seeing Rose.

'How long will you stay at the manor, lass?'

'Until the end of August, and then I don't know what I'll do. What about you, though? What are your plans?'

'John Laybourne seems pleased enough with what I'm doing and he's promised that he'll consider me for under manager within a year. Once we've got the new shaft opened up and the South Ridge workings producing he wants to spend more time on the other mines so he'll have to appoint a new manager. He reckons I might be the man, Lizzie, but don't tell anyone about that, not yet.'

'Seems like you're going to do well, lad. You're already talking like a manager.' He saw the way she avoided looking at him. 'So have you managed to talk to Nancy yet?'

'I haven't seen much of her lately. We agreed to play

things a bit quiet, like.' He was pleased that Nancy had left him alone for the past few weeks, and even more pleased that when they had seen each other she had not said anything more about getting married.

'I see. You both agreed, did you?' Lizzie said sharply, and he did not admit that he still had not told Nancy they would never be married.

'No one in your life at the moment?' he asked, knowing the answer but trying to shift the conversation away from himself.

'Of course not!' It was not simply the way she said it that surprised him but also the way she asked, 'Why? What have you heard?'

'Nothing, lass, nothing,' but he could not resist teasing her, 'but John Laybourne's always asking after you, like, and you going up there to live . . .'

'You mustn't say things like that.' She spoke sharply again. 'Especially with me working at the manor. What'd people think?'

'I'm sorry, lass, I was only joking.'

'Well, it's not something to joke about, Edward. The Laybournes might get the wrong impression if they heard.'

They drove in silence until he turned the cart through the manor's high gates and saw the lodge for the first time. 'Look at that, Lizzie. It's six times the size of our house and it's left to ruin.'

'Aye, lad, and it could be a beautiful home, done up, like.'

He reined the nag in and they sat and looked at the lodge for a few minutes.

The building had been left to the elements: a fallen tree had crashed through the roof and a small tree must have seeded inside the house because it was growing out through another part of the roof. The house was built with decorative brick panels set between large wooden beams and although the structure seemed sound the only thing that did not need attention was a wooden paling fence which enclosed a large overgrown garden.

'Beautiful,' Elizabeth said again, 'don't you think so, Edward?'

'Aye, but not as beautiful as that.' He nodded up the curved drive towards the manor, a quarter of a mile away. 'Still, I don't envy you, living there, like, with the Laybournes.'

'It's only somewhere to live, Edward, and they're only people, like you and me.'

'No, lass. They're people, all right, but not like you and me and you mustn't forget that. You just take care of yourself, and don't let them bully you. You're here to teach, not to skivvy. Nor anything else, for that matter.'

'What do you mean by that?'

'You know, lass.' He felt awkward. 'John Laybourne, and his father. You away from home, like, living under their roof. Don't let them take advantage, that's all I'm saying.'

'I doubt either John Laybourne or his father would think of me in that way,' she said, but he noticed a slight tremble in her voice and thought she needed reassuring.

'Well, lass, be careful and don't get taken in by any sweet promises, like. If they try anything, you just leave and come home. We'll sort something out. Just don't feel obliged to them, that's all.'

The cart crunched over the final few yards of gravel and stopped by the steps which led to the front door.

'Edward, I'm not sure we're right to use the front door,' she said urgently, and he felt her squeeze his hand.

'Well, lass, I don't think we can just step into the kitchen like we would at home.' He stopped talking as he heard Rose and John's voices coming from an open window.

'I can't do it, John. I can't.'

'Just try, Rose, just do your best. It'll help Miss Forrester to know that you really do appreciate her coming here to teach you.'

'But why this piece. It's so long that I keep forgetting the words.'

'Because it's the piece I remember Miss Forrester reciting. Come along, try.'

Edward stared at Elizabeth and they waited for the silence to end.

'The quality of mercy is not strained, it droppeth as the gentle rain from heaven. Oh, John, I feel silly.'

'Try again. She'll be here soon.'

The front door opened and Charlotte Laybourne called out, 'Miss Forrester, Mr Forrester, good afternoon.' She glanced across to the open window. 'John was sorry that you've been deprived of the usual St George's Day recital and he and Rose are preparing a special greeting for you, but Rose seems to be having some difficulty remembering the words.'

Two faces appeared at the window, immediately disappeared, and moments later John and Rose Laybourne followed their mother down the flight of steps.

'I'm sorry, Miss Forrester, but I can't remember all the words.' Rose laughed and stood by the cart. 'Good afternoon, Mr Forrester. I'm pleased to see you again.'

He greeted her quietly, trying to control the confusion of thoughts which seeing her sent tumbling through his mind.

Then he nodded to John Laybourne, watched him help Elizabeth down from the cart, and heard his drawling, 'We thought it would be rather nice to offer you a special welcome.'

'John thought it would be nice,' Rose said sharply. 'He remembered hearing you recite the piece, but I'm sure you can do it much better than me.'

'It is a difficult piece,' Elizabeth sympathised, 'and I'm not sure I could do it now.'

'Come on, Miss Forrester,' John challenged, 'try. Show Rose how it should be done.'

'I don't think so.' She glanced back towards the cart and shrugged, obviously looking for support.

'Try, Lizzie.' Edward saw how embarrassed both she

and Rose looked and it seemed to him the easiest solution was for her to try. 'You can do it easily.'

'There's really no need,' Charlotte Laybourne began but John interrupted and asked Elizabeth to prove that she could still do it.

'If you insist.' She resigned herself and rattled through the speech as fast as she could, obviously embarrassed and finally turned to the cart to glare at Edward and mouth the word, 'Satisfied?'

Everyone applauded and he was glad he had encouraged her to respond.

'Well done, Miss Forrester.' John Laybourne laughed. 'Now it's your brother's turn.'

'I don't think so, Mr Laybourne.' He felt uncomfortable.

'Come on, man. Your sister's done her act and now it's time for yours.'

'John!' His mother turned on him. 'It's not fair to embarrass Mr Forrester like this.'

He felt awkward having her trying to protect him. 'That's all right, Mrs Laybourne. I'll do my bit, if Mr Laybourne'll do something as well.'

'Of course,' John Laybourne said brightly. 'We need some laughter, after all that's happened here. Go ahead, Mr Forrester.'

'Certainly.' He stood up on the cart and recited the piece he liked most. 'Once more unto the breach, dear friends, once more; or close the wall up with our English dead.'

He hesitated, suddenly remembering that Miss Smith had been buried only days ago and aware he had chosen badly, but everyone was watching him intently so he continued, reaching deep into the part as he spoke.

'In peace there's nothing so becomes a man . . .' He spoke on, King Henry at Harfleur, urging his troops on to battle; just as George Willis had taught him during quiet nights at home. He built to the finale, standing on the cart and ignorant of everything about him.

'Cry "God for Harry, England, and Saint George!" ' he roared.

And then complete silence.

It lasted several, uncomfortable seconds, and was broken by a spontaneous cheer from everyone who had heard him.

'That was wonderful.' Rose stepped forward, her eyes shining.

'Bravo, bravo,' Sebastian Laybourne called from the top of the steps, his hands coming together in slow, loud claps. 'I didn't realise we had such talent in Pincote. Such talent.'

Edward was happy to be drawn into the house and although it was his second visit he still found the inside even more intimidating than the outside. He realised now that the furnishings were much simpler than he imagined or remembered, but the rooms seemed enormous and everything in them seemed more substantial, more permanent than he had experienced anywhere. Rose strolled about, comfortable and at home, and her sense of ease unsettled him.

This was the sort of home she was used to, and nothing he could ever offer her would compare. He avoided looking at her any more than he had to, she was too beautiful, even when she was dressed in the clothes she wore to stay at home. He caught her looking at him several times, her big green eyes widening and smiling the way that had made him ache for her, but she made no real attempt to talk to him and seemed preoccupied, distant.

He realised that whatever there had been between them had changed. Perhaps she had begun to realise their differences.

He felt shabby and poor in her home, and supposed that was how she saw him now. He was not surprised when she disappeared; embarrassed, he supposed, hiding away until he had left.

He left, eventually, and Rose did not reappear to say goodbye. He kissed Elizabeth, quietly reminding her about what he had said, shook hands with John Laybourne and his parents, and was embarrassed to hear Sebastian Laybourne again praising him for his work and what he had achieved.

Then he was on the cart, Elizabeth and the Laybournes had gone indoors, and he was driving back towards the gates and the derelict old lodge, relieved to be free, half sorry and half glad that he had not said goodbye to Rose, trying to adjust to the thought that she did not love him after all.

It had simply been a silly, but enjoyable, adventure. He was glad that he had not told Nancy how he felt about Rose. Perhaps he should think more seriously about Nancy; he could do far worse for himself.

He did not see Rose at first, not until he was level with the lodge. She suddenly ran out and grabbed the nag's bridle. The horse turned its head, its white eye angry, and he knew how the horse felt.

'I found your handkerchief.' She held it up. 'It is yours?'

'Aye.' He had hers in his pocket and he took it out and offered it to her. 'I found yours. Here, you'd better have it back.'

'But I want you to keep it.' She sounded puzzled.

'Why?' he said gruffly, not caring if it upset her because he wanted the game, if it was a game, finished.

'To remember me by until I return from France.'

'Miss Laybourne' – he looped the reins around the cart's foot rail and turned to face her – 'isn't it time to stop all this?'

'I don't understand.' Her face dropped.

'I don't like being made a fool of. Especially by a young woman like you.'

'Made a fool of? I thought,' she began, and then turned away and started walking towards the manor.

'You thought what?' he called after her.

'I thought,' she began again, turned and walked back to

him. 'Here, you'd better have this. I don't need it any more.'

He took the folded paper from her and opened it as she walked away. It was the sketch she had drawn of him. 'Wait, Miss Laybourne, wait. Please.'

He jumped off the cart and ran after her and because she did not stop he grabbed her arm and turned her towards him. 'Why did you do this?'

'I told you. Because I don't need it any more.'

'No. I meant why did you draw it in the first place? When did you draw it?'

'The night after we'd met on King's Crag. Because I didn't want to forget how you looked. It's not very good, I'm afraid.'

'It's very good. I'm impressed, but I don't understand.'

She held up the rag handkerchief. 'I don't understand why you left this. With the primrose. It was a very cruel thing to do, if you didn't mean it. I didn't think you'd be like that.' She looked very sad, and then angry. 'Here, you'd better have this too.'

'Wait.' He stopped her from pulling away. 'I thought you'd been playing games with me. Teasing me, like. Trying to make a fool of me.'

'Does it look as if I have?' She began to cry and he slipped his arms around her and pulled her into him.

'I thought it did, lass. I thought it did,' he said softly.

'No one's ever called me "lass" before,' she said between sobs.

'No, lass, I don't expect they have,' he said, and wondered why, whenever he thought he knew how things were, they immediately changed.

'Let's go into the lodge,' she suggested, 'we can talk there.'

'I don't think that's a good idea,' he said warily.

'It looks like a wreck but it's quite safe.'

'No, lass, let's sit on the cart where anyone can see what we're up to.' It hurt to refuse her, but he doubted whether the lodge would be safe if they were alone there, out of sight.

He helped her up on to the cart's driving bench and sat close to her, his left arm around her shoulders.

'I love you,' she said suddenly, without looking at him. 'I always have. Even before I knew you.'

'That's daft, lass.' He tried to sound sensible but he knew exactly what she meant. 'I reckon I love you, but I can't see it doing either of us much good. I've seen how you live. I could never give you anything like that. Not on my wages and I wouldn't take any of your money. That wouldn't work either.'

'I've thought about that and it doesn't matter. I don't suppose I could marry you if you were a miner, but soon you'll be a manager and you'd be able to take on a manager's house.'

'I think you're looking a bit too far ahead,' he warned and stopped when he saw the way she was smiling at him.

'I knew you'd say that. I imagined this conversation so many times and I knew you'd say that, so doesn't that at least prove something? That we've only met a few times and I already know enough about you to know what you'll say?'

'Perhaps, but what about this school business? Two years away? In France?' He was surprised that he felt comfortable with her, comfortable enough to ask the question bluntly and expect an answer.

'There are three main reasons for that.' She held up her hand and extended three fingers as she spoke. 'Firstly, we've not known each other for very long and although I'm sure I love you I don't really think we should gallop into marriage. Secondly, I'm not old enough to marry anyway, not without my father's consent and I cannot imagine he would allow me to marry you, not at the moment. I'm sorry if I seem scheming or I'm assuming more than I've a right to but we don't have many opportunities to be together, especially alone, and we've so much to decide before I go away.'

She stopped the tumble of words and he felt her eyes taking him in, almost as if she was trying to absorb him.

He looked back at her. 'I give you credit for thinking it all out, lass. I even think Lizzie'd be proud of you, but you said you had three reasons. What's the third?'

'If I don't go away to school my father will make me marry Hubert Belchester.'

'Who's Hubert Belchester?'

'His grandfather and father are in some business with my father. Something to do with one of the London underground railways, and a few other businesses. The Belchesters are very wealthy and own a huge estate in Dorset and lots of land in London. Hubert is twenty-eight years old and he wants to marry me. And I don't want to marry him even though he could give me all the things you say you can't.'

'Then you're mad,' he said flatly and shifted his arm from her shoulders.

'Don't say that,' she pleaded and held his hand tightly. 'I don't love him. I love you, and you can give me so much that he can't.'

'If he loves you, I can't give you any more. And he'll always be there, mind. Even if you refused him and we did get married, he'd always be there, in my mind, and I'd know you could've had a better life with someone else. And one day you'd tell me that, after a row or when we couldn't afford to buy something you wanted.'

'I don't think so,' she said firmly, 'but that's why we need the two years. To be sure. Two years without seeing each other. We'll know if we love each other then. For certain, and if we do, nothing else will matter. Ever!'

He looked at her, and felt her confidence and determination seeping into him.

'If I go away for two years, will you wait for me?' She

looked deep into his eyes, so deep that he felt she was already a part of him.

He nodded because suddenly he could not speak, but it did not matter. He knew she would understand in the same way as he could understand what she could not say.

CHAPTER 14

Elizabeth stood and waved as Edward drove away, then turned back into the house before anyone could see the tears which were stinging her eyes.

'I'll show you your room.' Charlotte Laybourne was holding her arm and gently guiding her away from the rest of the family. 'Your bags have been taken up already.'

She followed Mrs Laybourne up the first flight of stairs, then down a long wood-panelled corridor set with doors on both sides, and tried to remember which room was which as Mrs Laybourne explained the layout of the house. Eventually they reached another flight of stairs that led up to an enclosed landing which she guessed ran from the front of the house to the back. The landing had a small window at each end and doors along one side; three doors, and the one nearest the rear of the house opened into her room.

'The servants all live at the other end of the house, Miss Forrester,' Charlotte Laybourne explained. 'This staircase is the only access to this end of the house and there are a number of store rooms between you and the servants so you should find it very quiet and peaceful living here. The schoolroom is next door and the room at the front is hardly ever used now, it used to be the children's day nursery. Miss Smith was very happy with her accommodation, and we hope that you'll also like it, Miss Forrester.'

'I'm sure I will, Mrs Laybourne.' She looked at her new room and immediately understood why Miss Smith had been happy to live here. The attic room looked comfortable and was much larger than her room in the Peebles' house. It had two dormer windows, one looking towards South Ridge and the other towards the gates and the lodge, both half hidden from view by spreading trees. The furniture was simple but looked comfortable: two large wardrobes, a dressing table, a huge chest of drawers, a writing table, several chairs, one enormous and padded, and an iron-framed bed which looked strangely out of place and as if it were trying to hide itself in a dark corner between the windows.

'I apologise for the bed, Miss Forrester, but it was the best we could find at short notice. We thought it best to burn Miss Smith's bed and bedding after she died,' Mrs Laybourne explained, and turned to the largest wardrobe. 'I hope you can manage with just one wardrobe for the moment, we appear to have lost the key to this one.'

'The one will be just fine, Mrs Laybourne. The room and everything looks wonderful to me. Thank you very much.' She peered behind a screen and saw a washstand complete with bowl and a jug of steaming water. 'You're very kind.'

'Not at all.' She sensed Mrs Laybourne felt embarrassed. 'I suggest that when you're ready you come down to the music room where we'll have a little tea and discuss what arrangements need to be made.'

'The music room?' She was not sure where the music room was.

'The room we've just left, Miss Forrester.' Mrs Laybourne

laughed. 'Rose will show you around and explain how the house is planned. It is a jumble, I know. It's been added to so much that any orderly plan disappeared years ago. Centuries ago, probably.'

The door shut and she was alone in the room's stillness. The only sound she could hear was the water jug's glaze chinking from the warmth of its water. Nothing else.

She washed in the warm water, used the scented soap which had been provided for her and dried herself on the soft towel which hung from a rail on the washstand. Luxury.

It was a new sensation and she was determined that she would remember what it felt like for the rest of her life.

New sensation followed new sensation throughout the rest of the afternoon and evening.

It seemed to take ages to find the music room and when she arrived the family had already gathered there.

'I'm sorry if I'm late,' she began as John Laybourne and his father both stood up.

'Please don't apologise, Miss Forrester.' The father smiled. 'We hope you'll feel at home here.'

'I doubt I'll ever feel that, sir,' she admitted and added quickly. 'It's so big I wonder if I'll ever find my way around.'

'I'm sure you'll soon adjust.' He smiled with his eyes. 'And Rose is charged to help you. If you're unsure about anything, or need anything, please don't be frightened to ask. Think of yourself as our guest for the next few months, and try to enjoy yourself whenever you can. We have a large library upstairs, so please use it. John and Rose will explain our family history to you and I'll be delighted to show you all the family portraits you'll see hanging on walls all over the house. Enjoy the gardens while you're here. They're magnificent during the summer months.'

'Thank you, sir,' she said and felt awkward as a maid served her with tea and small sugared buns.

To make her feel more like a guest she was told to call Rose and John by their first names, and the whole family called her Elizabeth. Rose had written out a list of the servants' names and positions to help her understand how the household was organised and John had drawn simple plans of the room arrangements for each floor so that she could easily find her way about.

That night she wore her best clothes and joined the family for dinner, already worried that her table manners would not match the event, but she was not prepared for the real problems which confronted her.

She sat next to Rose and opposite John, with their parents at each end of the long polished table, and as she sat down the array of cutlery spread out each side of a stiff white linen table mat unnerved her. At home she was used to a knife and fork and possibly a spoon, but here she had as much cutlery as the whole family might use, each knife and fork slightly different to the one next to it.

'Our first meal together, Elizabeth,' John said to her, and she saw him wink. 'I'm afraid my parents think that a couple of years in America has turned me into a savage, so I hope I don't embarrass you too much.'

He had anticipated her confusion and guided her through the mass of cutlery by innocently playing with the correct implements before each course was served.

She had never eaten so much or so richly, and although she sampled the wines that were served she was careful to sip slowly so that she did not drink too much. Even so, by the end of the meal she felt bloated and a little hazy.

'Cigar, John?' Mr Laybourne asked and she saw Rose and her mother move to leave.

'Thank you, Papa, but I think I'll take one for a stroll in the garden,' John said easily, and asked, 'Would you care for some air, Elizabeth?'

'Certainly.' She almost leapt up, eager to take some exercise and air to clear her head.

* * *

They strolled along the drive, towards the lodge.

'Food a little rich for you?' he asked pleasantly.

'Everything's a little rich for me,' she admitted and tried to plant her feet more surely.

'You'll get used to it. You did very well, and I don't mean that in a patronising way.' The smoke from his cigar curled across her face and she breathed it deeply, enjoying another sensation that she did not want to forget.

'It is a different world, though, and I may find it difficult adjusting back to the real one,' she told him.

'But this is the real one, Elizabeth. This life is as real to me as yours is to you.'

'I hadn't thought of that,' she admitted.

'And you don't approve, do you?'

She felt embarrassed, and tried to think of something inoffensive she could say. 'I could grow to enjoy it, and I don't approve of that.'

He laughed. 'You're a Puritan. Cromwell would have been proud of you.'

'No, it's not that, not really.' She realised she had to explain. 'I've eaten enough food tonight for a family of four or five. I don't see how that can be fair.'

'It isn't fair.' His reply surprised her. 'But it has nothing to do with what's fair. There are people who'd think that your family of four or five are eating more than they need. All over the world people are starving, Elizabeth, and they're not going to eat any more if we eat less. Trade is the answer, international trade which helps to distribute wealth more evenly throughout the world.'

'Perhaps,' she conceded, 'but how do we manage that?'

'First of all we must sort out our domestic economy. The industrial nations, England, Germany, America and Japan, for example, must become more productive so that the standard of living improves in our own countries and so that ordinary people can afford to buy more. That will improve the trade of the poorer countries and the whole world will benefit, in time.'

'Sounds simple.' She had never heard anyone talk about trade in that way before.

'The theory's simple, it's the practice that's difficult. One thing we have to do in England is to break down the restrictions that the class system imposes on developing our industries. It's already happening in America.'

'So I've heard from my brothers. Joey and Paul leave for America next week.'

'I know. I'll be sorry to lose them, but I can understand why they're going. Edward could have gone but he decided to stay. Do you know why?'

'I'm not sure,' she said honestly, still wondering if Rose could have had any influence on Edward's decision, 'but I suppose he thinks there's not much reason to go halfway around the world if he has a future here.'

'I'm glad he thinks like that. He does have a future here, I'm sure of it, but what about you? What do you want from life?'

'Me?' She felt trapped by the question; compared to his ideas whatever she said would seem paltry or offensive. 'Once I thought I simply wanted to marry and have children, but now I'd like to do more. I still want a family, of course, but I'd like to do something first.'

'Such as?'

'I don't really know. I'd like to do something to help women and children have a better life. I think women should have the same rights as men and I think children should be better taken care of, better educated. I'd like to see everyone living in better conditions, eating better, having more time to enjoy life instead of working all hours then being too tired to do anything in their free time. I'd like to see more doctors, women doctors too, so women will be more willing to go for help. Better care of children's health.' She stopped when she noticed the expression on his face. 'I suppose you think that sounds revolutionary?'

'I do.' He nodded. 'But I think you're right. I'm surprised

because I thought you were only interested in the rights of the Pincote miners.'

'I believe in the socialist movement, and that's no secret.'

'Which is why you didn't go to Alnwick?'

'Partly,' she said and hoped he would not press for more details, 'but you don't?'

'No. I think socialism would be a disaster. The French have tried it, and it doesn't work. It never will, Elizabeth, never.'

They had reached the lodge and they both stared at it, John puffing on his cigar and she trying to organise her thoughts.

'Socialism,' she said slowly, 'would not accept that this house should be left to collapse when it could house four families.'

'And if it already housed just one family?' he asked quietly, and waved his cigar towards the manor. 'Our house could accommodate more people. Would your socialist friends fill it up?'

'No, I don't suppose so,' she admitted.

'So, where do you draw the line?' he asked, then added kindly, 'I'm sorry if I've sounded rude but it isn't often that I can have a discussion like this about the things that really matter to me.'

'Do these things really matter to you?'

'Of course they do.' He sounded offended. 'Don't think that because I'm against socialism I'm also against social justice. You socialists don't have exclusivity on caring, Miss Forrester. My family, for one, cares very much, and I would have thought that was obvious, but changes should come slowly or we'll upset the natural balance. I don't approve of our class system, but it's a reality and it's given us a history, a pedigree if you prefer, of people who know how to run industry, commerce, farming, the country. We also have a pedigree of people who know how to work for them. We mustn't mix them too quickly. The results would be disastrous.'

'But the Americans seem to be mixing, from what I've heard, and you've asked Edward to move from one to the other and he seems to be succeeding.'

'Yes,' he said and she knew she had him beaten.

'So, where do you draw the line, Mr Laybourne?'

He grinned at her. '*Touché*,' he said.

She smiled back and thought she should change the conversation.

'This could be a beautiful house.' She rested her hands on the fence.

'It will be.' She could see from the expression on his face that he was fond of the old building. 'I intend to repair it and live in it myself.'

'When you marry Miss McDougall?'

He did not reply, just stared at the house and puffed on his cigar.

'It's becoming dark, Elizabeth, and I think that we should go back.' He threw the cigar down and ground it with his shoe.

They walked back to the manor without speaking, but already comfortable in each other's company.

The house was warm and she suddenly felt so tired that she immediately excused herself and went to her room.

It had been an exciting and enlightening day, she thought as she locked the door behind her, undressed and slipped into bed. And tomorrow she would see John again, and the day after, and every day for months.

CHAPTER 15

'Sit down, Elizabeth, please.' She sat in the chair Sebastian Laybourne indicated, in front of his desk. 'You've been here less than two weeks and I've already heard good reports about Rose's progress.'

'She's very bright, sir.' She returned his smile.

'I'm happy to hear you say that, but I want to discuss something else.' He leaned forward and she thought he looked almost shy. 'I have to ask if you'll grant me a favour.'

'Of course, if I can.'

'I understand that you're spending tomorrow with your family. To see two of your brothers leave for America?'

'Yes, sir,' she said anxiously, wondering if he was about to ask her to stay at the manor. 'I did arrange it in advance, with Mrs Laybourne.'

'Yes, I know.' He smiled again. 'You'll be seeing young Edward, I expect.'

She nodded.

'I was very impressed by his recitation, and yours, and I wonder if you'd both consider giving a short performance for some of my friends. The evening before John's and Rose's ball.'

'But that's next week, sir, hardly time to practise.' She could not think of anything worse than performing before strangers and tried to find a way of refusing without seeming ungrateful for all he had done for her.

'Please consider it, Elizabeth. The house will be full of guests from London, Manchester and Liverpool, and I'm sure they think that Pincote's only good for producing coal and sheep. I'd like to show them that we can also produce our own cultural talent. Mrs Laybourne will play the piano and John has agreed to sing. Even Rose seems quite enthusiastic.' He paused, then added, 'As she should because it was her idea.'

'I'll certainly speak to Edward.' She knew she was beaten and she was interested to see how he would react when she told him it was Rose's idea.

'Thank you. Now there's one other matter.' His shyness seemed to increase. 'You do realise that you're invited to the ball?'

'Me, sir?' She was aghast.

'Of course, Elizabeth. You are our guest and we have been rather negligent in assuming you would attend.'

'But I can't, sir,' she said and felt ill as she tried to explain. 'I don't know how to behave and I'd hate to humiliate you in front of all your friends.'

'I'm sure you won't,' he said confidently. 'You've managed well enough since you've been here, and that can't have been easy for you. You speak well and intelligently, you have a natural warm charm and Rose and John can soon teach you all the niceties you may need. And they can also show you some dance steps, enough for you to manage with.'

'But I can't, sir,' she repeated as she thought about what she could wear.

'I hope you won't think this is impertinent of me, but I'd be pleased to ensure you're suitably dressed for the occasion. Mrs Laybourne will be too busy to assist, but she assures me that Mrs Lumley will manage something suitable, and of course you have a personal friend in Mrs Darling.' He smiled again. 'Please agree, and please forgive me and Mrs Laybourne for not thinking about this earlier.'

She knew she had no choice.

The train steamed out of the station and in minutes the carriage with hands fluttering at its window was pulled around a curve and out of sight.

It saddened her to see Joey and Paul leave, knowing that she would probably never see them again. It was almost as if they had died, worse in a way because they had chosen to go. But she was glad that her mother and father had not come to the station. It was bad enough to stand there with the three brothers she had left, none of them speaking. They all stood for several minutes, then Edward turned and took her arm.

'Coming on home then, Lizzie?' She nodded because she could not trust herself to speak.

They had passed the colliery and turned into North Hill before she felt able to talk. She explained what Sebastian Laybourne had planned and was not surprised to see Edward's mood change instantly.

'Of course I'll do it, Lizzie. I think we ought to,' he added, 'to repay the Laybournes for all they've done for us.'

It was a change of attitude she did not question. A few weeks ago he had been all for grinding the Laybournes into the ground, but she could not blame him for changing his views when she knew hers had changed as much if not more.

As soon as they arrived back home they told their mother about the performance and the ball but she hardly seemed interested.

'That'll be nice,' she said, without looking up from the fire which blazed even though the day was warm. 'You've settled in there, Lizzie?'

'Aye, Ma, I have. They're all very nice to me, very nice indeed.'

'Good,' her mother said, and hardly spoke again until it was time to say goodbye.

Edward arrived at the manor the next afternoon, Saturday, after taking the direct route over South Ridge. As he opened the rear gate into the walled vegetable garden he was nervous as well as excited.

He had pressed his only suit before he left, and polished his brown boots until they gleamed. He had even brought a rag with him so he could brush the dust off his boots before anyone saw him. His usual red choker had been replaced with a piece of silk, dark blue with small white spots, which George Willis had produced from somewhere and shown him how to knot as a floppy bow. And he carried a small bunch of flowers for Rose's mother.

This was his first real opportunity to be accepted into the Laybournes' house and he saw it as a test. He was determined they should see him as more than just another miner. He had to impress them, even though he was scared because he did not know how to behave and because he knew he would feel intimidated by the family and the house itself.

He used the rag to brush his boots then threw it into a nearby compost heap, and brushed his suit with his hands. As he turned towards the house he saw Rose watching him. His heart was already beating fast and when he saw her it thumped so hard he could not speak.

'Good afternoon, Edward.' Her eyes seemed to shine even more than usual. 'Can I call you Edward? We call Elizabeth by her name.'

'It's all right by me, lass, but I think I should still call you Miss Laybourne.' He thought it was a silly situation but he did not want to risk offending anyone. 'I'd not feel comfortable being anything except formal, with your parents and your brother around, like.'

'Then I'd better call you Mr Forrester,' she said, and he felt clumsy as he watched her stare at him. 'You look so different. So handsome. You look like Lord Byron.'

Mrs Laybourne appeared a moment later and rustled over to greet him. He held out the flowers and almost thrust them into her hands.

'Well, thank you, Mr Forrester.' He saw how taken aback she was and he was not sure whether it was his appearance or the flowers which surprised her. 'I can't remember the last time a gentleman gave me flowers.'

She held them to her face and smelled their scent. 'Aren't they divine, Rose? So nice of you to think of flowers, Mr Forrester.' She looked at him for a moment and took his arm. 'How is your mother? Is she any better?'

'No, ma'am, I'm afraid not.' He allowed her to lead him towards the house. 'Worse, if anything. I doubt she'll last much longer.'

'I'm so sorry to hear that. Is there nothing we can do to help? I'd gladly pay for the doctor.'

'Thank you, but we've had the doctor to her for months and there's nothing much seems to help.'

'That's awful,' she said and he was astonished when she hugged him and added, 'We already think of Elizabeth almost as part of the family, and you too, in a way. I just wish there was something we could do.'

He realised that a few weeks ago he might have told her she could help by improving living conditions, but things had changed and now he was more concerned that she had said he was almost part of the family. He felt guilty and excited, and when he saw the look in Rose's eyes his excitement built up so that he wondered if he should risk admitting that he and Rose were in love. But John Laybourne appeared and as they shook hands he contented himself with the thought that he was making good progress towards his ultimate goal. Anything more could wait.

They rehearsed in the music room, the flowers he had brought set in a trumpet-shaped glass vase placed on top of the piano.

He noticed how relaxed Elizabeth seemed, and as he and Rose gave each other short, guarded smiles, he realised that the same quick glances were passing between Elizabeth and John Laybourne. It occurred to him, selfishly, that if Elizabeth and John broke the taboo it would be easier for him and Rose to follow.

After the rehearsal was over and he was drinking tea from dainty china cups and eating small scones off delicate plates he was satisfied that he had done nothing to be ashamed of. He had been polite but not servile, and had joined in the conversation without being self-conscious or controversial.

'There's just one problem, Mama,' Rose said suddenly and everyone looked at her, waiting for an explanation which she suddenly seemed unhappy to give. 'We'll begin the soirée immediately after dinner, so we'll all be here. All except for Mr Forrester.'

He panicked. He had expected to come along, do his piece, and leave, perhaps after having a few minutes with Rose. Nothing more. Elizabeth had told him about the need to use the correct cutlery, about behaving properly, and admitted that she was worried about making conversation with people she did not know; and the prospect of being forced to endure dinner terrified him.

'You're very welcome to come to dinner, Mr Forrester,' Mrs Laybourne said warmly, but he could see the reservation in her eyes, and feel her embarrassment as she tried to find a reason for him to refuse. 'In fact I think you should come, but we'll all be dressing, of course. Do you have suitable evening dress?'

He laughed, hoping that might overcome everyone's

embarrassment. 'This is my evening dress, Mrs Laybourne, and my morning dress and even my afternoon dress if there is such a thing.'

'You could borrow something of mine,' John Laybourne offered.

'Thank you Mr Laybourne, it's a very generous offer, but I don't think your clothes'd fit me too well, like, us being different sizes. Anyway, and I don't mean to sound rude, mind, but I'd not feel comfortable wearing another man's clothes.'

'We could try to fit you up with something,' Mrs Laybourne offered, but he could see that she was simply trying to be polite and save him from humiliation.

'No, but thank you anyway. If I cannot dress myself as a gentleman I'll not pretend to be one.'

'Mr Forrester' – Mrs Laybourne rested her soft hand on his – 'clothes don't make a gentleman, and no matter how you're dressed, you will always be a gentleman. And now I'll ask Mr Hopkins to bring the trap around and take you home. We'll also arrange for him to collect you next Friday evening, and take you home afterwards.'

'There's no need, ma'am,' he said, but his objections were waved aside.

'Mr Forrester' – he stood up as Sebastian Laybourne appeared in the room – 'that's the least my wife can do for a gentleman who brings her flowers.'

He looked into Laybourne's face and could not decide whether he was being pleasant or critical. Suddenly the flowers seemed shabby and cheap.

There was a moment's silence, broken by John. 'Why don't you allow Elizabeth to show you her quarters while we're waiting for Hopkins?'

'Of course.' Rose stood up quickly. 'And afterwards I'll show you the schoolroom.'

'Lizzie!' He was impressed. 'I reckon you've as much space in here as we have in the whole house back home.'

'I reckon you're right, lad, and I'll tell you something else.' She put her arm around him and kissed his cheek. 'I was really proud of you this afternoon. It couldn't have been easy and you did really well.'

'It wasn't that difficult, lass,' he said. 'Mrs Laybourne made me feel as though she really wanted me here.'

'Aye, she's lovely, Edward, and very caring. And so's Mr Laybourne, though he tries to hide it sometimes. He's charming, when he wants to be. Really.'

'If you say so,' he said, and turned away as Rose ran up the stairs.

Elizabeth caught his hand. 'I noticed, lad. You and Rose looking at each other. Be careful, and don't even think about doing anything silly.'

She stayed in her room and left him to follow Rose into the schoolroom, simply reinforcing her warning with her eyes.

Rose pushed the schoolroom door closed behind her and leaned against it.

'I thought you were wonderful, Edward, Mr Forrester,' she said uncertainly. 'And so did Mama.'

'I'm not sure your father approved.' He looked at her, conscious that they were alone at last.

'He likes you really. He often asks how you're managing with your new job and you know how much you impressed him a few weeks ago.'

'That's what Lizzie said.' He felt reassured that he had not upset her father by bringing flowers for her mother.

'He likes Lizzie, too. He often asks me if she's happy here.'

'And your brother? Does he like Lizzie?'

She smiled, and glanced away from him. 'You must have noticed. I think he more than likes her.'

'Aye, that's what I reckon,' he said, and enjoyed the way her copper hair fell around her face and over her shoulders.

'I don't think Mama and Papa have noticed but John

takes Elizabeth out for a walk every evening, after dinner. They seem to stay out longer and longer each evening. John and Elizabeth,' she said, 'and you and me?'

He nodded and moved towards her, and as he did so she pushed herself away from the door and into him. His arms wrapped around her and his mouth settled against hers.

It was an inexpert kiss; her nose got in the way and her teeth caught his lip, but it caused no more than a moment's delay before the softness of her mouth overwhelmed him and he crushed his lips against hers and squeezed her so tight that she gasped for breath.

'Edward, I love you so much!' She said it with an urgency that set him reeling.

'I love you, Rose, and no matter what happens—' He was stopped as she kissed him again.

Their lips parted but they stood with their bodies pressed hard against each other until she moved across the room and stared out of the window.

'Hold me, the way you did on King's Crag,' she asked, and he followed her and wrapped his arms around her. 'That feels wonderful.'

He lifted his arms until he could feel the swell of her breasts and had just moved his hands to feel her better when he heard Elizabeth close her bedroom door. 'Mr Hopkins must be ready by now, Edward.' He heeded the warning and stepped away from Rose before Elizabeth opened the schoolroom door.

He asked Hopkins to leave him in Pincote Market, stuffed the silk bow into his pocket and started to make his own way home, but when he reached the end of Albert Street he hesitated. The afternoon had been the best he could remember and he wanted the enjoyment to last as long as possible; he was not in the mood to tell the family what had happened. They probably would not understand how he felt; could not understand without knowing he was in love with Rose, and he was not prepared to admit that to anyone other than Lizzie. Not yet. He would tell them all when the time came, but just now it was his secret. His and Rose's. Something to share.

He walked on up North Hill, the rutted surface dry now, crusty and firm. The air smelled of smoke and coal dust and the evening sunshine made the sky glow orange-yellow, rust-coloured towards the west. He did not see Nancy leaning against a gate until it was too late to avoid her.

'Edward.' He saw her smile and his mellowness made him smile back at her.

'Nancy. Beautiful evening.' He stopped.

'Aye,' she said, and stretched her arms along the gate like a comfortable cat. 'What are you doing up here?'

'Just felt like a walk,' he said simply.

'Feel like company?' she asked and he could not refuse so he nodded and waited for her to join him.

They strolled past the cemetery and up to the rocks near the top of the hill.

'Can we sit for a bit?' she asked. 'I feel tired.'

'Aye,' he said, and instinctively held out his hand to steady her as they climbed up a low bank, moved across some uneven ground and chose a flat-topped boulder to sit on.

The rock was warm from the day's sun. They sat for a while, as quiet and peaceful as the evening itself, and when she did eventually speak her voice was soft and conversational.

'Haven't seen much of you lately,' she said, without looking at him.

'Been busy, Nance.'

'Enjoying the new job?'

'Aye.'

She paused for a few moments, then, 'Wonder where Joey and Paul are now,' she said and he knew she was trying to make conversation without asking him outright if he had thought any more about her and their future.

'At sea, I reckon. It's a long journey.'

'Wish you'd gone with them?'

'No. Good luck to 'em, like, but I'm happy here.'

'Are you? Really happy?'

'Happy as I can be,' he said, and wished he had the courage to tell her it was all over between them.

She patted his hand and then held it. 'I'm sorry, Edward.'

'What about?' Perhaps she was going to say it for him.

'About your ma. She's bad, isn't she?'

'Pretty bad, I reckon.' He felt her squeeze his hand in sympathy, and wished she had not.

'Anything I can do?' she asked and snuggled closer. 'I'm here if you want me. I'll always be here, Edward. You know that, don't you?'

'Aye, lass. Thanks.'

They sat quietly for a few moments and she suddenly lifted his arm and put it around her shoulders, gripping his hand tightly and holding it close to her breast.

'Hold me, Edward, please.' She sounded frightened and desperate and he held her because he did not know what else to do.

He felt her free hand take his fingers and open them up, lay them on her breast and stroke them lightly. He tried not to react, he wanted desperately not to take advantage of her again, but she encouraged him to feel her, gently at first then with more and more urgency until his blood was pounding and he did not care any more. His free hand lifted to her other breast and she turned to lean her back against him, giving him easy access to her.

She was soft and warm, compliant and exciting, and suddenly it was not enough to feel her through her clothes. He wanted to feel her flesh, to see her and suck her. He fumbled at her buttons and she did nothing to stop him.

Seconds later she was stripped to the waist, lying soft and pale against the hard grey rock, her head turned towards the valley and resting on the pillow of her hair.

She had closed her eyes, and her lips were smiling. It was as if she was telling him that she wanted him to enjoy her, and that would please her, too.

She whimpered as he gently chewed her nipples, and he felt her hands in his hair, pulling his face close against her, pushing him down to kiss her belly and her hips but always bringing him back to her nipples and lips.

She unbuttoned his shirt and he felt her lips and tongue on his chest, and then on his stomach as his shirt opened down to his waist. His heart was pounding and surrounding him in a red mist. His trousers, tight and constricting, loosened suddenly and slipped down and she was holding him.

'No, Nance,' he murmured and tried to pull away but she held him firmly, stimulating him. 'No, Nance. No.'

But he did nothing to stop her.

She stopped at the last moment. 'I want you,' she shouted urgently and pushed her clothes down until she could wriggle out of them.

He was on top of her, thrusting her against the rock and she was crying out and running her hands through her hair.

Suddenly it was over, a climactic conclusion, simultaneous for both of them as far as he could judge.

He pulled away almost immediately. He felt ashamed of himself, until he saw the expression on her face. Sheer pleasure.

He pulled up his trousers, buckled his belt and as he fumbled with his shirt he watched her stretch out and eventually sit up. Her profile was silhouetted against the orange sky and she ran her hands over her body, lifting her breasts and allowing them to fall back, firm with her nipples erect; and he knew she had enjoyed him.

She had used him just as he had used her weeks ago. Somehow it seemed to even things up.

It was the end of something that he half wished had never happened. But only half wished had not happened.

* * *

Elizabeth fingered the swatches of material Mrs Lumley threw along the table. She was tempted to choose the shiny brass-coloured cloth but Rose took a length of satin, the colour of burgundy wine, and hung it across her shoulders.

'The deep red suits your colouring, Elizabeth.' As she saw her reflection in the mirror she agreed.

'Can you make it into something by Saturday?' Elizabeth asked Mrs Lumley.

'Can we, Mrs Darling?' Mrs Lumley smiled.

'If someone else can make the grey dress,' Mrs Darling promised, 'I'll finish it. Somehow. Depending on the pattern, that is.'

She had already chosen material and a pattern for a dress she would wear to the Friday night dinner, and now she had to choose a design for Saturday's ball gown.

Lizzie Forrester, she thought, who'd have reckoned you'd be here ordering dresses for a party and a ball?

Mrs Lumley led her and Rose to a small room where they sat and drank tea while they glanced through a sheaf of dress designs. She discarded most of them instantly as too fussy, but there were two which she and Rose thought might suit her.

'It's so difficult to decide.' She held both designs up.

Rose and Mrs Lumley were no help, they both thought different designs would suit her best.

'It has to be your choice, Elizabeth,' Rose reminded her, 'because you have to feel comfortable wearing it.'

'More tea, perhaps?' Mrs Lumley suggested as though tea might help her decide.

She thought that if John was there he could help; and immediately realised that was why she was hesitating. She knew what she preferred, a modest design with a high neck and puff sleeves, but she sensed John would like something more revealing; more, as she thought, in a style that an American girl might wear. The design Rose preferred.

'If only you were being accompanied you could ask your beau's opinion,' Rose said, as if she could read her mind.

Minutes later they heard Sebastian Laybourne's voice and realised he had come to collect them.

Rose laughed. 'We've been here for three hours and you still haven't decided what to wear. Why don't you ask Papa? I'm sure he'd be pleased to help.'

'Of course.' It would be polite to ask his advice anyway, especially as he was paying for both dresses; and besides, he was John's father and they might have similar tastes.

A moment later Mrs Lumley brought him into the room. He smiled as he saw the designs spread out. 'Ladies, are you ready to leave, or is Elizabeth still trying to decide what to choose?'

'Everything's so wonderful, Mr Laybourne, but of two possibilities I don't know which would suit me best. Which do you prefer?' She turned both designs around so that he could see them. 'That one.' His finger went straight to the revealing style.

'Oh.' She did not mean to sound disappointed but she was frightened of wearing something which was cut so low.

'You sound unsure,' he said, 'so choose the other one if you prefer.'

Mrs Darling brought in the material and handed it to him.

He draped a length over her shoulders and studied her. 'No, trust me, Elizabeth, and order that one. I'm sure we'll find a suitable necklace and some jewellery you can wear for the occasion.'

She felt like a little girl being treated by her father as he carefully lifted the material away and asked Mrs Lumley for samples of both dress materials so they could arrange for shoes to be made and dyed to match, then arranged for them to return on Thursday for a fitting.

During the next few days Rose's lessons took second

place, restricted to the mornings only. The afternoons and evenings passed in a flurry of dancing and etiquette lessons, interspersed with the need to carry out a multitude of tasks to help Mrs Laybourne prepare for the dinner and the following evening's ball.

Suddenly it was Thursday and Mrs Laybourne took her for the arranged fitting. Both dresses were nearly finished and only needed final touches to make them perfect.

'You've chosen excellently.' Mrs Laybourne looked impressed by what she saw. 'You've a fine eye for style, Elizabeth.'

'Rose and Mr Laybourne helped enormously,' she admitted, and added. 'You all have, in so many ways, and I'm extremely grateful.'

Mrs Laybourne shook her head. 'There's no need, Elizabeth. You've been a great help and we're very grateful to you for everything you've done, especially for Rose. She was quite depressed by Miss Smith's death but you've helped her to recover very quickly. Also we could never have managed to organise the ball without your help and hard work, so I think you should look on the clothes as our way of thanking you. We like having you at the house. You've brought new life into it and we're all going to be very sorry to see you leave.'

'I'll be sorry to go, Mrs Laybourne.' She realised that she already thought of the old manor house as home, and the Laybournes as an extension to her own family.

'We'll return for the dresses tomorrow,' Mrs Laybourne said, and added thoughtfully. 'Do you think it would be possible to visit your mother and show them to her? She might enjoy seeing you dressed up.'

'I'm sure she would. What a wonderful idea.' She was astonished that even though there were a thousand things to do Mrs Laybourne still made time to think about the small things which might make someone else happy.

Elizabeth woke early on Friday morning and was surprised

to find Rose was already about and had completed most of the chores allocated to her for the day.

'May I come into town with you, Elizabeth? It'll mean that Mama has less to do,' she heard Rose explain and guessed that she wanted to visit the house where Edward lived even though he would be at work.

'I'd like that.' She tried hard not to smile as she saw the glint in Rose's eyes, and then decided to tease her a little. 'But I believe your father's coming with me, so there's no real need.'

'But he's a meeting at the bank and that might delay him,' Rose said quickly. 'Besides, I'd like to meet your mother again. It's ages since I talked with her.'

'Don't expect her to say much, Rose. She's very ill and I wouldn't want to see you upset, especially so soon after Miss Smith, and as it's only the day before your birthday.'

'But I'd like to see her, Elizabeth. Anyway I have a present I'd like to give her.'

'A present? What sort of present?'

'Just something simple, but I hope she'll like it,' Rose said and looked away.

'I'm sure she will, but what is it?'

'You'll see when we arrive.'

As the carriage stopped outside her parents' home front doors opened and people stared out all along the street. She went into the house to prepare her mother for the visit while Rose and Mr Laybourne waited in the carriage.

Pru Wright was with her mother and they were both taken aback when Rose and Sebastian Laybourne finally trooped in laden with boxes.

'How lovely to see you both again.' Rose kissed both women and without being asked plopped down opposite Minty in the empty fireside chair. 'I've brought you a small present. I hope you don't mind. It's nothing much, just something I made myself.'

'That's really nice of you, Miss Laybourne.' Minty

brightened as she took the small parcel Rose offered.
'Lizzie, make some tea, will you, lass?'

'Aye, Ma, in a moment.' She waited to see what was in
the parcel her mother was already untying.

'Oh, they're lovely, lass, really lovely.' Her mother held
up two framed sketches. 'It's our Lizzie and our Edward,
Pru, look. And you, Lizzie, come and look.'

She studied the drawings for a moment, then noticed
the gratitude in her mother's face and escaped into the
kitchen before she made a fool of herself and started
crying.

'It's a sort of thank you,' she heard Rose explain, 'for
having Elizabeth and Edward and allowing them to come
to the manor.'

They drank their tea and enjoyed a conversation which
was remarkably easy considering the difference in all their
circumstances, and then she asked Rose to follow her
upstairs and help her change into her new clothes.

She wore the grey outfit first, a tailored neck to toe
dress, plain dark grey except for some pale grey piping
and a tiny lace collar. She kept her long black hair
gathered up in the loose netted bun she always wore, and
when she walked down to the living room she was pleased
by the murmurs of approval which came from her mother
and Pru.

'You look very tidy, Lizzie,' her mother said brightly,
and then added in her practical way, 'and when it's a bit
worn, like, you can easily make it up to wear for work.'

'Aye, Ma, that's what I thought, too.' She admitted her
own reason for choosing the style and noticed the sparkle
in Sebastian Laybourne's eyes and the tolerant smile on his
face.

She paraded for a few moments, showing how the fine
material followed her movements and asking her mother
and Pru to feel the weave which would not crush or crease
no matter how it was treated, then she climbed the stairs
to change into the ball gown.

She was about to leave the bedroom when Rose stopped her.

'Take your net off, Elizabeth, and I'll pin your hair up for you.'

'There's not time, Rose, and I've no . . .'

'We'll make time.' Rose was already producing hairpins from her small bag; obviously there was no purpose in arguing.

She sat down, slipped off the net which always held her hair in a loose bun, and Rose produced a hair brush and immediately set to brushing and arranging.

It was a strangely pleasant and intimate experience, almost as if they were sisters. 'Your hair's beautiful, Elizabeth. So heavy and curly, and long.'

'I know I should cut it, but . . .' But she could not admit she liked her hair so much she could not bear to cut it short. She stared at her reflection in the room's dim mirror. Her nose was far too big and her eyes were crooked, her eyebrows were too heavy, her lashes too thick and her skin was a shade swarthy; she had no beautiful features, except for her hair, and even that was unfashionably long. But it was beautiful and the one good thing she had inherited from her real mother and father, the only link she relished; so nothing would ever make her cut it short. Ever.

'There,' Rose said suddenly, and stopped fussing. 'I didn't have enough pins, Elizabeth, but they'll hold up long enough for your mother to see just how beautiful you'll look at the ball.'

Beautiful? No; one of Rose's exaggerations, but the gown's colour did show off her own colouring just as Rose said it would, and her figure suited the gown in a way she would not have imagined. She gazed at the amount of chest she was showing below her bare shoulders and instinctively hitched the dress up, but as soon as she let go it slipped back and emphasised her cleavage again.

'You don't think it's too daring?' she asked desperately.

'Only if you drop the sorbet.' Rose giggled and pushed her towards the door.

The fullness of the gown made it difficult to walk down the stairs with any grace so she pulled the hem up and descended sideways.

Her mother and Pru gasped when they saw her. She smiled at them then turned to see the effect she had on Rose's father.

He was smiling, obviously appreciating what he saw. 'You look quite beautiful, Elizabeth. Turn around.'

She did as he asked, at once enjoying being the centre of attention and also feeling embarrassed at being looked at; especially by a man she still felt a little in awe of and particularly because he could see so much that she usually kept covered.

'Please turn again,' he asked, 'fast enough for us to see how the gown will look when you're dancing.'

She did as she was told, and dipped and twirled again and again, no longer embarrassed but eager to please him and happy to hear her mother clapping her hands and calling out with pleasure.

She stopped twirling. The precarious pins had slipped and her hair had loosened. Now it settled, half hiding her shoulders, fringing across her breasts.

She turned to Rose's father and deliberately kept her eyes cast down as she waited to hear his final words of approval.

He did not speak.

She looked up and saw a man she had never seen before.

Sebastian Laybourne's face was drained of all colour. He looked all of his sixty years. He looked awful.

Catherine and her husband Walter were the first guests to arrive and three more couples followed an hour later. The Belchesters – Hubert, his parents and his grandfather – were not due until Saturday afternoon, as was Lillian

McDougall and her parents, but it seemed as though the large manor was already crowded as people spilled from room to room and over into the garden. Elizabeth was pleased that the bustle and confusion helped her get to know the guests and to find that they all affably accepted her into their company. All the men shared business interests with Sebastian Laybourne and seemed to spend most of their time discussing various projects, politics and the economy. The women chatted about the house, the gardens and the clothes they had brought to wear that evening and for the ball the following day.

John appeared late in the afternoon and took her aside to ask if she was coping and tell her that there had been a small collapse in the mine's main road. No one had been hurt and he had left Edward in charge of the repairs which were minor and should not interfere with output. He warned that the work might make Edward a little late arriving, then left her so that he could talk to each of the guests.

A small tea was served at four o'clock and by five the house seemed to be deserted, apart from the servants who bustled about preparing for the evening dinner. All the guests had gone to their rooms to rest.

She went to her own room but before she had time to settle she heard a knock on her door. Rose had come to talk.

'Are you looking forward to this evening, Elizabeth?'

'Very much so, apart from the recitation,' she admitted.

'That'll be fun.' Rose smiled and added, 'And it'll be nice to see Edward again.'

'Edward, is it?' She noticed the tone Rose used and the way her eyes shone when she said his name. 'I don't want to pry but he is my brother, and I am responsible for you, so can you tell me how you managed to draw my mother such a fine sketch of him when you've only met him a few times? Brief meetings, too.'

She saw Rose's embarrassment, but liked the way she

looked her in the eyes as she spoke. 'We did meet up on King's Crag, Elizabeth, only once and by accident. It was the day William Wright was buried and Edward had gone there to be alone and to think about whether or not he should accept Papa's offer of the deputy's job. He'd fallen asleep and I sat and watched him. Afterwards we talked for an hour or so, and I drew my first picture of him that night, before I forgot what he looked like.'

'Your first picture? There's more?'

'Only the one I gave your mother. And I sketched you from memory, too.'

'But you see me every day, Rose. Have you had any more secret meetings with Edward?'

'Only one, on the day he brought you here. I waited for him, by the old lodge. Just so we could talk, Elizabeth, that's all.'

They looked at each other for a few moments. It was obvious that she wanted to say more, wanted to talk to someone, but could not.

'You've done nothing more than just talk?'

'No, except we did exchange handkerchiefs as sort of love tokens.'

'Love tokens? Oh, Rose, you silly girl,' she said, sympathising with her but frightened of what might follow. 'You surely can't think you're in love with Edward?'

'I think I am, Elizabeth, and please don't tell me that it's ridiculous because I know of all the problems, and so does Edward. I like to think that when I come back from France he'll be waiting for me and that we'll find a way to be together, but I know it may be just a dream.'

'A dream Edward's sharing?' she asked but she knew her brother well enough to know he was prone to romantic dreams and she was not surprised when Rose simply smiled and nodded. 'Rose, you must be very careful not to let this thing get out of proportion. I can't think anything serious could ever come of it but I can imagine what your father would say if he found out about it.'

'Oh no, you can't.' She was taken aback by Rose's response. 'If he found out he'd make me marry Hubert Belchester.'

'He'd do what?' She was not sure she had heard correctly, but Rose repeated what she had said and quickly explained why she was going to France.

'I did not realise how strongly you felt about this, Rose,' she said, suddenly conscious of how important it was for Rose to be admitted to the school.

'It's worse than that, Elizabeth.' Rose told her how her father had only agreed to consider sending her to the school if she agreed to become engaged to Hubert Belchester.

'Are you suggesting that he wants you to marry this man whether or not you love him?'

'Of course, Elizabeth. For some reason he wants me to leave home almost immediately, and I suppose he thinks that if I'm married I'm not likely to return.'

'But why? And doesn't your mother have anything to say about it?'

'It's difficult for Mama to stop him when he makes up his mind, Elizabeth, but she and John have tried to help. I would not be allowed to apply for a place at the school if they hadn't persuaded Papa, and I overheard Mama telling John that she is trying to arrange for me to be offered a place whether or not I pass the entrance examination.'

'So whatever I do isn't really that important?' She felt betrayed and irritated that she was only being employed because of a family dispute.

'Of course it is, Elizabeth. It's important that you teach me as much as you can before I go to France. I hope you don't think we've deceived you, but tomorrow you'll meet Hubert Belchester and I'm sure you'll understand why I can't marry him, and how much I need your help.'

'Perhaps I will, Rose, but I find it difficult to believe your father could be so cold-hearted. He's always been so kind to me.'

'But you're not his daughter, Elizabeth. He sent Catherine away to be married when she was eighteen. He thinks eighteen is a good age for a woman to marry. He even married my mother when she was eighteen.'

It seemed an eccentric idea, almost as if he thought of his daughters as birds that would never learn to fly unless they were pushed out of the nest, but she knew it was not her place to comment any more on the relationship between Rose and her father.

'I'll help all I can, Rose, but please don't rely on Edward waiting for you,' she warned again. 'A lot can happen in two years. It's quite possible that both of you could find someone else.'

'That's possible, of course, and that's another reason for going away. But if, when I come back, we both feel the same way, then we'll do everything we can to be together because we'll have stood the test of being separated and proved to ourselves that we really do love each other. I don't want a loveless marriage, Elizabeth. I wouldn't want to live like my parents. I'm not sure if my mother loved my father when she married him, but I don't think they love each other now.'

'I'm sure they do, Rose. They seem very happy together.' She was shocked by what Rose told her.

'They're keeping up appearances, Elizabeth, and I'm afraid I'm too honest to do that. Which is why I must be sure before I commit myself.' It seemed a very mature thing for a young girl who thought she was in love to say. 'And, although I did not want to leave home at first, I think it may be best. The last thing Miss Smith told me was that I should leave. Moments before she died in this room.'

'Are you sure that's what she said?' It seemed to be a bizarre way to depart this world, to advise a young girl to leave home.

'Oh yes. She muttered something about the way I looked and then told me to leave. Poor dear. She was a hopeless teacher, but I'm sure she loved me, and John, and even dear Catherine when she took care of her years ago.'

Elizabeth went to the music room where all the guests were asked to assemble before dinner and found Catherine and Walter waiting alone. She was not sure how to greet them and decided she must be formal.

'Mrs Wyndham, Mr Wyndham.' For some reason she wanted to curtsy, but stopped herself.

'Catherine and Walter, please, Miss Forrester. Elizabeth, isn't it?' Catherine smiled warmly and invited her to sit with her on the small settee. 'I'm sorry we didn't meet properly when we arrived, but you appeared to be very busy and everything seemed so confused.'

Catherine was wearing a simple and modest high-necked black velvet dress which emphasised her violet eyes and fine grey hair. She had probably been very pretty, twenty years ago, and now she looked homely and comfortable and a little less than plump. Walter looked much older than Catherine, perhaps old enough to be mistaken for her father. He was quiet, obviously very refined, and looked at ease with himself and the formal evening clothes which made his unexceptional looks almost dashing.

'Are you enjoying life here?' he asked, almost shyly.

'Very much. Everyone's so kind.'

'Good. Excellent,' he said, and nodded, obviously genuinely pleased for her but not sure how to continue the conversation.

'Charlotte's told me that you've helped Rose much more than anyone thought possible,' Catherine said smoothly, as if she were used to continuing conversations when Walter foundered. 'I do hope Rose is accepted into Charlotte's old school. Pincote is so restricting.'

'Yes, it is,' she answered as evenly as she could manage, fighting back the temptation to say that Pincote was not only restricting for the likes of Rose, but a moment later she realised she had misjudged Rose's half sister.

'I understand that you grew up in Pincote and taught at the Lower School so you obviously know all about the strengths and restrictions of living here, and I cannot tell you how much I admire your abilities. There's not many young women who've been brought up here who could teach, and even fewer who could cope with all the challenges you must have faced coming to live in this house. What do you intend to do next? Surely not simply settle down with a husband and children. Not until you've really tested yourself?'

'I honestly don't know,' she admitted, and felt rather ashamed that she had no firm plans.

'Well, please don't waste your talents, Elizabeth.' Catherine paused. 'I know this is very presumptuous of me—'

'But of course you'll presume anyway, my dear,' Walter interrupted mildly.

'Yes.' Catherine smiled at him. 'I know a number of people who would be interested in a young woman with your abilities, and I'd be very pleased to help or simply offer you advice once your duties are at an end here.'

'That's very generous of you, Catherine.' She was astonished at the woman's offer.

'Not at all.'

A moment later Rose arrived and her appearance made Walter smile so much that she thought he suddenly looked ten years younger, and certainly sounded younger as he drew a long breath and said, almost wondrously, 'Rose, my dear, you look lovely.'

'Perfect,' Catherine agreed, 'don't you think, Elizabeth?'

She turned and looked at Rose, framed in the double doorway; a beautiful picture, almost too beautiful to be real.

Her eyes absorbed the detail in Rose's clothes, and it was several moments before she realised Rose's dress was cut to almost exactly the same pattern as her own. A high, lace collar, puffed shoulders over sleeves which were tight

to the wrist, a close-fitting bodice loosening slightly over
the hips and a ruffed bustle which helped to conceal a back
pleat that managed to give the skirt a tight, almost hobbled
appearance without making it too tight to take normal
steps. But whereas her own dress was fine wool, plain dark
grey except for pale grey piping, Rose's dress gleamed like
satin and faded from deepest blue at the neck to smoke
grey at the bottom hem. It was not simply a dress it was a
masterpiece of creation from the talent of the dyer to the
skill of the dressmaker.

Topped with Rose's burnished copper hair, the dress
gave the impression that she had not simply walked into
the room but that she had materialised out of the ground.

'Look how fine the stitching is.' Rose invited Catherine
to look closely. 'That's Mrs Darling's work. Elizabeth and
I went home with Mrs Darling to help her with her
husband. He's a cripple and can't work, and her thirteen-
year-old son had to work at the coal face to help her feed
them and three young daughters, Catherine. It seems so
unfair, don't you think . . .'

She listened as Rose told Catherine what had happened
the night of the accident and realised once again how
exceptional Rose was. Most wealthy young women would
simply accept that they were entitled to the best their
father's money could buy; they would not relate the
apparent cost of their clothes to the income the
dressmaker earned to support her family.

And she also realised that Catherine and Walter were
quite exceptional in their way, too. They were obviously
interested in what Rose told them, and although they had
no children they were enveloped in an umistakable aura of
domesticity; astonishing when she considered that Walter
was a director of one of the largest merchant banks in
Manchester and Catherine ran a town house with a full
complement of servants.

The music room slowly filled with men who wore uniform

evening dress and perfumed women who radiated colour and excitement, and who seemed so at ease with each other that she began to realise how out of place she felt.

Charlotte Laybourne appeared last of all, another vision of beauty although she wore plain silver grey contrasted only by a shoulder-hung sash which exactly matched the deepest blue of Rose's dress.

'I think we're ready to eat,' Charlotte said in a matter-of-fact voice which suggested they were about to sit down to a normal meal.

'Elizabeth?' John swept her arm into his and led her through to the dining room.

She almost stumbled when she saw the dining table; it was thoroughly daunting.

It had been extended to seat everyone and looked immense and splendid with its starched linen cloth and a stunning collection of gleaming porcelain, crystal and silver settings.

She noticed the cutlery in particular, and her heart thumped so much that she could not hear anything but its fast beat. She had become used to the array of knives and forks and spoons that were laid out for normal family meals, but now there were additional items she had never seen before and could not imagine what they were to be used for.

'Copy me,' John whispered, and she realised he knew how she must feel.

Sebastian and Charlotte Laybourne sat at opposite ends of the table and the guest couples were seated opposite each other. Rose partnered old Mr Sawtry, the Laybournes' lawyer whom Hopkins had brought up from Pincote Market before he left to collect Edward, and she was delighted and relieved to be seated opposite John.

The food was excellent, and seemed endless in variety and quantity. Course followed course, every one sumptuous. Her various glasses were filled with wine, refilled, and removed even though they were hardly touched, only for another glass to be filled as another plate was revealed and laden with more food. Her dress began to feel tight and she began to feel warm and thirsty and drank more of the wine to quench the thirst. It simply made her even more thirsty so she drank more.

After an hour or so the large room started to seem quite cosy and the company less intimidating. The conversations were light and amusing and she finally began to enjoy herself. She felt especially comfortable with John who led her through conversations with her neighbours and protected her whenever it seemed that she might be drawn out of her depth; so comfortable that she realised, happily, they were sharing secret looks and smiles when various guests who had drunk a little too much made mistakes which might have been embarrassing under other circumstances.

Then an elderly gentleman whose face was red with good food and too much wine leaned towards her and winked. 'Glad to have young John home again, eh, my dear? You'll be getting on with the wedding now he's finished with his travels, I expect.'

She felt herself blush with embarrassment. 'I, I'm not John's fiancée, sir.'

'You're not?' He did not seem at all embarrassed by his mistake and transferred his attention to John. 'You young scoundrel, John. One last fling, eh?'

'Mr Jamieson, sir.' John grinned. 'You do the lady a dishonour. She's far too respectable to wish to associate with a dissolute like me.'

They both laughed, and she was happy to join them in the joke, but then she heard Mrs Jamieson question loudly, 'Respectable? The girl's a servant, isn't she?'

The table fell silent.

She felt humiliated, did not know what to do, realised she had best do nothing, and looked to John for help. He smiled at her, nodded, and slowly directed his smile on Mrs Jamieson.

'Mrs Jamieson, please allow me to reassure you.' He turned around to take an open bottle of wine from a serving table behind him, and when he turned back his smile had gone. 'It's possible that your manners might offend Elizabeth and embarrass others, but unthinkable that Elizabeth's morals could offend or embarrass anyone. Now, would you like me to serve you with more wine, or do you think, perhaps, that you've already drunk enough?'

She saw Mrs Jamieson blush. 'No, no thank you, John. Too much red wine sends me to sleep.'

'Excellent.' John smiled, and carefully filled her glass to the brim before launching into a hilarious anecdote about a disastrous dinner he remembered having shortly after arriving in America. The relaxed atmosphere quickly returned to the table, everyone obviously attributing Mrs Jamieson's rudeness to the amount of wine she had drunk.

But the incident had changed the conspiratorial relationship she had been sharing with John into something more potent. She was very aware both of the way he kept looking at her and the amused way Rose looked at both of them. Something had changed and she began to feel hypocritical for telling Rose that she must forget Edward when there was such an attraction between herself and John.

And, although she tried to tell herself that she must ignore it, she knew now that there was a mutual attraction. Their evening walks had started innocently enough, but then they had occasionally linked arms, then he had held her hand to steady her as they climbed the steep paths leading up South Ridge. A week ago they had stood close together and watched the sun go down and his hand had slipped around her waist. It seemed so natural she hardly noticed until they parted, awkwardly and aware of what had happened. They had avoided touching each other since then; but now she sensed their restraint would end.

But she had been right in what she told Rose, and the same rules applied to her. She could not allow herself to be in love with John, especially as he was already engaged. It was impossible.

She concentrated her mind on John's parents; listened to Sebastian Laybourne's even voice and found it difficult to believe he would force his daughter to leave home, even more difficult to believe he would force her to marry someone she did not love. And she found it difficult to believe that Charlotte Laybourne would believe that the only way she could protect her daughter was to conspire against her husband.

But then other thoughts gathered themselves. Sebastian and Charlotte had separate bedrooms. They never touched each other as her own parents did. They never seemed to spend time alone with each other and when they were together in company they were overly polite towards each other; almost distant. She had noticed all these things before, but never really thought about them until that evening.

All eyes turned towards Sebastian Laybourne when he rapped his knuckles on the table and stood up. 'Ladies and gentlemen, we have a small cultural event for you. A home-made entertainment which we hope you'll enjoy and which will prove that there's more than just coal and wool in the Pincote Valley. If you would all care to adjourn to the music room my wife and her troupe will commence proceedings.'

Suddenly all her earlier impressions seemed to fuse together. He had called her his wife, not Charlotte or even Mrs Laybourne. The expression, my wife, carried an implication of ownership which she disliked instinctively. The Married Women's Property Act may have given women certain rights to retain their own property after marriage, but it did not help them retain their own identity if their husband chose to think of them simply as a chattel.

The thought preoccupied her as she followed the others into the music room and it occurred to her that it was impossible for any legislation to change human nature. She remembered the conversation she had with John during her first evening at the manor and realised he already understood this and that was probably why he believed that social changes should be made slowly.

'You seem nervous,' she heard him say, and she nodded.

She was nervous about reciting her piece in front of all the guests, but their kind reaction when Rose made a mistake during the duet put her at ease again.

Suddenly she was being introduced, the guests were applauding enthusiastically, and she was on her feet.

Then it was all over, the guests were applauding again, and John was smiling at her from his stance by the piano. He sang the lyrical 'Shenandoah', and, after shouts of encore which he shamelessly encouraged, he sang it again. Then, because Edward had not arrived, he sang two more American ballads, Charlotte played another piece and Rose recited some poetry.

Hopkins had been gone for nearly two hours and he still had not returned with Edward, so John explained that there should have been another item. 'We had arranged a very special contribution from one of our deputies, Edward Forrester, Elizabeth's brother.' He waved his hand towards her and she felt doubly uncomfortable because of the guests' surprise and her worry that Edward was so late in arriving. 'Unfortunately we had a small collapse underground and Edward was supervising the repairs. I can only guess that it's taken longer than we expected, so I'll finish with a recitation of "Jerusalem", by William Blake.'

She listened as John worked through the piece, worrying all the time about Edward, and aware of the fear in Rose's eyes. A look she had seen too often in the eyes of colliery women.

'In England's green and pleasant land.' John spoke the last line and as he did so wheels ground on the gravel in the drive.

Charlotte Laybourne leaped up to investigate and

moments later Edward was standing in the music room
doorway.

'Everything all right?' John called across the room.

'Yes, Mr Laybourne. Bit of unexpected flooding but it's
all cleared up now.'

'Let me welcome you, then, Edward.'

The use of his Christian name was a small gesture, but
as she looked at Edward she could see that he was relaxed
and smiling. She saw him glance towards Rose, and nod as
she smiled back at him. The smile showed that Rose's fear
had gone now she knew he was safe, but it injected an edge
of fear into her own feelings. There was something real
between these two, no matter how impossible it seemed,
which if it was allowed to get out of hand could only lead to
the trouble she had feared that night weeks ago, after the
accident, when she first saw the way they looked at each
other.

As Edward walked past her she smelled coal, and she
knew that clean as he seemed, he could only have washed
his face and hands and that under his clothes he would be
covered in black dust.

'Ladies and gentlemen' – she watched as John spoke,
his arm resting across Edward's shoulders – 'I think you
should know two things about Edward. First, he has had
no training as an actor. His talent is purely natural.
Secondly, he recently saved half a dozen men from certain
death underground, and risked his life in an unsuccessful
attempt to save two more.'

She felt proud as the guests called out their approval,
and nervous as she saw the pride in Rose's face.

'Edward Forrester,' John said simply, and as he sat in
the chair next to her he reached out, briefly squeezed her
hand, and murmured in his casual way, 'I told you there
was nothing to worry about.'

And in that moment she knew, for certain, that she was
in love with him. Everything he did made her love him
more. It was the most wonderful feeling she had ever

known, even if it was an impossible situation; so how could she really criticise Rose for thinking she too was in love?

She forgot her feelings as Edward began to speak, prowling around the room and taking on the identity of the King. She watched people watching him, then his spell captivated her even though she had heard him a hundred times before, and she simply watched him.

The guests were silent, immobile, everyone concentrating on the small miner who moved amongst them, stirring them into action in their minds. He persuaded them, cajoled them, entranced them with the words written centuries before.

'For there is none of you so mean and base that hath not noble lustre in your eyes. I see you stand like greyhounds in the slips, straining upon that start. The game's afoot.' His right arm lifted as though he were holding a sword, and his deep voice roared the climactic, 'Follow your spirit, and upon this charge, cry "God for Harry, England, and St George".'

They hesitated. He was not a miner, not any longer. He really was King Henry and they were his assembled troops. They hesitated for a moment, there was a united gasp, and suddenly everyone was on their feet calling out and clapping.

'Laybourne,' she heard someone say, 'this man should be on the stage for all of us, not cutting coal just for you.'

'He doesn't cut coal any more,' Sebastian Laybourne retorted, laughing, 'he's already a deputy, and from what John tells me it'll not be long before he's a manager.'

'Still a waste of talent, my man,' she heard the first man reply, and as some of the guests moved forward to thank Edward and shake his hand she glanced towards Rose.

She saw a gleam in Rose's eyes that told her trouble was inevitable, and when she saw Rose move towards Edward she thought it would start immediately.

'You look tired' – she heard Rose hesitate and wondered

if she would take John's lead and call Edward by his name
– 'Mr Forrester.'

'I feel tired, Miss Laybourne, and if Mr Hopkins can
take me home I think I'd better go now.'

'But have you eaten?' Rose sounded concerned as she
ignored his suggestion.

'No. There wasn't time.'

'Well, I suggest that Elizabeth and I find you something
to eat before you go. Don't you think that's sensible,
Elizabeth?'

'Of course.' She saw Rose had grabbed her chance to
talk to Edward, but she wondered whether or not she
should risk leaving them alone. She took Edward to the
cold greenhouse in the kitchen garden while Rose fetched
food from the larder.

'You've seen the drawings Rose gave to Ma?' she asked.

'Aye, lass. Ma showed them to me the moment I got
home, like. She's full if it, and the way you looked.'

'You will be careful with Rose, won't you?' she asked,
and risked upsetting him by adding. 'And what are you
doing about Nancy?'

'That's over, Lizzie, what there was of it. I want Rose,
want to marry her, mind. Look, I know it sounds
impossible, but if we still feel the same about each other
when she gets back from France, then I'll find some way
to make it happen. Somehow. Meanwhile, don't worry. I'll
not do anything stupid. You can be sure of that, lass. It's
too important.'

'You know her father wants her to marry someone else?'
she asked and was relieved when he nodded and told her
that he had told Rose to accept Belchester's proposal and
take the easy life it offered.

She looked at him and saw how eager he was to see
Rose again. On impulse she threw her arms around him
and hugged him.

'I love you, Edward, and I hope it works out for you and
Rose. I reckon you are made for each other, really, and

there's no doubt she could make you happy, but I cannot see how you're going to carry it off.' She felt a hand on her shoulder and realised that Rose had returned with the food.

'We'll manage, Elizabeth. Believe me, we'll manage somehow,' Rose said, put the plate down, and the three of them fell into a tight embrace.

The house seemed to be full of cigar smoke and brandy fumes and she was relieved when John suggested they take their usual walk in the gardens.

'Are you enjoying yourself, Elizabeth?'

'Much more than I thought I would,' she said honestly and breathed the scents that wafted through the warm, moonlit night.

'I hope the confusion over our supposed engagement didn't embarrass you too much,' he said and she thought she detected a slightly regretful tone in his voice.

'Will you mention it to Miss McDougall?' She wondered whether he would try to keep it a secret.

He did not answer, so she prompted him, 'Well?'

They had walked away from the house and were under the limbs of a large oak tree. The comforting, musty smell of rotting acorns overpowered the other scents. John still had not answered.

'Is there anything wrong?' She stopped and raised her arms above her head to feel the bark on one of the tree's lower limbs.

John's face was dappled by the moonlight which sifted down through the tree's branches and she could not see enough to judge his expression.

Neither did she see his hands as they reached out and gripped her waist. 'Marry me, Elizabeth.'

'Oh.' The surprise of his proposal and the grab at her waist broke her grip on the tree and as her arms fell they wrapped around his neck.

He took the initiative and held her tight, his lips coming

down on hers in a kiss that took all her breath away. She
felt weak and was aware that he was half carrying her.
Suddenly she was between the tree's trunk and John's
body, both hard and both warm.

She did not resist as he held her head and kissed her
again.

'Say you'll marry me, Elizabeth, say it.' His persistence
seemed to make him irresistible.

'Yes, John,' she gasped between kisses.

'Say it,' he insisted and she felt his lips warm against the
only part of her neck he could reach.

'I'll marry you, John. I'll marry you,' and because his lips
were straining the buttons on her high collar and making
it cut into her neck she reached up and undid them.

She gasped as he kissed her throat and turned her so
that he was leaning against the tree and she was hanging
against him, his arms locked around her waist and his firm
kisses bending her backwards. Instinctively she undid
more buttons as he kissed her lower and lower until she
had no more buttons to undo. Her petticoat was fastened
with small bows and she clawed at them, eager to feel his
lips against her chest and the tops of her breasts.

He nuzzled her and her heart pounded with excitement,
then he swung her off her feet and moments later she was
lying on a bench in a small open summer house that stood
back amongst the trees.

'I love you,' she said as he slipped her dress and petticoat over her shoulders, pinning her arms against her
sides so that she could not have stopped him even if she
had wanted to.

He pulled her remaining clothes down to her waist. She
felt her breasts come loose and heard him murmur with
pleasure. He immediately transferred his pleasure to her
and she whimpered in ecstasy as he kissed and sucked her.
It was the strongest feeling she had ever had, and without
speaking she willed him to peel all her clothes away and
take her, there and then, in the clear, pure moonlight.

She lay still and did not help him. He fumbled with her clothes, awkward and clumsy in his urgency, feeling every inch of her before he lifted her from the bench and laid her, naked, on to the worn wooden floor. She smelled the resinous wood, the scent of acorns, the earth below the summer house, and she looked up at the shining moon as he entered her with a gentleness that made silent and happy tears flood from her eyes.

'I love you,' she said again.

'And I love you,' he whispered into her ear, 'and tomorrow we'll tell the world.'

CHAPTER 16

She slept well, woke early, and went to her window to look down at the little summer house where she had committed herself and her future to John.

John! Her life had changed completely since he had come into it. The change had been fast, but not sudden; the urgency natural, not rushed. It seemed that perhaps destiny had taken over and was trying to make her recover the years she had used up dallying with Saul.

And it was not simply her circumstances which had changed; she had changed with them. A few weeks ago she had been so frightened of the future she had been willing to marry Saul even though she knew he did not love her, and, worse, knew she did not love him. She had even been frightened that the masters of Alnwick School, or their wives, would see through the self-confident façade she was able to maintain in Pincote and see her for what she really was: a nervous, worrying, awkward, illegitimate foundling from an insignificant mining village.

Now none of that mattered. Now she had enough confidence in herself to become the future mistress of the Laybourne Estates.

Elizabeth Laybourne! Mrs John Laybourne!

Her heart thumped. She would need all the confidence she could muster when John told his family, and when she told hers; Edward had agonised enough about taking the job John's father had offered him, but she was proposing to marry into the family!

Then, she realised immediately, her parents had changed their attitudes over the past few weeks, her father especially. He had mellowed more than she would have thought possible, perhaps because of the strength Edward had suddenly found or perhaps because he realised he would soon be left alone.

It occurred to her that it would be wonderful if her mother could live long enough to see her married, and the sadness that came with the thought put her in a different mood.

She thought about Lillian; she had waited two years for John to return from America. She would be devastated, and her family would feel humiliated and angry. And, of course, John's father would be angry. The McDougalls owned even more mines than him and the two families shared so many other businesses that there were sure to be serious repercussions if John and Lillian did not marry as everyone had always assumed they would.

It was not going to be easy; in fact it was going to be very difficult and she suddenly realised that John would have to curb his usual impulsiveness if they were not to make things even worse. He had said he wanted to tell the world about their plans but the world would have to wait, at least until after the ball. It would be unwise to declare themselves too soon, and unfair on both Lillian and Rose.

Energy rushed through her body and mind. She needed to walk to control it, needed to think calmly.

She washed quickly and dressed in a gypsy-style white

blouse and blue cotton skirt, and decided not to spend time netting up her hair until later.

As she stepped into the passage she noticed a short length of cigar ash on the polished floorboards. John must have come to her room and then decided against waking her; or perhaps he had knocked and she had not heard him. She smiled, half sorry that she had been too sleepy to wake up and let him in, and half glad that she had tantalised him by leaving the door locked.

Downstairs the staff were busy dusting and polishing, or preparing breakfasts in the kitchen and they did not seem to notice her as she let herself out through the back door.

She walked through the stable yard and saw old Hopkins helping the stable boy pull the main carriage out from the coach house. 'Good morning, Mr Hopkins, beautiful morning, don't you think?'

'Aye, it is that, Miss Forrester,' he called over his shoulder before he turned to look at her.

The expression on his face changed instantly.

'Mr Hopkins? Is there something wrong?'

He did not say anything, just stared.

'Mr Hopkins?' she said again.

'No, Miss Forrester,' he answered awkwardly, 'you just, just startled me, miss.'

'I'm sorry.' She touched his arm but he quickly drew away from her.

He peered at her for a moment longer, shrugged and shook his head as though he were coming out of a dream, turned and without saying anything more shuffled across to the coach house.

'Are you feeling all right, Mr Hopkins?' she called after him.

'Aye, miss,' he muttered and disappeared into the darkness of the coach house.

She stood still, wondering what was in the old man's mind, then left the yard and walked towards the oak tree where John had proposed to her. The smell of acorns renewed the memory of last night and after a few moments she turned towards the little summer house.

And stopped dead.

There was a pile of clothes lying on the bench, exactly where John had left her clothes when he undressed her last night.

For a wild moment she had the ridiculous thought that they were her clothes, that she had forgotten to dress afterwards. Then the panic passed but she did not move. She stood where she was, twenty, perhaps thirty feet from the wooden building, staring at the clothes, the awful realisation dawning that someone had watched John and her making love and had left the clothes there as a sign.

She shuddered, with shock and then with fear. Being seen was bad enough, but who would do something so bizarre as putting clothes on the bench? And why?

The magic of last night disappeared.

She felt guilty and disgraced, turned her back on the summer house and walked away, quickly and not caring where she was going. How could she go back to the house now that someone knew what she had done? How could she tell John what had happened? He would feel as humiliated as she.

She found herself at the lodge, standing by the fence where she had talked to John on the first evening she had come to the manor. Her mind began to clear and she started to think rationally.

It must have been one of the guests who had played the trick so all she had to do was to look closely at the clothes and try to remember which woman had worn them. And if she could not remember, or if none of them had worn the clothes the previous day, she might be able to guess who it was from the clothes' size and style. If it was one of the husbands who had played the trick, and she thought that was more likely, then his wife was sure to mention that some of her clothes were missing.

She left the lodge and walked back to the summer house.

The clothes had gone.

She returned to her room, washed again, dressed in her usual day wear and folded her hair up into its customary loose bun. There was no choice but to face everyone and hope that the culprit gave themselves away by some gesture or comment, but at the moment there seemed no reason to tell John and force him to share the humiliation and anger she felt.

This was simply someone playing a silly, boyish game, and there was no reason to allow them to spoil Rose's birthday and everyone else's day.

'Good morning, Elizabeth.' Sebastian Laybourne came from his study as she walked past on her way down to breakfast. 'Did you enjoy yourself last night? I thought that you and your brother performed exceptionally well. He was quite astonishing.'

'Thank you, sir. Yes I did enjoy myself, and I'm pleased you did.'

'Good.' He touched her arm in a gentle, fatherly way. 'And I was pleased to see you holding your own at dinner. I know that some of our friends can be a little overbearing, but you should know that everyone feels you're extremely charming.'

She was surprised that he could show her such kindness and gentleness if what Rose had said about him was true, so she smiled back and said simply, 'John helped me, sir, and everyone was very kind,' and hid the nervousness that had crept up and damaged her confidence.

'Good,' he said again, and nodded towards the small parcel she was carrying. 'I assume that's a present for Rose. I hope you haven't spent too much of your hard-earned wage on her.'

'Just books that I think Rose will enjoy,' she said, 'nothing expensive.'

'That's very considerate of you.' He smiled. 'I do worry about Rose being spoiled, and sometimes I suppose I'm too strict with her, but today is different. I've had an emerald necklace and matching earrings made for her.'

The breakfast room was already cluttered with people and presents, and the sound of Rose's excited laughter and chatter washed away the fear she had earlier felt about meeting the guests again.

John arrived several minutes later and made his sister close her eyes while he fastened a glittering bracelet around her wrist.

'Good morning, Elizabeth,' he said after Rose had finished kissing and thanking him. 'I trust you slept exceptionally well?'

'Yes, thank you,' she said, and thought his grin was meant to tell her that he already knew how well she had slept.

'I'm afraid I must leave you all for a few hours,' he apologised to the guests. 'I have to meet Edward to inspect the repair he made.'

He reached the door before he called back, 'Oh, Elizabeth, would you mind helping me for a moment?'

She followed him through the hall and down the front steps to the drive. His horse was already hitched to a post and as he unlooped the reins with one hand he held her shoulder in his other.

'I love you, Elizabeth Forrester.' He sounded serious. 'I spent all night thinking about you.'

'I see,' she said and smiled up at him, any remaining shame washed away by simply being with him.

'And this morning, Elizabeth' – she watched him as he frowned and seemed uncertain – 'I need to know if you still want to marry me?'

'More than anything.'

'Then I'll tell Lillian tonight. I'm not prepared to ignore you, and I want to be fair to you, but I also want to be honest with Lillian and I don't want to hurt her.'

'Wait.' She gripped his arm. 'Look, John, she's going to feel hurt whenever you tell her. She's waited two years for you to come home from America and whatever you say to her she's sure to feel you've betrayed her. We've plenty of time, so why don't you say nothing for the moment?'

He looked perplexed and unsure of her so she led him around the far side of his horse, where they could not be seen from the house, stood on tiptoe and gave him a brief kiss.

Her hand stroked his face, 'John, I want everyone to know we'll be married, although God knows what your parents'll say, but a few hours or days isn't going to make any difference. Don't risk spoiling the ball for Rose, please. She's been looking forward to it for months, and anyway, it'll be difficult enough for her when she tells Mr Belchester that she's going away for two years.'

Four large wagons distracted her as they trundled through the gates at the far end of the drive.

'I'd rather get it over with, Elizabeth.' He swung up on to his horse. 'But we can't talk now, not with the workmen coming to set up the dance floor and awnings. I'll try to see you before the ball and we'll talk about it then.'

She nodded, and as he wheeled his horse round her she saw Rose standing by the front door. They both waved to him as he rode away and Rose ran down the steps to wait for the wagons to arrive.

'When's he going to tell Lillian?' she asked astutely.

'You know?'

'I guessed, Elizabeth, from the way he looks at you. And Lillian isn't blind, she'll guess too.'

'Well, I hope she doesn't guess tonight, Rose. Not tonight. I don't want to hurt her.'

'No, I don't suppose you do,' Rose said and smiled before she rushed off to tell her mother that the workmen had arrived.

Charlotte Laybourne kept Elizabeth busy supervising a

number of chores and the morning passed quickly. The remaining house guests arrived during the afternoon and she saw Rose growing more and more anxious as the time neared for the Belchesters to arrive.

Hopkins left to collect them off the three o'clock train and Rose found an excuse not to accompany him, but she was waiting at the front door when the carriage returned.

The energy which had made Rose sparkle seemed to have drained away, and the moment Hubert Belchester stepped out from the carriage she understood why.

He was a tall, gracefully beautiful man, and was dressed immaculately. He was the exact opposite of Edward and it was obvious why, if Rose loved Edward, she could not bear to think of marrying Hubert.

He helped his mother down from the carriage and reached out to steady a tall, elderly man whom Elizabeth guessed was his grandfather. The old man shoved him aside, stepped down and immediately walked towards the front steps.

She noticed how warm his smile was as he called out to Rose, 'Good day, Miss Laybourne.'

He reached the top step as Charlotte Laybourne came through the front doors.

'Good afternoon, Mr Belchester.' She heard the dual response, and stepped aside as the grandfather's long arms reached out and hugged them both simultaneously.

'And who's this beautiful young lady?' He looked directly at her and she smiled as, with his arms still around Rose and Charlotte, he looked her over and winked flirtatiously.

She was introduced and let him kiss her, and as she felt herself pulled tight against him she decided immediately that she liked him even though he was an old scoundrel. He seemed as if he knew how to enjoy himself and she was sure that his flirting was nothing more than an old man's mischief.

She was introduced to Hubert's parents, who were

polite, but, she decided, were neither as warm as the grandfather nor likely to be as much fun.

Hubert seemed to linger before deciding to stroll up the steps. When he did arrive his manners were exquisite. He presented himself first to Rose's mother, enquired after her health, complimented her upon her appearance and politely thanked her for the invitation to the ball. He did all this in a slow, languorous manner, and she was so engrossed in the way that he spoke and acted that she hardly noticed him doff his hat to her and turn away.

'Miss Laybourne.' She watched how he gently lifted Rose's hand, brushed it with his lips, and settled it back by her side. 'I trust you are well. Thank you so much for inviting me to your birthday ball. I have been anticipating it for months.'

She saw that although Rose was trying to respond she was unable to interrupt the carefully timed greeting that Hubert had apparently rehearsed and was scared to divert from. There was no sign of any intimacy between them, nothing but a formality that seemed strained and unnatural for a couple who were supposedly considering marriage.

'And this is Miss Forrester.' Charlotte Laybourne led her forward.

The hat was doffed again, and she heard the practised greeting start all over, but it faltered when Hubert must have realised that she had no part in inviting him to the ball.

'I'm Rose's house tutor,' she explained as the silence became embarrassing.

'But I thought you had died?' Hubert said in a confused, slightly hurt tone.

'That was my prede—' she started to explain but Rose interrupted her.

'Noisiest corpse I've ever heard.'

There was a moment's astonished silence before Hubert's grandfather slapped his sides and roared with laughter.

'Well said, that girl, well said.' He grabbed Rose and they stood together, one roaring with laughter and the other giggling uncontrollably, both with tears streaming down their faces.

She tried hard not to laugh with them, especially when she saw Rose's mother cover her mouth with her handkerchief and pretend a sudden coughing fit. Hubert and his parents stood still, looking puzzled.

'My predecessor, Miss Smith, died some weeks ago,' she finished her explanation.

'I understand, now.' Hubert nodded. 'So you're not the tutor who's dead.'

'Not yet,' she answered, and heard Rose and the grandfather rise into new hilarity.

'I'm sorry I couldn't be there to see it for myself.' John laughed as she told him what had happened. 'But at least you can see why we can't let Rose marry the man. She'd be better off with the grandfather.'

'And talking of marrying' – she brought John back to the subject they had to discuss – 'I still think you should avoid saying anything to Miss McDougall tonight. And you shouldn't pay me too much attention, either. Rose has already guessed.'

'Is it that obvious?' he asked, and for a moment she was tempted to tell him about the clothes she had seen in the summer house. 'Is there something else, Elizabeth?'

'No. I just don't want to be the cause of any trouble, especially tonight.' She decided to leave the other matter until later.

'As you wish,' he said, then added quickly, 'although I want at least two dances with you.'

The temporary dance floor and the two large awnings had been erected on the lawns facing the front door and its sweeping step. A twenty-piece orchestra was tuning its instruments under one awning, and the other awning sheltered tables laden with food hidden under silver and linen covers. Rows of coloured candle lanterns were strung above the dance floor, and chairs for the guests to rest on between dances were placed around it.

The guests all gathered in the large hallway, and Elizabeth waited with them, chatting with people she had met the previous evening and nodding to the local celebrities she knew by name and reputation, and who seemed to recognise her but were too unsure to come forward and introduce themselves.

A few of the women wore dresses which were as revealing as hers, but their relative nakedness did not make her feel any more comfortable, particularly as she knew that someone amongst the guests had seen much more of her than she was showing now.

She saw Lillian McDougall, beautiful in a white dress which covered her from neck to toes and emphasised her slim figure and made her look sylph-like. After several minutes John's official fiancée noticed her and walked across to introduce herself again.

'Good evening, Miss Forrester. I trust that you've settled into the manor since we last met.' She glanced down as she spoke and it was obvious she did not approve of the burgundy gown's low-cut style.

'Good evening, Miss McDougall.' She suddenly felt ashamed again; then nervous that even now John might decide this was the night to break off his engagement, and immediately frightened that he might change his mind when he saw how beautiful Lillian looked. 'I have settled in, thank you. Everyone's been very kind to me.'

'I'm so pleased,' Lillian said in an airy manner which showed that she was simply saying the words to be polite.

There was a moment while they looked at each other without speaking, then someone called and Lillian McDougall went to join people she clearly felt were more to her liking.

Grandfather Belchester thrust his way through the

crowd. 'Good God, young lady, I thought you looked
beautiful before, but now.' He took both her hands and
squeezed them gently.

'Thank you, sir.' She smiled and felt comfortable again.

'Don't "sir" me, young lady, please.' He grinned and
shook his head. 'It makes me feel my age. And looking at
you, that's the last thing I want to feel.'

The implication was obvious but she was not shocked,
simply amused, so she smiled and shook her own head in
mock offence.

She turned and saw Sebastian Laybourne looking at her.
He did not speak, just looked, even more intensely than he
had the first time he had seen her wear the gown. His eyes
seemed to travel all over her, lingering. Her comfortable
feeling evaporated.

'Good evening, Elizabeth.' Catherine moved in front of
her father and blocked his view. 'You look most attractive,
especially with your hair dressed as it is. And I see you're
wearing my mother's rubies. It's rather nice to see them
being used rather than being left in an old drawer
somewhere.'

The compliments were genuine, she was sure of that,
and she wondered if it was the rubies that Sebastian was
staring at. Perhaps, with her hair down, she looked similar
to his first wife. Perhaps that was why old Hopkins had
been so startled.

The guests pressed towards the bottom of the stairs and
she decided she would ask Catherine later, when there
were fewer people around.

Moments later the guests started to applaud. Rose and
Hubert were standing at the top of the stairs, Rose in a
revealing green gown, her chest laid with emeralds and
her copper hair swirled up to show her ears and the
emerald earrings which dropped from them. She looked
exquisitely beautiful, far too beautiful and poised to marry
a coal miner, she thought desperately. Hubert wore the
palest grey tail suit, a soft, glistening white shirt and a

silver cravat. It should not have suited his pale complexion and his fine blond hair, but it did; and made him look even sleeker now than he had earlier.

'Don't they look perfect together?' she heard Sebastian ask Hubert's grandfather, but Catherine answered first.

'They each look perfect,' Catherine said, and added truculently, 'but not necessarily together.'

So Rose had another ally.

The couple moved down from the landing, slowly, stepping in time with the rhythm the guests set by clapping their hands. They reached the bottom step and the rhythm broke, faltered, and then the applause rose again, not just clapping but shouts and laughter, too.

John and Lillian were standing on the landing, ready to make their formal entrance.

She felt a hand hold hers and realised that Rose was standing beside her. 'Doesn't John look handsome, Elizabeth?'

'He certainly does.' She suddenly felt jealous that it was Lillian and not her who was standing beside him.

She stared at him. He was dressed in a rakishly cut dark grey tail suit that she guessed he had bought in America. It was trimmed with shiny black edgings that matched the thin ribbon bow he wore as a neck-tie over a ruffle-fronted white cotton shirt. The whole sombre outfit was set off by a violently multicoloured waistcoat that gleamed in any light it caught, but even this was outshone by his broad smile.

She watched him take Lillian's hand with overt gallantry and lead her down the stairs, his free hand audaciously accepting the applause and cheers aimed at him. Lillian smiled, but it was clear she was thoroughly embarrassed by John's sense of fun.

The applause was overcome by everyone's laughter but four steps from the bottom John raised his hand and called for silence. It was clear that he was about to make an announcement.

His twinkling eyes looked straight at her. She stared back, silently imploring him not to say anything which would cause trouble.

She knew that anyone else who looked at her would see her heart beating above the line of her dress; and as she prayed that he would not make the announcement now she heard him speak in the Southern States drawl he used to amuse people. 'I would just like to announce that I'm so very happy you could all come here to be with us tonight, so let the dancing commence.'

He was still looking at her and she could see that he had enjoyed teasing her, but all she could do was grin back at him and confirm their shared secret.

The guests stepped aside, the two couples moved outside to the dance floor, the orchestra began to play, the lanterns swayed in a warm breeze, and a special magic wafted over the manor and its gardens. Pincote Colliery, on the other side of South Ridge, could have been a million miles away, somewhere on another planet. She did not even think about it.

She danced, first of all with grandfather Belchester, and then with a number of other men, each of whom seemed to be enjoying themselves. She soon stopped worrying about remembering the steps; most of the men were no better dancers than her and those who were seemed to lead her so well that her inexperience did not matter anyway.

'May I have the pleasure of this dance?' a voice drawled and she turned and looked into John's chest; he seemed to have grown.

'Certainly, sir.' She let him lead her on to the dance floor and slipped happily into his arms for a waltz.

'It's the boots, ma'am.' He seemed to guess what she was thinking. 'Genuine dude cowboy boots. As worn by all sidewalk cowboys.'

He whirled her around the floor and as the lanterns floated past she thought that life with him would never be boring. It might be embarrassing at times, but never boring.

'You look beautiful, Elizabeth, and I just want to pick you up and carry you off. I want to live with you for ever and ever. Just the two of us, alone.'

'I don't think we'd be alone for very long,' she laughed, glad she had an opportunity to tease him, 'not if last night was anything to judge by.'

'God, I'd like to be with you now,' he grunted and she felt him pull her closer, 'making babies.'

'How many?' She laughed as he pretended to calculate how many.

'A dozen. A score.' He grinned. 'A hundred?'

'A few too many, I think.'

They danced on, looking at the guests, smiling when they were smiled at, and she realised again how comfortable she felt with him. Far more comfortable than Rose appeared to feel as she danced by with Hubert holding her at arm's length.

John followed her gaze. 'My sister seems quite happy. Has she said anything to you tonight?'

'We've hardly had time to talk.' The dance ended and she accepted John's slight bow and bobbed the faintest curtsy to keep matters formal. 'But she told me that Hubert has asked if they can talk together. Alone.'

'The famous proposal?'

'I suppose so.' She was about to tell him what Catherine had said when Sebastian Laybourne asked her for the next dance.

They moved awkwardly at first – she did not feel relaxed and he was a poor dancer – but after a few minutes they learned how to avoid each other's feet and did not have to concentrate on what they were doing.

'Are you enjoying yourself, Elizabeth?'

'Yes, sir, very much. I never thought that I'd ever see anything like this,' she admitted, conscious that she was not only careful to speak better when she was with the

Laybournes but that she was inclined to sound too subservient when she talked to Sebastian Laybourne.

'You look as though you were born to this life, my dear.' He smiled at her then grimaced. 'Much more than me. All this, the dinners, the dances and the interminable talking, makes me feel very uncomfortable.'

'You don't enjoy it?' She was astonished, he always seemed so relaxed.

'Not really. I never did and it becomes more of a chore as I grow older. I'd rather be out on my horse, or talking with the farmers. That's what I intend to do the moment John can take care of the mines and the other businesses. That's why it's important that he finds the right men to train as managers.'

'So there really is a good opportunity for Edward?'

'Of course there is, my dear, but what about you? What will you do when Rose leaves home? Leave Pincote?'

'I don't know,' she said warily, embarrassed because she could not give him an honest answer.

'I'm sure you'd have a better future away from Pincote, Elizabeth,' he said after a moment's hesitation. 'I could find you a suitable position and somewhere to live. In one of the cities, perhaps.'

'Thank you, sir, but I couldn't put you to that trouble.' She felt his hands hold her a little tighter. 'You've already been most kind to me.'

'I've done nothing, Elizabeth.' He pulled her tightly against him as the dancers all seemed to crush into one corner. 'Nothing more than I would for any other bright young woman or man I thought deserved some help. I know the people here misinterpret my motives or think that I'm too paternal, the dispute over the mine proved that to me, but I really do care, Elizabeth. I really do care.'

His earlier calm had gone and now his face was red and agitated. She was still crushed against him. His body felt warm and hard against her breasts, his heart thudded against her chest, and his breath smelled of brandy and cigars.

Something had changed him and, for some reason, although there were scores of people around, she felt scared. She tried to prise herself away but his grip was too tight so she danced on, frightened to struggle in case she lost her balance and fell and pulled him down on top of her. That would be the ultimate embarrassment. No, not the ultimate; she suddenly remembered the clothes laid on the summer house bench.

'I'm always expected to know what to do, Elizabeth,' he said suddenly, sighing heavily and swamping her with his breath. 'I know I frighten people, but I can't help it. I have to stand apart and sometimes I feel I'm an outcast. I'm sure, with your background, you know what I mean. I've seen it in your eyes.'

She did know what he meant. She did feel lonely sometimes. Even though her parents loved her as if she were their real daughter she had never forgotten that her real parents had abandoned her. Edward understood. He had his own reasons for feeling he was different from those around him, but his feelings were real to him and their shared sense of being different was why they were so close. But she was surprised Sebastian Laybourne had sensed her loneliness, and astounded that he felt the same. And she did not feel frightened of him any more.

'Yes, I do understand,' she said, and some instinct made her hold him tight, the way she sometimes held Edward for mutual comfort.

She looked away and saw Rose standing alone under a lantern, serene and lovely.

'You must be very proud of Rose, sir, she looks so beautiful.'

'She is.' His voice was softer again, he lessened his grip on her and his face lost its agitated look. 'She looks exactly as her mother did when I married her. Quite beautiful. I just wish she'd marry young Belchester. She'd be safe with him.'

'Safe?'

'Yes, Elizabeth. She's very beautiful, and very innocent and the world is full of men who might assume she's also very rich and take advantage of her. Hubert would never harm her, I'm sure of that, and his family could buy me out ten times over so she'd be safe with him. I hope she doesn't keep him waiting so long that he finds someone else.' The music stopped as he finished speaking but instead of letting her go he kept one arm around her waist and led her off the dance floor until they were standing in the darkness beyond the lanterns. 'You're also very beautiful, Elizabeth, and I want you to understand that I would be very happy to help you settle down somewhere away from Pincote.'

'Thank you, Mr Laybourne.' She watched him as he smiled down at her, and she realised how much John might grow to look like him.

She was glad they had talked. She felt she knew him better now. He did care about Rose, he had shown that, but he did not understand her and Rose did not understand him. He must have been more than twice Charlotte's age when he married her and he was so much older than his two youngest children that there were sure to be difficulties in them all understanding each other.

'I'm pleased that you're wearing my first wife's rubies,' he said quietly, and reached out to finger the arrangement of stones which lay against her chest. 'They need to be worn by someone like you.'

She felt the back of his rough hand against her exposed breasts but she did not pull away from him; it was an innocent move on his part and there was no reason to feel frightened any more.

She stood close to him for several moments, one of his hands still around her waist and the other fondling the jewellery, and she was about to ask him if she looked anything like his first wife when he sighed and stepped away.

'I'd better talk to my other guests.' He bowed slightly, took her arm and walked her back towards the lantern-lit dance floor.

They passed John and Lillian and she was left to talk with them but the conversation had hardly started before John's mother appeared.

'Elizabeth.' Charlotte touched her arm, and as she turned she saw Edward.

'Ma's dead,' was all he said.

CHAPTER 17

Minty was buried on Wednesday morning. It was a windless day and the layer of smoke and steam which hung across the valley glowed white, showing that the sun was shining above it.

Edward watched his mother's coffin being lowered into its grave. It was difficult to relate his mother to what was in the box, and impossible to feel sad for her.

He had found her crumpled on the living room floor, her hand holding a broken mug, and he had the feeling that she had simply discarded her body the way she would have taken off a set of dirty clothes. She had obviously made herself some tea, the first she had made for weeks, and then collapsed as she walked back to her chair by the fire. It seemed as though she had tried to claw her way up to the mantelpiece after she collapsed, but she must have died suddenly and fallen on to the rag mat in front of the hearth. She was quite cold when he found her and closed her thin lids over her pale green eyes.

He thought that the last thing she would have seen was Rose's sketch of Lizzie. At least she died smiling.

He did not feel shocked, but he knew he had been numbed when he saw Rose standing with her mother at the rear of the mourners and the usual surging excitement did not come. Rose's face was veiled by a dark net but he could see enough to know that she was crying and he hated not being able to walk across and comfort her.

Adam said a few words and then ushered everyone except Rose and Mrs Laybourne away so the family could have a few moments alone by the grave.

'I'm terribly sorry.' Mrs Laybourne moved forward and he saw her touch his father's arm. 'If there's anything we can do for you . . .'

'Thank you, ma'am,' his father answered in a thick voice. 'The only thing I want is to be down there with her.'

He watched as Mrs Laybourne took his arm and stood with him, silent and still.

'Edward, Elizabeth.' Rose stood by them.

'Thanks for coming,' he said and noticed how gruff his own voice was. 'I didn't expect it.'

She shrugged and he reached out and took her hand, squeezed it and turned away before she might see the tears he suddenly needed to cry.

Simon and Thomas were already following the mourners out of the cemetery, and Elizabeth moved across to her father's side and took him in her arms.

Edward heard her say, 'Come on, Da, it's time to go,' and he watched how defeated his father looked as he was led away.

'I'd better go too.' He looked at Rose, saw her raised eyebrows and knew what was on her mind. 'If I can,' he said, nodded to her mother, and followed the others.

The mourners went back to the Wrights' house where Pru had prepared some food but no one stayed long and Edward was glad when the last of them left.

His father stood up. 'Thanks for everything, Pru, but I think I'll go too.'

'Let us know if there's anything you want, Josh,' Pru said quietly and kissed his cheek before Elizabeth led him back to the empty house next door.

He watched them go then wandered into the kitchen to help Nancy with the washing-up.

'Lizzie going back to the manor?' she asked.

'Mrs Laybourne's told her not to hurry back, but I think she will, for a few months anyway. Until Rose leaves, that is.'

'She's definitely going to France, then?'

'Aye.' He sighed, and tried not to let his feelings show.

'I'll help wherever I can, Edward,' she said quietly, 'with cooking and washing, like.'

'That's good of you, lass, but we'll try not to trouble you too much.'

'It's no trouble, Edward,' she said anxiously, 'you'll need a woman now.'

He nodded. He knew she wanted to help and he thought it would be unfair to point out that they had been sending out the washing for months and had all taken to cooking when Lizzie was not there.

'Aye, thanks, lass, we'll ask if we need you.'

They finished the chores and as he left she gripped his arms and kissed him on the lips. 'I'm always here, Edward. I always will be, for you. I'm not going away.'

He held her for a moment, even when her mother came through the door and smiled at him.

'Thanks, Nance, Pru,' he said and left, his brothers still talking in Pru's living room.

He walked into his back yard as Elizabeth came out through the kitchen door.

'How's Da?' he asked.

'Crying his eyes out, lad. Leave him be for a bit.'

'Aye, poor bugger. Don't know what he'll do without Ma.' He slumped down on to the rough wooden bench his father had made years ago. 'What are you going to do, Lizzie? Once Rose leaves, like.'

'I'm not sure, yet, but I know what you should do.'

'Aye?' He listened as she told him what Sebastian Laybourne had said to her during the ball.

'So you were right to take the job, Edward. Mr Laybourne seems to think you're the right man to manage Pincote, and from what John's said I reckon you've a good chance of running all the mines before long.'

'And Rose?' he asked quietly.

'Her father's not the tyrant most people think he is. Give it the two years, lad, and see what happens. I reckon you and Rose are both going to be busy during that time so it'll go fast enough, and if you both feel the same when it's over, well . . .' She shrugged, and he nodded, understanding what she was saying.

'Look, Lizzie, I'm sorry if I was a bit blunt the other night. When I came to get you.' It was an apology which was overdue, but there had not seemed to be the right opportunity to speak before. 'I was upset anyway, about Ma, like. But to be honest that wasn't all of it. When John Laybourne asked me to take on this job he promised that although he wouldn't sink a second shaft he would find and open up the original mine entrance which was lost years ago. Hundreds of years back. It means clearing one of the spills and he says the company can't afford it yet. When I saw the ball I reckoned Laybourne could have spent the money better.'

'Was that all?' she asked and he realised that she had already guessed there was more.

'No. I'd seen Rose, seen how really beautiful she is when she's all dressed up, like, and I saw how much she was enjoying herself dancing with one of those rich bastards. And the way he was looking at her. Then I saw you wearing that frock and all those jewels, and I got a bit mixed up.'

More than a bit mixed up. He wanted to walk on to the

dance floor, grab Rose and run away with her. But that was impossible. Then Lizzie, looking like he had never seen her before; all he could think was that she was not really his sister. She was another beautiful woman who was enjoying her beauty, beauty that only money could bring. The sort of money he was never likely to have.

He stood up. 'I think I'll go for a walk, lass.'

'Aye.' She stood up beside him, a head taller than him, and hugged him tight. 'You're right, lad, and I think I understand, but you've got to let it go. It'll do no good to let it fester.'

He watched her go back indoors. She was still Lizzie, but she had changed since she had been living at the manor. She was more willing to compromise now. Still, he was in no position to judge. He had compromised more than anyone. And he knew he would keep on compromising until he had what he wanted.

He was about to turn out of the alley when he heard Nancy calling him. He almost ignored her, pretended that he had not heard her, but that would have been unfair so he turned around and walked back to where she was standing by her open back gate.

'Aye, lass?'

'Going anywhere special?'

'Not really.' He tried to hide his reluctance to spend time with her when Rose might already be on her way to King's Crag.

'Mind if I come with you?'

He could not refuse but he needed to warn her. 'Not the old barn.'

'Of course not,' she said, closed the gate, took his arm and led him along the alley. They turned down North Hill and nodded to men coming off shift.

'I've got to tell you I'm expecting your baby,' she said without warning.

The world seemed to blow up in his face.

What could he say? What should he say?

Suddenly nothing had any reason any more.

It was hours before his mind cleared, and even then the reality was overlaid by Pru and Ned's understanding smiles and the family's plans for a hasty wedding. Early June. Nancy had already missed twice, he remembered her telling her mother, so there was no time to waste if they were to convince the neighbours that the baby's arrival was premature, and even then there were those who would guess the truth.

In early June he would be married to a woman who was expecting his baby, shackled for life. All those years when he had walked away from lusty situations rather than risk what had now happened, all those years and the first time he took the risk he was hooked. And he had not even been thinking of Nancy at the time. He had been thinking about Rose.

The guilt flared up again, and behind it he could hear the voice that had been quiet for so long. The soft, ironic laughter from his conscience.

It was unfair; not to him, he deserved whatever happened to him, but it was unfair on Nancy because she deserved better than a husband who did not really love her. And it was unfair on Rose; perhaps most of all on her because she was completely innocent of everything that had happened.

Rose! He had to tell her, and he climbed South Ridge with a picture of her in his mind.

He climbed through the smoke which shut out the sun and when he reached King's Crag he saw her. She was still dressed in black but her hat and veil had gone and her copper hair was hanging over her shoulders.

'Edward! I was frightened you mightn't be able to come.' She did not hesitate politely as she had always done before, but came at a run, and he steadied himself as he felt her arms wrap around his neck and her lips push against his in a firm, loving kiss. 'How are you? I wanted to hug you at the cemetery.'

'I'm all right, lass.'

'I know you probably don't feel much like staying, but can you stay for a while? I've brought some food. Look.'

The food was laid out on a small white cloth, and she had also brought a rug for them to sit on.

'I wanted to hold you earlier, at the cemetery,' she said again as she led him towards the rug and pulled him down. 'How are you?'

He felt himself shrugging, and although his throat felt blocked he forced out some words. 'We've got to talk, Rose.'

'After we've eaten. I promised myself the other night that even if I couldn't dance with you I'd at least share some food with you. Just the two of us, alone up here. My last birthday present, to myself, sharing something with you. I feel a little guilty, under the circumstances, but I'm sure your mother wouldn't mind.'

It was miserable seeing her so excited and knowing that she would be in tears within minutes, but he tried hard not to spoil the treat she had looked forward to, and he told her that she was right, his mother would not mind.

'Oh, I nearly forgot,' she said suddenly and he watched her lean across to the bag she had brought with her and lift out an almost full bottle with a cork standing halfway out of the neck.

'Wine, is that, lass? I've drunk water, tea and ale before, but not wine.' He took a mouthful of the red wine she poured into a tumbler; it tasted sour and left his mouth dry. 'Very nice, lass. Very nice.'

It tasted awful, but it did seem to take the raw edge off his feelings. The next glassful tasted better and the third better still. Pincote and Nancy and his troubles seemed not to be so bad after all.

The food was eaten and there was no more than an inch or so of wine left in the bottle. Rose was stretched out flat on the rug, her hair fanned out below her head. He leaned over her, tracing a blade of grass across her face so that she wrinkled her nose. He wanted to kiss her.

'Kiss me, Edward,' she said as if she could read his thoughts, so he did; a long passionate kiss that brought her arms up around his neck. 'I wish you could have been at the ball.'

'I was, if you remember.'

'I'm sorry, I didn't mean . . .'

He placed his fingers against her lips and felt her kiss them.

'I saw you,' he said stiffly, knowing what he was leading up to, 'and you looked beautiful.'

'It was the gown, Edward. Did you like it?'

'I liked what I saw in it.'

'Good,' she said, and he felt her hands move and realised she was unbuttoning her dress.

'No, lass.' He tried to stop her but she gripped his hand and held it against her.

'Please, Edward. Please touch me. I wouldn't have wanted Hubert to, but I want you to know what I feel like before I go.'

'Hubert?' He was muddled.

'Hubert Belchester.' She worked his hand through her clothes until his fingers touched her breasts. 'The man Papa wants me to marry. He proposed again. Hubert still wants me to be his wife, Edward.'

Suddenly the jealousy of the other night swept back and instead of resisting her he reached deeper and further with one hand while he undid more buttons with the other.

'And what did you say?' He pulled her into a sitting position so he could loosen her clothes easier.

'I said "yes", of course, so I can go to France, but that's the only reason. I'm going to marry you, Edward. When I get back from France.'

The comforting effect of the wine seemed to ebb, then drain away. He pulled his hands back and stared at them.

'No, Rose. You're not. I'm going to marry Nancy Wright. In a few weeks. She's expecting my baby.'

He looked at her and saw her face stiffen.

'But,' she said and he stopped her by holding her shoulders.

'But, nothing, lass. I'm sorry. I didn't mean it to happen.'

'You said you loved me,' she whispered and he wanted to hold her but knew it would be the wrong thing to do.

'I do love you, Rose, and I always will, and that's what's wrong with it.'

'But why did you . . . ?'

He shrugged. 'Because you weren't there, Rose. I'd got all steamed up over you, but you weren't there and Nancy was.'

'So she gets the prize?'

'I'm no prize, lass.' He had expected her to be angry or cry, not to ask for explanations. 'Your Hubert's the prize.'

She stared, and then asked suddenly, 'Are you "all steamed up" now?'

'I reckon so.' He was and he could not deny it without hurting her more.

'Well I'm here now, Edward, and I still love you.' She started to wriggle out of her dress.

'No, Rose, no.' He tried to stop her undressing but she pushed him away.

'Do you prefer her to me? Is that why?'

'No, Rose. God, I want you more than anything in this world, but I can't risk making you pregnant too.'

'But I want your babies, Edward. Please. Please love me once, just once for me to remember. And for you to remember me.'

She laid back and he knelt by her, lowered his face to hers and kissed her lips tenderly.

'Love me properly, Edward.' Tears ran down her face and he tasted them on his lips. 'Just once. Please.'

'I'll always love you properly, Rose. And for ever.' He shoved himself to his feet. 'And I want to make love to you, here and right now. I want you more than I've ever wanted anyone. But it wouldn't be right. Not now. Not as things are.'

He turned his back on her and walked away.

'Edward!' He heard her call but he did not look back, he would be lost if he did. 'Edward! I love you!'

A train shunted coal trucks down in the valley bottom and he concentrated on the sound so that it shut out her calls. Then he began to run and the steepness of the hill took him away from her, faster and faster.

He did not look back until he had reached the bottom of the ridge, and then the layer of smoke which hung across the valley had shut out the sun and King's Crag and the world she had shown him.

Elizabeth felt herself staring at Edward. She had heard what he said but she was not sure that she understood him correctly.

'You've made Nancy pregnant and you're going to marry her?'

'Aye, lass, what about it?'

'But why, for God's sake? Why when you had everything you wanted?'

'I didn't have everything, Lizzie, and I didn't plan it this way but I'm stuck with it now, so let it rest, will you.'

His attitude triggered her temper. 'No I won't. It's not just you that's affected. It's Nancy and her baby, Pru, Ned, all of us and not least of all, Rose.'

'For Christ's sake, Lizzie, do you think I don't know that? Haven't you ever done something on the spur of the moment and then wondered afterwards why you did it, or are you so bloody perfect you always think before you act?'

'I've more sense,' she began and then thought about the way she had let John make love to her.

It could be her turn next; she could be the one to come home and say she had to get married.

'Oh, Edward, don't let's argue. Not us, and not today.' She reached for him and was glad when he hugged her back.

They stood holding each other for several minutes,

listening to their father's exhausted snores coming from the bedroom above, and glad that Simon and Thomas had gone out for the evening.

'You'll have to be careful how you tell Rose,' she said, and ruffled his hair as though he was a small boy.

'I've already told her. We met up on the ridge this afternoon. I told her before anyone, apart from Pru and Ned.'

She heard the finality in his voice and knew he felt defeated. There was no point in making him feel worse.

'Oh well, lad, it may be for the best. She was going away and she might have changed her mind anyway, or you might. And Nancy thinks the world of you, she always has.'

'I told Rose to marry Hubert Belchester, Lizzie. He obviously wants to marry her.' She heard his teeth grind together as he paused. 'You've met him. What's he like?'

'Nothing at all like you.' She tried to avoid describing him in case he was the man whom Edward had been jealous of.

'But he loves her?' The question was asked urgently, as if he desperately needed to know that Rose would be cherished and cared for.

Under different circumstances she would have said that it was difficult to know whether or not he really loved her or simply liked the thought of having her as an accessory, but she knew she had to lie. 'There's no doubt he loves her, Edward, none at all.'

'Good, then that's that,' he said, and turned away into the kitchen.

She sat down heavily in her mother's chair. She had expected to stay at home to watch over her father for a few days, until Sunday evening, but now she was torn. Her father needed her but Rose also needed her, and it was probably more important that she went to Rose and talked her out of making any hasty decisions.

Hubert was not the man for her to marry. He was weak, characterless and he had no real sense of humour. Life with him would be unbearable for someone like Rose, but she might not see there was an alternative, especially if her father could influence her. But she could not leave now so she would have to meet John at the mine the next morning and ask him either to take her back to the manor or arrange for Hopkins to collect her.

The next day she was surprised to find her father up and dressed and ready to leave for work.

'Are you sure you want to go, Da?'

'Aye, Lizzie. There's no point brooding and I'll be better doing something,' he said wearily and she noticed the redness in his eyes.

'Besides, now Ma's buried we need to get back to normal, whatever that's going to be.'

'I'll walk down with you, then,' she decided, then thought she should ask him if he wanted her to stay any longer.

'No, lass. I reckon you've got your own life to lead, and it's better you get back to work, too. But will you come over on Saturday? Stay for the weekend, like?'

'Of course, Da. I'd like to.'

'Elizabeth!' John was alone in the manager's office and she could see he was pleased she had come to him. 'I'm sorry I couldn't see you yesterday but there was too much going on here. How are you feeling?'

She let him hold her and enjoyed the feeling of his hand stroking her hair which was still hanging loose.

'I'm all right, John, but I'd like to go back to the manor. Can you take me, or ask Mr Hopkins if he can?'

'Of course Hopkins can take you. He'll be here sometime this morning. He's bringing my mother and father into town.'

'Is Rose coming with them?' she asked warily.

He shook his head and she could tell he was worried about something. 'Rose isn't very well. Her asthma seems to have come back. After your mother's funeral she insisted on walking on the ridge and the doctor thinks she over-exerted herself, but he says she'll be all right if she rests for a few days.'

'I think there may be more to it than that.' She told him the whole story.

He listened carefully after his initial surprise, and then said simply, 'I hope she doesn't take Edward's advice.'

'Whatever she decides, John, I don't think we should tell anyone about us. Not just yet,' and she was glad when he nodded his agreement.

'But I don't want to wait too long, Elizabeth. I think Lillian's noticed there's something wrong and she might already have guessed that it's something to do with you.'

'I don't want to wait much longer either, especially' – she almost told him that someone must have seen them on Saturday evening but then she changed her mind – 'especially after the other night.'

He smiled and she kissed him, then sat down to wait for Hopkins.

She was pleased to see Hopkins arrive with the family's brougham, the small two-seater carriage which was drawn by just one horse. She always felt more comfortable in the brougham because it attracted less attention than the family's large four-horse carriage.

She stopped just long enough to exchange a few words with John's father, and after Hopkins had taken her to her own father's house to collect her bag she climbed up on to the driver's bench so she could sit beside old Hopkins and enjoy the warm morning air.

They talked easily, but she noticed the quick glances he gave her when he thought she was looking away from him.

'Is there something wrong, Mr Hopkins?'

'No, Miss Forrester, nothing wrong.'

'Did I upset you the other morning? By the coach yard?' She tried to draw him out.

'No, miss,' he said, and stared ahead at the horse's back.

She could see that he was thinking and she left him alone in the hope that he would volunteer an explanation for his behaviour. When he did speak it was not about her.

'I understand Miss Rose is leaving the manor, miss.'

'Yes, but not until August, Mr Hopkins.'

'I think, maybe, that's been changed, miss. I heard she's leaving next week. Going south with the mistress. Then she's marrying Mr Belchester.'

'When did you hear this, this rumour?'

'It's not rumour, Miss Forrester. I heard the master and mistress talking about it this morning.'

She rushed to Rose's room as soon as she arrived back at the manor.

'Is it true, Rose?' she demanded as she sat beside Rose's bed.

Dull eyes and a slight nod confirmed the story.

'But why? Why not go away as you planned and decide what to do in two years?'

'Because I need to be loved now, Elizabeth. Edward wouldn't love me, even though I asked him to. He said he loved me but he didn't want to touch me, Elizabeth, I could tell. And if I don't marry now, no man will ever want me, and I couldn't bear that.'

'But you're beautiful, Rose. You could choose any man you wanted,' she insisted, and sat back quickly as Rose reacted.

'No, you don't understand.' She sounded almost hysterical. 'I'm too beautiful. I'll frighten men away as Mama did when she was young. That's why she married Papa.'

'Calm down, Rose. You're not talking sense.'

'Elizabeth, listen. Mama lived with her uncle and aunt in London where there were thousands of young men, but she was so beautiful that they were all scared of her. If Papa had not taken her away she'd have become an old maid.'

'Who told you this, Rose? Not your mama?'

'Miss Smith,' Rose gasped.

'Miss Smith? When?'

Rose seemed to think before she answered. 'Last year. Just after Hubert proposed for the first time.'

'I understand,' Elizabeth heard herself say, but she did not understand at all.

It seemed to her that Miss Smith was as concerned as Sebastian Laybourne to see Rose marry Hubert Belchester. Since the ball she could understand why Rose's father was acting as he was, even though she thought he was misguided, but she could not understand why Miss Smith, who seemed to have loved Rose, would try to intimidate her into marrying a man she did not care for by using an incredible story about her mother.

She remembered Miss Smith's last words to Rose, the words she stayed alive just long enough to deliver personally.

'You're a very beautiful woman, Rose. Leave here before it's too late.'

And Sebastian Laybourne's obsession with eighteenth birthdays. Somehow she had a feeling that it was all linked to the person Sebastian Laybourne had thought about when he first saw her wearing the red ball gown, and the person Hopkins had remembered when he saw her on Saturday morning. And she was not sure that was the first Mrs Laybourne.

An idea occurred to her. 'Rose, is there a portrait of your father's first wife anywhere in the house.'

'Only one. In his bedroom, Elizabeth. Why?'

'I simply wondered what she looked like.' She tried to sound no more than slightly curious.

'Well, go along and have a look,' Rose said. 'I'm sure Papa won't object. Besides, I should like to sleep, if you don't mind.'

She shut the door quietly as she left, and walked along the passage to Sebastian's room.

The door was locked. She knew that a door from his study led into his bedroom so she tried his study door but it was also locked. She half remembered seeing a door in Charlotte's bedroom which must lead into the study, but although her bedroom door was open, the door leading to the study was locked. She would have to wait for another opportunity, but meanwhile she might ask John if he had seen the picture.

Dinner that night was a sombre affair, and she guessed that the mood was not only out of deference for her own loss, but because a depression had settled over the house in anticipation of Rose's leaving.

After dinner she was invited, with John and Charlotte, to go to Sebastian's study to discuss plans for the next few weeks. Rose was not invited; it seemed that she would play her part later and had nothing to do with what was being discussed that evening.

It was tantalising to be sitting in the study, only yards away from the portrait she wanted to see, and her thoughts kept drifting away from the detailed discussion which was taking place.

So much had happened over the past few months, but even more had happened in a few days. Now there was more to come if Rose insisted on marrying Hubert. Then, perhaps, there would be her own wedding; plans to be made, things to do.

'Elizabeth! Do you feel unwell?' John's voice brought her attention back to the discussion.

'A little tired, that's all,' she said to hide her distraction.

'A feeling we'll all share before long,' Sebastian Laybourne said wearily. 'I imagine this is the first marriage ever to be arranged via the telegraph system.'

'That's progress, Father,' she heard John say, and was surprised he sounded so light-hearted about a serious matter.

'Is it really, John?' his father answered sourly. 'I'm not

sure I approve of such forms of progress. I simply hope
that Rose really has made her final decision. Only days ago
she was insisting that she wanted to wait for two years, and
now it seems she can't wait to leave and settle down. I
suppose she misses him, or something similar.'

'I don't think Rose will change her mind again, and she's
quite adamant about leaving, Sebastian.' Charlotte
confirmed her daughter's intentions. 'She even wanted to
spend time on the estate before the marriage, so that
Hubert can court her properly. The Belchesters have
arranged for us to join them at the end of June but Rose
insists on leaving here before then. Doctor Roberts has
suggested that some sea air would be good for her, so I've
arranged to take a steamer from Newcastle to London.
Then we'll travel down to Bournemouth and stay there for
a few weeks so that Hubert can pay us some visits.'

Sebastian nodded his agreement. 'When do you intend
to leave?'

'We'll leave from here a week on Monday, if Elizabeth
agrees,' Charlotte said, 'but we mustn't forget that
Elizabeth has her father to consider.'

She concentrated as she heard her name mentioned.

She was frightened that she would be asked to leave
John and join Rose and her mother and she listened
attentively as Mrs Laybourne explained what was
proposed. 'We'd like you to join us, Elizabeth, but I need
someone to run the house while I'm away. Would you be
prepared to do that? And perhaps, during that time, you
might consider remaining here for a while after Rose is
married, as my companion? I'm sure that I'll miss not
having Rose around and I'd appreciate another woman's
company.'

'Yes, Mrs Laybourne,' she said, relieved that she need
not be parted from John and that she could stay in Pincote
to watch over her father, 'I'd be pleased to run the house
while you're away.'

'And the future?' She saw the concern in Charlotte

Laybourne's face. 'Would you become my companion?'

'Perhaps we can discuss that when you return.' It was an exciting offer and she tried to conceal her feelings and avoided looking towards John in case either of his parents noticed.

Later she took what had become a customary evening walk with John.

'It all seems to be working out rather well, Elizabeth.' He squeezed her hand.

'Apart from Rose marrying Hubert,' she answered, avoiding any further reference to Edward.

'Don't worry about that. I know Rose. She'll change her mind before the wedding.'

'I wouldn't be too sure about that,' she warned him. 'Anyway, what'll happen if she does? Will your mother still be able to get her into the school?'

'Perhaps, or perhaps she'll just come back here and things'll go on as before. Except that she'll have to forget this daft idea about Edward. Romantic idea, maybe, and I happen to think they're quite suited in some ways, but I can't really believe anything could ever have come of it, Elizabeth.'

'A Laybourne marrying someone from the colliery?' she asked bluntly, scared of how he might answer.

'No, just Rose marrying Edward. She doesn't understand what it'd mean, Elizabeth. They'd be dependent on whatever he could earn, and I think she's too young to understand how little, relative to her idea of income, that would be, even though he's a good future ahead of him. And, what's more, I think Edward's sensible enough not to let her make that mistake and far too proud to live off any money she has.' He looked down at her and they stopped walking. 'Our situation is different. You have to adjust to my way of life, and although that won't be easy for you I'm sure you'll manage.'

He suddenly grabbed her and she felt his lips firm against hers.

They stood under the trees and kissed for a long time. She could see the summer house half hidden amongst flowering shrubs and she knew then was the time to tell him what she had seen.

'The clothes were gone when you returned?' She was surprised that he did not seem at all concerned. 'Are you sure they were women's clothes, or could it have been one of the gardener's boys taking a nap? They'd been working hard to get everything ready for the ball, and it wouldn't surprise me if one of them thought they could have a short rest without being seen. Especially at that time in the morning.'

It was a solution she had not thought of, and suddenly she wanted to believe that was what had happened. After all, no one had said anything so the matter was probably best ignored anyway.

'There's just one other thing, Miss Forrester.' She followed him as he pulled her towards the old lodge. 'I rather thought that we still might do the old place up a bit and live here rather than in the house. I know it's what I'd planned to do when I married Lillian, but it could be a wonderful home and it'd be more private, if you understand what I mean.'

She understood exactly what he meant, and told him she thought it would be a lovely idea.

During the next few days, as May merged into June, the warm weather turned hot. The valley was stifling and it was difficult to decide whether it was cooler above ground or below. Then on the first Saturday of June the weather broke.

Thunder had been rumbling all morning but the lightning flashes only glowed in the clouds, showing that the storm was a long way off, but at exactly one o'clock a tempest hit the valley. The first lightning bolt struck St George's Church and the second toppled the iron tower that stood above the larger waste spill on South Ridge. The third set fire to some of the ridge's bracken and gorse, but the rain which followed extinguished the flames almost instantly.

Edward had never seen or heard rain like it. It hammered on the roof and filled the back yard six inches deep, enough to make him force a sack into the gap under the back door to stop the flood coming into the kitchen. When he looked out of the windows he could not see the terraces at the rear or the front of the house. He made one attempt to go out but the force of water and the bruising size of hailstones that were fired at him changed his mind.

It rained hard for four hours, and when it stopped he stood on the front doorstep and breathed air which was fresh and clear and smelled clean.

'Edward!' Nancy's brother Albert was pounding along the street, shouting, 'George Willis needs you underground.'

He grabbed his coat and followed Albert down North Hill. As he ran he could see that the tower supporting the highest chain of waste buckets across the river had fallen and the cable and buckets were spread across the valley floor.

When he arrived in the yard he saw Ben Clements and his maintenance men already untangling the cable and fallen buckets from the winch gear that pulled them on their continuous round from the mine to the spill and back.

'Many men below, Ben?' he yelled.

The shift always finished at noon on Saturday to allow the deputies and the maintenance crews to check the mine for safety and make any repairs that might not be possible while coal was still being cut, but that meant there were always a score of men underground until late on Saturday night.

'George sent everyone up, Edward, but he's still down there watching the repair you did on the main road.'

'I'll go down too,' he yelled back and raced to the lamp room, collected two lamps and signalled to the winchman to drop the cage as soon as he was inside.

The mine was eerie when it was quiet and the noise made by the pumps and dripping water were the only sounds. He made his way along the main road until he saw a pinprick of light far away at the end of a straight stretch where the road sloped away towards the face.

'George!'

'Careful, you're coming into water.' He heard George's warning too late and water spilled into his boots.

Before he reached George the flood was over his knees and he could hear water splashing like a small waterfall. 'Patch leaking?'

'Aye, lad.' George sounded puzzled more than worried. 'Aye, it's leaking a lot but I'm surprised the water's found its way down here so fast. I reckon we've got a bloody great underground river running above us and all that's stopping it flooding the workings is this patch of yours. The watercourse might even be connected to the one that flooded the lower face back in March.'

'Christ, George! The patch'll never take that sort of pressure.' He felt his old fear running back to him.

'May not be too bad, Edward, if the crack's not too wide.'

'But there's only one way we'll know if it's dangerous, man, and that's if it collapses.' He tried to sound calm but knew he sounded scared.

'One other thing, lad.' He saw George point to a marker he had placed against the tunnel wall. 'Difficult to say, mind, but I reckon some of the water's draining off, somehow. The road rises about forty yards on so the flood's contained in this dip. It's a bloody big puddle, but it's not getting any deeper and it should be considering the amount of water that's coming in, like.'

'Running off to the bypass like it should?' He thought it was a reasonable suggestion but George waved his hand in disagreement.

'No, if it were running off there, lad, it either wouldn't

have flooded at all or it'd still be rising. No, it's going
somewhere else. But I'm buggered if I know where, mind.'

'So what can we do, George?'

'You go and tell John Laybourne what's happened and
I'll stay here and see what happens next. Oh, and you can
leave me that spare lamp.'

'Don't you want me to wait with you?' He tried not to
sound too relieved at being sent up.

'Do you want to?' He heard a laugh caught in George's
voice.

'Not much.'

'Well, I only wanted you here so you could see it for
yourself before you talked to Mr Laybourne. You've seen
it now, so you can bugger off, man. Besides, you've got a
woman and a new bairn to think of.'

'Who told you about the baby?'

'I guessed. Healthy lad like you, pretty lass like Nancy.
Quick wedding, like.' George reached out for the spare
lamp. 'Don't worry, Edward, I'll not say anything, but I like
to hand out the dangerous jobs properly, like.'

'How dangerous do you reckon it is?'

George shrugged. 'Like you said, lad, we won't know
until we find out. Go on now, and don't worry about me. I'll
be out of here if I reckon it's getting worse.'

'Thanks, man.' He waved his lamp and walked back
along the road; and wondered if he could find a way of
visiting the manor without seeing Rose.

The storm had moved on and the early evening light
was bright after the mine's gloom. He stepped out from the
cage and mistook John Laybourne for one of Ben
Clement's men.

'Edward! Where are you going?' He recognised the
voice instantly and was relieved that he did not have to go
to the manor.

'I'm sorry, Mr Laybourne, but I didn't expect to see you
here, like.'

'I came over to see if there was any damage done after

that storm, and to check on the river. And I brought Elizabeth over to see your father.' He looked embarrassed as he explained why Elizabeth was visiting on a Saturday. 'I know she usually spends Sunday with you but Rose is leaving on the first train on Monday morning, and Elizabeth wants to spend tomorrow with her.'

'I understand, Mr Laybourne.' He nodded and explained what was happening below.

'Well, I think we'll leave that in Mr Willis's capable hands. I'll go down and have a look myself in an hour or two. Meanwhile I'll see how much damage that fallen cable's done and I suggest you go home to Elizabeth and your father. Perhaps, tomorrow, when the surface water's run off, you'll inspect the spills to see if they're stable. The river's rising already so an awful lot of water must have fallen on the ridge and we need to be sure it's not disturbed the waste too much. We don't want the spill sliding into the river and damming it, or it might back up across the valley and flood the yard and pithead and then we could lose the workings for good.'

'What's happening about the second entry, Mr Laybourne? The men'll be asking, after the storm, like.'

'I'm sorry, Edward, but you heard what my father said about the cost, and now we're going to have the tower and all this wreckage to make good.'

'Mr Laybourne' – he stood his ground – 'you promised me that if I got the men back to work we'd open up another entrance. Besides, you've spent a lot of money on boreholes and planning to open up a new face under South Ridge, and it'll not be possible to work that without a second entrance, whether it be a drift or shaft. The men and me are standing by the word we gave, I think it's time you did your bit too.'

'I'll do what I can as soon as I can, Mr Forrester.'

It was obvious that he was angry, but there was something in his voice that made it difficult to know who he was angry with.

Edward guessed that John was angry either with his father for stopping the investment, or with himself for not being able to make his father listen to him. It was a dilemma he recognised, so he simply nodded, assured John that he believed he would do his best, and walked through the lamp room and away from the workings.

He opened the back gate and saw Lizzie sitting on the yard bench, a bowl on her lap, peeling potatoes.

'Bit different to the way you looked a fortnight ago.' He grinned at her.

'Is that all it is? Two weeks.' He saw her frown in disbelief.

'Aye, but a lifetime all the same.' He flopped down beside her. 'I've just been talking to your John.'

'My John, is it? Better not let him hear you say that.'

'Come on, Lizzie, there's no use trying to pretend there's not something going on between you. It's been obvious for months.'

'It's not been going on for months,' she snapped back and he saw her realise her mistake.

'So it is serious?' He watched her blush and knew it was.

'Aye, lad. The real thing this time. Remember the old lodge? He wants to repair it so we can live there rather than the manor.'

'Rose said that's what he'd do,' he remembered suddenly. 'She'd planned for us to take on the manager's house down by the river.'

'Oh, I'm sorry, lad, I didn't think, like.'

'It's all right, Lizzie. I try not to think too much meself.'

'But you still do?'

'Aye, and I reckon I always will. But I've only meself to blame, lass, and I cannot take it out on others.'

'But you will, won't you. You'll take it out on Nancy, and on the baby, especially if things get hard.'

'So what are you saying, lass? You telling me to rescue Rose off the train on Monday? Abandon Nance with the baby?' He tried to make it sound as though he was joking.

'Perhaps. Nancy's a good-looking lass, Edward. She'd find someone else to take care of her.'

'Doesn't sound like you, Lizzie. Not talking like that.'

'Maybe, but I didn't realise how much you and Rose mean to each other, or how much you were prepared to go through to be together. If you marry Nancy you'll hurt her, and Rose, and yourself. If you run off with Rose it'll be difficult for you both, but you'll only hurt Nancy. And I'm sure John and I could find some way to take care of her and the baby if necessary.'

'Might be twins, lass. They run in both families.'

'Don't joke about it, Edward. I'm serious.'

'So am I, lass. I'll stick by Nancy because it's as much my fault as hers, more probably, and because I can't hurt her any more. I've already cost her a brother. Two if you include Henry.'

'But, Edward.' She began to argue but he stopped her, and then he told her exactly what had happened the day William was killed.

'So you see, Lizzie, what a hero I really am. I'm a fake, lass, so I'll carry on being a fake for as long as I can get away with it. And if it means I can make Nancy happy by pretending I love her, then that's what I've got to do.'

They jumped as their father banged the door open and asked how much longer they would be, and neither of them heard Nancy crying on the other side of the yard wall.

CHAPTER 18

The previous day's storm had cleared the air but left it full of a strange, potent energy. Rose noticed it the moment she woke up; and it made her restless.

The artificial normality of her last family Sunday and Vicar Franklin's lengthy and apparently pointless sermon made her even more restless to the point where she fidgeted so much she dropped her Bible five times. She finally forced herself to sit still and diverted her mind by wondering why the lightning bolt which had struck the church tower had not done a better job and demolished the church altogether, by listening to the birds singing outside, and by wishing she was on South Ridge where she always felt closer to God than she ever did in His church.

She was overtly charming to all the people who stopped to talk after the service, and was careful to smile and to ask the appropriate questions, but she used her eyes to show that she was not really interested in what was being said and each conversation died quickly from mild embarrassment. And as Hopkins drove the carriage through the town on the way home, she did not join the family in waving back to the ladies who nodded and the gentlemen who doffed their hats.

She could see that both her mother and father were furious with her but for the first time in her life she did not care. She had no great feeling for pretentious Pincote Market or the people who lived there, and as she was leaving and would never return she saw no reason to be hypocritical any longer.

Within minutes of arriving back home she changed out of her church dress and into a skirt and blouse, chose a pair of boots suitable for walking and wrapped herself in a woollen cloak.

'Where are you going, Rose?'

'Just walking, Mama.' She waited for the objection and prepared to argue.

'I don't think you should go out alone, Rose. Not as you've been ill.'

'But, Mama . . .'

'I'm walking with Rose, Mrs Laybourne. If you've no objection. A long walk may help prepare her for tomorrow's sea air.'

Elizabeth, the saviour, appeared; dressed and ready to leave. Moments later they were outside.

'It seems a very peculiar day, Elizabeth. Everyone's trying to behave as if this is just another Sunday, but it's the last Sunday I'll spend here as me.'

'You'll always be you, Rose. That won't change.'

'Oh yes it will.' She was sure of that; she would have to compromise and become Mrs Hubert Belchester. 'And it's already started. Let's go up on to the Ridge.'

'Are you sure? It's a hard climb and you have been ill.'

She did not bother to answer, just looked into Elizabeth's eyes and trusted her to understand. It might be the last time she would walk up there, up above the world, up in the sky where imagination was currency and anything was possible. Up there where Edward was a prince. Up there where lovers stood on top of King's Crag and looked over their own private world and picnicked in the little valley between the rocks.

Pincote Colliery looked small and cramped on the opposite hill, and she said what she always thought when she saw the town: 'I don't know how those tiny cottages can each house so many people. How people can live in them.'

'They don't have any choice, Rose, and it depends what you mean by live,' she heard Elizabeth reply and she knew what she meant.

'Do you think Edward's down there, somewhere?' It was an idle thought but she might never be even this close to him again.

'Maybe,' Elizabeth answered, 'but John did ask him to check the waste spills. To see if the storm had loosened them at all.'

And suddenly there he was, a tiny figure nearly a mile away and hundreds of feet below her but she knew it was him. She watched him walk away from the spills, past the Dead Lakes and towards the flat iron bridge which carried the railway line across the river. She waved. She knew he would not see her, he had his back to her, but she waved anyway because they had never said a proper goodbye.

'He talked about you a lot yesterday, Rose,' she heard Elizabeth say, and knew the only real friend she had was trying to make her feel better; trying to lessen the pain that made her throat and her heart feel rigid. 'He told me about your plans to live in the manager's house by the river, and about how much he loved you and wanted you, and the real reason why he can't abandon Nancy and marry you.'

'The real reason? Nancy Wright's expecting his baby, isn't she?'

'That's not the whole story, Rose.' Elizabeth told her how William had been injured, and why Edward had never told anyone but her why he was not the hero they all assumed he was.

It was difficult to believe but she was inclined to believe it because it was Elizabeth who told her.

'Elizabeth, you don't think this is another one of his stories? Just something he's made up to make me feel better?'

'No, Rose. It all makes too much sense, and it explains his moods and the reason he was so rude to you the night of the accident.'

She remembered that night, the way he had looked at her after he apologised, and the feelings she had for him that night. It was almost three months ago, a lifetime.

'So, Elizabeth, we're agreed, are we, that he's a coward, a liar, a cheat, a philanderer and an all-round fraud.'

'That's how he sees himself, Rose.'

'Well, he's wrong, Elizabeth. He's so terribly wrong.'

If he had tried to stop her loving him then he had failed. Rose loved him more now than ever before. And there was nothing she could do about it. Tomorrow she would take the ten o'clock train away from Pincote. But that was not all she had decided; she had made two other decisions.

She had vowed she would never return to Pincote. She could not bear the thought of being in the same town as Edward. If she came back she would want to see him and that would not be fair on Hubert, Nancy, Edward or even herself.

And she would make her father understand that he had not caused her to change her mind about marrying Hubert. She had made her own decision, not because she loved Hubert but because she could not marry the man she wanted; and she would leave her father wondering just who this other man was. He would never guess it was Edward, she would make sure of that.

She watched the distant figure until it disappeared behind the colliery buildings. 'Goodbye, darling. I hope Nancy makes you happy.'

*   *   *

Edward lay on his mattress on the floor and stared at the patch of grey sky he could see through the window. Monday morning.

The house was silent. He had been awake when Thomas and Simon clambered down from their bunks and trampled over him to get to the bedroom door, but he had not opened his eyes or spoken to them. He did not want to speak to anyone this morning, and because he did not have to go to work with the first shift he did not need to let anyone know he was awake.

He had worked all day Sunday checking the spills and helping Ben Clements's men stop the leak in the main road. He had to check the waste spills again this morning, but there was no point in doing that until the overnight rain had drained off them, so he had time to lie in bed and think.

He heard a train shunting coal trucks and thought about Rose. Her train would probably pull those coal trucks away from Pincote; but unlike her the emptied trucks would come back. She never would.

He had not spoken to her but he sensed that she would not return to Pincote. The thought of never seeing her again added to the misery he was trying to contain, added to the bleakness he saw as his future. He clambered off his mattress and started to dress, anything to occupy him until he had work to do.

He rinsed his face and shaved in cold water, the pull of the razor punishing him but not enough to stop the desolation he felt. He ate a hunk of dry bread washed down with lukewarm tea and wandered into the living room. The sketches Rose had drawn looked down from above the fireplace and he could not help fingering them, his only contact with her.

Rose!

It was almost as if she was there with him; he could hear his mother telling him how kind Rose had been.

As he looked at the drawing of Elizabeth he remembered what she had told him on Saturday.

If he stayed he would make everyone unhappy, but if he ran away with Rose . . .

His mind began to race. There was not a man in town who would not be happy to take care of Nancy, better care than he could. He had even seen Adam looking at her in a way he never looked at any other woman. There were good men who would love her more than he ever could. Was it fair to tie her down to what would become a miserable marriage?

Rose's train left at ten o'clock. Plenty of time to check the spills, report to George, and make some excuse to return to the surface. He could easily hide away on one of the coal trucks, stay hidden until the train reached Shearton then make his way to Rose's carriage. Even better, wait until the train reached Newcastle. They could run away from there and no one would know where they had gone.

He did not have much money but he had saved some so he could send his mother on the holiday she never had. He ran upstairs and packed a few clothes and half the money into a canvas bag. He would leave the remaining money for Nancy, but he would not leave a note. It would be obvious what he had done, and anyway, he did not know what to say.

Nancy. He had not seen her on Saturday because after he took Lizzie back to the mine to meet John he decided to go back underground and relieve George, and he had worked all day Sunday. When he finally called to see her on Sunday evening she had gone out alone.

And now he would never see her again; never see the baby he had sown in her.

He trembled as he picked up his bag, took one last look around the living room and kitchen he had grown up in, and walked out across the back yard. He shut the high gate for the last time and turned down the alleyway without looking back.

He was halfway along the alley when he heard Pru scream, 'Edward. It's Nancy. She's bleeding terrible. Will you come? I think she's losing the baby.'

He did not hesitate. 'I'm coming, Pru, don't worry.'

They burst into the house and he followed Pru upstairs. Nancy was on her bed in the back bedroom. She looked as if she had been drained of blood and when he saw a half-filled bowl underneath the bed he thought at first that it was there to catch the blood she was losing.

'She's lost all that?' He was scared.

'No,' Pru said sharply. 'Mostly it's water. I've been washing her. Just saw you through the window. I didn't realise you were home or I'd have called you earlier.'

'Have you sent someone for the doctor?'

'Aye. He should be here soon.'

'Nancy.' He leaned over her and touched her clammy face.

She half smiled at him, then screwed up her face and clamped her eyes shut.

'Bring me another bowl.' He felt Pru pulling him away.

He clumped back down the stairs, found another bowl in the kitchen, half filled it with warm water from the range and carried it back up the stairs.

'Get rid of that, will you, lad?'

He exchanged the bowls and seconds later he was back downstairs, wondering what to do with the bloody water.

The lavatory. He rushed down the alley to the first brick closet and poured away the bowl's contents. Something white and stringy slid out of the bowl and into the earth closet. He saw it and was puzzled, but did not realise what it was until he was halfway back to the house.

'Oh Christ.'

He rushed back to Nancy and saw Pru leaning over her, trying to explain why she needed the doctor. 'Nancy, I can't stop you bleeding lass. I've had to send for the doctor.'

'No, you mustn't!' Nancy looked hot and agitated. 'No doctor! He mustn't see me!'

'Why ever not, lass?' he asked, and saw Pru's face stiffen.

'I want to talk to Edward, Ma.'

'Go on, Nance. I'm here.' He knelt down by the bed and smoothed her hair.

'Alone, Ma. Please,' Nancy begged.

'I can't leave you, lass,' Pru argued.

'Please, Ma. There's not much time. Please. Just me and Edward.'

He nodded to Pru and saw she looked even more worried than before.

'All right, but just a minute, mind.' Pru backed away but left the door open.

'Shut the door, Edward. Quickly.'

He did as she asked.

'I haven't miscarried. I got rid of the baby. Mrs McDonnel did it for me. Last night.'

He felt guilty and sick.

'Why did you go to her, Nance? Why do it at all? We're getting married in a few weeks.'

'I overheard you telling Lizzie about us. Heard it all, Edward. You're free this way.' She spoke in bursts and in between she screwed up her face with pain.

'Oh God, Nance. I wouldn't . . .' He jumped back as an awful ragged scream came out of her.

Pru rushed back into the room and felt under the blankets.

'Where's the sodding doctor?' She sounded hysterical. 'I don't know what else to do, Edward!'

'Neither do I.' He felt useless and responsible and scared.

'You've done enough already.' Pru lashed out and caught his face.

'Stop it!' Nancy screamed. 'It's not all his fault. She got me drunk first so I didn't know what she was doing.'

'Mrs McDonnel,' Edward heard himself start to explain but he stopped when Pru raised her hand.

'I thought so.' She turned to Nancy. 'What did she do to you, lass? You must tell me so I can explain to the doctor.'

'Gave me lots of gin and stuck knitting pins into me. I didn't start bleeding at first. Not until I was sick in the night. Then I got a pain.'

The front door banged open and moments later Doctor Roberts pushed his way into the room.

'You'd better stay, Mrs Wright, but you, young man, out.'

Edward sat downstairs and listened to the half-muffled conversation and the doctor's verdict. 'Someone made her lose the child. Was it you?'

'No. Mrs McDonnel,' Pru answered.

'Old witch.' The doctor obviously believed her. 'Should have been a butcher. She's made a terrible mess here but I think we can stop the bleeding.'

There was the sound of instruments being pulled from his bag.

'You'll have to help me, missus. Should be done in the infirmary but I daren't move her.'

He waited. Half an hour passed, then the doctor walked downstairs. Pru followed him. They both had bloodstains over their hands and wrists and they both looked worn out.

He followed them into the kitchen and watched them wash their hands.

'What did you have to do with this, young man?' the doctor asked sternly.

'Nothing, Doctor.'

'Hmm.' Doctor Roberts looked dubious.

'He's telling the truth, Doctor.' He was relieved to hear Pru defending him. 'I called him this morning.'

'Why him?'

'Because he was the only one here, Doctor,' Pru said sharply. 'Besides, they're getting married soon.'

'Did you know about the baby, lad?'

'Aye, Doctor, I knew.'

'It was your baby then?'

'Yes. Yes, it's my baby,' he answered.

'No, lad,' the doctor said in a bitter voice. 'It was your baby.'

'Aye, of course,' remembering again that the skinny piece of scrag he had thrown into the lavatory had been what was left of his child.

'You know it's against the law to do what she did?' The doctor rolled down his sleeves.

'Aye,' he answered shakily, unsure what the penalties were for obtaining an abortion. 'But do you have to report it, Doctor? Does that matter now?'

'It may matter if the lass dies.' The doctor put his coat on. 'Yes, you can look worried. She may die yet. Don't let her get out of bed and don't leave her alone for more than a few minutes at a time. I'll be back later to have another look at her.'

Pru showed the doctor out through the front door. She came back and sat at the kitchen table, spread out her hands and stared down at them. When she spoke her voice was heavy and rough.

'Doctor reckons she's been damaged too much to have children even if she lives.'

'All right if I sit by her for a bit?' he asked, unsure what to do or say.

'I don't think so, Edward. I heard what she told you and I don't think I want you in my house any more.'

He looked around for his bag, picked it up and walked to the back door. 'I'm sorry, Pru. Really sorry, like.'

'You will be, when Ned and the boys catch up with you.'

'Aye,' he said, and left.

Rose sat at the breakfast table and listened to the clock ticking. It was the only sound. No one had spoken for five minutes and she wished that it was already nine o'clock and time to leave. The waiting was irritating and there was another hour and a half to endure. She moved her food about the plate but did not feel like eating any more.

'Make sure you eat a full breakfast, Rose,' her mother warned, 'because it'll be a long time before we eat again.'

'Yes, Mama.' She forced down a few more mouthfuls. 'Elizabeth, you are still coming to the station to see us leave?'

'Of course.'

'And you, John? Are you coming?'

'I must go to the colliery, first, but I'll be at the station before you leave, I promise.'

'Do you have to go to the mine?' she asked, hoping she could wheedle him into changing his plans. 'I'd hoped to ride into town with you.'

'I should be at the mine now, Rose, but I thought I'd have my last breakfast with you.'

'You make it sound as though I'm to be hung.' She managed to say it with a measured amount of petulance.

'I must go, Rose. Mr Trenchard and the deputies will want to discuss the flooding with me. And I want to know if we've to do anything about the waste spills.'

'Oh, the waste spills. How exciting,' she said and enjoyed the irritated look on her father's face. 'However will I live without discussing waste spills?'

She saw the grin John disguised by stuffing food into his mouth, then turned as her father spoke.

'Rose, I can't tell you how pleased I am that you've given up this nonsensical idea your mother and brother had to send you away to school. You wouldn't have been happy there. You'd have been out of place and longing to come home within a week. Much better to get married.'

She tried to tell him it was her idea to go to school, but he interrupted her. 'It'll do you good to marry young Belchester.'

'And if it doesn't, Papa?'

'Doesn't what?'

'Doesn't do me good? You make marriage sound like a

dose of medicine, Papa. What if it doesn't do me good?'
Now she was leaving she found the courage to talk as she
chose.

'Words. Words and nerves,' he blustered. 'I'm simply
telling you that I'm glad you've seen sense, my girl, and
you are doing the sensible thing marrying young
Belchester.'

'They're two separate things, Papa. I've seen the sense
in marrying Hubert, or his money anyway, but I'm not sure
that it's really the sensible thing for me to do.'

Her mother sat back and asked in an exasperated voice,
'Are you saying that you've changed your mind again,
Rose? If so you've left it a little late. The train leaves in an
hour or so.'

'I'm sure it would wait, Mama. After all, Papa does own
it.'

'Rose!' She looked back as her father spoke. 'This is
most unlike you.'

'No, Papa. This is me.' She took a deep breath and said
what she had rehearsed. 'This is the real me and it's the
first time you've ever seen the real me because you've
always scared me so much that I couldn't be myself. And
this is the last time you'll see the me you know because
soon I'll have to stop playing the role of your daughter and
start playing the role of Mrs Hubert Belchester. Papa.'

He slammed his knife and fork down on the table.
'You're talking rubbish, but you haven't changed your
mind about marrying Belchester?'

It pleased her to watch him stand up and take a few
strutting steps towards the window, but she was not
prepared for what he said next. 'There isn't someone else
you'd rather marry?'

The ruse had gone wrong. She had wanted to make her
father believe there might be someone else, but she
wanted to do it as the last thing she said before leaving so
he did not have time to bully her into admitting too much.
Now she did not know what to say or do. She instinctively

looked towards Elizabeth and when she looked back at her father she saw that he had noticed.

'Well, I assume by your silence that there is someone else,' he said heavily. 'Well, are you going to enlighten us?'

'There is no one else, Papa.'

'I can tell that you're lying to me, Rose. Now who is it? Or do I have to beat it out of you?'

'Father.' John was on his feet and she was glad he was there to defend her. 'This is rather pointless, isn't it? Even if there was someone else, which is unlikely considering the limited opportunities Rose has to meet suitable men, does it matter now that she's leaving?'

'Well, young man.' She watched her father turn on John. 'I will go to the colliery to undertake your duties, and I suggest that you accept the responsibility of ensuring that your sister leaves the town without creating any embarrassment or scandal. And you'd better not mention this to the Belchesters. God knows what they'd think. Or do.'

She watched him storm out of the room without saying anything further to her or her mother, not even goodbye.

'An excellent way to leave home, Rose,' her mother said sarcastically, and left the table.

John turned on her, his face red with anger. 'That was damned foolish, Rose. You've made Papa furious.'

'I really don't know why he should be so upset, John,' she said coolly, 'he's got exactly what he wanted, as usual, and he isn't the one who's going to marry Hubert Belchester. I am.'

'Come on, Rose.' She was surprised that John sounded so dismissive. 'We both know that you're not going through with it. You'll not marry that prig, not even to better Papa.'

'John' – she made sure she had his attention – 'Papa has nothing to do with my decision. I'm going to marry Hubert because it makes sense. Because he can provide for me and because although he loves me I don't love him.'

'But that doesn't make sense, Rose.'

'Yes it does. You see, if I don't love him, he can't do anything to hurt me.' She thought about Edward and knew that it made sense.

CHAPTER 19

———————

Edward reached the spill and sat on a rock for a few moments' rest. He was breathless, his clothes were covered in mud and his legs, back and arms ached.

The path up to the spill was steep, a difficult climb even in dry weather, but the storm had loosened the ridge's thin soil and, overnight, whole sections of the slope had simply slipped away, taking turf and bushes and the path with it. He was glad he had left his bag in the lamp room at the colliery; it meant he had his hands free and he needed both of them when he finally resorted to crawling up the hillside.

He looked across the valley and identified his own house, smaller than a matchbox, and Nancy's next door, but they were both just houses to him now. They were nothing to do with him, he would never go back to them.

There was no future for him in Pincote. Nancy did not want him any more; she had even killed their baby to give him the freedom to leave.

His father would not want to know him once the truth came out and his brothers would be ashamed to call him brother. Lizzie would stand by him, as Lizzie always had, but he could not drag her down with him, and that was what would happen if he stayed.

But he could not stay even if he wanted to. Ned and the boys would kill him if he stayed.

A small locomotive shunted coal trucks.

Rose might understand, if she really loved him, if he could talk to her and explain that he was going to run away with her even before he knew what Nancy had done. It would have to be her choice but he would be fair with her, explain how hard their life together would be, how much easier it would be for her to forget him and marry Hubert Belchester and his money.

He began to shake with fear and shame and frustration, and for once the voice inside his head was sympathetic.

He was still shaking when he stood up and scrambled further up the slope. He had one last job to do before he left: to make sure he reported back on the condition of the waste spills. He could not leave without knowing that he had done all he could to protect the lives of the men working in the blackness underground.

The waste looked unusual. Normally the slag stayed on top and the dust settled or blew away, but now the surface was a sodden mixture of both. He tested the surface by pressing down with one foot; it felt spongy and when he lifted his foot the impression left by his boot quickly filled with water. The spill was saturated, and that meant it was dangerous; it might become too heavy, slide down the steep slope and dam the river.

He looked down towards the Dead Lakes and imagined them spread across the valley bottom, imagined the river flooding until it poured down the shaft into the mine.

'Hell,' he said out loud and scrambled further up the slope.

He reached the line of markers he had laid out the

previous day; posts set in a line across both spills and the firm ground between. The first posts were still in line, showing the nearer spill had not moved, but from where he was standing he could not see the markers on the second spill, and to reach them he needed either to go around or across the first one.

He glanced down at the colliery and saw the little shunting locomotive was pushing filled coal wagons down the line, ready to be hitched to the ten o'clock train. It had taken him much longer than he expected to climb this far and he knew that if he had to climb even higher to get around the nearest spill he would not have time to go underground, report to George and get back to the surface before the train left. He looked back at the waste's saturated surface and realised he had to risk crossing it.

He moved slowly. The waste stuck to his boots and made them heavy to lift, but he kept going even when he sank halfway up to his knees and had to use his hands to pull his feet out from the mess.

The waste was piled higher in the middle of the heap and by the time he reached the crest he was sinking deeper. He rested for a moment and felt the waste close around his thighs, squeezing his muscles, and it was only then that he realised how fast the waste could suck him down.

He grabbed his left knee and pulled, and sank deeper. Pulled again. The waste pulled back. He felt its cold close around his waist. He slapped the surface and water rose up, and the waste pressed against his ribs.

Shock and fear. He could not move his legs!

He pulled his jacket off, spread it in front of him. The jacket turned black as water soaked it but it did not sink. He pressed down on it, the backs of his arms flat, and slowly he eased himself up. A slurping sound and his left leg came free. He knelt on his jacket and pulled his right leg free, stepped on to the sludge and struggled on, too scared to risk stopping for breath and unable to turn back.

He still had over a hundred yards to go before there was solid ground. He tried crawling but his hands sank even faster than his feet.

He looked back. The holes he had made were already filled with black water. He prayed the waste was stable, and not only for the sake of the men working below; if it started to move it would carry him with it.

He found he could run, a stumbling, sliding run that carried him down the slope as much as it took him across the spill. He fell on his back. The waste held him, sucking him down again. He rolled sideways, over and over until he could feel he was pulling himself free, then he was on his knees, scrambling until he could get to his feet and run on to the solid ground between the spills.

He could see that the tower which had collapsed was half buried and the huge buckets its cable carried had all but disappeared under the grey black surface, but when he reached the line of markers he saw that even this spill, on the steeper slope, had not started to move. Not yet.

He turned back towards the colliery and ran, keeping well below the bottom of the first spill, enough distance, he hoped, to allow him to run clear if the waste suddenly began to move.

He reached the manager's office and cursed when he found it locked. He guessed John and his father were probably going to the station to see Rose leave but he had hoped that Trenchard would have been there so he could report to him rather than go below to George. He had less than an hour now before the train left.

He ran across the yard and up the steps to the lamp room. 'Do you know where Mr Trenchard is?'

'Mr Laybourne sent him below to see George Willis,' the supervisor answered and made some comment about the condition of his clothes.

'Mr Laybourne's here?' He was surprised.

'Aye. Senior, that is. And in a bloody foul mood, man.'

'Where is he now?'

'I don't know, Edward, but Trenchard went down about ten minutes ago.'

He glanced through the window and saw an empty coal tub being wheeled into the cage. 'Give me a lamp. I'll go down with the tub and see if I can find him.'

The cage dropped fast and minutes later he was in the underground office telling Trenchard how dangerous the spills were, and suggesting someone should set charges which could be used to scatter the waste if it started to move.

'I'll see to that, Edward.' Trenchard nodded. 'Now go and have a word with George. The repair's leaking again.'

'Again?' It was dry when he left it last night; concern conflicted with the need to leave.

'Aye. It's not much, but George is worried and he's asked Mr Laybourne to close the workings for a few hours while he looks at it.'

'George wants to close down? It's that serious?'

'He's probably being too cautious, Edward. That's what Mr Laybourne thinks, anyway, so he's refused permission. He's keeping the workings open.'

He hurried down the main road, conscious that he was running out of time if he was to leave with the ten o'clock train.

He passed two men working a hand pump and found George standing by the repair, a thin jet of water pouring out from the roof. 'Doesn't look too bad to me, George.'

'Maybe not, lad, but I'm a bit uneasy, like. I don't want another bloody disaster on me conscience.' George stared up at the roof as if he were trying to see through hundreds of feet of rock. 'I reckon we're right under the ridge now, and we know it's riddled with caves and springs and God knows how many underground rivers. I'm worried something's happened to make one of 'em change course. Maybe that's why we had so much flooding last time. Maybe the water's found another way through . . .'

'Aye.' He remembered how much rain had fallen, how

much water the waste spills and the surrounding ground
had soaked up; all that water had to drain off somewhere
and not all of it would flow off into the river.

'Maybe,' George said quietly, almost to himself, 'there's
a bloody big underground lake filling up above our heads.
That'd account for everything, even why your repair keeps
leaking.'

He suddenly felt very scared. 'So you reckon the
workings could flood? If the repair breaks, like?'

'Aye, and look.' George pointed to the leak. 'It's getting
worse, I reckon.'

It was difficult to judge. They looked at it for several
minutes and still could not decide.

Then George made up his mind. 'I'll get the face
cleared. You tell everyone else to leave, as a precaution
like, and tell Mr Laybourne what I'm doing.'

'Right.' He turned away, then turned back as he
remembered to ask about yesterday's flooding. 'There's
hardly anything left from yesterday. I'm surprised the
hand pump could clear it so quick, with more water
coming in, like.'

'Aye.' George shrugged. 'And I still don't know where
it's going – but you get up top, lad, and speak to Mr
Laybourne.'

Edward turned and walked back towards the porch,
warning men quietly that the workings were being cleared
as a precaution against another rock fall in the main road.
He did not mention the danger from flooding in case he
started a panic. Everyone grumbled and he did not argue
with them. He did not even argue with those who said they
would keep working. He wanted to get to the surface to let
Mr Laybourne know what was happening, and then run
away with his daughter.

Neither Laybourne nor Trenchard were in the
manager's office so he went to warn the winch driver to get
ready to bring the miners to the surface.

The winch room overlooked the railway line and while

he was explaining what was happening a locomotive pushing a single carriage backed through the yard, a guard walking along the rails signalling to the engine driver. The guard's flag dropped, the train stopped hissing, and its wheels turned very slowly until its iron buffers clanked against the leading wagon.

'You all right, Edward?' He heard the winch driver ask, but his attention was taken up by watching the guard and another man lifting the chains and loops that hitched the wagon to the carriage. 'Edward?'

'Yes.' He hesitated, and turned back to the winchman. 'Do you understand what you've got to do?'

'Aye?'

He could see the man was puzzled but he left him and ran back towards the lamp room to collect his bag. There was no time to explain anything more to Trenchard or Laybourne. George would have to cope as best he could when he came up. There was no time to do anything more if he was to get on the train before it left the sidings.

There was a crush of men in the lamp room and he pushed his way through. 'Can I have my bag, please.'

'Just a minute, Edward.'

'I don't have a minute, man. Now! Please.'

The supervisor glared at him. 'Bit of a hurry, Edward?'

'Aye.'

'I'm not sure what we did with it. Wait a minute.'

He groaned. His money was in the bag, as well as a spare set of clothes. He could hardly run away with Rose in clothes that were stiff with coal waste and without even a penny in his pocket.

Outside, wheels screamed and slid as the locomotive pulled away.

'Here we are.' The supervisor tossed the bag at him.

He grabbed it and ran. Across the yard, on to the rails ahead of the train, and out through the wide wooden doors into River Street. The train was moving slowly but he could hear its speed building so he sprinted on to the flat iron bridge which spanned the river and ran another hundred yards or so before he turned and looked back.

The train was passing through the doors and edging across River Street. The coal wagons it pulled were trundling along the rails under the winch room window. He could see the winchman operating the long levers which controlled the direction and speed of the cages as they lifted or fell, and he suddenly realised that would be his last sight of the colliery. He would never see it again. Or his family. Or Nancy. Or Lizzie.

The last of the wagons cleared the colliery yard and the engine's front wheels touched the flat bridge.

He steadied himself to jump on to the last wagon. The locomotive passed him in a shuddering flurry of steam and heat. The wagons' wheels thundered across the bridge and began to whirr against the smooth rails.

Then he heard the other sound. He heard it quite clearly in spite of the distance and the noise made by the wagons, and he heard it because he had been trained to hear it whatever else was happening.

Five bells on the underground telegraph.

A serious accident.

He ignored the warning, turned away and started to run alongside the last wagon, matching it for speed until he could get his hands on something solid and lift himself aboard. Then he was on it, standing on its buffer, the rails and sleepers dashing past below his feet. He looked up, back towards the colliery moving further and further away as the train carried him towards Rose.

And he knew he had to go back.

CHAPTER 20

————

Elizabeth stood beside John and they both waved as the train left the station. Rose and her mother leaned out of the carriage window and waved back until the train rounded the curve and took them out of sight. The train hooted all the way, warning men who were working along the track to stand back.

She stood and listened to the train's whistle, and thought about the day her brothers had left. The memory added to the sadness she felt. Then she heard the other whistle, louder than the departing train, and suddenly her sadness was overtaken by fear.

John was already running and by the time she reached the carriage he had given Hopkins instructions and was holding the door open ready to pull her inside. Hopkins drove off before the door was shut and they reached the colliery yard in less than ten minutes.

Murdock Street and the yard were awash with people, frightened women, nervous men and a few crying children who were too young to be in school and were confused and scared by what was happening.

She followed John up to the office, aware that everyone was watching her and John and that shortly she might have to explain what had happened to everyone standing in the yard.

John had a quick discussion with his father and she asked a few pertinent questions of her own, then John left to go underground and she found herself standing alone on the platform outside the office.

'What's happened, Lizzie?' a woman called up to her, and the noisy crowd settled and waited to hear what she said.

'A large section of the roof has come down and blocked the main road. It's about a mile in so it's nowhere near the face, but the face is cut off behind the fall. Water's pouring through the roof and flooding the main so it's going to be difficult to clear the fall. I'm afraid that several men have already been killed and a list of their names will be posted near the steps to the lamp room. Edward, my brother, is already underground supervising a rescue, and John Laybourne is on his way to join him. That's all I can tell you for now, but Mr Laybourne will keep me informed and then I'll let you all know what's happening.' She did not invite any questions because she had told them all she knew.

She went back into the office. John's desk had been taken over by his father, and she slumped into the chair placed in front of it.

Sebastian Laybourne stared at her. 'You must be very worried, Elizabeth. You've had an eventful few weeks.'

She shrugged. She could not think of anything to say. Her mother was dead and now her father and brothers were in serious danger. For the first time she was grateful that Joey and Paul had gone to America. She might never see them again, but at least she knew they were safe.

The silence lasted a minute or so, then she heard Mr

Laybourne ask, 'I assume my wife and Rose departed before the accident?'

'Yes, sir. We heard the alarm moments after the train left.'

'Good. At least this business shouldn't distract Rose again.' He spoke as if the collapse and the flood were small irritations. 'I was extremely upset with that young lady this morning, Elizabeth.'

His comment infuriated her and she was about to tell him there were more important things to worry about when she saw something frightening in his face, in his eyes; and instead of ranting at him she tried to make excuses for Rose's earlier outburst. 'I think Rose was rather scared, Mr Laybourne, and I don't suppose she meant half what she said.'

'Nevertheless, Elizabeth.' He paused and she watched him concentrate on putting several very precise folds into a piece of paper before he spoke again. 'I think there was some truth behind her comment that she would have preferred to marry someone else. Given that she has met very few young men, as John quite correctly reminded me, I believe I know to whom she was referring.'

He was intimidating, blue veins bulged in his temples and his eyes had shrunk and turned hard.

'I don't think . . .' she began but his raised hand stopped her.

'Your brother Edward, Elizabeth. I had no inkling that Rose took him so seriously, almost as seriously as he takes himself.' He laughed, a quiet, scornful laugh. 'He is so gullible, Elizabeth. I saw that immediately. So gullible and so honest that others believe him. The men would never have conceded so much if they'd been led by Henry Wright, I'm sure of that. And, of course, Edward is quite entertaining in his own way, his rather pompous posturing as King Harry and that silly business of bringing flowers for my wife.'

She was stunned, did not know how to react to what she

saw as a betrayal, but she managed to ask, sarcastically,
'And have I also proved to be quite entertaining? And
useful?'

'Your situation is entirely different, Elizabeth.' He spoke
quickly, showing that she had irritated him. 'You're strong.
I can see that, but Edward's weak and his worst weakness
is his vanity. He really thinks he matters enough to be able
to take advantage of the position I put him in, and I suppose
my foolish daughter was taken in by him. I told you she
was very innocent and vulnerable. That's why she must
marry young Belchester.'

Her mind raced as she tried to understand the
implications of what had been said, tried to adjust her
thoughts to what she saw as a changed situation.

'But you don't think I would take advantage of the
position you've put me in?' she asked hotly.

'Of course not, my dear. How could you?' He smiled at
her and she wondered what he would say if she told him
that John wanted to marry her, but she did not say
anything.

He stood up and walked around his desk until he was
standing close behind her, one hand resting on her
shoulder. 'I've already asked you to consider a somewhat
better offer, my dear.'

'As Mrs Laybourne's companion?' She could see his
reflection in a mirror and looked into his eyes as he rested
his free hand on her other shoulder.

'I can give you far more than that, dearest Elizabeth.
Away from here, of course.' His hands moved slightly, his
thumbs hooked around her neck and his fingers pressed
against her breast bone.

She suddenly remembered the way he had held her at
the ball and realised what he had meant when he offered
to find her a suitable position away from Pincote,
remembered the pile of clothes on the summer house
bench, and wondered . . .

'Do I remind you of your first wife, Mr Laybourne?' She

asked before she realised what she had said.

'Not at all.' She felt him smile, the tips of his fingers ruffled her blouse and she sensed he had forgotten all about the disaster that was happening underground. 'Why do you ask that?'

'You said I reminded you of someone you knew a long time ago, and I thought that perhaps . . .' She tried not to react to his probing fingers as they pressed down and rubbed against her upper chest.

'No, you're nothing like my first wife.'

'May I ask who I remind you of?'

He hesitated, as if he was not sure whether or not to tell her, then he nodded. 'Miss Smith.'

'Rose's tutor?' No one else had mentioned any likeness to Miss Smith.

'And John's. She was more than a tutor to them, more a nanny when they were younger. And she was a wet nurse to Catherine.'

'A wet nurse? Then she had a child of her own? What happened to it?'

'It died,' he said bluntly, the fingers of both hands running along the top few buttons of her blouse. 'She was about your age when she came to us. A little younger perhaps. About eighteen, I think. I forget exactly.'

There it was again, eighteen. 'I think I'll wait outside, in the air,' she said, stood up and walked towards the door.

She was scared and did not want to be alone with him, and she left without looking back.

She shut the door firmly and stood on the landing outside the office, looking across the crowd for someone to wait with, and felt very alone.

During the last accident, back in March, she had felt she belonged with the waiting women as she stood with her mother and sisters-in-law, and Rose, Pru and Nancy. Now she felt isolated from everyone; her mother was dead, Flo, Mary and Rose had left, and she could not see Pru or Nancy anywhere.

That was strange; they should have been there.

She looked towards the gates, half hoping to see them arrive late, and was surprised to see Henry running into the yard. She waved, he waved back, and she ran down the steps to talk with him.

'Haven't seen you for a while,' she said awkwardly, knowing that he had left the mine and was working as a labourer on a farm near Shearton. 'What are you doing here?'

'Brought a cartload of stuff over for tomorrow's market and I thought I'd stop and see Ma and Nancy.' He did not look at her, his eyes were on the winding wheels. 'What's happened, Lizzie?'

She ignored his question for a moment, 'Where are your ma and Nancy?'

'Don't know. I came straight here. Well? D'you know?'

'Aye.' She sighed and told him everything she knew.

'Sounds bad.' He looked frightened. 'I'll see if they'll let me go down and help.'

Then he was gone, running across the yard and up into the lamp room. She saw him seconds later, lamp in hand, ducking into a cage seconds before it was dropped.

Moments later she felt a hand on her shoulder and turned as Annie Darling spoke. 'I thought I'd look for you, Lizzie. Doesn't seem long since last time, does it?'

She shook her head. It did not seem long, but so much had changed.

'Is it really true what they're saying about Edward?' Annie asked quietly.

'Edward?'

'You haven't heard?' Annie looked embarrassed.

'No.' She shook her head again, her throat closed by fear. 'Is he hurt?'

'No, no. They're saying he's threatened to kill Mr Laybourne.'

'What?' Her heart thumped; Sebastian Laybourne had not told her about this, surely it could not be true.

'First thing this morning George Willis wanted to clear the workings but Mr Laybourne wouldn't let him. Then when the accident happened Edward asked him to sound the general alarm but Mr Laybourne said it wasn't necessary. Edward told him that if any of your family died he was going to come back and kill him.'

'Oh God, the fool. But that's all, Annie,' she said quickly, imagining what could have happened. 'He probably just lost his temper. He's been a bit short lately.'

'Aye.' Annie nodded. 'But the word's gone round and everyone's talking about it.'

'Let 'em talk.' She had more important things to worry about, her father and brothers were trapped. 'You haven't seen Pru or Nancy?'

Annie shook her head. 'Not since yesterday.'

It was strange that they were not in the yard. She decided she would go to look for them in an hour or so, sooner if there was some news.

The only news which reached her was that the situation was becoming worse, the workings were still flooding, and Edward and John were trying to find a way either to stop the water flowing in or to allow it to drain off. She did not understand the second option; how could they drain the water out of a mine? She was sure someone had made a mistake.

The hours passed, marked as before by the unfeeling chimes of the Town Hall clock. Her legs and back ached from standing; neither Charlotte nor Rose were there to organise places for the women to rest and she did not feel inclined to ask Sebastian Laybourne for any favours.

The clock struck three. There was still no news of any of the men trapped behind the rock fall; the flood made it impossible to reach them. She began to wonder if it was already too late. Perhaps they were already dead.

She remembered she had not gone to see Pru and was about to leave when the wheels started turning. Perhaps there would be some news, something encouraging to improve her mood before she went to see her friend and Edward's wife-to-be.

She moved across the yard and stood by the landing stage. The cage latched into position and even before the gate was opened she saw Edward inside and waved to attract his attention. 'Lizzie,' he called from the landing, and a few moments later he was running down the lamp room steps. 'How are you, lass?'

'I'm fine, but what about you, lad? You look worn out. Is there any news?'

'Well, a big length of roof's fallen into the main road and shut off the way to the face but we cannot even get to the fall because of the flood.' He paused for breath. 'John Laybourne and I went to see if we could find a way of draining the flood off, like, and we've found an old dried-up watercourse which goes under the main road. John reckons it might have been the original entrance to the workings. Roman, maybe. Anyway, it's been plugged with stones and waste then capped but the flood might drain off if we can shift the capping.'

She understood immediately, but noticed the caution in his voice. 'The flood might drain off if you can shift the capping? How're you going to do that?'

'We're not sure if we can, lass, especially as it's under about four feet of water.' He paused. 'We're going to try blasting the plug out, and we hope the pressure of water'll wash the rest of the filling away.'

'It sounds dangerous. Is it?'

'No, not really, lass. No more dangerous than any other blasting, and we do enough of them.' She could tell from his eyes that he was lying.

'Don't lie to me, Edward. What you're going to do is dangerous, isn't it? I've heard Da talking about blasting under water. You'll have to use a short fuse and so much explosive that the blast could bring down even more of the roof. That's right, isn't it?'

'Aye,' he said simply.

'So who's going to fire the charges? You or John, I suppose.'

She saw him squirm before he answered, 'John. He thinks he should.' Then he added quickly, his hand on her arm, 'But he'll be in a side channel and we're building a blast wall to protect him.'

She stared for a moment. 'Take care of him, will you? If you can.'

'Of course, lass.' They hugged each other, and she thought it was time to be honest with him.

'He's asked me to marry him, Edward. And I've agreed, but don't tell anyone.'

She could see that he did not know what to say. She was marrying a Laybourne? It did not seem likely, or possible, or even fair given his situation with Rose and Nancy; but now was not the time to discuss it.

'He'll be all right, lass. I'll keep an eye on him.'

She smiled and nodded, then said quietly, 'I haven't seen Nancy or Pru.'

'I don't suppose you will, lass.'

She listened, horrified as he told her what Nancy had done. He did it quickly but without missing any of the details. She felt sick.

'Anyway, Lizzie, does Mr Laybourne know about you and John?'

'No,' she said quickly. 'No one knows, except Rose. I told her yesterday.'

'And what else is wrong, Lizzie?' She could no more hide her feelings from him than he could from her; they had always been able to see into each other's minds.

'I had a bit of a talk with John's father. I don't trust him any more, Edward, and you shouldn't, either. He told me how he tricked you into helping get the men back to work, and how he's been using you since. John doesn't know so I think he's been lying to him, too.' She squeezed his hands. 'And he's guessed about you and Rose. I think you should leave here once this is over. To be safe, Edward.'

She thought he was about to say something but they were interrupted by people who wanted to know what was happening, so he asked her to explain, kissed her good-bye, and ran back to the cage.

He waved just before the cage dropped. She waved back, head and shoulders above most of the crowd; she realised how he had seen her so easily when he came up. Now she wished she was shorter, anonymous, so no one could see her crying.

It was early in the evening and she was waiting alone.

Annie Darling had offered to call on Pru and Nancy, and under the circumstances she had let her go; Pru might not have welcomed her anyway, not as Edward's sister and someone who had played a part, however passive, in Nancy's decision to go to an abortionist. Annie had left some hours earlier and she had not returned; she had probably gone home to make tea for her husband and daughters as there was nothing she could do for Billy, still somewhere under the ground.

Elizabeth had sat herself down on the lamp room steps. It was the best place to wait for news; no one could pass without her knowing. Anyone with any news had to come down those steps.

She sat, elbows on knees, chin resting in her cupped hands, listening to the machinery which was either pumping air into the mine or water out. The winding gear was ominously quiet.

Some of the men who had come up earlier had gone home to rest and their women had gone with them but the yard was still crowded. Doctor Roberts was there with a handful of nurses ready to give immediate help to those who needed it, and a row of wagons had been lined up to take seriously injured men to the infirmary. Somehow two newspapers had heard about the accident and had

managed to get five bowler-hatted reporters to Pincote on
the four o'clock train.

Across the yard she could see Sebastian Laybourne
sitting on his own in the office, and she felt he deserved to
be on his own.

A small group of policemen had been sent to control the
crowd if it got out of hand, but the crowd was docile and
quiet. The policemen sat in a group on anything which
could be used as seats, and they seemed to respect the
mood and smoked and spoke quietly amongst themselves.
They had even taken their helmets off and held them in
their laps, out of sight.

The high wall and the tall brick buildings which
surrounded the yard seemed to enclose a world of grey-
dressed people with nothing to do. A world which seemed
to have slowed down and finally stopped.

'Lizzie.' Henry called her name as he walked from the cage
to the lamp room, and she did not notice the awkward way
he was holding his arm until she walked up to the lamp
room and saw a nurse bandaging his wrist.

'Henry, what happened?'

'Edward broke it.' She saw Henry wince as the nurse
pulled the bandage tight. 'But he saved me life, lass.'

'How was that?'

'I was helping Adam Marriott dig out a hole under
water, so we could fix a charge, like, and a slab of rock
slipped and trapped me hand. Thought I was done for,
Lizzie. Even Adam couldn't shift the rock and then more
stuff started falling in on top of us. Next thing I knew
Edward was there, pulling me arm about until me wrist
snapped, and then I was back above the water.'

'Is he safe?' Fear churned up her empty stomach.

'Aye. Only just, like. He could have been killed trying to
help me, Lizzie.'

'But is he safe?'

'Aye, lass. Bit confused that's all. Got me mixed up with

William and Gordon, but he's all right.' He looked past her, down into the yard. 'Ma and Nancy not here?'

'No.' She told him what had happened.

'Well, I hope Nancy's all right, lass, but I cannot grieve for the baby.' He shook his head. 'I'm more frightened for Da and all the others. It doesn't look good, Lizzie. Even if we blow the capping, mind, there's still an awful lot of water and rock to clear before we can get up to the face.'

She helped him down the steps and watched him walk towards the gates; wondered how Pru would react to him telling her that Edward had saved his life, then put the thought out of her mind.

She sat on the steps again, tried to imagine what John and Edward were doing and prayed they were safe. Prayed that both they and all her family were safe, but something in the evening air told her they were not.

John watched the glow of the men's lamps disappear back along the main road, watched their reflections on the floodwater, then turned and splashed back into the narrow channel that had been cut and worn smooth by centuries of water passing through it and was now flooded again. He was alone but he did not feel alone. He sensed he had the support of every man who had helped, perhaps even the spirits of the men he thought had originally used the channel as their means of reaching the coal.

He had admitted some of the obvious risk to Edward but he had deliberately understated the full danger of what he was about to do. There were two charges. The first was in a hole in the channel where he was standing, and if that loosened enough rock it would not be necessary to blow the second charge in the main road. He hoped the first charge would be enough; the second one might clear the plug but it might bring down more of the roof and seal the workings for ever.

Now the time had come he was frightened; not only because within minutes he could be blown apart or crushed to death, or even because any gas trapped below the capping could ignite and roast him like meat, but because for just a few moments he would know what was going to happen to him. Just a few seconds before he died. He was more frightened of those few seconds than he was of dying.

He started counting. He had smashed his watch earlier and had forgotten to ask if anyone else had one he could use, so he had to count away the thirty minutes he had allowed for Edward to get the men clear.

He sat down on the low blast wall the men had built to protect him and tried to concentrate, but suddenly he felt weary and the boredom of counting made him drowsy. He studied the fuse, felt it in his hands, let his eyes trace its route down the channel until it disappeared into a length of wide canvas hose which led to the waterproof explosives buried in the underwater hole the religious Adam and the reformed troublemaker, Henry Wright, had dug.

He listened to his lamp hissing and wondered what time it was; whether it was light or dark, dry or raining. There was no reason for wondering, it was just that he would have liked to know.

He thought about Elizabeth, and immediately put her out of his mind in case his courage failed and he found an excuse not to blow the charges.

He lost count and started again. And again and again. And still he lost count and had to restart; he did not know how many times. He was not concerned, it was better to blow the charge late than early when there could still be men in the main road. He patiently started counting again and this time he concentrated hard so as not to lose track again.

Edward stood under the big lintel which marked the entrance to the main road. John was late blowing the charge. Half an hour late. Something must have gone wrong and all the time the flood was rising, maybe flooding the face, trapping and drowning his father and brothers and the other men waiting for help.

He had to find out what had gone wrong.

He glanced towards the underground office. Adam and the others were slumped on chairs or on the office floor, dozing off their exhaustion, and Henry had been taken up to the surface.

He wondered if he should wake Adam and tell him what he was going to do, but decided not to. Perhaps John's courage had failed; he could not blame him if it had, and it would be better if no one else knew.

He lit a fresh lamp and started back down the main road. The debris that had littered the floor had been cleared from between the rails before the tub with its load of waterproof gelatinous dynamite had been pushed into position above the capping. Now he was able to move reasonably fast even after he waded back into the flood. For some reason the water did not seem so frightening, not even as it closed around his chest and its weight forced him to slow down.

His eyes stung from the gritty sludge which splashed up, and his lamp lit up no more than three feet of black roof and even blacker water, but as he rounded a gentle curve he recognised the straight stretch of main road which led to the submerged tub with its big charge. The channel where John would blow the smaller charge was about forty yards away.

John squeezed himself down behind the blast wall and fingered the fuse.

'Work, damn you. Work!' He fired the charge.

There was a slight delay, then his world exploded.

He gasped as the blast shoved the air out of the channel. His lamp went over him like a comet leading a trail of fire he knew was blazing oil. He felt it burn him, then suddenly it was dark. The blackest darkness he had ever known. And airless. He choked on dust.

Then the blackness gave way to white light and mad
shadows and noises that chased him.

Yards away Edward felt the air move and went deaf. An
immense flare lit up the entire main road.

One moment the rocks covering the tub were where he
had left them, the next they had disappeared under water.

The flare died. The tunnel went dark.

Then it lit with brilliant white light. The glare clung to
the roof, intensified, seemed to contract, expanded again
and charged at him, screaming. He ducked under the
water but the water did not want him. It lifted him up and
threw him backwards. His lamp had gone but he could see
a huge torch burning where the tub had been.

Suddenly, over his deafness, he heard the second
explosion.

The tunnel flared again and he saw the iron wheels and
axles from the tub blown back up against the tunnel roof. One
of the wheels broke off its axle and skimmed towards him.
A flat stone bouncing across a pond. Coming right at him.

He saw a wave rise up as the wheel came down but he
did not hear anything as the two touched. And he did not
feel anything, not instantly; the pain seemed to come
moments later and by that time he was swallowing water
and trying to stay balanced as his shoulders were shoved
back and his legs pulled forwards.

He splashed about in the dark, blind, trying to swim,
always colliding with rock, and then there was something
pulling at him and a light in his eyes.

Then there was nothing.

Except the loud gurgling roar of the devil laughing.

The world she thought had stopped started violently. She
heard the explosion, muffled, a long way away, but still
frightening.

She sat up sharply. Stood up as the crowd took in one
united breath and held it, waiting.

Elizabeth was high enough on the steps to see everything that happened in and around the yard; how people edged together, reached out hands and touched each other, not knowing or caring who they held. How quickly the nurses moved towards the lamp room and the way the policemen all stood up and put on their helmets. She saw the reporters take out their notebooks and pocket watches and she flinched when a flashgun lit up the yard as one of the photographers made a permanent record of the moment.

Everyone had been waiting for the first explosion, but they had still been surprised when it came.

The second explosion was a total shock.

The steps trembled. The ground heaved, or seemed to. Horses shied and whinnied and were immediately quietened by jacketless drivers.

The extraction fans sucked out the smell of the explosive and sent a column of dust into the evening air. The dust settled back on to the shoulders and heads of those who waited. No one brushed it off. It was the only thing that had come up from underground which seemed to unite those on the surface with those below.

The winchman's telegraph clanged and diverted the tension for a moment. Surely now there would be some news.

A fresh team of rescuers, men already in the lamp room waiting for orders to go down, began to shuffle along the walkway to the cage.

'What's happened, Lizzie?' a woman yelled, expecting her to know.

'They did say they were going to blast,' she said, trying to keep calm as she thought about the explosives Edward had said they were keeping in reserve. 'I'll go inside and let you know when there's more news.'

She ran up to the lamp room but no one could tell her anything more than not to worry.

'Can I go down?' She had never been underground but

now seemed to be the right time to do it.

'No, lass.' The supervisor shook his head. 'You'd only get in the way, and they'll send news up here as soon as they can.'

She knew he was right, and turned to leave but he called her back. 'Miss Forrester, there's a spare chair in here if you'd like to stay. And we might be grateful for your help, later. We've got help for the injured men, like, but there's no one here for the women and I reckon there's going to be a few lasses who'll need comforting before the night's through.'

'Of course.' She sat down, and immediately felt closer to the men working in the dark tunnels hundreds of feet below her.

The supervisor sent someone off to bring her a cup of tea but the girl brought soup instead. Soup and a hunk of bread. She realised that she had not eaten since breakfast. Rose and Charlotte would be on their ship by now, steaming off the coast without any idea of what had happened. Was happening.

'Miss Forrester, wake up.' She came to slowly. She was still sitting in the hard upright chair and did not remember falling asleep, but the girl who had brought her soup instead of tea was shaking her shoulders. 'Some of the men are coming up, Miss Forrester. They'll know what's been happening.'

'Thank you.' She smiled and the girl smiled back.

'You were having a lovely sleep, miss. Been out for two hours.' She nodded towards the clock and Elizabeth saw that it was ten minutes past ten. It was dark outside but the lamp room was well lit with lamps which popped and spluttered and smelled, and reminded her of evenings at home in Albert Street.

She heard the cage lock into place and the gate swing up, then the dragging sound of men's boots scuffing along the gantry. She watched the lamp room supervisor open the door and a big, tired man heave himself inside, half carrying a man with a bad head wound. A nurse took the injured man away for treatment and moments later all the nurses seemed busy as more men were brought in, some on stretchers. She stood up and offered the big man the chair. He sat down heavily and she could see through the black crust on his face that he was exhausted. She recognised him but did not know his name.

'What's happening down there?' she asked.

'Mr Laybourne blasted a big hole into the floor of the main road and shifted the flood all right. Water just started to pour away, so I was told. Anyway, by the time we got down there the water was dropping real fast. Like water down a plug hole, but the blast must have loosened the roof because another section had caved in and we were clearing that when more came down on top of us. I got five dead and twenty-one injured. Nine of them bad. And I still got ten missing.'

She did not know what to say. It did not seem right to ask if John and Edward were safe, not outright, so she stated what seemed to be obvious. 'So we're no nearer to clearing the original fall, then?'

'That's right.' The man peered at her. 'You're Elizabeth Forrester, aren't you? I didn't recognise you at first.'

'Aye.'

'Your brother Edward's safe, miss. He's been hurt but it can't be too bad because he's trying to get through to Mr Laybourne.'

Suddenly she was crying, 'Trying to get through to him?'

'Aye, Miss Forrester. Mr Laybourne might be trapped in a side channel that collapsed, or he might have got sucked out when he blew the hole. Don't reckon much on his chances meself, like.'

More injured men filed into the room, dirty, bloody, bandaged; some of them moaning with pain, but, she thought, at least they were free and alive.

'What's happened, Lizzie?' Annie Darling had come back to wait for Billy. 'Are you all right?'

'John Laybourne's missing. Trapped. Maybe dead.' She knew Annie would not understand fully what that meant to her. 'It seems the flood's going down but there's been another collapse and several men have been killed. A lot injured.'

'So they haven't got through to the face yet?'

'No. Nowhere near it.'

'Someone ought to tell the . . .' Annie nodded towards the women crowding the steps and the yard. 'Shall I?'

'No Annie, I'll do that.' It was better to have something to do.

She walked to the top of the steps and coughed to clear her throat. The nearest women told others to be quiet and within moments the crowd was silent. No one spoke as she explained what had happened. The silence lasted for several minutes more, then a cage clanged into position and men started to carry bodies out and along the landing to the lamp room. Women pushed up the steps and closed around the injured men and the crushed bodies.

She heard a woman scream, 'My boy last time. Now he's killed my man.'

Suddenly everything changed. A sullen rumbling swept through the once-docile crowd and in seconds the rumbling grew to an angry roar. A group of men surged towards the manager's office.

She was still standing at the top of the lamp room steps and could see right over the mass of people and through the manager's office window. There were lamps left alight, but the office was empty. Laybourne had gone. Then she noticed Henry Wright standing on the edge of the crowd, his bandaged arm held awkwardly in the large white sling. He was shouting but there was too much noise for her to hear what he was shouting.

Someone threw a stone. It smashed the office window and the noise of glass breaking seemed to ignite fury in the crowd. A small group of men rushed the steps leading up to the office and a scuffle started as the policemen tried to stop them; then the whole crowd seemed to heave itself towards the office steps and the police disappeared in a sea of ragged jackets and caps and shawls.

Three men clambered up the girders which supported the steps, kicked the office door down and rushed inside. Seconds later the office was ablaze. The crowd cheered, stopped fighting with the policemen and stood back to catch the arsonists as they leapt down from the landing. Flames flicked out through the broken window and door, then seconds later the remaining glass exploded and showered shards over the crowd.

She thought that if Sebastian Laybourne had still been there the crowd would have lynched him, or burned him alive. She shuddered. It was an awful thought.

More awful because at that moment she would not have cared if they had.

Suddenly, for no obvious reason, everything went quiet and everyone pulled back. Some of the policemen staggered upright, waving their long sticks to protect their injured colleagues. Flashes showed that the newspaper men were taking more photographs.

Someone called for fire buckets or a pump.

The crowd's fury was already spent. She was surprised to see how fast the mood changed and within minutes a score of men had formed a chain to pass buckets up to the office, and women were helping the injured policemen to reach the nurses.

'Sounds like someone laughing, Edward,' Adam said, and Edward listened to the mocking sound echoing along the main road and knew what he meant.

'Aye, man. I thought it was the devil come to get me.' But it was the sound of running water. The flood had gone, and when he saw the size of the hole that had been blasted in the tunnel floor he understood why the water had drained off so fast and very nearly sucked him away, too.

The hole was the full width of the main road and eight or nine feet long. He stepped on to the simple bridge that had been thrown across the hole, held his lamp low and peered down the opening but he could not see the bottom, even if it had one. Water was pouring out from the rocks which littered the tunnel floor beyond the hole, and cascading into the opening like a waterfall; and the hole just seemed to swallow it all, throwing back nothing more than an empty, echoing noise.

'How long was I out?' he asked, and Adam frowned.

'That's the third time you've asked me, Edward. I don't know, but no more than seconds, I should think. You still had enough wits to be hanging on to a prop when I found you, and I was only just round the corner when the charges blew . . .'

'No, I mean the second time. After you found me.' He half remembered Adam finding him minutes after the explosion and carrying him back to the shaft, but then he had passed out and he needed to know how much time had gone by.

'Two, three hours.' Adam held up his lamp. 'My opinion, my friend, is that you should go up top. I reckon you're still a little concussed.'

'No!' He stood on the bridge and thought he could see where the entrance to the channel had been. 'Reckon he's in there, Adam?'

'I don't know, Edward. There's a good chance he was washed out when the water drained away.'

He turned and saw Trenchard, filthy dirty and sagging with exhaustion.

'How long do you reckon before we get through the original fall?' he asked, concerned that so much time had gone by without anyone getting any nearer his father and brothers and the other trapped men.

'Glad you're on your feet, Edward.' He thought Trenchard looked surprised to see him. 'We'll never reach the face if we try to shift all the rock that's collapsed, so we're trying to tunnel our way over the top of the fall. I reckon we'll reach the original fall in about three hours if we don't have any more accidents. I'll let you know when we get through.'

'Aye, thanks, but what about Mr Laybourne?'

Trenchard came across the bridge. 'We reckon the first blast cleared the channel enough to weaken the floor in the main road, and then the tub with the big charge just fell through and detonated itself on impact. The blasts must have made the channel collapse. I don't reckon John Laybourne stood much of a chance, Edward.'

'Aye.' He stared at the fallen entrance and wondered what was beyond the jumble of rocks. 'No one's tried to get through, yet?'

'No, Edward, we've been concentrating on the main road and the men trapped near the face.'

'I'll do it.' He saw Adam and Trenchard look at each other and guessed what they were thinking. 'I'm all right now, so just bring me some timber and a couple more men and I'll get going. I'll take care of this, Mr Trenchard, while you concentrate on getting through to the main fall.'

'Don't be a fool, Edward,' Adam said bluntly, 'you're in no condition to dig through that lot.'

'Watch me.' He pulled a chunk of rock out of the fall that blocked the channel entrance and handed it to Adam. 'If you have to, then you can pull me out.'

He did not wait for Adam or Trenchard to agree. He took off his shirt and started to lift the largest pieces of rock and coal out from the blockage, and within five minutes he was able to work in the space he had cleared.

Perhaps John was dead, but what if he were still alive?

His head pounded as if it were ready to burst and his brain seemed to be loose in his skull, but he worked steadily, grateful that the dust and the dim light stopped Adam from seeing how ill he felt. He had to be the one who broke through the blockage. He had to be the one who found John, if he was there. It was the only way he could repay him for the risk he had taken. The only way he could face Lizzie. The only way he could silence all the demons that were shouting at him. He tunnelled forwards, away from the noise of the devil laughing, lying on his belly, clearing an opening two feet high under the firm roof. The air was hot and the dust stuck to his sweaty skin, made his eyes gritty and his nose and throat sore, but he ignored it, prised away more rocks and passed them back for Adam to clear.

'Come out for a rest, Edward,' Adam called. 'You've been going for more than an hour, boy.'

'I'm all right for a bit longer,' he grunted back, and shoved back a large rock to prove he could carry on.

Suddenly there was a cool draught.

'Anyway, we're almost through,' he said quietly.

One large rock, too heavy for him to pull, stopped him. He tried to judge whether or not it was supporting the remaining rocks hanging above his head, and decided that the only way to find out was to try to shove it forward. He paused, shoved, felt the rock move a little, and shoved some more. The rock shifted, stones rattled down on his head, the roof groaned; and air moved past him. He pushed a few rocks forward and heard them roll away.

The channel had not collapsed. John might still be safe.

'John! Can you hear me?'

No answer. He pushed away more stones to clear an opening big enough to crawl through, reached for his lamp and scrambled forward until he was clear of the fall and standing in a rock-filled depression he guessed was all that was left of the hole where the first charge had been laid.

'John! Where are you?'

He clambered over a mound of rocks and found John lying behind what was left of the blast wall.

'Oh Christ!' He understood the situation immediately.

A huge slab of stone had been blown out of the roof and one end was resting on what was left of John's left leg. The other end of the rock rested on the blast wall six inches above John's head.

He hesitated, then reached under the rock and placed his fingers either side of John's throat. There was a pulse but it was very weak.

He moved his lamp along the rock; it was impossible to move it enough to pull John free.

There was only one solution. He scrambled back to the opening. 'Adam, get a surgeon down here quick, and tell him to bring a saw. John's bleeding badly. His leg's crushed and trapped by a big rock. There's only one way to get him out and we'll have to move fast.'

The night was just a little lighter.

Elizabeth stood near the bottom of the lamp room steps. Someone had told her that John was still alive, but he needed a surgeon. That was all they knew.

She clasped her hands tight together, thumb knuckles pressed hard against her breast bone. Her neck and back and legs were rigid. Her only movement was a metronomic sway as she moved forward, then back, then forward again, boots clunking on rounded cobbles, the sound marking off the seconds that bridged her past and her future.

Someone had wrapped a grey woollen shawl around her and it was still over her shoulders, its long fringe adding a measure of grace to her movements as it trailed forward and back again, forward and back again; following her never-ending, never-relenting movement.

The cage gate clanged open and grated across the platform and a nurse and two men carried a stretcher towards the lamp room. She rushed up the steps and saw the stretcher but Doctor Roberts grabbed her and pulled her away.

She heard him explaining what had happened but the words did not mean anything. All she could think of was that the doctor was much shorter than her and that he was covered in coal dust as though he were a miner. Then she saw the bloodstains on his tweed jacket and waistcoat.

'I'm sorry,' he apologised. 'I didn't have anything to cover my clothes with.'

'What's happened, Doctor?'

'Well, your brother Edward's battered but all right. He's still working down there. Insisted on staying down until he found your father and brothers.'

'Thank you. But John? John Laybourne? Is he all right?'

The doctor half turned as the stretcher was carried past them and down the steps into the yard.

'He's alive but only just.'

'Will he live?' She spoke very quietly; afraid of the answer.

The doctor shrugged. 'I can't say. He's very badly injured.'

She ran after the men carrying the stretcher and saw John's bandaged head. Then she saw how flat the covering blanket lay where his left leg should have been. Doctor Roberts followed her and she looked at him and understood the grimace he gave her.

'Can I go with him?'

'If you don't get in the way. But I think the best thing you can do is tell Mr and Mrs Laybourne what's happened.'

'I don't know where his father is and his mother's not in town. Left this morning, with Rose.' She reached towards John's bandaged head but the doctor pulled her hand away.

'He's very badly burned, my dear. Very badly burned.'

'I see.' She felt inordinately calm now that she understood better. 'Is that why you think he . . .'

She couldn't bring herself to say the awful words.

The doctor nodded.

Edward guessed he was standing near the place where he had last seen George Willis. It frightened him to think how fast everything had happened; how much danger could build up without anyone knowing about it.

The roof was much higher now because what had once been the roof had collapsed. The rocks had fallen and left a natural dome above the shambles below.

Water was still pouring through the roof but much of it flowed along the main road until it drained down the hole John had blasted. The rest flowed behind the rock fall, and some of it, at least, drained back through the rocks and joined the torrent in the hole.

But it was impossible to know how bad the flood was behind the rock fall, whether or not the water had reached the face. He thought about his father and brothers, imagined them crouching back there in the dark, sweating in an airless tunnel, watching the water rising. He remembered how he felt months ago, waiting in the dark, the water creeping up his body, and the feeling of total fear which made him critically alert to everything, every sound, every smell, every sensation.

He shook himself to throw off the feeling. 'Mr Trenchard, any sounds from the other side of the fall?'

'No.' Trenchard looked uneasy. 'But we've only just cleared a way over the top and we can see the flood's still high on the other side.'

'Up to the roof?'

Trenchard shook his head. 'Not quite but we'll know better once we've cleared enough of the rocks to drain more water off.'

That could take hours when seconds might be critical. 'I'm not waiting, Mr Trenchard. I'll go through now.'

'But there could be gas, the roof could be loose and . . .'

'I'm going, Mr Trenchard. I'll need two fresh lamps.'

'No, Edward. You're not thinking straight, man.' Trenchard gripped his arm.

'I said I'll need two fresh lamps, Mr Trenchard.'

'Make that four,' Adam said. 'I'm going with him.'

* * *

The water shocked him.

It was bitter cold and it reached up to his chest.

'Edward?' Adam yelled from somewhere behind.

'I'm all right, man. And you?'

'Don't you worry about me, boy. You just make sure you don't rush on too fast and prove Mr Trenchard right,' Adam shouted back.

'Someone call my name? We're right behind you both,' Trenchard yelled, and there were scrambling sounds as Trenchard led other men over the fall.

At least the rescue was moving after all this time.

Someone had given him a jacket to keep him warm, but it was a nuisance now he was in the water so he took it off without dousing his lamps, and felt the flood pressing against his bare skin. He shuffled forward, his head hurting from the blow he had taken, his arms aching from the effort of holding up the lamps, and his legs and body aching from the chilling water.

Apart from water and floating debris the road was empty.

'This is Edward Forrester,' he shouted into the gloom. 'Is there anyone there? Anyone?'

His voice rolled down the tunnel and came back to him. There was no answer. Just a murmuring echo and the slopping sound the water made as he pushed forward. And the sound of Adam bellowing details about the condition of the tunnel so that Trenchard knew what his men had to do to make it safe.

He pushed on for half an hour or more, shouting out every few minutes, but no one called back. He was disappointed there was no one there but not too worried. The tunnel had been flooded up to the roof but the main road climbed as it neared the coal face. There was still a chance that everyone had moved back as the flood rose and still a chance the water had not risen enough to flood the face. Still a chance of finding everyone safe, if they had enough air to breathe. The water inched up above his shoulders, then began to slide down his body so gradually that he did not notice the level was falling. It was not until he realised he did not have to hold the lamps up so high that it occurred to him that the flood was back around his chest. He pushed forward, moving slowly but as fast as he could, his feet feeling for the rails to guide him.

'This is Edward Forrester. Is there anyone there?'

No answer.

The water was down to his belly when he found the first drowned men. The corpses floated face down. As he reached them their dead hands brushed against his bare stomach and made him vomit. He turned away, spewed up bile and some of the water he had swallowed, then steadied himself for what he had to do.

He held both lamps in one hand and lifted each man's head up to look at the face, preparing himself for the sight of his father or brothers and feeling both relieved and guilty when he did not see them.

'Bodies.' He yelled back a warning to Adam and the other men who were following on.

More bodies and a dead pony, still harnessed to an overturned tub. He did not know how far he had walked but now the flood was around his knees and wading was easier.

He stepped over another corpse laying face up and then his feet lifted above the floodwater. A few minutes more and he was completely clear. He began to run, not bothering to check whether the props were still solid enough to hold up the roof; only concerned to reach the face. Adam ran alongside him.

They stopped. The roof had come down and blocked the road completely.

They were already scrabbling at the rocks when the rest of the rescuers caught up with them.

The men worked fast, passing the boulders backwards and stacking them out of the way.

'Reckon they could have brought this lot down to stop

the flood rising?' someone asked hopefully.

'Possible. Looks a bit like that,' someone else answered.

He prayed that was what had happened. Prayed that it had worked; but as the debris was cleared more water gushed through the rocks and the men had to stop work for a few moments as they heard the unsupported roof above and beyond the fall groan under its own weight.

'Get some more props in,' he yelled. 'Quick!'

There were enough broken props lying around to shore up the dome which had formed above the fall and as soon as there was room he climbed up into the gap which had been cleared. 'There's still a lot of water in here. Clear some more of the fall.'

He hauled boulders back to the men who were working behind him. Adam worked with him. The roof groaned again and cracked.

'Back away!' he yelled and dived after Adam as slabs of rock dipped.

The rocks crashed down. Dust and stones filled the air and closed down the light from the lamps.

'That were close, boy,' Adam said, and he heard the nervousness in the big man's voice. 'I thought we'd had it then, Edward.'

'Pray, Adam.' He touched Adam's shoulder. 'Pray for us and the men who're stuck behind that lot.'

'I've been doing that ever since I came down, boy.'

'I just hope He can hear you, Adam,' he said earnestly.

'He can hear me, all right, Edward. You and I wouldn't be here now if He couldn't.'

He might have argued if the circumstances had been different but he started shifting rock instead.

It took nearly two hours to clear a way through.

He was still working at the front and he was the first to drop down into the flood on the far side. The water reached his waist.

'Clear it!' he yelled back. 'The flood's only up to my belly. Clear it! Clear it! Quick!'

He heard one of the men accuse him of panicking, and Adam defend him. 'No, he's very scared, but he's still all right. Do as he says.'

Adam was right, he was very scared. Scared of what he might find now he was that close to the face.

'Is there anyone here?' he screamed desperately, and the foul air made him cough.

And he found another body.

The water was sinking lower and he began to run, stumbling over hidden equipment or rocks but always managing to keep his lamps high.

'Anybody alive?'

'Over here, man!'

He stopped. He was not sure whether the voice was ahead or behind him.

'Over here,' the unseen voice repeated. 'Three of us.'

He held his lamps high and saw a ledge which had been cut out as an equipment store. 'Are you all right?'

'We're alive.' A man raised an arm.

'Better than some,' he said, and asked immediately, 'How far to the face?'

'Couple of hundred yards. Roof's loose, though.'

The roof groaned as if to emphasise the warning.

'Anyone alive up there?'

'Don't know,' the man said and lowered himself from the ledge.

The roof groaned again and suddenly Adam was beside him. 'Careful, Edward. Sounds as if it's ready to fall.'

'Maybe,' he said and they looked at each other for a moment, nodded simultaneously, and rushed on, panting because of the effort and the stale air.

The flood was only knee-deep but he could feel the current as the water drained away through the last blockage. He splashed through it as fast as he could, Adam right behind him.

'Anyone else alive?' he yelled as he ran.

'Aye. Ten of us here.'

'Three more over here.'

'More of us up here.'

He stopped some men who were coming down from the top of a small dam that had been made from coal turned out of tubs. 'Anyone seen Josh Forrester and his sons?'

The men shook their heads.

'The face? What's it like?'

The men shrugged, but none of them seemed able to speak.

Suddenly the tunnel seemed crowded with men who had survived and others who had come to rescue them. He pushed himself on, yelling for his father and brothers. He saw Adam stop to talk to a few men but he did not stop; it was more important to reach the face.

CHAPTER 21

'Miss Forrester, are you sure you don't know where Mr Laybourne might be?' Doctor Roberts seemed unable to understand that she honestly could not help him find John's father.

'No, Doctor. I've sent a messenger to the manor, but he's not there. And I don't know how to contact Mrs Laybourne, or even if it's possible to contact her before she reaches London in a few days' time.' She looked around the doctor's office and noted, ironically, that most of the pictures hung on the walls were of ships under sail.

'Is there anything they could do that I can't?'

'Yes, Miss Forrester, there is.' Doctor Roberts rubbed his hands hard against his face. 'John Laybourne is a very important man, he's the heir to the Laybourne Estates, and he's very ill. I need to operate on him and carry out certain treatments which may or may not save his sight. Even his life. But I've treated injuries like this before, as an army surgeon, and I know the risks. I don't want to take them without his parents' agreement.'

'You're scared of being blamed if it goes wrong?' It seemed incredible that the doctor was willing to wait for permission before trying to save John's life.

'Yes, Miss Forrester. I'm very tired and not even sure if I'm capable at the moment.'

'Isn't there anyone else you could ask for advice, another professional opinion?' she suggested.

'No, sadly. There's no one else experienced enough to help.'

'Then you must do what you think is right, Doctor Roberts. I'm sure John's father won't thank you for letting his son die without even trying to save him.' She pointed out the simple truth, and added, 'You didn't ask permission before you cut his leg off. If you're not going to treat him now you've got him here, then you might as well have left him to die in the mine.'

'Perhaps it might have been better if I had, Miss Forrester. He'll be a cripple for the rest of his life, possibly a blind cripple, and he'll certainly be disfigured, very ugly, I imagine. That's the best he can expect, if he lives.' He stood up and walked across to an oil painting of troops resting after a battle. 'He was a good-looking man, very active. Possibly he would rather be left to die than be saved and forced to spend the rest of his life as some sort of monster, Miss Forrester.'

'You don't know him very well, Doctor, if you think that,' she said.

'The man we brought up from the mine, Miss Forrester, isn't the same man who went down. The same body, true, or at least some of it, but a different mind.' He tapped the painting. 'Miss Forrester, I spent years as an army surgeon and I've seen how serious injuries change men, believe me. I've seen too much, too many men who lost the will to live when they saw how bad their injuries were. And I've seen strong men who fought back through all the pain the

injuries, operations and treatment gave them, who
recovered from the most awful injuries only to succumb to
drink or suicide or go mad later, when they found out just
how the world and the people in it treated them.'

She saw the pain in the doctor's face and began to
understand his dilemma, but if there was a chance to save
John she wanted it taken; she would worry about the
consequences later. 'I think I understand what you're
saying, Doctor, but I know John. I know he wouldn't want
to run away from a fight, no matter how much pain he
suffered. I promise you, if you can stop him dying, I'll take
care of him for the rest of his life. You won't regret helping
him, I can assure you of that, so please try. Please!'

Her sudden outburst and the tears that followed
embarrassed her and she could see that the doctor was
embarrassed, too.

'Forgive me, Miss Forrester, but that's an easy promise
to make, and I know because I've heard a hundred women
promise the same. What you say in an emotional moment,
and what you are able to do year in, year out, day after day
as your life ticks away, might be two different things.
Anyway, I don't know how you can make such a promise.
You're not his mother, his sister, or even his fiancée. He's
engaged to Miss McDougall, isn't he?'

'They are engaged, yes.' She wished her own
relationship with John was clearer, public, then perhaps
the doctor would listen to her. 'Doctor, if John's fiancée
asked you to operate, would you do so?'

'Probably.'

'Then, if we can get a message to her, a telegraph
message, and she replies the same way, would that do?'

'I think so, Miss Forrester, if you can arrange it.'

She could arrange it. The Laybournes and the
McDougalls owned the railway between them, they both
owned mines, and the mines' and the railway telegraph
were all connected; John had explained it all to her. She
could have a message sent from the mine; it would be

public and might shock Lillian when she learned about John's accident, but at least it should get results.

The telegraph transmitter was in an office alongside the railway siding, a few yards from the winch room. The operator listened as the message he had sent was played back to him, confirmed it was correct and signed off.

'All done, Miss Forrester.' He sat back in his chair and looked at her, and she thought he looked a little like her brother Paul. 'Pardon me for saying so, Miss Forrester, but you look worn out. Why don't you sit down here and get some rest. I'll let you know as soon as we get a reply from Miss McDougall.'

'Thank you, I think I will.'

She had just sat down when she heard a bell ring over in the winch room, then a shout from the winch operator followed by more shouts from other men.

'What's happening?' she asked, nervous and frightened again.

'They've broken through the blockage,' the telegraph operator said quietly, then urgently, 'They've broken through and found men alive!'

'Oh God!' she yelled. Perhaps her father and brothers were all right. 'I'm going to the lamp room. Can you let me know when you hear?'

'Of course, miss.'

She ran into the yard and up the lamp room steps. The supervisor told her that the first survivors were being brought up in a few moments so she ran on to the gantry to see who they were.

Down in the yard the crowd was silent, expectant. The police guard had been doubled to protect the mine buildings against any more damage but it was clear that the people who were waiting had more important things on their minds and the policemen looked relaxed as they sat on the office steps, their helmets once again held on their laps. The newspaper reporters had moved away from the shadows and into positions which gave them good views of whatever happened next. One man with a camera mounted on a tripod stood under the lamp room steps and photographed the waiting crowd.

She saw Prudence Wright and called out, 'How's Nancy?'

'Stopped bleeding. Weak and sleeping a lot,' Pru called back. 'Henry's sitting with her a bit so I could come here.'

The winding wheels started to turn and cables gave out long metallic groans. Nurses and a young doctor moved on to the gantry which joined the lamp room to the platform where the cage would stop. The crowd held its breath. The first cage lifted into sight and the draw bolts which held it at the top of the shaft grated into position. As the gate clanged open the doctor and nurses crowded around the men who were waiting to get out and hid them from the women who were waiting.

Women shuffled forward, anxious to see who had come up. A ripple of angry voices told the doctor and nurses to get out of the way and give a clear view.

One by one the men passed into the lamp room, some on stretchers but most walking and helped by a nurse or a mate. Every man who could turned his face towards the yard to look for his family.

The women who waited stood on tiptoe and stretched their necks to get a glimpse of the men they were longing to see.

'There's my Jim!'

'There's Henry!'

'Thank God I can see him!'

The women did not shout in celebration; they spoke quietly and with consideration for other women who were still waiting and did not yet know if their own men were safe. Nevertheless the words were spoken and once released they floated across the crowd, plumes of relief that gave temporary comfort and hope to everyone who heard them.

No sign of Edward or her father or her other brothers. She stemmed her disappointment and watched the empty cage drop out of sight.

Women who had seen their men eddied through the crowd and gathered at the bottom of the steps as the men walked down. Some were emotional, others were able to contain their feelings, some scolded their husbands for causing such worry; but they all led their men away, secure in their possessiveness and nodding unspoken thanks to the other women who still waited and worried but who said how pleased they were to see this man or that man was safe.

They walked away but then they all gathered by the gates, conscious that they were no longer a part of the waiting sisterhood. The men ignored each other as they held quiet conversations with their own women and one by one they walked back into the crowd to break bad news to women they knew would never see their own men walk down the steps.

She watched it all from her position on the gantry.

The cages kept dropping and rising and more men and bodies came up. A tense, depressed silence spread through the crowd as it divided into three groups: one made up of women whose men were safe, one of those who still waited, and the last, wretched group made up of new widows and saddened mothers and sweethearts.

She felt her heart thump unsteadily, looked down at Pru and saw that she had bitten her bottom lip enough to make it bleed, and decided to go back into the yard and wait with her old friend and neighbour.

She had just joined her when the cables wailed again and pulled another cage back to the surface. The hard clanging of the gate seemed to represent a male world which was separate from the hopes of the waiting women. More men shuffled out along the bridge and she watched them disappear into the lamp room to reappear moments later at the top of the steps.

No sign of Edward or her father or the boys. She felt sick but she stiffened her body and resigned herself to waiting even longer. Her mind drifted back into the protective isolation which had brought her through the night.

She came out of it as someone touched her shoulder. It was Annie Darling, her arm wrapped around Billy.

'Miss Forrester.' Billy smiled at her. 'I didn't want to leave without speaking to you. I heard we've all got Mr Laybourne and your brother to thank for getting us out.'

'Thank you, Billy. That's kind of you,' she said and could not stop the tears from rolling down her face. 'Have you seen Edward, or any of mine or Pru's family?'

He shook his head. 'Sorry, Miss Forrester. It's chaos down there, and I don't know what's happened, not really.'

'Would you like us to wait with you?' Annie offered, but she declined the offer; Annie looked as tired as she felt.

A moment later the man from the telegraph office appeared, waving a scrap of paper and calling to her, 'Miss Forrester, I've got the answer from Miss McDougall.'

Annie hovered as she read the scribbled note. It told the doctor to do all he could to save John and said that Lillian was on her way to Pincote and would arrive by train as soon as possible.

'Billy, Annie' – she hesitated to ask them for help, but she could not wait at the mine and go to the infirmary – 'I need to get this message to Doctor Roberts as quickly as possible but I don't want to leave here. It is very important, possibly a matter of saving John Laybourne's life.'

Billy reached out for the note and looked towards a wagon being loaded with injured men. 'I'll take it, Miss Forrester, it's the least I can do. I'll ride on that wagon, it'll be quicker than walking.'

He started to run towards the wagon which was already trundling towards the gates.

'Make sure you give it to Doctor Roberts, Billy,' she called after him. 'No one else.'

He shouted back something she couldn't hear properly, grabbed the tail gate of the wagon and hauled himself on board as the wagon passed through the gates and turned along Murdock Street. 'Are you sure you wouldn't like me to wait with you?' his mother offered again.

'No, Annie, but thank you. Go home, I think you've probably enough to do.'

She watched as Annie Darling smiled, nodded, turned away and left.

'Must be terrible for her,' Pru said, 'with all she's got to put up with.'

It seemed a very kind thing to say, considering all Pru had to put up with, and it helped her control her own fears.

There was a long delay, maybe an hour or even more, and the next time the cage came up it carried nothing but dead men. The scenes were awful and she shut them out.

There was still no sign of the men she and Pru were waiting for, and worse, no message to say they were alive.

The cage that brought up the dead men stayed up for a long time, locked into position, the second cage sitting below in the porch. There were fewer women waiting now and she and Pru moved forward so that they were only yards away from the raised platform where the second cage would stop when it came up. Then the bolts were pulled, the winding wheels began to spin, the first cage dropped and the second was lifted back and locked into position.

She heard the bolts secure it safely against the platform but she kept her eyes tightly shut. The fear of what she might see overcame her need to know what was happening.

The enormous, uneasy sigh which broke out from above made her look up. Adam Marriott stood head and shoulders above the waiting nurses. He pushed his way through them and leaned over the platform's rail.

'Elizabeth. Pru.' His tone told them what they did not want to know.

Elizabeth stumbled as she walked towards the lamp room steps but Pru held on to her and she saw how rigid her older friend was. Adam was the first man to come down the steps and he reached out and held both her and Pru in his long arms.

'I'm sorry. Ned, Joshua, all the boys too.' He shook as he cried.

'All of them?' she whispered, unsure that she had heard him correctly.

'Apart from Edward. We managed to get to him moments before it all fell in.'

'Where is he?'

Then she saw him at the top of the steps. He was held upright by two nurses and his hands and head were wrapped in blood-soaked bandages, but he was there. And he was alive. She felt unsteady as an immense sense of relief unlocked her tense muscles.

She was aware of a pop and flash as a photographer took a picture.

'Go away and leave us alone.' Adam pushed the newspaper man aside and climbed the steps to help Edward down. 'This man's a hero. If it hadn't been for him and John Laybourne, the owner's son, we'd never have got to all these men you've seen come up. Put that in your papers, but leave these people alone.'

Other men, the last ones to come out alive, let go of their wives and grouped themselves around the reporters, pushing them away.

Adam half-carried Edward down the steps and brought him to her. She put her arms around him. Edward was only half conscious and he did not react to her touch. She held him tight but she did not speak. There were not any words to say.

'He's concussed but he'll be all right once he's had a good sleep,' the young doctor said and told her to take Edward home.

'Come on, my boy.' Adam lifted Edward on to his back

as if he were a bag of coal. 'Let's get you away from here.'

Adam tramped towards the gates and she turned to follow but suddenly caught sight of Pru Wright standing alone.

'Are you coming, Pru?'

'You go on, lass. I'll wait here for Ned and my lads.'

'But Pru . . .' She felt awkward.

'I know lass, I know.' Pru nodded. 'But I've got to see them. I'll wait till they bring them to me. You go on home, Lizzie.'

'No, Pru, I'll wait with you.' She called out to Adam to explain.

'There's no point in waiting,' he said quietly and padded back to where they stood. 'They're not bringing them up, Pru. None of them. They were all dead when we got to the face. The roof collapsed again before we could get them out and now it's not possible to get anywhere near them. At least you've got Henry and Nancy.'

Pru stared and her mouth opened but she did not speak.

'Elizabeth, it's the same for Josh and Simon and Thomas too.' She saw the anguish in Adam's face as he tried to explain. 'Edward found your father. He wanted to bring him out for a proper burial and we almost made it but then the roof caved in. Edward was hurt and it was either him or Josh's body. I couldn't bring both of them, Elizabeth.'

She reached up and softly touched his cheek, her fingers leaving pale marks in the coal grime.

Then Pru began to sob.

'I need to see them again. Need to bury them and know they're safe and they can't be hurt any more!'

She put her arm around Pru's waist and pulled her away.

'They're safe now, Pru. And out of pain.' She wanted to say that they were the lucky ones; for them it was over.

For Pru and herself it had only just begun.

No one spoke as they plodded up the hill. The streets were almost empty and even the housewives who usually gathered in groups around each other's front steps had migrated indoors. There was a strange atmosphere about the back end of town; a mood of desolation, a primeval rawness, as if everyone had retreated into the depths of their caves to lie and lick their wounds. A tangible need for privacy. It was almost as though the whole town had gone to bed and drawn covers over its head to shut out a chill night; but it was noon on a warm summer's day and the atmosphere was unnatural.

It was frightening, explosive.

She saw Henry standing in the front doorway of Pru's house. He was leaning back against the door frame and he did not say anything as Adam carried Edward past him; his eyes were on her and his mother.

'I'm sorry, Henry,' she said and although he still did not speak she saw him gulp and stiffen his face against his emotions.

She followed Pru indoors and told Henry what had happened. Pru sat down in a chair by the fireplace and stared at the wall. She had not spoken one word since her outburst in the yard.

'I'll make some tea, Lizzie,' Henry suggested and she went into the back kitchen to help him.

'How's Nancy?'

'Sleeping, I think. Will you go and have a look at her?'

She felt heavy and exhausted as she climbed the ladder-like stairs and she hoped that Nancy would still be asleep. She could not bear the thought of having to tell her what had happened.

Nancy was asleep, deeply asleep, rolled up in a ball like a small child, and it was shocking to see how pale the girl looked, almost transparent. The room had an awful smell of death about it so she opened up the sash window to let in air before she went back downstairs.

Pru was sitting in her chair, crying silently, tears sheeting down her face and dripping off her chin on to her shawl.

'Tea, Lizzie?' Henry asked but she refused, shrugged him a silent goodbye and patted Pru's shoulder before she left them to their grief.

Adam had undressed Edward, washed him and put him into the bed Josh and Minty had shared for most of their lives.

'I'd best be getting home now,' he said quietly.

'It's too far, Adam.' She held his arms. 'Get some sleep first. There are beds upstairs in the other room.'

He hesitated for a moment before he accepted the offer. She followed him up the stairs, showed him where he could rest, then went into her parents' bedroom.

Edward was tucked up under the covers, already fast asleep. She lay down beside him and listened to him breathing. The sounds coming up from the mine were muted by the heavy afternoon air, and the quiet and her exhaustion put her to sleep.

She woke up several hours later. Adam's snores sawed through the wall and Edward was breathing heavily in his deep sleep, but there was another, faint sound which made her uncomfortable. A thin, whimpering sound. The miserable noise a small child makes. The sound came from next door. It was Pru crying.

She shivered in her own loneliness. She needed comfort and slipped under the blankets to cuddle up against Edward the way she often had when they were children. He turned to face her and she put her arm around him and held him tightly.

Her face rested against his and although a patch of dried blood in his bandage scratched her face she did not pull away. She needed his comfort too much. If John died he would be all she had left.

She woke up, hot and sticky. It was early evening and the air was heavy as if another storm was building up. Adam had left; a note thanked her and said he would call back the next morning. Edward was still sleeping.

She washed, drank some cold water and wrote Edward a note saying that she had gone to the infirmary to see how John was, and she would go on to the manor to collect some fresh clothes but she would be back with him before dark.

The streets were empty, even the children were indoors. She walked to the colliery, hoping to find John's father, but as she approached the yard she saw the gates had been padlocked shut and a dozen armed policemen were standing guard.

'What do you want, miss?' the police sergeant asked.

'I'm looking for Mr Sebastian Laybourne.'

'Are you now? Well you won't find him here.'

She looked past him and saw the burned-out office with black streaks marking the walls where the flames had licked out from the smashed window. The yard was empty, as if the mine had been abandoned.

'Thank you.' She turned to go.

'Wait!' The order was snapped and the sergeant's hand reached through the gates and caught her arm. 'You're Miss Forrester, aren't you? Edward Forrester's sister?'

'Aye.' Pulling her arm free. 'Why?'

'Tell him we don't want any more trouble. We're guarding the workings and there's more of us up at the manor.'

'Why should he want any more trouble? He's had enough already. We all have, Sergeant.'

'Don't get clever with me, miss.' He pulled a newspaper out from his tunic and flicked it open so she could read the headline.

COLLIER THREATENS TO KILL MINE OWNER.

'He's not going to kill anyone, Sergeant. He's at home in bed, half dead himself, and even if he wasn't I can't think he meant what he said. Not Edward.' The words tumbled out but she could see the sergeant did not believe her. 'He said it in the heat of the moment, Sergeant. He wouldn't kill anyone. He's seen enough death in the last few hours.'

'Maybe, but we'll be keeping an eye on him anyway. And guarding Mr Laybourne.'

'I'll tell him when I see him, but now I'm going to the infirmary to see the man he risked his life to save. Mr Laybourne's son, John.'

She walked away, furious that the newspaper had chosen to print Edward's threat instead of recording what he had done to save the trapped men, but not worried that he could be in any real trouble.

When Elizabeth arrived at the infirmary she was told that the doctor had tidied up the stump left when he amputated John's leg, and had cut away the burned and irreparable flesh from his hands and face so the next phase of treatments could begin when John was strong enough. She could not see John because he was unconscious and his wounds were still open, but she was allowed to sit in a corridor outside his room in case he recovered sooner than expected. She waited a long time, but he did not wake up so she gave the nurses a message for him, and arranged to return the next morning.

She was half asleep when she walked out of the infirmary and collided with Mr Hopkins, the Laybournes' coachman.

'Mr Hopkins, what are you doing here?'

'Looking for Mr Laybourne.' The old man looked worried. 'His horse, Saxon, has come home by himself, like. The police found him loose in the grounds, but there's no sign of the master. Where's your brother?'

The obvious implication made her angry and she curtly repeated what she had said to the police sergeant.

'Aye, makes sense.' Hopkins scratched his chin. 'I'm sorry, Miss Forrester, but what with everything people's saying . . .'

She could see how upset he was, but she was worried now. 'What things?'

'It doesn't matter.'

'It might do. Please tell me.'

'Well.' He shuffled and looked awkward. 'The staff reckon there was something between your brother and Miss Rose. That's why she was sent away to marry Mr Belchester.'

It was obvious that there was something else on his mind but although she asked him he denied it, and as she needed his help she did not want to antagonise him.

He had brought a gig into town so she asked him to drive her to the manor to collect her clothes and then return her to Edward. Within a few minutes they were on their way back to the manor. The horse was fractious and when she mentioned it he said it was probably because the animal sensed there was a storm building. They were the only words they spoke on the entire journey.

A loud hammering on the front door woke Edward. His head hurt and he was unsteady as he clambered down the stairs and opened the door to Sergeant Craddock and two constables.

'Edward Forrester?'

'Aye, you know I am, Sergeant.' He did not mean to sound rude or arrogant but he knew the sergeant should remember him from their exchange at the colliery gates a few weeks earlier.

'We've come to take you to the station.'

'The station?'

'The police station,' Sergeant Craddock explained. 'To discuss your threat?'

'What threat?'

'You threatened to kill Mr Laybourne.'

'God, did I?' He could not remember. 'When did I do that?'

'Are you denying it?'

He tried to think. 'I cannot remember it, Sergeant. I cannot even remember getting back home, like. I've been underground ever since the accident and had a couple of bashes on me head.'

'I can see that, Mr Forrester.' The sergeant seemed to mellow. 'You feeling rough, lad?'

'Bloody rough, man, but I'll get meself ready if you can wait a few minutes.' He stumbled as he turned away.

'Steady, lad.' Craddock grabbed him and helped him to a chair. 'We'll have to walk. Do you think you can make it?'

'I'll have to, won't I? If we're going to sort this out, like.'

'Maybe, but you reckon you can't remember making any threats, Mr Forrester?'

He shook his head and winced as the pain hammered him. 'Don't be daft, man. I've just seen enough dead men to last me a lifetime. I don't remember threatening Laybourne, and if I did, well, I didn't mean it.'

He could see the sergeant considering what he had told him.

'All right, Mr Forrester, I believe you and I don't reckon you could do much anyway, at least not just now. But so as you know, like, there's men been brought in from Shearton and from Byford in case there's any more trouble like we had yesterday. There's an armed guard on the mine, and on the manor, mind, so don't you or any of your mates get any ideas. Understand?'

'Aye, Sergeant, I understand, but I won't be causing anyone any trouble. I can promise you that.'

'Good. Don't make me come to get you again.' The policeman walked back to the door, signalled the others to leave, and added quietly, 'I'm sorry to hear about your da and your brothers, son. And I hope you get better soon. Can't have been very pleasant down there.'

'It wasn't,' he said as the door closed.

And it was not much better since he had come up, he thought to himself. He realised he was going to be sick and rushed into the kitchen to vomit into the sink. All he brought up was an acrid grey bile but the effort of vomiting made him feel even weaker. He slumped on to a chair, rested his head on the table and saw Elizabeth's note.

He read it, once he could focus his eyes, and after a few

minutes' rest crawled back upstairs. But he could not sleep. Too much had happened too fast: Rose leaving, Nancy, the accident and everything that went with it, and now he was accused of threatening Laybourne. He wished Elizabeth was still there, he needed to talk to someone who would listen and not make any judgements.

He found himself waiting for the hidden voice to start up again, but it did not, and he realised that at last he felt at ease with himself, almost.

Nancy. He would have to see her and find out how she was. Talk about their future, if they had one. Rose had been a diversion from reality, an impossible dream. Nancy was his future now. He owed her all the loyalty he could muster.

'Mr Forrester.' The call from downstairs roused him from his doze. 'Mr Forrester, are you there?'

'Aye.' He sat up on the bed. 'Who's there?'

'Billy Darling. Mrs Wright sent me.'

He was down the stairs in moments and found Billy standing in the kitchen. 'What's up, Billy?'

'Can you come next door?' He looked anxious.

'Nancy?'

'Can you come? Now?' Billy was already out of the back door and halfway across the yard.

He followed him into Pru's kitchen and saw her and Nancy at the table. They were both pale and dishevelled.

'What's wrong?' He put his hands on Nancy's shoulders and she closed her hands over his. 'Shouldn't you be in bed still?'

'It's Henry.' She sounded shocked. 'He's leading a gang to burn down the manor.'

'Oh Christ! Lizzie's gone back there.' He remembered her note and immediately recalled what the sergeant had said about an armed guard but did not mention any of that to the women.

Nancy looked up at him. 'Can you stop him, Edward? We don't want any more trouble.'

'When did they go?' He tried to think how he could possibly catch them up.

Billy answered, 'Quarter of an hour ago. They went along the Market road. We could get there first if we go over the ridge.'

'We?' He saw Billy was eager to help.

'I can't stop 'em, Mr Forrester, not without you, but I don't reckon you can get there on your own,' Billy said.

Billy was right. Henry would not listen to the boy, and the climb over South Ridge would be hard.

'Please, Edward.' Nancy stood up and looked into his eyes. 'Please. For Ma and me. We don't want any more trouble.'

'Aye, we'll have a try, lass, and afterwards we'll sit down and talk.' He slipped his arms around her waist and hugged her tight to him. 'Now go back to bed and rest. I don't want anything else happening to you. Not after all this.'

Elizabeth was surprised how many policemen were guarding the manor. She counted twelve resting around the lodge and the gates and a further dozen stationed near the manor itself. They all carried pistols in brown holsters strapped over their uniforms, and most also carried cudgels in place of their usual truncheons. None of them looked familiar and she guessed they were the men the sergeant at the colliery said had been brought in from one of the nearby towns.

The officer in charge came over to the gig and asked who she was.

'I'm Elizabeth Forrester, Edward Forrester's sister. I live here.' She noticed the man's confusion. 'You must think my brother's a very determined man if it takes this many of you to protect Mr Laybourne from him.'

'It's not just your brother, miss.' The officer looked embarrassed by her outburst. 'We've been told to watch out for any of the miners who might come up and cause trouble. Like they did at the colliery yesterday.'

'Oh, I see.' She felt foolish that she had been so outspoken. 'But I reckon they've all had enough trouble without looking for any more.'

'Maybe you're right, miss, and I hope you are, but we've been told not to take any chances.'

She nodded and Hopkins drove the gig towards the house. He left it under cover and followed her through the back door into the kitchen. She thought the staff might be hostile towards her because of the way they felt abut Edward, but they had already heard about her father and brothers and were very sympathetic. They were also very concerned about John, and the master who still had not returned.

'I know you all think my brother may have harmed Mr Laybourne' – it was best to bring the matter out into the open – 'but I can assure you that he hasn't. He's either been helping with the rescue underground or with me, and if you saw him you'd realise he's in no condition to hurt anyone, least of all someone as big and strong as the master. He did lose his temper and threaten Mr Laybourne, but the newspaper has distorted the story to make it more dramatic than it really was. He risked his life to save John, and now all he wants is a little peace and quiet. I think all this business with the police is completely unwarranted.'

'Aye.' Hopkins supported her and told the staff what the policemen had said.

She politely refused the meal Cook offered her, arranged for Hopkins to be ready in an hour or so after he had eaten, then went upstairs to her room. Her mind was full of all the things she had to think about and it was not until she had passed Sebastian's study that it occurred to her to try looking inside to see if he was telling the truth about her not resembling his first wife.

She turned back and tried to open his study door but it was locked. His bedroom was next door. She tried the

large brass doorknob, and it turned. She opened the door
slowly in case anyone should hear, stepped inside and
closed the door behind her.

The room was large, even larger than her own room,
but she was more surprised to see it was plushly furnished
in soft, feminine colours, a complete contrast to the decor
she expected. And there on the wall, opposite the foot of
the four-poster bed, she saw the portrait of the first Mrs
Laybourne.

Sebastian had not lied to her: his first wife was fair-
haired, small and delicately beautiful, not at all like her.
But there was something familiar about her.

She studied the portrait closely, looking at the details of
the woman's face and poise. There was a vague similarity
to Charlotte Laybourne, but only vague, and a tendency
towards Lillian McDougall, although the similarities were
only in colouring and bearing. But there was something
else.

She stepped back and leaned against the bed while she
thought; studied the hair, eyes, nose, mouth, hands,
figure, even the jewellery. Nothing helped. Then she
noticed the dress.

It was the dress she had seen on the summer house
bench. She was sure.

Her skin crept. She felt sick.

Sebastian had watched his son make love to her. He had
seen her at her most intimate, and he had let her know.

Her heart beat fast. She felt cold then hot and dirty.
Violated as if Sebastian himself had taken her. She thought
about the way he must have watched them, hiding himself
in the shadows, and the feelings he must have had as he
held her against him when they danced together the
following night. She remembered the way he had
immediately chosen the most revealing dress for her to
order, the feel of his hands against her breasts as he had
used the excuse of fondling his first wife's necklace, his
offer to find her a position away from Pincote; and she

wondered what might have happened that night if Edward
had not arrived to take her away.

Then other things came to mind, almost unnoticed
things that had somehow lodged in her memory: the way
he had steadied her when she used the library steps, his
fingers sliding from her waist under her arms and over the
sides of her breasts. The way she sometimes had to brush
past him because he did not allow enough room, the way
she sometimes found him looking at her. None of the
incidents seemed significant at the time, they were never
frequent enough to be noticed as deliberate.

Suddenly she remembered Edward's warning when he
had first brought her to the manor, and the way she had
dismissed it. Dismissed it only because she trusted the
kindness and generosity Sebastian had shown both her
and Edward, and now she felt betrayed. Both of the
Laybourne men had enjoyed her, just as Edward warned;
John with love and her consent, his father with perversion.

She thought about the way he had spoken to her in the
office when they were alone yesterday, how he had rested
his hands on her shoulders and how his fingers had
brushed her chest.

Then all the other coincidences and odd happenings
began to collect themselves into a sort of logic. Just how
perverted was Sebastian? He had married both his wives
when they were eighteen. He told her she reminded him
of Miss Smith when she was eighteen. Catherine had been
sent away when she was eighteen. Sent away or taken
away from him? Was that why Charlotte was so concerned
to send Rose away? Had Catherine warned her? Then she
remembered what Rose had told her about Miss Smith's
last words. Leave the manor.

She shuddered and decided to pack all her clothes.
Once she had left she was not coming back. Not even as
John's wife. Not unless Sebastian was dead.

She walked to the door and pulled it. It did not open.
She tried the knob furiously. It turned but the door did

not open. Someone had locked it.

She tried again, her sweating hands sliding on the big brass door knob. She used both hands. The lock clicked and the door opened.

It had not been locked, it had simply stuck for a moment, but it was enough to scare her and she ran all the way to her own room, shut the door carefully behind her, then threw herself on her bed and burst into tears.

She cried for John, for her father, her brothers, and for herself. A few weeks ago, the night John asked her to marry him and made love to her, everything had seemed wonderful. But it had not lasted. Everything had started to go wrong the very next morning, when she saw the clothes on the bench.

And now she realised how much she had deceived herself. She had accepted John's explanation that the clothes were really a sleeping gardener's boy because she wanted to believe that was all they were. She did not want to think someone could spoil everything, but she had known. She had known there was something wrong, and she had ignored it because she wanted to.

None so blind as those who will not see, she reminded herself, and cried even harder now she had to admit her own stupidity.

She cried until she could not cry any more and then stood up and dried her eyes. She felt better for shedding the tears, but tired, so tired she wished she had time to sleep before Hopkins took her back to Pincote.

But there was not time.

She emptied all the drawers from the tallboy on to the bed, crossed to the wardrobe and pulled the handles to open it. The doors did not open.

Her heart missed a beat, then she relaxed. She must be tired, she had tried to open the wrong wardrobe, the one that had always been locked and had no keys. She moved to the wardrobe alongside, lifted out her clothes and spread them out on the bed beside her other possessions.

Her bags and her bonnet were stored on the top shelf, she took them down. She moved stiffly, knowing this was the last time she would use her room, wondering what the future held.

It was not until she had started packing that she realised she had not washed properly or changed her clothes since first thing the previous morning. Her eyes fell on the fluffy white towels that hung close to the washstand, the scented soap, the first luxuries she had enjoyed when she came to the manor.

Hopkins would not be ready yet, and it made sense to wash and change before she left. She locked the bedroom door, undressed, folded her dirty clothes into her bag, and washed herself all over, the cold water refreshing her, the scented soap pleasing her, the soft towels drying her without scratching.

She left the wet towel on its rack and padded back to her bed, ready to dress.

Then she heard him.

'Not yet, Elizabeth. We haven't played our game yet.'

A man parodying a child's voice but she knew it was Sebastian Laybourne.

She did not know what to do, and because the room was empty she did not think he could see her, did not think of covering herself.

'Are you ready to play? I hope you are,' the voice whined.

'What game is that?' She guessed it was dangerous to encourage him but it might be even more dangerous to break his mood.

'You know the one. Don't tease me.'

'I'm not teasing you, really. I don't know which game it is.' She was listening hard, trying to decide where he was, edging towards the bed and her clothes.

'You're Isobel and I'm my father. You remember.'

'I don't think we've played that before. What do we do?'

'I'm me and you're Isobel. You're cuddling me in your

bed, then my father comes in and locks me in the wardrobe
and I watch you and him through the keyhole.'

'You want me to lock you in the wardrobe?'

'No! Don't be silly. I'll be my father. In bed with you.'

'Cuddling?'

'No. You remember, don't you? I make you take all your
clothes off and you scream and I hit you until you stop.'

'I don't think I like that game, Sebastian.'

'You do. Everyone does.'

'Everyone? Who have you played it with?'

'Isobel, of course.'

'Who's she?'

'You know Isobel.'

'Let's pretend I don't. It's a new part of the game,
Sebastian.' Anything to keep him talking until Hopkins
came up to collect the bags.

'But I don't want to change anything. I like it as it is.' No
reaction to being called Sebastian.

'You'll like this, Sebastian. I'll ask you who else you've
played it with and you'll tell me. Then you can tell me
exactly what you, your father, did to them and you'll enjoy
it much more. I promise. You'll see.'

'Promise? I don't want to spoil it.'

'I promise you, Sebastian. You'll enjoy it much more.'
Anything to keep him talking while she reached for her
clothes and dressed.

'Oh, yes, but don't dress. I like looking at you.'

Good God, he could see her. 'It'll be better if I put some
clothes on.'

'Promise?'

'I promise.' Anything to keep him away.

'But you'll stay near the bed.'

'If you want me to.' Promise him anything to keep him
away. 'Who's Isobel?'

'Mrs Jarret's daughter.'

'And who's Mrs Jarret?' Dressing quickly.

'My governess.'

'And how old is Isobel?' She knew before she asked.

'She's eighteen.'

'And how old are you?'

'I'm ten years old, almost.'

'And you went to bed with her?'

'When I was frightened. She used to make the monsters go away and show me the way to the light. She was the only one who could stop the bad dreams from coming back.'

'And your father raped her while you watched.'

'Oh yes.'

'And you enjoyed watching?'

'Oh yes.'

'And did he rape Miss Smith?'

'No. She was different. He never hurt her. She was special.'

'Why didn't he hurt her? Why was she special?'

'I kept her secret. I liked her, kept her safe. Away from him.'

'Who else, Sebastian?'

'I can't remember.'

'Catherine?'

'Oh yes, Catherine. She was naughty. She wouldn't play properly. She just cried and asked for her mother.'

She felt sick. 'Did her mother come to her?'

'No she'd left us. She went to sleep and we had to put her away. In the ground.'

He was mad, totally mad.

'Who else, Sebastian? Who else did you play with?'

'Willow. You look just like Willow. You've got hair like Willow. I've been looking for her, but her mother said she's gone away, too.'

'Into the ground, Sebastian?'

'Yes. Into the ground.'

She pulled on a stocking, only one more stocking to go and she was fully dressed. 'Who else? Rose?'

There was a long pause. 'No. Not Rose.'

The voice had changed but she noticed it too late. The wardrobe door that had always been locked swung open and he was there, and behind him she could see through into the schoolroom.

'No, I sent Rose away,' he said in his normal voice. 'I had to, before my father could hurt her.'

'But your father's dead.' She moved away, ready to run, fight, anything.

'He comes back. He's here now.'

'No, he isn't.'

'He's inside me. He makes me do things.'

'He's dead, Sebastian. He can't make you do anything.'

'He can. You don't understand. He can do anything he wants to. He told me that.'

There was nothing to gain from trying to delay him any longer. Hopkins would not be able to help even if he came in time.

But the house was surrounded by policemen. If she could get to the window and smash it they might hear and come to investigate.

'You were correct, Elizabeth, it is better this way but now I want you the way I saw John have you.' He lunged.

She jumped away from him, on to the bed and across it. Her foot slipped on a loose rug. She slammed into the tallboy, reached for the window beyond it.

She felt him grab her hair and pull. She flailed at the window and missed. Grabbed at the tallboy. He yanked her hair and she was on her knees but hanging on to the tallboy. It tipped. A candle holder thudded on to the floor. She let go of the tallboy, grabbed the candle holder and threw it at the window. Heard glass shatter.

Then she was on the floor, being dragged by her hair. Saw her bag, grabbed it and swung it at his legs.

He laughed. A kick across her knuckles opened her hand. The bag fell away and its buckle cut her face as he dragged her across the plank floor.

She clawed and kicked without reaching him. He jerked her hair, laughed again.

'Don't. Sebastian! Please.' It was an instinctive plea but she knew it was wasted.

She was spun around on the floor, then lifted and thrown. The bed stopped her, and knocked the breath out of her. Then he dropped on top of her and flattened her before she could breathe again. She gasped for air as his chest covered her face.

'He's ten years old, you whore.' He moved to sit astride her and the ugliness of his face distracted her so she did not see the punch which split her lip and knocked her half senseless. 'You want a man, whore? I'll give you a man.'

His fingers were in her hair, his mouth over hers so she could not breathe. She felt weak and could not move her arms or legs. Blows seemed to rain down on her until she could not feel them any more.

Then she thought she was screaming but it could have been someone else. No one came to help her.

'That's good. That's right. You're doing it properly now,' he said, once again in his parody of a child's voice.

Her head shook from a punch. She passed out for a moment but when she revived she was still on her back and Sebastian was on top of her, his stinking breath sweeping over her face, making her sick. She could feel one of his hands holding her wrists above her head and his other hand tearing at her clothes.

Everything stepped away. Whatever was happening was not happening to her.

Somewhere there was a lot of shouting and short sharp sounds like whips being cracked, but she knew they were not whips. She remembered the police had pistols. The sounds must be gunshots. She concentrated on the cacophony outside. Anything other than understand what Sebastian was doing to her.

Then there was another sound, a crackling, roaring sound, and she smelt smoke.

She screamed and screamed and screamed.

'Edward, they're burning the house!' Billy was on top of the ridge, fifty yards above him, and dancing like a puppet. 'Come on, quick!'

Quick! He could not do anything quickly, least of all run up a steep slope. He was weak and ill and his head seemed as if it were split down the middle.

He struggled up as fast as he could, aware that it had already taken much longer than he had expected to climb this far.

He saw the flames for himself as Billy helped him over the crest of the ridge.

'I think we're too late, Billy.'

'Aye.' Billy did not say any more.

He needed to get closer, to see how much of the house was on fire; if it was the house itself or if Henry had burned the stables or one of the other buildings. To see where the police were, if they really were guarding the house.

He began a stumbling run down the slope, between the gorse bushes, following a path he thought was the one he had used to get to the house the evening he had rehearsed for the Laybournes' party. Billy followed, urging him on, reminding him that Elizabeth might be in danger, as if he needed to be reminded.

He breasted a knoll, and stared down into the manor's kitchen garden.

'Oh Christ!' He saw the eastern wing of the house was ablaze; the fire was spreading below the room where Lizzie lived.

Then he saw the mob, and the policemen; saw flashes from their guns and seconds later heard the shots.

'Stay here, Billy. And keep out of sight!' He began to run, fell, clambered to his feet and ran again, his eyes loose and unfocused, the pains in his head jagging through his body.

He reached the yard and saw bundles of straw burning,

miners fighting with policemen, and Hopkins trying to lead panicking horses out from stables where the straw strewn on the floor was smouldering and smoking.

'Have you seen Lizzie?' he yelled at Hopkins and saw the shock and fear on the old man's face.

'She's in the house,' Hopkins yelled back and was swung off his feet as the horse he was leading tried to bolt.

'In her room?'

'Aye.' Hopkins rolled away from the horse's hooves and let the animal run free.

'You bloody old fool,' he cursed Hopkins and wondered what sort of man would take care of the horses before he went to find a woman who might be trapped in the fire.

He raced across the kitchen garden and through the door into the kitchen, came face to face with a large woman wearing a white apron.

'Have you seen Elizabeth? Miss Forrester?' He watched the woman dither. 'Is she still upstairs?'

The woman nodded and he ran into the house and hoped he could remember the way up to Lizzie's room.

All the corridors looked the same. The first one he tried came to a dead end so he raced back to the stairs, climbed another flight, and ran towards the eastern end of the house. A door at the end of the corridor opened on to a flight of stairs and he bounded up, sure these were the ones that led to Elizabeth.

He recognised the enclosed landing as soon as he saw it. Then he heard the screams.

'Lizzie! Lizzie! Is that you?' He ran to her door and tried to open it; it was locked.

Another savage scream.

'Lizzie! Open the door!'

'Edward! I can't. Sebastian . . .' A thud and she was silent.

He threw himself at the door. It shuddered but it did not open. Again. He still could not break it down.

'The schoolroom!' Another thud.

He bounded back to the middle door and threw it open. Smoke was wafting into the room through the open window but Lizzie was not there. Then he saw a high bookcase that had been pulled away from the wall and the opening behind it. He ran through, was half aware that it led to a wardrobe, then he saw Sebastian Laybourne lying on top of Lizzie.

He lunged. His fist drove into Sebastian's head and half pushed him off the bed. He followed, dragging him on to the floor, kicking and punching as he fell. He saw Sebastian's hand come up, fingers outstretched, but he was too slow.

He felt the finger hit his eyeball. The pain paralysed him. A swiping cut across his throat choked him and a chop on the back of his neck made his throat dry up. A knee in his face knocked him back into a kneeling position and although he saw the next full punch he could not avoid it. It did not knock him completely unconscious, but it was enough to put him on his back and stop him doing any more.

Sebastian stood over him, foot raised ready to stamp on his head, and there was nothing he could do to stop him.

Then behind Laybourne he saw Lizzie, her dress ripped open and her petticoat torn. She was holding her bonnet, tugging at it.

Sebastian laughed down at him. 'You think you're so special, Laybourne, but I'll show you.'

The boot came down, he moved slightly and it grazed the side of his face, lifted again, paused . . .

And Laybourne screamed.

Lizzie was stabbing at him with a long pin. Her hat pin!

Laybourne fell and he grabbed him, swung his own boot into Laybourne's face. A retaliating kick knocked him away. He struggled to sit up, saw Laybourne swipe backwards at Lizzie and knock her over.

There was a crash from below and the room seemed to shake. Smoke poured up through the cracks in the floorboards.

'Lizzie, the house is going up. Get out!' He grabbed for her but she was confused and slow. 'Lizzie!'

He pulled, and she followed him across the room. He was only half aware that Laybourne had already gone as he pulled her through the door and down the enclosed staircase. He reached out to open the door at the bottom of the stairs, and heard Laybourne laugh through the door.

'It's locked, Forrester. And there's no other way out.'

'Isn't there?' He turned to Lizzie and saw her shake her head. 'Come on, Laybourne. What've you to gain by killing us?'

'What have I to gain by letting you go? I've had all I want from both of you.'

Smoke rolled down the narrow stairway.

'There must be a way, Lizzie. Think.' He passed his choker to her so she could breathe through it, and tried to kick the door open.

'It opens inwards, Edward.' He felt her hand on his arm and noticed how calm she was. 'We're trapped. There is no other way out.'

'No, Lizzie. We're not trapped. Not yet.' He ran his hands over the door panels. 'Is there anything heavy upstairs? Something I can use as a hammer?'

She thought for a few moments. 'In the schoolroom. A poker with a big brass handle?'

'That'll have to do. Let's get it.'

He led her back up the stairs, up into the smoke. It was so thick that he could not see along the short passage, but when he looked down at the floor he could see the glow from the fire shining through the cracks between the floorboards.

'We'll have to be quick, Lizzie. The floor'll catch any minute.'

He held her with one hand and felt along the wall with his other, found the schoolroom door still open and pulled her inside. The room was hot but draughts from the open windows and the chimney were drawing the smoke out and he could see the long, brass-handled poker in the fireplace.

'Stay here.' He left her by the door and ran along the room, grabbed the poker and started back.

'Edward, stop!' He heard her and saw a smouldering rug burst into flames.

A moment later the rug and large table disappeared as the floor collapsed.

'Edward!' He could not see her, she was behind a huge sheet of flame that burst through the hole in the floor.

Now he was trapped; there was no way around the hole. He could not reach the door.

He gripped the poker, ran, and jumped.

The flame seemed to hold him. He kicked at the air, felt the heat. And hit the floor on the far side of the hole. The floor sagged under his weight but he was already skipping towards Lizzie and the door. He grabbed her as he passed and suddenly they were in the passage, tumbling towards the stairs.

He crashed down, dragging her with him, coughing and spluttering as the smoke filled their throats.

'Stand back.' He pushed her aside and swung the poker at the door.

The heavy handle dented a panel. Another blow and the panel splintered. Another blow and a sharp twist and a hole appeared.

He reached through, found the doorknob and felt for the key.

It was still in the lock! He turned it, twisted the doorknob, and the door opened. He yanked it back, pushed Lizzie through, and saw Sebastian.

'No!' He heard Laybourne's shout and saw him lurch forward. A fist smashed into his face and before he could recover another punch sent him sprawling against the door. The doorknob crunched against his spine and the pain stopped him reacting. Another punch winded him and another hit the side of his head and seemed to break his skull open.

He could not see. Another blow caught his head again, and another. He swung the poker up, felt it hit something and heard a crunch. Then something heavy leaned against him.

'Edward!' He heard Lizzie scream but he could not see her. 'Edward!'

The weight slid off him. There were no more blows. He stood still, waving the poker blindly. His sight cleared and he saw Laybourne crumpled on the floor, staring at him, blood pumping out of his nose and mouth. There was a large dent in his left temple.

He knelt down, but even before he touched him he knew Sebastian Laybourne was dead.

'Oh God!' He looked down at his clothes; they were drenched in blood. 'Jesus! I've killed him.'

'Edward! What are we going to do?'

He did not know.

There was a tearing crash and sparks blew out of the doorway. He slammed the door shut to stop them.

'Lizzie, no one's going to believe I didn't kill him deliberately, especially if they know what he did to you. You've got to be brave. Go downstairs and don't say anything about any of this. Your clothes are torn, but they're burnt as well so you can pretend that happened as you escaped from the fire. No one's going to suspect anything because you're upset, it's what they'd expect. Don't admit that you've seen me or you'll be in trouble too. Go on. Be brave. For me.'

'But what are you going to do?'

'The staff saw me arrive so the police'll know I killed him. I need to get away before they find him or catch me here. Go on, Lizzie. Help me. I need you to give me time to get away.'

'But where will you go?'

'I don't know, but I'll get in touch when it's safe.' He

went to hug her but remembered the blood on his clothes, and instead simply held her hands. 'Go on, Lizzie, please. Be brave, and remember I love you.'

'And I love you, Edward. I always will. Take care of yourself.'

She walked away, then began to run. He watched her until she had disappeared down the stairs at the far end of the corridor.

His head bandage had come off during one of the fights and he threw the bloodstained jacket up the stairs where he hoped it would be burned. The police were downstairs telling the staff to leave, and with nothing to draw attention to himself he found it easy to mingle with the turmoil the house was in and walk out without being recognised. One of the policemen even told him to join the other staff and help carry water to douse the fire.

It was almost dark when he walked out of the house. The fighting had stopped and there were no miners and very few policemen about so he guessed Henry and the others had been rounded up and were being held somewhere. He was halfway across the stable yard when Hopkins saw him.

'Mr Forrester? Did you find your sister?'

He was tempted to ignore the question but he knew that would only make the old man suspicious. 'No, Mr Hopkins. I went up to her room but she wasn't there, man. Just as well, looking at that lot.'

He nodded towards the fire and the row of men chaining buckets of water to throw on it in a hopeless attempt to control it.

'The police have sent all the women down to the lodge.' Hopkins shuffled his feet and looked at the ground. 'I'm sorry I didn't go after Miss Elizabeth meself, like, but I didn't think. All I could think about was the horses.'

'Well, it doesn't matter now, man.' He wanted to get away but Hopkins grabbed his arm.

'I could take you to Miss Elizabeth if you want. Just to

make sure she is safe, like?' he offered.

'I don't think so.' This was awkward. 'Look, if the police see me here I'm in trouble. I've been warned to stay away.'

'Aye, of course, I'd forgotten that.'

'Well, then, I'd better get going.' He tried to pull away but Hopkins held on tight.

'Over the ridge?'

'Aye, it's quicker than the road, like.'

'Don't. Some of the miners escaped up on to the ridge and the police are up there looking for them. They've got guns, and I reckon they're keen to use them. Quite a few of 'em got badly bashed about and I reckon they'll take it out on anyone they see.'

Billy Darling was up there waiting for him!

'I could hide you in the stables for a bit, until things quieten down, like,' Hopkins offered.

It was a tempting offer, but what about Billy? The longer he waited the more chance there was of Billy being caught, if the police did not have him already.

'No, I reckon I'll take me chances, Mr Hopkins.'

'You're sure, lad?' Hopkins tightened his grip.

They both turned as a constable rushed into the yard. 'Sergeant! Sergeant! Quick! I've just found Mr Laybourne. Someone's killed him.'

There was not time to think or argue. He shoved Hopkins away and ran.

'Hey, stop,' the policeman yelled. 'I said stop!'

He ignored the constable and made for the corner of the coach house, running as fast as he could but lurching about to make himself difficult to shoot.

'I told you to stop.' There was no shot; all he heard was the policeman who seemed to be annoyed he had been disobeyed. 'You. Do you know that man?'

And then he heard Hopkins's needlessly honest answer: 'Edward Forrester, Constable.'

Then he was sliding on the muddy path which led behind the coach house and the stables and up towards the knoll where he had left Billy. He did not look back; the sound of police whistles told him what was happening.

Although it was dark he remembered exactly where he had left Billy and found him hiding under a thick gorse bush. 'There's been a terrible accident, Billy. Laybourne attacked me, tried to trap me in the fire. We had a fight and I killed him.' There was no time to explain all the details. 'By accident, mind, you've got to believe that, but now the police are after me and if they catch me I'll hang for sure. And so will you if you're seen with me. So stay here, all night if you have to. Stay hidden and don't move. Do you understand?'

'Aye.' Billy's eyes were wide; suddenly he began to take his jacket off. 'Take my coat, Edward. It'll keep you warmer than just your shirt, like, and you won't look so obvious if anyone sees you.'

He thanked him, took the jacket and pounded up towards the top of the ridge.

The air had been heavy all evening and as he topped the ridge a fresh wind came up from the valley, carrying the smell of Pincote Colliery and the sound of policemen shouting. He settled down in a clump of gorse and tried to judge where the police were, and decided after a short while that they were spread out all along the north slope of the ridge and making their way to the top.

There was a chance that if he stayed where he was they would walk right past, but it was a chance he could not afford to take. He could not risk moving down the hill towards the police, or going back over the ridge towards the house. The safest plan seemed to head east, close to the top of the ridge, and hope that there were no more men waiting near the open ground beyond the gorse.

Then, above the sound of the shouting men, there was the patter, patter, patter of rain. Within minutes the shower turned into a downpour.

He started to run; not eastwards but straight down the hill. It was impossible to see more than a few yards, but he was used to moving in the dark and he guessed that gave him an advantage over the police. Unless he was unlucky enough to run right into a policeman he should be able to get through their line.

Lightning blazed across the sky; not the fork lightning which had done so much damage days before but vivid sheet lightning which lingered and glowed like a million lamps.

And caught him below the line where the gorse bushes stopped and where there was nowhere to hide.

The cry went up instantly. He was almost level with the line of policemen, ten yards away from two of them, both with their revolvers held ready.

'Stop!'

Darkness as the lightning faded. He ran between the men, heard a buzz like a huge bee, stumbled and fell.

'Stop!' Another shout.

Back on his feet, running again. The valley lit up blue as the lightning flashed again, flashed and lingered. He ran on, the downpour drenching him.

'Stop!' Shouts coming from all along the line, then shots.

Stumbled again, and fell on something soft and spongy. The spill! He had run into the spill, the spill which had nearly killed him days ago. There was nowhere to run, not now.

He staggered upright, and saw a policeman standing yards away, his gun ready to fire.

'Stop or I'll shoot,' the man warned.

'Don't fire.' He dragged his feet out of the sticky waste and walked forward with his hands raised in surrender.

'What's your name?' the policeman asked.

'Edward Forrester.'

'You a miner?'

'Aye, I'm a miner.'

'You in that business over the hill? At the manor?'

'Not exactly, Constable.'

'Well, I'm arresting you anyway. For resisting arrest for one thing.'

A second policeman came out of the torrential rain, handcuffs swinging from one hand, a stick held in the other. 'Hold your hands out, Forrester.'

He did as he was told. The policeman stepped towards him, and the ground exploded.

The pouring rain turned solid. And black.

The ground moved again, and again, and the black rain grew thicker. Lightning flashed. The world was ending.

Explosions and fires all around. Ground heaving. Men running, shouting. Solid black rain pouring down.

He was on his knees, alone; the policemen had gone, too concerned for their own safety. And all around him the world exploded.

Then he realised: Trenchard had set off the charges to scatter the waste before the torrential rain could make the spills slide down the slope and into the river.

He knelt on the ground and laughed. Timid Trenchard, who had disappeared for hours when he should have been underground, had been setting charges on the hillside.

He looked up as the lightning lit the valley again, and he saw the overhead cable which carried the waste buckets across the valley, across the river and back to the mine. If he could climb the pylon he could escape along the cable and no one could reach him. They would not even think to look for him, not up in the air.

Another charge exploded, and he felt himself lifted off his feet.

PART TWO

CHAPTER 22

When Elizabeth thought back over the months which followed that evening she was shocked to realise how close she may have come to being seriously ill, mentally ill. At the time everything seemed normal; it was not until later, when her perspective altered, that she realised the subtle changes that had taken place.

During those months she felt unprotected and exposed, as if someone had carefully peeled off all her skin and left her flesh and nerve endings uncovered so that everything which touched her, emotionally, left a raw feeling which went direct to her soul. She saw everything with a new perspective; everything that happened was seen with a new and simple clarity which made understanding easy and she wondered why she had not thought so clearly before.

Her mind worked on two different levels: one level frightened, vulnerable and eager to hide behind the other level which enjoyed a false confidence and a briskness meant to fool people into believing she was tough enough not to be affected by what had happened.

Also, her memory did not seem to work properly: it discarded irrelevances immediately and it was not until years later that certain small incidents came back, and then they were as clear as if they had happened yesterday.

Finally, desolation; that was how she saw the aftermath of that evening, a summer's evening when she had every right to expect to have been walking in the gardens with John, smelling flowers, listening to birdsong and planning her wedding.

Instead, her mother, father and her brothers were dead, John was lying in hospital, one leg amputated, his face and hands horribly burned, possibly blind, probably dying; and she had been beaten and raped by his father. She was alone in what seemed the aftermath of a battle.

But whatever led up to it, John, her father and brothers, Sebastian terrorising her, raping her, the fight which followed, the real shock did not fall on her until they told her Edward was dead.

She remembered the solid feeling as the policeman's words sank into her mind.

The shock was physical, audible and visual, the words an axe thudding into a log and being left.

Edward was dead. And she wished she was dead too.

Sebastian had slaughtered her, ripped out her life and left her empty, a carcass. But she was not dead.

She remembered seeing scissors on a table, grabbing them and seeing the shock on the policeman's face as she hacked at her hair; just her hair. Looking down, seeing it dead, lifeless, separated from her, on the floor by her feet; her treacherous hair that she had loved so much for so long until it led her into Sebastian's . . .

That was when she knew she had to stun her emotions if she were to survive.

From that moment on she was practical in everything she did; everything had to have an object and she did everything she could to keep herself busy because she did not want time to think.

Even when she found she was pregnant she did not think about it, just put it aside until she had time to deal with it.

One morning a month later, when she woke up in agony and saw she was lying on a bed soaked in blood, she simply cleaned herself, did what was necessary, burned the bedding and all it contained, and thought that was another problem resolved.

She did not even wonder if it was John's baby or his father's. It did not matter, not now it was not going to grow into a real baby any more. She was not glad or sorry or shocked by the miscarriage. It was just something else that happened.

And in retrospect she realised that more than anything it was Charlotte Laybourne's kindness, even love, which helped her to retain her self-respect, to regain her confidence, and not to go insane with desolation.

The only light during those days was to visit John every afternoon. He had recovered consciousness but he was in a deep trance; his eyes were covered, he never moved, never spoke, never acknowledged her; but she read to him or talked about everyday things, carefully censored and in an artificially bright voice because she believed that he might be able to hear her and that hearing her might help him to hang on to his life. But even then she was careful not to allow her emotions to rise. He was still very ill, and she knew his death would destroy her if she let it.

Doctor Roberts had made it clear that he would prefer to send John to a hospital where he could receive more specialised treatment, but Charlotte was adamant in bringing specialists to Pincote whenever it was necessary; and although she visited John every day she could not bring herself to read to him or talk as if he could hear her, but she wanted him kept as close to her as possible.

Lillian McDougall visited him occasionally, by

arrangement. Her journey was long and difficult and
John's lack of response made her efforts seem pointless
and always made her cry.

The summer passed away during a chill and windy August
and it seemed that even the seasons were in a hurry to put
that day behind them. The leaves fell off the trees and the
grass was thick with dew which lasted throughout the
days. Fires were lit in the manor's main rooms and she was
glad she had accepted Charlotte's offer to stay with her in
the house; it meant she could live without having to find a
job and that she had someone to share the evenings with,
even if they were quiet evenings spent doing meaningless
small jobs that the staff would normally have done.

She and Charlotte were able to comfort each other just
by being together. There was no discussion about the
circumstances of Sebastian's death other than a single
acknowledgement that Edward must have had his own
reasons for killing him, no questions, no recriminations,
just companionship and a shared need to put everything
behind them.

She could not share the same companionship with Rose.
Rose had come home and seen her father buried, but she
could not settle; could not accept that Edward had killed
her father and died escaping from the police who were
hunting him. She spent hours alone in her room or on
South Ridge, dressed in black, apparently mourning her
own lost hope as much as her father or Edward; and then
without any discussion she wrote to Hubert to say their
marriage had been postponed long enough and suggested
he arrange another date for early September.

Despite all the arguments her mother put forward for
delaying the marriage Rose refused to change her mind; it
was as if by continuing with her plans and leaving Pincote
Rose hoped to shut out all that had happened and begin a
new life with no ties to the past.

The wedding took place in Dorset and because John
was still very ill and could not attend the service Charlotte

asked her to arrange railway tickets for just the three of them, herself, Charlotte and Rose to travel to Dorset and for only herself and Charlotte to return. Catherine and Walter were to make their own arrangements.

Catherine had been travelling abroad when her father was buried so she could not be contacted in time for his funeral; and although she had been back in England for six weeks she had made no attempt to visit her father's grave or to visit John or offer Charlotte any more solace than two letters could convey. It was not surprising that she did not want to see her father's grave, but it was surprising that the friendly, warm Catherine she remembered from months ago had abandoned all that was left of a family she seemed to love.

The thought of meeting Catherine again made her anxious. They would, inevitably, talk about Sebastian, and she was not sure she could look into Catherine's eyes without giving herself away.

She was probably the only other person alive who knew what Catherine had been through; it was unlikely she had ever told Walter, and she was not sure that she could treat her simply as Rose's half sister because she no longer thought of her only as Rose's half sister. She thought of her, perhaps, almost as her own sister, someone with whom she had shared the most intimate of experiences; and she had an almost overwhelming need to tell her what they shared.

Also, she wondered how Catherine would behave towards Rose. Catherine had made it quite obvious that unlike her father she did not think Rose and Hubert Belchester were a good match; she was almost certain to comment on the total irony of Rose choosing to marry Hubert now her father was not there to manipulate her, and that might upset both Rose and Charlotte.

And finally she wondered how Catherine would respond to her, the sister of the man who had allegedly murdered her father.

*   *   *

Her anxiety proved unnecessary. Catherine and Walter
appeared only moments before the marriage service
began, both muffled up against the blustery Dorset
weather, both barely recovered from influenza and almost
unable to talk because of chesty coughs. They left
immediately after the service, wrapped in furs inside the
hired carriage which took them directly to the railway
station.

She thought they had made an effort, a very real effort,
to support Charlotte and to acknowledge Rose's choice of
husband; but there was something worrying Catherine,
she could see it in her eyes. And she knew Catherine was
aware that she had noticed.

Rose wore white on her wedding day, a symbol of her
purity and a contrast to everyone else who wore black. The
wedding was quiet, in deference to her father's death, and
her bouquet of white lilies and the glass vases of white
lilies which decked the Belchester estate's chapel marked
the deeper than usual solemnity of the occasion.

Hubert's grandfather represented her father and gave
her away, three of Hubert's cousins were her bridesmaids
and another of his cousins acted as pageboy. The wedding
service was kept brief, the congregation was small and the
hymn singing was drowned out by the chapel's organ.

The wedding breakfast was simple and eaten from a
plain white service set out on an undecorated table. There
was no wine drunk with the meal but the few guests, all
family, drank three champagne toasts: one to the newly
married couple, one to absent friends, and one to the
Queen. Immediately afterwards they all said their
goodbyes and left.

There seemed to be a communal sense of relief that it
was done with; no feeling that any wrong had been done,
as such, simply an unspoken sense that Rose's desire to be
married so soon after her father's death was flouting
decency.

It seemed to Elizabeth that the wedding emphasised the bleakness of that period.

But it also marked its end.

Elizabeth was sleeping as the return train pulled into Pincote Market; the long journey to Dorset had been tiring, the circumstances of the wedding had been trying, and the Dorset air seemed to have drained all her energy even before she began the return journey with Charlotte. As a result she had slept through most of the journey back to Pincote, and even slept heavily during the overnight stay in a noisy railway hotel.

Charlotte woke her as the train stopped and suddenly Mr Hopkins was standing by the open compartment door, greeting her and Mrs Laybourne and organising porters to carry luggage to the carriage parked outside.

He asked about the journey and the wedding but it was obvious there was something he was impatient to tell them.

'Is something wrong, Mr Hopkins?' Charlotte asked warily.

'Not wrong, Mrs Laybourne. It's good news.' He paused. 'Doctor Roberts told me to tell you that Mr Laybourne's started talking.'

The relief was immense, it rose and spread like a wide fountain. The long sleep, the best she had enjoyed since the awful day, had already begun to give Elizabeth strength, and Hopkins's news stimulated her even more.

'What did he say? Do you know?' she asked and slipped a comforting arm around Charlotte's waist.

'He asked where you were, Miss Elizabeth, and why you weren't reading to him.'

She heard Charlotte sob, and felt guilty that John's first words were to ask after her and not his mother, but like a child waking up on Christmas morning, she felt a thrill running through her. She had been reading to him for weeks, reading aloud from novels, but he had never acknowledged her or even shown that he could hear her.

Suddenly she thought of all the other things she had told him when they had been left alone by the nurses. How the eastern end of the manor had been burned and demolished and a new end wall had been built. How helpful Lillian McDougall's father had been in arranging for surveyors and engineers to find and enlarge the original monks' entry to the mine. How she had gently told him that his father had died, and, most important, how often she had told him that she loved him and he was still the only man for her so he had to get better and marry her as soon as he could.

She suddenly thought that perhaps Rose was right; if you were determined enough, and ruthless enough, perhaps you could make a fresh start, cut away the past and begin again.

They drove directly to the infirmary but John was asleep and Doctor Roberts warned them against waking him.

'It's a good sign, Mrs Laybourne,' he said carefully, 'but don't build up your hopes too much. It shows us that his brain can work properly, but just a few lucid moments doesn't mean that he'll recover fully. His stump is healing quite well and fresh skin has grown over his burns but he'll always be horribly scarred. We don't know what effect those things might have on him. When he realises what he's like, well, it's difficult to know how he'll react.'

'Do you think he'll be able to see, Doctor?' Charlotte asked.

'I think he'll be able to see a little, just light and shade, maybe more in time, but he'll never see properly.'

'But he'll live?' She heard herself ask the question she had avoided since the first day John had been brought into the infirmary.

'I think so, Miss Forrester.' Doctor Roberts nodded, then smiled at her for the first time. 'And I think that's as much, and maybe more, due to you than anything we've done. All those hours you've just sat here talking to him and touching him, that's probably kept him interested in living.'

Charlotte kissed her, suddenly and without hesitation. 'Thank you, Elizabeth. You've been quite wonderful through all of this.'

'It was nothing, Mrs Laybourne. I was happy to spend the time with him.'

'Yes.' Charlotte nodded, a new expression on her face, an expression that suggested she might have guessed the truth. 'I think I understand what you mean, Elizabeth.'

She decided then that if Charlotte asked her outright she would tell her about the plans she and John had made, and risk John's reaction when it came.

It was dark as they drove back to the manor; dark except for the light reflected off a large silver moon and a million stars.

She sat in the carriage opposite Charlotte. They did not speak, except to comment on how clear the sky was and predict the likelihood of frost; they were both too occupied with their own thoughts to bother with conversation.

Something, the crispness of the air, the long, refreshing sleep, the news about John, or the possibility that she could soon admit her love for him, charged her with energy, and the moment the carriage stopped by the front steps she bounded up them, eager to be back inside the house that alternately scared or entranced her.

The staff welcomed her and Charlotte home, diffidently at first and then with enthusiasm when they were told that John should live. The bags were taken upstairs and Charlotte rifled through the post that had accumulated.

She extracted one envelope with big, bold handwriting on it. 'For you, Elizabeth.'

'Really?' She had no idea who might be writing to her and did not know the handwriting so she opened it carefully, as if slow movements might make bad news or further trouble easier to deal with. 'It's from Adam Marriott. He's going to marry Nancy Wright!'

'Isn't she the girl Edward . . .' Charlotte asked and stopped awkwardly.

'Yes.' She nodded absently, reading the rest of the letter as fast as she could. 'Adam's asking if I intend to take on the lease to my parents' house, and if not whether I'd be willing to clear the house and recommend him as a tenant.'

'Well?' Charlotte asked. 'What are you going to tell him?'

She had not made any plans for the house, or for herself for that matter. She had agreed to stay with Charlotte for an indefinite period, and had neither dared nor wanted to think too far into the future; it seemed so bleak.

Charlotte motioned to her to sit down, 'No doubt Mr Marriott wants the house so that he and Nancy can have some privacy but still be close to Nancy's mother. It sounds ideal to me, Elizabeth, if you don't have any plans to use the house yourself. You haven't been back to Albert Street more than half a dozen times during the past few months, and each time you went only to visit Mrs Wright and Nancy, not to stay in your old home.'

Her 'old' home. That was how it seemed to her now, more than ever, and by implication Charlotte Laybourne also considered the manor was her new home, her real home now.

'Are you suggesting that I'll always have a home here, Mrs Laybourne?' She needed to know exactly where she stood.

'Elizabeth, I'd be pleased if you'd do two things for me. First, stop calling me Mrs Laybourne and start calling me Charlotte. We've been through enough together to be friends rather than employer and employee, and friends should be informal with each other. Secondly, please feel that you have a home here for as long as you want one.'

'Thank you, Charlotte.' It was difficult to use her first name after all the months of being formal, and Charlotte's generosity made her want to cry.

'There is a third thing I'd like you to do, but we'll leave

that until some time later, when the time is right, and in the meanwhile I don't want you worrying about it; it's just something to put a mother's mind at rest.' Charlotte smiled.

'Is it about John and me?' Again, it was important to know where she stood and Charlotte's attitude might change when she knew the truth.

'Of course it is, Elizabeth. Do you love him very much, my dear?'

Charlotte's frankness took her aback, but she recovered quickly and answered without any embarrassment. 'Oh yes, there's no doubt. I think I fell in love with him when he nearly knocked me over on the day he came back to Pincote.'

'And do you love him enough to take care of him in his present condition, and to help him through the inevitable scandal and the business repercussions of his jilting Lillian?'

'Oh yes. I've thought about all the implications and I've no doubt at all, Mrs Laybourne. Charlotte.'

'And finally, does he love you in the same way?'

'He asked me to marry him the night before the ball. He wanted to tell Miss McDougall then, but I persuaded him to wait because I didn't think it was fair on him or on Rose, or on you and your husband—' She stopped quickly.

She stopped because she was aware she was walking on forbidden territory, but also because she could feel herself trembling and could not stop. The trembling grew and grew until her whole body was shaking violently, uncontrollably.

'Elizabeth! Whatever's the matter?' Charlotte was on her feet, holding her, arms tight around her, one hand smoothing her hair.

'I don't know, but I can't stop.' She found it difficult to speak.

'Don't worry, my dear, it's probably the strain of all that's happened coming out at last.' Charlotte held her very

tight and talked soothingly, exactly the way her mother
used to when she woke from a nightmare. 'Talking about
the ball probably reminded you of things. It'll pass. It'll
pass. Whatever's happened has happened and now it's
over. You can try to forget it or if you want to you can talk
about it, but only if you want to, my dear.'

She did not want to talk; she did not even want to think,
but she could not stop. She was not thinking only about the
night of the ball; she was thinking about the night John
asked her to marry him, and about making love and being
watched by John's father, and what it had led to;
intimidation, a beating and rape. But she could not tell
Charlotte any of that. Not ever.

She stood for several minutes, held in Charlotte's arms,
terrified that the spasms would never stop; but they did.

'Well, my dear, if you and John are determined to marry
each other I'll stand by you both. Happily. But you're quite
correct in believing that any announcement should be
handled very carefully. Lillian has been very loyal and
waited a long time for John. I wouldn't want to see her hurt
any more than necessary, and I certainly don't want to see
her disgraced.' Charlotte returned to her chair. 'Now,
think about Mr Marriott's request. You must make up your
own mind, of course, and I'll follow any line you
recommend. I trust Mr Marriott would make an honest
and reliable tenant?'

'I doubt you'd ever find anyone better,' she said, smiling
at the thought that anyone would even ask that question
about Adam, but still uneasy about breaking her last ties
with her past life, her parents, and her brothers, especially
Edward.

'If you're worried about clearing the furniture and
contents we can easily arrange for Mr Hopkins to take a
few of the stronger gardener's boys over on a cart and
bring everything back here. We've any number of rooms
to store furniture in and a plethora of cases and chests to
put small items in. We could bring everything back here,

and then, when you're ready, you could sort through it all and keep whatever you want.'

'Thank you, but there's not really that much to clear.' She had to admit that all the possessions her parents had managed to accumulate during their whole lifetime did not amount to even one very small cartload. 'And it's not worth going to all the trouble of bringing it back here. It was part of my home when I was a child, a part of my life and I love it all for that reason, but that's all the value it has. There are four or five things I'd like to keep for sentimental reasons, but Adam and Nancy can keep the rest if they want it.'

'I assume that you've made up your mind, then.' Charlotte smiled at her.

'Oh, yes, I think so.' She nodded. 'It was a good home for me. I hope Adam and Nancy enjoy it as much as I did. I'd be happy for Adam to take over the tenancy, if you agree, and I'd like him and Nancy to keep whatever furniture and bits they want. If I kept them they'd only become clutter, and perhaps it's time to clear out all the clutter with its memories of the past, and start afresh.'

'I think it is, my dear Elizabeth.' Charlotte reached out and held both her hands. 'I think it's time for us all to do that, and not only the belongings which clutter up our lives. Other things tie you to the past much more than possessions. What's gone is gone, there's no going back, no means of retrieving the past whether it was good or bad. Perhaps you and I should make a pact to agree that the past doesn't matter any more. Agree that our new friendship was born of today, and take a leaf from Rose's book and promise ourselves that we'll do all we can to make our future lives happier than our past.'

'I think that is a very good idea, Charlotte.' She moved towards the fireplace and watched as a burning log slipped down on to a bed of glowing cinders and shot red sparks up the chimney.

Tomorrow that log would be grey ash, forgotten as a

log, and the ash would go on to the compost heap to help something else grow in time. Charlotte was right about the past; what had happened could not be changed and could not change the future. The worst of the past could not hurt her unless she allowed it to, but the best of the past could be remembered and something good could be made to grow out of those memories.

She knelt before the fire and felt its heat on her face and chest, and the chilling desolation which had shrouded the past few months started to melt away.

CHAPTER 23

―――――――――――――

'Thank you for everything you've done, Elizabeth.' Nancy smiled and nodded towards the small bag containing a few sentimental treasures. 'Is that all you're taking? Don't you want any of the furniture or the pots?'

'No, lass, you're welcome to whatever's left. I reckon it'd please my ma and da to know you and Adam can settle down with their things the way they did. There's a lot of memories here, Nancy, most of them are happy and I hope you can be happy here too. I'm really glad things are working out for you, lass.' She hugged Nancy to show she meant what she said, and that all the old misgivings were gone. 'Adam's a fine man, one of the finest either of us'll ever know. You both deserve to be happy, and I'm sure you will be.'

'Aye.' Nancy returned the hug. 'Who ever would've thought I'd end up with the Old Prophet?'

Nancy laughed, and it was obvious she was happy. 'But you're sure there's nothing else you want to take, Elizabeth?'

'Well, there is just one thing, if you come across it. It's a
book of Edward's, called the *Histories of William
Shakespeare*. It's got a faded red cover and it was given to
him by Uncle George, George Willis. Now they're both
gone it'd be nice to have it, but I can't find it anywhere.
Edward probably tucked it away somewhere, so if you
come across it . . .'

'Of course.' Nancy looked sad for a moment. 'Poor
Edward. He wasn't very lucky, Elizabeth, was he?'

It was a question which did not need answering, so she
did not try, but changed the subject to a happier one.
'When do you plan to get married and move in here?'

'Adam'll move in as soon as he can, and we expect to get
married just before Christmas. You will come, won't you?'

'Of course, lass. I'll look forward to it.' She hugged
Nancy again, and took a last look around the living room
her mother had sometimes called the kitchen and
sometimes the parlour, and the kitchen she had called the
back kitchen or scullery; the rooms seemed to have
changed already even though nothing had been done to
them, except to remove the people who had lived their
lives out there.

She walked out through the back yard and closed the
gate behind her as she had thousands of times before, and
a lump grew in her throat so she could not call back a reply
to Nancy's parting promise to invite her to the wedding.

As she walked along the alley she hoped it would be a
happier occasion than Rose's wedding, and wondered how
Rose was. Charlotte had only received one non-committal
letter from Rose since the wedding, and she had not
received any at all.

Rose looked out of the window at the unseasonable
Christmas weather and thought that the ground around
Pincote would be white with frost if not snow. It would be
impossible to climb the steep paths up South Ridge until
the weather was warmer.

But at least it was only the weather which was cold up there, so far away; the people were warmer.

'Now then, Princess, what's wrong with you this morning? Feeling a little sick?'

She turned quickly and smiled at the only person who did show her any warmth or affection. 'No, Grandpa, just thinking about the weather back at home.'

'Still think of Pincote as home, do you?'

'It was my home for a long time. I didn't mean—'

'I'm just teasing you, Princess,' he interrupted her and smiled, put one arm around her shoulders and patted her stomach with his free hand. 'Looks to me as if you're losing weight, my dear. Thought you'd have been putting it on by now.'

She smiled her best apologetic smile; it was not her choice not to be pregnant yet but she could not tell him she was never going to become pregnant until Hubert slept with her. 'My name's Rose, Grandpa, not Mary.'

He laughed, as she knew he would, and she was pleased with the retort herself even though the reference to a virgin birth could only be her own private joke.

'Of course, my dear Princess, of course.' He chortled again and winked mischievously. 'You'd have had to marry a lot sooner to give us a Christmas baby. Still, any signs yet? I'd like to see my great-grandchild before I go.'

'Go? Go where?' A moment's alarm at the thought of losing his company.

'The Happy Hunting Ground, Princess, as the American Indians call it. Heaven, or hell perhaps if St Peter's really got a record of everything I've done in me life.'

'Don't talk like that, Grandpa, you've years ahead of you yet.'

'Maybe, my dear, maybe not. But don't keep me waiting too long will you, just in case.'

'I'll try not to.' If she could do it alone, she would give him his great-grandchild in nine months' time, but she needed help from Hubert and he was either unwilling or unable to give it; she was not sure which.

She fingered the Christmas card which had arrived from her mother. There was no letter enclosed, not even a personal message written on the card, simply a formal note wishing her and Hubert a happy Christmas. It was her mother's subtle way of reprimanding her for not having replied to her last letter; but how could she reply? She could not write down her problems and worries in a letter, and she would not lie and pretend that everything was perfect; so it was best to say nothing, not to write at all.

For the first time since she had started visiting him Elizabeth was glad to leave John. He was so depressed that she had found it difficult to maintain a conversation without sounding falsely cheerful.

Doctor Roberts had reduced the amount of painkilling drugs he was giving John and even after all these months he could still feel pain from his face and his stump. Also, he had tried to walk on crutches and had realised how incapable he was. He was weak from months of lying in bed, the skin on the backs of his hands was tight and stopped him gripping the handles of the crutches with enough strength to control them properly, and his sight was so poor that he could not see where he was going even when he did manage a few steps.

He had hoped he would be home for Christmas, but the doctor had told him the best he could hope for was to transfer to a hospital which could give him the exercise treatments he needed to build himself up and to lessen his need for painkilling drugs. Another blow to his morale was being told that he should expect to remain in hospital for another six months at least.

Finally, he had overheard someone visiting another patient say how ugly he looked, and how people like him should be shut away in case they frightened children.

She could not blame him for feeling depressed; seeing him as he was depressed her too.

It was snowing as she left the infirmary, and Hopkins drove her through the snow to the railway station to meet Catherine who had come to stay for the Christmas holiday a week before Walter was due to arrive.

'You don't look at all well, Elizabeth,' Catherine said as they settled into the carriage, and for the first time in weeks Elizabeth found herself crying.

She explained why and saw the concern on Catherine's face, then noticed there was more than concern, there was something else on Catherine's mind. She looked worried, much as she had at Rose's wedding.

'What's wrong, Catherine?' She took her usual direct approach. 'You look worried.'

'Worried, frightened, even guilty,' Catherine admitted. 'I was hoping to talk to you about something, well, unpleasant, before we reached the manor. Something I need to discuss with you before I meet my stepmother.'

'Go on. I'll be all right.' She wiped her eyes and tried to prepare herself for more trouble.

Catherine took a bundle of papers out from a small leather bag she was holding close to her. 'I don't know how much you know about Miss Smith, but she and I were very close and after she died I received a parcel from her solicitors. It contained some of her diaries, years old, some of them. Certain pages were marked, and I've torn them out so you can see them. I want your opinion as to whether or not I should show them to my stepmother.'

She reached out to take the pages but Catherine pulled them away. 'Elizabeth, you should prepare yourself for some horrific reading. They're most unpleasant. That's a terrible understatement,' she added quickly. 'They show that my father was a very sick person, mentally. I already had experience of that, the worst sort of experience, but I thought that what happened to me was an exception. It wasn't.'

Catherine offered her the papers but when she reached out to take them her hands began to shake, so much that several minutes passed before she could hold them. 'I know, Catherine. At least I think I know what you're trying to tell me. He beat me and raped me as well. That was how Edward came to kill him, in a way.'

It was an immense relief to be able to tell her what had happened and within minutes the whole story was out: the intimidation, the beating, the rape and how Sebastian had tried to kill her and Edward. How Edward knew nothing could be proved and how he had begged her to keep it a secret. And how awful she felt about denying him, about betraying him even when he was dead because she could not face telling the truth about what had happened.

'Oh God.' Catherine was ashen. 'I didn't think you were in any danger. I thought you'd be old enough to be safe from him. I didn't think he'd do that to you.'

'Because I'm older than eighteen?'

Catherine nodded. 'From what Miss Smith says in her diaries he even did it to a young gypsy girl who was about fourteen. I honestly thought you were safe, Elizabeth, or I would have warned you, somehow. I didn't receive these, didn't know how bad he was until after he was dead, and I still can't forgive Miss Smith for not trying to protect me or Rose.'

'Miss Smith warned Rose and she escaped. Perhaps that's why he turned on me, although it might have happened anyway. He said I reminded him of someone called Willow, whoever she was. He said he went to look for her but her mother told him she was dead, "in the ground" he said.'

'You don't need to read these pages then, Elizabeth. You know as much as I do, more even, but there's nothing about Willow in there.' Catherine pulled the papers away and tucked them back in the bag. 'Did you know that Miss Smith had his child, but it died?'

'He told me she had lost a child but he did not say it was his.'

'It happened just before I was born, and Miss Smith

loved him so much that she came to live in the house as my wet nurse because my own mother couldn't feed me,' Catherine said stolidly. 'Can you imagine loving someone that much? So much that you're willing to go through all she did just to be with him even though she knew he would never acknowledge her as anything more than a servant?'

'It depends just how much you love someone, I suppose, Catherine.' She wondered just how much she would be prepared to go through to be close to John. 'But I don't think there's any need to tell Charlotte about all this. I think she may have suspected something, not to the extent we know about, but it's all past now. It's something we've got to put behind us and it won't help Charlotte to know how evil he really was.'

Catherine nodded. 'I think I agree, but I'm glad I talked to you. It helps, doesn't it, to know you're not alone, that you're not to blame.'

She was relieved to hear Catherine admit to feeling guilty, a feeling she realised she shared but had not recognised as guilt, but there was something else she had to share. 'I had a miscarriage, Catherine. You're the only one who knows. I wasn't sorry about it, I was glad. Is that awful?'

'No.' Catherine did not hesitate. 'Maybe it was God's way of making things right.'

'I hadn't thought of it like that,' she confessed, and felt she had to be completely honest if she was to clear the memory once and for all. 'It could have been John's child, though.'

Catherine looked stunned, more so than she had throughout the conversation. 'John's child? My half brother?'

'I know he's engaged to Lillian McDougall, but he asked me to marry him and I agreed. Charlotte knows all about it, but she's the only one. We're waiting for the right time to tell Miss McDougall. We don't want to hurt her too much. It's very difficult.'

Catherine began to laugh, a quiet, ironic laugh. 'I can imagine, but I must be honest, Elizabeth. I never thought John would actually marry Lillian. I think my father almost forced him to become engaged to her because he saw certain advantages where business was concerned. And I think John agreed partly in order to appease my father and partly because Lillian is very beautiful and he saw their engagement almost as a means of reserving her while he was away for two years. Anyway, what you've told me makes an offer I was going to make you sound rather ridiculous, now.'

'What offer was that?' She was glad to have Catherine as an ally, but the offer sounded intriguing.

'I'm a director of the National Women's Mission, and I was going to tell you that if you ever wanted to leave Pincote and were interested in missionary work in one of the cities I'd be pleased to find you a position and accommodation.'

It was strange how life changed. Before she met John she would have been happy to consider such an offer, but now she could not think of doing anything other than marrying John and taking care of him, whatever that demanded of her; so perhaps she could understand how Miss Smith felt. In her heart she could not blame the old lady for not making Sebastian's madness public.

Nancy and Adam were married in the Inkerman Street chapel.

Nancy chose not to wear white but instead wore an ankle-length deep green flannel skirt and matching waistcoat over a dark red blouse. The outfit was finished with a shawl knitted by her mother from fine wool, cream-coloured, with a deep hood which fastened around her neck, and with a long fringe made from strands of wool mixed with lengths of glittery silver and green threads donated by Mrs Lumley. She carried a sheaf of green and silver ferns wrapped in a cream lace doily.

The effect was Christmassy and stunning and astonished Adam so much that he gave an audible gasp when he saw her walk down the chapel aisle.

Nancy's brother, Henry, was still in prison for his part in the attack on the manor so Ben Clements gave her away. Elizabeth attended her and young Billy Darling, looking older than his years, supported Adam.

The wedding was popular and happy and the congregation filled the chapel and sang the hymns and carols so lustily that they drowned out the piano which played the tunes.

After the service everyone moved into the hall alongside the chapel, ate simple sandwiches and toasted the couple with cups of tea.

Elizabeth found the honesty and simplicity of the service touching and when Adam insisted on giving her a small present she cried.

She unwrapped the brown paper parcel and took out the present, a new copy of the *Histories of William Shakespeare*, bound in bright red cloth.

'We couldn't find Edward's copy,' Adam said apologetically, 'but we thought you might like this one anyway.'

'It's wonderful. Thank you so much.' She looked inside the cover and saw the flyleaf had been inscribed by Adam; it read: 'With love from Nancy and Adam Marriott and in thanks for all you have done for us.'

'But I did so little, Adam,' she said, clutching the book with one hand and wiping away tears with the other.

'You did more than you'll ever know.' Nancy kissed her. 'You're Edward's sister and your total support and forgiveness for what's happened means more to us than we can say, Elizabeth.'

She left them to talk with other guests, and turned as Jacob Frith, the lamp room supervisor, touched her elbow. 'Elizabeth, maybe this isn't the time to mention this, but I haven't seen you to ask before . . .'

He hesitated, so she prompted him. 'Go on Jacob, say what's on your mind.'

'Well it's a bit awkward, like, but have you had Edward's bag?'

'His bag? What bag?'

'The day of the accident.' He paused again, then went on, obviously embarrassed by what he had to say. 'Edward came in late and left a bag with me. I don't know what was in it, mind, not much, probably just a few clothes, like. Anyway, he left it with me when he went to check on the spills. Then he went below to see George Willis, came back up a bit later and made a real fuss because he wanted the bag and I couldn't find it. Said he was in a hurry, like and started blowing up. Well, I found it and gave it him and he rushed out with it. Then we had the collapse and minutes later he was back, threw the bag at me, went below again, and, well, that was the last time I saw him until he was brought up the next day. I forgot to give the bag back to him then, but I put it on a shelf so I'd know where it was because I reckoned he'd be asking for it, like.'

'And he didn't come back for it,' she said to save him any more embarrassment.

'No, but it wasn't there the next day. I thought someone must've given it to you, so I asked them all but no one had, so then I thought that as no one was likely to steal it, well, you must have it.'

'No, Jacob, this is the first I've heard about it. Someone else must have taken it,' she said quietly, saddened that someone should have stolen something which would have no value, except perhaps to her.

'Well then, I'm sorry, Elizabeth. I should have taken better care of it.' Jacob looked downcast.

'Don't blame yourself, Jacob. We all had more important things on our mind that day. You weren't to know we had a thief amongst us.' She smiled.

It was a false smile, and the day had been spoiled, not only because of the theft. She guessed why the book could

not be found. It was in the missing bag, probably along
with some of Edward's clothes; and the only reason he
would have packed the bag and been in a hurry to leave
with it just before the accident was because he had planned
to run away with Rose. If he had not gone back to the mine
he might still be alive; but then Sebastian might also be
alive and John might be dead. The past she had so willingly
let go suddenly came back with a rush.

She managed to control herself and spent the next half
an hour talking with Pru and a few other friends, aimless
chatter she would have preferred to avoid, but in order not
to spoil the day for anyone else she did not mention the
theft to them. Later she saw Mr Trenchard, now the acting
manager, stroll into the hall with a present for Nancy and
Adam, and as soon as he was alone she asked if they could
talk.

'It's the first I've heard about the bag, Miss Forrester.
I'm surprised that anyone would be so mean, but there's
not much I can do now, not six months later.' He shrugged
and sighed. 'Not that I could have done much back then.
Given the mood at the time I'd only have stirred up more
trouble if I'd started asking people if they'd taken it. They'd
have seen it as an accusation, and it's not the sort of crime
I could have asked the police to look into either.'

'No, I understand,' she said quickly. 'I just hoped that it
might have been put away somewhere and been forgotten.'

'No, I'm sorry.' Suddenly he looked puzzled. 'There is
one thing, though. Something I thought was odd at the
time but I forgot, what with everything else that was going
on.'

'Yes?' She could almost see his mind working as he
tried to remember the exact details.

'Because we half expected trouble from Henry, Nancy's
brother, we locked the gates and had the police guard the
yard. We didn't bother to lock any of the buildings so the
police could move about easier, but a few days after the
accident someone reported that a rear window leading into

the lamp room had been forced. The glass wasn't broken but the frame had been levered open. I thought it was strange because the lamp room wasn't locked so there was no need to go to all that trouble, not unless someone wanted to get in without being seen by the police in the yard. But there wasn't anything of any value in the room, and anyway nothing had been taken, or so we thought. Perhaps whoever broke in saw Edward's bag and stole it because he thought there might be something in there he could sell.'

'If that was the case, then I'm sure he must have been desperate to have gone to all that trouble and risked being caught by the police,' she said, genuinely sorry for the thief. 'Anyway, he must have been disappointed when he opened the bag. Edward did not have anything worth stealing.'

An hour later Hopkins appeared and she knew it was time to leave. She wished Nancy and Adam every happiness, promised to visit them and Pru soon after Christmas and stepped into snow-covered Inkerman Street.

She thanked Hopkins for calling for her, apologised for bringing him out on such a cold afternoon, and stepped up into the small carriage, glad to be alone with thoughts and feelings that had come back with talk of the disaster.

John would never be the same again. He would never again look as smart and handsome as he had on the night of the ball. He would never again be able to carry her the way he had before they made love in the summer house. She would never again be able to run her hands over his face or hold his hands without feeling the scars. But he was alive, unlike so many others, and that was something to be thankful for.

Hopkins drove the brougham along Inkerman Street to the junction with Murdock Street and River Street, where there was enough space to turn the carriage around without making the horse back up on the slippery cobbles.

She glanced along Murdock Street, and remembered the service Edward had organised to avoid the miners' humiliation in chapel; glanced up River Street which led to the flat iron railway bridge and remembered standing on South Ridge with Rose, watching Edward, far below as he crossed the bridge after inspecting the spills.

Suddenly she sat up. Her heart was beating fast and her skin crawled with excitement.

Mr Trenchard was right; there was no reason for anyone to break into the lamp room, not unless they were looking for something specific. The only thing that had been taken was Edward's bag, but apart from Jacob, Edward was the only one who knew it was there.

She tried to organise her thoughts. Several policemen had seen Edward disappear when a charge exploded alongside him, but although they made a detailed search after the remaining charges had been exploded nothing had been found and they all assumed he had either been blown apart or his body had been buried by the spill.

But what if, by some chance, he was still alive? He would not go home, that would be too dangerous, but he might have gone back to the mine to collect the bag he had left there.

If he had been planning to run away after Rose he would have packed spare clothes into his bag, would have taken enough money to meet his immediate needs, and being Edward he would have taken the volume of Shakespeare's plays with him.

But he was already hurt and the explosion would have hurt him more, so how far would he have gone?

And what would he do if he found he was too late to stop Rose marrying Hubert? What would Rose do if she learned he was still alive?

The questions and probabilities kept tumbling into her mind as Hopkins drove her home to the manor, and when she arrived it was all she could do not to admit to Charlotte and Catherine that she thought there was a possibility that

Edward was not dead after all.

But it was a hope she had to keep to herself. If the police thought he was still alive they would look for him, and if they captured him he would stand trial for murder.

She had begun to adjust to his death; she did not know how she could cope with the hope that he might be alive.

CHAPTER 24

Rose lay awake, listening. The March wind rattled the
windows and shutters and boomed down the tall chimney,
bringing the smell and the sound of the sea into her room.
And it whined her name: Rose, Rose, Rose.

She turned and pulled the blankets over her head, but
the wind called louder: Rose, Rose, Rose, and seemed to
rattle the windows more determinedly. And suddenly,
louder than the wind, the sound of the sea breaking over
the boulders at the base of the cliffs and running back
across the pebble beach.

The night was agitating, noisy and confusing; it was
impossible to relax, impossible to sleep.

She slipped out of bed, wrapped her dressing-gown
around her, crossed to the shutters and opened them,
fastening the brass hooks to hold them back and stop them
rattling.

A full moon lit the world. The grass that reached to the
clifftops was silver, the sea dark grey, dull in places, shiny

in others, laced with lines of white froth. The sky was a paler grey, almost luminous, scattered with racing black clouds with ragged edges thin enough for the moonlight to shine through.

She fastened her dressing-gown, opened the full-length window doors and held them as they bucked and pulled in her hands. The cold air poured into her lungs. Perhaps, if she stood on the balcony for a few minutes, the air would also pour into her mind and clear it enough to let her sleep.

She stepped outside and closed the doors behind her, crossed the balcony and leaned against the rail, her hair and nightclothes flapping in the gusts of salt-smelling air. On impulse she unwrapped the dressing-gown and undid the bows and buttons that held her nightgown closed. The wind pulled both open and she felt the damp cold of the night feeling her like invisible hands.

The sensation wakened her even more; made her as restless as the sea thudding against the cliffs a hundred yards away.

'Oh, Hubert, why won't you love me?' The wind tossed the whisper into the night, turned, and lifted both her dressing-gown and nightgown off her shoulders.

She let the wind undress her, stood still as her clothes slid down her body and gathered over her hips and hands.

The night wrapped itself around her and the sea roared, and still she stood, wondering if this was the closest she would ever come to enjoying her body, wondering what she could do to break through Hubert's shyness and reserve.

Another gust hit her hard and she jumped as the doors crashed open behind her and banged backwards and forwards. She stepped back inside, locked the doors shut, and stared at the beauty of the night through the glass; but it was not the same as standing outside, feeling the night, enjoying the physical sensation, the stimulation of the elements touching her skin.

Eager to go out again she reached for the door handles, but stopped. That was not the answer. She could stand outside all night but that would not solve the problem she had with Hubert, it would simply be yet another way of avoiding it.

Better to go to him now, slip into bed beside him. She was cold; he might be persuaded to hold her and if he held her he might be encouraged to do more.

She let her clothes fall and stepped out of them, opened the door between her bedroom and his, and crept into his room. His window shutters were open. The room was bright with light from the moon and she saw him asleep, lying on his back, his left arm outside the covers, his right tucked away beside him.

He was beautiful; his gracefulness was obvious even when he was asleep. He was beautiful and he was kind and considerate, and she realised quite suddenly that during the six months she had been his wife, even though it was in name only, she had fallen in love with him.

She looked down at him, willing him to wake up and see her and pull her into bed beside him. Even if he did no more, just held her, that would be enough encouragement for now, enough to give her back some hope that soon he would want to love her properly.

'Hubert,' softly, so that only he might hear, not his mother sleeping in the next room. 'Hubert.'

He did not wake. She nuzzled her head close to his, her mouth next to his ear.

'Hubert.'

He stirred, turned slightly; that was all.

'Hubert,' quietly again, but still no response.

The moment passed; the urgent need for him passed, and she went back to her own bed and lay awake until dawn.

She did not see him until they sat down to dinner that night, sitting opposite each other across the broad table, his mother next to him, his father next to her, his grandfather at the table head.

The conversation was exclusively about business,

complicated discussions she could not take part in because
no one had thought it necessary to explain even the
rudiments of the family business to her. There appeared to
be a number of minor crises which needed to be settled,
and the conversations carried on after dinner when the
family was gathered in the warm withdrawing room.

She sat and listened and tried to learn more from what
she could understand, but she did not interrupt; she did
not want to be thought of as interfering in something she
knew nothing about.

The evening wore on, the conversations and arguments
endless and incomprehensible. Her concentration drifted.

The wind was still buffeting the house, still carrying the
sound and the scent of the sea, and the moon was still
bright, still silvering the world. She had been married six
months. Most women in her position would still be
enjoying their bridal period. The beauty of the night and
the privacy of the location would have encouraged most
men to take their new wife on a moonlight walk; the
warmth of their love all the protection they would need
against the buffeting wind.

She looked at Hubert. He looked romantic but he was
practical, and if there was any romance in his soul she had
not found it yet; but perhaps that was because there was
something lacking in her. Perhaps she failed to raise his
romantic spirit. Perhaps she was the problem, but if she
was, then why would he not tell her? Why did he treat her
like a fragile doll, something to be dressed and admired,
cared for and put back into its box? Something to be
handled carefully in case it broke.

They would have to talk, when they could have some
time alone together.

She must have fallen asleep because she woke up
feeling a hand gently pressing her shoulder.

'Rose, Rose, wake up, dearest.' He was crouched in
front of her. 'I'm sorry, but we'll be talking for hours yet. If
you're tired you should go to bed.'

'Mm.' She nodded, still sleepy, then remembered. 'I'd like to talk to you. Will you come and see me before you go to bed?'

'Of course.' He helped her stand up, kissed her cheek, and immediately rejoined the discussion with his family.

She went to her room and was tempted to go back out on to the balcony but resisted and satisfied herself with opening the shutters and spending a few minutes looking at the night before sliding into bed. She tried to stay awake but sleep crept up and the next thing she knew it was morning.

She left her bed and crossed to the door connecting her room with Hubert's, knocked on the door, and when there was no answer, went inside. He was not there. She washed, dressed and went downstairs. Hubert had already left the house.

'Did you want him for anything in particular?' his mother asked.

'I need to talk to him.' She tried to hide her disappointment and the anger that was beginning to grow.

'He mentioned something about that to me,' his mother said in a voice which suggested she was curious to know more. 'I'm sure I can help with anything you might wish to discuss with my son.'

My son! Not Hubert or even your husband. My son.

Her anger rose until she could feel her cheeks burning. 'No, I'm afraid this is something I need to discuss with Hubert.'

'I hope we're not going to start having secrets in our home, Rose. We've always been a family which could discuss anything between ourselves. I'm sure I know Hubert well enough to answer for him, whatever you wish to discuss.'

'It's not important,' she heard herself say, and despised herself for not telling his mother that there were some things a wife could discuss only with her husband.

* * *

He came home late that night, after dinner, and she was already in bed when she heard him moving around his room. She did not knock on the door this time, but walked in, her dressing-gown open and her low-cut nightdress exposing her chest and the upper parts of her breasts.

'Good evening, Hubert.' She crossed the room and startled him with a moist kiss full on his lips.

He was bare-chested and warm and it was pleasant to feel his skin next to hers, so she wrapped her arms around him and held on.

'Let me put a shirt on, Rose.' He tried to move away.

'No, please. Not for a moment.'

'Please, Rose. I feel cold.'

'You feel warm to me. Anyway, I'll soon warm you if you are cold.'

'Rose!' He sounded shocked.

'It's quite respectable, Hubert. We are married.'

'Of course, but . . .'

She waited for him to say more but he did not, so she prompted him, 'But what?'

'It's just that it doesn't seem quite, quite' – he hunted for the word he needed – 'quite proper. Not yet.'

'We've been married six months, Hubert. How long will it be before it is proper?'

'Rose, you're still recovering from the shock of, well, what happened. You're very young and very innocent, and I love you and respect you very much.'

'Don't,' was all she could think of saying, and she saw immediately that she had confused him. 'I can't help being young, Hubert, and it isn't my fault that I'm still innocent. I love you, too, and I'd love you more if you didn't respect me so much. I'm your wife, and I'd like to be treated as such.'

'But I do treat you as my wife.' His confusion seemed to have turned to surprise.

'Not entirely, Hubert. You're wonderful with me, you're gentle and considerate and you take care of me, but you don't treat me as if I'm your wife.'

'I'm not sure I understand what you mean, Rose.'

There was no alternative but to be blunt. 'We've been married six months and we haven't yet slept together, Hubert. We haven't yet consummated our marriage.'

'But, Rose, we know each other well enough, have done for years. And we love each other and trust each other implicitly. Surely we don't need to . . .'

'Perhaps we don't need to, Hubert, but I want to!' It came as an outburst, frustration, humiliation and desperation all mixed up together. 'I want to feel you enjoying me as a woman. I want to enjoy you enjoying me.'

'Rose!'

The door leading to the hallway opened suddenly and she saw his mother standing there, peering in at them, sniffing disapproval. 'You disturbed me. Is anything wrong?'

'No, Mother. I'm sorry if Rose disturbed you. She's just going back to her own room, aren't you, Rose?'

She did not answer immediately, not until Hubert turned his face towards her and she could look him in the eye. 'Only if you insist, husband.'

'I think it's probably for the best.' He looked away from her.

'Then I'll probably go.' She swung around and flounced back to her room, satisfying herself by slamming the connecting door as hard as she could.

The fury subsided into blind anger almost immediately, and because there was no other way to relieve her feelings she cried; but she cried silently because she could hear Hubert talking to his mother in the next room and she refused to give either of them the satisfaction of knowing they had upset her.

She cried herself to sleep, humiliated, alone and bitter.

And she cried because she felt disgraced for wanting something that was base and primitive.

For the first time in months she dreamed of Edward. She was in his arms up on King's Crag; and when she woke up she cried again because the dream was only a dream and because she remembered he was dead.

She strolled aimlessly along the clifftop path, her hat in her hand, the wind flapping her flared coat and skirt and tugging her loose hair.

The same wind carried the sound of the sea, the noise of the incoming tide. Gulls wheeled and screeched; thin birds making thin calls, nothing like the heavy hunting buzzards that mewed over South Ridge. She stopped and stared out across the sea; grey and shifting, restless, always moving, nothing like the placid farming plain that stretched away from the manor she still thought of as home.

Beyond where she stood the land curved out into a point like the prow of a giant ship, and the apex of the point was cluttered with giant boulders worn round and smooth by the wind and weather. She walked towards the rocks, the nearest thing she could find to King's Crag, and stood on the very edge of the cliffs, staring down at the sea dividing and breaking two hundred feet below.

When she first came here she loved the sea, its endlessness, its changing moods, its power; but now she hated it, its constant motion, its constant noise. She hated it during the day and hated it more during the night when its noise came roaring or whispering into her bedroom, taunting her, making her feel more lonely than ever.

She picked up a small rock, hurled it over the cliff edge and watched it fall. The sea consumed it without even noticing. The cold, arrogant sea.

She was irritated by the way it casually ignored the small rock so she lifted a larger, flat rock, staggered to the edge of the cliff and dropped it. It struck an outcrop in the cliff face, bounced out over the water and fell flat on to the shoulders of a large wave. It left a hole that the sea filled angrily with frothy white water but at least she had the satisfaction of feeling that she had made some impression on the beast that postured below.

She turned and walked away, lifted her skirts to step on

to a small boulder, and saw a clutch of primroses already in flower and hiding in a crevice.

'Oh, Edward.' The cry came out without thought. 'Why, Edward, why?'

He would not have waited six months to take her. He would not have waited six minutes if she had only let him know she could have been his the first time they had met on King's Crag. It was all so stupid. Such a waste.

He was dead and if Hubert would not love her she might as well be.

She may as well be dead!

She listened to the sea crashing against the cliffs. That was the answer. Better to die young and tragically than live long and miserably.

She picked the primroses, kissed them and tucked them inside her coat, next to her heart, jumped off the boulder and ran to the cliff edge and stared down. A huge breaker hunched itself and began its run at the cliff. The wind lifted her hair.

'Rose. Rose.' She heard her name, felt her heart pounding, stood on tiptoe ready to jump.

'Rose!' Strong arms grabbed her from behind, wrapped around her and held her.

For a moment she was back on King's Crag and Edward was holding her.

The breaker smashed into the rocks and its death sounds rolled up the cliff.

'It's dangerous to be out here on your own, Princess.'

'Oh, Grandpa.' She let him pull her away and sit her down on a rock a safe distance from the cliff edge. 'Oh, Grandpa. I'm so unhappy. I wish I'd never come here.'

'Now then, young lady, tell me why you're so unhappy.' He still had one arm around her, warm and comforting, and the fingers of his other hand were brushing away her tears. 'Don't worry about not having a baby yet. Sometimes it just doesn't happen that easily, but it will once you settle down here.'

'It won't, Grandpa, not if Hubert doesn't make it.' The words came out in desperation, not because she wanted to betray her husband, the old man's grandson; but once they were said she felt relieved to share the reason for her misery, and guilty that she had revealed a marriage secret.

'Are you saying he hasn't' – the old man paused, looking embarrassed – 'he hasn't consummated your marriage?'

'I've tried to encourage him, really, I have, but he just won't touch me.' She could not speak properly through her sobs.

'He shouldn't need encouragement, Princess. No normal man would.' The grandfather was suddenly angry. 'He needs a whipping. That's what he needs.'

'No, please. Don't. He mustn't know I told you.'

'I can't understand it.' The old man shook his head. 'I've been some things, Princess, and in my time I've done a lot I'm not proud of, but I'd never lose an opportunity with a pretty girl, let alone a beauty like you.'

'Perhaps I'm just not attractive enough for him.'

'What? You're the most beautiful young woman I've ever seen. I always thought Sebastian had a filly when he married your mother, but by God, you're even more beautiful than she was at your age, I remember.' He paused. 'No, never mind that, but I'd have been happy to marry you meself, if you hadn't minded having Hubert as your stepgrandson.'

The thought made her laugh, the first time she had laughed in months, and she thought she knew the old man's humour enough to risk a joke which others would have taken in bad taste. 'Perhaps, if I had married you instead, then Hubert might have been waiting for an uncle to be born.'

'By jove, Princess, he would have been.' The old man roared with laughter and hugged her so tight they nearly fell off the rock. 'But what are we going to do, Princess? Do you love him? Want him?'

'Of course. That's why I'm so miserable.'

'It may be just that he's shy, Princess, so here's what we'll do to make him a bit braver.'

Life in the London house was entirely different to life on the estate. Even though the house was smaller than the house on the cliffs, smaller than the manor she had grown up in, it was still large; and it seemed to be constantly filled with people Hubert and his family knew.

They called during the afternoons, and in the evenings there were theatre parties and invitations to dine out at restaurants or at private homes. Some nights family friends were invited back to the house for dinner and drinks. The social life was exciting, the people amusing and interesting; and there was not time to feel lonely or any reason to feel neglected, until she went to bed alone each night.

Although Hubert began to change, to relax and recover his sense of humour, he still insisted that they slept in separate rooms. His restraint had not been broken even after two weeks, but she was less worried now. He was changing, they had another two weeks before they had to return to his family in the country, and she was determined that she would win him over during that time. She was so happy she even wrote to her mother suggesting she and Elizabeth should come to stay for a few days.

'It seems that we're to spend this evening alone together, Rose.' She did not think he sounded too disappointed. 'Would you like to go out somewhere, a theatre or dinner?'

'No, thank you.' She had refused several invitations already. 'I'd like the two of us to spend this evening alone together. It'll be the first time since our wedding.'

She was relieved when he did not object, encouraged because it seemed he wanted to spend time alone with her.

During dinner she put his grandfather's plan into action. She had dressed in a pale grey suit and a modest, high-necked white blouse, and she dismissed the servants immediately they had served the main course and placed the dessert and fruit and cheeses on a side table.

'I've been enjoying myself more than I ever thought possible,' she explained, 'but I can't be bothered with all the fussing tonight. Let's just talk and enjoy ourselves without any interruptions.'

He nodded, and accepted the wine she poured into his glass.

She filled her own glass and lifted it. 'A toast to us, the Belchesters.' She sipped her wine and watched the satisfying way he drank from his.

She filled his glass again and again, encouraging him to drink far more than she did, and when he finished his main course she dutifully cleared his setting, placed his pudding in front of him and served him a fine golden Madeira.

He talked and ate and drank; and when he had finished she served him cheese and port and suggested he finished the meal with a cigar and a large brandy.

'I feel a little unsteady,' he said as he stood up, the brandy and cigar finished.

'You're probably just tired,' she said smoothly, stood beside him as she cleared his empty glass and the open brandy decanter, and somehow contrived to spill a good quantity of brandy over her blouse. 'Hubert! Do something! I'm soaked and it's burning me.'

He was on his feet, his napkin pressed to her breasts, dabbing at her.

'It's soaked through my blouse. It's burning me,' she cried desperately, helpless with her hands holding the decanter and crystal glass.

He hesitated, seemed confused and unsure what to do. With her hands still full she hooked her fingers between the buttons which closed her blouse and yanked. Buttons flew off as the blouse ripped open. She saw his pupils dilate, felt his napkin wiping the brandy off her chest.

'It's running down me. Stop it. Quick!' Her clothes

ripped, her breasts came free. 'Water, Hubert. Wash me with the cold water.'

She nodded to a jug of iced water but was not prepared for its coldness as he tipped it over her chest. She gasped; and gasped again as he tore off what was left of her blouse and clawed off the rest of her clothes.

The sudden frenzy frightened her, but she did not stop him; she had waited too long for this. He pushed her on to the floor, rolling her over and over, feeling her, squeezing her, kissing her and biting her; praising her and cursing her, one moment telling her he loved her, the next calling her a whore. Then she was on her back, and he was on top of her, his body between her legs, thrusting at her but not entering her. She tried to help him but he was not ready.

'Hubert, Hubert, I love you.' She kissed his shoulder as it moved above her, and then, quite suddenly, his weight crushed down on her and he stopped moving. 'Hubert?'

He lay still. She rolled him off her and he did not move.

He was asleep, in a drunk's sleep; but at least he had made a start.

'A little too much drink, I think, Grandpa,' she muttered and hoped that the next night might be different.

She managed to put him into her bed and helped him when he was sick several times during the night. He slept restlessly, sweating and grinding his teeth, and she lay beside him, happy with the thought that they would wake up beside each other.

She woke up first and turned so she could look at him. She was still looking at him when he woke.

'Good morning, darling.' She stroked his face.

'Rose?'

'Don't look so surprised.' She snuggled close. 'Don't you remember?'

'Some of it,' he said uncertainly, and then urgently, 'Did we . . . ?'

'Of course,' she lied. 'It was wonderful.'

'Oh.' He seemed puzzled. 'I feel awful.'

He recovered during the day and was well enough to be charming and amusing to the friends who came for dinner that evening. Their guests left as the hall clock struck eleven.

'Would you care for a last drink?' she asked him. 'Just the two of us. Alone?'

He nodded, and she saw a look in his eyes that suggested her worries were over.

Her instinct was right. She drank one small cognac and went upstairs to her bathroom, washed, walked naked into the adjoining dressing room and caught sight of herself in a full-length mirror.

'Hmm.' She held her hair up and turned this way and that before the mirror, quite happy that the weight she had lost over the past six months was being replaced already and that the drawn look which had pulled her face out of shape had almost disappeared.

She heard Hubert open her bedroom door as she dabbed herself with perfume and selected her most revealing nightgown. She did not have time to slip it on before the dressing room door swung open.

She stood still, naked, and watched him looking at her.

'I love you, Hubert. I love you so much I . . .'

He grabbed her and his mouth covered hers, a smothering kiss which pushed her head back; then his mouth travelled down over her throat and shoulders and breasts and suddenly she was off her feet, being carried to her bed. The silk quilt cover felt cold for a moment, then her own warmth made it snug against her back and she lay still and watched him undress in front of her, something he had never done before.

He was tall and slim, and what little hair there was on his body was fine and soft and pale.

'I love you, Hubert.'

He lay down beside her and she felt his hands on her body, gentle and smooth, stroking, feeling; heard his breathing, quick and light at first than harsher as he became more excited.

She grunted and gasped as his handling became firmer, more urgent, more exploratory.

'Hubert, love me. Please.' It all seemed about to happen at last.

He continued to handle her, roughly at times, squeezing harder, pressing more firmly.

'Now, darling.' She looked into his eyes, dilated eyes, and begged him to take her properly. 'Please! Now!'

Suddenly he was on top of her, spreading her legs, pushing her; groaning and muttering but not entering her. She tried to help but he was not ready. He groaned louder, pushed harder and harder. He still did not enter her.

She heard the clock in the hall strike twelve as he rolled off her and lay down by her side. She slipped her arm under his shoulders and held him, understanding why he had been so reluctant to share her bed. He was impotent.

'It's all right, darling, I understand,' holding him, kissing him, wondering how to help him overcome whatever was wrong. 'Let's lie here, together, and try to sleep. Don't worry. You'll find a way.'

He did not speak, and holding him, she realised how much she really did love him.

She fell asleep and woke up alone. He had gone back to his own room.

They both tried to act normally the next day but there was a tension she could not break. She tried to discuss the problem but the hurt look in his eyes stopped her and she decided it was best ignored, for the time being.

That evening a married couple Hubert was friendly with invited them and another couple to a theatre. As she climbed down from their hosts' carriage she noticed a crowd gathered on the pavement outside the theatre.

'What's happening?' She was not tall enough to see through the crowd.

'Buskers,' one of the party answered. 'People entertaining the queue waiting to go in.'

'Can we watch?'

'Not if we're to have a drink before the performance.' Hubert stared over the crowd. 'Anyway it looks as though they've almost finished.'

'Oh.' She let Hubert lead her up the steps but there was a crush as they tried to enter the theatre foyer and she stopped and looked back.

She still could not see the performers but she heard one man's closing speech: 'Cry God, for Harry, England and Saint George.'

The words stunned her. She ran back down the steps but the pavement was crowded as the queue moved and people milled about the buskers, calling out their appreciation and throwing pennies to them.

'Rose. Come on, we're waiting,' Hubert called, and she turned and ran back up the steps, felt his hand reach for hers and tow her through the throng in the foyer.

She sat through the performance but she could not concentrate on what was happening; her mind kept slipping back to Pincote, the day Edward brought Elizabeth to the manor, the evening they all rehearsed for the after dinner party, the party itself. Just hearing someone speak those words had brought it all back.

'Are you feeling ill, Rose?' They were back home and Hubert was helping her with her coat. 'You've been very quiet all evening.'

'Yes.' She made herself smile. 'I'm tired, that's all.'

'Are you sure?'

'Yes.' She nodded, excused herself and went upstairs to bed.

She sat in bed, took her diary out of the bedside table and unlocked it but did not make her usual daily entry; instead, she pulled out a piece of paper and unfolded her first sketch of Edward, the one she had made the evening after she had met him on King's Crag.

'You didn't deserve to die, Edward,' whispered as if she were having an intimate conversation with him. 'And I'm partly responsible and I'm sorry. So sorry.'

She cried, not the sobbing tears she had cried when she heard that he was dead and that Nancy had killed his baby, but gentle tears shed more in sorrow for him than for herself.

'Rose? What is the matter?' She had not heard Hubert come through her still-open door. 'What are you looking at?'

'Only a drawing I made a long time ago.' She dried her eyes and let him take the sketch.

'Fine sketch and an interesting-looking fellow.' He held the drawing close to the bedside lamp. 'Who is he?'

'Someone I knew. Once. He used to recite poetry and pieces of Shakespeare. He's dead now.'

'Rather young to die, wasn't he?'

'An accident. He died in an accident,' she explained quietly, and noticed that Hubert had a full glass of brandy in his other hand. 'Don't make yourself ill again, will you?'

'Just something to relax me.' He handed back the drawing and sat on the edge of her bed. 'I thought it might help.'

She saw the look in his eyes and knew what he planned to do. She would rather he had gone to his own bed, but she could not refuse him if he wanted to try again, not after all she had done to encourage him.

'I suppose it might.' She slipped the sketch back into her diary, snapped the lock shut, and put the diary back in the drawer where it belonged.

Hubert finished his drink, washed in her bathroom, and was naked when he came back to her.

'I do love you, Hubert.'

He nodded, told her he loved her, slipped into the bed, and moments later she felt his hands inside her nightgown. He was gentle and loving, complimentary and considerate. She had to make herself respond at first but after a few minutes she was excited enough to respond eagerly.

She was hot and the excitement grew and grew until she thought she would burst if he did not relieve her properly.

'Love me, darling. Now. Please.' She pulled off her nightgown and pushed down the covers so he could look at her.

'You're so beautiful, Rose. So beautiful.' Then he was on her, thrusting at her.

She reached down and tried to help him, held him and prayed that somehow he could overcome his impotence. His closeness, his urgency, his movement against her compounded her feelings. She cried out and grunted and groaned, wished him to enter her, moved into a level of frenzy she had not known before.

'I love you, Rose. I love you so much. I always have.'

Her frenzy built up and up. 'And I love you. I love you so much, Edward.'

'Edward?' He pulled back, kneeling between her legs. 'Edward?'

She felt cold. Her frenzy, her emotions, everything, drained away and left her feeling cold and sorry and ashamed. She lay still, watching his face change.

'Edward who?' His voice was hard, cold and hard like iron.

'I'm sorry. I don't know why I said that,' but it was too late, it had been said, and at a most intimate moment.

'Edward who?' The question was repeated, his voice and expression even harder.

'I'm sorry, Hubert. It doesn't mean anything.'

'Edward who?' His hands gripped her upper arms, his thumbs pressing hard into her muscles, paralysing her with pain. 'Edward who?'

Suddenly she was being shaken so hard her neck was hurting.

'Who, Rose? Edward who? Tell me.'

'Stop it, Hubert. You're hurting me.'

The shaking stopped. 'Edward who?'

'It doesn't matter, darling.'

'It does to me, and you'll tell me even if I have to beat it out of you.'

He hit her.

The punch in her stomach shocked and winded her; she could not have answered even if she had wanted to.

'Who? Who is he, Rose? Who is he?' Another punch and another and another until her stomach and ribs felt bruised and smashed.

Screaming at him, 'It doesn't matter. Please stop. You're hurting me.'

'Who is he? Did he give you a taste for this?'

'No, of course not.'

'Then who? Who? Who?' Each question was marked by another punch. 'Were you thinking of him all the time? Was it him you were thinking of? Did he do what I can't?'

'Please, Hubert. Please don't hit me any more,' crying and pleading, trying to move away but being yanked back. 'Please, Hubert, please don't hit me any more. Please.'

Then his hands pinned her down so she could not move and, unbelievably, she felt him in her, rough and fast, uncaring.

He cried out, she felt wet, and he pulled away.

'Was that good enough for you?' She saw his snarling expression as he asked. 'Well? Was it?'

She knew she had to answer but she could not speak so she nodded.

'Better than him?'

'We never,' she started to say but knew it was useless to try to make him understand. 'I love you, Hubert. Only you.'

He did not speak, just stared at her, then walked away.

He insisted on returning to Dorset the next day. She packed her own clothes, but when she opened the drawer in the bedside table it was empty. He had taken her diary, and she was too scared of the consequences to ask him to return it.

CHAPTER 25

'Doctor Roberts is downstairs?' Elizabeth asked sharply, thinking the girl must have made a mistake.

The young girl nodded, and looked wary, as if she were scared she might be blamed for bringing bad news. 'In the music room, Miss Forrester. Madam asked you to come immediately. I'm sorry. Miss.'

'Thank you.' She stood up and poked her hair with her fingers. 'No, I'm sorry if I sounded rude, it's just that . . .'

The girl smiled as if she understood the worry that the doctor's sudden appearance had caused, and backed away, holding the door open. 'May I go, miss?'

'Yes, of course.' She needed a moment to compose herself. 'Please tell Mrs Laybourne that I'll be downstairs in just a few minutes.'

The girl left, closing the door softly.

Oh God. Her hands were trembling. Doctor Roberts was a busy man, he would not call unless it was necessary. He had called only once during the ten weeks that had passed since he had finally managed to convince Charlotte to send John away from Pincote for specialist treatment.

Ten weeks of misery for both her and Charlotte. Ten weeks which had passed so slowly, seemed so much longer to her because after seeing John every day for months she was not allowed to visit him at all, was not even allowed to write to him. The doctors at the hospital said he had to work hard at getting better and learn to accept what disabilities he could not overcome; visitors, even letters, were an unwanted diversion. And he was expected to be there for several months more; but spending months apart no longer seemed important. Not now.

'Doctor Roberts.' She could not see his face, he was looking out of the window. 'Good morning.'

Her voice trembled. Charlotte reached out and pulled her down beside her on the settee. They held hands, both shaking. The doctor turned around.

'I apologise for coming without notice, but I received this letter this morning.' He pulled a fold of paper from his jacket pocket. 'It's about John. My old colleague at the hospital has written to say he's done all he can for him and can see little value in John remaining there much longer.' The doctor wrinkled his forehead, and added, 'However, he has agreed to keeping him there for a few more weeks if you don't feel you can bring him home and want to find him somewhere else to stay.'

'What does that mean?' Elizabeth heard Charlotte ask quietly. 'Does that mean he can't be cured?'

'We can't cure disabilities, Mrs Laybourne, especially those resulting from the type of injuries your son has suffered.'

'Then what does it mean?' Elizabeth found her own voice. 'We expected him to be away for several more months. Please be honest, Doctor, we need to know.'

Doctor Roberts looked her full in the eyes. 'Elizabeth, we agreed that if John was to recover as much as possible he needed both to be helped by doctors and nurses who were experienced in treating injuries like his, and to meet other men with similar injuries. It's important that he doesn't see himself as a freak.'

'Yes, I know we agreed to all that, Doctor,' she said, her voice sharp again, 'but what—'

'Elizabeth,' Doctor Roberts interrupted her, 'we managed to have John cared for in a very special hospital. The doctors and nurses believe they've done all they can to repair his body and we must accept what they say. He's ugly, he's lost a leg, he can't use his hands properly or see properly, and he's not going to get any better. He'll always be in some pain, and all of that will have changed him.'

'We understand all that,' she objected, but the doctor held up his hand.

'No. With respect, you're aware of the problems but you don't understand them. You cannot understand them until you've lived with them, and once you've brought John home you'll be committed to living with him for the rest of his life.' Doctor Roberts sounded angry and she did not dare to interrupt him again. 'During the past ten weeks John's lived with men who have similar injuries to his own. He's started to accept how he is, but once he returns home, and is living amongst things that remind him of how he was before the accident, he'll realise the extent of his disabilities. That might well lead to bouts of depression or violent tantrums. He might even want to slide back into the trance he lived in for months, alive but unaware. Are you positive you can cope with that? Don't you have any reservations at all about bringing a total stranger into your home?'

'But he's not a total stranger, Doctor,' Charlotte began, then stopped as the doctor raised his hand.

'No, he's worse, Mrs Laybourne. He's a stranger in what's left of your son's body.'

Elizabeth saw Charlotte blanch, and suddenly remembered how Annie Darling had to cope. She shuddered. 'What's the alternative, Doctor?'

'Let's worry about that after you've seen him.' The
doctor smiled for the first time.

'We can see him?' Charlotte asked excitedly.

'Of course. He's not a prisoner, but please don't expect
too much. You may not be able to see any actual difference
in his condition.'

'When' – Elizabeth noticed how excited she sounded –
'when can we see him?'

'You must let me know, Elizabeth, but allow yourself a
few days to adjust to the situation, to prepare yourselves
for what you'll see. There'll be others around who look far
worse than John, and they'll be just as sensitive to your
reactions as he'll be.'

As the train slowly chuffed its way through the sunlit
Borders countryside Elizabeth noticed how often
Charlotte fiddled with her clothes or cast surreptitious
glances at the watch she was holding in her pocket. She
guessed what was on her mind. They would shortly see
John for the first time for more than ten weeks, and
Charlotte, like her, was wondering what they would find.

They were visiting him to decide if they could endure
living with him again. It seemed a cold and callous thing to
do, but both she and Charlotte had enough confidence in
Doctor Roberts to consider his advice.

Elizabeth read the name above the station platform. 'We've
arrived, Charlotte.'

'Yes,' Charlotte said, but did not move.

'Come on,' she said gently, and helped her down on to
the platform. 'Doctor Roberts said he's improved
remarkably well.'

'Yes, but he also said we weren't to expect too much.'

'I know but there's only one way to find out how well he
is.' Elizabeth tried to sound confident but her stomach was
churning with fear.

When John left Pincote he was weak and bitter,

depressed so much he hardly spoke except to complain about the constant pain or things he could not do. What was he like now, ten weeks later, and what would he look like? Would he be able to see any better, move any easier? Would he be anything like the man they both loved, or would he be a stranger, someone who was unlovable?

She approached the first cab waiting outside the station and asked the driver if he knew the hospital.

'Aye, ladies.' The cab driver nodded. 'I know the hospital right enough. Settle yourself in now, it'll take us about an hour but at least the countryside's nice in this sunny weather.'

An hour! The drive seemed to take much longer but she tried to relax herself and Charlotte by discussing the unfamiliar countryside, exchanging inane comments about the likelihood of the good weather lasting all day, the possibility of an early spring, the size of the lambs which crowded the fields, and anything else that occurred to her.

Eventually the cab passed through a large village which seemed to be centred around an army barracks, and on the outskirts of the village it turned through a pair of wrought-iron gates similar to those at Laybourne Manor, and headed along a sweeping white stone drive between well-kept lawns.

What she saw on the lawns shocked her: trains of uniformed nurses pushing limbless men in wheelchairs, men with one leg missing walking about on crutches, men with no legs lying out on rugs on the grass, men with no arms, and, worst of all, men without proper faces.

She felt sick, glanced at Charlotte and saw that all the colour had drained from her face. Charlotte looked awful, and she guessed that she looked just as bad. The only consolation she could find was that all this had prepared them before they saw John. He might not be able to see their expression, but there was no doubt that he would notice any hesitation or doubt in their voices and the way they touched him.

'Steady yourself, Elizabeth,' Charlotte said, and it was obvious that she was having similar thoughts.

The cab left them by steps leading up to an ornate front door, and the driver joined a rank of cabs waiting to take visitors back to the station.

'Well, Charlotte.' She stiffened herself for the ordeal which was to follow. 'Are you ready?'

Charlotte did not speak, she just nodded and they climbed the steps together, stopped at a reception desk inside the main hall and introduced themselves.

'Mr Laybourne?' The pretty young woman behind the desk smiled. 'He already has two visitors, his fiancée and her father.'

'I didn't know they were coming.' Charlotte sounded annoyed.

'They arrived an hour ago,' the woman said, and asked them to wait while she found someone to take them to John.

Minutes later a large, muscular, stern-looking nurse arrived, her starched uniform crackling as she walked. 'More visitors for Mr Laybourne? I hope this isn't tiring him too much.'

The nurse led them along a passage and opened a door into a large, plant-filled conservatory. 'He's in there,' she said, and left without another word.

There were several patients entertaining groups of visitors in the conservatory and although Elizabeth could not see John she did recognise Mr McDougall. She led the hesitant Charlotte forward and as they moved between two large potted shrubs Lillian saw them, stood up to greet them and said, in a voice an adult might use when speaking to a child, 'Why, John, it's your mother and Miss Forrester.'

John was sitting in an upright chair with his back towards them and he made no attempt to stand or turn around so they could see his face.

'Come on, Charlotte,' Elizabeth said, and put on a bright smile.

'Mother and Elizabeth?' She heard John's voice, hesitant and strange but sounding as if he were relieved as much as glad to see them.

'How are you, John?' She walked forward, almost pulling Charlotte along, moved around his chair and was about to bend down and touch his hand when he stood up.

'I'm well, and much better for seeing you.' He kissed her cheek lightly and too fast for her to see what he looked like, then Charlotte was there and he was kissing her, his arms around his mother's neck, squeezing her tight.

'That's a nice coat, Elizabeth,' he said as he turned away from Charlotte. 'And I like that clasp, sorry, brooch.'

'A Christmas present from your mother,' she said quickly, then realised what he had said. 'You can see it.'

'With my left eye. You're a blur with my right.' He grinned, an awkward grin through battered lips that looked as if they were not part of his shiny, stiff-skinned and disfigured face. 'And I can walk, with a crutch of course.'

To prove it he lurched away to a table laden with cups and saucers, picked up a cup and lurched back.

'Can't manage to carry a cup on a saucer, yet. Trail of smashed crockery to prove that, but a lot better than the last time you saw me, eh?'

It was, and the relief made her cry.

He was broken and he was ugly and his speech was difficult to understand even though his voice was strong, but at that moment he was the most beautiful man she had ever seen and his voice was more moving than the best music.

She wanted to hug him and tell him she loved him, but with Lillian and her father present she knew she could not. Not until they could spend a few minutes alone.

'How are things at home?' He took the initiative, pointed to two empty chairs and waved an arm towards the table holding the tea things. 'Help yourselves to tea. The service here's appalling, you have to do everything for yourself. They say it's part of the treatment, but I reckon it's because they just can't be bothered. I keep telling them that if things don't improve I'll leave, but old Boadicea, one of the nurses, big strong woman, reckons she can't wait to see the back of me.'

'Shameful,' she heard Lillian say, shaking her head and not understanding John's awful sense of humour.

She poured tea for Charlotte and herself, settled on a chair and studied him. He still looked as battered as when he left Pincote, but he had put on weight, he was wearing ordinary clothes with one trouser leg pinned up so it did not flap loose below his stump, and he constantly clenched and opened his fists.

'Exercises.' He smiled at her. 'To stretch the skin and build up my strength. That's all we do here, exercise, sit in foul-smelling baths, eat and sleep. That and read and throw small balls to each other.'

'It seems to have done you good.' She smiled back, wondering why Doctor Roberts had warned them not to expect too much; it seemed that the hospital had worked a miracle.

They talked for half an hour; often awkward, stilted conversation, relieved only by John's stories about what had been done to him and the mischief he and a few others caused to get some sort of revenge on the staff. Lillian and her father listened intently, accepted his wild exaggerations as fact and occasionally tutting their disapproval when he told them about his pranks.

Lillian's father stood up during one of the silences. 'Miss Forrester, would you care to join me in a stroll around the grounds? Leave John with his mother and Lillian for a while?'

She was reluctant to agree but did so because it would have been embarrassing to refuse his suggestion. They walked away from the conservatory and along a path between high clumps of rhododendron.

It was several minutes before he spoke. 'It's quite

obvious that you're very fond of young John.'

'Yes, sir.' She wondered what he might say next.

'More than fond, I'd guess.'

There was no point in denying it. 'Is it that obvious?'

'Oh, yes. My daughter and I have discussed it.'

They had discussed it? There was nothing she could say so she said nothing, and waited a minute or so for him to continue.

'Very difficult subject, this, my dear. You know that Lillian and John have been engaged for three years now?'

'Yes, sir.'

'Well, it's clear that you've been instrumental in helping John to recover. I understand that you spent hours sitting by him when he was in Pincote infirmary, reading to him and talking. You even told him his father was dead, and that must have taken a lot of courage. Your sort of devotion is highly commendable, my dear, and you deserve the utmost praise,' he blundered on and she wished he would get to the point. 'Reminds me rather of Miss Smith and Sebastian. Stayed with him for years, helped to bring up his children. Most unfair, really. Devoted her life to him even though there was no chance of him reciprocating her feelings.'

'Is that so?' No need to tell him she knew any of the unpleasant truths about their relationship.

'Well, my dear, admirable as that sort of devotion is, and if I knew how to brew the sort of loyalty the Laybournes attract I'd bottle it and make my fortune, but, admirable as it is, Lillian and I would not want to see that situation repeated.' He paused and turned to her. 'We fully understand that you may wish to devote the rest of your life to John, and my daughter wants you to understand that she has no objection to that.'

What did he mean? Was he saying that Lillian would make John free to marry her?

'I don't understand what you mean, Mr McDougall.'

'Simply this. If you wish to remain in the house to take

care of John, then Lillian has no objection, but if you wish to leave, then we'll understand.'

Disappointment, anger, and then a cool fury flooded through her. 'Forgive me, Mr McDougall, but I find that very offensive. What right do you or your daughter have to be so, so patronising?' She noticed a blue colour rise up in his pudgy face. 'May I remind you that Charlotte is still the mistress of the manor and the estates, that she considers me as a friend rather than an employee, and that I am her companion, not your daughter's skivvy.'

'I don't think I understand your meaning, Miss Forrester.' He heaved his shoulders and thundered at her.

'I think you understand fully, Mr McDougall, but if you wish . . .' He charged off before she could finish.

She stood and watched him go, tried to compose herself and failed, and decided that she needed to be alone until her temper had cooled.

'Miss Forrester?'

She turned and saw the stern nurse who had taken her and Charlotte to find John. 'Yes, I'm Elizabeth Forrester.'

'You're upset.' A kind voice came out from the intimidating face. 'Is it because of Mr Laybourne?'

'No, not at all. I'm relieved to see him looking so well, considering how ill he was the last time I saw him. He's improved so much.'

'I know your secret, Miss Forrester. He told me when I was treating him one day. He's determined to be able to walk down the aisle and speak clearly during your marriage service. We try to get the men to set themselves targets, and that's been his. He's a remarkable man, like so many we see here, but he owes a lot to you and he knows that.'

'He owes more to you and the others here, nurse.'

'Don't call me nurse. Call me Boadicea. He does, even though he doesn't realise I know.' The nurse smiled. 'I'm sorry, but I couldn't help overhearing part of your conversation. Stick to your guns, as we say here. You'll win. You'll see.'

'Thank you. When do you think the doctors will allow John to come home?'

Boadicea shrugged. 'He's as fit as he's going to get here. Take him back with you, if you think you can manage. Take him back so he's with you and that other silly woman and her father can't influence him.'

'Can't influence him?'

'They've been here before. Twice.'

'But I thought visitors weren't allowed?'

'It's difficult to refuse someone who's on the hospital board, Miss Forrester. Particularly someone like Mr McDougall and especially when his daughter is to marry the patient they wish to visit.'

'But he didn't tell Charlotte, John's mother, that he had been here.'

Boadicea shrugged. 'I suppose he had his reasons, but if Mr Laybourne is at home he won't be able to visit him without your knowing. Take him, if you think you can manage.'

'Do you mean that? What'll the doctors say?'

'They'll probably thank you. Mr Laybourne's taking up room we can use to help someone else.'

'I'll discuss it with his mother.'

She walked for twenty minutes or more, nodding and smiling at the men she saw, steeling herself not to show the revulsion their appearance made her feel, and when she was in control she returned to the conservatory.

John and Charlotte were alone.

'Thank you,' John said as she walked up to him.

'For what?'

'I don't know what you said to Lillian's father but he looked furious when he came back from your walk and insisted it was time he and Lillian left.'

'I'm afraid I was very rude to him. I lost my temper and said things that might've been better left unsaid, especially when I think how helpful he's been over the past few months.'

'Don't worry about it. I don't know why they came, I didn't ask them to.'

'Have they been before?' Charlotte asked, not bothering to hide her annoyance.

'Twice, two or three weeks ago. I refused to see them the first time, but I could hardly refuse again.'

'But he's seen me since then and he didn't mention his visits,' Charlotte said angrily.

'He wouldn't,' John said awkwardly, then added quietly, 'Well, what do you think of me? Do you want me back home or do you think I'll frighten the staff and the horses too much?'

'I want you home as soon as possible,' Charlotte answered without hesitating.

'Elizabeth?' She saw the doubt in his eyes and wanted to cry again.

'Why don't you come back with us? Today. Your friend, Boadicea, told me there's nothing more they can do for you and the doctors would be pleased to see the back of you.'

'Do you really want me back, Elizabeth?'

She leaned towards him, put her hands on his face and kissed him full on his scratchy, misshapen mouth. 'As soon as possible. I've missed you terribly.'

'Mother's told me she knows about our plans, and she's happy to see us married. Do you still want to go through with that? I'll understand if you don't. Lillian and her father are sure to fight, there'll be a lot of bad feeling, and anyway I'm not much of a catch, not now.'

'Just you try to stop me, Mr Laybourne.' The tears were flooding down her face and people were staring at her, but she did not care.

'Well, there's something you should know before you really commit yourself, Elizabeth.' He hesitated, and she could see from the look in his eyes that there was something terribly wrong. 'There's damage you can't see. I breathed in a lot of very hot smoke and dust. My lungs can't be repaired. I don't know how long I've got, but I'm not going to be an old man.'

She looked at him, the progress he had made, all his hard work; it seemed so unfair.

She knew that for once he was not exaggerating; this time he was understating the problem. If he said he was not going to be an old man he really meant that he did not have very much longer to live; that was what Doctor Roberts had meant when he warned her not to expect too much.

It was cruel; and there was only one answer she could give him.

'Then we'll just have to enjoy whatever time we can have together, John.'

CHAPTER 26

'I'm bored, Elizabeth.' She smiled at him; he had been home for two days and already he was restless. 'Let's go for a walk.'

'A walk?'

'Well, you walk and I'll hop alongside you.' He laughed and she laughed with him because she was happy to be with him and glad he had learned to laugh at his injuries.

They walked towards the lodge. She could not relax; she was waiting for him to fall, but he managed, helped by a crutch and grunting with every step.

'Don't try to go too far,' she warned.

'Wait until I get my Anglesey, then you'll have to run to keep up.'

His Anglesey was a wooden leg which hinged at the knee and ankle and which he was to be fitted for in two weeks' time.

'Then I suppose you'll want to go underground again,' she said quietly.

'As soon as possible. I have to, Elizabeth. You understand why?'

'I suppose so.'

'Anyway, I want to look at the new entry.' He stopped. 'I don't think I can go any further. Do you mind if we go back to the house?'

'Of course not.' She turned, walked a few paces, then realised he had not moved. 'Are you all right?'

'Yes.' He was staring at the manor, where the new end wall and the newly slated roof marked the damage done by the fire. 'I find that rather comforting, somehow.'

'Comforting?'

'Yes. It makes me feel as though I'm in good company. The house has had a bit lopped off it, like me, and it's been patched up like me, but it'll go on, like me. Don't you feel that, too?'

It was a view that had not occurred to her before, but she understood, walked back to him and put her arms around him. 'I love you, John. I can't tell you how much.'

'You can try.' He laughed and she enjoyed the way he hung on to her so he could kiss her.

Elizabeth was pleased when, after dinner, Charlotte left them alone in the music room. She was reading and John was running his fingers over the piano keys, exercising his hands rather than playing a proper tune.

'We haven't talked, Elizabeth, not properly,' he said suddenly and turned on the stool so he faced her.

She put her book down on the table beside her; this was the moment she knew had to come but had been prepared to wait for. 'No, we haven't. Not properly.'

'It must have been awful for you.' He spoke gently and she could see how concerned he was not to upset her more than he had to. 'Everything happening at once like that, and with no one to turn to.'

She did not speak for a moment. He did not know everything that had happened and she did not want to say anything which might make him suspicious. 'Your mother was very kind to me.' It sounded trite under the circumstances, but it was true.

'And you were very good for her. She told me she couldn't have coped if it hadn't been for you. Rose doesn't seem to have helped very much.'

'Don't blame her,' she said quickly. 'She's very young, she had enough to think about on her own account, and there wasn't much she could have done anyway.'

'You were here so I'll accept what you say, but do you think she did the right thing in marrying Belchester?'

'Probably not.' The opinion slipped out unconsciously. 'Oh, I don't know, John, it's difficult to say. We didn't hear from her for months but when she wrote her last letter she seemed very happy.'

'But you think she would have been happier married to Edward?'

'We'll never know, will we?' A lump formed in her throat.

'I can't believe he's dead, Elizabeth.'

She did not want to keep any secrets from him, she wanted to tell him she thought Edward might still be alive somewhere, but first she had to tell him how both his father and Edward had really died; she had led him to believe that Edward had died underground and his father had died shortly after the accident and the fire.

'John, I've an awful confession to make to you. I lied to you about your father and Edward, how they died, because you were very ill and I was scared the shock might kill you too. But I must tell you now, before you find out from someone else.' She looked directly into his eyes and saw his head shake slightly as she rushed through what had happened. 'Edward was hurt during the rescue, he wasn't killed until later. And the fire wasn't an accident, it was started by Henry Wright or one of the mob he brought here after the men had been rescued from the mine.'

'I see, but . . .' He scratched his head. 'Never mind, just carry on.'

'Billy Darling told Edward that Henry was going to burn the house and he came to stop him, or to try, but the house was already on fire when he arrived, so he came looking for me, to try to save me, John. Your father didn't just die, he was killed while Edward was here and the police believe Edward killed him. Edward died shortly afterwards. He was near the spills when the charges that had been set to scatter them exploded.'

John was silent for a minute or so. 'Good God, Elizabeth! I'm, well, stunned.' He stopped again, obviously shocked and confused. 'It'll take me a while to understand all this, but why do the police think Edward killed my father?'

This was going to be the worst part to explain. 'Your father was killed with a poker which was found by his body. The police believe it was Edward because, in the heat of the moment, when the main road collapsed and the mine was flooding, your father refused to sound the general alarm and Edward threatened to kill him. Some men overheard and told a newspaper reporter. The newspaper even used the threat as a headline to its front page story the next day.'

John did not say anything, just sat slumped on the stall. She walked over to him and wrapped her arms around him.

He held her tight, his face pressed against her breasts until she pulled away when he spoke. 'Do you think Edward killed him?'

'Yes, but I can't believe it was deliberate.' That was the best she could offer Edward without explaining the whole story, and she could not inflict that on John, not on top of everything else, and she would not risk ruining her own intimacy with him by telling him that his father had raped her.

'I don't understand any of this, Elizabeth. It's a

nightmare, but if Edward did kill Father it must have been an accident. I can't believe he was a cold-blooded killer.'

'No. Your mother and I agree.'

He paused and hugged her tightly. 'Where's he buried? North Hill?'

'His headstone's there. I had one put up and Adam Marriott said a few words for him.'

'His headstone?'

'They never found his body. The police assumed it . . .' She could not finish.

'My poor darling.' He struggled upright and hugged her tightly. 'And I thought I was the one who needed sympathy.'

'Don't, John,' she pleaded, 'don't make me cry any more.'

'Come on, let's sit down.' He grabbed his crutch and they moved on to the settee and sat cuddled together for several minutes.

It was a warm, wonderful feeling, to be held and loved and treated gently. 'I love you, John. So much.'

'You must do, still to be here after all that's happened to you.' He hugged her tighter and kissed her hair.

'Of course I stayed. You're all I've got left.' She kissed his face. 'Well, maybe . . .'

'Maybe?' he asked when she stopped.

'Well, I think there's a possibility Edward may still be alive.' Now she had seen his reaction to the truth she knew she could tell him what had happened at Adam and Nancy's wedding, so she explained everything that had been said.

'I can understand why you think that, but I can't believe he could have escaped from the ridge without being seen, especially as he would have been tired and hurt.'

'But his bag was taken from the lamp room.'

'Perhaps, but perhaps it was lost or stolen. Don't hope too much. People do, you know, if they've lost someone and they haven't had a proper funeral. It's difficult to adjust to losing someone anyway, without all you've had to put up with.'

'But I've just got this feeling, John,' she said, knowing he was right and half thinking about Pru Wright who still talked sometimes as though Ned and the boys were below ground, working a shift.

'Perhaps you are right, Elizabeth, but don't be too hopeful that you'll ever see him again if he is still alive.' He hugged her and kissed her again. 'He'll probably stay in hiding rather than risk being caught by the police.'

'I know. That's why I haven't told anyone else.'

'And mustn't, Elizabeth, ever. It's got to stay our secret. If he is alive it's the only way we can help him.'

Elizabeth was pleased that the weather, although cold, was dry and sunny, because it allowed her and John to walk outside every day. By the end of his first week at home he could walk all the way to the lodge, and it was while they were sitting on a bench in the lodge garden that he told her that Lillian and her father were coming to stay for a few days.

'Catherine and Walter will be here too,' he added quickly.

She grimaced. 'I can't say I'll look forward to meeting either Mr McDougall or his daughter, John, especially after the row at the hospital.'

'You'll have to face them sometime, Elizabeth, and as Catherine and Walter will be here it may be the right time for me to talk to Lillian and tell her and them that we're getting married.'

'I've already told Catherine,' she blurted. 'I can't remember how it happened now, but she knows.'

'And?'

'She's very happy for us. She even said she did not think you would actually marry Lillian.'

'How perceptive.' He shrugged. 'Look, I don't mind that you told her, or my mother of course, but does anyone else know? Any of the staff?'

'They shouldn't. Why?'

'Old Hopkins.' He frowned. 'He's been a little odd with me since I came back home. Not unpleasant or surly or anything like that but, well, distant, I suppose. I thought it was something to do with the way I am now, but I've noticed the way he looks at you sometimes. I thought that he may have heard something and doesn't approve of my philanderings.'

'Hardly philanderings.' She laughed falsely, suddenly on edge, and old memories and fears made her shudder.

'You're cold.' John lurched upright. 'Come on, let's go back indoors.'

She did not argue; she wanted to go back to the house and find Mr Hopkins and insist he told her what was on his mind.

She found him in the coach house.

'I'm glad I've found you alone, Mr Hopkins.' She closed the door behind her so he would find it more difficult to escape. 'I'd like to talk with you for a few minutes.'

'Aye, Miss Elizabeth.' She thought he looked nervous as she approached him.

'I've noticed you looking at me in a rather, I suppose, furtive manner.' She stood directly in front of him, making it clear that he had to stay and talk. 'I first noticed it a long time ago, before last year's ball, and I should have approached you before but whenever I began to broach the subject you always avoided answering me. Now Mr John has also noticed, so I think you owe me an explanation.'

He looked at the ground and shuffled his feet, but made no attempt to speak.

'Mr Hopkins, you've always been very kind to me and I promise that whatever you say won't make me angry. Whatever you say will remain between us, if you prefer, but I must know what's been on your mind. It's beginning to worry me that I may have done something you disapprove of.'

'Oh no, Miss Elizabeth,' he said quickly. 'It's nothing like that.'

'Then what is it?' Asked gently with an intonation of puzzlement. 'Please say, whatever it is.'

'It's just that' – he spoke slowly, avoiding her eyes, obviously embarrassed to say anything – 'well, sometimes, when you let your hair down, well, you remind me of someone.'

Her stomach knotted itself, and she asked sharply, 'Who?'

'Are you coming to the Horse Fair?' he asked, looking directly at her. 'It's in a couple of days' time.'

'I know when it is, Mr Hopkins, but what has that to do with my question?'

'Everything, miss, or maybe nothing.'

'I don't understand.'

'There'll be someone there I'd like you to meet, miss.' She could see he was sweating even though the coach house was cold.

'Who? And what do they have to do with this?' The knot had turned into real fear.

'I'd rather not say until you've met her, Miss Elizabeth, but I think you should come. I'll introduce you, but you should see her alone.'

'Very well.' It was obvious that he was not going to say any more so she did not pressure him further, simply turned away and left.

The Horse Fair was an annual Pincote Market event. The town was packed with visitors, and the Victoria Gardens, the town's recreation ground alongside the river, became a camp for gypsies who brought horses to sell, and for a circus and fair.

Catherine and Walter were happy to accompany her to the fair but Charlotte was busy supervising the staff and arranging accommodation for Lillian and her father who were due to arrive the following day, and John decided that the fair would be too tiring and stayed at home with his mother.

The moment they arrived at the fair Elizabeth suggested Catherine and Walter go off and explore while she helped Hopkins with some small chores, and she arranged for them all to meet near the bandstand in an hour's time.

'Come on, Mr Hopkins.' She took a firm grip on his arm. 'Introduce me to your friend.'

'Weddy Hedge isn't really a friend, Miss Elizabeth,' he explained nervously, 'she's sort of related to me. My parents were gypsies and there's a family connection somewhere, mind, but I'm not really sure exactly what it is.'

'Does that matter?'

'Not really,' he admitted, and she realised he was talking because he was nervous.

He led her to a weary-looking caravan and asked her to wait while he climbed up on the driving board and disappeared inside. He reappeared a moment later and helped her climb up.

'Miss Elizabeth' – he moved aside so she could duck through the small door – 'this is Weddy Hedge.'

A short, wide, brown-skinned old crone stared at her through the dim light.

'Come in. Come right in, my dear.' A hand pulled her inside and made her sit on a wooden bench in front of a plank table.

Hopkins excused himself and left the door open so a little light could filter into the dark caravan, poorly lit by a single candle. 'So you're Elizabeth Forrester?' the crone said in a wheezing voice.

'Yes.' She drew back as the gypsy picked up the candle and moved it close to her face. 'I'm Elizabeth Forrester.'

'Brought up by Joshua and Minty Forrester?'

'Yes.' Hopkins must have told her that.

'And you're living up at Laybourne Manor now?'

'Yes. Why?'

'A minute. A minute.' The old woman sat back and

seemed to think. 'Your hair, all tied up like that. Undo it. I want to see it loose.'

Her fingers trembled as she pulled her net off and shook her hair free.

'I can see. Oh yes, I can see.' The old woman lifted the candle again.

'What can you see?' she asked, her voice trembling like her hands.

'Tell me, my dear' – the gypsy ignored the question – 'a few things about yourself.'

'What things?'

'Do you have the sleeper's eye?'

'What's that?'

'Sleeper's eye!' the old woman said impatiently, as if she were talking to a fool. 'Your left eyelid drops when you're tired.'

It was a surprise to be told that by a complete stranger. 'Yes, I do.'

'And you've got two little holes in the top of your left ear?'

'Yes?'

'Well, anyone who's been close enough to you could know that, my dear, but they wouldn't know this, not unless they'd been real close,' and even before the old woman told her she knew what she would say next. 'There's a red blotch, shaped like a pear, right at the top of your right leg. Inside like, where nobbut a husband or a mother should see it.'

'Yes.'

'Then you're Willow's girl, all right, just like Laybourne said. But you've got the Laybourne nose, though for your sake I hope that's all Sebastian Laybourne gave you.'

'Gave me?' An awful fear crept through her: Willow, gypsy girl?

'He's your father. Sebastian Laybourne sired you through me daughter, Willow.'

Oh God! She was Sebastian Laybourne's daughter.

Then an even worse shock hit her. She was John's half sister.

The shock and the musty smell of the enclosed caravan made her vomit over the table.

She was sitting on a seat near the riverbank and did not hear Catherine approaching. 'Elizabeth! I've been looking everywhere for you. Walter's still looking on the far side of the ground. We were worried you might have had an accident. You were supposed to meet us an hour ago.'

'I'm sorry.' She did not look up, not even when Catherine's arm slipped around her shoulders.

'Are you ill? You look awful.'

'I know who Willow is. Was.' She stared into Catherine's face and saw it turn pale. 'She was my mother.'

'And your father?' Catherine stammered.

She did not answer, simply nodded, and knew Catherine would understand.

'Oh, Elizabeth!'

They sat together, stunned, two daughters who had both been raped by their father.

'How did you find out?' Catherine asked eventually, and Elizabeth told her everything Weddy Hedge had said, including the detailed account of how Hopkins had inadvertently introduced Willow to Sebastian, how Willow had died giving her life and how Weddy had abandoned her where she knew the baby would be found.

Catherine listened without interrupting, and when the story was finished held both her hands and squeezed them. 'Elizabeth, this means we're half sisters. You understand what that means?'

'Only too well. I'm John's half sister, too, and that means I can't marry him.'

'You could keep it a secret,' Catherine suggested, adding gently, 'After all, it may not be for long, Elizabeth.'

'No. There are too many secrets already. One of them's bound to come out and then the whole thing would collapse. Besides, I couldn't live with it. John's already made it clear that he's quite capable of being a proper husband and I couldn't refuse him so there could be a child, or children, to consider.'

'Then what are you going to do?'

'Well, I'm not going to marry John so I must leave as soon as possible. I don't know beyond that.'

'It'll devastate him, Elizabeth.'

'He'll survive if I handle it properly, but it'll kill him if he ever finds out the truth.'

'What will you tell him? How will you tell him?'

'I won't tell him anything. I can't. I can't tell him the truth and I couldn't lie to him, not convincingly, so I'll simply leave. No letter, no goodbyes. Simply go.'

'When?'

'Now. I can't face him this evening. Or Charlotte. I've got to go now, while I still feel strong enough. If you'll help me.'

Catherine looked unsure, then seemed to make up her mind. 'What do you want me to do?'

She could not remember the station-master's name but she was sure he recognised her. She hoped he had. John was sure to ask at the station when he realised she had left Pincote, and when he heard she had purchased a through ticket to London and left without any baggage he would probably assume that the strain of the past months had led to a mental aberration. That was the kindest thing that could happen.

She stood still as the locomotive came growling and hissing into the station, filling it with steam and smoke, suddenly reminding her of the day she had waited for Saul and met John. Perhaps she should have married Saul and settled down comfortably as a schoolmaster's wife. At least she would have had a warm home and security.

Now she was off to God knows where to do God knows what; and she was scared.

'Oh, John!' She had always had him to think about since everything started to go wrong, and now she was alone; completely alone.

Even her relationship with Catherine would have to be kept secret, and she could never see Rose again.

A whistle blew, the locomotive chuffed. She stepped forward, opened a carriage door, stood with one foot on the step and the other planted firmly on the platform.

Was there an alternative? Could she stay and marry John and live with the possible consequences?

Or perhaps she could find a way to persuade him to marry Lillian and she could still stay in the manor as Charlotte's companion? Miss Smith had managed for all those years; would it really be any worse than never seeing John again?

She stepped back on to the platform. A whistle blew again, the locomotive gathered up steam. Wheels spun against the rails. The carriage started to move slowly away.

She stood and watched, heart beating fast, and began to tremble.

The train was leaving. She had to decide now.

But there was no choice, not really.

She began to run.

PART THREE

CHAPTER 27

The scraggy little tree outside Number Fourteen Angel Street was just breaking into bud.

'Looks lovely in the summer, dear, and real beautiful in the autumn. You must be Miss Forrester?' A friendly voice spoke up.

She turned away from the tree and looked across the pavement, across the front garden which could not have been more than five feet deep and twelve wide but was arranged with its own system of tiled paths and black soil flower beds, and across the white-stoned step to the open front door. A pair of bright eyes seemed to glow in the evening gloom; there was a rustle and a tiny wren of a woman stepped forward. She was tiny; less than five feet tall, narrow, fragile-looking, and grey from her neatly swept-back hair, her blouse under an encompassing overall to her stockings and soft shoes. But the sun seemed to shine out of her smile and its warmth reached down to her outstretched hand.

'I'm Evie Roper. Come in, dear. I've got the kettle on.'

'Thank you, Mrs Roper.' She followed her down the narrow hall, careful not to bang her new bag against the wallpapered walls.

'No, call me Evie, dear. No need to be formal if you're going to be living here.'

'Oh thank you.' She was grateful for the stranger's friendliness. 'I'm Lizzie.'

No need to stand on ceremony here, she already felt at home and Lizzie was much more homely than Elizabeth.

'Well, come into the kitchen, Lizzie, and sit down. You must be tired after your journey.' She followed Evie into the kitchen at the back of the house; a room as big as the parlour in her mother's little cottage and a real kitchen with a black kitchen range, a large table pushed against a wall, three dining chairs, a sideboard and two easy chairs either side of the range. 'We'll have a cup of tea and a chat then sort your room out, and after that we'll have some dinner.'

The room smelled of stew and boiling potatoes, washing and polish.

'Here, give me your bag.' Evie dumped the bag on one of the dining chairs. 'Hang your coat up on the hallstand, dear. If you want the toilet it's up the first flight of stairs, the left-hand door on the landing. If you want to wash you'll have to drain off some water and use the sink in the scullery. That's down the stairs, out the back, in the addition.'

'It's a lovely house, Evie.'

'Not bad. Moved here with my Sidney twelve years ago. He died three years ago this July. It's a bit big for me on me own, so I'm glad to have a bit of company.'

It was big, bigger than she had expected; terraced but three stories with a two-storey back addition. She quickly worked out the number of rooms: two on each storey of the main building, a scullery and another room above that. Eight rooms and an inside toilet. Her mother would have thought it was a palace.

'No one else lives with you?' It seemed such a waste.

'No, not now. I did have a lodger until three weeks ago, nice girl called Mary. She did the job you've taken on, but then she left to get married. Moved over to Hornsey.' Evie chattered as she made the tea. 'I feel a bit guilty sometimes, when I think about how some people have to live, but Sidney and me bought and paid for this place and he left me with enough money so I don't need to let out rooms to make ends meet. We always liked our privacy, if you know what I mean, and I wouldn't feel comfortable with a lot of strangers trooping in and out. Don't think Sidney'd like it either. Bit silly, really, I suppose. Milk and sugar?'

'Yes, please.' She suddenly remembered the evening she moved into the manor when she had a conversation with John and they disagreed about housing; and she realised how much her attitude had changed since then. 'I don't think it's silly at all, Evie. This isn't just a house, is it? It's your home and I don't blame you for not wanting to share your home with strangers. I wouldn't either, and I suppose that's why I feel I've been lucky to come here.'

'You've not had an easy time, so Mrs Wyndham tells me.' Evie sat down and leaned her elbows on the table.

'Catherine, Mrs Wyndham discussed me with you?'

'Oh yes, she's not silly, you know. She had you earmarked for this job months ago, before Christmas. She wrote to me around September, I think, telling me all about you and asking if I'd make a home for you if you wanted to come. Then it all went quiet and I reckoned you didn't want it, and then, out of the blue, there was this telegraph thing saying you were on your way.'

Earmarked months ago! So Catherine must have thought she could handle the job even before she mentioned it just before Christmas.

'I didn't realise she had this all planned so well,' she admitted.

'I don't say it was planned, Lizzie, not really.' Evie sipped her tea. 'We get a load of girls and women volunteering for missionary work, most of 'em religious and thinking they're going to do God's work. They just don't understand what they're letting themselves in for. They either get taken for a ride by some of the crafty bitches they come across, or they get knocked about and robbed, or they go all queer when they see how some people live. Some of 'em like to quote the Bible at prostitutes, some of 'em just can't face the girls, and most of 'em can't understand that a lot of women'd prefer to spend their money on ale or gin than buy their children a pair of recovered shoes or some better rags to wear. They're good at going to church on Sundays and praying and singing hymns, but they ain't much good at being Christian. I hear your young man threw you over because you wouldn't pretend you weren't working class. Is that right?'

'Well, yes, but—'

'But nothing, dear. You sound just the right sort. I don't think you'll be taken in too easily. I reckon you're a good judge of character, and that's what's needed. Help those that don't mind helping themselves and leave the rest to stew. You can't help everyone and you're wasting your time if you try to convert them. You don't strike me as a time-waster.'

'No.' She said it emphatically. 'I hate wasting time. There are always too many things to do.'

'You'll be all right, Lizzie, I can tell.' Evie's eyes twinkled. 'And I reckon we're going to get on like a house on fire.' It was an unfortunate choice of words, but she knew what Evie meant and she was sure she was right.

The next day was Sunday and Evie took her to the Methodist chapel at one end of Angel Street for the first morning service, showed her the outside of the Angel Inn at the other end of the street and then showed her around the immediate neighbourhood before Sunday dinner. After dinner they walked to the Hoxton Mission, a grim building on the outside and functional and crowded inside, but after she had met several of the families living there while they waited for permanent accommodation she knew she had made the right decision to accept the job. She had made it because she had no choice, but she had no doubts that she had done the right thing.

This was something worthwhile, something where she could use her abilities properly. Something that promised to be more satisfying even than teaching. Something that would certainly be more fulfilling than being Charlotte's companion.

And a month later, after she had seen the worst that London could throw at her, she still felt the same. Even the pain of losing John had begun to fade.

CHAPTER 28

Rose sat in the train, staring out of the window, trying hard not to look at Hubert. Neither of them spoke; she because she was scared to say anything, and he, she imagined, because he was either ashamed of himself or still furious with her.

She cursed herself for speaking Edward's name at such an intimate moment, and wondered why she had said it. He was not on her mind at the time; she was thinking abut Hubert, grateful that he had finally found the courage to try to make love to her. So why had she suddenly murmured Edward's name? Why?

It had ruined everything. Now she would have to start all over again, only now it would be harder because there was something between them; resentment on his part and shame and fear on hers. How could she expect Hubert to make love to her if he was always wondering whether or not she was thinking about another man?

But, just thinking about Edward generated a sad, warm

sorrow which in turn offered comfort; it had ever since she knew she could never have him to herself. Now he had come between her and her husband she ought to try to forget him, but to deny his memory now would deny that she had loved him when she was still free to love him, before her marriage made it wrong to do so, and she knew she could never do that. Even though nothing had come of their love for each other, even though they had both turned away from each other in the eyes of the world, she would never forget how much she had loved him because that would be a betrayal both to Edward's memory and to Hubert as her husband.

She had to make Hubert understand that she had chosen him and that now she loved him above anyone else in the world.

It would take time, but she had time. She had the rest of her life if necessary.

'Didn't expect you back this soon.' Grandfather Belchester hugged her tight and kissed her. 'Only received your letter this morning. Assumed you were enjoying yourself so much you'd stay on as arranged.'

He winked at her, slyly letting her know that he had understood the hidden meaning in the letter she sent days before she had almost seduced Hubert.

'Rose felt unwell, Grandfather,' Hubert answered vaguely as she hesitated. 'London life is too much for her so I don't suppose we'll go up again.'

The words sounded like a sentence and told her he was not ashamed with himself, he was still angry with her. Well, if that was the case she could not blame him; she would simply have to work harder to convince him of the truth.

'Get your bags taken up, lad' – the old man winked at her again – 'but not to your old rooms. I've had things rearranged and moved all your things into the empty rooms at the far end of the house. Where the guests usually sleep.'

More privacy! Away from Hubert's mother and her interfering ways. She should have been grateful, but a sudden doubt nagged her and she realised that she had unconsciously thought she would be safer back at the house; safer because Hubert would not dare beat her if they were close enough to his mother to be heard. It was only then that she realised she was scared that last night was not an exception, that Hubert might beat her again. No one would hear them if they were in the rooms at the far end of the house but she could not refuse to move there, not without giving his grandfather a valid reason.

'Anyway' – Grandfather Belchester took her arm and led her towards the morning room – 'I'm glad you're back because it means I've seen you again before I leave.'

'Leave?'

'Yes, me dear. This winter's got into me bones so I'm going away for a few months in the sun. Going down to Jerez for a while, to sort out a few problems down there.'

The family owned two vineyards near Jerez. She had hoped Hubert would take her there immediately after they were married but he had said it would not be decent to take a wedding journey so soon after her father had died. He suggested they might go later; visit Seville and see the Giralda and the Torre Doro, possibly go on to Cordoba and the famous mosque, maybe even travel as far as Granada and visit the Alhambra Palaces. It all sounded so exciting, so romantic, but if his grandfather was going to visit the vineyard there would be no excuse for Hubert to go later and take her with him.

'I'm sure the sun will do you the world of good, Grandpa.' She patted his arm and smiled, trying hard to conceal her disappointment and the sharp nagging fear that the only person she could talk to was going away from her. 'When do you leave?'

'Tomorrow, Princess. Early tomorrow morning. Will you see me off?'

'Of course I will, Grandpa. Of course I will.'

* * *

She was asleep when she felt the bedcovers pulled back.
'Hubert?'

'Who else did you expect?' The way he spoke told her
that he had not come out of love or compassion. 'Take your
nightgown off, you bitch.'

She did as she was told and lay still, trying not to show
how scared she was.

He stared at her, then leaned close and hissed into her
face, 'It's Edward Forrester, isn't it?'

She did not answer.

'Isn't it?' The first punch into her belly made her sit up
and the second into her chest knocked her flat. 'Isn't it?'

'Yes, Hubert,' she whimpered even though she tried to
control herself, 'but we weren't real lovers. Please believe
that, even if you won't believe me when I say that now I
love you and only you.'

'You bitch.' He pressed his thumbs into her until she
screamed with pain. 'You love the man who killed your
father? Your father's murderer? A coal miner?'

'Yes, if that's what you want to believe.'

'You need punishing, you whore.'

He hit her again and again, always around her stomach
and ribs, hitting the same point time after time until she
ached so much she could not feel the blows any more. It
was a dream, an awful, endless dream.

'I ought to tell your mother what you did with the man
who murdered your father. What do you think she would
say? Her and your precious brother? How do you think
they'd feel if they knew? Shall I tell them, Rose? Should I
take you to see them and make you admit that you keep a
drawing of your father's murderer in your diary? And you
call out his name when we're in bed together?' He hit her
again. 'Should I tell them that? Should I? Answer me, you
lying little whore woman.'

'No, Hubert, please don't do that. I'll do whatever you
want, but please don't tell them anything.' It would destroy

her mother and John after everything else that had
happened.

'Then we'll keep it our secret, but I'll have to punish you
for it, Rose. And I'll have to keep on punishing you. You
understand that, don't you?'

'Yes, Hubert.' There was no point in arguing with him,
not if he was to keep the secret. 'But please let's talk, when
you've calmed down.'

'I am quite calm, Rose, but I don't think there's anything
left to discuss. I know it all now. I understand everything.'

'You don't, Hubert. You don't understand at all.'

'But I do, Rose. I know why you married me, why you
lied to me, why you wanted me to make love to you. I
understand it all, Rose, every thought that goes into your
head. I can see your mind, Rose, so never think you can lie
to me again.'

There was a distance in his eyes, a blankness that was
not him, and it was terrifying. He was not Hubert, not in
this mood. He was someone she did not know. She felt him
inside her, satisfying himself and hurting her more, but
now that did not matter; it was more important to get it
over and be left alone.

She refused to cry until after he had gone, and then she
covered her face with her pillow so he would not hear.

He came to her every night for the next week. He entered
her twice, brutally, after he had excited himself enough by
hitting her, but he did not seem to take any satisfaction
from the act. The only thing that seemed to satisfy him was
to see her in pain so she learned to hide the pain, forced
herself not to resist his attacks, and her passiveness
seemed to spoil his pleasure; the attacks became shorter
and after a week he stopped coming to her but he kept the
key to her room, and every night she lay awake for hours,
waiting for the creak as the door opened.

She hardly saw him during the days, and in the evenings
they dined and sat with his parents and behaved as if there

were nothing wrong. The only way she could stop him telling everyone about her secret love for the man who had killed her father was to maintain the illusion that nothing had changed, but everything had changed.

Kind, considerate Hubert had changed; or perhaps she had forced his real character to surface. Whatever had happened to him had affected her feelings for him. She had liked him, then loved him, and now she was close to hating him.

And there was no one she could talk to. If his grandfather had been there she might have risked telling him, even showed him some of the hidden bruises as proof, but she could not tell Hubert's doting mother or his distant father. The only person she could tell was Elizabeth. Elizabeth would understand, and she would know what to do, but Elizabeth was in Pincote.

'Hubert, would you mind if I travelled to Pincote and stayed with my mother for a few weeks?' She asked the question over breakfast.

He stared at her, suspicion sharpening his eyes so she felt the need to justify her request. 'I haven't seen her for over six months and John's at home with her now. I'd like to spend some time with them, if you don't mind.'

His mother spoke first. 'You've not been looking well of late, Rose. I think it would worry your mother to see you looking so pale and thin. You should wait a month or so and allow the spring weather to benefit you first.'

'Hubert?' She turned to her husband for support, but she knew he would agree with his mother.

'No. Mother's talking sense, Rose, and you know that, really. It's warmer here, much more clement than the weather in Pincote, and your mother has enough to contend with taking care of one invalid. She won't thank you for giving her more worry.'

'You're telling me that I can't go?'

'Not yet. We'll discuss it when you feel better,' he said flatly without looking at her.

'Excuse me.' Her eyes were hot with tears she refused to shed in front of him or his parents so she abandoned her half-eaten breakfast and almost ran from the room.

Before she closed the door behind her she heard Hubert's father make his only contribution to the conversation. 'Whatever is the matter with that girl, Hubert? She's sullen, bad-tempered, picks at her food and nothing we do ever seems to satisfy her. She's thoroughly spoilt and it's about time you dealt with her. Knock sense into her if necessary, but do something about her and do it soon. I'm tired of living in the same house as her.'

'Perhaps we should build the other house we've discussed, Father,' Hubert suggested. 'At least she wouldn't be under your and mother's feet all day if we had our own house on the estate.'

'Oh no, Hubert,' his mother cut in quickly, 'we wouldn't see so much of you, then.'

She stood outside the door, waiting to hear Hubert's response, but a maid interrupted. 'Excuse me, madam. There's a letter for you.'

She took the letter, smiled as the maid gave the bobbing curtsy the family insisted upon, and glanced back into the room as the girl opened the door to deliver the remaining letters. Hubert and his parents were eating their breakfasts as if nothing had happened or been said.

She read the letter and its news stunned her so much she read it again, hoping that she had made some awful mistake in the way she had interpreted the words. The second reading told her the same as the first: Elizabeth had left Pincote without telling anyone where she had gone and without taking any of her clothes or other possessions. The station-master reported seeing her board a train and confirmed that she had purchased a through ticket to London. Beyond that nothing was known.

Above her fear for Elizabeth's safety and concern for her friend's health, and beyond her feeling for the desolation she knew John must be suffering, there was her own misery. The only real friend she had ever had, the only person she could turn to, had disappeared without explanation.

The breeze was blowing off the land and carrying the noise of the receding sea away to the horizon, creating the impression that the clifftop was contained in a soundless vacuum. The waves licked at the rocks scattered below the ship-like point, and the gulls glided on the breeze, coal black eyes searching for scraps; but there was no sound other than the wind over her ears.

The cluster of rounded boulders sheltered her and kept her warm under the thin sunlight, and it was probably their warmth which had protected the clump of primroses snuggled down in a crack. She picked some of the faded leaves. A few weeks ago those primroses had prompted her to think of suicide; now they gave her the strength to make the decision she knew she had to make.

Pincote; she would go back no matter what anyone said. Her marriage to Hubert was over.

There would be a scandal but she could live with that. The story of her love for Edward might be made public, but it was an innocent love and she could learn to ignore the accusing fingers that would be pointed at her. What she could not learn to do was to live with Hubert and his parents. She could not learn to accept being beaten whenever Hubert cared to come to her. She could not live a lie in order to retain society's respect for his family, nor to protect her own family from an imagined sin.

Tomorrow she would take her jewellery, all except the few pieces Hubert had given her, and all her money, pack a few things into a small bag, make an excuse to go shopping in Dorchester and instead catch the London train. When she did not return home Hubert would almost certainly guess what she was doing and would have someone waiting at the railway station to intercept her before she could board the train to Pincote, so she would

stay in London long enough to avoid them and catch a train
to Pincote a few days later. Once she was in Pincote she
would be safe; her mother and John would not turn her
away, not once they saw the bruises.

When Hubert came to her that night she struggled so that
he hit her more; the bruises would last for a week or so and
she could use them as proof of the way he ill-treated her.
The beating hurt, but she did not cry after Hubert left her;
she smiled because she had controlled him this time and
it would be the last time he ever laid a hand or his eyes on
her.

CHAPTER 29

Rose slept well until she heard the servants moving about at five o'clock; then she dozed, eager to get on with the day but knowing it would be a long one and that she should rest while she could.

A knock on her window stopped her dozing. Her new room had a small balcony facing the sea but the only way to reach it was through the room and the shutters were still closed from inside. She lay still and listened. There was a small noise outside, then silence.

Who could have reached the balcony? Who would have wanted to? She slipped out of bed, took a small poker from the empty fireplace, crossed to the shutters and carefully opened only one. The balcony was empty. She stared towards the sea, shifting grey and soundless in the early light, then saw a gull waddle across the balcony and collapse in a shaking heap, its feathers ruffling in the breeze.

The bird must have flown into her window and stunned

itself. She pulled back the second shutter, swung the
window door open and stepped outside. The gull stared at
her through bleary eyes and made no attempt to fly away.
She picked it up, felt its heart beating fast against her
fingers, and stroked it gently until it recovered and tried to
flutter its wings.

'There, there,' she said soothingly, 'don't be frightened.
I won't harm you.'

The bird screeched and craned its neck forward, trying
to break free. She held it high and opened her hands and it
fluttered its wings again then flew away.

She watched it go, thinking its flight was symbolic of
what she was going to do that day, and somehow it gave
her more confidence to do what she knew she must. As
she turned back indoors she saw a white feather lying on
the balcony, a single quill, and suddenly she realised what
else she must do before she left. She had to steal her diary
back from Hubert. Without it and the drawing of Edward
he would not have the proof he needed to carry out his
threat.

There was a writing desk in Hubert's room and he was
sure to have hidden the diary in one of its drawers. He
always kept his bedroom locked but the servants had keys
and she would simply have to find a reasonable excuse to
enter the room before they finished cleaning and to remain
there after they left.

Energy surged through her, excitement at the thought
of fighting back.

Now she was fully awake it seemed sensible to prepare
another plan which would allow her to leave the house with
a bag full of clothes without arousing any suspicions. She
undressed and stood before her full-length mirror and was
satisfied with what she saw. The red marks would turn to
bruises and weals during the day and provide the evidence
that she had been beaten, but, more important, her hip
bones and ribs showed through where once they had been
covered with soft flesh. She had lost weight and her

clothes were now too big for her, and that was her excuse to go into Dorchester with a bag full of clothes; she was taking them to the dressmaker's so they could be remade in a smaller size. It was the sort of economy Hubert's mother would approve of.

She washed and dressed in the largest frock she could find, one that hung from her shoulders and emphasised how much weight she had lost, then packed a bag with the clothes she intended to take home to Pincote.

Breakfast was eaten with customary silence. Afterwards she waited until Hubert and his father had left for a meeting before explaining to her mother-in-law that she was going into Dorchester to have some clothes remade.

She returned to her own room as the servants were moving into Hubert's, waited until they had almost finished then simply walked in and made an excuse that she was looking for something her husband had borrowed from her and forgotten to give back. The maid hesitated until told she could go, and then scuttled off to the other end of the house.

Every drawer in the desk was locked. She thought it was typical of Hubert's need to hide his belongings, and realised the house was almost silent, dangerously quiet if she were not to be heard forcing her way into the desk. She looked around for tools to help, found a strong paper-knife and took a pillow from Hubert's bed to muffle the sound of breaking wood.

It took only seconds to break into the top drawer. Her heart beat fast and her hands trembled as the wood splintered. Now she was committed. There was no way to repair or conceal the damage. There was no going back, not now.

'Mrs Coles!' It was her mother-in-law calling the housekeeper.

Footsteps clumped along the corridor outside the room. 'Yes, madam?'

'Have you seen . . .' Her heart was thumping so much she did not hear what was missing.

'I think Master Hubert took it, madam. Shall I fetch it?'

She rifled through the drawer, did not find the diary, stepped back and realised anyone entering the room would immediately notice the damaged drawer front. Mrs Coles's footsteps clumped back along the corridor. The bedroom door swung open.

'Oh, Mrs Belchester.' Mrs Coles paused in the doorway. 'I didn't realise you were here, madam.'

'I'm looking for something I think I left in here last evening.' She stood in front of the desk, hiding the damage, brazening out the situation. 'I don't suppose you've seen my diary, Mrs Coles? It's bound in brown leather and it has a clasp.'

'No, madam.' Mrs Coles stared at her, did not move, and Rose was sure the woman was suspicious.

'Are you looking for something?' she asked the housekeeper to divert her attention. 'Or have you come here to clean?'

It was the sort of insult she knew would make the woman bridle.

'I don't clean, madam. We have people to do that and this room had already been cleaned, quite meticulously I think you'll find.'

'Of course, Mrs Coles, of course.' She tried to sound a little apologetic, but not enough to encourage the woman to stay. 'Can I help you look for whatever it is you need?'

'No, thank you, madam.' Mrs Coles walked stiffly to a small table and picked up a thick ledger-like book. 'I know exactly where it is, thank you all the same.'

Mrs Coles turned and cast a quick look around the room. 'I'm sure that even the meanest examination won't reveal the tiniest speck of dust, or anything out of place.'

She watched the housekeeper stomp out of the room, and was grateful that she had not noticed a pillow missing from Hubert's bed.

The door was left open and she knew she would only draw attention to herself if she closed it, so she retrieved the pillow from under the desk, thrust it against the next drawer and inserted the knife into a crack. The lock broke and she opened the drawer. The diary was resting on top of a pile of papers, the sketch folded inside the front cover.

She used her handkerchief to dab a mixture of red and black ink on to the splintered wood, stepped back to see if she had hidden the damage well enough not to attract immediate attention and decided she had. Before leaving the room she returned Hubert's pillow to his bed, spitefully happy that several jagged splinters should give her some revenge before he went to sleep that night.

The Belchesters' surly coachman, Mrs Coles's husband, loaded her bags into the brougham, drove her to Dorchester and left her outside the dressmaker's shop. She told him to collect her in four hours, guessed he would spend the interval in one of the town's inns, and enjoyed the thought of him waiting for her and then worrying about explaining her absence when he returned to the house without her. She tried to imagine how events would unravel, how long it would take Hubert to realise she had run away and taken her diary with her, and how he would react when the truth became apparent. The thought of the disruption and embarrassment she would cause thrilled her; at last she would have wrought some revenge on the miserable family that had never really showed her any warmth, much less love, and had always treated her as a stranger thrust upon them by circumstances they could not control.

Her only sorrow was the effect it would have on Hubert's grandfather, and she decided that she must write to him at the vineyard in Jerez and hope he received her letter before he began his journey home. The thought of writing to him reminded her to post the letter she had written to her mother, a short letter simply saying that she was coming home and would explain everything when she arrived, and asking her mother not to acknowledge any enquiries Hubert or his family might make until she understood the circumstances. She posted the letter in Dorchester minutes before she boarded the London train.

She watched the countryside rushing past and recognised landmarks which had become familiar during her journeys to and from Dorchester, landmarks she was not sorry to see pass behind, and hoped never to see again.

The noise and smells and bustle of London excited Rose but they also frightened her a little now that she was alone, and she was glad when the cab driver stopped outside a small hotel he recommended as being a suitable place for her to stay for a few days. It looked a quiet and respectable place to rest until she was ready to complete her journey.

It was not until she went down to dinner that night and noticed the curious looks the other guests gave her that she realised this was the first time in her life that she had ever been completely alone and totally responsible for herself. She was nineteen years old, married, and she had never been alone before. The feeling gave her a fresh appetite for life and for food, and she ate her meal with a relish she had forgotten.

Hubert and all that had happened to her was behind her now; she had a new life to look forward to, a difficult life, probably, but one she was determined to remain in control of. She would never go looking for love again. If she found it, real love, she would be happy. If it never came her way then she would remember Edward and at least have the consolation of knowing that she had enjoyed being loved by someone, even if that love was never allowed to flower into total fulfilment.

The next few days passed in a curious kind of bliss; life seemed to be suspended, decisions postponed, her only interests being a self-indulgent enjoyment of having no one to answer to and the opportunity to do as she wanted without much restraint. She visited sights she had read about or heard of, spent hours sitting in squares and parks either reading or simply watching what was happening around her, and deliberately avoided going to places she had visited with Hubert. The only real restraint was the amount of money she had; she carefully put by enough to pay her hotel bill and buy the railway ticket on to Pincote, and counted out the dwindling remainder every morning to ensure she did not overspend.

The guests eating in the hotel dining room changed during the few days she was there, except for an elderly American couple and their son who reminded her of her brother, John. They nodded acknowledgements to each other, and even exchanged a few words about the weather or other insignificant matters, but as she entered the dining room on her final evening at the hotel the son left the family table and strode across to her.

'Excuse me, Mrs Browning' – she was using a false name to make it more difficult for Hubert to find her – 'but we've been watching you eat alone and wondered if you'd care to join us for dinner tonight. Please say "yes", I'd enjoy some younger company.'

She hesitated, not sure if she wanted company, but his hand rested gently on her arm.

'I'll be real offended if you refuse, ma'am,' he said in the sort of voice John imitated so well.

'Of course.' She smiled and allowed him to lead her over to his parents' table.

His father stood up as they approached. 'Mrs Browning, I'm pleased you can join us. I'm Ernest Parker from Great Falls, Montana, this is Edith, my wife, and the man who just abducted you is Matthew, our youngest son, just finished at Philadelphia University. Please sit with us, we'd be honoured by your company.'

She accepted the chair opposite Mrs Parker. 'Thank you for your hospitality which I'm very happy to accept.

Great Falls, that's on the Missouri, I believe.'

'Why, yes it is.' Mrs Parker seemed delighted that she knew something about their home town.

'I always think of it as a wonderfully romantic river,' she said politely, 'rising in the north-west and flowing down through the centre of your country.'

'Mrs Browning, it sounds to me as though you've travelled in the United States.' Mr Parker beamed at her.

'No, I haven't, much to my regret, but my brother has. He spent two years working in coal mines, several in Montana.'

'Forgive me, my dear.' Mrs Parker smiled. 'But you don't look like a coal miner's sister.'

'I'm not, not exactly. My family own several coal mines and my brother went to America to learn new methods.' She suddenly realised she was telling them more than perhaps she ought, so she changed the subject quickly. 'Do you mind me asking why you're visiting England?'

'We have English roots,' Matthew told her, and explained his family background and how he and his parents had travelled on the Continent and intended to investigate a little of their family history before returning home.

The Parkers were very outgoing and told her a number of fascinating stories about their travels. Their company was relaxing; it was a relief to be with people who accepted her as she was and were happy to talk openly and intelligently about places they had been to and the different cultures they had seen. She found that she was not expected to contribute much to the conversation, but when she did speak they actually listened and took her opinions seriously.

'I can see that you're a young lady with strong views,' Mrs Parker said. 'You said that your brother has travelled in Europe and the United States, but have you, yourself, travelled much?'

'Very little. I haven't had much opportunity, I'm afraid.'

'That's a pity.' Mr Parker shook his head. 'You'd enjoy it, obviously. What does your husband do, Mrs Browning?'

The question, although she was sure it was innocent, caught her off guard. She hesitated while she tried to think of a plausible answer which would not encourage any more questions, and as the delay lengthened, one which would account for her hesitation.

'I'm afraid he's dead,' she blurted out and felt sorry for her hosts as she saw their embarrassment mount, then felt the need to fill the silence by explaining more. 'He died a year ago, in a house fire.'

'Oh no.' Mrs Parker almost wailed with sorrow for her. 'That's awful and you're so young to have to face that. To bury your husband at your age.'

For some reason she could not understand she added quickly, 'There wasn't a proper funeral. His body was never found.'

'Oh my God!' Mrs Parker clasped her hands to her chest, and added softly, 'We wondered why you were travelling alone, my dear, but we didn't mean to pry and we certainly wouldn't have wanted to upset you by reminding you of something best left to lie.'

'Please don't apologise. I'm quite over it now and I still enjoy thinking about him,' and to give the kindly woman some comfort she added, 'Quite honestly it's rather nice to be able to talk about Edward without people feeling awkward.'

'That's a very healthy attitude, my dear.' Mr Parker patted her hand in the fatherly way that her own father never would. 'You must have been very happy together to want to remember him still.'

'We were, although we were only married a matter of months. I'd known him most of my life.'

'His people were in mining, too, I guess,' he said seriously, and for a dangerous moment she wanted to laugh.

'Yes, his whole family were in mining, but Edward was

an actor. A very promising young Shakespearean actor. His Henry the Fifth was breathtaking.' It was so good to be able to talk about him, and so easy to lie, that she could not stop.

'Look, Mrs Browning' – she noticed the glances and nods that passed between Mr Parker and his wife just before he spoke – 'this isn't Shakespeare, it's opera, but we do have a box at Covent Garden tomorrow evening and we'd be honoured if you'd come along with us.'

'Yes, please do, Mrs Browning,' Matthew, who had been very quiet, added enthusiastically.

'I'm sorry, I can't. I'm leaving for home tomorrow morning.'

'Can't you delay leaving for just one night, Mrs Browning?' Matthew almost begged her to stay.

'Surely you can get a message through to your folks to say you'll be a day late,' Mr Parker added. 'If you want to come with us, of course.'

She did want to go with them, but she was not sure if she could afford another night at the hotel, so she told them she would like to go if she could contact her mother, and that she would talk to them again the next day.

She bade Mr and Mrs Parker goodnight and turned to do the same to Matthew. 'Goodnight, Mr Parker, and thank you for being such pleasant company.'

'Goodnight, Mrs Browning.' As he kissed her hand she saw a look in his eye which made her feel flattered and a little uneasy.

The next morning she found the hotel bill was less than she expected; dining with the Parkers had saved her enough to stay one more night. She turned away from the desk and almost collided with Matthew.

'Good morning, Mrs Browning. Now, is it going to stay a good morning or are you going to spoil it for me?'

'I can stay just one more night, Mr Parker.'

'That's wonderful.' His joyful shout made everyone in

the hotel lounge turn to look. 'Now then, I guess you don't have anything else planned for today, not as you were reckoning on going home. Is that right?'

'Yes.' She grinned at his enthusiasm, and nodded to emphasise what she had said.

'Then, ma'am, place yourself in my hands for the day. The weather looks fine to me so I've booked a buggy for a ride through the parks. We can find somewhere for a quiet but pleasant midday meal, follow that by taking a boat along the river, and then come back to the hotel in time to change for the opera. After Covent Garden we'll take dinner somewhere or other before finishing the day back here.' He rattled out the itinerary so quickly that she could hardly take it in and it was not until she was sitting in the open carriage he had ordered that she realised they would be spending the day alone.

'Your parents aren't joining us, Mr Parker?'

'No, ma'am.' He looked crestfallen. 'Does that mean you won't come with me?'

She paused, remembering the way he looked at her last night.

'Ma'am, honestly, believe me.' He held his hands up in a sign of openness. 'I'm quite safe to go out with. I've already had lectures from both my father and my mother this morning. I admit that I think you're extremely attractive, I'd have to be blind not to think that, but I do respect you, honestly, believe me, and all I'm looking for is some good company for today. And if the company also happens to be charming and beautiful, then that's a dividend I won't refuse. But I do understand your particular circumstances and I won't be at all offended if you decide you can't spend the day alone with me. I'll be disappointed . . .'

She held her hand up to stop him. 'Please! I'd like to spend the day with you. Let's go.'

'Honestly?' He looked surprised.

'Honestly, believe me.' She mimicked him and enjoyed

seeing him laugh. 'You remind me so much of my brother, John. He doesn't stop talking either.'

As the carriage moved into the traffic she spared a moment's thought for John. Perhaps he did not talk so much now. Perhaps he was not as much fun as he used to be. Not after all he had gone through. Perhaps that was why Elizabeth had left so suddenly, perhaps she had simply run away because she could not face him any more.

'You look sad, Mrs Browning,' Matthew noticed.

'A passing thought, Mr Parker. Just a passing thought,' and she put all sad thoughts out of her mind; there had been enough sadness and today offered an opportunity to have some innocent fun.

She did have fun and it was all entirely innocent; they did not even use each other's first names. She often noticed him looking at her, and when she caught him out and their eyes clashed he always grinned like a young boy caught secretly admiring something he wants but has been told he cannot have. There was nothing furtive about him, he was open and frank and honest.

She was grateful that throughout the entire day he touched her only once, when she slipped stepping into a boat at Greenwich and he grabbed her tightly around her waist. The pressure on her bruised skin and muscle hurt and although she managed to stop herself shouting she stiffened against the pain and she could see that he misinterpreted her reaction as offence at being touched.

Even that incident encouraged her; the whole day had not only been enjoyable, it had given her back some of the confidence that the past year had stolen. She knew Matthew Parker found her attractive, not only by what he said but by what he did, and not simply attractive to look at but someone he wanted to spend time with because he enjoyed her company. It was obvious that his parents had similar feelings, and before she left for the opera she made a note in her diary that a chance meeting with this

American family seemed to be a good omen with which to begin what she saw as her new life.

She studied the meagre collection of clothes she had managed to bring, held various dresses against her and looked in the mirror, and decided nothing was really suitable to wear to an opera; but she had to choose something.

Instinctively she decided it was better to wear something that was not fussy, and chose a simple day dress made from hard-wearing lawn dyed to moss green. She ran her fingers over a motif her mother had embroidered in a mixture of silks and tiny beads: a peacock's feather which crossed the bodice from her right hip to rest its colourful eye against her left shoulder, and sniffed back tears that threatened to make her eyes red.

She wiped her eyes and fastened a green enamel brooch to the dress's high buttoned neck, selected a pair of pale green gloves, and planned to complete the whole makeshift outfit by hiding as much as possible under a silk shawl made from slightly darker grey.

Then she concentrated on her face and on brushing and pinning up her shining copper hair high. She had already decided to show off her eighteenth birthday present, the emerald earrings, in the hope that she could avoid embarrassing the Parkers by distracting attention from her unfashionably dressed body to her head.

As she left the room she caught sight of herself in a full-length mirror; an accident, but she realised that although the outfit was far from fashionable it did reflect something of her own character.

The Parkers were waiting for her and when she saw how well they were all dressed she felt bound to apologise for her own outfit.

'I'm sorry, but I had not planned on anything so grand as the opera and I brought very few clothes with me.'

'My dear.' Mrs Parker looked her over, then said with her usual directness, 'If I had your body, hair and face, I'd have chosen exactly that dress to wear for the opera. You look ravishing, Mrs Browning, and I cannot imagine you could find anyone on this earth who'd disagree with me.'

Her confidence surged, and she happily accepted Matthew's tentative hand when he offered to help her up into the carriage ordered to take them to Covent Garden. 'Thank you, Matthew.'

It seemed right to use his first name, a chance to show him she did not resent him touching her earlier, and she took the opportunity to spend the time riding to the Opera House to tell his parents how much she had enjoyed everything they had done that day. Matthew looked pleased and after a few hesitating attempts allowed himself to speak her first name, and she smiled to show him that she was happy for him to use it.

Nothing could come of all this, and after tomorrow she would never see any of them again, but it would do no one any harm to be extra charming and it would add just a little more magic to the evening; she had begun to think that life needed just a little more magic.

Their carriage joined a slow-moving queue of cabs and carriages waiting to pull up by the Opera House.

'Come on, it's a fine night. Let's walk the last few yards,' Mr Parker suggested, 'if you ladies don't mind, that is.'

'Not at all, dear.' Mrs Parker stretched out her legs and prepared to leave. 'Matthew, you walk ahead with Mrs Browning, with Rose. We'll follow you in a moment.'

'If that's all right with you, Rose.' Matthew smiled at her and she nodded.

She allowed him to help her down from the carriage, and did not really object when he wrapped his arm about hers and escorted her along the crowded pavement.

'Do you really have to leave tomorrow, Rose?'

She paused before answering; she could stay longer if she had more money and perhaps she could raise a little more by selling some of her jewellery, but she did not know how to do that and she sensed that it would somehow make the stay seem tawdry. Anyway, at that moment she was not sure that another delay would be good for either Matthew or her.

'I do have to leave, Matthew, but I'd be happy to take your address so we can write to each other.' It seemed a sensible compromise.

'Well, I suppose that's better than nothing, Rose, but across the Atlantic Ocean? That's not much contact.'

Her heart pounded. He had fallen in love with her, she was sure.

His arm tightened against hers. 'Rose, you're leaving London tomorrow, but maybe I could come up to your home and visit you before I leave England. It won't be for a week or so.'

'Matthew, I'm sorry if I've misled you, but I don't think that's a very sensible idea. You know nothing about me and—'

'You haven't done or said anything to lead me or mislead me, Rose,' he interrupted, 'and I'm asking for nothing more than to see you again before I leave your country.'

She allowed him to slide his arm around her as he guided her through the crush on the pavement, past the vendors selling food along the kerb, and she was a little sorry when his hand slipped back to her arm. 'I've had a wonderful time since I met you, Matthew, but let's not spoil the memory by arguing. Please?'

'I won't argue with you, Rose. I know you've had a hard time, but I also know you were happy today. And knowing that made me feel happy too. That's all. But I've had more fun today than I've had in years and I'd like to try to have just one more day like that before I go home.'

She stopped walking and grabbed his arm with her free hand. 'Matthew, please listen to me without interrupting. I've grown very fond of you during the few hours that I've known you. You and your parents, but you know very little about me and I'm in no position to invite you to my home . . .'

'I know you're recently been widowed, Rose, and I respect your position but I've grown very fond of you too and I can't allow you to walk . . .'

She was not listening to what he was saying. Her head was swimming, she felt ill with shock.

'Edward!' She staggered between two cabs and across the street towards a man standing under a gas lamp. 'Edward!'

It was him; the way he was standing, shoulders back, hands in his pockets, head to one side. 'Edward!'

His back was towards her but it was him. She knew it was him. She did not see the cab until it almost hit her.

'Rose!' Matthew grabbed her and held her, then hurried her across the road between two more cabs.

'Edward!' She broke away from Matthew and ran along the pavement. 'Edward!'

The man turned suddenly and she saw his face, puffy and bruised and scarred with fresh cuts.

'Rose!'

Matthew caught her and held her arms but a moment later he was pushed aside.

'Edward! I thought you were dead!'

'Not quite, Rose. Not quite.' He wrapped his arms around her and through her tears she saw Mr Parker run up to her, and Matthew looking stunned and confused.

'Mr Parker, Matthew, this is Edward. My husband,' she added quickly.

'Mr Browning,' Matthew said lamely and held out his hand. 'Your wife thought you were dead.'

'Browning?' Edward looked puzzled. 'My name's Forrester.'

'Good God.' Mr Parker clapped a hand on Edward's shoulder. 'Don't know what you've been through, boy, but your name's Browning and this beautiful young lady's your wife. I saw things like this during the war, men coming back from the dead, or so we thought. Never reckoned on seeing it again, though.'

'Edward, it is you, isn't it?' she cried and held him tight.

'It's me, Rose. It is me. But what's all this?'

'Mrs Browning.' It was Mr Parker speaking again. 'I don't know what's happening but it's obvious you need to be alone with your husband. If you're sure you're all right we'll leave you here. Is that what you want?'

'Oh, yes please. Yes please.'

'We'll see you back at the hotel tomorrow morning. You can introduce us properly then.' He turned to his son. 'Come along, Matthew. I left your mother on the far side of the street. Let's find her and go to the opera. I think we'll just get in the way if we stay here.'

She kept her tight hold on Edward as she watched a shocked Matthew follow his father across the road, and when they became lost in the crowd she stepped away from Edward, turned and looked deeply into his eyes.

She felt his hands rest on her shoulders, then slide down her arms, the tips of his fingers tracing across the backs of her hands as if he was trying to prolong contact with her for as long as possible. She turned her hands over and gripped his, enjoyed feeling the hard roughness of his hands, and stood, silent, looking deep into his eyes.

A strange sense of timelessness bathed over her; they were standing precisely as they had when he had apologised to her for being rude more than a year earlier. It was as if fate was giving them a second chance. She remembered exactly how she felt that night; she had thought about it often enough, and now her emotions were identical. She wanted him, to hold him and kiss him and to feel his body against hers.

In an instant of clarity she understood why she had called out his name when Hubert was trying to make love to her.

He was the lover she had dreamed of; he was the only man she wanted. The cry was an instinctive call from one mate to another, one soul to another.

'Edward, I love you. I love you more than life itself.' She

said the words she had never said to him before, and she
saw the tears run down his face, washing over the cuts and
weals which crossed his cheeks.

He did not speak as their hands parted. He stood still
and silent, staring back at her.

'Edward.' A young woman with a baby in her arms
tugged at his sleeve. 'Eddie's tired. You coming home?'

CHAPTER 30

God! He was alive. Alive! But married, with a child.

The cruelness of it all outreached her.

Nothing that had happened shocked her more than this. Not even when they told her he may have killed her father – not even when they said he was dead, too.

'Ada, this is Rose. Rose Browning, an old friend of mine.' She saw the confusion and embarrassment on his face, and the indignant, possessive way the young woman looked her over; and then she could not see anything because she was crying.

'I'm sorry, Edward.' She tried to sound dignified, felt awful, turned and walked away as fast as she could.

'Rose, stop!'

She heard him call but she did not stop. This was the cruellest thing of all: to find him still alive but with another woman and with a baby named after him. The baby she had wanted to give him.

'Rose. Rose!' She ignored his calls and pushed her way

through the crowd, walking blindly, colliding with passers-by, just wanting to get away.

'Rose! Wait!' She tried to escape across the road but the traffic was too heavy; then a hand gripped her arm. 'Rose! Wait. It's not what you think.'

She turned to him, her chin up, ready to defend herself against anything he said.

'Ada's just a friend, Rose. Just a friend. And I love you, too.'

'And the baby? Eddie?' She could not hide the hurt in her voice.

'Her baby brother. Ada's baby brother.' He held on to her and turned as the young woman walked up to them. 'Isn't that right, Ada?'

'Isn't what right?' Ada asked petulantly.

'Eddie. What's he to me?' She saw the anxious look in his face and his irritation as the girl hesitated. 'Rose seems to think he's my son.'

The girl hesitated a moment longer, then looked down and kicked a scrap of paper into the gutter. 'No, Mrs, 'e's me baby brother. But 'e is named after Edward.'

Ada added the last words defiantly, but it did not matter.

'So you're not married, Edward, or anything else?' She needed to be sure before she risked unleashing her feelings again.

'No,' Ada answered for him. 'No, Edward looks after me and me brothers and sisters. We ain't married, or anything.'

It was obvious that Ada would have liked to be married, or something, to Edward, and she suddenly felt a huge surge of sympathy for the girl.

'Ada, take Eddie home,' Edward ordered, and handed her some coins. 'Get some hot food, too, for you two and the others. I'll be with Rose for a while. We've got a lot to talk about.'

Ada shuffled off without argument.

'We can't talk here, it's too public.' He grabbed her arm

and laid it under his. 'There's a coffee house nearby, it'll be quieter than a pub.'

She let him guide her through a maze of quiet alleyways. Neither of them spoke, but she sensed the magic she had wanted earlier was there and she felt happier than she ever had before, even happier than when she had stood in his arms on top of King's Crag.

The coffee house was warm and busy. While he ordered coffee and food she sat down at a table in a small stable-like booth and listened to the burble of a dozen conversations, the chink of crockery and cutlery, the plopping hiss of gas jets, and tried to think of the simplest way to explain to him what had happened to her and how much she loved him. But first, she wanted to know his story.

'And that's about all that's happened, Rose.' He sat back, his plate empty, and she poured him another cup of coffee while he summarised all he had told her. 'The explosions stunned me but they frightened the police away and I escaped across the valley and the river by using the overhead cables. I avoided the police in the yard, grabbed my bag and hid in one of the coal heaps until I could get on a train. I came to London because I thought it was the best place to hide and get work. I've done a lot of different things to earn me crust and moved around quite a bit until I found a room near the docks.'

'And your face,' she asked, 'how did that happen?'

'A gang tried to black me, attacked me in the street and tried to take me money, that's all. It happens a lot where I live.' He shrugged. 'But you? Mrs Browning? What's been happening to you?'

She told him all she thought he needed to know, not the details of Hubert's beatings but enough for him to understand why she had run away and was never going back.

'The bastard,' was all he said but she laid her hand on his and smiled at him.

'It wasn't entirely his fault, Edward. I tried to pretend that I loved him, even tried to convince myself, but I think we both knew the truth. I shouldn't have married him, it wasn't fair on either of us.'

'Lizzie? And John and your mother?'

She told him what she knew, and added that Nancy and Adam were married and that the mine had a new entrance which led directly down to a rich seam below the one which had been worked.

'So Lizzie's gone missing as well?' he said after a long pause. 'I hope to God she's all right. She's been put through enough. You all have.'

'So have you, darling.' She risked using the endearment to see how he would react.

'I deserved all I got, Rose. I've got no right to complain, I caused all the trouble in the first place.'

'Don't say that. You saved dozens of lives by going back. How would we have felt it we'd run away together and then read about the accident in newspapers?'

'No worse than we feel now, lass.'

'But I feel happier now than I ever have. I've found you at last, and I'm never going to let you go again. Never.'

There was a long delay before he replied, and when he spoke his voice was rough and strained. 'You're still dreaming, Rose. We can't stay together. It's impossible. More so now than before.'

He saw the hurt in her face as he told her they could not stay together, and noticed how fleeting it was. The expression no sooner appeared than it was pushed aside, replaced by a firm-lipped determination that reminded him of the way she looked at him moments before she made him climb to the top of King's Crag.

King's Crag. That was in a different world, a different life which had nothing to do with how things were now; and she was part of that life and could never be a part of this one.

Circumstances had changed; he had changed them. He

had changed them irrevocably when he killed her father. He had cut himself off from everyone the moment he did that. The police were not looking for him because they thought he was dead. If they found him alive they would arrest him for murder and he would be convicted. And if she or anyone who knew what he had done was found with him they would be arrested and tried beside him.

She was speaking, arguing, saying something about love.

Love? She was in love with an ideal; an ideal he could never achieve, not in this life. She was wealthy and secure, used to plenty, regular food, a warm home, quiet and comfort. She would never adapt to poverty; shivering in a damp bed, hunger, sharing a house with twenty dirty and foul-mouthed adults and smelly children, cold that ate into your bones until you could not think of anything else. She could never adapt to living with the constant noise the poor lived with, the constant fear of falling ill or not finding work.

'No, Rose.' He had to make her understand. 'You don't know what it's like to live the way I do. It'd make you sick in your stomach and in your mind. I know you've gone through a lot, but it's nothing to what you would go through if you lived with me.'

'How do you know, Edward? How can you possibly know what I can do? You hardly know me at all. I can—'

'Stop it! I live in one room. I have a chair and an iron bed with a mattress which is so thin I can feel the bed's netting through it. The floor is bare boards stained with God knows what and I hang what clothes I have on a hook on the door or over the back of the chair. I have to eat in pubs or places like this when I can afford it because I've nowhere to cook, and I share a lavatory at the end of an alley with a hundred people. The lavatory is so dirty most people don't even bother with it, they use the alley or a yard instead. I find it hard, and I come from a poor background. You couldn't live like that and don't fool yourself that you could.'

'It can't be that bad, Edward.' She spoke as if she were talking to a child. 'You've enough money to bring me here and you gave Ada some to buy food for herself and the baby.'

'Only because I've been working today, the first time for a week. And I gave Ada a shilling. A shilling, Rose, a shilling to feed herself and her six brothers and sisters. How much food do you think that'll buy?'

'I have some money, not much now, but a few shillings and I've got my jewellery to sell.' She was not looking at him as she spoke. 'That could raise quite a lot, enough for us to find somewhere better to live and perhaps . . .'

'Stop dreaming. This is my life, Rose, not yours. I couldn't let you live the way I do, and I certainly wouldn't take your money from you.'

'I don't care. I want to be with you and I don't care what I have to do to prove it.'

'You don't care what you do? God, Rose, you've no idea . . .'

'Then let me see. Let me see for myself, Edward, and stop making my decisions for me. People have done that all my life. My father told me I should marry Hubert. You, even, told me I should do that . . .'

'You can't blame me for that, Rose.'

'I don't blame you, Edward. You said what you thought was right for me, but you were wrong. My father was wrong, and I was wrong to let you all bully me into it. I know we can be happy together. I know it won't be easy but—'

'Won't be easy! God, that has to be the understatement of the century.'

'But, if you'll let me finish, I know I can make you happy and I know I can help you to change things.'

'Rose, I'm running away from the police because they think I murdered your father,' he whispered in case anyone overheard.

'Well, I don't know what happened but I know you're not

a murderer. Anyway, the police aren't looking for you, they think you're dead. Your problem, Edward, is that you're feeling sorry for yourself. You've made a mess of your life and you're punishing yourself. I think you're frightened to try to do better in case you fail.'

The nerve of the girl!

'Look, Rose, if I'm such a bloody hopeless case why do you want to bother with me?'

'Because I love you, Edward. I told you, I love you more than life itself. And I think you've a lot to give me, much more than anyone else I've ever known. And I think I've been a fool and treated you badly. I should have been honest with you and everyone when I first realised I was in love with you. Nancy, Elizabeth, my mother and father, even Hubert, I've hurt everyone because I was selfish and stupid. I can't put that right, but at least I can make the best of it, and so can you. But we can only do it together, Edward, so please, let's try.'

'But, Rose' – it did make some sort of illogical sense – 'you don't know what you're letting yourself in for.'

'No, you're right, I don't know.'

The fact that she had stopped arguing was strangely unnerving. Had she seen reason and changed her mind? He looked at her, desperately trying to hide his own feelings while trying to judge hers.

Was there some sort of destiny which controlled, or at least influenced life? The rock fall which had dammed the tunnel and saved his life and Adam's and the other men who were trapped in number one pit? The tub wheel which had injured him and meant he was not working in the main road trying to rescue John when the roof collapsed and killed the men who were there? Nancy overhearing his conversation with Lizzie, the charges which exploded all around him and convinced the police that he was dead? Rose finding him in the world's biggest city when she should have been on her way back to Pincote?

'Edward, it seems to me that we're fated to be together.'

It was as if she could read his mind.

'Aye, lass, maybe you're right.' He looked at her properly for the first time since they had met again, and realised how much more beautiful she was now than a year ago. 'You've lost weight, but it suits you.'

'Does that mean you're willing to try?'

There was a way to avoid making a commitment so soon. 'What would you say to coming home with me now? Just to look, like, no funny business. See what you think, like. Then decide what you want to do.'

It was embarrassing to look at her, even worse when she did not answer. Then he felt her hand rest on his, and when he did look he realised why she had not spoken. Tears were flooding down her face and washing over her smiling lips. She nodded and gripped his hand tightly.

Outside, away from the scent of coffee, the air was cool and damp and smelled of horse dung and rot off the river. The damp and the smells settled on his face and he looked at her to see how she would react. She caught him looking and smiled, a bright, confident smile that made her glow. He guessed that they had about three miles' walk to Shadwell where he lived and he wondered if she would still be smiling at the end of the journey.

He walked at a pace Rose seemed happy with and because he was too tired to walk at his usual speed. He had worked hard that evening and been paid exceptionally well: five pounds, much more than he could admit to earning. He felt mean to have given Ada only one shilling of that, but to have given her more would have drawn attention to her and him and there were people who would murder for much less money than five pounds.

His body ached from the bruising he had taken and although Rose had noticed the cuts and marks on his face he was glad she had believed his story about being attacked by a gang which wanted to steal his money. Bare-knuckle fighting paid well for those who stayed on their feet, but it was dangerous and illegal and he knew he could not tell Rose that he earned money by beating another man senseless. She might understand later, if she stayed around long enough to realise what he had to do to live, but there were limits as to how much he wanted her exposed to that night. Anyway, prize fighting was not something he was proud to do.

Rose thought he seemed distant at first, in mind and body, not saying much and walking apart from her, as if he still were not sure of his right to walk close, even hold her hand or arm; but then the damp air drew the smoke down, and as the fog grew thicker and the streets became narrower and smelled more and more foul he wrapped his arm around her shoulders and held her tight, and she felt safer than she ever had in her life.

She was surprised how easily he found his way through the streets and alleys, especially after the soot-smelling fog closed around them and hid anything more than an arm's length away. The streets sounded empty and she could hear nothing much more than the noise of their footsteps crunching along the pavements and thudding over the wooden blocks which lined the roadways.

Shapes reared out of the fog. Some passed by without speaking; others, cursing or singing and smelling of ale, stumbled against her and lurched off into the night. A few hung on to her clothes and breathed their foul breath into her face until Edward pushed them away. Moaning shapes that stank worse than the night air lay on the ground and had to be avoided. Voices called out, begging for money, cursing when they were ignored.

'Warm enough?' he asked.

'Yes, thank you.' She was warm from walking and the closenesss of his body, then they walked down some steps and she heard water slopping nearby and the sound of it made her shiver.

'Sure?'

'I'm sure.' The groaning sound of ships at anchor told

her they were near the river's edge. 'Is it much further?'

'No. We're nearly there.'

He turned her into another alley, guided her up a dozen slippery steps, then turned again, crossed a roadway and stopped.

'We're home, Rose, if you can call it home.'

He pushed an unlocked door open and a rush of warm air brushed against her face. The house was dark and it smelled awful: the combined stench of boiled cabbage, damp, and dirty bodies.

'Follow me up the stairs but be careful. There's no banister and don't touch the wall. There's ants and maggots and Christ knows what living underneath the wallpaper.'

She shuddered and climbed carefully, hanging on to his jacket until they reached a landing where he told her to wait. A moment later a key unlocked a door, a match flared and a candle glimmered.

'Come in. This is where I live.' He closed the door behind her.

He used the candle to light an oil lamp and she saw how small the room was. She had hoped he had exaggerated when he told her how he lived, but now she saw he had told the truth.

The room was small. A little iron bed reached from the door to the end wall with its window. A small upright chair stood under the window and the bed and chair reached more than halfway across the room. A tiny fireplace with an empty grate was set into the wall opposite the bed and a packing case which he used as a table filled an alcove opposite the door. A cracked china water jug, a small bowl, a single plate, two mugs and a few pieces of cutlery stood on the packing case.

This was his home. And hers, if she stayed.

It was awful.

'You look shocked,' he said bluntly. 'I told you what it was like.'

'I thought you were exaggerating, to put me off.'

'Now you've seen it I'll take you back to your hotel, if you like.'

'No.' Determined to spend at least one night there. 'You promised to let me stay if I wanted to.'

'Do you want to?' He seemed surprised.

'It's your home, Edward. Of course I want to stay.'

'But it's awful, Rose. It's far worse than even I'm used to, let alone what you're used to.'

'Yes, but that doesn't matter. Not tonight.' She jumped as she heard a row break out in another room.

A woman was screaming abuse at someone. It was impossible to understand what was being said but the tone and volume made understanding unnecessary.

'Aw, shut up!' A thud and a crash then silence until a child started to scream. 'You too!'

Another thud and the child stopped.

'What's happening, Edward?'

'Just the usual.' He shrugged and pulled the thin curtains shut. 'You get used to it in time.'

'I'd like to use the toilet.' Surely that could not be as bad as he had told her.

'I'll take you.' He opened the bedroom door.

'Just tell me where it is.' Hiding the embarrassment that suddenly welled up at the thought of him taking her to do something so private.

'No, it's outside and God knows who's out there in the dark. I'll take you, unless you want to use the pot under the bed.'

'Show me where it is, then.'

He relit the candle and held it as she followed him back down the two flights of stairs they had climbed, turned through a narrow passage and walked out into a rubbish-filled yard.

'Watch where you walk,' he warned. 'Most people use this as their toilet.'

She lifted her dress above her ankles and studied the

ground before stepping forward, and realised that once again he was telling the truth. The lavatory was as bad as he had promised, and once he had shut her in and was standing guard she was not surprised to hear him urinating outside. The thought of the smart manager's house by the river in Pincote flashed through her mind, and she stayed in the lavatory longer than she needed because she did not want him to see that she had been crying.

She slept fully dressed for a few hours, but the feel of the iron netting through the thin mattress and the bone-chilling cold woke her up long before daylight.

Edward had stretched out on the floor and she could hear his steady breathing and occasional snuffle or groan. The house was quiet apart from faint squeaking sounds and the rapid scuffle of clawed feet. Rats! She shuddered and pulled the thin bedcover around her.

He was right; she could not live like this and she was amazed that he could. Amazed that anything could have brought him down to living like a rat himself.

She had not realised how much he had changed until they had sat down in his room and talked. His energy and enthusiasm had gone, he was physically and mentally listless. He was not the man she remembered, but then, she thought, she was not the woman he probably remembered.

So much had happened to them both that there were certain to be changes in their attitudes and ambitions, but as they talked she began to realise that whereas finding him made her more determined to make their old dream come true he seemed determined to prove it was impossible.

At first she had made allowances, he was simply trying to protect her, but then a more sinister realisation dawned: he really was scared. She remembered the way he had bridled in the coffee house when she had accused him of being scared of failure: 'Look, Rose, if I'm such a bloody hopeless case why do you want to bother with me?'

He would rather give up than try. That was not the real Edward, she was sure of that. It was as if he were deliberately shutting out his feelings, not only for her but for life itself.

They would not have a chance to live together unless she could do something to change him, but she could not make him change, he would have to want to change, so she lay still and thought harder than she had ever thought in her whole life.

By the time grey light started filtering through the rag curtains she had a plan.

'Good morning, darling.' She spoke as soon as she saw him begin to stir. 'What are your plans for today?'

'Plans?' He rubbed his eyes and stared at her.

She was sitting on the small chair under the window and she moved on to the floor beside him and kissed him on the mouth. 'Is there anything you must do? You said you had no work unless you could find something in the docks or the market.'

'That's right.' His lack of commitment annoyed her but she hid her feelings.

'I must go back to my hotel, collect my things and pay my bill before I do anything else. Then I thought we could come back here and tidy up, then sit down together and made some plans.'

'You're stopping?' She could not decide whether he was surprised or disappointed, or both.

'Of course I am, if you'll let me. I've nowhere else to go and even this is better than sleeping on the streets.' She rushed on, eager to show that she was committed to staying with him.

'Don't be ridiculous, Rose.' He sat up. 'I'd have thought a night here would have shown you how impossible it is for you to stay here.'

'If it's good enough for you then it's good enough for me, Edward.'

He stood up and walked to the window, pulled back the curtains and turned to her. 'It's not good enough for you, Rose. Nothing like good enough.'

'You're right. Of course you're right, and of course I want something better for us, but it's all we have at the moment and at least we can be together while we decide how we're going to get something better.'

'And just how do you think we're going to do that?' He sounded desperate. 'You don't realise what life's like here.'

'I'm beginning to understand, Edward, but what I don't understand is why you stay here if it really is as awful as you say. You're intelligent, you're young and you're healthy, so why do you put up with it if you hate it so much? I don't believe you would stay unless you had a reason. Other men might, but not you.' She sat on the floor and emphasised what she said in a way which she hoped would make him believe she thought he really had a reason for staying. 'I don't expect you to tell me, not yet, not until I've proved myself to you, but—'

'You don't have to prove anything to me, Rose,' he interrupted sharply, 'but you must understand—'

'No, don't tell me.' She cut him off before he could deflate himself. 'I don't want you to explain yet, not until we've had time to get used to each other. We had all those vague plans a year ago, made all those immature promises, but everything's changed now. We were playing then, I realise that now. It was a sort of game where we could say whatever we liked because I was a princess locked up in a castle and you were shut outside and we used that as an excuse not to face facts, but we don't have that excuse any more. I've been thrown out of the castle and now I'm dependent on you to take care of me. I'm not blaming you, it was my fault as well, but I wouldn't be in the mess I'm in if it wasn't for you and the way you made me feel about you.'

'You're not in a mess, Rose, not really. You can go home to Pincote and your mother's sure to take care of you, much better than I can.'

'Not really. Not for long, anyway. I'd be a burden on her and the Belchesters would put pressure on her to send me back. I couldn't stand that. A few months ago I was so miserable I nearly killed myself. I'd found some primroses growing on top of a cliff and they reminded me so much of those we saw on King's Crag that I knew I couldn't live without you and I would have jumped off the cliff if Hubert's grandfather hadn't grabbed me.' The slight distortion of what had happened seemed justifiable. 'That was even before Hubert started beating me, and the reason he beat me was because I called out your name when he was trying to make love to me. I still have the sketch I made of you. I keep it in my diary and I kiss it every night before I go to sleep. I'd rather kiss you.'

It all sounded silly and childish, but there was a small change in his expression, a shift in the way he held his shoulders, and when he spoke there seemed to be a little more authority in his voice.

'I think you're making a mistake, Rose, but I'll go along with you, for a while anyway. Until we see how things work out.'

'Elizabeth told me why Nancy had her abortion, Edward. Because she overheard you telling Elizabeth that you loved me and not her. It'd be wrong to have put her through all that and not try to stay together now we've found each other again.' It was moral blackmail and she hated hurting him by using it, but it was a weapon she was glad to have. 'Nancy's very happy now, married to Adam Marriott, so Elizabeth said in a letter to me, but she told Elizabeth that her greatest sadness was that you had not come after me so we could be happy together. Don't you think that was a nice thing to say?'

He did not speak, just dropped to his knees and wrapped his arms around her, and she knew she had won

the first battle. The next one might be more difficult; she
had to find a way to show him the damage Hubert had
inflicted on her.

Matthew Parker was pacing about the hotel lobby
when she appeared with her arm locked tight around
Edward's.

'Mrs Browning, Rose!' He greeted her with a mixture of
shock and disappointment overlaid with relief. 'I was
worried about you being out all night. I reckoned I'd go to
the police if you didn't show up by ten o'clock.'

'It's very kind of you to be so concerned, Matthew' – she
smiled and clutched his arm – 'but I spent the night at my
husband's home. I was quite safe.'

'Yes,' he said and she could see the sorrow in his eyes.
'I'm very happy for you. For you both.'

'Thank you.' She watched as Edward held out his hand
to greet the young American. 'Thank you for taking such
good care of Rose for me.'

There was a possessiveness in Edward's voice that
made her tingle.

They collected her room key from the clerk behind the
reception desk, thanked him for the concern he expressed
and his congratulations and wishes for their happiness,
and walked upstairs to her room. She noticed its size; it
had seemed small when she had taken it but now,
compared to Edward's tiny room, it seemed large. The
deep double bed, the wardrobe, dressing table, writing
desk and array of chairs seemed to take up very little
space, and the adjoining bathroom smelled sweet and
perfumed and inviting.

'Seems a pity to waste all that soap and hot water,' she
said carefully, hoping he would not feel she was being
critical of the lack of amenities in the house at Shadwell.
'Why don't we take a bath before I pack my things?'

'Aye, you can if you like.' He nodded.

'I thought we both might, if you want to.'

'Aye, go on then. You go first.' He settled into an easy chair.

'I thought we might take one together.' She noticed the shock on his face and wished she had not made the suggestion.

'No, lass, not yet. Bit too soon, I reckon.'

Perhaps it was. Perhaps he felt she was pushing him along too fast. She nodded, walked into the bathroom, left the door slightly ajar and undressed quietly. She had never worn her clothes for so long between changing and it felt good to take them off.

There was a mirror above the hand basin and she suddenly caught a glimpse of herself. As she had expected, the last beating Hubert gave her had covered her ribcage and the tops of her legs in large bruises. Her breasts were ringed with smaller marks where he had grabbed her and squeezed until she screamed, and where his fingernails had scratched her there were long raised weals. She had to let Edward see what damage had been done, if she could entice him into the bathroom.

'Edward, can you help me, please. I can't turn on the bath taps.' It was a plea he could hardly refuse and a moment later the door swung fully open.

'I didn't realise,' he stammered and although her back was towards him she knew he was embarrassed to see her naked. 'Oh, my God.'

She had turned, colouring with her own embarrassment at standing naked before him, and avoided his eyes until he spoke; then she looked directly at him. 'I wanted you to see how much he had hurt me, Edward. Perhaps it'll help you to understand why I need you to protect me. He did more and more every night and . . .'

'God, Rose, I'm sorry. I'd no idea.' His arms came round her and held her tight and his lips kissed her hair as she laid her head against his chest. 'I had no idea.'

They stood still for several minutes, then she felt his hands stroking her back, comfortingly at first and then with a firmness which pushed her even closer to him. She reached upwards, her lips kissing his throat and chin, then pulled his face down so she could kiss him properly.

It was the longest, softest kiss she had known, and she felt secure in his arms as she leaned back and began to unbutton his shirt, unbuckle his trousers.

She was everything he thought she would be: soft, warm, and, above all, passionate. It seemed natural to make love to her, slowly and gently, kissing the bruises and praying that he could take away the pain she must have felt, telling her how much he loved her, promising her anything to make her happy. And when it reached the moment of total love and she cried he knew she was crying in ecstasy not sorrow, and her tears and hot moist kisses meant more to him than anything he could remember.

They lay in each other's arms, still, not speaking, and drifted into a form of sleep which shut out all life's problems and miseries.

CHAPTER 31

The wooden jetty was deserted apart from the two of them standing there, leaning against the worn guard-rail, staring, but not speaking.

The lightermen had stopped working; the sun was low and the twilight and shadows made it too dangerous still to be unloading cargoes. Most of the men had gone home but a few sat around on jetties or in boats, small congenial groups just chatting or enjoying a final pipe of tobacco, their murmured voices and the occasional sharp scent from their smoke or a foreign cargo adding to the mellowness which was settling. Pale clouds coming from the east reflected a yellow sunset down on to the bridges and warehouses surrounding the docks, softening sharp features and somehow making the shabbiness and the river stench less noticeable.

Edward put his arm around Rose's shoulders and pulled her against him, felt her hair ruffle against his face, smelled her freshness, sensed her decency; and for the second time that day felt he was at peace, the first peace he had known for more than a year.

'What are you thinking about?' She slid between him and the rail and nuzzled the back of her head under his chin.

He did not answer immediately. His arms around her, he ran his hands along the worn wooden rail until his thumbs touched, and enjoyed the feeling that he was surrounding her, holding her tight, secure and protected without his hands touching her. Earlier he had needed to touch her, to run his hands all over her, and he had sensed that she needed that too; but now the initial passion, or curiosity, or need to possess, was satisfied he was happy to shelter her with his body and know that she was there for him, and he was there for her.

The sheer thrill that ran through him closed his eyes, but in his mind he could still see the river. It was filled with a hundred or more vessels waiting to load or offload cargoes. The ships and barges were queued end to end, beam to beam, a bobbing forest of masts and spars above wooden decks which reached almost across the river and would have blocked it if there had not been a gap left to allow local river traffic to travel up and down. The mass of ships had seeded an idea in his mind but he did not want to tell her about it yet, not until he had thought it out properly, so when she asked him again what he was thinking about he told her what had been on his mind minutes earlier.

'We're both runaways, Rose, but you ran in more style than me.' He grinned and spoke lightly so she would not take him too seriously, would not interpret his concern as being any doubt of her commitment. 'I sat in the back of a coal truck, you rode in a first-class carriage. I carried my own small canvas bag, you had a porter carry half your wardrobe for you. I had a penknife and a tattered book, you brought your jewels.'

She laughed. 'Not half my wardrobe. I left most of my clothes behind.'

'Thank God for that.' He pointed to her two bags dumped close to where they stood. 'If you'd brought any more you'd have needed a mule train or a herd of elephants.'

She laughed again and turned to face him, kissed his lips then settled her head against his chest.

'I love you, Rose.' He squeezed her, and his heart thumped.

'I know,' she said softly, and her arm tightened around his waist, 'but please try to ignore the differences between us. Neither of us can help our backgrounds, but now we're together that doesn't matter any more. I've always thought of us as being one, and now we can be. Let's think about what'll keep us together, not about what almost kept us apart.'

He nodded, glad he had broached the matter, happy she replied as she did because it confirmed a feeling that had grown in him since they had made love that morning. They had surrendered to each other in the truest sense; shown their real feelings, dropped all their defences and committed themselves to each other no matter the consequences. That commitment was enough for him, and now she had told him it was enough for her, too.

He had felt a moment's guilt about making love to another man's wife, but Rose did not have a proper marriage; her bruises proved that. Then he had thought momentarily about Nancy but by all accounts she was happy, and he was sure she would have approved if she had known; anyway, his first concern was to take care of Rose.

'I'm growing cold, Edward. Can we go home soon?'

Home! Home with her! Yes, he would take her home, but not yet.

'In a few minutes, but first there's something I want you to see.'

In a moment the sun slipped away and the light quickly turned through shades of yellow to brown; shadows became deep purple, the river grey. Gulls stopped wheeling and fell silent. One by one the ships lit lamps to see their crews through the night; a thousand yellow stars which settled above the water and transformed the workaday scene into something magical.

'It's beautiful,' Rose breathed quietly.

'And time to go,' he said, glad she saw things with his eyes and understood why he had made her wait.

'Home?' She nuzzled against him.

'Aye, lass. Time to go home.'

Ada was on the landing outside his room when they returned. He saw her look at the bags he was carrying, and then at Rose.

'You're staying?' She sounded surprised and upset.

'Yes, Ada,' he said quickly.

She hesitated, then held out her hand. 'I'd better give you this, then.'

He took the key she offered. 'Thanks, lass. Have you finished?'

'Yeah, and I've cleared up for you and fetched clean water.'

'We'll have a talk, Ada. Tomorrow.'

'Yeah.' She looked glum, nodded, then walked away and up the next flight of stairs.

The room smelled of carbolic. The thin curtains flapped in a breeze from the open window. He laid Rose's bags on the bed and lit the lamp.

'Ada cleans for you?' Rose sounded surprised.

'Yes.' He would have to explain why but it might be difficult for her to understand. 'I told you she looks after her brothers and sisters. Her mother died giving birth to the youngest.'

'The baby she had with her last night?'

'Yes, the one you thought was mine.' He stared out of the window because suddenly he could not face her. 'Her father works on the docks most days, and drinks most of the money he earns each night. Ada keeps the children on what he gives her, or more like what she can steal from him without him noticing, and whatever she can earn besides.'

'From cleaning?'

'No. Not by cleaning. Sometimes, when she can, she goes out begging. Sometimes she fringes, finds a troupe of buskers and pretends she's with them so the theatre queues give her money.' He turned to face her. 'But most of the time the only way she can earn what she needs is by prostitution.'

'You mean she sells herself?' She sounded more surprised than shocked.

'Aye. Half the women in this house are prostitutes. It's why they live near the docks. There's a steady trade from the sailors, and that's one reason why I won't let you wander about alone.'

'I see.' She nodded.

'No you don't, not all of it. Ada lives up in the loft, under the roof in a space divided up by bits of curtain. She can't take men up there, not with her little brothers and sisters around, so I let her bring the men in here.'

'She brings men in here? On that bed?'

'Aye.' He watched her pulling at her fingers, noticed how her lips pursed to make her mouth thin and tight as she moved about the tiny room. 'I'm sorry, Rose, I should have told you but things happened so fast.'

He could see her picking up her bags and walking away, in his mind, but his eyes told him something different. She was angry, so angry she could not speak; so he grabbed the bags himself.

'I am sorry, Rose, but I can guess how you feel. I'll take you—'

'What are you doing with those?' Her eyes were blazing, green and furious.

'I can see you're upset, angry, and I don't blame you. I'll see you get back to your hotel.' He saw her anger turn into confusion.

'I'm not angry with you, Edward. I'm angry with the world. How can people like me live the way we do when young girls like Ada have to live like she does?'

He was stunned. 'It's the way life is,' was all he could think of to say.

'I never knew, Edward. I never knew,' she said vehemently, as though she was trying to make excuses for herself. 'The night I first met you again, the night your friend William and all the others were killed, I stood in the yard with Elizabeth and I felt separated from all the other women there. It was as if I didn't belong in their world.'

'You didn't, and you don't belong in this one either.'

'No one belongs in this world, Edward. No one actually belongs in a world which makes them live like this. It's wrong. It's all wrong and we've got to change it, so put my bags down, I'm not going anywhere.'

'Are you sure, Rose? Really sure? I won't blame you if you want to go. I can't give you what I'd like to, let alone what you're used to.'

'Oh, Edward!' She sounded exasperated and he was not sure whether it was with the situation or with him, then her arms slipped round his waist and hugged him. 'Of course I'm staying with you, but somehow we're going to change things, for ourselves and girls like Ada. Someone's got to do something, and I can't help if I run away.'

'You're beginning to sound like our Lizzie.' He dropped her bags and held her tight. 'But we cannot change the world on our own, lass. Believe me, I tried to change one small town and failed. Remember?'

'Yes,' she said firmly, 'but we can try to change things for a few. Starting with Ada and her family.'

'But we don't even know how to change our own lives, Rose, let alone take on Ada and six young children.'

'Then we'd better start thinking about what we're going to do.' She tore her coat off and threw it on the bed.

'I've already got one idea.' He sat on the bed as she sat down on the chair. 'Seeing all those ships in the river made me think. My brothers went to America. We could go, too.'

She did not hesitate before answering, 'Run away, you mean?'

Her bluntness hurt; there she went again, accusing him of running away.

'I didn't see it as that. I saw it as a challenge we could face together. An opportunity to do something worthwhile with our lives.'

'Perhaps, but we could do much more by staying here. Not only for ourselves but for others, too.' He could feel the energy burning out from her. 'And as I've said, we can't do anything by running away.'

'Now you do sound like Lizzie, but how, exactly, do you think we can do that?'

'I don't know yet, Edward, but I promise I'll think of a way, you'll see. Tonight.'

And he could see from her expression that she would.

The idea which had been forming since she woke up that morning was almost complete, a way of devising a plan Edward would see as something they shared, not something she was forcing on him.

'Three lists, Edward' – his smile showed he was humouring her, treating the idea as if it were a parlour game – 'but you must take it seriously. Three lists, one for all the things we'd like to do or have, one for the things we already have, abilities and talents as well as belongings, and one for any ideas of how we might get what we want. We'll take it in turns to say what we want and I'll write everything down. Then we'll do the same for the other lists.'

'And then?' He sounded sceptical.

'And then we'll refine our ideas until we have a plan.' It was quite simple. 'You start. What do you want most in the world?'

'To spend the rest of my life with you.' He stroked her arm.

'And I'll write down the same for me. I want to see you

every day for the rest of my life. Where do you want us to live?'

'Anywhere, so long as you're there.'

'Not good enough, Edward. Be more specific. Do you want us to live in this room for the rest of our lives? Somewhere better? In London, the country?' His blank expression bothered her; either he had no idea or he did not really care. 'Or in an igloo, perhaps?'

He grinned. 'No. I'd like to live in the country. In a house like the old ruined lodge near the manor.'

His answer was encouraging; he was willing to talk about the past and was not trying to ignore it, and it confirmed something else they had in common: the lodge as an ideal house.

'So, Mr Forrester, you want a half-derelict house with a tree growing through the kitchen?'

'Mind now, lass. You were the one who said we were supposed to take this seriously, and all you've done so far is joke.' There was something intimate in the way he pretended to scold her, and did not worry about hiding his natural accent.

'I know, but I haven't had anyone to laugh with for so long I couldn't resist it. I'll try to be more serious, now. Promise.' She grimaced. 'I'd like a house like the old lodge, too, but not somewhere that's isolated. I want to be near people we can get to know, really know, and I'd like children.'

'How many?'

'Four or five. Enough to make a real family.' She paused and looked into his eyes. 'I really do want your children.'

'Good,' he said and touched her arm again, then went on with another thought. 'And I want to work for myself. Employ other men, perhaps, but I don't want to work for anyone else.'

The list grew, three pages listing their ideal life. The list of what they had was much shorter; possessions least of all, their talents and skills not much longer. Finally they came to trying to decide how they could achieve all they wanted. Breeding a family was top of the list, that was the easiest to arrange. The rest was more difficult.

'A house in the country isn't going to come that easily, Edward. We need to start off with something less ambitious, decent rented rooms, perhaps. In London, to start with. Then a rented house in London, then buy a small house in town, then, once we're established—'

'Whoa,' he interrupted. 'How're we going to rent decent rooms? We don't even have any money coming in on a regular basis. We cannot dream ourselves out of here, Rose.'

He was taking it seriously. She stopped and thought about finding a solution, walked to the window, stared out through the grime and across the dark yard. How could they get started, preferably in a way which would not divert them from their main aims? The solution offered itself immediately.

'Windows, Edward.' The answer was obvious. 'There must be millions of windows in London, and they all need cleaning. It wouldn't cost much to set up a window-cleaning business and it would bring in regular money. You could do that, you're fit and strong.'

'Aye, lass, I reckon you've got something. It'd be a start right enough.'

'I can sew quite well.' She saw her own contribution. 'I could learn to make clothes. Perhaps, when we had a house, we could buy a piano and I could teach. I might be able to teach elocution, there are always people who want to talk properly, and perhaps drama as well, if you'd help.'

'Slow down, lass, before you run off the rails.' He stood up and put his arms around her. 'We can't do everything, especially if you're going to have four or five children to look after.'

'But we've found something to be getting on with, haven't we, Edward?' It felt good to hug him, exciting to be making plans with him. 'I told you we could find a way.

How much do you think we'll need to start us off?'

'A few pounds, I suppose. Not much, anyway.'

'Do you have enough now?'

'No, not if we're to eat and pay the rent, but I reckon I can manage it in a week or so.' He sounded as excited as she was.

'How?' It was a reasonable question but she saw his face change.

'I'll find a way, don't worry.'

'But how?'

'Leave it to me, Rose. I'll do it. I promise you.'

'But how?'

She noticed the way he hesitated before answering, and when he did speak he was cautious. 'Just leave it to me, lass. There are a few people who owe me. It's only a matter of collecting. Just give me a couple of weeks, maybe not even that long.'

'I'm only asking, Edward, because there's always my jewels. I don't need them and they're probably worth quite a lot.'

'No!' His vehemence frightened her. 'We'll do it on what I can make. I'm not living off you, not now, not ever.'

'But they'd give us a good start.'

'No, they wouldn't. They'd give us a very bad start because I'd always wonder if I could have managed without them to set us up. I'd feel that I'd taken the easy option, Rose, and that'd spoil it for me. I couldn't respect meself, and maybe that's what's been wrong with me all these months.' She did not resist as he wrapped his arms around her. 'I've been living some sort of half life down here, but you've changed all that in a day. One day. God knows what you can do for me in a lifetime.'

She kissed him back as hard as he kissed her, then told him how she felt she had changed since she had found him. 'It's been the same for me, Edward. My life seemed to have gone out. You've rekindled it for me.'

'I'm glad, lass, but it's not going to be easy, and as far as your beads and things are concerned I'd rather you kept them safe so you've got something to fall back on if you need them any time.'

'No, Edward. That's not fair.' He still did not understand. 'If we're to stay together then we must share the risks as much as anything else. I think it's insulting for you to refuse to use the jewels, then expect me to keep them as insurance against things going wrong. If we succeed, then we succeed together. If we fail, then we starve together. If you can't accept that then tell me, now.'

'I just thought . . .'

'No, you didn't think at all, Edward. Why can't you understand that I love you? I always have. I always will, no matter what happens.'

'Aye, lass. I believe you. Now.' His arms wrapped around her again and squeezed her until she could not breathe, and when she pulled away, gasping, he caught her again and turned her so her back was against his chest. 'I know when I fell for you, really fell for you. It was that day up on top of King's Crag.'

'Really? Was it really then?' If she had known then, that day, then maybe everything would have been different. 'I thought it was all in my imagination.'

'Imagination?' She felt him breathe the word, felt his heart thumping against her back, his arms under her breasts, and noticed the ragged edge to his voice. 'My imagination played havoc with me after that day. Thinking about you and me up there all alone, no one to see or care what we did.'

'Well, just imagine we're still there.'

The tiny room did not matter any more, not for a while, not while she could believe they were back on King's Crag living the dream she had dreamed so often.

They made love on the floor and she gave herself to him, followed his lead, totally submissive and safe and happy in his care. He did care, that was obvious from the gentle way he handled her and the way he spoke, quietly, reassuringly. His kindness was warm and protective but behind it there was a sense of danger which made loving him exciting. It had frightened her at first, when they made love that morning, but now it was obvious that his passion was just that; it was a part of him, something that was within him and motivated him, not something that came from without and dominated him. Unlike the destructive energy Hubert had unleashed, Edward's passion was constructive, healing, rebuilding.

Afterwards she felt him wrap her up in his arms, and she was happy to sleep on the floor with him, her head resting on his chest, her heart measuring its beat with his. She wanted to be that close to him, to be so close she was inside him, a part of him.

It was a vision of heaven to be held by him after they had made love, but even if he had turned away from her she would still have slept on the floor. She could never think again of sleeping on the bed where Ada earned money for giving men what she and Edward shared so willingly.

'One guinea?'

'Yes, Forrester. One guinea. Your price has gone down. You finished off Carter too fast, before the betting got going. Mr Penn likes your shape, but he told me to offer no more'n a guinea if you wanted another fight,' Scraggs said firmly, then looked slyly around and added in a whisper, 'but if you take this I might be able to fix you up with something better for a second ring.'

'How much better?' A guinea was not worth the risk of being hurt or fined if the police stopped the fight and took him to court.

'Five?' Scraggs grinned his toothless grin. 'Five to fight Bull O'Leary, and if you beat him I might, just might, be able to fix you up against the Frenchy.'

He did not answer immediately, he needed a few moments to think about Scraggs's offer. O'Leary did not enter bare-knuckle prize fights because he needed the money, he fought because he enjoyed fighting.

Bull O'Leary was a big man, and strong, with fists bigger and harder than swedes. During the day he was a foreman on one of the Irish gangs that laboured for the railway and road builders; at night he worked for slum landlords who wanted their properties cleared. The landlords who owned properties that were in the path of a new road or railway knew the constructors would pay more for a trouble-free empty property than for an occupied one; O'Leary and his gang were paid to frighten tenants away, or simply throw them out and wreck the buildings so they could not go back.

O'Leary was a violent man, he did not follow any rules, and he had crippled several men in the past year, but his stomach had been stretched and weakened by beer and a few good punches on the top of his paunch might be enough to stop him quickly.

A fight with O'Leary might be worth considering.

The Frenchman was a different proposition. He was a fair fighter but even bigger than O'Leary, six feet six, he had heard, and he used his strength and stamina to draw fights out for an hour or more. Penn and the other men who organised the illegal rings were sure of good profits when the Frenchman fought because he drew out the big gamblers and they took a commission from all the money which changed hands.

'Well?' Scraggs asked impatiently. 'Do you want the fights or not?'

The money from the first two fights could be enough to set him and Rose up in business. He did not want to fight the Frenchman but he was sure that if he admitted that to Scraggs the offer of the five guineas to fight O' Leary would be withdrawn, so he pretended to be interested. 'How much to fight the Frenchman?'

'Ten, twelve, maybe, and perhaps a prize of another twenty if you win.'

He hesitated, still unsure about O'Leary. Scraggs would

probably find him an easy match for the first fight but tell him to make it look difficult so he would not be seen as a good bet against O'Leary; but that meant he would have to take some hard punches which would weaken him. He might not have enough strength left to fight O'Leary and win.

He was not sure it was worth the risks, especially as he could not tell Rose what he was doing to earn the money he needed.

'I'll fight, but only if you guarantee both purses even if I lose, and double to win,' he said and watched Scraggs's expression as he thought about the conditions.

'All right, but we'd better see some blood in the first ring or Mr Penn'll do me for it.'

'You'll get your blood, if that's what you want,' he said, wondering how he was going to explain away even more cuts and bruises to Rose.

It was dark. He took off his shirt and walked to the middle of a yard paved with uneven flagstones and lit by small oil lamps hung from wall brackets. The yard served an ale house, a match factory, a row of tenements and an enclosed market; it smelled of ale, sulphur and rotting rubbish.

Milligan, his first opponent, was at least a head taller than himself, an ugly broken-nosed shaven-headed man about thirty years old and around fifteen stones in weight. Milligan was very broad and had long arms that reached almost to his knees. He had a paunch which lolloped over his thick leather belt, and even before the fight started he was puffing and running with sweat. He wore heavy boots which were covered with clods of grey clay, London clay.

Scraggs was standing to one side, a handkerchief raised, and men wearing smart suits and tall hats stood in groups in the shadows around the edge of the yard. Each man clutched a sheaf of paper money, ready to pass notes to stewards who handled the betting.

He looked at Milligan, then at the gentlemen, smelled their cigars and drinks, and realised, as he always did, that they did not think of him as a person. In their eyes he was no different to a pit bull or a fighting cock. His heart thumped, he felt sick and weak, and ashamed of himself for having to resort to this to earn a living.

Scraggs fluttered the handkerchief, the gentlemen roared, and he shut his mind and concentrated on the fight.

He circled and ducked and weaved. He punched Milligan whenever he could, hardening himself against the pain in his hands and knuckles when he hit bone, and he took the shock when Milligan hit back.

The fight seemed to go on for a long time but he had no way of telling how long. Then he was aware of the crowd yelling for blood; and then it was over.

He had beaten Milligan, in more senses than one, but he did not feel victorious; he felt sick.

'A win for Fighting Forrester,' Scraggs yelled.

He stepped back, heaving air into his lungs, easing his fists open and closed, glad it was over; and watched as the gentlemen collected their winnings or shrugged because they had lost. No one spoke to him or attended to Milligan.

He used a thin towel to wipe away his own and Milligan's blood, and the sweat which was pouring from him, then fetched a jug of water, flicked some on to Milligan's face and poured a little over the man's split mouth. It was three or four minutes before Milligan came around enough to be trusted to drink from the jug without choking himself. Milligan did not speak, but the yard was loud with the chatter of frock-coated gentlemen exchanging views and opinions on how they thought the fight might have been better fought.

Penn, a tall, thin man, came out from a crowd, a leather saddle-bag tucked under his left arm and made secure by a strap which ran across his chest and over his right shoulder. Penn tapped the bag and made his thin lips smile. 'Well done, Forrester. Blood, that's what I like to see. It builds the odds nicely for the next ring.'

'Aye, Mr Penn.' He pulled Milligan to his feet and helped him towards a bench laid out with buckets of water.

Bull O'Leary stepped through the crowd and lifted Milligan's weight off him. 'Leave Patrick to me, Forrester. He's one o' my men and I take care of me own. You'll understand that, when I've finished with you, you bastard.'

'Hold on, man. I finished him fair.' He stopped when O'Leary glanced towards Scraggs and he saw the almost imperceptible nod Scraggs gave the Irishman.

'Aye, so you reckon, but your man there told me to watch you, Forrester, and it's him who decides what's fair.'

'I'd rather fight clean, O'Leary, but if you try anything queer . . .'

'You're frightening me already, Forrester.' O'Leary laughed, dumped Milligan down on a chair and washed the blood off the man's face and chest.

The next fight was between two dwarfs who used their feet as well as their fists and heads. Edward was too disgusted to watch, and walked into an alley so he could let his head clear. He heard footsteps behind him but did not take any notice until the man who had followed him spoke.

'You fought well, my friend. And cleanly.'

The deep voice was unmistakable; he spun around and stared up at the huge figure who stood in shadow four yards away. 'Adam? Is that you?'

The figure stepped forward, an enormous hand thrust out. 'No, my name's not Adam, but I'm pleased to meet you, Mr Forrester.'

'I'm sorry.' He shook the man's hand. 'Your voice reminded me of someone I once knew.'

'A prize fighter?'

'No.' The thought of Adam fighting, especially for money, made him smile. 'No, Adam Marriott's a coal miner and a lay preacher.'

'Marriott? Adam Marriott?' the man asked urgently.

'Aye. Do you know him?'

The man ignored the question but pulled him a little way along the alley, away from the door. 'Where was this, and which church did he preach in?'

'Pincote, a small town north of Durham. He preached in any chapel that asked him, or on street corners, in market places or even down the mine if he thought it was the right place. Why?'

'You don't know who I am, do you, Mr Forrester?'

He shook his head, but he could see the man clearer now and there was something familiar about his goatee-bearded face.

'I call myself François Marot, better known in these circles as the Frenchman. My real name's Francis Marriott.' He paused. 'If your friend looks anything like me, Mr Forrester, then I think he may be my Uncle Abraham.'

'Aye, there's a good similarity in your face, and build.' He could see how Adam must have looked twenty years ago. 'But why would he use a different name?'

'A long story, Mr Forrester, and I'm sure that if he wanted you to know it he would have told you himself.'

'Aye, but if you want to contact him I can give you his address. He's living in Pincote, in the house I grew up in meself. Seventeen Albert Street, Pincote.'

'Thank you, my friend, but I'll not be writing to him. Perhaps though, when you next see him, you'd mention that I asked after him?'

'Of course.' Prudence told him to make the promise even though he knew he would not keep it, but then he realised he might betray this man's trust in Adam if he did not tell the truth. 'But it's not likely I'll see him again. I left in a bit of a rush, like, last June, and I cannot see meself going back, ever.'

'Oh.' He thought Francis Marriott sounded disappointed. 'Why's that? Or perhaps I shouldn't ask?'

'Like you said, it's a bit of a long story, but I'm very

pleased I met you, Mr Marriott.' He felt he could trust this
stranger exactly as he would Adam, but sensed it was best
not to say too much.

'The same goes for me, my friend. Now, have you
fought Bull O'Leary before?'

He had not, and he was grateful for the warnings and
advice the Frenchman offered him as they strolled back
down the alley. He did not notice Scraggs standing in the
shadows until he had passed him, and even then he did not
think much about it.

He took the Frenchman's advice and went on to the
attack the moment Scraggs's arm began to move down,
then, as usual, he shut away his senses and concentrated
on winning the fight. He knew he had to end this fight fast,
otherwise O'Leary would bite, gouge and do anything else
to cripple him.

They circled each other, punching when they could,
bluffing and feigning when they could not land a clear
punch. He realised O'Leary was deliberately slowing the
fight, and he felt his concentration slide.

Suddenly O'Leary was on him and he was trapped in a
clinch he could not break. O'Leary's fingers clamped over
his windpipe and the veins that ran behind his jaw bone
and carried blood to his brain. His sight blurred.

Scraggs should have broken the clinch but he did not,
he simply stood by, grinning at him.

'I'll do you, Forrester.' O'Leary's words seemed to come
from a long way off.

He was on the floor, Scraggs leaning over him, counting
slowly to prolong the fight; O'Leary hovered beside
Scraggs, ready to come in again the moment he clambered
to his feet.

'Get up, you coward.' O'Leary spat on him.

He crouched, balancing unsteadily on his shaking legs
as Scraggs counted nine, then O'Leary hit him and
knocked him flat. Scraggs was counting again, but much
too slowly so the fight could be made to last and more

money would be laid down. Up on his feet again on the count of eight, but he could not breathe properly, could not see clearly, could not do anything more than shuffle his feet and could not raise his arms because they were too heavy.

This time he had to endure watching O'Leary taunt him before the first blow came.

The crowd were yelling for blood, his blood. He shut his mind, put his head down, and charged.

The next few minutes were a blur of pain, the smell of sweat, and a vision of lights swaying around him.

He thought about Rose; standing with her on the quay as the ships lit their lamps, the sweet smell of her body, her father trying to kill him in the manor at Pincote.

Then he heard Scraggs counting.

He shook his head, his eyes cleared and he saw O'Leary crumpled on the flagstones.

'Ten,' Scraggs said quietly, almost as if he did not believe what he was saying.

The gentlemen in the crowd went wild.

'Best let me look after you, I think.' It was Francis Marriott, the legendary Frenchman, who steadied him and helped him to the bench with its buckets of water. 'You should call yourself David, my friend. Little fellow like you didn't stand a chance against O'Leary, I'd have said. Penn'll have made his money on this fight, I'd say, and you'll have no trouble demanding a good price after this.'

'That was my last fight, man. No offence to you, like, but I reckon it's a disgusting way to earn a wage. I've made what I need, and I'll never hit another man again, not unless he forces me to.'

'That's what Abraham said.'

'Adam was a prize fighter?' It did not seem possible.

'Down in Taunton he was. Big name down there, but as I said, it's a long story and he would have told you if he'd wanted you to know.'

* * *

'Edward, what happened?' He saw the horror on Rose's face when she opened the door.

'Not as bad as it looks, lass, and I've got the money I went for. Twelve guineas.'

'Eighteen,' Francis Marriott corrected him and followed him into the room. 'I "persuaded" Mr Penn to double the prize money.'

'Prize money? Who is this man, Edward?'

'François Marot, madam.' He heard the Frenchman introduce himself.

'Bonsoir, monsieur. Est-ce que—'

'Forgive me, madam, but I don't speak French. I simply use a French name for, for professional purposes,' Edward heard Francis explain.

'Professional purposes?' Edward could see Rose's confusion; he would rather have explained what he had done in his own time, not have Francis Marriott thrust him into a situation where he knew Rose would be upset.

'I'm a prize fighter.' He watched Francis bow slightly as he spoke.

'A prize fighter? Edward, have you been . . .' He held up his hand to stop her.

'I'll explain later, but let's eat first. Francis, that's his real name, has some hot food. He's been a good friend to me, to us, today, and I'd like him to share our little celebration.'

'Celebration! We have to celebrate your success as a prize fighter?'

'An ex-prize fighter,' he said firmly. 'We're celebrating finding a new friend, ending our old life, and having the money to begin our new one.'

'I can assure you that Edward's no prize fighter, madam.' Edward saw Rose soften as Francis spoke quietly and laid out the food on the tea chest that served as a table. 'He's much too fair and gentle, and it was obvious that he hated what he had to do tonight.'

'What, exactly, did you do?' Rose demanded, but he could tell she was forcing herself to sound severe;

Francis's lightness of touch was having an effect and now he was grateful for his presence.

'He had two fights,' Francis Marriott cut in before he could speak. 'Two illegal, bare-knuckle fights with men who were half as big again as him and who used every false trick they could to win. He beat them both, fairly, and still insisted on apologising to them for hurting them. I can't understand why he did it, and even though he tells me he had his reasons I still think he was mad to take on two bruisers like that. The odds were far too high for my liking, madam. If I'd been him I would not have fought.'

'I see,' Rose said quietly, and Edward saw her looking at him. 'It's just that it's rather a shock to see you like this, Edward.'

'I know, lass, but it's the only way I could think of to get out from here quickly.' He passed her a plate filled with chops and a baked potato. 'Anyway, it's over now, or it will be once me hand's mended. I think I've broken some bones.'

'Well' – she smiled at last – 'if Monsieur Marot weren't here I might have broken your skull for frightening me like this.'

The next day they gave Ada two guineas in small coins which she could spend without attracting attention, promised they would contact her when they were settled, and took a cab to Islington. Francis Marriott had written a note introducing them to a house agent who, he promised them, would offer them clean rooms in a respectable area at a reasonable rent. They broke the journey for Rose to post a letter telling her mother that she had fled from Hubert's beatings but had decided to remain in London rather than return to Pincote where she would be an embarrassment. She could not mention Edward, but to put her mother's mind at ease she hinted that she was staying with a kind family who would take care of her, and she promised to write regularly so that her mother need not worry.

CHAPTER 32

———————————

Charlotte read Rose's letter, and sighed. How much had Rose's imagination exaggerated the problems she had with Hubert? And it was far from reassuring for Rose to announce she was now living in London with an unknown family at an address which she had not disclosed.

'Something wrong, Mother?'

She glanced across the room at John, then walked to the door and shut it in case Hubert, who had arrived unannounced two days earlier, returned from his afternoon walk. 'Yes. I've received a letter from Rose.'

'How is she? Where is she?'

'She says she's well, no thanks to Hubert if she's to be believed. And she's living in London with a "kind" family whose circumstances and address she declines to give me. I'm worried. It's not like Rose. Not like her at all.'

'At least she's written.'

'She's hiding something, John, I can tell.'

She watched him as he spoke slowly, manipulating his

scarred lips in an attempt to sound clear. 'Hubert did say he's been worried because she's been acting strangely, being secretive, hiding things from him, exaggerating problems. Perhaps it's a delayed reaction to everything that's happened, a form of grief.'

'No.' She was sure. 'Let me read the letter to you. Give me your opinion.'

She read the letter carefully, looking for clues to support her feelings, then folded it back into its envelope. 'Well?' she asked.

'Starting with the important part.' She waited as John moistened his lips. 'She does sound as if she's happy, which is surprising considering the circumstances. That's something we should be grateful for. As to her not coming home, well she may have guessed Hubert would arrive here and if she is running away from him it's not surprising she's decided to stay away for a while. But as to him beating her, well, I can't imagine Hubert beating anyone, least of all Rose. He's more likely to bore her to death and maybe that's the trouble. Maybe she's sorry she married him and she's just making up an excuse for running away.'

'My thoughts exactly, but there is something else, I'm sure of that.'

'Possibly,' John said and she moved forward ready to steady him as he lurched to his feet and stumped over to the window. 'Perhaps she does think she'd embarrass us by returning, but perhaps she simply wants time alone to think things out. We won't know until she tells us.'

'We could try to find out.' She followed him to the window and put her arm around his waist.

'London's a large city, Mother, and we'd be lucky to find her even if we knew the area she was living in.'

'But we could employ someone who knows the city.' An idea was already forming in her mind. 'A private detective, perhaps.'

'Expensive,' John said flatly, reminding her that they must be careful with their money. 'I don't know how much it would cost but I doubt we could afford it.'

'Not even to find your sister?'

'I wasn't going to tell you, not yet, but the bank has refused to underwrite any more cheques unless we can offer more security.'

'What?' That was another shock on top of all the others that had come over the past few weeks. 'But we own the bank.'

'In name, Mother, not in practice. We need to talk, urgently and without Hubert interrupting.'

She sat in Sebastian's study and listened to what John had to say, and felt with each new revelation that the hole Sebastian had left her in was growing deeper and wider by each day. After an hour she simply wanted to cry and walk away from it all. There was no answer. No possibility of avoiding even more worry and frustration, and humiliation. The great Laybourne family tradition, founded centuries ago and built on by each generation, was bankrupt.

'Father was telling the truth when he said we couldn't afford to sink a second shaft into Pincote Colliery.' John brushed the fingers of his right hand along the scars on his face, something she had noticed he did quite often. 'The mine's working quite profitably now but we owe the McDougalls tens of thousands for the money they put into the repairs, and we don't have the money to pay them. Also, the market price of coal has fallen sharply so the Byford and Shearton Collieries are working at a loss and our income from the Newcastle field is substantially less than we expected. The mills are already working short time because we don't have enough orders to meet, but at least they're working, unlike some of our competitors.'

'The farms, John. What about the farms?' There had to be some good news.

'They're very productive but there's a slump and that means there's little demand for what they're producing. The tenants can hardly manage and they certainly couldn't afford to pay higher rents. We can't even sell the land because Father mortgaged most of it to pay for improvements and to raise capital, and the slump means that all the farms together are currently worth less than the money borrowed against them. Father also invested vast sums in two of the London underground railway companies and because of poor dividends the shares are almost worthless.'

'Anything more? You may as well tell me the whole sorry story, John.'

'Well, Mother, the builders who repaired the house last year are pressing for payment. So are the musicians who played at last year's ball. We can't pay either account. However, the bank has agreed to honour my personal cheque settling all the bills for my hospital treatment and a payment I've made to Mrs Lumley for Rose's ball gown. Mrs Lumley refused to charge for Elizabeth's clothes.' She noticed his face harden as he spoke Elizabeth's name; it was the first time he had mentioned her since she left. 'I've also settled the account for the jewellery you and Father presented to Rose for her birthday, a matter of a few pounds only, which rather surprised me. Did you know he returned the originals in exchange for paste copies?'

She shook her head, grateful for once that her husband had been mean. 'Anything more, John?'

'Only details, but they mount up. The remaining major matter is a promissory note Father gave Hubert's father as a guarantee of Rose's dowry. We can't meet it, but Mr Belchester has agreed to return it in exchange for a debenture on the mining business. That means we would still owe him the money but we would have to make annual interest payments, and if we could not pay he could force the company to close. In that event his claim on any remaining company assets would rank higher than ours or any other shareholders'.'

'But that's outrageous.' This was too much. 'It would place everything we own under his control, and anyway

Rose has left Hubert. I'll talk with the old man. The Belchesters don't need the money and as far as I'm aware they haven't yet started building the house the money was meant to help fund.'

'The note's still a legally binding document made in favour of Belchester's bank, and we can't afford to argue because the bank holds the mortgages on all the farms and if it forecloses we would be forced into bankruptcy. Anyway, Hubert's grandfather is in Spain for several months, and is very ill, so Hubert tells me. I wouldn't like to impose on him even if we could find him.'

'It sounds hopeless, John,' she whispered; the shock of hearing everything explained made her breathless. 'We're going to lose everything, aren't we? The businesses, the land, the house. Everything. What was your father thinking of?'

'In hindsight we can see he made mistakes, but he was trying to correct them and he couldn't have foreseen the slump that's sweeping this country and Europe. The foreigners, America, Germany and Japan, in particular, are attacking our traditional markets and destroying our export trade by improved production methods which cut costs. Father knew that, at least, which was one reason he was so opposed to too much change within our own country. He was frightened that our costs would increase and add to our problems, make us less competitive. Don't be too hard on him. I'd have done just as he did.'

'But what do we do now, John? How do we manage with all these debts?'

'Our main creditors are three banks.' She listened as he explained his proposal, and was glad that he had thought it all out in advance. 'First off I'd say the Belchesters have nothing to gain by bankrupting us, and I can't believe they would want to risk the inevitable scandal. Secondly, I must resign from the board of our own bank to avoid any charges of duplicity, and if we can introduce some cash or security I'm sure we can avoid trouble from that quarter.

Finally, our biggest creditor is the McDougall's bank which could put us outside the gates with nothing more than our clothes and a shilling apiece. But Mr McDougall is hardly likely to bankrupt his own son-in-law.'

It took her a few moments to understand the implications of what he had said. 'You're going to marry Lillian?'

'We are engaged, Mother.'

'I know, but what if Elizabeth returns?'

'Elizabeth Forrester walked out on me, Mother. It's unlikely she'll return, and I wouldn't marry her even if she did.'

'Wouldn't or couldn't, John? There's an important difference.'

'The end result is the same, Mother. I'm going to marry Lillian.'

He seemed so wooden; Elizabeth Forrester had done that to him. Her son had been hurt by Elizabeth just as her daughter had been hurt by Edward Forrester. And her husband killed by him. How could one family cause so much havoc with another?

The tears she had been holding back began to flow and she reached into her pocket for her handkerchief. It was several moments before she realised that the handkerchief was all that was in her pocket.

'Oh God, John. I've left Rose's letter downstairs. What if Hubert sees it?'

She ran downstairs and found the envelope where she had left it, but she could see immediately that the letter had been taken out and replaced.

'Mrs Laybourne.' She dropped the letter, frightened by Hubert's sudden arrival.

'Oh, Hubert. I've received a letter from Rose. I think you should read it.' She passed the letter to him and watched how fast he scanned the words and turned the pages; it was obvious that he knew the contents.

'My, my. This is very strange, Mrs Laybourne. Do you

have any idea where she's staying, or with whom?'

'You know as much as I do, Hubert. I did think that perhaps I ought to engage a private detective to look for her.'

'Yes, I think we should.' He sounded very concerned, distracted, even desperate. 'I'll make the arrangements myself, leave this afternoon. The sooner we find her the better, before any harm can come to her. She must be very ill to have written a letter such as this, Mrs Laybourne. Really, can you imagine me beating her? I adore her, always have, ever since she was little. She's always been special to me, you know that. My special little friend.'

'No, Hubert, I can't imagine you beating her.' She hugged him and tried to console him, a part of her relieved to see him so sad and worried. 'But in a sense it would have been less worrying if you had beaten her. At least we'd have known she was telling the truth, that she had a valid reason for leaving you.'

'Yes, but I simply want her home again, where I can care for her and ensure that she's safe.' She felt the anguish in his mind.

'Yes, Hubert, of course.' She hugged him, the importance of Rose's overdue dowry and the debenture put back into perspective.

'I'll leave today. Find a detective, the finest I can. Don't know why I didn't think of that before.'

But as she watched him climb the stairs there was something which did not seem quite right.

'Here is the initial cheque for the investigation, Mr Speedwell. Simply send me weekly reports and monthly accounts and I'll arrange to furnish you with any further information which comes into my own hands.' Clarence Speedwell, the sole proprietor and senior investigator of the London Discreet Investigation Agency, remembered Hubert Belchester's words well.

He had resigned from the police and founded his

business in order to accept commissions from the likes of Hubert Belchester, who invariably considered discretion more important than the amount of money they would be asked to part with. He particularly enjoyed looking for people who had gone missing because those enquiries almost always uncovered scandals that the clients wanted kept secret, and because gentrified folk were usually much easier to find than the clients believed. Both circumstances gave him the opportunity to increase his earnings for very little extra effort.

The fact that Rose Belchester was so memorably attractive made his task even easier than usual. He knew she had come to London from Dorchester, and was carrying two bags. He guessed she would have travelled by train, so he started his investigation at the obvious London rail terminus. He simply showed a small picture of Rose to every cab driver he could find until he discovered a man who remembered taking her to a hotel.

The hotel staff remembered her well, as Mrs Browning, and it seemed as if the lucrative investigation would come to an unexpectedly sudden end, until the hotel manager mentioned that she had disappeared with a man she claimed was her husband.

'You're sure you've no idea who this mysterious gentleman could be, sir?' He watched Hubert Belchester's face as he replied, and knew he was being told the truth.

'I've no idea, Mr Speedwell. Mrs Belchester knew no one in London, other than friends of mine and there is no possibility of her being with any of them. Are you sure the hotel manager isn't lying?'

'What would be the point, sir? Unless he's hiding her away somewhere and that's not likely. I hesitate to suggest this, sir, because of the not inconsiderable cost involved' – he knew exactly how to make his clients prove they could afford his services – 'but the only way to find out any more about this mysterious gentleman is to talk with the Parker family. They got to know your wife quite well, it seems, and

were with her when she was supposed to find the man she
called her husband, the mysterious Mr Browning. I could
write to them, of course, but in my experience in other
situations like this a letter don't do enough. I need to talk
to them like I'm trying to find the lady for her own good,
and tease information out of them, if you understand me
meaning, sir. Trouble is they're in America and it'd be
fares and hotels, and I'd have to pay somebody to do me
other work while I was away, hold the fort, as it is.'

'I'll give you an advance to cover your costs, Mr
Speedwell, and reimburse any other expenses. Just make
sure you make it worth my while and find my wife for me.'

Mr Speedwell sailed for New York two weeks later,
wondering if all he had to do was ask the Parkers if they
had Mrs Browning's current address, and sure he could
draw out his absence for three months at least. Work was,
as he told the landlord of his local, 'thin on the ground', and
he was sure that the young man he employed as his sole
assistant would be more than capable of 'holding the fort'
until he returned.

In the event his assistant held the fort for more than four
months. A ruptured appendix and further complications
kept his employer away from England until the last day of
October.

CHAPTER 33

'You're putting on weight, Rose.' There was approval in his voice and she smiled as he grabbed her around her waist and pulled her to him. 'Pretty much back to the shape you were when I first knew you.'

'Not when you first knew me, Edward. I was a child then.'

'And talking of children.' She understood his raised eyebrow and shook her head; she had thought she might be pregnant but this morning had proved she was not.

'There's no hurry, Edward. We're young and healthy and happy. A baby's sure to come soon.'

'Aye, you're right. Anyway, can't stand around talking to you, I've got windows to clean.'

'It's Sunday, Edward.' Surely he was not going to work today; he already worked dawn to dusk six days a week. 'You need a rest and I . . .'

'No.' He held his hands up in mock protest. 'I'm cleaning our windows, and old Mrs Crow's, downstairs.'

'Oh.' She glanced at the window and saw how dirty it looked in the late September sun. 'Purely as a point of interest, does Mrs Crow pay you for cleaning her windows each week?'

'I've never asked her to. It only takes a few minutes and I wouldn't feel right cleaning ours without doing hers too. Besides, there's only the three of us in the house and she's our landlady, and I wouldn't want to cause any bad feeling between us. We never know when we might need to ask a favour from her.'

'You're soft, Edward Forrester, and I wouldn't love you if you weren't, but I think she takes advantage of you. You look after her garden, carry coal, do odd jobs for her, but she never knocks a penny off the rent. She still expects to be paid in full every week.'

'Aye, I know you're right, lass, but she is a widow, and I reckon it doesn't cost us anything to be helpful.'

'I'm not complaining, just commenting so we don't let her go too far. Anyway, yesterday I overheard her telling a neighbour that she doesn't believe we're really married.'

'Ah, so that's what's behind it.' She smarted under his overly tolerant smile. 'Anyway, she's right. We're not married, and not likely to be either. It doesn't matter, does it?'

'Yes, it does.' She had not realised before just how much it did matter. 'I want us to be married. I want to be your wife.'

'Rose.' She hung on to him as he hugged her again. 'We live together, we sleep together, you cook and clean and take care of me, and most of all we've planned our futures together. If that's not being married, then what is?'

'A ceremony, even a simple one in a register office, a certificate and a ring. That's how people see being married, Edward, how other people see it. I'd simply like to be able to stand up and say we're married without feeling that I'm lying. I'd like to be able to call you my husband without thinking that my real, legal, husband is Hubert, not you.'

'Well, lass, marriages can be ended. It's not easy, mind, but it can be done, if that's really what you want.'

'What do you think?' She needed to know if he would be happy to support her through the scandal of divorce. 'Tell me, honestly.'

'I think I understand how you feel, and of course having children when we're not legally married might cause problems for them, but personally, I don't feel we're not married. We are, as far as I'm concerned, and as long as Hubert stays out of our lives I cannot see any real reason to change things.' She was watching his face and noticed his earnest expression change slightly. 'There's another point to this though. You'd have to go through the courts, and as I seem to be the reason Hubert started beating you, I cannot see him standing by and not telling the police who I am. They're not looking for me because they think I'm dead, but . . .'

'Oh God, I'd forgotten that. I'd forgotten all about it.' She was stunned that her new life and current happiness had made her overlook all that had happened in Pincote only a little more than a year earlier. 'Of course we can't risk that. You're right, we can't let Hubert find us.'

The following Saturday, the first Saturday in October, it poured with rain all day. Edward could not work and apart from an hour spent shopping for food they stayed indoors all day doing small chores, reading and talking. They went to bed early, but at ten o'clock there was a commotion at the front door and they heard Mrs Crow calling.

'Mr Forrester, Mr Forrester! Come down, please!'

'On my way, Mrs Crow.' He leaped out of bed, pulled on a pair of trousers and a woollen slipover, and ran downstairs barefoot.

'There's someone at the door, Mr Forrester. He says he's looking for you, and I think he must be drunk because he's fallen over.'

'I'll take care of it, Mrs Crow. You go back into your

living room and shut your door. Don't worry.'

He waited until she was out of sight, then padded to the front door. 'Who's there?'

'Francis Marriott, Edward. I'm hurt. Can I come in? I need to see you.'

The Frenchman was slumped on the doorstep. His hair, his hands, his face and his clothes were covered with dried blood. He had been beaten badly, but not in a prize fight.

'Good God, Francis! What happened?' He helped him into the narrow hallway, up the stairs and into the back room which he and Rose used as their kitchen. 'Who did this to you? Why?'

'Penn and Scraggs. Or rather their men. O'Leary, Milligan and four more caught me in an alley and thrashed me. Careful with my side and shoulder.' He winced with pain. 'They twisted my arm out of its socket then kicked in a few ribs for good measure.'

'For God's sake, why?'

'Looking for you. Reckoned I'd know where you're living.'

'Did you tell 'em?'

'No. They'd've been here if I had.'

'What do they want me for?'

'They've got a big fight lined up, they said. They want you to take on a killer called Pugh, a big Welsh miner.'

'Why me?'

'They'd got someone else and a lot of money's been put down already, more'n a thousand I heard. But their man's got himself locked up and the fight's next Saturday. No one else'll fight Pugh. I wouldn't, but they reckon you'd give him a good run. Plenty of blood, plenty of money, for them.'

'But they know I've stopped. I've told 'em I'll never fight again.'

'They know who you are, Edward. Someone must've overheard us talking about Abraham and Pincote. They say you killed someone and they're threatening to tell the police where you are if you don't agree to fight.' Francis stopped as Rose came into the room.

'Rose knows all about me, Francis. We've no secrets from each other.' He explained to Rose what had happened, helped her clean up Francis's cuts and bruises, and when they had finished he offered to take the Frenchman to hospital.

'No, but thank you anyway, my friend. You'd best not get involved with me. Just watch yourself, though. If you can lay low until after the fight you might be all right, Edward.'

'Aye, until the next time.' He patted Francis's good shoulder. 'I'm sorry they did this to you, and I owe you a big favour for keeping quiet about where we live.'

'No, Edward. I think this makes us even. Talking to you that night, then seeing you fight O'Leary, well, somehow some of what you said rubbed off on me. I could see myself repeating my uncle's—' He stopped and gave a thin smile, then stood up to leave. 'Well, my friend, I gave up the illegal fights that night. Now, you watch out for yourself and Rose, but if Penn does find you, I suggest you agree to the fight but flit before it starts. Pugh'd kill you. He's done in two men already this year.'

He saw Francis out to the street and turned back up the stairs. Rose was waiting on the landing and he guessed what she was going to ask even before she spoke.

'Well, Edward, what are you going to do?'

'Carry on as usual, lass. I've two new jobs to start this week, both of them branches of banks, and if I let them down I'll risk a lot of work which could make all the difference to us. I reckon that if we can tie up a few more business premises we'll be on our way. We'll need to employ one or two men to help me but once I'm sure the clients are happy with the service we give them for window washing I'll see if I can get the general cleaning contracts for the offices. Then we'll have to start looking for reliable cleaning women.' As he led her into the bedroom he could feel her shaking with fear. 'I can't afford to let them frighten me into hiding, Rose.'

'It might be better if we moved on, Edward. Away from London, perhaps. We've proved what we can do here, we can do it somewhere else just as well.'

'Run away, you mean? Never thought I'd hear you say that, lass.'

'No, neither did I, but I'm frightened for you. I couldn't bear anything happening to you, especially when it could be avoided so easily.'

'Rose.' He squeezed her hand. 'I've spent most of my life running away in one form or another. It's never led to anything other than even more trouble. The only time I've been happy, really happy, is the last few months when I've stood me ground and worked hard for what I want. I'm not being bullied into giving that up. Not now, not ever.'

'No, I didn't think you would, but be careful, darling. Please be extra careful.'

He was cleaning the windows on the second floor of a building in Holloway Road when he felt his ladder shake.

'Forrester. We need to talk.' He recognised Scraggs's voice. 'Come down before you fall.'

He was in no position to argue so he climbed down and turned round on the pavement to see Scraggs, O'Leary, Milligan and two other men.

'A sparrow told us we'd find you around here,' Scraggs said coldly, 'after a bit of persuasion.'

'Aye?' He wondered who they had hurt this time and guessed it must be Ada or one of her brood because apart from Francis no one else knew where they were. 'What do you want me for?'

'We've got a fight lined up for you.'

'Not interested.'

'Rather be hung for murder, would you?' Scraggs grinned.

'I don't understand what you mean.'

'You look real healthy, for a dead man.' Scraggs's grin widened and the other men laughed at his joke.

'You've lost me, man. What're you talking about?'

'I heard you talking to the Frenchman, about a place called Pincote. A man was murdered there, and you killed him.'

'Rubbish, man. You've been drinking too much.'

'We'll let the police decide then, shall we?'

'Do what you like, man. I've no idea what you're talking about.' He knew he could not carry on the bluff indefinitely so he went on the attack. 'If you like we could go to a station now, and while you're telling the police what you think you know about me I can tell 'em what I do know about you and Mr Penn. And O'Leary, of course. Wouldn't want to leave him out of it.'

'Just one fight, Forrester, that's all.' Scraggs sounded less confident when he heard the threat. 'One fight and we'll forget all about everything we know.'

'You know nothing, man. You've got me confused with someone else. Sure, I lived in Pincote all right, but I left because I couldn't stick cutting coal any more. I'm damn glad I did because a few weeks later the bloody mine collapsed and killed all my family. Aye, I heard about Mr Laybourne, the mine owner being killed, but there was a riot where he lived and one of the rioters must have killed him. That or someone who worked in his house. No one liked the bastard.'

'No, Forrester, no,' Scraggs said patiently. 'Mr Penn went up there and checked for himself, months ago. Pincote, Newcastle, Durham. He's seen the newspapers. You were quite a hero, he says, until you murdered your governor.'

'Well, he certainly went to a lot of trouble.' There was no reason to lie any more.

'You never know when a bit of information like that'll come in useful, Forrester. Once a killer, always a killer, we reckon. Useful men to know if you need a job done well, if you understand me.'

'I'm no killer, Scraggs, but if you push me I'll tell the police all about you and Penn, and the sort of tricks O'Leary and his gang get up to. I've got others who'll back me, mind, you can be sure of that.' It was another bluff, but he could see it was enough to make Scraggs think about the possible risks. 'I'll not fight for you, so shove off and tell Mr Penn what he can do with his fight, and what I'll do if you or anyone else tries to make trouble for me.'

Scraggs stepped back but O'Leary pushed himself forward. 'You're a dead man, Forrester. I'll do you, you bastard.'

'Go away before you make me angry, O'Leary. I've thrashed both you and Milligan before and I'll do it again if you make me.'

'You're frightening me, Forrester.' O'Leary pretended to be scared. 'Look, I'm shaking like a leaf.'

'That's what you said last time we met.' He smiled as the Irishman realised he had made himself look a fool. 'And look what I did to you then. I broke your nose, your jaw, punched your teeth out and made you lie down like a baby. And I'd already floored your friend there minutes earlier, so don't threaten me, man, I've work to do.'

He turned round and started to pull down his ladder, and by the time he had finished Scraggs and the others were a hundred yards away. He was trembling so much that he could hardly lift the heavy ladder on to his barrow.

'Mrs Forrester! Mrs Forrester! There's someone at the door for you.'

Rose heard Mrs Crow call out and her heart thumped. She was already frantic; it was nearly ten o'clock and Edward should have been home hours ago. She raced down the stairs and even before she reached the front door she could see her caller was Francis Marriott.

'Rose.' His tone told her there was something very wrong.

'Edward?' She could not say any more.

'Yes. Get your coat. He's in the Royal Northern Hospital, seriously ill.'

'How did you . . .' She was shocked and confused.

'He had a message sent to my address, asking me to collect you. It was sent this afternoon but I didn't get home until an hour ago. I've got a cab waiting. It'll be quicker than the buses.'

The hospital was gloomy and its endless tiled corridors echoed and smelled oppressively clean. She sat on a hard bench and tried to make sense of what the nurse was telling her.

'Your husband has had a very bad accident, Mrs Forrester. He fell from a second-storey window on to some iron railings. He broke his right leg and his right arm, probably against the parapet of a ground-floor bay, but his worst injuries were caused by the railings. A spike went right through him. I'm afraid he was impaled for some minutes before he could be lifted off the spike, and it's fortunate that he was just around the corner or he might have died before he could be brought here. He has lost an awful lot of blood and he's very poorly, I'm afraid. Very poorly.'

'You think he'll die?' She had to know.

'We can't say. He is very badly hurt, but fortunately it was a straight spike, not one of the ornamental types like an arrow head which would have done far more damage.'

'Can I see him?'

'Of course, provided you're quiet. There're other patients around him, you see. And he's sleeping at the moment so be careful not to wake him.'

'Did anyone see the accident?' she heard Francis ask, and knew why.

'Yes, apparently several people did, which again was fortunate for him because they were able to support him until he could be lifted. I understand that the bottom of his ladder was in the gutter and a cart hit it.'

'Did the driver stop?' she asked quickly.

'I'm not sure, but I don't think so. Mr Forrester was brought in here on his own barrow.'

She saw the quick frown cross Francis's face and guessed what he was thinking. Best not to say anything, though. Not yet.

Rose did not sleep that night, did not even try to. All she could see was Edward's bloodless face, so white she had thought he was already dead. All she could smell was the ether and the hospital's cleanness, and all she could feel was a sense of death waiting in the hospital ward, hovering by the door, waiting to be called. And hear? All she could hear, inside her head, was Edward screaming in pain as he hung backwards across the spiked railings; in pain and alone and frightened.

He was just a man, mortal, and his mortality frightened her more than anything else ever had. He could die and she would live, but she could not imagine life without him; without her dream of living with her prince. A prince who told fairy stories and could transform himself into King Henry. A prince who cleaned windows to give her a better life, who stood up to bullies, and was kind and loving and cuddled her to sleep each night.

She needed a friend but she had only two, Francis and Ada, and they both lived a long way away and she was scared to go to either in case the hospital called for her. If Edward was going to die she wanted to be with him so he could hear her tell him how much she loved him and say goodbye. She did not want him to die alone in a hospital in a strange and unfriendly city.

She told Mrs Crow what had happened but the widow just shrugged. 'It's a worry, dear, no doubt, but 'e'll get better, you see if 'e don't. I'm off out now, so make sure you take your key if you get called to the 'ospital,' and the house was silent again.

In a strange moment she was able to see herself as if her

mind and body were separate; not yet twenty years old and she had left one husband and been widowed by another. What would she go through before she was forty, sixty? She saw she had changed into Mrs Crow, and she shuddered.

Francis Marriott called for her at six o'clock and took her to the hospital on a bus. The evening was cold and a wet wind made her feel even more miserable as they waited for the traffic to part so they could cross Holloway Road and walk up the steps into the hospital.

They gathered with other visitors in the corridor outside the ward. There was no nurse to talk to them or treat them specially, and the sheer normality of the situation made her feel even worse; guilty that she felt so sorry for herself when there were women who obviously had children to support who were visiting their sick husbands.

Edward's eyes were open.

'Edward? It's Rose, and Francis.' She leaned over him, scared to kiss his white, lifeless face.

His lips moved. She read the words even though there was no sound.

'No need to be sorry, darling,' she whispered and wiped away her tears. 'I love you.'

'I love you too.' She read his lips, then watched his eyes close and listened to his breathing change as he fell asleep.

The next few days were fragmented versions of the first. He was lingering, not properly alive but not yet dead. On the Wednesday Mrs Crow reminded her that she had not paid the previous week's rent, due on Friday, and she paid her minutes before Francis called to take her back to the hospital.

They did not speak during the journey, talking seemed pointless and too much effort. This time, as they waited outside the ward, a sister called her name and came to talk to her.

'There's been a change in your husband's condition, Mrs Forrester.'

She heard the words and waited for the bad news she had been expecting. 'Yes, sister?'

'We need to perform another operation.'

'Another? Why?'

'We need to remove some of the stitches which stopped his internal bleeding before they cause further problems for him. We think he's strong enough, or will be in a day or two.'

'You mean he's recovering?'

'Yes.' The sister sounded surprised to be asked the question.

'I thought he was dying.'

'He very nearly did, but he's been making reasonable progress although we think he may have an internal infection which we must treat before the poison makes him worse. We'll know better after the surgeon's seen him. Go along now. He's been asking after you.'

'I'll wait here,' Francis said, and when she walked into the ward she saw Edward sitting up, propped up by pillows.

His face was grey, not white, and when he smiled at her she could not stop herself crying.

'Hey, lass, don't cry. I'll be up and about soon, you'll see.'

'Oh God, I love you so much and I've been so worried about you.'

'Cannot get rid of me that easy, lass. How're you keeping?'

It all seemed so natural she felt ashamed of herself for worrying so much.

It was four days since Rose had first seen him sitting up, and a day since the second operation.

'Francis did not call for you again.' He sounded unusually edgy.

'No. It's strange. He was supposed to come last night and when he didn't I thought he'd been delayed and I'd find him waiting when I returned home. But he wasn't, and he didn't arrive tonight, either.' It was unlike Francis not to send a message, and Edward's nervousness made her uneasy. 'You haven't heard from him?'

'No, darling, I haven't.' He did not look at her as she answered and she knew he was lying.

'I thought I might call on him tomorrow, in case he's ill. I'm going to see Ada, anyway, although I can't afford to take her any money, and Francis lives quite close, doesn't he?'

'No, don't do that.'

'What, call on Francis? Why not?'

'No, don't call on Ada.' She saw him wriggle and knew there was something he was keeping from her.

'What's happened, Edward? What aren't you telling me?'

'Look, don't get upset, but Francis has been to see me a couple of times in the afternoons. We didn't tell you because I didn't want to worry you. The accident wasn't an accident, I'm sure of that. I'd already had a run-in with Scraggs.' She listened as he told her what had happened an hour before the cart hit his ladder. 'I was worried that maybe Scraggs had forced Ada or one of the children to tell him where he might find me but I was too ill to think much of it until this last few days. I told Francis that we'd been giving Ada money each week but that had stopped when I came in here. I asked him if he could help her with a shilling or two, and also if he could find out if she'd seen Scraggs.'

'And?' She hardened herself against what she thought he might say.

'Scraggs had called to ask her if she knew where we were, and when she told him to get lost he let O'Leary loose on her. She still wouldn't tell 'em, knowing Ada that probably made her more determined to see 'em off, so they dangled the baby, Eddie, out of a window and threatened to drop him into the yard. She had to tell 'em where they might find me.'

'Oh, Edward.'

'That's not all, lass. They took Eddie away with 'em and told her to keep quiet or they'd send him back in a pie. That's why she didn't warn us. Poor kid feels awful, worse than me, I reckon.'

'This is horrible.' Her mind was racing but not making sense of anything, then a thought occurred to her. 'Where's Eddie now? Back with Ada?'

'I don't know. They hadn't returned him but Francis found out where they were keeping him and was going to get him back and move Ada and the brood to another address. That's all I know. I haven't heard from Francis or seen him since he came here with you two nights back.'

'What a mess.' There was nothing else to say.

'Aye, and best left alone, I reckon.' He gripped her hand. 'I don't want you going over there and getting involved in any nasty stuff, Rose.'

'I'm already involved in the nasty stuff, darling.'

'Aye, but don't get more involved. Whatever's happened has happened, and there's nothing you can do to sort it out. Nor me, for that matter, not stuck in here like this. Anyway there is some good news.' He grinned but it was a false grin. 'They reckon I can probably come home next week.'

'That's wonderful.' It was, but after learning what had happened to Ada, it did not thrill her as much as she thought it ought.

The next morning she ignored Edward's warning and went back to the house in Shadwell. It was as disgusting as ever, worse, if anything, because the cold weather and a permanent mist off the river made it even more damp and the cold discouraged the tenants from going even as far as the yard to relieve themselves.

She went up to the loft where Ada lived but there was no one there, so she climbed back down to what had been

Edward's room and listened to the sounds of ecstasy, or agony, that came through the thin door. When the noises stopped she called out and a half-dressed woman with an Oriental-looking man draped over her opened it just enough to talk.

'A young girl lives upstairs with—'

'Yer mean Ada,' the woman interrupted impatiently and shoved the man backwards, cursing him and telling him he would have to pay more if he wanted more.

'Yes, Ada. Do you know where—'

'Gone. With her kids.' The door banged shut.

'With the baby? Eddie?'

The woman did not reply so she pushed the door open. 'Did she have the youngest baby with her?'

The man was lying on the floor and the woman was already astride him. 'I dunno. Didn't see 'er go, did I? Now, bugger off unless you wanna pay to watch.'

She shut the door and made her way back into the street. As she walked away she thought that at least something positive had come out of the affair: Ada had left her useless father; but Rose realised immediately that she might now be in worse trouble than she had been before. And what about the baby?

Edward had told her not to come here, and he had told her not to go to Francis's lodgings, but Francis was the only one who could tell her what had happened and whether Ada and all the children were safe. She walked fast, partly because she was eager to talk to Francis, but mainly because she wanted to get away from that awful Shadwell street as quickly as possible.

The woman who opened the door looked at her suspiciously. 'Yes?'

'Please pardon me for disturbing you, but I'm looking for Mr Marriott.'

''oo ain't?'

'I beg your pardon?'

"e's gone, miss. Flit yesterday, 'e did, in a real 'urry.
Paid 'is rent though. Shame to lose 'im. Good payer, and
quiet. Told them that. 'ope it 'elps 'im, whatever trouble 'e's
in.'

'Told "them"? Who're . . .'

'Law, miss. Five came lookin' fer 'im. Big feller, you see.
Takin' no chances, that lot.'

'Did he have anyone with him when he . . .'

'No, miss, and I don't wanna get involved.' The door was
slammed with an impatience that made it rattle.

She walked away. Francis was in trouble, and she was
sure it was all connected with the troubles she and Edward
had. They seemed to have a knack for involving innocent
people in their problems.

The moment she turned into the road where she lived she
saw an overcoated man with five uniformed policemen
waiting by Mrs Crow's front door.

'Oh, God, what next?' She was too weary to turn back,
and she knew it would do no good anyway; if they wanted
to talk to her they would keep coming back until they
found her.

She pulled out her front door key as she approached the
house, and forced herself to smile as naturally as she
could. 'Good afternoon, gentlemen. Are you looking for
someone?'

'We've been knocking but no one's answered. Do you
live here, miss?' the man wearing the overcoat asked,
without returning her smile.

'Yes, I have two rooms upstairs that I rent from Mrs
Crow, a widow who lives on the ground floor.' Best to
volunteer as much information as quickly as possible.

'Inspector Windsor, miss. May we come inside?'

'Of course, Officer, but may I ask why?'

'We'll tell you inside, miss, if you don't mind. Is there a
back way?'

'Only across the garden wall and out through another

house. It's an enclosed block.' It was obvious they thought she was hiding Francis Marriott, but why?

She opened the door and was immediately pushed aside. 'Inspector!'

'Sorry, miss. Just wait here, please.' He stood with her by the front door as two uniformed men crashed into Mrs Crow's rooms and another two raced up the stairs.

'Inspector!' She flew at the inspector. 'I don't know what you hope to find but I am very pleased Mrs Crow isn't here at the moment. She's quite old and you might have frightened her to death.'

'No one downstairs, sir.' A constable reappeared from the scullery at the back of the house. 'And the back door's bolted from the inside so no one left that way.'

'Empty upstairs, too, sir,' a second constable shouted from the top of the stairs.

'Inspector, do you mind telling me what this is all about?'

'Do you associate with a man called Francis Marriott, or François Marot, or sometimes called the Frenchman?' The inspector waved his men out into the street as he asked the question.

'Associate with him? No. But I do know him. Why?'

'In what context do you know him, miss?'

'He was a prize fighter, took part in illegal fights. I couldn't persuade him to stop entirely but I did persuade him only to fight in legal bouts.' It was surprising how easy it was to distort the truth a little.

'Do you mind me asking, miss, are you a missionary?'

'What makes you ask that, Inspector?' It seemed a strange question.

'Pardon me for saying so, miss, but you've got the smell of the slums on you and this house looks clean and respectable. And, of course, miss, you sound and look far too respectable yourself to be meeting with the likes of Frankie Marriott.'

'Well, thank you, Inspector.' She avoided answering

with a direct lie. 'Why did you come here and why are you looking for Mr Marriott?'

'We searched his rooms and found this address on a slip of paper caught down the back of a chair, miss. I'm sorry we troubled you, but we need to find him and he's not the sort to argue with.'

'You still haven't told me what he's supposed to have done, Inspector.'

'Murder, miss. Three men, no less.'

'Oh God!' She felt weak and slumped down on to the stairs. 'I can't believe that.'

'He did it, miss. Four witnesses to say so.'

'Who, why?'

'Messrs Penn, Scraggs and O'Leary. We reckon O'Leary just got in the way, but we'd been watching out for the other two because they organised illegal fights, amongst other things. Perhaps Frankie hadn't given up after all, miss. Perhaps he went back to get some money Penn wouldn't pay.'

'I'm shocked,' she said truthfully and for a moment wondered if she should say more, but realised it would not help Francis and it would draw attention to Edward.

The inspector walked out through the front door and she saw the crowd of neighbours who had come into the street to see what was happening.

He turned to her and apologised for the intrusion, then closed the door himself. She took off the mittens that she had been scared to remove earlier in case the policemen saw her ring and asked about her husband, closed the doors to Mrs Crow's room, then went upstairs and made herself a cup of very sweet tea.

'But Mrs Crow, we've always paid our rent on time, and considering all the things my husband has done for you I'd have thought you could allow us a little credit. My sewing only earns me enough to live on, and anyway, Mr Forrester will be home next week.'

'Never a borrower nor a lender be, Mrs Forrester, that's my way and it's never done me wrong in all my years. Anyway, even when 'e comes out of 'ospital 'e's not going to be fit enough to climb up ladders, is 'e, so 'ow're you going to pay me?'

'You're a very uncharitable woman, Mrs Crow.'

'That's what you say, but the money ain't all of it. I can't take all these goings-on, not at my age. Blood-soaked drunks turning up on me doorstep at all hours, police calling, and all that. Puts me in bad with me neighbours, it does. I was going to ask you to go anyway.'

'But where can we go? We don't have any money.'

'Sleep on the streets for all I care, or under the arches!'

A thought suddenly occurred to her. 'If I pay you double the rent, will you let us stay then?'

''ow're you going to do that? You can't pay me even one week.'

'I have some jewellery I can sell.' Surely Edward would not mind, not under the circumstances.

'Jewel'ry. Bits and pieces, I suppose. Even your wedding ring's a fake. Wedding ring? Huh! Brass curtain ring I reckon, and you ain't never been married.'

She did not argue about the ring. She had given her real wedding ring to Ada to sell to buy food for her brood, and Mrs Crow was right about the ring she was wearing.

'I'll show you if you don't believe me. It's jewellery my parents gave me to wear for my eighteenth birthday ball.'

'Birthday ball. Birthday ball.' Mrs Crow laughed scornfully. 'Miss high and bleedin' mighty, you've come down a bit since then, ain't you?'

'Wait here, please. I'll show you.' She ran upstairs, found her jewellery box and rushed back down to show Mrs Crow what she had.

'Glass, you can't fool me. Bits o' glass they are, I'll be bound.'

'No they're not. They're worth a lot of money.'

'Sell 'em then, and when you've got your fortune you come back and we'll see.' Mrs Crow turned into her back room and shut the door.

'Pawn or sell?' The jeweller looked at her over his half-glasses.

'I want to sell them, please.' Mrs Crow was right about being neither a borrower nor a lender; pawning them would not realise their value, and she would have to pay interest, she knew that much.

'Not worth much.' The jeweller screwed a magnifying glass against his eye and inspected the necklace and earrings. 'Four pounds for the lot, mrs.'

'Four pounds! They're worth much more than that.'

The man gathered up the items again, held them up against the light, then carefully inspected each setting individually. 'No, four pounds, and only because you look like a young lady who's in trouble.'

'That's ridiculous and you know it.'

'Take them away then.' He handed the pieces back to her. 'I don't really want them anyway. They're too expensive for most, and not good enough for the others who've got real money to spend.'

She sailed out of the shop, trying hard to hold back her tears, and walked along two streets until she reached another small jeweller's.

'Three pounds, missus.'

'But they're worth much more than that.' How could they both be wrong?

'No, they're just dress pieces, made for the stage I should think.'

'But they were an expensive birthday present from my father.'

'I'm sorry, mrs. Perhaps you should take them back to him. If he thought they were genuine, then he was done, no mistake.'

'I can't. He's dead.'

'Then keep them for sentiment. You won't get more than three pounds for this lot.'

'Someone else offered me four pounds,' she said with a mixture of hope and desperation.

'So you know they're not worth much. Take them back there, then.'

'No, I can't. I made a fool of myself because I thought they were worth much more. Much more.'

'Three pounds then?'

'I suppose so.'

'All right then Mrs Forrester.' She could see Mrs Crow gloating. 'Pay me ten bob and you can stay until next rent day. Then you go.'

'But that's only tomorrow. I'll give you a pound if you'll let us stay another two weeks.'

'Make it three and you can.'

Three was too much to ask, in value and principle. 'Go to hell, Mrs Crow. You will one day.'

Half an hour later she was on the street, her bags at her feet, thrown there by the next-door neighbour's husband.

She walked to the agent who had found the accommodation with Mrs Crow, but he refused to help. It seemed that Mrs Crow had already complained about her and Edward. He told her to try Hoxton. There was always cheap accommodation in Hoxton, he said, where landlords were not particular about the sort of people who rented their rooms.

'I'm sorry it's on the top floor, Edward. It was the only room I could afford.' She opened the door to the dingy little room she had done her best to clean and brighten.

'The exercise'll do me leg good, lass,' he said, but she could see he was in pain from the climb.

She settled him into the room's only soft chair and stiffened as he recognised the material which covered it.

'This looked better on you when it was a dress, lass.'

She knew he meant to sound grateful for the effort she had made, but she could not stop herself crying. 'Never mind, Rose. Never mind. It's better than the room we had to start with, so we've made a bit of progress. And I see we've got a pet, too.'

A rat stared out from the empty grate. She recoiled, then started as Edward flattened it with his walking stick.

'I'm sorry, Edward. I'm sorry, but I might as well tell you now. We could only afford this because I sold my jewellery. For three pounds. It was fake.'

There was a moment of silence when she studied his face trying to guess what he was thinking.

'Oh, Rose.' He held his arms out and she knelt beside him, grateful to be held close after so long apart. 'I'm sorry you had to do that, and grateful you did. And I'm sorry that you had to find out that . . .'

'Go on. What were you going to say?'

'Nothing, it doesn't matter.'

'That my father was a cheapskate?'

'I'm sure he either didn't know or he had his reasons, Rose. I had good reason to hate him but I think he really did love you and that's why he didn't want you to get involved with me. He could probably see what I'd bring you down to.'

'Never say that again!' She did not want Edward to blame himself for what had happened to them, that was due to Scraggs and Penn and O'Leary, and they were dead.

'I'm sorry, I didn't mean to upset you.'

'Never, ever apologise to me, Edward. I knew it was going to be hard to achieve what we want, but we will, one day, and at least we're together. I never want to be apart from you again.'

'Mr Speedwell, I'm very happy to see you're home safely, after so long abroad.'

'Thank you kindly, sir. Thank you kindly. A long time indeed, and none of it wasted, I can assure you of that, sir.'

Speedwell cringed; now it was time to justify the length of time he had spent in America, the evidence he had collected seemed trivial. 'When I arrived I was informed that the Parker family was travelling, and it took quite a lot of trailing about to find them, I can tell you, sir.'

'Please don't bother me with details, Mr Speedwell. Just tell me what you found out. And briefly, please.'

'Right, sir. Right ho. It don't seem much now, but it took a lot of—'

'I have no doubts it did, Speedwell. But hurry, man, hurry.'

'Right you are, sir. Mr Browning's an actor, sir.'

'An actor? Mrs Belchester has never had any contact with any actors, man.'

'Well, sir, that's what I've been informed of.' The client's doubt made it seem prudent to refer to the little notebook in which Mrs Parker's exact words had been copied. 'A promising young Shakespearean actor. His portrayal of Henry Five was quite outstanding.'

'Henry the Fifth?'

'Yes, sir. I suppose that's who she meant, if you think so. Came from a family that was in mining, owned a number of mines around where Mrs Browning, sorry, Belchester was born.'

'Really?' He noticed the way the client seemed to perk up. 'A name for this mysterious Mr Browning? Not Edward, by any chance, Mr Speedwell?'

'How'd you know that, sir?' All the way to America and back to be told the client already knew his choicest piece of information.

'But no address, I assume, Mr Speedwell?'

'Not quite, but I have copied out a letter which Mrs Browning, sorry, Belchester, wrote to the Parkers to thank them for their attention and concern. She says she hasn't given an address because they were in temporary accommodation but promised she would write later advising a permanent address. The Parkers promised to let me have that.'

'Is that all?'

'No. The letter said they were living between two recreation grounds which they visited on Sundays, and she described the grounds. I think I know them both, and if I'm right, then they are, or were, living somewhere in Highbury.' He could not help making himself sound triumphant.

'So, Mr Speedwell, you think you'll be able to find them, now?'

'Undoubtedly, sir, and because you kindly agreed to pay my costs when my return to England was unavoidably delayed because of my illness, brought on by the strange food, I might say, I'll put my whole team of investigators into scouring the Highbury area until we find the missing lady. Even if she has moved on, sir.'

'Good man, Speedwell. Good man. I take it you'll also enquire at all the theatres?'

'Of course, sir. That's already in hand.' He made a mental note to tell his sole assistant to do that next.

He did not tell Hubert Belchester that once he had discovered a little more he intended visiting Pincote where the woman's mother lived, and asking a few questions about Edward Browning. The locals must know something abut a man who would give up the family mining businesses to go into acting. There was more to this investigation than he had been told, he was sure of that, and it might be well worth his while to find out what that was.

The oil lamp swayed in the wind, and Rose held her hands close to it to capture some warmth, then rubbed them together briskly to get her blood running back into her fingers. Her skin was rough from working out of doors and handling the vegetables but she did not mind; at least she could spend all day with Edward and feel that she was doing something to help them recover from the disaster that had struck them.

The rent for the barrow and the pitch took a large portion out of their daily takings, but they still had enough to pay for their room and to buy food and a daily bucket of coal, if nothing else.

'It's quiet now, Rose. Go home if you're cold.' Edward coughed as he spoke and she thought he sounded worse than he had that morning.

'No, I'm all right, but I think you should go, darling. Get inside, out of this wind before it makes you worse.'

'No, I'm all right.'

'You're not. You've been getting worse all week. I think you should go to a doctor before that cold turns to pneumonia.'

'I'm all right!' He turned away to serve another customer and she saw the way he held his side, where the railing had speared him.

He was not all right. He had a heavy cold, his leg had stiffened up so that he could not bend it, and his skin was turning yellow. He could not eat without suffering pains in his stomach and back, and he was growing more irritable each day. She had to make him rest, but she did not know how.

And she did not know how they would manage if he did rest. They earned only enough money to live from day to day and although she could manage to haggle with the wholesalers who sold them vegetables, she needed him to push the barrow to and from the market where they bought their stock. She could not work without him, and if they did not work they would still have to pay rent for the barrow and pitch or risk losing it to someone else.

A clock struck eight, then quarter past, and the evening trade died to a trickle of latecomers who knew they could argue about prices because anything that was left on the barrow would probably have to be thrown away. By nine it was pouring with rain and the street was almost empty.

'We may as well go home, darling.' The first time she had spoken to him for more than an hour.

He did not answer, simply dumped the remaining vegetables into a large wooden box they had fitted with a handle and two wheels, took down the lamp and turned it out, and began to push the makeshift trolley away.

She turned up the collar on what had been her best coat and was now stained with mud from the vegetables, and followed him, her feet sore inside the remade boots she had bought for sixpence.

The next morning she woke up at four o'clock as usual. The wind was rattling ice pellets against the window and she was cold even though beside her Edward radiated damp, feverish heat. She lay still for several moments, hands poised ready to wake him, then decided to let him sleep on. If she could wash and dress without waking him she could find some way of getting the barrow to the market and back to the pitch, even if it took until dawn; and he could stay in the warm for a few more hours.

She quietly riddled ash through the fire basket and laid the last pieces of coal on top of the glowing cinders in the hope that she could keep the room warm for as long as possible, then wrote a brief note telling him to stay at home even though she guessed he would ignore it and come to find her as soon as he woke up. Her coat was still damp from last night's soaking but it was all she had to wear against the wind and sleet. She slipped it on and left the room without making a sound, carrying her boots out on to the landing where she pulled them on and tied the string laces in a slip knot she could undo even if the string shrank in the wet.

The sleet stuck to her coat and froze in a layer. She was glad when she reached the shelter where most of the costers stopped for a morning mug of hot soup, their customary breakfast.

'On yer own, luvvy? Where's yer ol' man?' the jolly woman who served the soup asked brightly.

'I left him in bed, Mrs Perkins. His cold's settled on his

chest and I'm hoping he'll stay in the warm for today.'

'How you gonna manage the barrer?'

'I don't know, but I'll manage somehow. I've no choice,' she said confidently, unwilling to admit that she felt excited she had stolen the chance to prove to Edward that she was capable of hard physical work.

'Well, you be careful. Don't do yerself an injury or you'll both be laid up.'

True, that wouldn't help them at all, but she did not have any choice. She walked to the barrow, removed the lock and chain that kept it secure, and started to push it towards Spitalfields Market to buy stock. Most of the other costers had already moved on and she felt alone and frightened as she trundled the heavy barrow through the almost empty streets. The leather satchel which contained the money she needed to buy produce was slung over her shoulders and her vulnerability made her push it inside her coat so nobody could see it.

She had always helped Edward push the barrow, each of them taking one of the wooden shafts, and it seemed easy to manoeuvre the heavy, flat trolley when they were both there. It was not easy on her own. The shafts were too far apart for her to hold both of them at the same time and pushing the thing one-sided made it skew across the road if she was not careful, but she soon learned to use the slight camber on the road surface to help her keep it straight. The barrow was heavy, much heavier than she expected, and she began to wonder how she would manage the return journey with a load of vegetables on board.

She did, somehow, helped by the way the wholesalers loaded the barrow to keep it balanced over its two wheels, and by men who took pity on her and helped her push it up the few inclines which otherwise would have beaten her. She arrived back at the pitch glowing with warmth and with her coat dried out.

'Rose. How the hell d'you manage that?' Edward did not

look pleased and his mood irritated her.

'Why have you come out in this wind? Why didn't you stay in bed as I asked you to?'

'I'm not a child, Rose, and I can't have you working for the both of us. It's too much for you.'

'I'm not a child either, and you can see that I'm not doing too badly, Edward. If you go down with pneumonia I'll have no choice but to work for the both of us, so go home.'

'I'm all right. Stop nagging, woman! It's not your place to be doing my job. Trying to make me look a fool.'

'I wasn't trying to do that, Edward. I was trying to help.' It hurt to be talked to like that, especially when other people could hear. 'And you won't help us by making yourself more ill.'

A racking cough stopped him arguing.

That night he became delirious. As soon as it was light she went to bring the nearest doctor to him.

'What's wrong with him, Doctor?'

'Very bad influenza, Mrs Forrester. And he's developing bronchitis. And he may have a liver infection.'

'What should I do for him, Doctor?'

'I'll recommend some medicine, but you can help by giving him plenty of hot drinks, broth would be good, and you need to keep this room warm and dry. You must keep the fire going all day and all night, and he needs to stay in bed for a week at least, two probably.'

'You wouldn't take him to the infirmary, Doctor?' She was surprised how willing she was to be parted from him again.

'Not for what he's got. We need the infirmary for people who're really ill, Mrs Forrester.'

'But he is ill, isn't he?'

'He is, but the infirmary couldn't do any more for him than you can do here.'

'But I've got to go to work each day.'

'Then you'll need to find someone who can come in and look after him, Mrs Forrester.'

'But there isn't anyone, Doctor.'

'Then you'd better stop working and apply for relief, young lady. Plenty do, and it looks to me as if you need it. In fact, I think I ought to look at you, too.'

'I'm quite well, thank you,' she said quickly and tried to avoid the doctor's direct stare.

'If you say so,' he answered quietly, 'but there's a good chance you'll catch this too, and it sounds to me as though you're already having some difficulty breathing.'

'Asthma, Doctor. Nothing serious, though, I've had it ever since I was small.' She did not realise that he had hold of her hands until it was too late.

'Good grief, young woman, what've you been doing to get hands like that?'

Even though handling vegetables had made her hands tough, pushing the cart had made them blister and during the day the blisters had burst and left a pulp of soft skin which had split and made her hands raw and bloody; she told him what she had been doing.

'Pushing a coster barrow loaded with vegetables then standing out in the cold all day? Good God, woman, are you trying to make yourself ill?'

'I've no choice, not if we're to eat and keep a roof over our heads.'

'Apply for relief, young woman, today, or you'll both end up dead before Christmas. I'm serious, so listen.'

Clarence Speedwell felt his heart thump; he had not been this excited for years, not even going to America at Belchester's expense. His nose picked up the unmistakable smell of scandal and extra money as the house agent handed him back Rose Belchester's picture.

'Yes, that's Mrs Forrester, all right, and the man you've described is definitely Edward Forrester.' He shook his head. 'I made a mistake, Mr Speedwell, I can tell you that. I always ask for references when I'm recommending tenants to my better customers, people like Mrs Crow. But the Forresters came recommended to me by someone I've known for years, and they seemed respectable enough, her especially. All right for a few months, it was, then no end of trouble and rent arrears so Mrs Crow threw 'em out. Even then the woman came to me for help but I turned her away. Told her to go over Hoxton, they'd be at home there.'

'You don't know their current address, then?'

'No, but they hadn't got any money. She even sold her jewels, as she called them, bits of glass really, and they're still stuck in the window in a shop along Blackstock Road. Try the costers down Hoxton Street. Someone might remember 'em. She wasn't the sort you'd forget. Stuck out like a sore thumb around here.'

'Rose, you've got to face it. I've been like this for two weeks now and I'm not going to get better.'

'You will, Edward. You will.' He would get better, she would make him better, somehow.

'No, lass. Me ma was just like this. Smelled just like me at the end. Poison in me lungs. I can feel 'em filling up.' He coughed so much his red eyes bulged and his veins stood out blue against his jaundiced skin. 'You've got to go. Before you get too ill to leave.'

His clammy hand ran across her face and her own chest tightened so she could not speak and could hardly breathe.

'You've got the flu already, lass, and it's going on to your chest, I can hear it. You've got to go before this place kills us both.'

'No, Edward. I'm not leaving you, ever.' The effort made her whisper the last words, and she lay back, pulled the blanket around them both, and cuddled him for warmth.

The afternoon bore slowly into the evening and then the night.

It seemed a long time before daylight showed through the thin curtain that only just covered the window. It was relief day, the day she could collect a few shillings to get them through a few more days, but first she had to get to the relief office and the sound of pouring rain made the bed seem warm and even comfortable.

She slipped back to sleep, anything to put off the walk to the relief office and the humiliation of queuing for the necessary charity.

The street below was noisy with traffic when she woke.

Unsure of the time she sat up and stepped out of the bed. There was no need to dress, she wore her clothes all the time so she could keep warm. They had not had a fire for two days, had not eaten more than thin soup for three, and they owed two weeks' rent to a rentman who was not due to call again until after the relief had already been spent on food and coal. The thought of all that gave her the urgency to rinse her face in cold water, prod her hair with her fingers, and try to feel human before she went out on to the street.

'Mr Forrester. Mr Forrester!' The voice woke him but he did not recognise it.

'Who's there?'

'Let me in. Quick!'

He felt for Rose and realised she was not there, remembered it was relief day and guessed she had gone to collect some money. 'Door's open. Come in.'

The few words set him coughing, a slow wheezing cough that hurt his lungs and ribs and back and made him feel bruised all through his body.

A man he did not know stood by his bed. 'Mr Forrester?'

'Aye. Who're you?' Rasped out of mucous-filled lungs.

'Sid Perkins. Me and me missus run the soup stall but we 'aven't met 'til now.'

'Soup stall? Oh, aye,' he remembered.

'There's someone been asking after you, Mr Forrester, and Mrs Perkins reckons he's police. Detective. She 'asn't told 'im nothin' but she reckons 'e's askin' around, sort of, and he says 'e's willin' to drop a few bob to anyone who can tell 'im where you are. You in trouble?'

'Sounds like it, Mr Perkins, doesn't it?'

'Yeah. Mrs says it's you 'e's lookin' for, all right, 'cos 'e's got a bit of a newspaper with your picture on the front. Your 'ead's all done up, but she's sure it's you.'

'It's me. Thanks for the warning.'

'Can I 'elp?'

'No, best if you don't get involved, but thanks anyway,' Edward whispered because it hurt too much to talk louder.

Perkins left, apparently eager to get away.

Penn! It had to be Penn even though he was dead. He must have told the police before Francis killed him; not that it made much difference now.

'Rose?' She froze; the voice was unmistakable. 'Rose, I've a present for you.'

The first thing she saw was the necklace, then Hubert, then the tubby, round-hatted man who almost danced a jig by her husband's side.

'It is Mrs Belchester?' the man asked.

'It certainly looks like her, but not exactly at her best.' Hubert smiled and held the necklace against her. 'Doesn't quite suit your outfit, my dear.'

'How did you?' No need to finish the question; how he had found her did not matter now that he had.

'I've come to take you home, Rose.' He eased her into a shop doorway.

'I won't go with you, Hubert.'

'Then we'll hand Forrester over to the police. I'm sure they'd like to meet again.'

'You wouldn't.' The words came instinctively, but she knew he would.

'Come home with me and we'll forget all about this little adventure, Rose, and I'll make sure Forrester is taken care of and goes free. I understand he's quite ill and needs treatment.'

'It may be too late for that.' It was the best defence she could offer.

'Then I'll pay for his funeral.'

'I hate you.'

'But I'm your husband, and from the way you look I'd suggest you need some attention, too.' He paused and pushed the necklace into his pocket. 'It's your choice, Rose. Either you come with me and let me take care of you and Forrester, or I'll hand him over to the police and abandon you. Think what the scandal'll do to your mother and your brother. They've enough trouble already, trying to avoid bankruptcy. A scandal will certainly finish them off completely.'

She had no choice. It was over.

That was all she could think of. Her life with Edward, it was over. They had lost everything. They had been beaten by circumstances, by bad luck, by life. And now they were going to be parted again, this time for ever, she was sure of that. It was over.

She did not reply, simply let Hubert take her arm and lead her back along the streets until they turned into the road where she lived.

'Let me warn Edward, please,' she pleaded. 'Just give me five minutes alone with him. To explain.'

'Of course.'

She found the energy to run up the stairs, tears flowing down her face, her mind not knowing how she was going to explain.

'Edward, darling.' She burst into the room.

It was empty.

'Edward?' There was nowhere for him to hide, the room was too small.

Then she saw the scrawled letter lying on the bed.

Darling Rose,
I love you more than I could ever tell you and I hate myself
for having put you through so much. I'm not good for you.

*Perhaps we're not good for each other. Anyway, the
dream's over. The police know I'm alive. It's only a matter
of days, even hours before they catch me. If they find you
with me they'll charge you as my accomplice even though
you had nothing to do with my crime. I couldn't bear for
you to hang or go to prison so I've given myself up. Please,
darling, you must use the relief money to buy your fare
back to Pincote. Your mother and John will take care of
you. I hope your life improves and implore you to forget
me.*
All my love,
Edward

She was too stunned to cry any more. He had given himself
up because he thought the police had found him; but it was
not the police, it was Hubert. He had given himself up for
nothing.

'Rose?' Hubert was beside her. 'Forrester's gone out?'

'He's given himself up to the police, Hubert.'

'He's a fool.'

She heard the words and rounded on him. 'Maybe,
but . . .'

'What about me, Mr Belchester? About our
arrangement?' the round-hatted man asked urgently.

'Your bonus, shall we call it, Mr Speedwell? Bonus
sounds so much better than blackmail, doesn't it?'

'What about it, Mr Belchester? You promised me—'

'Go away, you impudent little scrounger. We're too late
to stop Forrester now, so you can be satisfied with
everything else you've taken from me. I'll not pay you a
penny more than I already have, so go away, before I
report you to the police for concealing information about a
wanted man. Go on, get out of my sight.'

'You're a bastard, Belchester,' she heard the man curse,
and silently agreed with him as he backed out through the
door. 'And I'll make you pay. Somehow. You bastard.'

She was alone with her husband and she watched his

eyes as his hands undid her coat and squeezed her hips. 'Well, Rose, you've lost weight.'

She nodded. She had lost weight, but she would soon regain it and more; more weight than Hubert might expect. There was nothing else she could do for Edward but she could make sure his love lived on in the baby only she knew she was carrying.

CHAPTER 34

As Elizabeth opened the front door the low afternoon sun blinded her, and she shaded her eyes as she greeted the silhouette standing on the tiled path. 'Good afternoon.'

'Good afternoon, Elizabeth.'

'Catherine!' It took a few moments to recover from the surprise, then, 'Come in. Do come in.'

A quick shout over her shoulder to tell Evie that Catherine was visiting, a few moments' confusion in the narrow passage as greetings were exchanged and Catherine's coat was taken and hung on the hallstand, and then as Evie went off to make the inevitable pot of tea Elizabeth led Catherine into the front room and settled her on the settee.

'It's lovely to see you, Catherine, but what's happened to bring you here like this?' Something must be very wrong for Catherine to have travelled unannounced to London.

'Several things, Elizabeth.'

'Is it John? Is he ill?'

'No, he's very well and quite robust. He's also married, to Lillian McDougall, last month.' Catherine paused, then added quickly, 'I didn't write to tell you before because I wasn't sure . . .'

'I'm pleased, Catherine. Really pleased for him. I've felt awful about just walking away from him.'

'You shouldn't,' Catherine said in her usual brisk way. 'You had no choice. It's been far more difficult for you, Elizabeth.'

'Well, to be honest, Catherine, I'm glad I left him and came here. I can see now that I wasn't ready to settle down with him, or anyone else. I'm still not, but at least I can say that something good has come out of what happened.' She felt better for speaking openly. 'But I can't believe you came all the way down here just to tell me John's married.'

'No, Elizabeth, you're quite right.' She listened carefully as Catherine revealed how close Charlotte had come to bankruptcy and how the McDougalls and Belchesters had bought up all the farms and other interests, leaving only the manor and its immediate grounds in the Laybourne name.

'Also,' Catherine continued, 'I didn't tell you before but Rose disappeared for several months. She's returned to poor Hubert now, much to everyone's relief. The doctors think it's possible that the shock of everything that happened, John's accident, Father's murder, Edward's death, all combined to unbalance her for a while. Unfortunately her asthma's returned and she's still quite ill, poor thing . . .'

'Good God, Catherine. That's awful. I wish I could see her.'

'Please, Elizabeth.' Catherine raised her hand. 'Hubert's taken her off for a belated wedding journey through Europe. They'll be away for some months and they don't have a planned itinerary so there's little purpose in writing.'

She thought Catherine looked relieved when Evie

appeared with the tea and settled down beside her on the settee. Catherine sipped from her cup then seemed to take a very deep breath before speaking in a slightly trembling voice. 'Actually, it is rather convenient that they're out of the country because something else has happened and it's best Rose doesn't hear of it, never if possible.'

She noticed the way Catherine hesitated before looking directly into her eyes, and she knew why Catherine had called. 'It's Edward, isn't it, Catherine? He's alive, isn't he?'

'Yes.' Catherine continued her steady gaze. 'He's been arrested and taken to Durham to stand trial.'

It seemed inevitable, somehow. Everything that had happened followed a natural, almost predictable course, and Edward's situation was no different.

'I'd better go to him, see if I can help in any way.'

'I'm sure he'd like that.' Catherine reached out and squeezed her hand. 'You can travel with me if that suits you, but you'd better prepare yourself for another shock when you see him. He's been very ill in the prison hospital. Apparently he nearly died and he looks awful.'

'Now, lad, I cannot make you see your sister, mind, but think on. She's been coming here every afternoon for five days now, and for what my opinion's worth I reckon that she'll just keep on coming, like, until either you agree to see her or they hang you. Now, come on, lad, be fair and let her talk to you. I cannot bear to see her cry again.'

'No. I don't want to see anyone. Tell her not to come back again, please.'

'I've already told her that four times, lad, but she doesn't listen to me. She might listen to you, if you'd only talk to her.'

'No.'

'Well, I'll not turn her away again, Forrester. She wants to see you so I'll break the rules and let her come to you. She's a fine-looking lass, mind, and I reckon your neighbours'll be right happy to see a woman again.'

'No, don't do that.' He knew how the other prisoners would react to a woman in the wing and he could not let Elizabeth hear the things they would shout at her.

'Well, you come and talk to her then.'

He hesitated, wondering if he could call the senior warder's bluff, and decided not to take the risk. 'Aye. I'll come.'

He stepped back as the cell door was opened, then followed the warder along a brown-tiled corridor until they reached a small room with bars dividing it in two. The warder sat on one of two chairs and motioned for him to sit on the other, a yard away from the bars. A similar chair faced him on the far side of the bars. A door in the other part of the room opened and he stood up involuntarily as he saw Lizzie.

'Edward!' She ran forward.

He stood against the bars, his arms through the gaps so he could hold and kiss her. She felt good and he wished he had agreed to see her days ago. Thankfully the warder did not complain or order them to stand back.

'How're they treating you, Edward?'

'Well enough, lass. I've only been here for a week or so. I spent the first six weeks in the prison hospital.'

'You look well.' He knew she was lying, he still looked awful. 'Better than I expected anyway.'

'Especially as you thought I was dead?' It needed to be said.

'I did at first, it was awful. Then I heard you'd taken a bag to work but it had gone missing, and I'd already realised your favourite book was not in the house. I began to wonder, Edward . . .' Her voice trailed off.

'Best forget it all now, Lizzie. Do you want to sit down?'

'No, I want to hold you.'

He was glad. The last time they had held each other was the night he had come up after the accident a year and a half ago. He remembered waking up and finding her in bed with him, fully dressed, holding him the way she often had when they were children.

'I'm sorry I didn't see you sooner, Lizzie.'

'It doesn't matter. It doesn't matter at all,' she said and he felt her tears against his face.

'It's just that I wasn't ready, lass. Nothing against you, like,' he tried to explain, but nothing could have explained how guilty he had been feeling.

'What've you been up to, lad?'

'All sorts, nothing that matters.' Careful not to admit that he had been with Rose, not when the warder might overhear. 'But what about you? You look so different. What are you doing now? Where are you living?'

'I'm a home visitor, sort of an inspector, working for a women's mission in Hoxton. Catherine arranged it all for me.'

'Catherine?' The name did not mean anything to him.

'Catherine Wyndham. Rose's sister. Half sister.'

'That was kind of her, I suppose.' The mention of Rose stunned him for a moment, stirred up feelings he was trying to keep down.

'It was very kind of her. She's done a lot for me, Edward, and I'm very grateful to her. And' – he noticed her hesitate for a moment – 'she wants to help you by paying for a good defence.'

'Bit of a waste of money, that, lass.' It was an instinctive reaction and he was sorry the moment he spoke; he could see he had hurt her.

'Please don't say that, and please don't refuse her offer. It'd hurt her, and me. Please, Edward, don't refuse her help.'

He could see from her expression how much his acceptance would mean to her, but he did not want to accept Catherine's offer, especially as he could not understand why it had been made. 'I can't see why she would want to help me, Lizzie, considering I killed her father.'

'It's a long story but she does have good reasons, believe me. Let her help, Edward. Please.'

'Aye, lass, all right. Tell her I'm grateful to her.' He was pleased to see her small smile.

He wanted to ask her if she knew how well Rose was, but he could not think of a way to do it without embarrassing her. A few moments passed.

'Rose?' she asked suddenly, and he was so surprised that he wondered for a moment if he had spoken his thoughts out loud, then he felt embarrassed in case she already knew about the months he spent with Rose.

'D'you know anything?' he asked as vaguely as he could.

'A little, though I haven't seen her for over a year, not since her wedding, lad.' He noticed the way she watched for his reaction, and he tried not to give her any hint that he already knew. 'She married Hubert, eventually, and then, according to Catherine, she disappeared for several months. Some sort of temporary madness, it seems.' She paused and he thought her words, a temporary madness, were a good description of his months with Rose. 'Anyway, she's back with Hubert now.'

The shock was like a punch in the face. He was stunned. 'She's gone back to him?'

How could she have gone back to him? Why? Why not safe, with her mother at Pincote?

'Yes.' Lizzie was deliberately looking away and had not noticed his reaction. 'And it seems their problems are over and they're very happy together. They're travelling around Europe. A delayed wedding journey.'

Everything seemed to move away from him. A soft helmet closed over his head, muting all sounds and distorting his sight; a sense of depression far worse than any he had known before swept over his shoulders and lay on his chest. Rose had done exactly as he asked. She had forgotten him.

He felt unsteady, lost, drowning, absolutely without hope. Nothing mattered now. There was no life without

Rose, without the hope, no matter how faint, that one day they would be together again.

There was a moment's awkward silence, and he heard the question, 'Do you know when your trial's going to be, lad?'

'Six weeks, they reckon. I'll be glad to get it over, lass. Get it done with, like. I'm pleading guilty so there's no reason for you to give any evidence and the whole thing shouldn't take too long.'

'Guilty?' He noticed her surprise and gave her a quick glance to caution her against saying too much in case the warder heard.

'No one's going to believe I didn't do it deliberately, so it's best for all concerned to admit to it and try to get it over quick, like.'

'You're not going to fight, then?' She still sounded surprised.

'I've no fight left in me, lass, not any more.'

'I see.' It was clear that she did not, but he knew she could not understand unless he told her everything; and he could never do that. Too many people had been hurt already.

The warder stood up. 'Your time's over, Forrester. I've got to take you back now, lad.'

He was glad it was time to go; it was difficult to talk any more.

'Edward, I've got to go back to London first thing tomorrow, but I'll come again, as soon as I can. As often as I can.'

'Thanks, lass, but don't worry too much. It's a long journey from London, all the way up here.' It would be something to look forward to if she came again but good as it was to see her, it was also painful; she brought back thoughts and emotions he would prefer left to lie.

'I will come back. I promise.' She was crying again.

He kissed her through the bars, hugged her until the warder's hand touched his shoulder.

'Goodbye, Lizzie.'

'I love you, Edward.'

He did not trust himself to answer, just nodded and turned away.

He watched Mr Joseph, his barrister, stroll around the room. Joseph was a grey man, silver grey, tall and slim with a long, fine face and large, expressive, long-fingered hands. He was a quiet man, softly spoken, given to periods of thought-filled silence.

It was interesting to watch him move because he did not stroll as other men did, he seemed to flow; everything he did flowed as though he were fluid.

'There's something about your case which bothered me, Mr Forrester, and still does. Something I felt was wrong and which I simply could not understand. And now I do.'

'Aye, sir?' Trying to end the unsettling silence which followed the statement.

'You're accused of murdering Mr Laybourne, but although it's quite clear that you're no murderer, Mr Forrester, you've never denied the charge nor offered any defence or even proffered any excuses.' Edward felt Mr Joseph's mild eyes washing into his mind, softening his resistance. 'Your poor sister told me exactly how you came to kill him, Mr Forrester. You obviously killed Mr Laybourne by accident, but for some perverse reason you wish to be punished as if you actually had murdered him. That puzzles me, Mr Forrester. Why do you wish to be punished for a murder you did not commit?'

'I did kill him, sir.' He knew that was not the answer Mr Joseph wanted, but it was the only answer he could give. He could not explain the guilt which overwhelmed him; he could not understand it himself, he certainly could not explain it to someone else. And he could not explain why he believed the feeling could only be purged if he were punished for killing Sebastian Laybourne. He only knew that in his mind he could understand how the martyrs must have felt as they took their punishment: a sense of cleansing, of purification, a rebirth of hope.

He was determined to be found guilty, no matter what the consequences were. It was better to be hanged, even, than live with this guilt and the sense of hopelessness for the rest of his life.

'Mr Forrester, it is my brief to defend you, and that is precisely what I intend to do, whether or not you approve. My position, and my inclination, demand that I defend you as best I can.'

'You must do whatever you feel is right for you, sir, but don't expect me to co-operate where you conflict with what I believe is best for me.'

'Mr Forrester' – Mr Joseph sounded exasperated – 'I know you wish to plead guilty, and if you do I could argue some mitigation be considered because of your emotional and physical condition at the time of the deed. However, having met your sister and learned exactly what happened that evening, I think it would be more honest of you to plead not guilty. That does mean, ironically, that you may receive a harsher sentence if you're finally found guilty, but I believe that ultimately both you and your sister will be happier with that plea.'

'Whatever you say, sir, but not if it means involving Lizzie.'

'Good.' The barrister seemed relieved. 'And we won't involve your sister. The prosecution case is based on three pieces of evidence. Firstly, you publicly threatened to kill Mr Laybourne. Secondly, that after you killed Mr Laybourne you deliberately moved his body in order that it would be destroyed in the conflagration. Thirdly, you ran away from the scene even though a policeman ordered you to stop.'

'I understand.'

'The policeman who issued the condemning statement about the position of the body cannot be traced. He's emigrated, apparently, and I'm assured that exhaustive investigations have failed to trace him. However, I could ask for the trial to be delayed until we've had an opportunity to locate him. Would you prefer that I did that, or would you rather I agree to his original statement being accepted as evidence?'

'I'd rather you get on with it, sir.'

'Even if I tell you that I believe the statement is false?' The soft eyes hardened. 'Mr Forrester?'

The statement was false if it said he had moved Mr Laybourne's body, but he was the only one who knew that.

'I'd rather get on with it,' he repeated after a moment's thought.

'So be it, Mr Forrester.' He was surprised that Mr Joseph did not argue. 'Although I must tell you I've had clients who've been more co-operative in helping me to preserve their futures.'

He felt unnerved by the silence which followed, and knew he owed the barrister some sort of explanation. 'I've done some terrible things in my life, Mr Joseph, and I'd feel better if I was punished for them.'

'Perhaps you have done terrible things, but with regard to your killing Mr Laybourne I believe life had already punished you enough.' Mr Joseph stared at him as if he were trying to see into his mind. 'I think you're punishing yourself unnecessarily, Mr Forrester, and you should learn to stop, though I doubt you ever will.'

Prison routine was a sponge which absorbed anyone who touched it. It was an ordered, planned, predictable life which was not unattractive. It was like being a child again; everything provided, everything organised, and because he was awaiting trial he had a cell to himself and could spend the days reading or simply doing nothing. He had lived in worse ways.

Elizabeth visited once more. She looked worn and tired. Her face was drawn and marked with dark lines under eyes that seemed to have lost their sparkle. It was a difficult meeting, too painful to be repeated, and although she argued at first she finally agreed not to come again and wrote weekly letters instead.

He had one more meeting with Mr Joseph, two days before the trial was due to begin in the Durham courthouse, and he was relieved when Mr Joseph said the hearing should not last more than three or four days.

Elizabeth was already very grateful to Catherine and Walter for insisting on retaining Mr Joseph and paying his fees; she was overwhelmed when Catherine promised to join her for the trial and booked them into a two-bedroom suite in one of Durham's finest hotels, only ten minutes' walk from the courthouse.

Catherine insisted that as they were obliged to watch the trial of an innocent man they should not feel ashamed and hide themselves away; particularly as Lillian's father was sure to make a show of reserving first-class accommodation for himself, Lillian, John and Charlotte.

'We'll eat and sleep better in a good hotel, Elizabeth, and that'll help us to appear more confident when Edward sees us. Our confidence might rub off on him, and the jury will notice. Such small things do matter, my dear.'

She could not argue with Catherine's logic, or generosity, but one aspect did worry her, and she raised it as they sat together in the suite's drawing room the evening before the trial began.

'Won't you find it difficult sitting with me, where Charlotte and John can see you? Won't you feel you're betraying them, just a little?'

'Why should I?' The question was asked with a sort of mild aggression.

'Charlotte's your stepmother and John's your half brother. Edward killed your father. They're sure to think—'

'Elizabeth! Charlotte's the woman my father married

after I'd left home. I respect her and I feel sorry for her, but I wouldn't even class her as a friend, not really. It's true that John is my half brother, but you're my half sister and my friend and we've both been through so much that you mean far more to me than John ever could.'

Catherine's warmth and honest affection made her cry. She did not think of Catherine as being her half sister any more than she thought of Rose in that vein; they were both friends, close friends, especially Catherine who had done so much to help her.

'But no one knows we're half sisters, Catherine, and I don't want them to know because it would hurt Charlotte, I'm sure, and I hate to think what it would do to John.'

'Perhaps it might be best if they did know, Elizabeth,' Charlotte said quietly. 'Perhaps it would be best if the whole matter was brought out into the open.'

'No!' She knew she owed Catherine an explanation, but she was not sure, even now, why she wanted the truth kept secret. 'I'm sorry, but my instinct tells me they should never know the truth. Especially as we can't prove it. Anyway, it's better left to lie. Better for John to think that I left him because I couldn't face marrying him after his accident. He's married now, and we shouldn't risk opening up old wounds. I don't want to cause even more trouble, there's no purpose in that, and I especially don't want to be the reason for trouble between you and your family.'

Catherine nodded. 'You mustn't worry about that. Excepting Rose, there's never been any real warmth between me and my father's, our father's, second family.' Catherine paused, seemed to think and then come to a decision. 'I've never told anyone this, Elizabeth. Walter and I love each other very much and in a very special way. He is much older than me, of course, and because we have no children we both have to face the fact that when he dies I'll be left alone without a family. We know that my father in particular, and even Charlotte and John at times, have been quite disparaging about Walter's assumed inability to make me pregnant. They've always regarded him as rather pathetic and weak, but Walter's actually very strong. He's never once spoken out, or complained that it's not his fault we don't have any children, or criticised me for never allowing him to sleep with me. I cannot abide the thought of sleeping with any man, not even Walter, although I love him very much. You must be able to understand why, Elizabeth, even though I could never explain the reason to him.'

She nodded, and remembered the dismissive way Sebastian always treated quiet Walter, remembered how even Rose, in her innocence, had once said that Catherine had married a man who failed her. It occurred to her that Sebastian Laybourne's legacy of horror lived on, even though he was dead. Walter was yet another innocent, and apparently ignorant, victim.

'We'll fight for Edward, Elizabeth. We'll fight and win, because it's all we can do. Edward mustn't be allowed to suffer because he killed our father. If I'd had the means, or the courage, I'd have killed him myself.'

With Catherine beside her she was first in the line of people queuing outside the courtroom. An attendant opened a door and she stepped into the room, high-ceilinged and grand; and its hush and ornateness imposed itself immediately. She felt trivial, and frightened for Edward whom she knew would feel the same.

She took an end seat in the front row of the gallery, thirty feet away from the dock but as close as she could get to the place where Edward would stand. She had the wood-panelled wall to her left and Catherine sitting to her immediate right, protecting her from anyone else who might choose to sit in the front row. Surprisingly, no one did.

During the next half-hour the room filled with the public, with officials and with some of the robed and wigged characters who would play a central part in the drama which seemed remote from real life. Sunshine poured in through a large round window, trapping a column of sparkling dust and throwing an oval of light on to the polished floor. Mr Joseph stood in the oval and looked towards her. She smiled, nodded, relieved she had been able to sit exactly where he told her to, and he nodded back but if he smiled at her she did not notice. He looked solemn, and the spring sunshine seemed out of place.

The barristers and officials shuffled papers and talked amongst themselves and hardly seemed to notice Edward being brought in by two policemen. He was not handcuffed to them and their presence seemed unnecessary; they simply pointed to the dock and left him to climb the steps, let himself in and close the door after him.

Mr Joseph had obviously told him where to look for her because he looked directly at her and smiled his quiet smile. She mouthed the words 'I love you' and he nodded.

'Mr Forrester, you are charged that on the ...' Elizabeth listened to the accusation being read and watched Edward's face, tried to sense his feelings. 'How do you plead?'

She saw him pause, glance down to where Mr Joseph sat waiting, and then at her.

'Not guilty.'

A murmur of anticipation raced around the courtroom and she whispered, more to herself than Catherine, 'That's better, Edward. Put up a fight, lad.'

She listened carefully as records were noted and the proceedings began. Mr Snipe, the prosecution barrister, stood up and she noticed how short he was, and how unusually thin. He had an exceptionally large Adam's apple, a long neck and a small sharp face. Compared to the sleek Mr Joseph he looked untidy under his scruffy wig and dusty black gown, but there was something in the way he stood, head thrust forward, and something cold in his eyes which frightened her even before he spoke.

'It is my duty to put before this court evidence which will

prove beyond any reasonable doubt that Mr Forrester, the defendant, entered Mr Sebastian Laybourne's home on the day noted with the deliberate intention of executing the threat he had previously made.' She listened to the way Snipe delivered the words quickly and in a thin, clear voice aimed directly at the men sitting in the jury benches, and thought she could hear a hint of maliciousness in the way he spoke.

Snipe continued, his voice rising and falling like an actor's, and for some reason she found herself comparing him to Shylock, in *The Merchant of Venice*. Snipe used a particular, quite disparaging, tone whenever he mentioned Edward, and she realised she was quietly snorting with disgust every time he used it. She listened to what he had to say, thought it was all exaggerated nonsense, and wished she could simply stand up and tell the court the truth and then take Edward back home with her.

Her mind drifted. She saw Edward as a small boy playing by the river, caring for a rabbit which had been injured in a trap, sitting close by a candle, reading late into the night.

Her concentration returned quickly when she heard the public murmur and saw everyone sit forward, listening keenly as Snipe continued his opening.

'The defendant took a heavy fire-iron from his victim's own hearth and used it to batter Mr Laybourne to death while the victim was distracted by a considerable house fire raised by a mob of the defendant's workmates. The defendant then attempted to drag his dead employer's body into a part of the house which was aflame, with the obvious intent to disguise his act and create the impression that Mr Laybourne's injuries and death had been a result of the fire which ultimately destroyed a large section of the victim's house.'

She wanted to shout out that these were lies but common sense and the imposing courtroom stopped her. Mr Joseph had warned her that the prosecution would distort the truth, but she had not believed him, had not believed that would happen in an English court.

Now she wished, more than ever, that she had insisted on standing up and telling the truth whatever the consequences might be for Charlotte and John, for Rose, Hubert, the Laybournes' reputation or her own. But it was too late, too late to do anything but sit and listen, and hope that Mr Joseph could unsettle the opinions she could see were already forming in the jurors' minds.

'Mr Forrester was cunning, gentlemen.' Snipe turned back to the jury. 'He chose to commit murder at a time when the victim's house was burning and when ordinary, decent people were running for their lives, no less. He deliberately chose such a moment to kill, unmercifully, with several blows to his victim's skull, smashing it as one would a breakfast egg. He did this in secret, where no one would see, but a lack of witnesses need not cause you any concern when you find him guilty of this heinous crime. I will provide you with witnesses enough to prove his threat was made in earnest, and that this man, who stands before you now, has a history of violent acts which would make any decent person sleep badly, very badly, knowing they were in his presence.'

She watched Snipe sit down and wondered how he could sleep at all, how his conscience, if he had one, would allow him ever to rest. Then, as Mr Joseph stood up and smiled at her, she forced back the depression she felt creeping up and concentrated on what he had to say in Edward's defence.

'I thank my learned colleague for his dramatic interpretation of what he believes my client's motives were.' Joseph stood in the beam of sunlight so that it cut across him, his black-gowned body disappearing into shade while his head was illuminated in a halo of light, and unlike Snipe he took time and did not rush his words. 'My client does not deny killing Mr Laybourne, gentlemen. But his act wasn't one of planned murder. Murder, gentlemen, is a deliberate act, and to understand how accidental this act was I must first enlighten you as to my client's physical condition at the time, and the terrain and geography of the area in which the events transpired. Moorland crossed by deep valleys.'

Joseph painted a picture of the valley in her mind. He described it simply, led her down from the house in Albert Street, across the river, up and across South Ridge and down to the manor. She felt the mud sliding under her feet as she mentally climbed the steep ridge, and she was surprised when Joseph told her exactly how far they had gone together, and exactly how high South Ridge was.

Then he imposed on that picture a rough sketch of a man who was injured and exhausted from the disaster which had killed the other members of his family, a man who had seen enough death and who was so ill that even a policeman sent to arrest him had believed he was not capable of causing trouble.

There was no sound from the public gallery.

'Mr Laybourne had disappeared the previous day. The police guarding his house against possible attack were not aware that he was at home. Even his servants who lived in accommodation in his house were not aware that he was at home. So why did my client make this long and hazardous journey to Laybourne Manor? The answer is quite simple.' Joseph crossed the floor and stood directly in front of Snipe, staring into his face. 'My learned colleague omitted to tell you that my client's sister lived and worked in Laybourne Manor as Mrs Laybourne's trusted companion. So trusted that she continued to live and work there until approximately one year ago when she travelled to London to undertake missionary work amongst the poor. The reason my client undertook the journey to Laybourne Manor was not to kill Mr Sebastian Laybourne, it was to save his sister because a neighbour had warned him the manor was to be attacked by a force of men bent on burning it down.'

Mr Joseph had given no indication that she was in the courtroom but she felt exposed, prominent, as though everyone knew she was there, and she tried hard not to respond to her feelings; not to say something to support Mr Joseph's words.

As Joseph turned away there was a sound from the public gallery, a rumbling sound as people made their own immediate judgements, accepting or refuting his argument. She listened to the noise, and looked back across the tiered seats to assess what she could from the expressions on people's faces.

One face stood out, the beautiful Lillian McDougall, now Mrs John Laybourne. She felt a treacherous tweak of jealousy at seeing her but the circumstances reduced the importance of what she felt and she looked for John out of interest only, all emotion removed. Lillian had been leaning forward, but she sat back and there was John, his face shaded and lined like an old parchment map, his hair grown long and left loose to cover some of the worst damage.

He turned towards her and she started but held her eyes on him, waiting for his sign of recognition, but it did not come. Then she realised he could not see her, probably because his eyes were not strong enough. A moment later she recognised the bullish head of Mr McDougall sitting beside his daughter but Charlotte was not there, and she was surprised how relieved that made her feel.

Elizabeth concentrated as Snipe built his case. He called a number of witnesses who heard Edward threaten to kill Mr Laybourne, and several who claimed they had heard previous arguments between the two men when the promised improvements were not made to the mine. He called Sergeant Craddock who confirmed exactly what had happened when he arrived to take Edward to the police station. Immediately afterwards he threw suspicion on the sergeant's assertion that Edward appeared in poor condition by calling several of the Laybourne family friends who were present at the dinner party nearly two years earlier and who could confirm how good an actor Edward was, easily capable of misleading an honest man like Sergeant Craddock.

In his turn Mr Joseph questioned some of the witnesses to establish that Edward might have made his threat in the heat of the moment, but otherwise he remained seated and took little part in the proceedings.

The court rose for lunch.

'Catherine. Miss Forrester.' She heard the accusation in Lillian's voice and felt sorry for Catherine who was obviously seen as being in the enemy camp. 'I didn't realise you knew each other so well.'

'It's a long story, Lillian,' Catherine said stoutly, but did not bother to explain, other than to add, 'We have common interests beyond Pincote.'

'Elizabeth,' John said quietly and she smiled at him and was relieved when he smiled back. 'Have you settled in London?'

'Yes, I have, thank you.' She felt hot and pink and embarrassed, was tempted to apologise but knew it was no use; this was not the place and anyway, apologies would mean nothing without explanations and she could not offer them. 'How are you, John?'

'Well. I suppose you know that Lillian and I are married?'

'Yes. I hope you'll both be very happy.' She hoped she sounded as though she meant it. 'Catherine, I think we should find somewhere to eat.'

She noticed a little confusion in Catherine's eyes but the need for lunch seemed to offer an opportunity to escape from the embarrassing situation. She was thankful that Mr McDougall had already gone off somewhere, and she nodded goodbye to John and Lillian and turned away.

'Elizabeth?' An old woman whom she had hardly

noticed in the gallery caught her arm. 'Elizabeth?'

She turned back and was horrified by what she saw, too embarrassed to hide her shock. 'Charlotte? I didn't see you, I'm sorry.'

'Didn't see me, or didn't recognise me?' There was no reproach in Charlotte's voice. 'I've changed since we last met. Grown old.'

'No . . .'

'I'm sorry to embarrass you, Elizabeth. My heart and my liver . . .'

'We were afraid that Mother might die last winter,' John explained quickly. 'She was very ill. Then all this . . .'

He shrugged, turned away as his father-in-law called out that he was waiting to take them to lunch, gathered up his mother and Lillian and shepherded them away.

'I'm sorry, Elizabeth,' Catherine apologised. 'I should have warned you. Charlotte's gone through so much that it's hardly surprising she's ill.'

'Does Rose know?' It suddenly occurred to her how selfish Rose had been to abandon her mother, abandon her husband, then return to Hubert and go abroad while her mother was so ill.

'No. Hubert knows how ill Charlotte is, and how weak Rose is, and he believed that meeting would probably make them both worse. I think we must trust his judgement. Perhaps you can understand his concern, given Rose's instability?'

'Yes, I do understand,' she said and thought Rose was fortunate to have a husband who was so considerate and protective.

Elizabeth watched Snipe turn to the witness box. 'Mr Milligan, am I correct in stating that you are currently serving a prison sentence for grievous assault?'

'Yes, sir.' She saw the smile on Milligan's face and thought he seemed proud of his sentence.

She listened as Milligan told the court how good a prize

fighter Edward was, and although she found it impossible
to believe everything the man said she could see from
Edward's reactions that there was some truth in the
stories.

Snipe used the stories Milligan told to show Edward
was callous and brutal. 'I would, of course, have called a
second man, a Mr O'Leary, to give evidence to this fact,
but there are reasons why I cannot do this. Mr Milligan,
would you please explain why Mr O'Leary cannot attend
here today?'

'He's dead. Murdered.'

It was a shocking statement which seemed to stun
everyone in the courtroom.

'And how was he murdered? Poisoned, strangled, shot,
stabbed?'

'No, sir. O'Leary was beaten to death at the same time
as two other men, shortly after Forrester threatened
them.'

'Of course you're not suggesting that it was the
defendant who actually beat these men to death with his
bare hands,' Mr Snipe said quickly, and apologised to the
judge for having placed the witness in a position where he
could make such harmful remarks about the defendant.

'I most humbly apologise.' She saw the smile on Snipe's
face as he asked for Milligan's last comment to be ignored,
but the damage had been done: Edward had been cast as a
violent and calculating killer.

She was surprised that Mr Joseph did not question
Milligan. Two policemen came and made a display of
handcuffing the convict before they led him away, grinning
and slyly pulling faces at Edward who stood impassive in
the dock.

She leaned forward as Snipe introduced his next
witness, a coarse-looking woman with clothes which
appeared too expensive for her to have bought herself.
'Miss Bell?'

'Mrs,' the woman said bluntly.

'Mrs Bell. I apologise. You're a prostitute, I believe.'

'Was,' Mrs Bell corrected him again and there was some laughter which died out immediately.

'I apologise again, most profusely, Mrs Bell.' She watched Snipe playing up to his sympathetic audience. 'You were once resident in a house which address you shared, amongst others, with the defendant and a Miss Ada Cox. Is that correct?'

'Yes.'

'This house was in the Shadwell area of London? Close by the docks?'

'Yes.'

'An area frequented by rough sailors who required female company?'

'Yes.'

'Which you and other women in the house were content to provide.'

'Yes.'

'All of the women in the house?'

'Yes.'

'Including Ada Cox?'

'Yes.'

'Who was a child, around fifteen years old at most?'

'Yes.'

She already knew enough about Snipe's tactics to know he would pause in order to allow the statement to have the effect he wanted, and she looked along the rows of men and women in the public gallery. They all looked concerned, as she guessed they would, and she wondered if they really were so naïve as to be shocked to learn there were child prostitutes, or were they all pretending.

'I assume that Ada Cox did not take men back to the room she shared with her widowed father and her brother and sisters. I assume she took them somewhere else. Is that correct?'

'Yes.'

'Where did she take them?'

'Into 'is room.' Mrs Bell nodded towards Edward.

'That seems to be a strange arrangement. Did you ever see money exchanged between the defendant and the child prostitute, Ada Cox?'

'Often.'

There was uproar and even though the judge hammered his gavel the noise continued.

'Oh, Elizabeth.' Catherine grabbed her hand. 'They'll hang him for that alone.'

'I know, I know.' She stared across the room into Edward's eyes and tried to read the expression on his face, then he shut his eyes and she felt locked out and lost to him.

Edward wanted to shut out what was happening around him. Mr Joseph had not told him it would be like this. He thought he would come to court, the facts would be discussed, considered, and a decision would be reached. He did not think they would try to discredit him this way.

He would not have cared what they had said about him if Lizzie had not been there, but she was there and he could not stand seeing the hurt in her eyes and on her face.

He opened his eyes again, avoided looking at Lizzie, and concentrated on the other people sitting in the public gallery. There was no one from Pincote, no one that he recognised, although there was an old woman who looked a little familiar and a man sitting near her who looked something like John Laybourne but was far too old and small.

'This court is adjourned until ten o'clock tomorrow morning. Please be . . .'

Edward was relieved that the first day was over, and he risked a quick glance towards Lizzie and saw an expression on her face which told him she must feel the same. Then he looked along the gallery and noticed how the man who looked like John Laybourne stood up, awkward and lop-sided. The man brushed his long hair back off his face and showed a mottled puzzle of red and yellow skin, then turned and lurched clumsily past the row of seats.

'John.' He mouthed the name but did not say it.

John Laybourne looked old and used up, and that was more of a shock than seeing his injuries. John was lying under a fallen rock the last time he saw him, his leg crushed, half his face and the backs of his hands burned away. Now he wondered if he should have left him there, wondered what sort of life he had condemned him to by helping to save him.

He realised immediately that he knew who the old woman was. She had been beautiful the last time he saw her, older but as beautiful as her daughter. He always felt comforted by knowing that Rose would stay beautiful as time passed, but now . . . Charlotte Laybourne was old and ragged and ugly, her face pulled out of shape by something which had happened to her, her body fumbling and slow and no longer sleek and graceful.

She reminded him of his own mother, and he had not thought about her for months.

Then his eyes came down to the policeman who stood ready to take him away, and he knew that all he wanted to do was to go; to get away from this room and these people who forced him to think about things he wanted to forget.

Elizabeth stood up with everyone else, glad that the awful day was over, scared that the quiet Mr Joseph could do nothing to stop Edward being hung. She stared as Edward was taken away, and her anger turned on him when he did not bother to look back at her.

'If it's been difficult for you, Elizabeth, think how much worse it's been for him,' Catherine reasoned.

They waited until everyone else had left the courtroom before they turned to go, and she was astonished how weak her legs felt as she climbed the steps towards the exit.

Elizabeth thought that the first day had been bad enough,

but the second promised to be worse.

Mr Snipe explained to the court that the police could not
trace the whereabouts of the policeman who found
Sebastian Laybourne's body, and then read the statement
which Constable McClusky had submitted on the night
Sebastian was killed. Her spirits fell further. The statement
was untrue, and she knew it was a critical piece of
evidence. She had no idea why, but the police were lying.

'Sergeant.' Snipe turned to the policeman who would
corroborate the false evidence. 'Please tell the court what
you saw when Constable McClusky called you to inspect
Mr Laybourne's body.'

'The victim's head had been crushed by repeated blows
to both his temples, sir.' She listened as the man lied, and
wanted to shout out the truth but knew no one would listen
even if she did.

She found it hard to contain her fury as she heard a
concocted story telling how Edward had moved the body
back through the door which Sebastian locked when he
tried to kill her and Edward, and how the two policemen
had endangered their own lives to recover the body and
save the evidence which proved Edward was a callous
murderer.

She found herself wondering if Sebastian would have
been tried for murder if he had succeeded in killing her
and Edward, and she knew that their deaths would have
been treated as accidents. No one would have suspected
Sebastian of any crime, because he was Sebastian
Laybourne; above suspicion of anything.

She was so angry she stopped listening while the
sergeant talked, and only concentrated again when Snipe
moved across to the witness box and marked the next
development of his case against Edward. 'Tell the court
what happened immediately after the body was found,
when the defendant heard that the body had been
discovered.'

'The defendant ran away, sir. Even when Constable

McClusky told him to stop he still kept running. He ran up on to South Ridge where we already had a number of officers searching for the rioters who'd set the manor afire. There were coal waste spills on the far side of the ridge . . .' He explained in detail what had happened up to the time the charges exploded. 'The charges exploded and the defendant ran away. He was not pursued because it was thought that he had himself been killed by the explosions.'

'Thank you.' Elizabeth watched Snipe carefully as he walked away from the witness box to stand close by the jury benches, and she saw the triumphant look on the prosecutor's face. 'I cannot imagine, as I doubt any of you can, why an innocent man, a man with nothing to fear, would run away, particularly when a policeman asked him to stop.'

She remembered how she had questioned Edward's decision to run away, and realised now why he made that decision. He had said then that no one would believe the killing was an accident.

She looked across to where Edward stood, and wondered what thoughts were in his mind, how he felt.

Edward saw the despair on Lizzie's face and wanted to walk across to her, to tell her not to worry. Snipe had built a strong case against him, but it did not matter to him, so it should not matter to her.

The lies irritated him, but that was all they did. He would rather be found guilty because the true circumstances made him look guilty; the lies were unnecessary and might prolong the hearing because the conscientious Mr Joseph would try to refute them. If he could have told him to accept the evidence without complaint he would have done so, but when the barrister rose to question the witness he could tell from his crisp tone that Mr Joseph was not going to give in.

'The house was on fire when you went to inspect Mr Laybourne's body. Is that correct?'

'Yes, sir.'

'Were you in danger of being burned by the fire?'

'Yes, sir. It was an extremely dangerous situation.'

'I can understand that it must have been most frightening, particularly as the body was behind a door leading off the landing where the killing had taken place.' Mr Joseph plodded through the words, making the mental journey from landing to the staircase sound long and complicated. 'I imagine you were pleased to move away from the situation you found yourself in?'

'Yes, sir.'

'Then how closely did you inspect the injuries Mr Laybourne had sustained?'

'Very closely, sir, once we had moved away from the immediate danger the fire imposed.'

'I see. I see.' There was controlled patience in Mr Joseph's voice. 'You moved the body very quickly, I imagine, in order to preserve it as evidence. I assume you simply dragged it from behind the door and out on to the landing.'

'No, sir. We lifted his body out.'

'Oh, I see. Which one of you moved the body out on to the landing, you or Constable McClusky?'

'It took the two of us, sir.'

'Of course. Pardon me, I wasn't thinking very clearly. Mr Laybourne was a very large man. It would have taken two of you to move his body.' Edward watched Mr Joseph lapse into one of his silences, and wondered what he was thinking. 'You then inspected the body for injuries. Were you aware that you had banged Mr Laybourne's head against the door jamb or something similar?'

'No, sir!'

'Well, the doctor's report, as accepted by the coroner's court, states that Mr Laybourne died from a single blow to his left temple and that the damage occasioned to his right temple was caused by a blow to or by an angular instrument or obstruction. Something similar to a door jamb, Sergeant.' Edward saw the light in Mr Joseph's eyes, and realised the man was actually enjoying himself now he had his victim cornered. 'Do you think, in retrospect, given the fact that you had just risked your life to recover the body and that a serious fire was raging only feet away from you, that you could have been mistaken in your assessment of Mr Laybourne's injuries?'

'I suppose we could've made a mistake, sir.' The policeman squirmed.

'It takes courage to make an admission like that,' Joseph said smoothly, 'particularly as it rather changes the circumstances of the killing. It changes it from a frenzied killing requiring many blows to one committed with a single blow. Also, the blow to the temple must have been made by someone standing in front of Mr Laybourne. A frontal attack with only one blow and not a cunning attack where the killer sneaked up behind his victim and battered his head as one would a breakfast egg, as the prosecution has stated?'

Elizabeth heard Mr Joseph refuting the policeman's evidence, and found herself admiring the quiet way he had gone about establishing the truth. Perhaps all was not yet lost.

'Well, Sergeant. A single blow from someone confronting Mr Laybourne?' Mr Joseph waited for an answer.

'Yes, sir. I suppose so.' She heard the policeman hesitate, and she was almost sure that Mr Joseph turned to her and winked.

'Are you sure that you did not crack Mr Laybourne's head against a door pillar or something similar when you moved his body?'

'Certainly, sir.'

'Then I would suggest that injury was sustained as he fell from the blow which killed him. Ergo, when he was attacked he was standing facing his assailant. But he was a tall man, at least a foot taller than the defendant. How do you think the defendant was able to deliver a single blow powerful enough to kill the victim when the victim was so much taller, was facing him, and presumably was able to defend himself?'

'My lord' – Snipe leapt up, his face red and sweating – 'counsel is asking the witness to conjecture on something which is impossible to resolve. No one but the defendant knows exactly what happened.'

'I agree, Mr Snipe.' She thought the judge looked even more solemn than usual. 'I must ask you to reword that last question, Mr Joseph, but as it is very nearly time to adjourn for lunch I feel we should continue upon our return.'

'My lord, I beg your permission to continue now in order to make best advantage of the court's time and to enable this witness to be released and go about his normal duties.' She could see from the expression on Mr Joseph's face that he was desperate to continue. 'Five more minutes, my lord, is all I ask of you.'

She watched the judge fumble in his robes and take out his pocket watch, and wondered if he was delaying deliberately; there was a perfectly reliable clock at the rear of the public gallery.

'It will make us late, Mr Joseph,' the judge demurred.

She noticed how quickly Mr Joseph strode across to the judge, and how quietly he spoke the next few words, so quietly she could not hear what was said.

Edward found himself leaning over the edge of the dock, his ears straining to hear what Joseph was asking.

'If we were to continue now, my lord, it may save me the embarrassment of having to request the court to restrain the witness in the sole company of the court's officers and prevent him from having contact with any persons present in this court, including the prosecution.'

Good God! Joseph was almost accusing Snipe of conniving to give false evidence.

He saw the judge begin to rise, then settle back into his

seat, to mutter, 'Such an appeal would carry very serious implications, Mr Joseph.'

'Indeed, my lord. Five minutes is all I ask, my lord, to avoid unnecessary unpleasantness.'

'Granted.'

'Please tell me,' Joseph turned directly to the witness who now looked ashen. 'How do you think such a blow could be delivered by a short man against a tall man who was facing him and standing up?'

'It couldn't, sir, not unless the shorter man was standing on a box, or a stair.'

'You saw no convenient boxes left lying around on the landing?'

'No, sir.'

'The stairs, of course? But I believe you stated that the attack took place on the landing, some way from the stairs?'

'Yes, sir.'

'So, how else do you think a man as tall as the victim could have been hit on the temple by a man as short as the defendant?'

'He must have been leaning forward, sir.'

'And why would he do that? He'd hardly present himself for a blow on the head.'

'Perhaps the defendant hit him in the, well, you know where, sir.'

'Perhaps, but then the defendant would have been close enough for Mr Laybourne to have grabbed him, and that would have made the blow even more difficult to deliver.'

'A kick, sir?'

'It would have been a very high kick, I would have thought, which in turn would have thrown the defendant off balance and stopped him developing enough power for a killing blow. Can you think of any other reason why the victim would be leaning forward, in a crouching position, perhaps?'

'No, sir.'

'Oh come now, I can think of several. I'm sure you can think of one or two, if you try.'

Snipe rose to complain but the judge waved him back before he spoke.

'I crouch down when I'm playing with my children, sir.'

'I don't think that could be the reason. Have you ever played any sports?'

'Football, sir.'

'And what position did you adopt when you ran for the ball? Show me.'

The policeman looked embarrassed and crouched down in the witness box.

She heard a sigh pass around the courtroom and this time she knew Mr Joseph winked at her.

'So Mr Laybourne could have been running towards the defendant when the fatal blow was administered.' Joseph walked slowly towards the jury. 'And why would he be running towards a man who had threatened to kill him, had already entered his house which was surrounded by armed police meant to keep him out, and was wielding an object capable of causing death?'

She saw the puzzled looks which broke out on each of the jurors' faces, and waited for Mr Joseph to offer an explanation, but he did not. He simply walked to his table, carefully closed the folder left open on his desk and looked up at the judge.

'I thank you for your indulgence, my lord,' he said respectfully.

'Well, Mr Joseph.' The judge frowned. 'You've raised a question. Are you not going to provide an answer?'

'I would not wish to overexact your lordship's or the court's indulgence, my lord, and I believe that any answer I could give would, quite correctly, be construed by my learned colleague as a matter of conjecture which it is impossible to resolve.'

There was a spontaneous guffaw of laughter from the public gallery and the jury, and she saw several court

officials smiling before she looked at the judge and saw
that even he was trying hard to control his lips.

'You look happier, Elizabeth,' Catherine said and offered
her another of the apples she had brought to eat in a small
garden shaded by Durham's cathedral.

'It looks more promising now. I was desperately worried
earlier this morning, but now I've a feeling that Mr Joseph
is winning.'

'Don't start counting your chickens, Elizabeth. It's not
over yet, and Edward has confessed to the killing.'

'The killing.' She repeated Catherine's last words. 'It's
strange but I feel quite remote from all that happened that
evening, except where Edward's future is concerned. I've
been so engrossed in mine and Edward's problems that I
rather forgot that Sebastian Laybourne was your father.'

'Yours too, Elizabeth.'

'Yes, but because I didn't know that until after he was
dead, I don't think of the man I remember as my father.
They seem two different people, somehow, but it must be
different for you.'

'Don't worry about that, Elizabeth. I've no grief or
sorrow. I hated the man and I'm glad he's dead. It's just so
typical of him to cause all this heartbreak even though he
is dead. I don't think I'll really be free of him until after this
is all over.'

'I won't be free even then, Catherine, not unless Edward
is released.' She gave an involuntary sigh. 'And I suppose
there will always be thoughts of what might have been.
John and me, given a little more time. Edward and Rose,
even. No, I'll never be free of your father, our father, not
until I die.'

Elizabeth watched Hopkins give evidence, but he was old
and shaking, deaf and inclined to ramble and he made a
poor witness. Snipe did not pursue some of the questions
the retired coachman seemed unable to answer, and she

thought the prosecutor had lost heart since Mr Joseph had
thrown so much doubt on the police evidence.

The judge confirmed that Hopkins was the last
prosecution witness, then asked Mr Joseph to introduce
his first witness.

'I thank you, my Lord. I have only one witness. I call Mr
Edward Forrester.'

Edward felt nervous at first but settled as Mr Joseph led
him through the events which accounted for him being at
the manor.

Eventually they reached the question they had
discussed in great detail: 'Did you intend to kill Mr
Laybourne?'

'No, sir. It was an accident. I was trying to protect
myself. I didn't even realise I had killed him at first.'

'Did you try to hide the body?'

'No, I panicked and all I could think of was to get away.'

'Why did you think you had to get away if Mr
Laybourne's death was an accident?'

'Because everyone knew I'd threatened to kill him, and
I didn't think they'd believe it was an accident.'

'Are you sure that in your panic you did not try to hide
Mr Laybourne's body?'

'I am sure of that, sir. Anyway, Mr Laybourne was a very
big man and I couldn't have moved his body even if I'd
wanted to.'

'How, then, do you account for the police finding the
body had been moved and hidden behind a door at the
bottom of an enclosed staircase?'

'I cannot, sir.'

'Quite.' Joseph turned to the jury again. 'Remember, the
police witness stated that it needed two large policemen to
move the body away from the area which was on fire.
Presumably, therefore, it would have taken two men to
move it towards the fire.' He turned back to Edward. 'Why
do you think Mr Laybourne attacked you?'

'I suppose he remembered my threat and thought I was

there to kill him, sir. I suppose he thought he was defending himself.' He saw Mr Joseph smile as he gave the answer they had rehearsed, the answer Mr Joseph thought would reassure the court that he was a reasonable man taking reasonable actions to defend himself against a man who seemed bent on killing him.

He watched Mr Joseph walk half the way to his table before saying to the judge, almost as if he had nearly forgotten to keep him informed. 'And that, my lord, concludes the defence case. The defendant killed Mr Laybourne in self-defence, panicked and ran away. He then voluntarily surrendered himself into the mercy of the court, and asked that he be suitably punished. I submit that these are not the acts of a murderer, my lord.'

Edward heard a loud murmur spread around the courtroom and when he looked at the jury he guessed that Mr Joseph had achieved his object, he had introduced enough doubt for the jury to reach a verdict of not guilty.

His heart sank. He had not meant to kill Mr Laybourne, but he was not sorry he had. He held no grudge against Laybourne for the fact that his father and brothers had been killed, he blamed God or the devil for that; but Laybourne had raped Lizzie, and that was why he deserved to die. He deserved to die a thousand times for that.

Then Snipe was on his feet, his small, vulture-like head thrust forward, his thin voice asking him question after question.

He gave Snipe direct answers, simple answers, always aware that a careless word might implicate Lizzie or Rose in what happened before or after he had killed Laybourne.

The questions seemed relentless, then suddenly Snipe said, 'There is just one final question, Mr Forrester.'

Just one more and it would be over. His mind blurred as he waited, his eyes fixed on Lizzie's eyes.

'Do you regret killing Mr Laybourne?'

Mr Joseph stood up and objected to the judge that the question was unreasonable, or words to that effect, but he

was not concerned about that. He was only concerned with
the hurt he saw in Lizzie's eyes and he did not listen to the
judge's response.

'No, sir. I certainly don't regret killing him.'

Elizabeth heard the words and the roar which filled the
room, and the pounding her heart sent through her body.
She had pleaded with Edward, with her eyes, to forget
what Laybourne had done to her and to lie, to say he did
regret what he had done; but stupid, proud Edward had
told the truth.

It was an appropriate climax to two days of drama and
she expected the judge to make some comment, but he
simply looked at the court usher and announced that the
court was adjourned until the next morning.

As the court cleared she sat still, leaning forward on the
rail which divided the public gallery from the official court
area. She was weary and felt that somehow she had been
cheated. Then she remembered to look up; Edward was
being led away. She managed to smile even though she
was crying, he smiled back, a policeman opened a door
and he was gone.

'Miss Forrester' – Mr Joseph had come to sit behind her
and Catherine – 'he should not have answered that last
question.'

'He was being honest.'

'He was being incredibly stupid,' Mr Joseph said
bluntly.

'No,' she defended him. 'You have to understand that in
a way this whole business started because once, two years
ago, he didn't tell the truth.'

Mr Joseph looked puzzled so she quickly told him how
Edward's friend William had died and how Edward allowed
everyone to think he was a hero, how he had concealed the
real reasons which led to William's death; and how from
that moment on one disaster seemed to follow another.

Catherine asked what would happen next.

'Summing up tomorrow, and then the jury will retire to

consider its verdict.' Mr Joseph rubbed his face and she
thought he looked tired.

'And what will that be?' she asked.

He shrugged. 'I'll do my best, of course, and try to
convince the jury that he did not mean to kill Mr
Laybourne. I still believe the police evidence is false but I
can't prove it, and anyway juries don't take kindly to people
like me claiming the police tell lies. It can do more harm
than good, Miss Forrester.'

'Perhaps if I had been a witness . . .' She voiced her own
feelings of guilt.

'No, Miss Forrester.' His certainty astonished her. 'No
one would have believed anything you said. You'd have
been seen as a woman who was trying to save her brother,
a man she loves. Your evidence would have been worth
less than a blade of grass.'

'But surely . . .'

'No, Miss Forrester. You had no part in this game.'

'Game? A murder trial?'

'Of course it's a game, and like any game luck plays an
important part. Perhaps I can find us some luck for
tomorrow.'

'I do hope he can,' she said to Catherine as Mr Joseph
left. 'I have a feeling that Edward needs all the luck
possible.'

She slept badly, went out for a walk instead of eating
breakfast, and arrived in the courtroom feeling drained
and ill. She took her usual seat, Catherine beside her. The
gallery filled with members of the public who had come to
see the events of the last day.

'Wonder they didn't bring their knitting.' She saw
Catherine looking around. 'That's what they were said to
do around the guillotine.'

'Don't, please,' she implored Catherine and saw her
friend's embarrassment when she realised how
unfortunate her words were.

Her heart lurched as Edward was brought in. He smiled at her and mouthed the words, 'Don't worry,' but she could see how drained he looked, and it was obvious from the way he avoided her eyes that he could not trust his own restraint.

Elizabeth winced as Snipe began his summing-up speech with a direct attack on Mr Joseph's main argument in Edward's defence.

Snipe faced the jury, walked slowly past each member, then retraced his steps and studied each man's face as if he never wanted to forget what he looked like. 'It has been shown that the police evidence is mistaken, and it has been implied that the police were lying. Nonsense, of course. Ask yourselves, gentlemen, why should the police lie? There is no reason.'

She watched as the man steepled his fingers against his mouth and appeared to think deeply before he spoke again. 'I do, however, now believe that the statement made by the officer who found the body was mistaken. But imagine your own reactions if you had been on a smoke-filled landing which was in danger of bursting into flames under your feet, and you found a body which had suffered a number of serious head wounds. Would you not, quite reasonably, assume the man had been viciously battered about the head? The officer did not lie, he made a mistake, and which one of us could say that under those circumstances we would not make a similar mistake?'

It was obvious that the jury was willing to accept Snipe's argument, and she saw Mr Joseph chewing the inside of his mouth and guessed he was worried about what remained of his thin defence.

Snipe continued, 'The location in which the body was found is critical. The police have stated that it took two men to lift the body. Mr Forrester was supposed to be alone. He may, of course, have had an accomplice' – Elizabeth felt herself twitch, and wondered if anyone else had seen her or noticed Edward twist his head to look at her; then concentrated again as Snipe droned on – 'or he may have simply dragged the body without lifting it. Perhaps that was how the additional head wounds were inflicted.'

Edward had looked away from her and she was studying the expression on Mr Joseph's face. He was worried, that was made obvious by the way he tried hard not to show any emotion at all.

Snipe stepped back and appealed to the whole jury as he concluded his summing-up. 'We have been told, gentlemen, that the defendant surrendered himself to the police as a result of his growing remorse. May I remind you of three things. First, it was winter when he surrendered himself, and at that time he was a homeless and hungry vagrant suffering from a number of serious ailments. He went from the gutter where he may have died that day into a warm hospital bed. Second, it took him eighteen months to feel this remorse. Third, gentlemen, and this is most important. Only yesterday, in this very court and in spite of his supposed remorse, the defendant admitted that he did not regret murdering Mr Laybourne. You have no alternative but to find the defendant guilty of murder.'

Mr Joseph stood up as Snipe sat down, and Elizabeth guessed that Snipe's closing remarks had made him revise his own speech because he started hesitantly, as if he was unsure what to say.

'Death, any death, is regrettable and emotive. Violent death is particularly so because it incites basic emotions such as horror and the need for revenge. As a part of our society I know how I . . .'

Her concentration ebbed as she listened to Mr Joseph trying to rebuild the defence Mr Snipe had discredited, trying to appeal to the jury's emotions. She studied Edward, and was alarmed by the aura of guilt which she sensed surrounded him.

Edward listened to Mr Joseph blustering and felt sorry

for him, felt guilty that he had destroyed the defence the man had built for him. He tried to console himself with the thought that Joseph was being paid handsomely whatever the outcome. Mr Joseph would, no doubt, feel depressed as he left the courtroom, but tomorrow he could concentrate on another case, and then another and another until his defeat in this court was forgotten, or became insignificant in his mind.

He looked across to where Lizzie sat and caught her eyes. She looked sad, desperately worried, and he felt guilty again because he was responsible for the way she felt. If he had not given himself up to the police, if he had co-operated better with Mr Joseph, if he had not told the truth yesterday. But he knew he could spend the rest of his life wondering what might have happened if he had not done as he had. Whatever happened now, and maybe they would hang him, whatever happened would cleanse him, purge him of the sins he had been carrying for too long.

He saw Lizzie trying to look brave, and he knew that she was so scared her hands were beginning to shake. If they hung him, well that was it, but if they sent him to prison he would have to make her believe he never wanted to see her again. She must not waste any more of her life on him; not only for her sake but for his, too.

The cleansing would not work if he knew she was waiting for him; if he was still spoiling her life.

At least he did not have to worry about Rose any more; she had escaped from him before it was too late.

He heard the judge speaking and realised that Mr Joseph had finished his summing-up. He had taken less than ten minutes.

Elizabeth watched the judge closely, trying hard to find any clues as to his opinion as he instructed the jury, 'The defendant admits to killing Mr Laybourne. There appears to be no question to that regard and you therefore have three considerations to debate amongst yourselves. Firstly, was this killing a matter simply of self-defence? In that case you must find the defendant not guilty. Secondly, did the defendant go to the house with no intention of killing Mr Laybourne, but in a fit of rage or revenge seize the opportunity to kill him when it arose? Or did the defendant deliberately set himself out to kill Mr Laybourne and later escape justice for his crime? If you should find either . . .'

She stopped listening as the judge imparted legal details the jury had to consider, and as the heat built up in the room. She longed for the court to rise so she could go to the cathedral where it was cool and she could be alone and think. And pray.

Then people were standing, she excused herself from Catherine, had a brief conversation with Mr Joseph, and walked out into bright sunshine where ordinary people went about their ordinary ways; and eventually made her way to the cathedral.

'Elizabeth? May I talk to you?' The words were whispered but the cathedral caught and magnified them.

'Adam!' Adam Marriott was sitting in the pew behind. 'I didn't see you. Were you here when I came in?'

'No, I came to the hearing today, then followed you here. Mostly because I wanted to talk to you about Edward, but I didn't want to say anything in front of anyone else. Can we talk? Privately?'

'I see.' She was not sure that she did. 'Catherine's gone off to make peace with Charlotte and John, and Mr Joseph, Edward's barrister, won't come looking for me either here or at the hotel until the jury returns, so where would you rather talk?'

'Here's fine with me.' Adam moved around the end of the pew and settled down beside her. 'In a sense it's quite apt, Lizzie, to tell you what I've heard here, in Durham Cathedral of all places. More'n three hundred criminals sought sanctuary in here during the Middle Ages, and most of them were supposed to be murderers. And it was used as a prison for a while, to hold Scots the Puritans had captured. Very particular people, Puritans. Take things a bit far, sometimes, like Edward.'

'Aye.' She nodded, glad to be with someone else who understood Edward. 'I wish he was here with me, Adam. I'm scared and I reckon he must be, too.'

'He won't be scared, Lizzie. I'm sure.'

'How can you be?'

'Believe me, he'll have learned how to close his mind by now. He might be getting impatient to know the verdict, but he won't be scared, not at the moment.'

'But how can you be so sure?'

'I know, lassy. I know.' He said it with such confidence that she did not argue. 'Elizabeth, how much do you know about what he got up to in London?'

'Not much more than I heard in court. Why?'

'My nephew, Francis, came by. Don't ask why or where he is now because he's gone, but he came across Edward when he was in London. Edward and Rose. They were living together.'

She could not answer. The surprise, shock, confused her for a few moments; then, even before Adam explained any more, she began to understand everything, why Edward did not defend himself as well as he might have.

'I thought you ought to know,' Adam said simply when he finished telling her everything that Francis had told him.

Mr Joseph came to her hotel at four o'clock to tell her that the jury had reached a verdict and it would be announced when the court reconvened the next morning.

She could not eat dinner that night, and she did not sleep. She was too worried, both about Edward and about Rose. Somehow they had almost achieved what seemed impossible, but almost was not enough. Her mind kept going over and over what Adam told her. She tried to make sense of it all; were Edward and Rose destined to be together or not? So many things suggested they should be, but always they seemed fated to be kept apart. Perhaps there was no destiny. Perhaps life was all chance; maybe, but there was no sense in tempting fate. Edward had not told anyone so she, too, would keep his secret; and not tell even Catherine.

Anyway, it all seemed irrelevant now. Rose was back with Hubert, travelling in some distant country, and Edward was awaiting a verdict which could hang him or send him to prison for the rest of his life. Mr Joseph was not optimistic. Men who killed their employers tended to be found guilty, he said.

She was pleased she had both Catherine and Adam there to support her when she arrived at the courthouse. She took her usual seat, Catherine and Adam with her, and John, Charlotte, Lillian and Mr McDougall sat a few yards away. The public gallery was crowded with strangers whom she resented. Catherine's comments had been right, these people were like the women who watched victims go to the guillotine during the French revolution. Their presence made the proceedings obscene.

The formal rigmarole of opening the court irritated her. She simply wanted to know the verdict, not to listen to all the trivialities which preceded it.

When Edward was brought into court he looked astonishingly calm, just as Adam had said he would. Mr Joseph smiled up at her, but she could see he did not look confident and she wondered if perhaps he had advance knowledge of the verdict which had been reached.

'Foreman of the jury, have you reached a unanimous verdict?'

Stupid question, the answer was obvious, but at least things were happening.

'We have,' the foreman said with profound self-importance.

'Please advise me of your findings.'

'Yes, my lord.' The foreman stood and shuffled his feet. 'We find the defendant . . .'

Someone nearby sneezed at the critical moment and she did not hear what the foreman said.

'Thank you. You may sit down.' The usher motioned to the man to sit and turned to the judge. 'My lord.'

The tension was unbearable. What was the verdict?

The judge did not speak, simply made some notes while everyone waited.

'What was the verdict?' she asked Catherine who looked ashen and shook her head. 'Didn't you hear?'

'No.'

The judge looked up.

'The jury has found the defendant guilty of murder.'

She felt as though she were falling. The smell of the courtroom suffocated her. Guilty? Guilty? What would they do to him? What?

Edward stood absolutely still, staring ahead, not even blinking. She saw his jaw and throat work as he swallowed, and then heard the usher ask the foreman to stand again.

The judge thanked him for his attention, sat back in his throne-like chair, then leaned forward and fixed the man with a concentrated stare. 'You have found the defendant guilty of murder. I instructed you yesterday that you should advise me how you should decide the extent of that guilt. I must now ask you for your findings in this matter. Did the defendant journey to the scene with the express intention of committing murder, or did he use an opportunity which presented itself upon his arrival at the scene?'

The foreman did not answer. Mr Joseph had told her that the extent of guilt could be critical; the difference between Edward being hanged or sent to prison.

'Answer his lordship,' the usher ordered impatiently.

'We believe the latter is the case, my lord.'

'You believe that he did not plan in advance to commit this murder? You must clarify this matter and state exactly what you mean.' Now the judge sounded impatient.

'Well, sir, my lord . . .'

'Come now, man. Answer clearly.'

'We do not believe the defendant went out to kill, like, but did it when the chance occurred.'

'I understand. It now remains for me to pass sentence.'

Her heart thumped so loudly she could not hear the first few words the judge said; something about making allowance for the strain that Edward was under at the time and the fact that he had surrendered himself.

Perhaps, even now, the sentence would not be too severe.

The judge started talking, summarising the case, drawing attention to various matters; she yearned for him to announce Edward's sentence, and was scared that at any moment he would.

'So, after taking account of all these circumstances, I sentence the defendant to twenty years' imprisonment . . .'

Twenty years? The roar from the public gallery supported her own feelings that the sentence was too harsh, but when she looked at Edward she could see that he was satisfied with both the verdict and the sentence.

'Twenty years, Edward?' She held him through the bars the way she had the first time she visited him.

'I deserve it, lass. He deserved to die and I'm glad it was me who killed him, but I'm wrong to feel that way. That's what makes me guilty, you see.'

'But the police evidence was false, Edward, and if it hadn't been for that . . .'

'Of course it was false, but I knew it would be and that's why I ran away that night. They were bound to protect the Laybourne name and I was a God-given scapegoat. Anyway, it's over now. There's no good in worrying any more, lass, just get on with your life.'

'I'll have a home ready for you when you're released.' She made the promise she had rehearsed.

'No, Lizzie!' He pulled away from her. 'I've wrecked enough lives already. I don't want you wasting years waiting for me. I want you to carry on with your life the way you were before all this happened. You've got to promise me that.'

'I can't, Edward. I can't abandon you.'

'Then I'd rather hang!' She could tell he meant what he said.

'I thought you might,' was all she could say. 'Those people that Snipe found to discredit you . . .'

'You didn't believe any of that?'

'No, of course not. No one who knows you, knows the real you, would believe what was said.'

'But some of it was true, lass.' His quiet words surprised her. 'The men Milligan talked about, O'Leary, Scraggs, Penn. I didn't kill 'em, but I might have done if I'd caught up with them before . . .'

'Before?' She wondered why he stopped.

'Before someone else did, lass. Ada Cox, though. That wasn't the truth.' She listened as he explained what had really happened, and decided that perhaps she should try to find Ada and her siblings; and she decided she had to tell him she knew he had lived with Rose, and how she knew.

'So Francis is safe,' he said almost to himself, 'and Rose is happy with Hubert and sane again, after her temporary madness?'

She heard the irony in his voice but saw sadness in his eyes, and asked the question she most wanted answered. 'What happened to make you part, Edward? What drove you apart after you'd gone through so much to be together?'

'Poverty, Lizzie. I couldn't earn enough to support us both, so I left her and told her to go back to her husband.'

'Just like that?' It was hard to believe.

He shrugged. 'That's what happened, lass.'

'And Rose just left you? Just like that?'

'No, she took a lot of persuading, at first, but living in one room with no heat and no food and no prospects of it ever getting better helped to make up her mind. Especially when we both fell ill. Especially as I was hiding from the police for killing her father. Don't blame her, it was mostly my fault.'

'I see, Edward.' She thought she understood; Rose was not brought up to be uncomfortable. 'I think I understand.'

'Perhaps you do, Lizzie. Anyway, it's over now, once and for all. Lost in the past.'

He seemed to be lost in himself and she did not know what to say to comfort him, did not even know if he needed comforting, and then she felt his hands grip hers. 'Lizzie, up until a couple of months ago you thought I was dead. I want you to pretend that I am and promise you won't visit or write to me. I won't be able to bear it if I have to worry about you.'

'I can't just abandon you, Edward.'

'You have to, Lizzie. Look, I've been sentenced to twenty years' hard labour. I may not even come out at all. How many long-term prisoners do? And even if I do I'll be forty-four, forty-five years old, and have spent half me life in prison. What use am I going to be, lass, tell me that? Anyway, if you did visit me, just think how it'll feel when it's time for you to go. Better we part now, tidy like, and you carry on with your life just as you were before. And I don't want that just for your sake, it's for me too.'

'But you wouldn't be in here if it wasn't for me, Edward. If you hadn't come to get me from the manor.'

'Aye, and I saved you from the fire, Lizzie. There's no point to any of it if you waste the life I saved. I wanted you to live. Now I want to know that you'll use that life properly. I want you to be happy, lass. Can't you understand that?'

'Of course.' It made sense, but that did not make it any less painful.

'Well then, lass, promise me. Promise you'll not visit nor

write. Come on now, promise me that. It's the last thing I'll
ever ask of you.'

Eyes shut, she made the promise. It was the only thing
she could do for him now.

She felt his lips brush hers. 'Goodbye, Lizzie.'

He was taken away. She stood, leaning against the bars
for several minutes, tears and grief pouring out of her.

A warder led her to the door and when he opened it she
saw Catherine standing in the passage.

For an insane moment it was as if time had travelled
back to the day in January when she opened the front door
in Angel Street and saw Catherine, as if all this had never
happened.

'It's over, Elizabeth. Ended.'

'Maybe.' She heard her voice as if it belonged to
someone else. 'Catherine, will you do something for me?
It's important.'

'Of course I will, Elizabeth.'

'Call me Lizzie, will you?'

PART FOUR

CHAPTER 35

'Mrs Belchester.'

The voice was a long way above her. A long way. Faint.

'Mrs Belchester.'

There was light, a long way above. Must be where the voice was calling from.

'Mrs Belchester.'

Wet and cold. Aching. Was she in a well? Perhaps they knew she was down here and that was why they were calling for Hubert's mother. Did not remember falling in, and there was no water, just damp and dark.

'Mrs Belchester!'

Suddenly the voice and its face were hovering just above her.

'Mrs Belchester.' The face pulled away and she could see it properly, very brown with brown eyes, black hair; a man's face, about forty years old. 'You have been very sick, but I think that now you are recovering.'

Very sick? Oh, yes, he was right.

She tried to answer but could not. A woman leaned forward, a strange, old, gypsy-like woman, and offered a glass of water.

She drank it. It had a sharp tang and she curled her lips against the taste.

'Drink it,' the man said quickly. 'It will help your fever.'

She drank. 'Are you a doctor?'

'Yes. Doctor Mendez.'

'I haven't met you before, have I?'

'No. But I have met you several times. Several times each day for the past four weeks.'

'Four weeks! What date is it?'

'It is the first day of January, 1887.'

The sun was streaming through part-open shutters, and beyond a roof there was blue sky.

'January? Where are we?'

'Sanlucar de Barrameda, Mrs Belchester. Near Cadiz, Jerez. In Spain.'

'My God.'

'Yes, you should thank God, Mrs Belchester. You very nearly died, but he saved you, and your baby.'

'My baby?'

'You are pregnant. Two, three months. You did not know?'

'Yes.' She remembered more now. 'Are you sure the baby is well?'

The doctor shrugged and smiled. 'Appears to be. Happy?'

When Doctor Mendez called that evening she felt much better and was able to talk to him for an hour or more. Luisa, the old gypsy woman, sat with them all the time, listening, but not understanding a word. She was there for propriety, the doctor explained; it was not proper for the doctor to be alone with the Englishman's wife in her bedroom.

The Englishman, it seemed, had brought her to the

hacienda, called the doctor, and then left on business. He was due to return in two or three weeks. 'Did you tell him about the baby?' It was important to know.

'Yes. I told him I thought he was a little foolish to bring you on a long sea voyage when you were expecting a child. You were certain to become sick.'

'And how did he react?'

'Not very pleasantly, Mrs Belchester.' Doctor Mendez smiled. 'But he was under great strain, so I excuse him for his rudeness.'

Doctor Mendez reduced his visits to one a day. Luisa took motherly care of her and they somehow managed to communicate a little even though neither spoke the other's language. She was told to stay in her room for a week, resting in bed as much as she could, but after the third day she could not resist the temptation to look around the house.

House! Its grandness left her breathless.

The hacienda, the house itself, was a large two-storey building surrounding a central garden. It seemed as though four almost identical white houses had been joined at the corners to form a square which was open in the middle. All the ground floor rooms opened into the square, the central garden, and the first-floor rooms all opened on to a wooden gallery which looked down on to the garden.

The house was old, very old, Doctor Mendez told her that evening after she admitted she had been exploring. 'It was once the summer palace of a Moorish prince, Mrs Belchester. A very unimportant prince and a very small palace, compared to those in Granada for example, but very beautiful, I think.'

It was very beautiful, exactly the right home for the sort of man she thought Hubert was when she married him. It was easy to imagine colourful, silk-robed and slippered figures rustling through the arched doorways, stopping to smell the scented herb bushes or sitting by the central fountain, reading poetry while they listened to the water splashing.

It was a small piece of paradise brought down to earth. Different to the surroundings she had known in Hoxton.

'You look unhappy, Mrs Belchester,' Doctor Mendez noticed. 'Your husband will be home soon, I think. Also, I think you should perhaps take more air. Sit in the garden during the daytime, but keep warm. And if you need diversion, go to the top of the tower. You may watch the ships sail the river to and from Seville.'

He rattled instructions to Luisa and said goodbye.

It was pleasant to sit in the central garden, protected from all breezes, warmed by the sun and scented by small bushes of herbs; but there was nothing to do, nothing to think about except Edward and his baby and what would happen when Hubert returned.

Some diversion was necessary so she walked up the steps of the square tower, two storeys higher than the house, and Luisa carried a chair for her to sit on.

The views from the tower were stunning. Green, undulating, gentle countryside; not the harsh sun-burned plains she had expected to see. Startling white buildings with shallow, ochre-coloured roofs, a vivid blue cloudless sky.

From one side of the tower she could see the river. It was a long way away, halfway to the horizon, but there it was, fringed with sandy beaches, a wide blue roadway for the tall and elegant ships that sailed in lines towards the north or the south. Beyond the river there was a purple and silver haze that rippled, flowers growing on marshland, colours that deepened as the sun sank behind them and the sky turned yellow and orange.

In the evenings, after dusk, the ships that sailed to and from Seville sailed with lamps lighting their decks; and she ached to leave this piece of paradise and to stand on the jetty by the London docks and feel Edward's arms around her.

* * *

Night after night after night the line of ships lit their lamps and sailed past, slow-moving earth-bound stars that were yellow, unlike the millions of blue and silver stars that pinned the night sky.

Day after day after day the scenery did not change, the days did not change. There was nothing to do, no one to talk to. Hubert did not come as the doctor thought he might, and because she was well even the doctor reduced his visits to one each week and eventually stopped calling at all.

The sun rose earlier and lingered later. The days grew hotter. It did not rain. The greenness began to wilt. She grew bigger and bigger and longed for July when the waiting should end, when she could hold Edward's baby in her arms; but meanwhile she had nothing to do but sit and wait, and worry and feel guilty.

Guilt; she listed in her mind all the reasons she should feel guilty for what had happened, and every time she reconsidered the list she found more reasons. But there was nothing she could do. She had food and warmth and care, and all she could hope was that Edward had those things even though his circumstances were different. The authorities would take care of him, even if it was only to bring him to trial; but what then? Prison? How would he bear being locked up? He used to grow restless living in two rooms and had to go out to walk off his energy.

Maybe it would be worse than prison. He could be hung.

Maybe that would be best. Best for him and her. And their child.

Maybe he already had been. The thought shocked her; and a tinge of relief added to her guilt.

Whatever his situation was, it was beyond her help. She felt impotent. There was nothing she could do for him, except to care for the baby he did not know he had given her.

Somehow the guilt seemed to lessen if she concentrated on how their child should be raised, how Edward's best virtues could be developed and enhanced, how his weaknesses could be overcome. How to do all this without spoiling the character the child would inherit from its father.

The child would never know poverty, not first hand, and that would have pleased Edward. It was strange that Edward, her prince, would never live in a palace but one day his child would own one. A palace in Spain. It seemed so romantic, exactly the sort of story Edward would have told the child. The Princess and the Pauper.

'Rose. You look better. Certainly fatter.' He was standing yards away but she already felt frightened.

'Yes, Hubert.'

'And how is the little bastard?'

She did not answer. There was no answer to give, but at least she knew what life was going to be like from now on.

She watched him turn a chair with his feet so he could sit astride it as though he were riding a horse. He sat down without removing his coat or boots and he dangled his leather hat from his hands.

'I don't have long, I must get back to the hacienda in Jerez.'

'I thought this was the sherry vineyard?'

'No. We produce manzanilla here, but the real business, the sherry, is between Jerez and Cadiz. I must go back. We have a few problems which need to be controlled.'

'Can I come with you when you go? Is your grandfather still there?' Suddenly there seemed to be some hope that the awful boredom might end.

'Grandfather was taken ill and had to go home. That's why I, we, came here.'

'Does my mother know we're here?'

'She thinks we're on a belated wedding tour through Europe.'

'May I write to her and tell her that I'm well?'

'Of course, Rose, if you agree to abide by certain rules which your misconduct obliges me to impose.'

His arrogance surprised her so much she could not speak.

'Firstly, Rose, that you support everything that I've told her about you. That is that you became disturbed with grief, but when you recovered you immediately wrote to me and asked me to take care of you, which I did. That we are on an extended tour and very happy. Secondly, you tell her that you believe you are pregnant and that the baby should be born during October. Thirdly, you explain that rather than return to England after our tour we will remain in Spain until early next year, but you will be pleased to have her stay with us in Dorset for a few weeks when we do return. And fourthly, you make no mention of your dalliance with Edward Forrester.' He stared at her and she felt slow and clumsy as she tried to think before answering. 'You may as well agree, Rose. You have absolutely no choice. I can do exactly as I like with you. No one knows you're here. You don't speak the language and no one around here speaks English, apart from Mendez and he's gone off to Seville anyway. You have no money, no travelling clothes, no walking shoes, and you're heavily pregnant and would not last a single hour in the sun. You have no choice, Rose, but to do exactly as I tell you.'

'You're saying that I'm your prisoner?' It seemed to be what he wanted her to realise.

'Quite. But I believe this an extremely pleasant prison. And no, you can't come with me. I prefer to be alone.'

'Hubert, why did you go to all the bother of finding me if you don't want to live with me?'

'You're my wife, Rose. You're mine, and I intend to keep you.'

'But you don't want me.'

'But you're mine, Rose. You belong to me and I'm not going to let you go, ever.'

There was nothing to gain by arguing, but there was some consolation in not living with him; he could not hurt her or the baby if they lived apart. 'I agree to your conditions, Hubert, because I don't have any choice.'

It all seemed so melodramatic that it did not seem real, but the bright look in his eyes was real, frightening, somehow more than frightening: totally intimidating. Instinctively she held her hands in front of her to protect her unborn child.

'I'll bring notepaper and pens next time I call.' He slipped his hat back on to his head.

'When will that be?' She had hoped she could write the letter immediately.

'When I have time, Rose. I have many more important things to do.' He swung off the chair and made towards the door.

'Would you please be so kind as to bring me some books to read, Hubert, and some paper and pencils so I can sketch?'

'No, Rose. That would distract you.'

'It's distraction that I'm seeking!'

'Oh no. You must spend your time meditating on what you have done. What trouble you have caused.'

'I do that anyway, Hubert. I can't stop myself doing it, but if I do that all day and all night I'll go mad!'

'Then so be it, Rose. That may be God's punishment for what you have done.' He opened the door.

'One more thing, Hubert. You intend to pass yourself off as the father of my baby, and I understand that, and I am grateful for it.'

'Good,' he said and began to close the door behind him.

'But will you tell me how the baby's real father is. I'm sure you must know.'

'Yes, he was tried and found guilty of your father's murder. He was sentenced to twenty years' hard labour, so I rather doubt he'll be released alive. One consolation for you, though. He's in Portland Prison, helping to build the new Royal Navy dockyard. When we go home I'll take you to Weymouth and from there you'll be able to see his handiwork. We may even be using some of the stone he's quarried to line the roads and paths on the estate. You'll not be too far from him, Rose. On a clear day it's sometimes possible to stand on the point and see Portland. Strange place. They say it's full of mad people.'

'Thank you.' It was difficult not to react, but that was what he wanted and she was not going to give him that satisfaction.

CHAPTER 36

———————

The streets held on to the rumbling August thunder and seemed to grow hotter in spite of the rain which fell in vertical torrents.

'I hope this is the young woman you're looking for, Miss Forrester, because if it isn't I'll have no choice but to put her and the children in the workhouse or in council homes. That'll mean separating the boys from the girls, of course.' The welfare officer shrugged his shoulders. 'I'd have no choice, you see?'

She nodded her understanding. Separating a family could mean it split up for ever, brothers and sisters growing further apart as they grew older. She had already decided that even if this was not Ada Cox and her brood she would still try to take them into the mission until she could find them somewhere better to live and also help them to obtain some kind of income.

The welfare man led her across the road and pushed open the front door of a high, narrow house.

'Top floor, I'm afraid, Miss Forrester.'

She followed him up the banisterless stairs, walking in the centre of the treads so she did not touch the walls which were probably alive with vermin under the stained wallpaper. The house stank; these houses were always worse during the summer, unlike those near the river which were worse in the winter.

'How long have you been working for the mission?' the man asked and she worked it out before answering.

'Two years and four months.' It seemed longer.

They reached the top landing. A ladder led up through an opening in the ceiling.

'I'll lead, shall I?' he offered and she said she thought he ought.

The loft was boarded in and there was a dirty skylight which did not open but did allow some light to glimmer through. Several bundles of rags seemed to have been dumped on the boards nearest the eaves. The bundles moved together as she stepped off the ladder and on to the board floor.

'Wotcha want?' The largest bundle, a girl, covered smaller bundles with her arms, a hen protecting its brood.

The welfare man sniffed. 'You know me, I've been here before, but I'd like you to meet this young lady who's going to ask you some questions.'

'Wot for?' The girl stared at her, eyes nervous and suspicious.

'Are you Ada Cox?' Elizabeth asked, thinking there was no reason not to come straight to the point.

Alert, dark eyes stared back. No answer.

'One, two three, four, five, six.' She bent down and counted the children, looked closely into the scared eyes. 'Ada Cox has six children to look after. Are you Ada?'

'No. Why?'

'I'm looking for her. To help her.' She stood up. 'But if you're not Ada I'll leave you alone.'

'How you gonna help?'

'How's little Edward been since Francis brought him back to you?' She saw the surprise on the girl's face, and felt immense relief; it would be difficult enough to care for one family of seven urchins, to find two would make things impossible. 'I'm Edward Forrester's sister.'

'Edward's?'

'Yes. If you are Ada you'll know the name of the woman he lived with.'

'The lady, you mean. Rose?'

'Yes, Rose.' She smiled, her own relief at finding the girl who could tell her more about Edward and Rose seemed to be matched by the man who had helped her.

'Doesn't seem to be anything more I can do, Miss Forrester, so I'll leave you to get acquainted.'

She thanked him and watched him climb down the ladder before she turned back to Ada. A crack of thunder made the roof rattle and the children quickly clustered even closer to their sister.

'You're really Edward's sister?' Ada Cox asked, wonderingly.

'Yes I am, and I work for a mission which has a shelter quite near here. There's beds and regular food, if you'd like to come,' she explained.

'Workhouse?' Ada asked sharply.

'No, not a workhouse or a home. And you can all stay together until we find you somewhere permanent to live, still all together if we can manage it.'

'We ain't got no money.'

'I can see that, Ada. You won't need any. We'll supply everything, and in return you can do chores to help run the place. Maybe we'll be able to help you find work while someone else looks after the children for you.'

'You're really Edward's sister?'

'Really.'

'Where is he?' It was interesting to note how her accent changed when she did not feel threatened.

'He's in Portland Prison. Rose is abroad with her

husband.' She saw the confusion on Ada's face and thought an explanation would confirm the girl's trust. 'Look, it's too wet to go walking through the streets at the moment, so I'll tell you all about Edward and Rose if you'll tell me more about yourself and the children.'

Ada nodded.

Evie Roper smiled at her as she walked through the front door and hung her coat on the hallstand. 'I can see from your expression that you found her.'

'Is it that obvious?'

'Yes. I've just made some tea. We'll sit down and have a cup and you can tell me what happened.'

Evie listened to the whole story, only interrupting to ask minor questions.

Francis Marriott had found the loft home for Ada and the brood and took them there after he had rescued the baby. He left Ada with some money, enough to support herself and the children for several weeks, and a woman Francis knew brought her more money for a few more weeks, and also told her that the men who had kidnapped the baby were dead.

Eventually the woman stopped coming and Ada had returned to begging. The youngest children helped by dancing for strangers who seemed happy to pay a few pennies for their entertainment, and, in Ada's words, baby Edward helped by crying and sucking his thumb; and her father helped by not being with them. She had managed to get by without prostitution, and freed from it she never wanted to have to do that again.

'They're nice children, Evie, all of them. Quiet, well behaved, and clean if they're given the chance. I can see why Edward was so concerned for them. Ada's quite remarkable. She's strict but she doesn't hit them or shout at them, and she's very pretty, or will be when she's eating properly. I think she was almost starving herself so the smaller ones could eat.'

'You sound very taken with them, dear.'

'I am. I just hope they'll settle down all right. They've always lived on their own and there's no privacy in the mission, just three large dormitories . . .'

'No need to tell me, dear. Don't forget I worked there myself for seven years.'

She had not forgotten, she was dropping a small hint. Number Fourteen would be a much better home for the Coxes than the mission, but if she were to move them in it would have to be at Evie's instigation.

'I wish I could let Edward know Ada's safe. It might be just the thing which would make him see sense.' And, she thought, make her feel better about breaking her promise not to write to him.

Not that he had read any of her letters: they had all been returned unopened. The last letter she had written really would be the last, she had already decided. If Edward was determined to break off all contact it would be cruel to keep writing, even though it hurt beyond belief to abandon him.

'Perhaps I will write. Just one last letter. After all, I was lucky enough to find Ada – perhaps the luck'll last a bit longer and he'll relent.' She wished she could also let Rose know Ada was safe, but even though Catherine knew Rose's address and could be asked to pass a message, it might cause too much trouble if Hubert ever found out what had happened.

'I think that before you do that you ought to read the two letters which came for you, dear.' Evie handed her two letters from behind the clock on the mantelpiece.

She opened the one written by Joey first, and read quickly. The families were well, both Flo and Mary had given birth to baby boys, and there was the usual invitation for her to join them at Joey and Paul's expense. It was interesting but not what she wanted to know.

Immediately after Edward's trial she had gone to Pincote, found out from Sergeant Craddock where

McClusky, the policeman who had found Sebastian's body, had lived before he emigrated, and then asked his old neighbours if they knew where he had gone. None of them had his address but they all confirmed he had gone to America. Mr Joseph had told her that if she could provide proof that the police evidence was false there was a possibility that the court's verdict could be overturned; but first she had to find McClusky and persuade him to tell the truth.

She smiled as she read Joey's complimentary remarks about her detection work, and his shared astonishment that the police had not done as she had. Yes, he and Paul were trying to trace McClusky but America was a big country and without knowing which city or town or even state he was in it was an almost impossible task. They would have to rely on luck and, as Joey remarked, Edward's luck seemed to vary enormously.

The second envelope had been posted in Portland, Dorset. She knew what was in it before she opened it: another of her letters to Edward returned unopened.

Inside was not only her letter to Edward but an official prison letter addressed to her. She pulled the letter out from the envelope, fingers shaking, and a feeling of awful dread swept over her as she saw the heavily printed letterhead. What had happened to Edward now?

'Something wrong, dear?' Evie asked.

She did not answer until she had read half the letter, 'No, Evie, not really. The governor's written to me about Edward. Mr Hampton. Richard Hampton.'

'Nice name, dear.'

'It's a nice letter. He is actually apologising for not being able to persuade Edward to accept my letters. He says that it's not unusual so I should keep trying, that Edward is well, keeps himself very much to himself, and doesn't cause any trouble.'

'You should write back and thank Mr Hampton, dear.'

'Yes, I will.' It could be useful to build up a relationship with this man; he might possibly help to get Edward released if McClusky could be found and persuaded to tell the truth.

For the next week she avoided talking about Ada or the children unless Evie mentioned them first, and she noticed that by the end of the week she could hardly get through the front door before Evie asked her about them. By the end of the second week she sensed that Evie was building up to a suggestion of some sort.

'The weather looks settled for the weekend, dear.'

'Yes, I think it probably is.'

'Your children must feel real cooped up in the mission.'

'My children? You mean Ada's brood?'

'Of course.' Evie seemed cross with her. 'Why don't you invite them home here for Sunday? They can have dinner here and play in the garden or we could take them all to the park. Or somewhere.'

'If you're sure, Evie.'

'I wouldn't ask if I wasn't. Just for the day, mind.'

By Sunday teatime everyone was exhausted. Even Jack Cutler, the young man who lived next door, had somehow volunteered himself as games referee, storyteller and general dogsbody, and had been kept busy all day.

The children had run and laughed and played until the three youngest had simply fallen asleep where they sat, and Evie had taken them upstairs and laid them on spare beds to rest.

'Well, thank you very much, Mrs Roper.' Ada gathered the oldest three around her. 'It's been a wonderful day, the best I can ever remember, but I think I ought to take the kids back to the mission before they all get too tired to walk.'

'It's an awful long way for them to walk, dear, after such a long day.' Evie stated the obvious as she often did.

'But the sooner we leave the sooner we'll get back.' Ada stood up.

Evie made her sit down again. 'The smallest three are already asleep, dear, and you shouldn't disturb them now. Why don't you all stay here for the night? We've only got three spare bedrooms, but you won't mind sharing, will you?'

Jack Cutler was press-ganged into helping put the three older children to bed, but he still seemed to come downstairs with fresh energy.

'Miss Cox, Ada, I don't suppose you'd care to come for a walk, would you? Just down to the park, around the lake, perhaps?' He looked flustered, as if he was anxious she might refuse or make objection.

'I'd like to, but I can't really leave the children, Jack.'

'Of course you can, young lady.' Evie was on her feet, almost shooing her and Jack out through the door. 'I'll listen out for the children.'

'Well, thank you, Mrs Roper. You know, I've never been out for a walk without the kids before. Never.' Ada allowed Jack to take her arm.

Elizabeth sat back in a comfortable chair and did not take any part in the conversations. She pretended to doze, and made sure that Evie did not see the smile which she felt curling her lips.

CHAPTER 37

The ward stank so much that someone had asked a nurse to leave a window open, and now the tide had changed the window was rattling and sending great blasts of fresh air across the beds. Edward did not mind, the wind cooled him and made him feel better.

'Nasty infection, Forrester.' The doctor pulled a face and dropped the used dressing into a bin. 'Teach you not to swing a pick-axe at your foot, won't it? It was your axe, wasn't it?'

'Aye, sir.' No point in telling the truth and causing him trouble which would only escalate; best to accept that the other prisoners thought he was different and try not to get into a position where he had to fight back.

'Clean it up and then dress it again,' the doctor ordered a nurse, 'before Forrester receives his visitors.'

'Visitors? There's no one visiting me, Doctor. Must be a mistake.'

'No mistake, unless you're not Edward Forrester, in

which case someone else has a badly injured foot.'

'Aye, it's my foot but they're not my visitors. I don't have visitors.' The nurse sprayed carbolic into the wound and the stinging pain took his breath away and stopped him saying any more.

'Well, you're going to see these visitors, Forrester. It's near Christmas, they're clergy, and you're in no position to run away.'

'But I don't know any clergy, Doctor.'

'Don't tell me, tell your visitors when you see them.'

The nurse finished the painful cleaning, wrapped a fresh dressing loosely around the wound, and wandered off saying she would have to get a stepladder so she could reach the open window.

'Allow me, Nurse,' he heard a big voice boom and saw a giant dressed as a parson reach up and pull the window shut.

'Adam.' He held out his hand and the giant beamed at him and returned the handshake. 'You're a parson?'

'Not a proper parson, no, my friend. Bit of an honorary position. Nancy and me have taken on an orphanage near Taunton. We're on our way there now, and we thought we'd call on you in passing.'

'This is a long way out of your way, Adam.'

There was a rustle beside him and Nancy said softly, 'Not for a friend who needs talking to, Edward.'

As he turned his face towards her she bent down to kiss him, on his cheek he imagined, but their mouths brushed and she did not hesitate to continue the kiss full on his lips.

It felt wonderful, her lips were soft and warm and she smelled clean and looked beautiful, but he had to ask, 'Am I still a friend, Nancy?'

'The best there is, Edward. Remember, you brought Adam and me together.'

'Aye, but I could've made the introductions a bit easier, lass. Did you get me letter?' He had sent the letter three weeks ago, asking for Nancy's forgiveness for what he had done; she was the final person he needed to apologise to, and in some ways the most important.

'Aye, Edward, I got your letter, and that's why we're here. There's nothing to forgive you for, lad. There might be if I had any regrets, but I haven't, and you've got to believe that. I cannot have any children of my own, true enough, but I've Adam and we're being given fifty children to look after. And as they grow up and leave we'll be given more to replace them. And we've got a lovely house for ourselves and Ma to live in, so we're very happy, Edward. I was just as much to blame as you were for the troubles we had, but all that's past now. It did what it had to, that business, and good came out from it.' She was smiling all the time and it was obvious that she was happy, much happier than she would have been if she had married him.

'I'm real pleased for you, lass.' There was nothing more to say.

'Thanks, lad.' She bent and kissed him again, and her hair fell over his face the way he remembered it had once before, but that was in a different life. 'I'll go, but Adam wants a quiet few words with you. I know this sounds silly, in here like, but promise me that one day you'll come and visit us. We'd like that, both of us.'

'I promise.' It was easy to say; in nineteen years' time she would have forgotten.

'Nancy's right, Edward. Stop blaming yourself for what happened. You're serving a sentence, a harsh one I reckon, and that's your punishment. Don't add to it.' He felt Adam's grip tighten on his hand. 'Don't shut yourself away from your friends, Lizzie in particular.'

'The sentence wasn't harsh, Adam. Maybe I should have been hung. It's true I didn't go to the manor to kill Laybourne, but I was glad he was dead. And I wish they'd hung me for it, because then, well . . . I don't want Lizzie to spend the rest of her life waiting for me. I want her to be happy.'

'Perhaps she'll only be happy waiting for you, Edward.

We all think of her as your sister, but she isn't, is she? Maybe that's why she wants to wait for you, my friend, and if that's the case you shouldn't deny her the pleasure of seeing you once in a while, or at least reading a letter from you.'

That was something he had never thought of, and it made some sense, perhaps. But Rose?

'That'd be even more unfair, Adam. There's only one woman for me, and it's not Lizzie. Not in that way.'

'Ah,' Adam sighed. 'Rose.'

'Aye. Have you seen anything of her, Adam?'

'No. You do know she went back to Hubert?'

'Aye.' It was strange, he did not feel angry or betrayed, not even jealous; just puzzled as to why she had gone back and worried about her. Was she happy, was she safe? 'You haven't seen her but have you heard anything? Is she well?'

'We sort of heard that she'd had a baby, but we don't know much about it. During October, maybe early November, I'm not sure.'

That would mean it was Hubert's. He had made her pregnant.

Adam was still talking to him but he did not listen. Hubert had forced himself on Rose and made her pregnant! It was not simply wrong, it was indecent, obscene. The man was a monster and now he had forced her to breed what could be another monster. How could God let things like that happen?

'How can God do what?' Adam asked suddenly.

'I'm sorry, Adam. Just thinking and I must have thought out loud.'

'About God? That's a good sign.'

'Not in this context, Adam. I was cussing Him. That's not allowed, is it?'

'If it helps you to find Him, it is then.'

'Find God? In here? If he'd ever been here in the first case he's not here now, man.'

'Edward, my friend, I found God in prison.'

It was said so quietly he was not sure he had heard correctly.

'You were in prison? What for?'

'The same as you, my friend. I killed a man, and I didn't mean to do it, either.'

'Francis said something, but he wouldn't give me any details. What happened?'

'Nothing very remarkable, Edward. All the family, my father and three uncles, were all tenant farmers around Taunton. They had two bad harvests and a run of accidents and illnesses and none of them could pay their rents. My uncles were the first ones to be evicted but of course the landlord eventually came to collect rent from my parents. They did not have enough to pay what was due, partly because they'd given money to my uncles to help support their families. Now, I'd been living away from home for a few years, partly because I couldn't face the sort of lives my parents led on the farm and partly because there wasn't any work for me anyway. So, I'd gone off and done what big country lads do when they go to cities, earned money wrestling and prize fighting and generally using my strength. I didn't like it much but I did it and I took money home whenever I went back. I turned up at home as the bailiffs were evicting my folks and I gave them all my money but it wasn't enough. They took what I had and still tried to throw my mother out even though she was ill and in bed. I tried to stop 'em and I hit one man too hard. I was lucky I wasn't hung.'

'I'd no idea, man. None at all.'

'But that's not the point. You see, Edward, up until that time I'd read the Bible every day, gone to church every Sunday and I thought I was a Christian and believed in God. But when I thought I needed Him more than ever before and He did not come to help me I wondered just what sort of God this was. A bit like you are now, I reckon.'

'Aye.'

'Well, I spent ten years in prison brooding on it. God

didn't send down any messages to help me. He didn't seem to care much, so far as I could see, just expected us all to praise Him and build churches for Him and generally puff Him up and pay our respects, if you understand me, my friend. I can tell you I was literally hell-bent on proving to all the Bible-thumpers that it didn't matter whether you had faith or not because this God, if He even existed, simply didn't care. But I hadn't realised that I was thinking about Him every day, and although I didn't like Him, I believed He existed. Anyway, I was released and on my way home I found myself outside an old monastery, near Somerton, I think, in the valley. A quiet old boy called me over and gave me food and drink and after I'd finished it we sat down and talked and I told him how I felt. "What benefit is there believing in God?" I asked him, and he said, "Comfort. What benefit is there in not believing in God?" Then he took my staff and threw it about ten yards. "Order it to come back to you," he said, and he made me do it. And of course the staff just lay there.'

'I don't understand what you're saying, Adam.' This was one of his more confusing stories.

'That's the point, Edward. I didn't understand either, but I wanted to. God had made me so angry with Him that I wanted to understand why He would do that to me, so I stayed there until I did. They had a bit of a refuge there, a sanctuary if you like. It took me eight months to understand what God had been trying to tell me when I was in prison, Edward.'

'And what is it, Adam?'

'That faith is self-supporting, Edward, and it's free. If you believe, you get comfort from your belief. If you don't believe, you don't get comforted, so you may as well believe. Even if you're wrong, if there is no God, what have you lost? Nothing. You've had all the benefits that faith can give you, so in fact you're better off.'

'I suppose that makes a kind of sense, but what was the point about your staff?'

'You think about that, and when you reckon you know the answer you write and let me know, and I'll come back and talk again.' Adam stood up. 'I must be going, my friend, so you take care of yourself and don't let anyone else hit you with an axe. Turning the other cheek's a good philosophy in theory, Edward, but sometimes questionable in practice.'

'How did you know?' No one could have known how he had been hurt.

'Very difficult to put a pick-axe through your own foot, Edward, and I know you, my friend. I know you better than maybe you think.'

'I reckon you do.' One last thing to ask him. 'You won't tell Lizzie you've seen me? It'd hurt her to think I'd seen you but not her.'

'See her, Edward. See her before it's too late to do anything with what's left of your life.'

'Maybe.'

CHAPTER 38

They were sitting by the fire in the front parlour and the house was quiet, astonishingly quiet.

'Cup of tea?' She placed a cup and saucer on the table by Evie's chair.

'Oh yes please, Lizzie dear.' Evie opened her eyes. 'That was the best Christmas I've had for years, but I'm glad it's over.'

'But isn't the house quiet, now, with all the children gone? It's only about three months since they all moved in here but it seems as if they'd been here for ever.'

'I know but they're only next door, Lizzie. Do you think Ada and Jack have done the right thing, getting married so soon and taking on all the children?'

'Of course they have. You could see how Jack felt about Ada from the first time they met, and you could see Ada feels the same about him. Anyway, they're married now, and I'm sure Jack cares for the children just as much as Ada. They'll be all right, don't you worry.'

'I hope so. I hope you're right.'

'Anything wrong, Evie? You're not usually pessimistic.'

'Oh no, don't worry, dear. It's just me. One of me headaches. Had it for days and it won't go away, not altogether.' Evie sipped her tea. 'Have you written and told Edward about Ada?'

'I have. I've written telling him everything that's happened since he was locked up but he hasn't read the letters. Mr Hampton wrote to tell me.'

'I think I'd like to meet your Mr Hampton, Lizzie.'

'So would I, but he's hardly my Mr Hampton. He's probably old and married with a grown-up family.' An odd sense of jealousy and panic suddenly welled up. 'And he's probably very proper and boring.'

'I don't know, Lizzie, but I do think you should try to see him. He might be able to persuade Edward to see you if you actually visited the prison.'

'I promised Edward I wouldn't do that, Evie, and I don't think it would be fair on either of us if I broke that promise as well.'

'Maybe you're right, but at my age you see how little time there is to put right things that've gone wrong. Time, Lizzie, there just isn't enough of it to waste, and I'd just like to know . . .' She stopped talking as though she thought she should not continue.

'Carry on, you won't upset me.'

'What was I saying then?' Evie looked confused.

'About me visiting Edward.'

'Why? Is he going to see you?' Her speech was slightly slurred.

'No, Evie. Look' – standing up and wondering whether or not to ask Ada to come back for a while – 'I'm going to get you a doctor. I think you need one.'

'Don't be silly, dear. What do I need a doctor for?'

'I think you're ill, Evie, and I'd like a doctor to see you.'

'I'm fine apart from me headache, and I don't need a doctor for that. Anyway, it's Boxing Night and no doctor's going to come out unless someone's dying or giving birth, and I don't propose doing either.' She rubbed her face. 'But I am tired, Lizzie, so I think I'll go up to bed when I've finished this tea. Better still, you can top this one up for me. Come on, dear, sit down again and don't look so worried. I'm tired, that's all.'

They were both tired; it had been a hectic few months.

'Lizzie! Has the clock stopped?'

She woke up suddenly, startled by Evie's clawing hand. It was half past one in the morning. They had both fallen asleep in the easy chairs.

'No, it's working, Evie.' The clock was ticking as loudly as ever.

'Where are all the children?'

'They're next door, Evie, with Ada and Jack.'

'Next door? Why aren't they here?' She was beginning to panic.

'Calm down, Evie. Everything's all right. Ada and Jack got married on Christmas Eve. Don't you remember?'

'Christmas? Is Christmas coming?' The panic increased.

'We've just had it, Evie. Look, I'll make you a nice cup of tea, and then we'll get you upstairs to bed.' Tea might calm her down and help her to remember.

'Thank you, Lizzie, dear.' Evie sipped her tea. 'I do remember now. Must have been waking up sudden like that put it out of me mind. Hope I didn't frighten you too much?'

'Of course not, though I do worry about you. You've been doing too much.'

'It's what keeps me going, dear. Work and having you here. Next to marrying my Sidney, having you come here is the best thing that's happened in my life.'

'I'm glad, Evie, because it is the best thing that's happened in my life, my adult life.' She smiled at Evie, then she saw the tea spilling back out from Evie's open mouth. 'Evie, Evie!'

She could not reach the cup and saucer before Evie dropped them. They rested on the old lady's lap and the spilled tea stained her best overall and soaked into her frock.

The sharp, sparkling eyes still sparkled, but now there was nothing behind them. Evie was dead.

A week later a letter came from Catherine saying that Charlotte had also died on Boxing Evening, and by coincidence both Evie and Charlotte were buried on the same day. It seemed to augur a bad beginning to 1888, but life went on much as it had before, except that at times Number Fourteen seemed oppressively quiet.

The solicitor smiled at her and told her that the daffodils had opened in his garden, a sign of spring and new beginnings.

'New beginnings, Miss Forrester,' he continued, 'that's what you must think of now. Mrs Roper led a very full and happy life, and she thought of you as the daughter she never had. You helped to make her final years happy ones, when for so many childless widows those years are the worst of their lives. Accordingly she has left her entire estate to you. That consists of her house, Fourteen Angel Street, her furniture, all her personal effects which amount to very little, and a small amount of money, something less than one hundred pounds. There is, however, one restriction concerning the house, though it is more in the nature of a request than anything else.'

'Yes, Mr Simkins?' Even before she knew what it was she knew she would do whatever Evie wanted her to.

'She asked that you retain the house as your personal home for as long as you wish, and that you do not turn it into an extension of the mission other than to offer temporary accommodation to women you feel need your personal assistance and who would respect her own feelings for the house. She was concerned that your dedication, as she put it, might oblige you to open your refuge with the result that you would never be able to escape the trials of your work. That, she felt, would benefit neither you nor the mission.'

'I understand.'

Catherine's hand brushed hers and she was glad that her friend had travelled down from Manchester to spend a few days with her.

Mr Simkins smiled again and closed the folder on his desk. 'There will be documents to sign, which I'll bring around to you in a week or so. Meanwhile, please don't be sad. I'm sure that Evelyn Roper's with Sidney, and even now she's telling him all about you and the fun you had together.'

She thanked the solicitor for his kindness and followed Catherine out into the sunshine.

'Have you heard from Rose?' she asked, because all through the family's trials Catherine had somehow always managed to keep in contact with Rose.

'No. I've written a number of letters but she hasn't answered any of them. I even wrote to Hubert's grandfather and asked him if he could persuade her to reply but I had a very short letter back from Hubert's father saying the old man was too ill to intervene in family squabbles and if Rose did not wish to respond to my letters I should accept her decision.'

'Doesn't seem like Rose at all. Perhaps she's simply trying to shut out all the unpleasant things that happened to her.' It seemed necessary to offer Rose some defence.

'That's exactly what I thought. She wrote to Charlotte occasionally, but even that seemed to pass. She promised to come home early this year but there's been no indication that she will, and she didn't even make any attempt to come home after Charlotte died. From what I have heard through various contacts Rose and Hubert have a very full social life in Spain, and they live in a palace, would you believe? A small palace, but a palace, and I suppose life back here must seem very mundane. John refuses to have anything to do with her now and won't even allow her name to be mentioned.'

'It seems very strange to me, Catherine. Not like Rose at all.'

'I know, but I don't know what to do about it. Still, I'd like to have seen her again before I leave England myself.'

'You're leaving England?' Another shock.

'Yes, my dear, I have to admit that we are. Walter's reached the age where he can retire from the bank and as that's the only reason we've remained in Manchester we've decided to move to slightly warmer climes, to Deauville in Normandy. We've often been there on holiday and we've several sets of friends there, both French and retired English couples. But don't worry, Lizzie, I'll keep in contact with you, and perhaps you might come to stay with us sometimes.'

'Yes, I'd like that.' It sounded wonderful, and she was genuinely pleased for Catherine and Walter who had always been so kind, but it was another good friend who was leaving and she found it difficult to hold back the tears.

The letter waiting on the doormat when she arrived home did not help her mood. It was from Joey. After a year of making enquiries they were still no nearer to tracing McClusky, and because Joey took the trouble to explain in detail how the law enforcement system worked within the United States she understood clearly why he thought they might never find the officer.

She hardly spoke as she prepared a light meal for Catherine and herself, and her heart felt heavier as they left for the station where she would wave her half sister goodbye and know she might not see her again for a very long time.

'It's Edward who's in prison, Lizzie, not you,' Catherine said, and behind her the noise and bustle of the station reflected the life that was going on at the moment. 'Don't waste your life waiting for him. I'm sure he wouldn't want you to.'

'No, Catherine, he's already told me that.'

'Then don't be so stubborn. Get on with your life, everyone else has, even Rose.'

She thanked Catherine for all her help over the past three years, wished her a happy retirement, kissed her goodbye and waved as the train left the station.

Yes, life was going on. On and on and on, and because of Edward she was not a part of it, or so it seemed. Thinking about him, worrying about him, and trying to find proof which might free him or reduce his sentence was becoming an obsession. Other things happened around her, she reacted as needed, but her main concentration was on Edward. He had warned her this might happen. And asked her to avoid it. Made her promise not to wait for him.

Catherine was quite right in what she said; Rose had her life, John had his, and Nancy was exceptionally happy.

Apart from Charlotte who was dead, and Edward who was in prison and seemed content in his isolation, she was the only one of those who had suffered when everything went wrong who was not living her life, not properly.

She went home and tore up the letter she was preparing for Edward, and burned the pieces in the kitchen range.

Then she cried, because there seemed to be nothing else to do.

CHAPTER 39

'Although it wasn't possible to return to England when my mother was dying it is quite acceptable to go back now your grandfather's dying? Is that what you're saying, Hubert?' It was a fine point but one worth arguing about, an advantage to take in the bickering life they led.

'Rose, we didn't even know your mother was ill until after she was dead and buried. There was no reason to go haring halfway around Europe at that time, especially as it was during the winter and we would have had your two babies with us.'

'Ah, so it was really their fault. Everything seems to have been their fault ever since they were born.'

'Well, Rose, they've been damned inconvenient, even you can't deny that. One child would have been enough of a problem; two, quite frankly, is a ridiculous embarrassment.'

'Only because you're trying to pretend you're their father. Twins are born to families who don't have a history of twins, Hubert. If you could accept that there would not be quite as many problems as you imagine. Besides, being born twins has an advantage in that they're both still quite small and you can easily pass them off as being three months younger than they really are. Anyway' – another stinging thought came to mind – 'you should be thankful that you have both a son and a daughter, a complete happy little family. Your mother won't expect you to perform any more miracles.'

'That's unkind, Rose.'

'Perhaps, but your mother puzzles me, Hubert. I can't understand why, as she thinks you're so marvellous, she didn't have any more children after you.'

'She nearly died giving birth to me. That's why she thinks I'm so precious, Rose.'

The very fact that he could say it and mean it proved that nothing she could do would ever change him. He would for ever be a self-centred, jealous, vindictive sadist who could only inveigle himself into any form of civilised society by hiding his real self behind an opposite image.

But at least, even under provocation, he had not hit her. Perhaps it was the threat to tell his parents that the children were not really his, something which anyway might become obvious as they developed; perhaps it was the threat to find the detective he had employed and expose the fact that Hubert himself knew of Edward's whereabouts but had not informed the police. Perhaps it was that she had threatened to gouge out his eyes if he laid a hand on her again or ever hurt her children. It did not matter, not while the occasional tests proved that he would keep his fists to himself.

She turned to leave but he called her back.

'One other thing, Rose, before you start to pack. I had some news from England, about Forrester.'

She knew that she reacted too instinctively, too fast, and that was why he kept her waiting, forcing her to ask him to tell. 'Yes?'

'Rather ironic in a sense. You know how ill he was, well of course you do, you were there. He recovered for the trial, twenty years instead of being hung.'

'Yes, Hubert, you've told me before.' She knew she would beg for the real news if he wanted her to, but not immediately.

'Well, after all of that he was hurt in a prison fight. Someone put an axe through his foot.'

'That's awful.' It was, but she knew Hubert's smile hid something much worse. 'I suppose it could have been worse.'

'It was, Rose. The wound became infected and he died a month ago.'

'He's dead?'

'And buried. Natural justice, Rose. A good end for a bad lot.'

'How long have you known?'

'A few days, but I kept forgetting to tell you. After all, he didn't mean anything to you, did he, not in the end?'

It was not possible to measure the pain.

Nothing Hubert had ever done to her hurt as much.

The greatest pleasure would have been to have died there, on the spot. But then he would have total control of Edward's children. That was not acceptable. It never would be.

She walked away from him and her room appeared around her. It was very quiet, so quiet it seemed the children had stopped breathing.

It was not possible to cry because it was not possible to feel anything. Life had stopped, not only for Edward but for her. The children, they were all that mattered. Keeping them safe, keeping Edward alive in them.

She picked them up, one at a time, cuddled them, kissed them twice, once for herself and once for Edward, something she had done since they were born, told them she was sorry but their father was dead, and promised to do everything she could to lessen their pain and what they had lost by never knowing him. Then she lay down on the bed and tried to stop her mind.

Hubert opened the door a few minutes later. 'Started packing yet?'

'Tomorrow, Hubert. Tomorrow.'

'We'll have to leave by nine.'

'I'll be ready.'

'Make sure you are. I don't want you to keep me waiting or we may lose all our connections.'

Even in May the London skies were bleak and the wind smelled of soot instead of fragrant herbs, but the pleasure on Grandpa Belchester's face when he saw the babies made the miserable weather and long journey worth while.

'Are you happy, Princess?' She had to put her ear close to his mouth to hear him.

'Yes, Grandpa. I'm happy.' There was no reason for him to take a miserable truth to the grave.

'And Luisa. Is she well?'

'She wants to know when you'll go back so you can dance flamenco together, Grandpa.' That was the old gypsy's last message, translated by Doctor Mendez who called as they left. The laughter in the old man's throat and eyes made her want to cry.

It was the last time she saw him laugh. He died that night.

He had died in London because he said he wished to spend his last days where there was life but he wanted to be interred in the family crypt by the estate chapel.

On the day of the funeral a thick mist stood on the sea, and an unseen buoy rolled and rang its bell out beyond the point she would have jumped from if Grandpa Belchester had not stopped her. That was two years ago and now, having seen the grandchild, grandchildren, he had waited for, he was dead. It seemed ironic.

She thought his burying was an intolerably mean affair. A single prayer, the Lord's Prayer, accounted for some sort of service to mark his passing, and apart from herself, only Hubert, his parents and the local parson witnessed the old man's entombment in the family crypt on the mist-bound clifftop.

It seemed a cheap and uncaring way to treat a lovely and caring man.

The family walked back to the house but she asked to be excused and went to sit in the chapel for a few minutes. She thought back over all the things that had happened since she had pledged herself to Hubert in that chapel, and as it offered her no solace at all she left it to its own misery and walked along the cliffs and out to the point.

She stood looking down at the waves and felt the irony of the situation mocking her. She had almost died here, because she wanted Edward so much, but Grandpa Belchester had saved her. Now he was dead and if the day had been clear she could have stood where she was and seen Portland Bill where Edward, the man she had wanted, also lay dead.

She had no doubt that Edward died because of her, and she thought it was obscene that he had to die within sight of the house she was condemned to live in with his children.

She turned and walked to the house, her tears stifled because they would be seen as yet another sign of her weakness.

In her room that night, alone and desolate, she cried, not only for Grandpa Belchester but for Edward, and her mother and, she wondered, perhaps also for herself. Three of the people she most cared for had died within months of each other and she felt that as they passed they had each taken something of her, too.

There was still John; the once happy, caring strong brother who knew her as well as she knew herself, who was always there when she needed him. And Catherine. Now, they were the only remaining links with the past.

Except that they, too, had been broken.

She had been suspicious, unnaturally suspicious, Hubert and his mother had said, when Hubert told her that neither John nor Catherine wanted anything more to do with her; then John replied to her latest letter using the most formal tones.

His reply shocked her. He wished her well, but the letter's tone and wording implied that he thought she was largely responsible for her mother's premature death and that a visit by her would never be considered convenient.

If it had not been for her children, and Hubert's father's warning that John had changed for the worse since his marriage to Lillian, she would have taken a train to Pincote and if necessary stayed in the Station Hotel while she tried to reason with him.

Instead, for days after the letter and Grandpa Belchester's funeral, she sat and brooded, cursing the distance there was between her and John, both the distance in miles and the distance in feelings.

While she had been in Spain she had written so many letters to her mother and John, and Catherine, but only her mother had ever bothered to reply, and even then infrequently. It was clear that they blamed her for so much of what had happened, and in her heart she could understand how they must feel. Her love for Edward had made her act irresponsibly, and she had no one to blame but herself for the troubles she had caused.

If she needed any confirmation that John wanted to have nothing more to do with her it arrived a week after the funeral, carefully wrapped in a small parcel: her mother's hairbrushes and several other personal items with a note from John explaining that their mother had asked for those things to be sent to her at an appropriate time. He even asked her to sign and return a form stating that she had received the items and would make no further claim on the residue of their mother's estate.

She signed the form and sealed it inside an envelope,

and cried because there was no reason to enclose a covering letter. She placed the envelope on the hall table ready to be posted, and went to sit in the morning room where she could be alone with her thoughts and regrets.

Half an hour later Hubert appeared, her single envelope addressed to John in one hand and a bundle of envelopes in the other.

'I see you've replied to your brother.' He waved the bundle of envelopes in front of her and she saw they were letters she had written to Catherine. 'Unfortunately your half sister won't even offer you the kindness of opening your letters before she returns them.'

She felt her chest tighten. 'Catherine's been returning my letters? Why didn't you tell me?'

'I didn't want you to become ill, and I hoped I could persuade Walter to talk reason to Catherine and avoid you ever having to know.'

'That seems to be unusually considerate of you, Hubert.' She recovered a little and as suspicions rose in her mind she reached out for the letters, remembering how, in Spain, Hubert had always taken her letters for posting. 'May I have the letters anyway? Please, Hubert.'

She realised she was so short of breath she could hardly speak.

'No, Rose. There's no reason to torture yourself any further. You're already upset about the way John treated you. Catherine . . .' He stopped.

'Yes?' She watched him poke the fire, noticed the deliberate way he stabbed at the coals and turned them over so they glowed red and angry.

'Catherine discovered, somehow, that when you disappeared you lived with Forrester, the man who murdered her father. Yours too, of course. She's made certain threats, Rose, about revealing the truth and I don't need to tell you how much that sort of scandal would affect you and me and especially the children.' He paused and poked the fire so it burst into fresh flames. 'Rose,

Catherine and Walter have left the country and have not informed me of their address. Catherine has, however, informed me through my solicitors that she wants nothing more to do with you. I'm sorry, but you have rather brought all this on yourself.'

'That all sounds so unlike Catherine.' It was almost impossible to believe.

'Come now, Rose. You chose not to believe me when I told you about your brother, and you soon saw how wrong you were.' He waved the bundle of letters in the air. 'There's only one place for these, Rose.'

She gasped for breath and reached out to stop him throwing the letters into the fire, but too late. They rested at the back of the grate for a few seconds, turned brown, crinkled, and burst into flames. Now she would never know if Catherine had really returned them or if Hubert had never even posted them; but did it matter?

She watched them burn and thought their flames marked the end of her real life. It seemed she was destined to be Hubert's prisoner for ever, always friendless and always unloved, except for her two children.

But it did seem to be a suitable punishment for what she had done, the misery and pain she had caused so many people.

She was worthless. All that mattered was that Edward's children should grow up healthy and untarnished by Hubert's family.

That was the only way she could ever redeem herself, through his children, and she would do anything to protect them.

'Hubert, I don't need or want a nurse for the children.' It was an appalling idea and one which she would not stand for.

'Don't be selfish, Rose,' his mother interrupted even before he could answer. 'Think of the children. They need correct care taken of them.'

'Which is precisely why I want to look after them myself.' She squared up to the old woman. 'After all, I managed quite well in Spain and I have nothing else to do.'

'That, young woman, is quite irrelevant. Children need expert care. Are you experienced in raising children? How many have you cared for previously, tell me that, will you? None, of course, which is why I have selected Miss Godwin with the utmost care. Are you suggesting, young woman, that I'm incompetent?'

'Not at all, but they're my children and I have a right to decide how they'll be brought up.'

'You have a right?' The old woman raised her shoulders and glared. 'You have proved to be totally unreliable and incapable of taking care of yourself, let alone my son's children. If it hadn't been for my Hubert you'd have been dead in a gutter by now. You have forfeited all rights to bring up my grandchildren, Hubert's children, heirs to our estates.'

'Hubert?' It was a hopeless appeal and his reaction was predictable.

'My mother knows best, Rose. Besides, Miss Godwin's been appointed now so it's far too late for you to raise any objections or throw another of your usual childish rages.'

The sudden compression on her chest made matters worse. The asthma had passed completely in Spain, but now, in this awful climate, under the family's pressure, it struck again, much worse than ever before.

The medicine the doctor prescribed had an almost immediate effect, but the relief lasted only as long as she continued taking the draughts. In truth she was grateful for Miss Godwin's skills and patience. The children accepted their nurse and Miss Godwin seemed willing to take any amount of trouble to care for them.

It seemed odd at first to sleep in a separate room to the twins, but whenever she visited them during the night they were always sleeping well, which was something they had not done when they all slept in the same room. They began to grow faster, if they did look pale and at times even a little jaundiced. Sometimes they seemed to be too calm, especially during the days. They were losing their natural liveliness, not showing much interest in what was happening around them, but, Miss Godwin assured her, that was a natural part of their development.

During October Hubert announced that they were all to spend a month in London at the house in Leinster Place. The house had nothing but bad memories; it was where Hubert had first beaten her and where his grandfather had died, but at least it meant she could spend some time away from his overbearing parents.

They arrived on the first day of November. London was at its worst, cold, wet, and blanketed with fog. She had supplies of her medicine and Miss Godwin travelled with all the items the children needed for their welfare.

They had been at the house for three days when Miss Godwin came to her room as she was dressing for breakfast.

She looked awful. 'Excuse me, madam, but I think that I may have contracted influenza. May I ask you to look after the children. I don't wish to infect them. Influenza can be very dangerous at their ages.'

'Of course, Miss Godwin. Go back to bed and don't worry about the children. I'll send some food and medicines to your room, and I'll take care of the children until you feel better.'

It seemed to be a wonderful opportunity to enjoy herself, but she was surprised how much more tiring the children had become to care for even though they were lethargic in themselves. Fortunately Mrs Carter, the housekeeper, was happy to help and between them they washed and dressed the children immediately after breakfast, and after Hubert had left for the City office.

'The fog's rising, madam.' Mrs Carter nodded towards

the window. 'You've all been cooped up here for three days, why don't you wrap yourself and the babies up well and take them for a walk in Kensington Gardens or Hyde Park. It's lovely there, even at this time of year.'

'That's a wonderful idea, Mrs Carter. Will you make sure someone takes care of Miss Godwin while I'm out?'

Once everything was arranged it seemed sensible to take a draught of medicine before going out. For months she had hardly walked more than twenty yards; a long walk in the cold air and pushing the heavy pram might be enough exertion to bring on another attack and she could not afford to be taken ill while she was entrusted with the babies.

Mrs Carter was right, the park was wonderful. So was the sense of freedom, of not being watched; the feeling of being out alone with the babies.

The further she walked the more relaxed she felt, and she was glad she had taken the medicine to give her strength. The morning began to take on a dreamlike quality; silver dew-covered grass, silver bark trees still covered with yellow leaves, the thin golden sunshine which was not warm but which was bright and cheerful. Everything was so quiet, except for the quacking of ducks in a lake.

Ducks. The children might enjoy seeing the ducks waddling about beside the lake. She turned the pram off the path and across the grass, heading down a slope towards the water. The grass was slippery and the slope seemed to grow steeper. The pram was heavy and it pulled her forward, faster and faster until she could hardly keep her feet on the wet grass.

She stumbled, put out a hand to stop herself falling, slipped again and felt the pram open the fingers on her other hand and pull away. It was running away on its own, jolting faster and faster down the slope. She ran after it, stumbling on the slippery grass, sinking into the soft ground. The pram rolled further away, faster and faster. It was moving faster than she could run, bouncing but heading directly for the lake. The lake looked enormous. And close. Too close!

'Help! Help me!' A twig caught between her feet, the ground rose up and she was breathless, scrabbling to get upright.

The pram bounced again. It seemed to hang over the water. Silence. Even then the babies did not cry. Then nothing.

'Here, miss. Let me help you.' A man was hauling her to her feet.

'My babies! My children!'

'They're all right, miss. Mrs. Someone stopped the pram before it reached the lake. There, look.'

She looked. A well-dressed middle-aged man was wheeling the pram back across the grass towards her. She waited until he brought it to her then almost pushed him aside in her eagerness to see if the babies had been harmed. They were still asleep, but the man clutched her arm and held her for a moment, sniffing as if he had a cold or did not approve of her, then released her.

'Thank you, sir. Thank you so much.' She pulled her arm away. 'They might've drowned if you hadn't stopped them.'

'They might well have done,' the man answered sharply. 'And then what would you have told your mistress?'

'My mistress?' Confused for a moment, then she understood. 'I'm not the babies' nurse, I'm their mother.'

'Then you should be doubly ashamed of yourself. You're not fit to take care of children, madam. Not in your condition.'

'My condition?' She frowned and watched the man who had helped her to stand up walk away, then realised what the well-dressed man meant. 'I'm sorry, I understand what you mean. I suffer from asthma and that's why I couldn't catch the pram when it ran away.'

'Asthma? Ask yourself why the pram ran away from

you, madam. What were you thinking of, bringing it down a slope like that? You should have realised you could never hold it.'

She looked back at the slope. It was much steeper than she had thought and now she realised how stupid she had been, but before she could say anything the man started to berate her again.

'As I said, madam, in your condition you're not fit to take care of children. Opium is not something you should indulge in.'

'Opium?'

'I'm a doctor of medicine, madam, and it's obvious to me that you use opium quite regularly. Possibly you're addicted to it.'

'I'm sorry, sir, and I thank you for saving my children, but you are being quite ridiculous. I've never taken opium in my life. The only drug I take is the medicine prescribed to me by my own doctor in Dorset. Why should I use opium? It's a filthy habit.'

'It's one which many people indulge in, madam, and I can assure you that you are taking a strong opiate, even though you may not realise it.'

A frightening thought began to develop, and she needed this doctor's opinion in order to think about the new fear.

'I'm already obliged to you, sir, but could I ask for your help?'

'Certainly.'

'Perhaps you'd accompany me home in case I have another accident, and perhaps you could give me your opinion of the medicine which has been prescribed for me and my babies.'

The doctor frowned. 'Obviously, as I'm not your physician I can't offer you advice upon your treatment, but if I may inspect your medicine I may be able to advise you if I feel the chemist has committed an error when compiling the draught.'

* * *

'That is an extremely powerful opiate.' The doctor smelled the contents of the bottle she offered him. 'What effect does it have on you?'

She explained how she felt when she took the medicine.

'It's an opiate, and a strong mixture. That won't help your asthma other than to make you relax and send you to sleep. May I see the mixture that the nurse gives your babies?'

He smelled and tasted samples from each bottle.

'Yes, that also, although there's nothing unusual about that. Half the mothers in this country pour opium down their babies' throats without even realising it. I suggest you ask your physician why he has prescribed such a powerful dosage, and if you are not satisfied ask for another opinion.'

'But my doctor is in Dorset, sir, and I'm not due to return for three weeks or more.'

'There are certain ethical considerations, madam, but are you asking me for an opinion as the only expert medical advisor you can consult at this moment?'

'Yes.'

'It is important that you understand I cannot ethically give you unwarranted advice, and that without knowing your full medical history it would be irresponsible for me to prescribe treatment for you?'

'Of course.'

'In my opinion the amount of opiate your children are consuming isn't excessive, but you are taking an amount which will cause addiction, if it hasn't already. I again recommend you to obtain further independent advice.'

It was obvious that the doctor did not want to break the rules of his profession, and it was clear that he thought she should stop taking the medicine immediately.

'You're very restless this evening, Rose. You're probably over-tired. I suggest that instead of pacing around down here you go to bed.'

'Yes, Hubert.' He was right, but when he spoke he did not bother to look up from his newspaper and it was obvious that he was more concerned with his own peace than her comfort.

'Take an extra draught of your medicine. That should settle you.'

'Goodnight.' Said because he would expect some response and this was not the time to talk about the prescription.

She checked that the babies were happy, then asked Miss Godwin if she needed anything, and finally undressed, washed and crawled into bed.

Sleep did not come. Her mind was too busy trying to organise a jumble of thoughts and ideas, and fears. The downstairs clock chimed the quarters from ten through to twelve thirty, and the restlessness that Hubert had complained about began to build on itself. The bottle of medicine sat on the window table, lit by moonlight, offering peace, threatening the opposite.

The doctor who had helped her had implied that the family doctor was a country quack who had made a mistake; but was there something more sinister in over-prescribing the medicine? Hubert's mother had already accused her of being incapable of leading her own life and incompetent as regards the children; and a nurse had been introduced against her wishes. Were Hubert and his mother planning to prove she was an unsuitable mother by turning her into an opium addict?

She climbed out of bed, walked to the open window and stared down into the street below. The fresh air seemed to wash away the jumbled thoughts and she tried to reassure herself. 'Rose, you're being ridiculous.'

'And what are you being ridiculous about?'

She spun around. Hubert was standing by the open door; open because the babies were in the room opposite and both doors were left open so she could hear them if they woke.

'Being ridiculous about what, Rose?'

'Nothing, Hubert. I'm just restless, that's all.' It was humiliating to be found talking to herself, and perhaps incriminating if Hubert was trying to prove her incompetence.

'Have you taken your medicine?' He shut the door and came towards her.

'Yes, Hubert. Of course.' Better to lie than try to explain.

'Well, it seems ineffective. Let me pour you some more.'

'There's no need, Hubert.'

'But I insist. We can't afford to have you tired now that Miss Godwin's been taken ill.' He walked across to the table, picked up the bottle and stared at it. 'Are you sure you've taken medicine tonight?'

'Of course.'

He glanced into the empty waste bin under the table, then walked quickly into the adjoining dressing room and through to the bathroom.

'What are you looking for, Hubert?'

'The bottle you used earlier.'

'But you have it in your hand, Hubert.' Impatience showing, the only reliable way to counter his bullying and arrogance.

'I don't think so, Rose. This bottle has been opened, the paper seal's broken, but the medicine still reaches almost up to the cork. You haven't taken any medicine from this bottle and there are no other empty bottles around.' There was pleasure in his voice, obviously because he had proved the lie. 'How are you ever going to get better if you don't take the medicine?'

'I won't get any better even if I do. It's an opiate and it's too strong.' The words flowed, too fast, too carelessly.

'Is that your informed opinion, Rose, or have you taken medical advice?'

He had her trapped. She was not qualified to give an informed opinion, and if she admitted she had taken advice from a doctor whose name she did not even know she would have to admit to nearly having an accident with the children.

'You haven't answered, Rose.'

'I simply know that it's not helping to improve my health.'

'But it helps you to sleep and you haven't had any further attacks since you started the treatment so how can you claim that?'

'I just know, Hubert. Can't we leave it at that?'

'No, you're being hysterical. I've been reading about hysteria in women and I really think we must find you some suitable treatment. Somewhere pleasant of course, in the country, or perhaps even in Europe where they're far more advanced than we are here. After all, we have Miss Godwin to take care of the children for you.'

'No, Hubert. There's nothing wrong with me and you can't send me away. Not like that.'

'Then take your medicine and perhaps you'll get better and won't have to be sent away. Don't be difficult, Rose. I can't accept or condone your tantrums and childish complaints.' He poured half a glass of the brown medicine. 'Here, drink this.'

'No, Hubert, I won't.'

'Drink it!' Thrusting the glass towards her.

'No, I won't.' Her hand slapped his wrist and knocked the glass on to the floor but the contents stained the front of his jacket.

'You bitch! You ungrateful whoring little bitch!'

She saw his fist but could not avoid it and felt her left eyebrow split as his heavy signet ring tore across it. The power of the blow seemed to come a moment later, throwing her sideways against the brass frame at the foot of the bed. The next punch hit her cheekbone and smashed the other side of her head against a large brass bedknob.

Then he was pulling her hair, slapping her face, punching, kicking, thrusting his knee up into her stomach and chest and finally, when she fell, she saw him jump towards her. She rolled. Instead of coming down on her ribs one of his feet missed completely and the other landed between her ribs and her hip.

She caught her breath, too winded to scream with the pain, then suddenly her ear burned, her head snapped forwards; then nothing.

Later a sensation of something cold in her mouth, being made to drink, then everything seemed to go limp and warm and after a long while there was the impression first of being carried, then of falling, almost flying.

Stairs, banisters, paintings, carpet raced past. Then there was peace on the carpet. Time to sleep. Not restless any more.

It was cold. She shivered, and felt sick, and before she could move the vomit rose and rose again, and again.

Now she was cold and sweating, not sure where she was, what had happened; but then in the moonlight she saw the flight of stairs and blood-smeared wallpaper and one thought became clear. She had to get away before Hubert drove her mad or killed her. And she had to go now.

CHAPTER 40

It was raining and almost dark. A train rattled on the lines above her head and as Elizabeth pulled her collar up against the cold the wind sucked smoke down into her face and made her cough. 'This is a foul little backwater, Ada.'

'No worse than many, Lizzie.'

That was true, but this street always seemed darker and more dangerous than most. Its railway, its arches, a public house which had half burned down and was still boarded over, its puddle-covered tarred block road, and the stinking match factory opposite blackened houses; it had the feel and the sulphurous smell of hell. If the railway had followed a straight course this street would have been demolished, but the match factory saved it and instead the railway crossed the street and curved around the backs of the houses opposite the factory, through what had once been courtyards and a mews and stables.

'I think it's that house over there,' nodding across the street to a four-storey house with a half basement below and attic rooms in the roof, six floors all together. 'I've been here before. It's an overcrowded, filthy hole.'

Suddenly all the filth and meanness seemed personal, now that she had a personal reason to be here.

'Come on, Lizzie.' Ada stepped into the road and she followed, eager to finish with all this. 'Room on the fourth floor, at the back, wasn't it?'

The moment they opened the front door the stench grabbed her throat until she held a scented handkerchief over her mouth and nose. She passed a spare to Ada.

She found the small room she was looking for. It was more a large cupboard than a room and had probably once been used to store bedlinen. Its door had no lock and was half off its hinges. She pushed it and peered in.

The room had no fireplace and it was damp. A tiny single pane window rattled against its rotting frame and let in rain. The window glass was covered in soot from the trains which passed immediately behind the house. There was no means of lighting the room other than a candle which stood in a saucer on the floor.

The floor was bare boards and the walls had once been papered but the paper had rotted and given over to a green-coloured slime. Somehow a colony of big black flies had survived the cold and clung to one of the walls. They moved constantly, climbing over one another but never falling to the floor, never trying to fly.

One chair furnished the room. It had a padded back and seat which were hinged so the back could be reclined for sleeping. It had one wooden arm, the other had broken off.

There were two grey buckets; one was half filled with clean water and the other was used as a lavatory.

She saw all this before she saw the woman sitting on the floor behind the door, a child held close in the crook of each arm. The woman rocked backwards and forwards, crying silently, and did not seem to know there was anyone else there.

'Rose?' There was no response.

She did not look like Rose, she did not look completely human, but whoever she was she did not deserve to be left in conditions like these.

'Come on, I'm taking you away from here.'

No resistance. The woman was totally passive.

'Let me take your babies.'

Now there was a reaction. The woman stopped crying and clawed her children closer to her.

'Let me take your babies so you can get up.' Best to explain so she would not be frightened.

The woman's face came up, smashed and crusty with dried black blood, lips broken and running with sores, eyes bloodshot with pinhead pupils. A mixture of a hiss and growl came through lips that did not move, and the children were held even tighter.

But there was something in the sound, and the way the woman moved.

'Rose. Is it you, Rose?'

A grunted, animal-like response.

'It's Elizabeth, Rose. Is that you?' Fingering the woman under the chin to lift her face higher.

'I'll light the candle.' Ada crouched down, lit the candle and passed it to her.

She took it, held it to the side of the woman's face. 'It's Elizabeth, Rose. Edward's sister.'

A flicker in the eyes, the faintest reflection of green.

'It's her, I'm sure of it, Ada.' She handed her the candle, put her arms around the bag of bones on the floor, and lifted both her and the children until the woman was on her feet. 'Rose, I'm taking you home with me. Where you'll be safe. Where Hubert can't find you, ever.'

The bus dropped them outside the Angel Inn and she could feel the angel watching her as she passed the children to Ada and helped Rose down from the platform.

She left Ada to carry the children while she supported Rose who could hardly walk and hung around her waist, stumbling, half crawling alongside her until they reached

Number Fourteen. It was dark and raining and the street was deserted, but for a moment she felt her life was complete, fulfilled, and that she was surrounded by all the friends she had ever known.

'Angel?' She glanced along the street to where the angel sat in its niche and it seemed to send back a message; everything's going to be all right, Lizzie.

She left Ada to care for the children. Apart from being hungry and dirty they did not seem to have suffered, and safe in Ada's arms they were asleep within minutes of being cleaned and fed.

But Rose was a different matter. It took two hours to take off or cut off her clothes and clean the cuts and grazes that covered her, and then to bath and delouse her. And all the time Rose simply stood or sat or lay down, skin and bones, totally passive, not speaking, but looking grateful for everything that was being done for her. Once her hair had been washed and dried, then carefully brushed, she began to look human again, but beyond an expression in her grateful eyes there was no response.

She had put Rose in Evie's old room and sat with her until she had gone to sleep. Rose slept fitfully at first, threshing about and murmuring, suddenly waking, eyes wide open, but she relaxed gradually and after an hour or so she was sleeping so deeply it seemed safe to leave her alone and go back downstairs.

Ada had taken Rose's babies next door where she could care for all the children under one roof.

The house was quiet and after all the worry and excitement a wave of weariness seemed to well over her. She was halfway up the stairs on her way to bed when someone knocked at the front door.

'Who is it?' She was not expecting anyone, especially at this time of night.

'It's Mr Speedwell, Miss Forrester. I was wondering if you'd found Mrs Belchester all right.'

She opened the door and took him into the front

parlour. 'Yes, you were right. It was her, but God knows what her husband's done to her.'

'I don't think God's got much to do with it, Miss Forrester. More like the devil, I reckon.'

'Perhaps you're right, but anyway I must thank you again for going to all the trouble of finding me and letting me know about her. I'll always be grateful to you, Mr Speedwell.'

'No, miss, there's no need to thank me. As I said earlier, it wasn't until I was sitting in the courtroom at your brother's trial that I realised what I'd done, and I'm just glad I had a chance to put things right. Well, as much as I can, anyway.' He looked embarrassed. 'I don't mind taking money from the likes of Belchester, and I'm going to make him pay well this time too, but it was the way he came and told me Mrs Belchester had left him again, the way he just assumed I'd work for him even after he crossed me up last time. I'd pretty much decided what I was going to do even before I found Mrs Belchester, but when I saw her, or what I thought was her, well that just did it for me, miss. Anyway, you look worn out so I won't keep you up, but I will keep in touch, if you don't mind.'

She wished him goodnight and shut the door after him. He did seem to care about Rose, and about what he had done to Edward. She had felt violently angry earlier that day when he first called and told her how he was responsible for Edward going to prison, but now she felt grateful to him for telling her where Rose was, and even a little sorry for him. He was simply another person caught up in Edward and Rose's affair. Simply another casualty.

She bolted the door, checked that Rose was still sleeping, and went to bed.

The crash and scream woke her instantly.

She did not bother to wrap herself in anything or put slippers on her feet, simply dashed for the door and ran downstairs to Rose's room.

'Rose! What are you doing?'

Rose was looking into wardrobes and throwing out whatever she found.

'My clothes! My clothes, where are they?'

'Rose! You're safe. You're in my house. Elizabeth. Elizabeth Forrester.' She turned and lit an oil lamp so Rose could see her in the darkness. 'We found you. Don't you remember? Ada and I?'

'Elizabeth? And Ada? Ada Cox?' Her voice was broken and weak.

'Yes, Rose. Go back to bed. You're quite safe. Hubert can't get at you here,' leading her towards the bed.

'You know about Hubert?'

'We've guessed that he's been hurting you, but you're safe now.'

Sudden panic. 'My babies! Where are my babies?'

'Safe with Ada in the house next door. That's where she lives now that she's married. She'll take care of your children until you're stronger, then we'll bring them here for you, but you can see them any time, Rose.' She tucked her under the blankets, wrapped a spare around herself and sat in Evie's old cane chair. 'I'll stay here, Rose, don't worry abut anything. You and your children are safe now.'

'Elizabeth, can we talk?'

The question brought her out from her doze. 'Of course.'

It was still dark, still early in the morning. Rose had hardly said anything until then, but once she started she did not seem able to stop. The revelations of all that Hubert and his parents had done poured out of her like a feverish sweat. The more Rose revealed the more like herself she became, but not totally her old self. She spoke quickly, in bursts, then fell into long silences when she seemed to be trying to build up the courage to remember and speak again. Her eyes never settled, always flitting around the room, alighting here then there, never resting, always avoiding direct glances, the possibility of contact.

It was as if she wanted to pretend she was alone, talking out loud to herself. There was no value in talking back to her; she did not hear, or chose not to hear. It was best simply to let her talk, not to comment, not to interrupt, and not try to shorten the silences.

Then suddenly, at half past five in the morning: 'Elizabeth, I'm sorry about Edward. Dreadfully sorry.'

'Not your fault, Rose. You mustn't blame yourself.'

'The babies are his, Elizabeth. They're older than they look, eighteen months. The twins are his.'

'Are you sure?' Of all the shocks and surprises this was the most unexpected and the happiest. 'Did he know you were expecting his child, children?'

'No, I didn't tell him,' and gradually the rest of the story unravelled, piece by piece and not always in order, but complete by the time pale light shone against the thin bedroom curtains.

What Rose told her filled in the gaps left by Edward, Ada and Clarence Speedwell, and left her feeling exhausted.

'I must go to sleep, Rose, and I think you should, too. We'll talk again, later, when we've both had some rest. It's Sunday today so there'll be plenty of time.'

And as Rose nodded, already slipping asleep, she went upstairs to her own room.

Next door Ada was beginning to wake up her brood ready for breakfast and the first service in the church at the end of the road, and Jack was looking at Rose's two children and thinking it might be time for him and Ada to add to the family they already had.

Rose could not sleep for long. Restlessness, excitement and fear prodded her mind awake even though her body felt limp and lifeless. The restlessness could have been overcome by the medicine, but she had deliberately left that behind when she left Hubert; and the excitement was uncontrollable, as was the fear. Not only fear that Hubert might still find her, fear this was a dream. Fear that it would end.

Elizabeth, and Ada, living next door to each other, taking care of her and the children. It could not be true. It could not. It was one of her dreams. Sometimes they were so vivid they seemed real. This was one of them.

She knew she had to break it, had to wake up and move about the room. She swung her legs out of the bed. The rug felt real. She rubbed her eyes, drank water from a jug and glass beside the bed. It tasted cold, reviving. Splashed water on to her face, felt it running down her cheeks. The water felt real, too.

Perhaps this was not a dream. A test would be to look out of the window, to see what was outside the room. If it was an ordinary street, then perhaps this was not a dream.

She crossed the room and pulled back the curtains but kept her eyes shut. If this was a dream she wanted it to last for as long as possible. The reality might be too hard to face.

But she had to know; whatever the truth was. She took a deep breath, and opened her eyes.

It was an ordinary street. There were people walking along the pavement, going to church. Ordinary people, families, just walking and talking as though everything was normal.

It must be wonderful to lead a normal life, to forget princes and castles, to forget romantic dreams that can never come true; just be normal, a part of an ordinary family which does ordinary things like walking to church on Sunday and singing hymns, and perhaps walking in a park and watching the children run and play. To be free.

It must be wonderful to be ordinary, to be satisfied with life, not always striving for something that can never be.

That had been the best part of living with Edward in Mrs Crow's house; being ordinary. A housewife with no servants to distort reality.

The exhaustion came suddenly, similar to the feeling at the end of a hard-run race, but more so. Legs weak, she staggered back to bed, careful not to make a noise which might disturb Elizabeth.

The bed was firm and comfortable. It was dry and the sheets felt crisp. And there was still warmth from where she had lain before.

She snuggled down and as sleep slipped over her there was the sound of hymns being sung, ordinary people singing hymns as they always did on Sunday mornings.

'Rose?' A knock on the bedroom door. 'Are you awake?'

'Yes, come in, please.'

It was Elizabeth, carrying a tray with tea things and a plate of thinly sliced bread. 'I thought I heard you moving about.'

'Thank you. What time is it?'

'Evening. Almost eight o'clock.'

'The babies!' Sudden fear that they were hungry.

'Over there.' Elizabeth nodded towards too deep drawers lined with blankets. 'Jack, Ada's husband, made them up. He'll make something better when he gets time, but we thought they'd be better in here with you. We've fed them and washed them, and they're quite happy. What do you call them?'

'I'm going to call them James and Helen.' They looked comfortable and were sleeping quite happily.

'You are going to call them?' There was a query in Elizabeth's words. 'Don't they already have names?'

'Yes, but names Hubert gave them. I'm going to call them James and Helen because they're Edward's children and that's what he wanted to call our first son and our first daughter, if we had both.'

She saw Elizabeth's expression change, and guessed what she was going to say. 'Rose, we need to talk about Edward, when you feel strong enough.'

'Of course, but not yet, Elizabeth, please.'

'Don't worry Rose, I do understand.' Elizabeth smiled and made her feel safe again. 'But somehow we've got to let him know you're here, and he's got a son and daughter.'

What was Elizabeth thinking of? Edward was dead, Hubert had said so.

'I don't understand, Elizabeth. What do you mean?'

'We've got to let him know but I'm not sure how, not unless we ask the governor to tell him. I kept writing to Edward but he always refused to read my letters and the prison governor sent them back to me. I stopped writing about a year ago, to Edward anyway although I still write to the governor and he writes back to tell me how Edward is. That's all I can do, you see? He is well, physically, but . . .'

'He's well?' Elizabeth was not making sense.

'Yes, according to the last letter. You can read it later.' Elizabeth's expression changed once again. 'What's wrong?'

'Hubert told me he was dead.'

'Good God, Rose! No! He was very ill a year ago, but he's alive and well. So the governor tells me, and I've no reason to doubt him. He seems to have taken quite a liking to Edward, for some reason.'

'But Hubert told me he'd had an accident and the wound had poisoned him and he had died.'

'Hubert seems to know some of it, somehow, but Edward's alive.'

'Thank God.' He was alive; alive!

'Well, yes, he's certainly alive, Rose, though in some ways he might as well be dead.'

That was a shocking thing to say. 'Elizabeth! What do you mean?'

'He wants me to treat him as if he is dead, Rose. He forced me to promise him that. But now you're here we might be able to make him change his mind.'

'Perhaps.' This, on top of everything else, was too much to believe. 'I need to think, Elizabeth. Do you mind?'

'Of course not, but I'll bring you the latest letter to read. Perhaps then you'll really believe that Hubert lied to you.'

The letter proved Edward was alive. She was not living in a dream, but the nightmare she had lived in was over. So much had changed so quickly it was difficult to think; but it was easy to sleep, so easy to fall asleep and not be scared any more. So easy that she forgot how much she missed not having the medicine to quell her restlessness.

'It's strange, Elizabeth' – they were washing the dinner things in the scullery sink – 'but I feel as though my life only really began when you brought me here. But I don't want to be a burden on you. You mustn't let me stay too long. I'll find somewhere to live as soon as I can find work of some sort.'

'I was hoping you'd stay here, Rose, at least for a while. I know this isn't the sort of house you're used to but . . .'

'It's a wonderful house, Elizabeth. I know you'll think I'm being silly, but I can feel something in this house, something special. I've been wandering around it this past week or so, just touching things, the furniture and silly things like the doorknobs. It's real. It sounds real, smells real. It's the loveliest house I've ever lived in.'

'Then stay, Rose, stay. It's far too big for me on my own, and since Evie died and Ada moved out I've sometimes felt quite lonely here. Even though Ada and Jack are only next door and always make me welcome I sometimes feel I'm intruding when I go in there. Look.' Elizabeth took hold of her arm. 'You're tired. You've done too much too soon, so leave what's left and come into the kitchen and sit down so we can talk properly.'

Elizabeth led the way to the kitchen and opened up the range to boil a kettle for tea. They sat in the two easy chairs beside the range. It was a warm, cosy room, ordinary, filled with domesticity; intimate and safe.

It should have seemed strange staying in Elizabeth's home; a complete reversal of the situation in the manor when Elizabeth had come to stay. It should have seemed strange but it did not; perhaps because they had both been affected by all that had happened, perhaps because they both loved Edward. But there seemed to be even more than that, a sense of sharing, of belonging to each other in a way that was impossible to understand. It was almost as if Elizabeth were her older sister.

'A lot's happened to you, Rose, that people don't know about,' Elizabeth started hesitantly, 'but there's an awful lot you don't know about, too. You don't know how many lies Hubert told about you, how he turned your family against you so it seemed you were rejecting them. You don't know how much Lillian and her father have changed John, or how the Belchesters and McDougalls have taken almost everything which belonged to your family. Most important, you don't know how happy Catherine will be when she knows you're here. I've already written to her but I've asked her not to tell John in case the news finds its way back to Hubert's family.'

Rose knew she could trust Elizabeth implicitly but what she was saying sounded so strange, so different to the truths she thought she understood.

'You mustn't think you're a prisoner here, Rose, but you must be careful not to do anything which may help Hubert find you.' Elizabeth sat back and smiled. 'It's quite safe to tell Catherine, she's been wonderful. I've been so lucky, and it's all due to Catherine. She paid Edward's legal costs and stood by me all through the trial. If it wasn't for her I wouldn't have met Evie Roper who took care of me as if I was her daughter, and left me this house when she died. And, of course, Catherine found me my job, which I love.'

'It sounds like the ideal life for you, Elizabeth. You're obviously happy.'

'Happy? No, you can't do what I do and be happy, exactly. Too much misery rubs off, but I suppose I'm content with my life. I get lonely in the evenings when I come home and there's no one to talk to, no one to tell how frustrating the day's been or how sad something's made

me or even how happy I feel when something's gone right.
Sometimes I just sit in this chair and talk to the one you're
sitting in. Daft isn't it?'

'No, I think I understand how you feel.' It seemed that
for most of her life she had been surrounded by people but
still felt lonely. 'I've learned that it's not the number of
people that matter, Elizabeth, it's having the right people
to talk to. That's what matters.'

Elizabeth nodded. 'I suppose you're right. I've never
found the right person. I always knew Saul Beckett wasn't
the right man for me, but I nearly married him just because
he asked me.'

'And John?' The question slipped out quite innocently,
not as an accusation, simply as a question, but it was too
late to stop it.

'I wondered when you'd ask why I . . .' Elizabeth looked
embarrassed.

'I'm sorry, Elizabeth. It's none of my business and I
didn't mean to sound as if I were blaming you. It's just that
you seemed so much in love with him.'

'I thought I was, and in a way I do still love him, but not
enough to marry him. John was fun, exciting, even after
the accident, but there were reasons why I couldn't marry
him. Good reasons, Rose, you must believe that, and if I
had married him it would have been for the wrong reasons
and sooner or later I would have made him very unhappy.
It was tempting to ignore them, but I couldn't, not when it
came to it. You've seen the sort of life I enjoy. Could you
really imagine me settling down as lady of the manor in
Pincote?'

Rose looked into Elizabeth's eyes, and although her
friend did not look away she knew there were shutters
being drawn, secrets being hidden, but best to respect
Elizabeth's privacy and agree with the obvious statement.
'No, Elizabeth, I don't think you're exactly the sort who
could happily play lady of the manor. John told me, once,
how you and he argued about the rights and wrongs of

living in the manor when whole families were crammed into those little cottages like the one you grew up in. I don't think you would ever have been happy with the Laybourne life, not really.'

'So you understand why I had to leave the way I did?'

'Of course I do, Elizabeth, just as I think you understand why I did most of the things I did.' It seemed to be important that they both agreed they had made mistakes and that the past had to be forgiven; and as Elizabeth nodded and smiled it seemed that the slight tension which had existed, barely noticeable though it was, evaporated.

'Will you stay here, Rose? Make this your proper home. You and Helen and James?'

'Do you really want us to? It won't be easy, Elizabeth, not bringing up two children, and I don't know what your neighbours'll say.'

'I want you to stay, Rose. You're the nearest I have to a family, now, and it'd be wonderful if you could bring up the children under this roof.'

Yes, it would; Elizabeth was the nearest she had to a family, now, but there were practical considerations. 'I'd love to stay, Elizabeth, but I must find work of some sort. I can't be a burden on you, especially with the children.'

'I'm sure we can sort something out, Rose, but there are two more important things to agree on.' Elizabeth kept her waiting while she poured two cups of tea. 'Firstly, all my closest friends call me Lizzie, so I hope you will. Secondly, there's something I must tell you about Edward and your father. Something you don't know, but you should know about even though it's going to hurt you.'

'What?' Her hands were trembling so much she could not hold the cup and saucer Elizabeth handed her. 'What's wrong?'

'This is very difficult, Rose. Very, very difficult, because it's about your father, it's personal, and it affects everything that's happened. Even why Edward's in prison, and I'm not sure how to tell you or whether you're ready to hear it.'

What was she going to say? What could be so terrible that Elizabeth, always so practical and forthright, found it difficult to talk about?

'Please tell me, Elizabeth, Lizzie. If it concerns Edward I need to know about it, especially if it can help me to help him.' If Elizabeth had asked if she was scared she would have admitted she was, but nothing Elizabeth could tell her would hurt as much as all that had already happened. 'Please, Lizzie, tell me whatever it is.'

'Are you sure you want to talk about this now, Rose? It's your father's death we're discussing, and how Edward killed him.'

'Please.' Sipping tea to steady her nerves.

'Edward threatened to kill your father when the mine collapsed, but he made the threat in the heat of the moment. Later, he only went to the manor because he'd heard a mob was going to set fire to it and he knew I might be there. The house was already on fire when he arrived but when he came to look for me he found your father, well, hurting me, and there was a fight. Your father ran downstairs and tried to lock us in so we'd burn. Edward saved us but your father tried to stop him and that's when Edward hit him, but it was self-defence, not murder. I think your father had gone mad, Rose, I'm sure he had. Edward left your father where he fell on the landing, but the police statement says that Edward tried to move him into the fire. That's why he was found guilty of murder, because he supposedly tried to hide your father's body. But he didn't, Rose. I was there and saw everything, and if we can find the policeman who found the body and persuade him to tell the truth we may be able to get Edward released.'

It was not as shocking as Elizabeth had made out. Edward had always refused to discuss what had happened, saying it was all in the past. Now it was clear why. But there were still questions to ask, and now seemed to be the time to ask them.

'Lizzie, you said my father was hurting you. Did he try

to rape you?' The stunned look on Elizabeth's face was enough of an answer. 'I think that perhaps he had done that before. Perhaps he was mad, mad at times, possibly. I think that was why Miss Smith warned me to leave, perhaps why Catherine was sent away when she became a young woman, why, maybe, he wanted me to leave. Perhaps he felt he couldn't trust himself with me. I know he stopped cuddling me when I started to grow, and he used to get more angry with me after I changed than he ever did before. What do you think?'

Elizabeth was nodding her head. It was time to ask something else.

'Lizzie, you said something about finding a policeman? How can that help now Edward's been convicted?'

'The officer who found your father's body, a man called McClusky, has resigned from the police and left the country, but we're sure he left to join a police force in another country. The police said they couldn't find him and did not even know what country he had gone to, but by simply asking his old neighbours I found out that he's gone to America. Mr Joseph, the barrister who defended Edward, believes that the police didn't really try to find the officer because they thought he might change his statement. If we can find him and persuade him to tell the truth which is that Edward did not move your father, Mr Joseph feels that the court will overturn the guilty verdict and Edward will be freed. But first we've got to find him, and America's a big country.'

'I believe you, Lizzie, but I can't understand why the police would lie.' It did not seem to make sense.

'Mr Joseph thinks it's because Edward humiliated them, Rose. He didn't mean to, but he walked into a house which was surrounded by dozens of policemen sent there specifically to keep him out. Apparently the newspapers made a great deal of the police force's incompetence. Maybe, because Edward was supposedly dead and would never be brought to trial, the police thought they could save face by concocting evidence which would make it look as though he wasn't just an ordinary miner who'd made a threat, but was capable of planning and executing an almost perfect murder. The newspapers certainly liked the idea, and the natural justice which had Edward blown up by one of the charges he himself suggested should be laid.'

It made more sense now that Elizabeth had explained, and it seemed that finding the missing policeman was Edward's only hope.

'Your brothers, Lizzie?' The family seemed the obvious people to ask for help.

'They've been trying ever since Edward was sentenced, but they're no further forward and it's difficult because they've no contacts. Besides, who's going to bother with a couple of foreign railwaymen who're trying to free a brother imprisoned for murder in another country?'

'The Parkers might be able to help. They're Americans, and I should think they've lots of contacts all over the country. They're very kind, too, and they met Edward. I'd have to write and tell them the truth, of course, because I told them a pack of lies before, but I'm sure they'd understand, Lizzie. I'm sure they'd help. Sure of it!' Suddenly anything seemed possible; everything seemed possible.

'Can you remember their address?' Elizabeth asked, and even she seemed brighter.

'No, but I know who we can ask.' A shadow passed as she remembered the way Hubert had enjoyed taunting her, saying that if she had not encouraged Matthew Parker to fall in love with her Clarence Speedwell could never have traced her and Edward. 'Mr Speedwell, Lizzie. He helped you to find me, and he knows the Parkers' address.'

'Good. I'll try to ask him tomorrow, then you can write to your Mr Parker while I write to Mr Hampton, the prison governor, and ask him to tell Edward about you and the children.'

'No. Please don't do that.'

'But why not, Rose? It's just the sort of news which might make Edward see sense. Give him some purpose.'

'No, Lizzie. I've thought it out very carefully and it's better that Edward doesn't know about me or the children until he's free. Knowing we're here will only make him feel worse if he wants to be with us, and if he doesn't then it'll just make him feel more guilty than ever. It'll just pile up the blame he's already putting on himself, you see?' It was important that Elizabeth did understand.

'But, Rose, don't you think he deserves to know? That he has a right to make his own decisions? He may be in prison for most of his life, if we can't get him released. Don't you think he has the right to know you're here, and that he has a son and daughter?'

'Of course, if he has to stay locked up for a long time. But, Lizzie, if we can find the evidence we need to free him I want him to have total freedom. I don't want him to come back to me because he thinks he should, that it's his duty because of the children. I want him to be happy, and if he comes back I want it to be because he wants to, really wants to. I've had one false marriage. I don't want another. I'd rather stay on my own all my life, but I'll always wait for Edward because I think that one day he will come back to me. There's a part of me in him, and a part of him in me, little magnets which will always bring us together, just as they did before.'

'I hope you're right, Rose.' Elizabeth looked sad, on the verge of tears.

'The Princess and the Pauper, Lizzie. Do you remember Edward's story?'

'Oh yes, I seem to remember that's how this whole business started.'

'It was, and it's how it'll finish. I'm not a princess, not any more, and that's why it will work, Lizzie. You'll see. The children have made us parts of the same family. He'll come back. He will, and then we'll live happily ever after, just like the story.'

'It might be just a dream, Rose.'

'But dreams are important, Lizzie. I've lived without one and I know how hard it is.' It was difficult to explain why she felt so certain that Edward would come back, but it was important that Lizzie understood her reasons. 'I've never believed that Edward murdered my father. I couldn't have loved him if he had and even though he and I never discussed the details of what happened that night I always believed he was innocent. You've told me I was right to feel that. Mr Speedwell took trouble to find you and tell you where I was and you came for me. You found Ada. Constable McClusky went to America and I made friends with an American family just before I found Edward.'

'Yes, Rose, but . . .'

'One moment, Lizzie.' She wanted Lizzie to hear the full explanation. 'There must be a purpose to all that, Lizzie. I've changed tremendously from the girl who dreamed about meeting her lover on King's Crag, and Edward's changed too.'

'You've changed, Rose, I can see that, but I'm not sure Edward has, not even now. He still stays too much inside himself, or how else could he bear to be locked up in prison? And he'll stay there, Rose, unless Mr McClusky's willing to help if we find him, and we've already been trying for a year. So have faith but don't build up your dreams too much, that's all I ask.'

'I won't, but, Lizzie, what's faith if it's not a dream?'

CHAPTER 41

'Lizzie, do you think I was wrong to invite Rose on this holiday?' Catherine looked worried, tired.

'Which one?' There had been three holidays, one spawning the next.

They had started in Deauville on what was supposed to be a family visit, then, leaving Walter at home, they travelled down to Orléans until on impulse Catherine had taken them on a railway and sailing barge tour of the Loire River. Now they were sitting on an island in the middle of the wide, slow river, the children were playing by the water's edge and Rose was sitting apart from them, sketching the town and high château of Saumur.

'No, Catherine, you weren't wrong, but you have given her time to think.'

'It's just that she seems so lonely, Lizzie. And I'm sure she's become worse over the past few days.'

'The children are four years old today, Catherine. It's nearly five years since she's seen Edward and it's probably going to be another fifteen before he's free. She's been living for a dream, living off it almost, and now it looks as if she was wrong. We're not going to find Mr McClusky. I'm resigned to it, but Rose isn't. Not yet, anyway.'

Rose had been worse since Matthew Parker came to see her and Jamie asked if the American was his father. Neither of the children had asked about their father until then, but once the seed was planted it grew and they had asked daily until they became bored with asking the question that their mother never answered. And Matthew had not helped by telling Rose he would be happy to take her and the children back to America so they would have a father and so that she could live a good life, as he put it. She had been quite short with him, thanking him for all his help, but pointing out very bluntly that she had already had one marriage of convenience and it had proved to be a disaster, so she was not about to involve herself in a second; especially when she was still married to one man and still in love with yet another.

Poor Matthew; Elizabeth had felt sorry for him as he left. He was besotted with Rose, that was obvious. She could imagine him remaining unmarried for the rest of his life because he could not marry the woman he loved, while Rose lived without Edward who would spend the rest of his life in prison; and Hubert would live his life taking satisfaction from the knowledge that he had caused so much misery in return for what he saw as a betrayal. It was all such a waste and it brought a sense of desolation to what should have been a pleasant afternoon sitting in the sun beside a beautiful river.

'You haven't told her that we're all, well, half sisters?' Catherine asked, leaning back in her chair, eyes half closed.

'No. I did think about it, especially when I thought I might have to justify why I ran away from John, but she seemed to accept what I told her without my having to go into all the details so I felt it was better to let things lie. I don't think there's anything to be gained from telling her, and maybe it might actually spoil our friendship if she knew we were half sisters. She can get very depressed, very vulnerable, and I think there's a danger that if she knew she might feel that I'm only helping her out of a sense of duty.'

'You're probably right, Lizzie, although it must be an awful temptation to say something.'

'I very nearly told her a few months after she moved in with me. Some neighbours were asking awkward questions about our exact relationship and Rose panicked and told them that we were half sisters. She laughed when she told me how she'd fooled them into believing that they had uncovered an imaginary skeleton in our cupboard. I was sorely tempted to tell her then, but couldn't see the point.'

'We're none of us alike in looks,' Catherine said. 'Do you think we're alike in other ways? Has our father passed on something common to us all? Something we may have inherited from our outlaw stock?'

'I think we're all stubborn at times, even to our own cost. That's been passed down. And a sense of loyalty. We tend to look after each other where we can. And I think we're all able to adapt to whatever happens to us.'

'That's true, Lizzie, but I'm not sure if our adaptability is a strength or weakness.'

'It's a strength if you want to survive, Catherine. I wish Edward could learn to adapt to changes rather than resist them. He always has to find someone to blame when things go wrong, and usually he blames himself. It's his biggest weakness.'

'Which is why he still won't see you, or even write?' Catherine shaded her eyes and looked at her.

'Yes, and why Rose won't let him know she's waiting for him. She's trying to protect him, but you can't really protect someone from themselves, can you? I've been trying to persuade her to write to him and she's always refused, but I think she may have changed her mind over these last few days. Perhaps that's why she's been so preoccupied, but no doubt she'll tell us in her own time.'

Elizabeth was not entirely surprised when that evening, over dinner, Rose announced her decision.

'I'd like to know what you both think,' she said suddenly. 'Joey and Paul have spent more than four years trying to find Mr McClusky and the Parkers have spent over two years advertising and trying to locate him for us. Even with all that effort we still haven't found him, and I'm beginning to think that perhaps he didn't go to America after all, or maybe he's not a policeman. Perhaps he moved on to somewhere else, Canada maybe, or perhaps he's dead. Maybe he simply doesn't want to be found. I don't know. All I do know is it's unlikely that we're going to find him now. Do you both agree?'

They did, not that their agreement improved Rose's depression.

'I think it's time, Lizzie. Time to tell Edward about me and the children. At least he may agree to see us, and that'd be something, wouldn't it?' She paused for a long time. 'I'm scared that he'll die in prison, and I think that if he knows about us it may give him the strength to continue. We might have a few years together when he's released and we could visit in the meantime. What do you think?'

'It has to be your decision, Rose,' she said, unwilling for once to say what she thought Rose should do, and surprised by her own reluctance to advise.

'Catherine?' Rose asked.

'I agree with Lizzie, Rose, but if you really do love each other then I think you're right. You may as well share as much of your lives as you can. It won't be easy for either of you, especially Edward, but I don't think you've much choice. The only warning I'd give you, though, is that Hubert might hear, and that might cause you even more trouble.'

'That's a risk I've got to take.' Elizabeth noticed the determination in Rose's voice. 'It's been a wonderful holiday, Catherine, I've enjoyed it and it's helped me to think clearly. You and Walter have been extremely generous, but could we go home now, please? We've been away for nearly a month, and now I've made my decision I'd like to go back and get on with things.'

'Thank God you're all back. Where the hell have you been?' Walter shouted at them the moment they opened the front door.

'I sent you an itinerary, didn't I, Lizzie?' Catherine looked at her for support.

'Yes, before we left Orléans.'

'Well, I didn't receive it. I've been worried sick.'

'But you must have received the letters and telegraph messages I sent from each place we stayed at.' Catherine sounded annoyed with her husband.

'Yes, I did, but I needed to contact you and because you kept moving each day I couldn't find you anywhere. I've been trying for over a week. Read this, Rose.' Walter thrust a letter into Rose's hands, then turned back to his wife. 'It's no good giving people an address where you can be contacted if you promptly disappear.'

'We didn't do it deliberately, Walter.' Catherine was almost in tears.

'Lizzie, it's from Mr Simkins, your solicitor.' Rose's face was glowing. 'He's says there's news about Edward. Matthew Parker's found Mr McClusky. He's a Pinkerton investigator, whatever that is.'

'A big American private detective agency,' Walter explained. 'A private police force, in effect.'

For more than four years they had been looking in the wrong places, but that did not matter now. 'What about Mr McClusky, Rose?'

'You read it, Lizzie. I'm not sure what it means.'

She took the letter from Rose and read it quickly. It

appeared that Mr McClusky had thwarted a large bullion robbery and his name had appeared in the New York newspapers while Matthew was in the city on business. He had been to see McClusky who had already made a statement under oath and had offered some other proof that he had been coerced into making a false statement about where he found Sebastian's body.

She wondered how Matthew had felt when he realised he was in a position to give Rose what she dreamed of, Edward; but this was not the time to mention thoughts like that.

'It could be over soon, Rose,' she said, and turned to Walter. 'How quickly can we get home, Walter?'

'There's a cargo steamer leaving Le Havre tomorrow afternoon on its weekly voyage into London. If there's a free passenger cabin you could be home the following day. That should be quicker than travelling up to Calais and taking the cross-Channel boat.'

Fog. The hump of forested hills above Le Havre was already half hidden as the steamer pulled away from the dock. By the time it had turned its bows towards the open sea the fog had rolled down to the town's rooftops and as the ship steamed north the fog rolled out over the waves and Cap d'Antifer and all France was lost.

'Come inside, into the cabin, Rose. There's nothing to see out here and you'll catch your death in this dampness.'

'Just a few more minutes, Lizzie. You take the children, will you, and I'll come down shortly. I just need to be alone for a while.'

'Yes, but please don't be long. You sound as if you already have a cold starting and there's no point in making it worse, especially now.'

'The sea air'll clear my head, Lizzie. Don't fuss so much. You're worse than Catherine.' Rose laughed, and she laughed with her.

It was true, she did fuss, but Rose and the children

sometimes seemed so fragile. Both Jamie and Helen had caught colds while they were on holiday, simple children's colds which disappeared in a few days, but she had fussed over them to the extent that both Rose and Catherine constantly teased her about her concern. It was probably a reaction to what she saw in the slums, she told herself, where a simple cold could turn to pneumonia and kill a child or an adult within a week, or weaken someone so that the next outbreak of influenza or consumption would prove fatal.

The slums and the mission; she had not left them for more than a week previously, and four, nearly five weeks away was a special privilege. It was all thanks to Catherine, of course, who had made all the arrangements, paid all the bills, and had been wonderful company throughout the holiday. Holiday? More of an adventure, a wonderful experience, and so enlightening to see how different life was in another country, even one as close as France.

An hour passed before she realised Rose was still on deck. She found her standing near the bow, watching the ship cut through the waves.

'Rose, you're soaked. You must come inside.'

'Can't we go any faster, Lizzie? Look, we're hardly moving forward at all.'

The ship's siren boomed out and its sound rolled across the fog-bound sea.

'Think yourself lucky the captain sailed at all, Rose. I thought we'd have to wait until the fog cleared before we left Le Havre. There's no point in rushing ahead and hitting another ship, is there?'

'Oh, I suppose you're right,' Rose said, turning away from the rail, 'but I just want to get home. I want to see Edward so much.'

'You will, soon. It'll soon be over. You'll see.'

There was little to do other than read and listen to the sound of the ship's siren and engines. The engines beat steadily for the remainder of the afternoon but during the

evening they seemed to slow, and around midnight they
sounded as if they had almost stopped.

The ship rolled a little more than usual, the sloshing
waves sounded louder, and sometimes the sound of
another ship's siren came back through the foggy night, a
hollow sound, frightening because of the danger it implied.

The night seemed endless, the hands on the cabin's
mahogany clock hardly moving.

A bell began to toll, the languorous sound of a bell buoy.
It rang and rang, sounding louder all the time until it
passed and its sound faded into the night; but at least it
showed the ship was still moving forward, still sailing
towards England.

And over all other sounds was the noise of the siren
blasting out its warning of the ship's presence; both
comforting and frightening, and making sleep impossible.

'Three days! Oh dear.' Mr Simkins smiled his kind,
sympathetic solicitor smile. 'That is a long time to be at
sea, but thankfully you're here now. It's unfortunate that
you were away for so long. I received notification from
New York a week after you'd departed for the Continent.
That's, let me see, four weeks ago, Miss Forrester.'

'Yes, I'm sorry.' She apologised without knowing why.
'We've spent four years waiting for news each day, and the
week after we leave everything seems to happen. What's
the current situation, Mr Simkins?'

'In essence, you have precisely what you've been
seeking. Mr McClusky has not only issued a sworn
statement concerning where he found Mr Laybourne's
body, he has actually produced his original statement, the
report he was instructed to change. There will be an
enquiry of course, but that evidence alone was enough for
Mr Joseph to submit an application for your brother's
release from prison.'

'An application?' She noticed the fear in Rose's voice.
'Does that mean it could be refused?'

'There has to be a formal hearing and that could cause a slight delay, but it is simply a formality. Mr Forrester will be released and his criminal record erased, Mrs Belchester. It then remains for you to sort out your own affairs, and if I can be of any assistance in that regard I'll be only too happy to help.'

Rose looked confused. 'My affairs?'

'I think Mr Simkins means your divorce from Hubert, Rose, if that's what you want,' Elizabeth explained quickly, and Mr Simkins nodded. 'But before we think about that, Mr Simkins, what do we do next? With regard to Edward.'

'I suggest you visit him in prison as soon as you can and explain the whole situation to him. His release will come as something of a shock, I imagine, especially as he's had no idea of what's been happening. He'll have adjusted himself to the thought of spending his life behind bars and suddenly he's to be thrown out into the world again. He'll need a lot of support and understanding. The sooner you assure him that he'll receive it the better it'll be for him.'

'I can't go, Lizzie. I want to but I can't. Please try to understand.'

'I'm trying to, Rose, but it's difficult.' She could not understand; all this time Rose had been looking forward to seeing Edward and now she was refusing to go to him.

'I want him back, Lizzie, you know I do.' There were tears streaming down her face. 'But as I told you a long time ago I don't want to oblige him to come back to me. Will you go to him and tell him that you know where I am and I've left Hubert. Let him decide whether or not he still wants me. I don't want to oblige him to come, but I couldn't bear seeing him again if he doesn't still want me. I couldn't bear seeing him walk away from me, Lizzie. Do you understand?'

'Of course, Rose.' She reached out and held her, felt her body heave as huge racking sobs and fear shook her. 'But

I'm sure you've nothing to worry about. He'll still love you.
That's one of the things I am sure of.'

After having spent so much time with Rose and Catherine
it seemed strange to be sitting alone in a hotel tea room.

She looked out of the window, across the road to the
promenade and the pierhead and the rank of open
carriages waiting to give rides to holidaymakers. The
scene was colourful, gay, relaxed, but across the bay the
bulk of Portland Bill stood out, grey and imposing.

Elizabeth was pleased that Mr Hampton, the prison
governor, had suggested they meet in her hotel rather
than at the prison. The thought of walking through the
gates and seeing the conditions that Edward had lived in
for so long frightened her; the thought of being a lone
woman in a violent man's world made her feel sick, but Mr
Hampton's message had calmed her, allowed her to
compose herself, and now she was looking forward to
meeting the man she had been corresponding with for
more than four years.

She had built up a mental picture of him. His letters
showed that he was considerate as well as frank, but he
had to be tough to run a prison, especially one like
Portland. She imagined he would be at least forty years
old, a heavy featured brooding type of man, solidly built
and capable, confident that he could take care of himself in
his violent world. Probably he had once been a policeman
or a soldier, she thought.

His letters had never mentioned any interests he might
have but his handwriting had the look of a man who had
plain interests, an uncomplicated view of life, someone
who would think of art or literature as weaknesses of the
mind.

She sipped her tea and glanced at a clock hanging over
the door. He was late. Not a good sign if he could not be
bothered to arrive on time.

Twenty minutes later she ordered more tea and settled

down to read the book she had brought with her, but it was difficult to concentrate.

'May I sit here?' She looked up and saw a man perhaps five years older than herself, tall, slim, fine-featured with receding fair hair. 'May I?'

He was already pulling a chair back from under the table; she hesitated, unsure what to say, and glanced around to see if there were any free tables to direct him to.

'You are Miss Forrester?' He blinked, looked embarrassed as if he thought he had made a mistake. 'I thought this was the table the waitress pointed to.'

'Yes, I'm Elizabeth Forrester.'

'I'm very pleased to meet you after all this time.' His hand reached out and gently enclosed hers. 'I'm Richard Hampton. I'm sorry I'm so late but I couldn't get away.'

He sat down and a waitress brought fresh tea and clean cups and saucers.

'I hope you don't mind, but I ordered some fresh tea.' He smiled. 'I thought my lateness might mean that anything you had was stewed.'

'No, of course not, Mr Hampton,' she heard herself stammer; he was wearing a pale grey suit and a silk tie the colour of forget-me-nots that exactly matched the colour of his eyes which were mesmerising. 'And I'm very pleased to meet you. I'm glad of the opportunity to thank you personally for your letters, and the concern you've shown for Edward.'

'Well, thank you. I don't usually become quite so involved with prisoners, Miss Forrester, but your brother interested me from the moment he arrived. If there is such a thing as an ideal prisoner, he's it. He always co-operated with my staff, kept out of trouble whatever the provocation from other prisoners, even when one of them put a pick-axe through his foot, and worked hard at whatever task he was set. His only fault was that he didn't seem to think his sentence was punishment enough and seemed determined to punish himself even more, but I suppose that's almost inevitable if we put very intelligent men into places where they can't use their minds. That's one reason why I encouraged him to write, even though it seemed strange to have a man convicted of murder writing children's stories.'

'He's been writing children's stories?' This was something she did not know.

'Oh yes, and quite enchanting stories too. The first was one about a princess who fell in love with a prince who'd had all his money and land stolen by his wicked uncle . . .'

'Ah, the magic tree with golden leaves.' She smiled; even in prison Edward was still a dreamer.

'Obviously you know that story, but there were others. Thirty or so, I think. I enjoyed reading them, and illustrating them. I gave him all the drawings the stories inspired me to do.'

'You're an artist, Mr Hampton?'

'Hardly, but I do enjoy drawing and painting when I have the time. And reading. And going to concerts when possible. One needs diversion, Miss Forrester, otherwise life becomes so mundane.'

'Yes, I agree. Do you read Edward's stories to your own children?' It was a clumsy question, put artlessly, but he did not seem to notice.

'No, Miss Forrester.' He laughed, a self-mocking laugh. 'I've no children. I'm not even married. I can't imagine anyone wanting to put up with me.'

She smiled, that was the only way she could think to answer.

'Anyway' – he smiled back and looked embarrassed again – 'enough about me. I imagine you're here to talk about your brother. I must say how pleased I was when I heard about his release, although I was sorry I was taking leave when the advice was received. I'd like to have been there to tell him about it.'

'That's very kind of you, Mr Hampton. When do you think he will actually be free?'

There was a long pause and she saw a puzzled expression change the governor's face. 'He was released ten days ago, Miss Forrester. You didn't know?'

The table, the tea room, the whole world seemed to rock. She heard a cup smash and realised she had dropped the one she was holding.

'I think you need some air, Miss Forrester.' He was behind her, steadying her as she tried to stand, but her legs were too weak to support her and all she could manage was to wonder how she was going to tell Rose.

A waitress scurried over and cleared away the mess and she heard the governor apologising, explaining that she felt unwell, and saw him leave coins on the table in payment for the tea and damage. Then they were outside, his arm around her waist, supporting her across the road until they reached an empty bench where he sat her down before sitting beside her.

'I thought there had to be an official hearing before he could be released?' She remembered what Mr Simkins had said only two days earlier.

'There was, but it was very informal under the circumstances.'

'I don't understand. What circumstances?'

'The hearing was in Durham where your brother was convicted. Unfortunately his legal representative, Mr Joseph, is abroad on holiday but as there was no doubt that your brother should be released it was agreed the hearing should not be delayed until Mr Joseph's return. It was all done in absence to ensure your brother wasn't detained for any longer than necessary.'

'Then where has he gone?'

'I'm afraid that my deputy rather assumed he'd go home to you, or back to Pincote.'

'But unless you gave him my address he doesn't know where I live, and there's nothing for him in Pincote. Our family's dead. Edward even wanted me to treat him as if he were dead and that's why I stopped writing to him. Even if he knew where I live I don't suppose he'd come without being asked, and by now he probably thinks I've given up on him.'

'Then I don't know where he is, Miss Forrester. I didn't give him your address, I assumed he knew it, and I'm almost sure my deputy would have thought the same.'

A little boy screamed for his father. He was pointing up into the sky. He had let go of the string attached to his toy kite and now the wind was carrying the kite out to sea.

'We'll buy you another one, a better one,' the father consoled the little boy, and she wished life was as simple as that.

'The release' – there was one last hope – 'would that have explained why he was being freed? Does Edward know it was because of our efforts to find new evidence?'

'I'm afraid not. It simply stated that the police evidence on which your brother had been convicted had subsequently been refuted, that there would be an enquiry into the manner in which the evidence had been collated, and that the sentence had been overturned. Your brother probably gained the impression that the police had volunteered fresh evidence.'

'May I speak to your deputy? He may remember something Edward said. Something which may give me a clue as to where he's gone.'

'Certainly, but not before tomorrow morning. He's off duty until then and I can't contact him.' She saw him pause and consider something. 'Miss Forrester, I'll quite understand if you refuse, but as you're going to be staying in Weymouth this evening, may I invite you to dinner. I'll quite understand if you say . . .'

'Thank you. Yes, I'd like that, Mr Hampton.'

'Oh.' He seemed surprised. 'Oh, good.'

It was a warm evening with soft breezes blowing in off the sea. After dinner they walked along the promenade and sat listening to a string quartet playing chamber music in a beach-side garden. Coloured lanterns were strung up amongst the trees, and behind the music the waves lapped against sand and pebbles.

She realised she was quite relaxed, even though she was worried about Edward and Rose. Richard Hampton seemed in no hurry to leave when the musicians packed up their instruments and left, and she was happy to sit in the quiet and talk to him.

He was very easy to talk to, a quiet man, reserved and considerate. In some ways he reminded her of Edward, his interest in books and poetry, a tendency to dream, an inclination to talk about change but an easy willingness to accept the inevitable. And she thought he found her interesting; he wanted to know about her work, what she thought could be done to improve lower-class living conditions in London, and he even asked about her personal ambitions.

He told her a little about himself, how he had failed to become a doctor like his father, how malaria had ended his career in the Foreign Service and how he had almost by accident fallen into the Prison Service. He admitted that he did not feel well suited to his job but said he had no regrets other than not being in a position to introduce many of the reforms he thought were necessary.

They talked for a long time until they noticed there were few people still about and were astonished to see how late it had become. He escorted her back to her hotel and after making arrangements to meet at the prison the next day, they parted in the lobby.

'Thank you, Richard. It's been the most wonderful evening.'

'I should thank you, Elizabeth. It has been a wonderful evening. The most enjoyable evening I've had in years.'

As he turned and walked away she knew exactly how he felt.

She slept badly, worrying about Edward; and when she managed to put Edward out of her mind Richard Hampton

appeared, stirring her emotions, keeping her awake for
other reasons.

Richard Hampton's deputy was a big bear of a man, exactly
the type of man she had imagined Richard would be, and
although she was sure he sympathised with her and tried
to remember every word Edward had said, he could not
help. He had not passed on her address and he had no idea
what Edward intended to do with his unexpected freedom.

'He might turn up, Miss Forrester.' She saw the concern
in Richard's blue eyes and guessed he was finding it
awkward to be formal in front of his deputy. 'I'll accompany
you back to Weymouth and wait with you until your train
leaves.'

'Thank you for your offer, Mr Hampton, but there's no
need. Not if you're busy. I've been enough of a nuisance
already.' She hoped she had used enough guile to satisfy
his deputy without convincing him.

'It's the least I can do under the circumstances.' She saw
him stand, and her heart beat a little quicker.

The engine puffed steam along the platform. Nearly time
to leave.

She looked down from the carriage window and smiled.
'You have my address?'

'Yes.' He nodded and smiled back at her. 'We've been
exchanging letters for years.'

'Of course.' She had forgotten; their friendship seemed
so new. 'Three weeks?'

The train began to move and he followed, walking so
that he stayed by the open window. 'Yes, Elizabeth. Three
weeks. Sooner if there's any news.'

He was stopped by a barrier, and she waved until he was
out of sight then closed the window and sat down. He had
said he was coming to London anyway, to a meeting which
had been planned for months; but he had not mentioned it
until her train was about to leave.

She slept for most of the return journey, but each time she woke she remembered Richard and a pleasantly unsettling warmth spread through her. She realised it had been a long time since she had felt like that.

The euphoria had died by the time she stepped off the bus by the Angel Inn.

She looked up at the gilded angel. 'Help me, please. Anything. Anything to bring him back to Rose. You promised me it would all come right.'

'Talking to yourself, Miss Forrester?'

'Oh, Sam. Yes, I've been doing a lot of that lately.' She laughed off her embarrassment and strode down Angel Street, stopped to look at the little lime tree for a moment, and turned indoors.

Rose came out from the scullery, anticipation all over her face. 'Well?'

'I think you'd better come and sit down, Rose, in the front room if the children are in the kitchen. I've got a lot to tell you, and some of it you won't want to hear.' It was necessary to tell her the truth about Edward, but it was not necessary to tell her all about Richard Hampton; that would have been unkind under the circumstances.

Rose listened without saying a word, then after a short silence: 'It's all my fault, Lizzie. I should have let you tell him about me and the children. He would have come back then. I'm sure he would have.'

She saw the anguish on Rose's face and decided not to say anything. It would have been cruel to remind her that the reason for not telling him was to give him his freedom, the freedom he was now taking advantage of.

'And if we hadn't gone away for so long.' Rose wrung her hands. 'If only we'd been here.'

'There's no good in blaming yourself, Rose. There's been a mix-up, that's all.' It was easy to say but she knew that she would feel as desolate as Rose did now if she had not met Richard and suddenly had something to look forward to in her own life. Angel, she thought, help me. If ever I needed you it's now.

But there was no flash of inspiration, no miracle or enlightenment, just the sight of the little tree outside on the pavement.

'Maybe he's waiting until the autumn, Rose, like the prince in his story.' It was a silly thing to say and she regretted it immediately.

'Don't be stupid!' She could see the anger in Rose's eyes. 'He doesn't even know we're here, does he?'

A moment later the children burst in.

Richard's first visit was over and she was standing on the platform with him, waiting for his train to leave. 'I'm glad you could come, Richard, and I hope you don't catch Rose's influenza.'

'Thank you for inviting me, Lizzie. It's been a wonderful weekend, but over too soon.' His arms squeezed her against him. 'We must find a way of spending more time together if we're . . .'

'If we're what?' she prompted when he did not continue.

'If we're to get to know each other better.'

'I think we already know each other quite well, especially as we've seen so little of each other.'

'Yes, but I want to see you more often, Lizzie.' She felt him squeeze her again, and knew from the embarrassed look that crossed his face he would change the subject. 'Now I've met Rose I can understand Edward even better. She is enchanting.'

'Yes, and she's not even at her best at the moment. She's obviously worried about Edward, and she just can't shake off this flu. It's pulling her down. She's not usually this depressed.'

'I don't suppose the situation with Edward is helping,' he said quietly. 'It's been more than a month now, hasn't it?'

She nodded, and jumped as the train's whistle blew.

'I must go, Lizzie, though I don't want to.'

'Go on.' She kissed him. 'I'll write.'

'Do, and let me know if you hear from Edward.'

'I will.'

'I love you, Lizzie Forrester,' and he was gone.

She made her way home, miserable without him, and even forgot to smile at the little angel on the corner of the street.

'Have you fallen in love with Richard?' Rose asked when, as usual, they sat down in the kitchen before going to bed.

'Yes. I'm sorry.'

'Why are you sorry? He seems rather nice. Not what I expected of a prison governor.'

'I'm sorry to have, well, you know.' It should not be necessary to explain.

'Because of Edward?'

She nodded, of course it was because of Edward.

'I'm happy for you, Lizzie, and I should be happy for Edward because he's free, not locked up any more, but I'm not. I wish he was still in prison because at least that gave me something to dream about. I didn't think it would be like this, me here, not knowing where he is, how he is. Worst of all not knowing whether or not he's ever going to come back to me.'

'You're not feeling well, Rose. That's why you're so depressed, that and the shock of all that's happened. It'll work out, you'll see. I've written to everyone I think he may go to and asked them all to tell him we're here, waiting for him, and asking them to let us know if they see him. I've even spoken to Mr Speedwell. If Edward comes back to London Mr Speedwell should know. It's difficult, Rose, but there's not much else we can do but wait.'

'The trouble is, Lizzie, I've never been very good at waiting.'

Elizabeth read Richard's letter thanking her for the

weekend and suggesting he could visit again in two weeks, if it was convenient.

'Of course it's convenient.' Rose smiled when she told her about the letter. 'Will he stay in a hotel again, or will you ask him to sleep here?'

'No, in a hotel, I think.' It was better to keep him away from the house at night; she was finding it difficult enough to cope with the pace their relationship seemed to be developing without putting any more of a strain on it. 'You won't mind him being here, Rose?'

'Not at all. I'd rather have him here talking about Edward than have no contact at all.' Rose spoke brightly, but there was a falseness to the words, a brittleness which suggested she might be about to break.

Elizabeth had only just returned from posting the letter to Richard confirming he could come for the weekend when the postman delivered a letter from Catherine. She opened it and read quickly.

'Rose, it seems we're to have a crowd over the weekend Richard's coming. Catherine's invited herself, which is lovely, but she's also asked John and, as she calls her, his wife, to visit on Saturday afternoon.' She saw the worry on Rose's face. 'Don't worry, they don't know you're here. Hubert's told them you're living in Spain, permanently, because of your health. And she says that when she's finished talking to them they'll be happy to support that belief.'

Rose clasped her chest and when she spoke there was a hint of wheeziness in her voice. 'I hope there won't be any trouble, Lizzie. And I hope John's not been drinking too much. Catherine told me he's getting worse.'

'Trust Catherine. Anyway Richard'll be here.'

'Perhaps Edward will be, too.'

'Yes.' Perhaps he would, and then the fur would really fly.

Edward was not there when Catherine arrived, nor when Richard arrived a few hours later.

'I'm sorry, Lizzie,' he apologised immediately. 'I wouldn't have suggested coming if I'd realised you had other guests coming.'

'Nonsense.' She held his arm tightly. 'I invited you, and I want you to meet Catherine anyway. She's more than a guest, she's certainly one of my closest friends, a real friend who stood by me when no one else would.'

She saw the way Richard and Catherine found immediate rapport, and the sly way Catherine looked at her and smiled a smile which asked if he was the one; and felt herself blush a little as she nodded and mouthed words which said she hoped so.

Pleasantries completed, she thanked Catherine for coming and for asking John and Lillian to visit at the same time. 'That must have been quite difficult to arrange, Catherine.' She frowned. 'But why did you say John and his wife? Why not Lillian?'

'Because I cannot abide the scheming little wench,' Catherine said haughtily.

She laughed, not so much at Catherine's indignation but at the thought of anyone calling the beautiful and fragrant Lillian a wench; and Lillian's likely reaction if she ever found out.

'I assume from that, Catherine, that you don't like her.'

'No, I don't like her or her father, or any of the Belchesters either, for that matter. Never have, apart from Hubert's grandfather. He was a likeable old rogue and thought the world of Charlotte and Rose. Fortunately' – Catherine smiled – 'because it offers me the opportunity to incite a little mischief, Lizzie, and to offer Rose some insurance.'

'I don't understand.' She was puzzled and could see Rose was, also.

'Allow me to explain.' Catherine smiled. 'But perhaps we should first of all explain some of this to Richard, or the poor man'll think we're a conniving bunch who can't be trusted.'

*   *   *

Richard had suggested he should go out and not return
until half an hour or so after John and Lillian were to arrive.
It should reduce embarrassment and confusion, he said,
and Elizabeth agreed even though she would have
preferred him to be there when she first saw John.

It was Catherine, sitting on the settee in the front room,
who saw John and Lillian turn through the front gate.
'Ready? Rose? Lizzie?'

She was as ready as she would be, but she saw Rose
press her hand against her chest and was worried it might
be a signal for another breathing attack. 'Are you all right,
Rose?'

Rose nodded, and took up her position in the hall. 'Yes,
Lizzie. Let them in.'

She reached the front door as the knocker rapped,
opened the door and immediately stood aside.

Lillian stared at her, then past her to Rose; and some
sort of understanding flickered across her intelligent face.

'A little different to the Belchesters' houses or their
castle in Spain.' Lillian's glance flicked along the hall. 'But
I see you still have staff.'

Elizabeth heard Rose's quick reply and smiled. 'I like to
do the cooking and cleaning, Lillian. My contribution to
the way we live. This is Lizzie's house, you see.'

'Yes.' Lillian sniffed and entered the narrow hall
carefully as if trying not to brush her coat against the walls.
'One can tell.'

'And I'd like to welcome you,' she heard herself say
without any feeling, then paused as John stopped in front
of her, leaned his head down and kissed her cheek. 'And
you, John.' His kiss meant nothing to her.

'Elizabeth.' He nodded and turned to Rose. 'Rose. What
a surprise to see you here.'

'John.' Rose nodded and stepped forward to kiss him but
he turned and walked into the front room where Catherine
was seated on the settee and did not bother to rise.

'Isn't Rose looking well?' she heard Catherine say, but did not hear any replies.

She ushered Rose into the room and almost directed her to sit beside Catherine while she remained by the door. 'Will you all take tea?'

'I'm not sure we have sufficient time for such niceties,' Lillian said in an obviously false apologetic tone. 'And we don't wish to be any trouble. We're here simply to please Catherine.'

Catherine smiled graciously. 'I'm very pleased to see you both, and I'd love some tea, please, Lizzie. If it's not too much trouble, of course. And then, perhaps, John and his wife won't feel that they're being such a nuisance after all.'

She left the room quickly and while she could still contain her grin; if Rose saw her she was sure to start giggling at Catherine's rudeness and then the whole purpose of the visit would be spoiled.

Elizabeth watched Lillian carefully inspect the rim of her cup before putting it near her lips, and she hoped the tea was hot enough to scald her.

'John' – Catherine shook her head in her half brother's direction – 'you not only allow Hubert to dupe you into believing Rose has been living in Spain for several years, but I understand you've allowed his father to trick you into paying him exorbitant interest on a debenture which should never have been raised.'

'I beg your pardon?' It was not John who spoke, it was Lillian.

'The promissory note our father made for Rose's dowry,' Catherine explained. 'It was payable to Hubert's grandfather, not his father, or the estate, or their bank. Personally to the grandfather, and he tore it up before he died. It's a little complicated but Walter's bank was involved in an exchange of guarantees, and it received a letter from Hubert's grandfather stating that he considered the note had been fulfilled and he had destroyed it. I have a copy of the letter here, and its accuracy has been attested by a commissioner of oaths.'

'May we have it?' Again it was Lillian who spoke.

'Possibly.' Catherine turned to her. 'Your family and the Belchesters have taken everything from John, except for the house and the immediate estate. I propose offering John a substantial advance against the deeds of the house and grounds, and you will agree to him accepting it. He won't have to pay me more than one English pound for each year that he lives there. He'll gain a substantial amount of capital and therefore won't be quite so beholden to you, and you'll never get your hands on the house or estate.'

'Thank you, Catherine. I appreciate your help, really,' John murmured quietly.

'He'll only use the money to buy drink,' Lillian snorted and gulped down her tea.

'Perhaps he needs it' – Catherine levelled her eyes into Lillian's – 'to keep out the cold.'

She watched Lillian put down her cup and half rise, but Catherine stopped her with one word: 'Stay!'

Lillian sat down again, like an obedient dog.

'I'm concerned that Rose's whereabouts are not revealed to Hubert or anyone who has contact with the Belchesters. You are both in regular contact with that family, as is your father, Mrs Laybourne.' Elizabeth found herself admiring Catherine's initiative in never speaking Lillian's name. 'Your families have many joint interests and there has always been a deal of competition between you. Since Walter retired from banking, and is therefore no longer restrained by professional ethics, we have been purchasing substantial quantities of shares in companies where your joint interests are dominant. The shares have been bought in the names of various holding companies which will make them extremely difficult to trace and the quantities are not sufficient to have attracted attention or obliged us to reveal the extent of our holdings, but they are enough to distort the levels of control that currently exist. I must warn you that if Rose is ever approached by any member of the Belchester family, all our holdings will be offered to the Belchesters at prices which will enable them to destroy you and your family, madam.'

Lillian looked as if someone had hit her.

'Do you understand?' She saw the fury Catherine was holding back.

'Yes,' Lillian said softly.

'Then you may go, if you wish.' Catherine made it clear she did not want Lillian to stay, and John's wife rose and left without a word to anyone. Catherine turned to John, and smiled. 'I'm sorry, John, but I simply don't like her.'

She half hoped John would stand up for his wife, but he did not. 'She can be very difficult, Catherine.'

Then Richard appeared in the doorway. 'The front door was open, Lizzie, so I came in. A young woman went past me like the breeze . . .'

'Lillian,' she said.

'Mrs Laybourne,' Catherine corrected her.

'Then you must be Mr Laybourne, Rose's brother.' Richard held out his hand to John, who took it timidly, then firmly. 'Richard Hampton. A friend of Lizzie's.'

'A close friend?' John looked at her and she felt awkward.

Richard smiled at her. 'I certainly hope so, Mr Laybourne. I certainly hope so.'

'Then, Mr Hampton, please take good care of her. She's a very special lady, and she still means a lot to me.'

She felt herself beginning to choke as emotion closed her throat, and she pretended to blow her nose to cover her feelings. John said goodbye to everyone, thanked Catherine again for her generosity and accepted her promise that he would hear from her solicitors, and he kissed Rose goodbye and promised to write. Then he turned to Elizabeth and shrugged, and she followed him out into the narrow hallway and closed the front room door behind her.

'How are you, John, really?'

He shrugged again. 'I could be a lot worse.'

'Your lungs?' She had noticed his breathing was harsh.

'Not too good, but all right if I don't try to do too much.'
It was obvious that he wanted to change the conversation.
'It's strange. Father had a dream, a Laybourne dynasty. He
thought that by marrying off his children into other
influential families, future generations of Laybournes could
spread and control whole areas of industry and farming
and transport. It's odd that he never bothered about
Catherine, and yet she's the one who's ended up with the
most influence. So much for dreams.'

'We all need dreams, John.'

'Yes.' He paused. 'Richard seems like a good man.'

'He is. I'm sure of that.'

'Good.' He hesitated and turned his burned-up face
away from her. 'Thank Catherine for me, will you. I
thanked her, but she might understand how grateful I
really am if you tell her.'

'Certainly.' Then she remembered something. 'The old
lodge? Did you repair it after all?'

He shook his head. 'No, Lillian wouldn't live in anything
that small. I still go there, when I want to be alone. And to
think about you.'

'John, don't.' Her fingers lifted instinctively and wiped
the tears from his face, and she prayed he would not ask
her why she left him.

Then he smiled. 'The summer house. You remember
the summer house, don't you? Where we . . .' His voice
trailed off and she nodded: yes she remembered the
summer house, that damned summer house.

'A tree fell on it. The woodmen were cutting down an
elm which had been killed by lightning, and for some
reason the tree fell the wrong way. No one knows why.' He
sounded as though he was still astonished.

She started to laugh; the story seemed a suitable end to

what really was a quite farcical interlude of her life. And he began to laugh with her, so much so that the front room door opened and the others stared out at them.

He bent his head and kissed her again, but this time he found her lips. 'I'm glad we met again. Goodbye, Elizabeth.' His hand reached for the door.

'Elizabeth?' she asked, 'Why not Lizzie.'

'I thought you reserved that for your friends.'

'I thought you were my friend, John. And more than just a friend.'

'Thank you.' He kissed her again, looked along the passage and waved, 'Thank you all.'

And he was gone.

'Well,' Richard grinned at her. 'It doesn't seem to have been quite as horrendous as you all thought it might be.'

'No.' She felt sad but tried to sound buoyant. 'Catherine and I can tell you all about it while the staff makes fresh tea.'

Rose bobbed a quick curtsy and disappeared into the kitchen, and Elizabeth led Richard and Catherine into the front room. Catherine quickly related what had happened.

'I've been thinking, while I was out.' Richard frowned. 'Buying shares like that, is it legal?'

'I don't know,' Catherine said simply. 'It doesn't matter anyway.'

'It will do if you're caught out,' Richard warned.

'Richard, please understand that Walter and I are quite wealthy, very wealthy, I suppose.' Catherine smiled secretively. 'But we couldn't afford to buy enough shares to support the threats I made to Lillian.'

She was stunned by Catherine's calmness. 'Do you mean you were lying, Catherine?'

'Yes, I was lying, although I would prefer you described my actions a little more tactfully. Bluffing, perhaps?'

'What happens if they find out?' Richard asked.

'They won't. They don't know what to look for, or

where, so how can they find out anything? Especially as there's nothing to find. Its total emptiness is what makes the threat so substantial. They'll check, of course, and when they don't find anything they'll think Walter and I have been exceptionally clever, and that'll make them even more nervous. They won't say anything to the Belchesters, and anyway, relations between the families won't be particularly friendly once the business of the fraudulent debenture is aired.'

'It's wonderful, Catherine.' She could not help clapping her hands with the pleasure of understanding the trick Catherine had played.

'You're a bandit, Mrs Wyndham,' Richard laughed.

'I know.' Catherine looked pleased with the description. 'Lizzie, do you remember when we were in France and you asked me what I thought we'd inherited from our father . . .'

She saw the look of horror on Catherine's face, and the puzzled stare on Richard's, and reacted quickly, sure that denials would not help. 'There are some things I must tell you, Richard, that I don't want Rose to know of.'

He nodded, and smiled as Rose came in with the tea.

'Catherine, it's very generous of you to help John,' Rose said as she poured.

'Not at all. He receives money I don't need, and I take control of the house I grew up in, and I stop the McDougalls taking it. Besides, John deserves some help. He helped save a lot of lives when he blew those charges in the mine, but he gave up so much by doing it. Whatever mistakes he's made since then have been a result of those few minutes. It's awful to think that what you do in minutes, or maybe seconds, can sometimes influence your whole future, and that of those around you.'

It was a sobering thought, and one they could all relate to.

His train chuffed out from the station and she stood and

waved him goodbye, and wondered if it really was goodbye. If he was going for good.

She loved him, she was sure of that. Real love, not the feeling she had for Saul, not even the strong feeling she had for John, but something much deeper that seemed as though it was already a part of the way she lived. And because of that she had to tell him everything, the little things and the big things that had happened in her past, and what she knew she had to have for the future.

Richard's family all lived in Cheltenham. His father was a doctor, his brothers were both doctors, and they all lived a life not unlike the one she would have had with Saul. But she knew now she could not live that life, not even to be with Richard.

She needed the mission as much as it needed her, more maybe, and she knew she could never give it up. Rose needed her, at least until Edward appeared, if he ever did; and if he never returned then Rose would need her even more. Ada did not need her, not now, but she did not want to live where she could not see Ada and the children every day. Everyone she shared her life with was, in a sense, in place of the family she had lost. Or perhaps the family she had never had; or might never have if she did not marry Richard.

And he had gone.

The story of her rape had pained him, she saw that, but he had to understand because if it came to marriage she might feel as Catherine did, and she could not marry him and expect him to accept that it was in name only; not without knowing the risks.

And she found herself telling him about the time with John, just so he might understand a little more about her, the real her, not the Lizzie she too often pretended to be.

Perhaps she had told him too much. He had left without kissing her, without saying that he loved her.

And that was frightening.

* * *

Rose was waiting for her when she arrived home.

'Well?' she asked in a careful voice.

'Well what, Rose?' She tried not to sound disheartened or irritated, but she felt both.

'I simply thought that you and Richard were giving each other such searching looks all weekend that perhaps he might have . . .' Rose shrugged lightly.

'Proposed? No, Rose. We did talk quite a lot, though. And I think I might have frightened him altogether. It's an effect I have on men.' She pulled a face that was meant to show she was not feeling sorry for herself.

'That's something we have in common,' Rose muttered and kissed her. 'Goodnight, Lizzie. I'm going to bed.'

She followed her up the stairs, climbed the extra flight that led to her own bedroom on the top floor, and lay on her bed, trying to sleep.

The night was airless, heavy with an impending storm.

She woke up suddenly at two o'clock the next morning. The sky was bright with constant lightning and thunder was shaking the house so much the windows rattled. It was not raining, but the air was moist and heavy, difficult to breathe, and she knew that if she found it difficult to breathe Rose might be finding it almost impossible.

She jumped out of bed and ran downstairs to Rose's room. 'Rose, are you all right?'

No answer.

She opened the door and immediately heard Rose gasping for breath.

The asthma always returned when Rose was worried, and that and the influenza and the airless night were all combining to choke her.

'Come on, out of bed, Rose. On to the chair.' She dragged her on to an upright chair and sat her astride it like a horse, arms hanging over the chair's back, the only way to help her breathe when she was having a bad attack.

'Mama. Mama.' Helen ran into the bedroom. 'Cuddle

me, Mama, I'm frightened of the big bangs.'

'Your mama can't come at the moment, Helen. Go back to bed and I'll be with you in a minute or two,' pressing Rose's back to help her take air in.

'Come on, Helen.' Jamie wandered in, looked at his mother and reacted exactly as his father would. 'There's nothing to be frightened of but I'll take care of you. Come on.'

She noticed the protective way his arm slid around his sister's shoulders as he led her away, typical of Edward, then she turned back to Rose. 'Is that any easier?'

Rose nodded her head and gasped and gurgled as she sucked air into her lungs. She was having an especially bad attack, the worst she had suffered since she had overcome the beating Hubert gave her and learned to live without the opiate medicine.

A draught of her new medicine, followed an hour later by cooler air that came when the rain started, helped ease the attack.

'I'm all right now, Lizzie, thank you.'

'Are you sure you're all right to be left alone?'

'Yes, the worst's over.' She paused and took several deep, gurgling breaths. 'It's four o'clock. Go to bed so you can at least get two hours sleep before work.'

Two hours! She walked back to her own room.

'Edward, Edward, where the hell are you? I need you here, now!'

The only answer was the sound of the rain drumming on the roof, and she was filled with an awful dread that had started when Rose insisted on staying up on the ship's deck in the fog; a fear that Rose was not destined to spend her life with Edward even though he was free. That the story would not have the happy ending the romantic Edward predicted because something in Rose would not allow it.

There was no reason for Rose to have stayed on deck in the fog. There was no reason for her to have married

Hubert. There was no reason for her, years ago, to have all but told her father she was in love with Edward. Rose had admitted earlier that she was no good at waiting, and it seemed sometimes that she had an unconscious eagerness to take risks, even to destroy herself rather than wait patiently for a chance of happiness.

Something of her outlaw heritage? Something their father had seeded in her?

Oh angel, she thought, fly off and find him. Bring him here before it's too late, please.

She sensed that if Edward did not appear soon he would be too late. She remembered the way Rose reacted to her comment about him coming back in the autumn, like the prince in his story.

It was a silly comment to make under the circumstances and it had made Rose angry; but Rose was not angry because it was a stupid comment, she was angry because it made her feel defensive. The faith she had wrapped herself in for years was about to be tested.

She was living the story Edward had told her when she was a child and she was totally dependent upon the story coming true. If Edward did not come in the autumn, as the story predicted, Rose was going to allow herself to die, as the princess in the story would have died.

She was certain of that, and no one but Edward could stop it happening.

CHAPTER 42

'You're a free man, Mr Forrester. You can leave here, today if you like.' He had been free for a day and a half but in his head he could still hear the words, and in his stomach he could still feel the excitement, and the fear. 'It seems that the court's decided you're innocent after all.'

Relief, satisfaction, even gratitude, but still somewhere a niggling feeling of guilt.

No longer for William's death because he had learned to accept that was the result of an accident, and if William had shown enough courage to sound the alarm when he first smelled gas then a score of lives would have been saved that day. Not even for pretending to be a hero when he was not, nor for the way he treated Nancy; because time to think had made him realise they were both typical human failings and, anyway, Nancy was happy enough now.

Not even for killing Rose's father; he had never felt guilty for that, only for feeling no remorse for the act, and prison had given him time to think and learn that he need not feel remorse for something he did not mean to do.

Nor did he any longer feel guilt for the misery he had caused Rose. He had warned her of the risks she was taking when she insisted on staying with him and she had agreed to share the risk, even seemed to enjoy it, but the main reason he no longer felt guilty was because he felt she had betrayed him. She had chosen to go back to Hubert when she could have returned to Pincote. That was something he could not understand, and until he understood he could not forgive.

Now he was free he had to see her, to talk to her for just a few moments. He had to find out if she really was happy and understand why she had gone back to Hubert because even though he felt betrayed the dream still flickered in his chest and he had to know for certain if the time had come to snuff it out. And to forgive her and try to forget her.

But in spite of all he had learned to come to terms with, there was something else that still made him feel guilty and he knew he had to discover what it was before he could ever feel entirely free and begin to think of the future.

He sensed that discovery would come in its own time, but meanwhile he had one other thing he had to do.

The Belchesters' estate was on the coast at Pyre, near Chideock, he knew that, but he had not realised just how close it was to Portland; less than thirty miles to the west. He was glad he had not known until he was free; there were times when knowing that he was imprisoned that close to her would have made life unbearable.

He walked along the narrow road which led from Portland to the mainland and turned on to the coast road which led to Pyre, and Rose's home.

He rode on the backs of carts, when rides were offered, and between rides he walked. He had one thought, that as a free man with nothing to be ashamed of he would simply stroll up the Belchesters' drive and introduce himself.

Then he reached Pyre and saw the gates that led to the Belchesters' estate, and his courage failed. He told himself that it was because he did not want to hurt Rose if she really was happy, but then admitted immediately that was not true. He was scared of seeing her again, scared of seeing her reaction.

Scared of finding her unhappy and even more scared that she might really be very happy; happy living with Hubert.

And he knew he could never look Hubert Belchester in the eye. He had tried to steal Rose from him, and he had failed.

He stood by the gates and looked at the distant house for a long while, but his courage did not return.

'What price freedom?' he asked himself, shouldered his bag and turned away.

'That's the Belchesters' house you been staring at, young man.' He was stopped by an old woman making lace outside a small cottage.

'Aye,' he said, and explained that he used to work for Sebastian Laybourne, Mrs Belchester's father, and wondered aloud if Rose still looked as beautiful as he remembered her.

'Oh yes, my dear, that's still fair to say. Young Mrs Belchester is beautiful all right.' The old woman put down her work. 'We haven't seen her here for a long time though. Lives down in Spain now, she does, because of her chest, poor thing. Can't live in England with the master, and neither can the children. They all needs the warmth, my dear, but the master goes out to her and the children whenever he can.'

His heart and his mind leapt in different directions and for one mad, fleeting moment, he thought about going to Spain to find her, but the moment passed as quick as it came. She had children now. Adam had said she had a child, but now she had more. She was married, she had children, and she lived in Spain. In a castle, the lacemaker added. A princess in a castle. It seemed right.

And it seemed fateful. She was the princess in the castle
and he was certainly a pauper. That was the story he had
told her when she was a child and lost. Now he was the one
who was lost because he could not have the one thing he
wanted more than anything: her.

He felt then that it really was over. He had to forget the
dream that had always stayed, even in prison; stop hoping
that the magic might bring them together again as it had
before. And because the magic could not help he was
grateful that the trees were green and autumn was still a
long way off.

He asked the old woman for directions to Somerton.
The old lady said she thought it was north, and pointed out
the right road. He thanked her and began to walk, and
even when she called out to him he did not turn but simply
waved his arm and kept walking. His tears were private.
The last thing Rose would ever give him.

Adam had said the monastery he had found was
somewhere near Somerton, and it seemed that the
monastery, dedicated to St Jude the Patron Saint of
hopeless cases, was the proper place to start his
unexpected new life.

Pyre, now a little way behind him, was where his old life
had ended.

After so long shut up and organised into a routine it was
strange to wander freely, listen to the sounds of animals
and birds hunting in the night, sleep under the stars and
wake up on a bed of grass or hay, and to barter labour for
food.

Where he was offered work for a day or a few days he
took it before moving on, and he lost count of the days he
spent working and walking north, becoming lost and
retracing his steps, sometimes alone and sometimes in
company; but time did not matter any more. He had time
to spare, time he had not expected to have. Time which,

when he was honest with himself, he knew he did not want.

He came to a crossroad where the signpost pointed to Taunton in one direction and Somerton in the other. He thought about turning towards Taunton and trying to find Adam and Nancy, but it did not seem time for that yet; and something told him that maybe it never would. Adam and Nancy were part of the past, the old life he had discarded, and if he was to have any future he knew he had to leave the past behind.

When he reached Somerton no one recognised his description of the monastery but there was an old priory back down Martock way, someone said. He turned around and retraced his steps and found the priory as dusk turned to night; but it was not the monastery he was looking for. Nobody there knew anything about the monastery Adam had described but the prior offered him rest for the night and promised that the next morning he would ask an old monk who was already asleep if he knew of St Jude's.

Yes, the old man recognised Adam's description. There was a monastery dedicated to St Jude, and he thought it offered seclusion to those who asked, but it was not near Somerton. It was a long way off, towards Shaftesbury. Adam must have been mistaken.

Aye, he must have been. He started eastwards, following the road, determined now to walk and not accept a ride even if one was offered. The journey to the monastery had suddenly taken on the feeling of a pilgrimage.

The surroundings changed from hedged fields to open country, almost downland, and when he woke on the third morning he felt a need to turn south. He found the monastery that night, nestled in a valley, half hidden by trees, and he wondered how Adam could possibly have stumbled across the place by accident. He thought that Adam would have difficulty in finding it again if he ever wanted to return there; it was about thirty miles away from where he had said it was.

*   *   *

It seemed strange to sleep under a roof again, and not just under a roof but in another cell even if it was one without a door.

The cell had a single wooden cot with no mattress and a covering of only a thin blanket. After sleeping on grass or hay the cot seemed hard and unforgiving; but the simplicity of the furniture and surroundings had a strangely calming effect.

The cell was small. It had no windows and the ceiling was low and arched and on it someone had painted a picture of St Jude at prayer, and a short inscription.

'Water and bread to succour your body, rest to succour your mind and peace to succour your soul.'

It was the first thing he saw on waking and the last thing he saw before sleep at night, and the more he read it the more it irritated him.

Rest did not succour his mind; it gave him time to think about things he wanted to forget. But the peace was doing something to his soul, which was why he stayed. Perhaps, if he stayed long enough, his mind and soul might come together and he might discover why he still felt so guilty, why he felt that there was something important that he should have done, something so important that it seemed to hold the key to his future happiness.

The trees were no longer quite so green, dusk came earlier, and dew made the grass wet to walk on in the mornings.

The slow, quiet, unintrusive life of the monastery had permeated him. He wore a monk's brown flannel cloak and hood and plaited rope sandals, but he did not wear the monk's crucifix nor one of the chain belts they each wrapped around their waist; he used a length of plain rope to keep his cloak closed.

The monks rarely spoke, never asked personal or intrusive questions, and expected nothing of him other than his work.

The water and bread, and the vegetable stews which succoured his body had to be worked for and he worked in the fields and orchards surrounding the monastery. The work was hard and tiring, but the near exhaustion he felt at the end of the day added to the peace the monastery offered.

An odd sense of almost unreal serenity came over him. Thoughts about the future were forgotten. Life was too peaceful to be disturbed. He had all he wanted.

Until he saw the child being tormented.

It was difficult to know whether it was a boy or girl. It looked about five or six years old but it was small and must have been partly crippled because it could not move properly. And it never spoke, never reacted to the other children from the village who poked it with sticks, screamed at it, kicked and pushed it until it fell, then threw pebbles at it.

'Get away!' The loudness of his own voice surprised him as he vaulted a gate and ran to the fallen child. 'Are you hurt?'

The child looked at him, puzzled, frightened; but did not reply.

'Are you hurt?' There was no answer. 'Where do you live? In the village? Where's your ma?'

Still no answer, just a stare which had no meaning.

He turned to the other children and asked them who the silent child was, where his or her mother was.

It did not have a mother, or a father. It had come to the village that day and it did not speak.

So why were they tormenting it? Because they did not want it in the village, that was why.

'Are you hungry?'

No answer.

'Do you like apples? Red, sweet apples?'

No answer, so he picked up the child and carried it to the orchard, sat it against a tree and handed it an apple. The child stared at the apple, but did not eat.

'Here, eat it like this.' He took another apple from the tree and bit into it. 'Eat it. It tastes good.'

He smiled and the child bit the apple and smiled back.

'It tastes good, doesn't it?' he said, but the child stayed silent. 'Would you like me to tell you a story?'

The child ate the apple and smiled; listened as the story was told and looked serious during the sad parts and smiled during the happy parts. But it did not speak.

He promised the child food and shelter for the night and told it to stay by the tree while he finished picking apples; but when he went back to the tree the child had gone.

The serenity that had built up shattered.

An awful foreboding rode up in his mind and he dropped the barrel of apples he was carrying and ran to the ditch near the spot where the child had been tormented.

The child was lying in the bottom of the ditch, staring upwards through two feet of clear ditchwater. Even though the child was drowned its mouth was opening and closing as though it were trying to speak; and somehow he knew who the child was and what it was trying to say.

'Why, Dadda? Why didn't you let me live?'

He plunged into the ditch and tried to hug the child but there was no child and there was no water. The ditch was dry and he knelt amongst the nettles and thistles and asked for forgiveness.

'I'm sorry. I'm sorry. I never meant to harm you. I know it doesn't help but you must believe I never meant you any harm,' and in his mind all he could see was a lavatory swilling with bloody water and something white and stringy sliding through the hole and on to the earth beneath; the child he and Nancy had created and killed.

And he knew what caused the guilt.

So much had happened immediately after that awful moment when he saw his child slide into the lavatory that he had managed to stop the memory settling into its own place in his mind, and now he knew why.

Because, of all the things he had done that was the worst.

He had caused Nancy to kill their baby even before it was born, and he had immediately seen nothing other than the opportunities the child's death gave him.

What opportunities? They had all slipped away, one by one, until he had nothing at all.

He walked away from the ditch, back into the orchard, and sat by the tree where he had told his child a story. He sat for a long time, shocked and numb, and when the numbness wore off he was left yearning for other children that he could love and cherish. Children he could take care of, protect. Children he could teach not to make the mistakes he had made. Children who could give a purpose and a direction to his own life. Other children who would help him redeem himself for what he had done.

But he could never have all that. He could never treat another woman the way he had treated Nancy. He could never again make love to a woman he did not love in his heart. And he only loved Rose that much.

And that was why he could not go to Lizzie, even if he could find her. If Adam was right, then Lizzie might expect him to love her the way he loved Rose, and that was not possible.

He lay on his cot and even though it was dark and impossible to see he could still read the inscription above his head because he could see it in his mind. And now it did not irritate him.

Remembering what he and Nancy had done to their baby, and knowing that in his mind he had tried to do all he could for the child who sat under the apple tree and listened to a story, seemed to have stemmed his guilt. The experience had been shocking and even twelve hours later he still sweated and felt sick thinking about what had happened, but also he felt more at ease with himself.

He had been a fool all his life. He had dreams which were impossible, which he had known were impossible from the start, but he had allowed them to influence everything he did.

But was he any more of a fool than, say, Adam? Adam had his dreams, dreams that he believed in, but Adam called his belief faith.

And that, of course, was the answer to Adam's riddle.

That was the purpose of telling Adam to throw aside his staff and to order it to come back. It was an illustration of faith.

A staff, or a faith, or perhaps dreams could support you through life, but you could not expect the staff to do that without your help. You could not order your staff to support you, you had to bend down and pick it up, to make the effort to embrace your faith or your dreams if you wanted their support.

He smiled in the darkness. Adam would be pleased with him for having found the answer to the riddle, so perhaps he should contact him now, as he had promised.

But perhaps not. He did not know where Adam lived so he could not write, and he was not sure that if he visited them he could face Nancy, not now he remembered so clearly what he put her through, what he did to her.

So perhaps he would leave here tomorrow, or the next day or next week. Soon anyway, before the autumn ended and winter set in, although where he would go and what he would do he still had not decided.

CHAPTER 43

Elizabeth sat on her own in the kitchen, and gave an involuntary sigh.

That was the story. She had gone over it all in her mind and she knew that as soon as Helen and Jamie woke and remembered she had promised to tell them about their father they would start asking questions.

But how could she explain all that had happened to two four-year-old children? It was clear in her own mind now, clearer than ever before, but how could she tell Helen and Jamie that their mother was going to die of a broken heart? She could not.

She walked into the front room and pulled back the curtains. Half a dozen straggly leaves clustered together on the tree. The slightest breeze would pull them off, and the autumn would be over.

And Rose would die.

She heard a noise from upstairs.

'Aunty Lizzie.' It was Jamie.

'I'm down here, Jamie.'

She heard him padding down the stairs, and the sound of Helen following him. They came to her in the hall, wrapped their arms around her and kissed her as they always did, and she waited tensely for the inevitable question.

Helen tugged Jamie's arm, prompting him to ask the question for both of them.

'You promised to tell us about our papa, Aunty Lizzie. About our father.'

'Yes, Jamie, I will after you've washed and dressed and eaten breakfast.' Anything to gain just a little more time.

'Oh, do we have to wait that long?' Jamie pulled a face.

'Yes, and you must feed Kitchener. He'll be hungry even if you're not.'

'Oh, yes.' Jamie remembered his pet. 'Yes, we must feed Kitchener, mustn't we?'

The diversion did not last long but suddenly another opportunity to delay things occurred to her. 'I think we ought to go to church and pray for God to help your mama to get better.'

This was dangerous because if they prayed and their mother died anyway they might never believe in prayer again, but it was a chance she was willing to take. Besides, prayer might help. Miracles did happen, sometimes.

'Yes, let's do that, Aunty Lizzie,' Helen said eagerly.

She prayed fervently, asking a God she only half believed in to be kind and give Rose the strength to get better, and she prayed that He would give her strength too, the strength to do whatever she had to. And she prayed that the leaves would stay on the tree for just a little longer.

They left the church together, her and the twins, Ada and Jack and their sibling family, and as they walked back along Angel Street she saw a familiar figure striding towards her.

'Richard, how lovely. I didn't expect to see you for another week.' But although she made herself sound bright his unexpected appearance worried her.

He looked awkward, embarrassed, as if he had been caught doing something wrong. 'I need to talk to you, Lizzie. I couldn't wait until next week.'

'Anything wrong?'

He did not answer, but asked, 'Where's Rose?'

She told him what had happened.

'Oh God!' He turned ashen. 'Is it consumption?'

'The doctor thinks it is. I'll know later, when I visit her in hospital.'

'Oh, well, perhaps I shouldn't have come.' He looked even more embarrassed. 'I never was much good at timing things.'

'Rubbish.' She took his hand and tried to act confidently. 'You're here now, and I'm very glad you are. I don't think I've ever needed anyone so much as I need you now. Come in and tell me what you want.'

She saw the way he looked at her, then at the children, and noticed the hesitation in his voice as he asked. 'Can we have a few minutes alone? Really alone? I've something important to say and it'll be difficult enough without interruptions.'

'Certainly.' Her heart thumped, this sounded serious and she wanted to hear whatever it was as soon as possible; things had not been the same between them since she had told him about Saul and John and Sebastian, and everything else which had shaped her life. 'Ada, can you look after the twins for a while?'

'Of course.' Ada tried to usher Helen and Jamie away but Jamie stood his ground.

'Aunty Lizzie was going to tell us about our father.'

'I will, after Uncle Richard and I have finished,' she said quickly, eager to be alone with Richard.

'You promise?' Jamie looked suspicious.

'I promise.'

He thought for a moment and then allowed Ada to whisk him into her house.

* * *

'Well?' She shut the front door and stood against it, frightened to hear what he had to say because she had guessed from the way he acted during his last visit that he was becoming tired of a relationship which could not develop beyond friendship.

'Can we go into the kitchen?' he asked. 'Have a cup of tea? I've been up most of the night. Caught the last train to London last night, stayed in a hotel and left before breakfast this morning.'

'Of course.' His delaying tactics were worrying.

She put the kettle on the range and sat down in one of the easy chairs, motioning him to sit in the other but he refused and walked to the window, stared out into the garden, his back towards her.

'Rose is seriously ill, is she?' he asked after a few moments.

'How serious is consumption, Richard?' There was a harshness in her voice which she regretted the moment he turned around and she saw the anguish on his face. 'What's wrong, Richard? What's the matter?'

'We're the matter, Lizzie.'

'Oh, I see.'

'I can't go on like this, living so far apart. Our lives are totally different. We can't go on seeing each other for a few hours every month or so. It's ridiculous, not fair on either of us.'

'I understand, Richard. I can't say I blame you, in all honesty. I know how difficult it is, I feel the same.' So this was the end of another romance, another chance of happiness snatched away just when it seemed she had found the man she wanted to spend her life with.

She had begun to suspect what was on his mind during his last visit, the comments about how her commitment to her job and to Rose and the children would prevent her ever living away from London. She had been tempted then to say anything to keep him, but that would not have been sensible. If she had learned nothing else from her experiences with Saul and later with John, she had at least learned that she needed her own life, to have her own identity and purpose and not simply become someone's wife, an accessory to another human being simply because she was scared she might one day end up lonely.

'Look, Lizzie, I can't carry on like this any longer. If I give up my job and find something in London, will you marry me?' The words poured out so fast she was not sure she heard him correctly.

'Pardon?'

'Marry me, will you? I know you can't move away but I can find work up here. I know it won't be easy, but . . .'

'Of course I'll marry you. I thought you were going to say you didn't want to see me any more.'

'Good God, Lizzie, why would I come up here like this to tell you that?'

'Because you're the sort of man who wouldn't do it by letter, Richard.'

'You will marry me then?'

'Of course, I've said so.'

'You're sure?'

'Of course. How many more times . . .'

Then he was kissing her and muttering something about being sorry it was not more romantic, and then the kettle boiled and she made tea. It seemed fitting, somehow, to become engaged in Evie Roper's kitchen, and drink tea to celebrate the occasion. She knew Evie would have approved.

He listened to what she said about the children's questions. 'Well, Lizzie, it's their welfare that's most important, whatever happens. If it comes to the worst we can always bring them up as our children, assuming Belchester doesn't get to hear of it and interfere, but I can't think how he could.'

'Well, that's a relief, anyway.' She sighed, happy that he would not object to raising two children that were not his.

'But I still have to give them answers, and I don't know what to tell them.'

'Leave it to me, Lizzie,' he volunteered. 'I read enough of Edward's stories to know how he'd do it. They don't need to know the full truth, just enough to satisfy them. When are you going to the hospital?'

'Straight after dinner. Will you come with me?'

'Of course I will, and I'll talk to the twins while you're cooking dinner. Let's get them and tell them they're so special that they're the first people we've told that we're getting married. They'll like that and it might distract them from worrying too much about their mother.'

'I love you.' It seemed the only thing to say under the circumstances.

They sat the children on the settee in the front room and being told that they were the first ones to know about the wedding did seem to impress them, especially when Richard told them they would play important roles as bridesmaid and pageboy, but it was not long before Jamie remembered that he still had not been told about his father.

'I know your father very well, Jamie,' Richard said, moved to sit between the children and lifted them both on to his lap. 'Did you know he writes stories for children?'

'No.' Jamie looked surprised.

'Did he write the one about the princess and the pauper?' Helen asked. 'The one Mama tells us?'

'Yes, he did, and lots, lots more, but that one's very important because it's very similar to what happened to your mama and papa, but their story's not over yet, is it? Do you know why?'

'Because papa's not come home yet?' Jamie suggested, already entering into the story.

'That's right. And do you know why he hasn't come home yet?'

'No.' Helen snuggled closer. 'Are you going to tell us?'

'Perhaps, but first let me tell you how your mama and papa met, when your mama was a princess and your father was a poor man.'

'Mama was a princess?' Helen squealed.

'Well, she was a sort of princess, in a kingdom full of high mountains and dark, dark forests. One day, when she was a little girl, not much older than you are now, she was out walking with her brother and they became lost in a dark, dark forest.'

The story wound on and on, imagined adventure following imagined adventure, never far from the truth, never so complicated that they could not understand. And it finished with their father fighting dragons and monsters in a strange land, always with a twig of golden leaves held in his hand to ward off the evil spirits, always striving to find the way home to his princess.

Dinner was almost ready by the time Richard had finished, but Jamie still had one question to ask. 'What does our father look like, Uncle Richard?'

Richard looked at Elizabeth, and she remembered the sketches Rose had drawn for her mother years ago; Catherine had taken them from the manor and given them to her shortly after she had moved into Angel Street. 'I've a picture of your father upstairs, Jamie. One your mother drew a long time ago. I'll show you.'

She handed the framed sketch to Helen and watched as she ran her fingers over the drawing of Edward's face, then suddenly bent forwards and kissed him. 'Come home, Papa. I miss you.'

It was an awful moment. Tears filled her eyes and closed her throat. She could see Richard was swallowing hard to stop himself crying.

There was a knock on the door and she was thankful for the excuse to turn away, but as she did so she glanced out of the window. Her heart fell.

The last leaves had fallen off the tree.

'Oh God!' she breathed, scared of what the caller had come to say.

'What's wrong?' Richard looked alarmed.

'The last leaves have gone from the tree.' She could see from his reaction that he understood the significance.

'I'll see to the door.' He started to move the children aside.

'No, stay here with them. I'll go.' She went into the hall, shut the front room door so the children would not hear what was being said, rubbed the tears from her eyes and opened the front door.

'Lizzie.'

She saw the leaf-covered twig before she recognised him. 'Edward?'

Suddenly they were together, arms wrapped around each other, kissing and holding on tight. She pulled him into the hall as the parlour door opened. Jamie and Helen were standing there holding hands, looking doubtfully at the commotion.

'Good morning, sir,' Helen said in her politest voice.

'Good morning.' Edward moved towards her, his voice gruff, his hand holding the twig of golden leaves.

Jamie tweaked his sister's arm. 'Helen, I think that gentleman's our father.'

Then Edward was on his knees, his arms wrapped around the children, repeating their names over and over.

'Where's Rose?' he asked, eyes red with tears.

'You'd better come and sit down.' She took his hand and ushered the children off to feed Kitchener and promised that they could talk to their father in a few minutes.

'Mr Hampton, sir.' Edward saw Richard and hesitated.

'Don't worry, Edward. I'm not here to take you back.' Richard held out his hand and Edward shook it. 'Lizzie'll explain. I'll go and keep an eye on the children. Your children.'

'Where's Rose, Lizzie? What's wrong?'

She explained quickly.

'Oh God. Can we go now? I must see her.'

'Of course, but how did you know where to find us? About the children.'

'Adam Marriott. I'm sorry, Lizzie, but he came to see me when I was in the prison hospital.'

'I know, Richard told me. I didn't mind, but that was years ago.'

'He mentioned an old monastery to me, a sort of sanctuary, refuge, where he stayed once, to sort himself out. I went there after I was released. I wasn't ready to go back into the world, Lizzie. It's difficult to explain. Anyway, Adam turned up two days ago. Nancy had reminded him that he'd told me about the place but because it wasn't where he thought it was it took him two weeks to find me. He showed me a letter he'd had from you, told me all you'd done for Rose and Ada, all you and Rose have done to get me freed. Told me about Rose and the children. I've been a fool, Lizzie. I know that now. I should have trusted you, all of you.'

'We've all been fools, Edward, but none of that matters now. Let's go to see Rose.'

'Thank you angel. Thank you.' They were outside the Angel Inn.

'What's that, Lizzie?' Edward looked around to see who she was speaking to.

'Just thanking my friend, Edward. My guardian angel if you like.'

He looked up. 'Looks identical to one in the chapel at the priory. I hadn't noticed it until the day Adam arrived.'

She looked at him and then at the angel, and smiled. It was going to be all right. She knew it was.

They crossed the road and began to run towards the hospital.

The tired doctor looked directly into his eyes. 'Mr Forrester, it's unfortunate that you could not have been here last night, when your wife was asking for you.'

'I would have come if I'd known, sir. How is she?'

'Well, your own doctor was quite right to have your wife admitted as he did, but she isn't suffering from consumption. She is very ill, though, both with pneumonia and asthma, but with medicine, rest and, if I may say, a lot of loving care, she'll recover. The nurse will take you to her.'

He followed the nurse along several corridors and finally into a ward with deep windows which filled it with autumn sunshine.

'Your wife's in the end bed where she can see out across to the park.' The nurse pointed along the ward. 'She's very weak, so don't excite her too much.'

'That might be difficult, nurse,' he said and followed Lizzie along the ward.

'Rose?' Lizzie said softly. 'It's Lizzie. Are you awake?'

'Yes, Lizzie,' Rose wheezed and hardly opened her eyes. 'I've been looking at the park. Not many leaves left on the trees, Lizzie. The autumn's nearly over.'

Lizzie moved aside and he stepped forward, opened Rose's fingers and pressed the sprig of golden leaves into her hand, 'Not in Angel Street, Rose. As far as we're concerned it'll always be autumn on Angel Street.'

ELIZABETH GILL

THE SINGING WINDS

Kate Farrer leaves London when her father dies in 1880 and travels north to County Durham to live with her uncle, a mine manager. Restricted by the rigid confines of polite society and hungry for education and honest company, she looks elsewhere for fulfilment and stimulation. This she finds – both by working in her uncle's office, unprecedented for a woman, and in the person of Jon Armstrong.

But Jon is a pit lad, tough and enigmatic, and not a man Kate should be consorting with. He's also engaged to a local lass, Lizzie Harton. And Kate's uncle has very different plans about who she should marry.

Then a sudden and shocking pit disaster destroys not only lives but Jon and Lizzie's future. Frustrated, both girls turn to other men for comfort until a second disaster threatens their carefully constructed worlds.

HODDER AND STOUGHTON PAPERBACKS

NORA KAY

A WOMAN OF SPIRIT

Susan MacFarlane had only a few months with David Cameron, but in that time he taught her the power of passionate love – its rewards and its punishments.

Then she returned to her duty: marriage to a man who could run the family's paper mill – the mill she loved and understood but could not have for herself.

Trapped in a loveless marriage with only her children to console her, her ambition and her ability thwarted by the conventions of the time, Susan seems destined to finish her life without ever knowing again the heady excitement of her brief time of freedom.

Then David Cameron comes back to Glasgow. Rich now, ready to avenge the slights of his youth. And the implacable enemy of Susan's family . . .

HODDER AND STOUGHTON PAPERBACKS

ELIZABETH LORD

STOLEN YEARS

Letty Bancroft is convinced that she has found the right man and is longing for the day when she and David Baron walk down the aisle.

But Letty's father has other ideas. Arthur Bancroft has decided that he cannot manage his East End shop alone now that Letty's mother has died, and turns his youngest daughter into a domestic drudge. Letty is to be tied to house and shop while her sisters find joy in their husbands and children.

So Letty, heartbroken, sees her love go off to fight in France, believing that she will never see him again. Then a shocking discovery makes her realise that she needs David more than ever . . .

HODDER AND STOUGHTON PAPERBACKS